Wish You Were Here

Vincent M. Wales

DGC PRESS   •   SACRAMENTO

ISBN 0-9741337-2-8

First DGC Press printing, August, 2005
Printed on acid-free paper.

ONE NATION 𝔘𝔫𝔡𝔢𝔯 𝔊𝔬𝔡

It's closer than you think...
...or fear!

[A] chilling book that reads more like something right out of today's headlines than an imaginative work of fiction. [The author] captures the danger of theocracy and our current government's abuse of the separation of church and state in a very unusual book that combines suspense with elements of social commentary.

　　　–BookIdeas.com

[This book portrays] the frightening downward spiral of American society in a future where today's popular mixing of religion and government have grown immeasurably worse. [Recommended] to anyone with an interest in our society, in the separation of church and state, in freedom of religion, freedom of conscience, or even personal growth.

　　　–A Book Lover's Book Reviews

[R]eading a book like this will help all of us who are different to draw together, and to remember what we have in common. We must guard our liberties lest they be lost to us. The book is sufficiently realistic that it could scare many of us...who need a good awakening.

　　　–Loving More Magazine

[The author] looks at numerous issues that are at the heart of social debate today and weaves them into his story seamlessly. When you finish reading the book you'll find yourself pondering these issues and thinking about people affected by such issues. You may not change your mind or stance, but at least you'll be thinking about it.

　　　–Atheism Awareness

One thing that is made absolutely plain is that our inaction now has desperate effects in the future, and those effects may be impossible to rectify later.

　　　–Daven's Journal

One Nation Under God
by Vincent M. Wales
ISBN 0-9741337-0-1
448 pp.　　$15.95
Available now from DGC Press.

Acknowledgments

My greatest appreciation goes to my family. Thank you for your unconditional support and for having always given me the freedom to pursue my dreams. A heartfelt thank you to Thia, for her wonderful cover art and advice. Mega-thanks to everyone who provided feedback and input along the way for this story, including (but certainly not limited to) Dale, Denise, Jeannette, Joan, Kay, Linda, Lorna, Lucy, Rich, Shannon, Sheila, and Tyler. Thanks also to those dear friends who provided inspiration for this book. You know who you are. And of course, my deepest gratitude to my wife, Lori, not only for her tireless editing, but also for seeing me through to the end on this massive undertaking. I love you.

Dedication

This book is dedicated to the memory of my father, one of the kindest, gentlest men I've ever known. His never-faltering belief in me was a source of constant motivation. And to the memory of my mother, who introduced me to the fantasy genre with the enchanting world of hobbits. Without her influence, this book might never have come to be.

Author's Foreword

When this book was first published, I expected comments to the effect that I was egocentric or some such thing for naming my protagonist after myself. Amazingly, not one review, not one fan letter, mentioned it. But now I'm going to explain it, anyway.

Many of the characters you're about to meet were created during my college days for use in a particular fantasy role-playing game. One of our group decided it would be fun to create characters who were rather idealized and exaggerated versions of ourselves. And thus, "we" became adventurers in our games for years to come. Due to this long history with the paper character, it would have been "wrong" to change Vincent's name for this book simply to prevent a few readers' raised eyebrows.

But there's a secondary reason the name was retained, too. All too often in fiction (whether on the printed page, or the big or little screens), characters named Vincent aren't exactly the good guys. A character named "Vinnie" often turns out to be a thug of some sort. And I've seen more than the average number of pimps named "Vince" out there. So to all the Vincents of the world who are neither procurers nor hitmen, but actually decent guys, here's one for you.

Wish You Were Here

Book One

What Am I Doing Here?

❧ One ❧

Darella's heart pounded in anticipation as she stood at the rear of the cave, her gaze fixed intently upon the huge object before her. Embedded in the solid rock of the cave wall, as though it were a door to the other side of the hill, was an oval shape, nearly ten feet high and five in width. Its polished surface was the dull grey of slate, bordered by a stone trim, intricately carved to portray the intertwined branches of trees.

Darella's right hand flexed at her side, preparing to wield the awesome energies she was soon to unleash. Her left hand clasped the blue crystal amulet that hung around her neck. The round stone glowed faintly, a hint of the power it would focus for her. She breathed deeply, mentally preparing her spell.

After so many years, she'd finally divined a way to initiate the portal's actions. She knew one day she'd be able to actually control it, manipulate it to do her exact bidding. For now, though, it was enough that she could cause it to operate on her own schedule.

Her schedule was important, for she was presently ripe. She'd seen to that. Now was the time for the future sire of her child to be summoned.

Darella firmed her grip on the crystal in her hand, and began her spell. Whispers of witchspeak echoed ever so faintly in the cave as she chanted, and the glow from her amulet sent streams of blue light from between her fingers. Her right hand shimmered as she wove a complex pattern in the air, sending waves of energy toward the grey face of the monolith.

Soon the portal began to shine with its own light. Darella completed her spell, and stood back to watch. The portal's face shimmered with a kaleidoscope of colors. Random bursts of golden light shot out into the cave.

Shortly, a shape began to coalesce inside the oval, gradually becoming more and more solid. She sighed in relief. The figure was definitely male. A female would have ruined her plans. As the figure fell forward, sprawling in the dirt on the floor of the cave, Darella stepped into the shadows and studied him, her jaw dropping in shock.

He was a mere boy! Still in his teens, from the look of him, complete with the innocence and ignorance of youth. And fat, as well. Whatever forces guided the choices of the portal, she thought, they had certainly chosen wrong this time.

But as the boy struggled to rise, she suddenly realized this was not the fault of the portal or her gods or whatever forces were behind the workings of the thing. It was her own. Her magicks had caused the portal to operate by her own command, not its own initiative.

In the years since discovering this cave, with its portal, Darella had seen it bring forth a series of courageous, powerful heroes. She now realized that the mechanism must require time to locate such a type. But now, her manipulations had caused it to summon the first being it could locate, which was this sorry specimen before her.

No, she thought with a shake of her head. He would never do. She would wait for the next one to come naturally. And yet, she thought with a sigh, years could pass before the next one arrived. And she was ready to conceive now and might not be, next time. The spells she used to control her cycle took far more time than the portal's spontaneous activation would allow.

She watched the young man dust himself off. He wore trousers of an unfamiliar blue fabric and a thin, black tunic. Over this, he wore a strange vest with bulging pouches sewn in. He had spectacles upon his face, but of a sort she'd never seen before. Darella shook her head. This would be distasteful, but she had to do it. Her curiosity about the end result of her experiment was simply too strong to ignore.

Before he could wander out of the cave, she made her move. Summoning her strength, she probed his dazed mind, searching for the physical traits he would find most appealing in the opposite sex. Based on these insights, she altered her appearance from that of a plain, middle-aged woman to that of a budding young beauty barely the age of the boy himself. Her hair became long and lustrous, rather than its normal unkempt mess. Her face would be lovely to him, fair of skin and wistfully beautiful.

When the transformation was complete, she stepped from the shadows, shedding her clothing as she approached the boy. Her sudden appearance startled him, but her beauty mesmerized him. She nearly laughed at the way he stared at her, his face flushing with embarrassment and lust. Her seduction of him was virtually instantaneous.

The following act was unpleasant. Darella wondered if the boy had ever been with a female before, so hesitant was he, and so awkward. The event took longer than she expected, too. The boy seemed more interested in touching and kissing than in intercourse. He would gaze into her eyes with what she had to interpret as longing. It made her want to throw up. But finally, he finished.

Once spent, he slept. Darella erased the memory of the deed from his mind, then grimaced at his sleeping form as she moved to her more comfortable part of the cave, in her more comfortable body. There she meditated. By the time the boy had awakened, dressed, and stumbled from the cave, Darella was certain she was pregnant.

The young man stopped in his tracks, closing his eyes against the wooziness that hit him suddenly. His mind was muddled, as though he couldn't quite come fully awake, and his body felt like he'd just walked into a wall of gelatin. He shook his head, opened his eyes, and resumed his walk up the street.

Then he froze again, as the bottom dropped from his stomach. This wasn't his street, he realized as he spun around, looking frantically in all directions. Gone were the single-family homes lining both sides of the cozy cul-de-sac where he'd lived his entire life. No asphalt lay beneath his sneakers. Instead, he stood in the middle of a narrow and muddy dirt road stretching to the horizon in either direction. "Holy shit," he croaked.

Panic surged inside him, driving away the muddled feeling. He looked down at his feet, soaking wet and mud-caked, then back down the road. There were puddles everywhere. But that was impossible! He hadn't been walking down this road! Where was he?

His feet ached, too, as though he'd been walking for miles. But that wasn't possible, either! He'd just left his house. That much was clear to him. He'd said goodbye to his dad, stepped out the door, descended the steps of their tiny front porch, cut across the lawn, and headed up the street. He'd been going to the pizza shop for a slice or two, and to play some pinball and video games with the gang. Maybe shoot a game of pool. Not the height of excitement, but it was a small town.

It couldn't have been more than a minute ago that he'd left the house.

"This can't be real," he said.

He looked around again. The land itself wasn't much different than the area around his home. Trees and hills were everywhere, and the air was fragrant and fresh. But there the similarities ended. He drew in deep breaths to calm himself. His heartbeat was finally slowing, but the sense of panic was still ringing in his head. He fought down the urge to yell. Obviously, no one was around. He'd be wasting his breath. The road must lead somewhere, though, he told himself. So he began walking again.

The sky was mostly clear and blue, with few clouds. The sun was low on the horizon, fitting the time of day when he'd left his house. Why, then, did his feet feel as though he'd been on them for hours? He cursed as he stepped into another puddle in the road, frowning as he stamped his foot to shake out as much water as he could. When he looked up again, he blinked. In the distance, he saw a small house. "Finally," he muttered, and began to run.

Being overweight and out of shape, he was soon too tired to keep up his pace. The wooziness had returned, too, so he slowed to a walk. He was close enough now to determine the house was a very small log structure, looking more like a tiny camping lodge than a residence. The only word that sprang to mind was "cottage."

The cottage, he saw, was shadowed by a large willow tree, under which were a table and two chairs. To his great relief, both seats were occupied. As he neared, he could see one figure was a tall man with black hair. Across from him sat a much shorter figure, possibly a child.

He came to a stop in the road, breathing heavily. "Hey," he managed to say before the world began to spin and he collapsed in the mud.

The next thing he heard was a gentle voice cutting through the fog inside his head. "Is he all right?"

"Yes," came a deeper reply. "Just exhaustion, I believe."

He came around slowly. With a shock, he realized he must have passed out. He felt the hardness of a chair under him as he tried to open his eyes. They wouldn't cooperate.

The slosh of pouring liquid made him suddenly aware of his thirst. A drink would be wonderful, he thought, just before the splash hit him in the face.

"Ghaa!" he blurted, eyes popping open. He wiped angrily at his face, sputtering and blowing water from his nose. Then he stopped, his attention captured by the tall man who stood before him. He was an intimidating figure, with a severe expression on his face. He estimated the man was about four inches taller than himself, making him probably six feet three or so. His clothing, however, was what really drew his attention. The man wore lace-up leather boots of a primitive design. His simple pants were dark brown and loose, tied with a drawstring. The pullover shirt was also loose, and of a natural hue. The clothes had the rough look of being hand-made, not mass-produced. A sheathed knife was at his waist, tied with a rope.

"That's better," he heard the other stranger say, and turned to look at the squat form standing near him. His eyes widened in surprise. This was no child, he realized. The figure stood less than four feet tall, had a wizened countenance, bright eyes that seemed slightly too large for his face, and long, silvery-gray hair. His nose was a bit on the bulbous side, but seemed to fit his face perfectly. He stood barely more than half the height of the other man. Despite the man's odd appearance, the boy couldn't shake the feeling that this was how he was supposed to look, rather than being the result of an unfortunate birth defect. The clothing he wore was similar to the tall man's, but in very bright shades of yellow and blue.

5

The young man shook his head. He removed his dripping glasses and placed them on what he now saw was a gaming table. It appeared the two had been playing chess before he'd interrupted them.

"Are you well?" asked the dark-haired man.

He closed his eyes and took a deep breath before opening them again. When the scene refused to change back to something more familiar, he sighed. "Not even remotely," he said.

"More water?" asked the other, proffering an earthen mug.

"No," he said slowly, his thirst now far from his mind. "Thanks." He blinked at the man. "I'm sorry. You are...?"

"Gnorrin," the little man said. "And yes, I'm a gnome." He reached out and lifted the eyeglasses from the table. "Why do you wear spectacles when not reading?"

"Because I need to," he said, too stunned to worry about getting them back. A gnome? No, he thought. He must have heard him wrong.

Gnorrin placed the glasses on his face, then looked up at his friend. His eyes crossed. "You *need* to wear them? But they make you blind!" He slid the glasses across the table.

The boy scooped them up and began drying the lenses on his pants. "Look," he said, trying to put the strangeness of the situation out of his head. "I'm hoping you can help me." He smiled sheepishly as he put on the glasses. "I seem to have gotten lost. Where am I, exactly?"

The tall man answered. "You are near the town of Glenmarsh. You would continue in the direction you were traveling," he said. "If you leave now, you would be there before sunset."

But the young man shook his head. "I'm sorry. I've never heard of Glenmarsh. What else is in the area?"

"Dynsa is to the southeast of here, but it is many leagues," the man said.

"Dynsa," he repeated. "I've never heard of a town called Dynsa in Pennsylvania." He saw the confused expressions on the faces of the men. "Don't say it," he whispered.

"Pennsylvania?" asked Gnorrin. "In what kingdom is that?"

He felt the blood drain from his face. Kingdom? He began to shake his head. "This can't be happening. You mean you've never heard of Pennsylvania?"

The gnome shrugged. "Sorry." He frowned. "You don't look well. Would you like to go inside? It is more comfortable there."

He didn't feel well, that was certain. The others escorted him inside, where he settled into a large, odd-looking armchair made of small logs and covered in soft leather. The tall man seated himself in another of similar construction, while Gnorrin climbed into an identical one in miniature, perfectly suited for his diminutive size.

The young man took a deep breath and licked his dry lips. "I don't know what to say. I have no idea where I am, and now you tell me you've never heard of Pennsylvania. It's like I'm in a different country or something, except we're speaking the same language."

"What is your name?" Gnorrin asked. "We'll start there."

"Vincent," he said.

The gnome raised an eyebrow. "An unusual name. Well, I'm Gnorrin, as I said." He indicated the taller man. "And this is—"

"You may call me Blade," the man interrupted.

6

Vincent saw Gnorrin give his friend a surprised look, then shrug. "Blade?" Vincent repeated. He was about to chuckle at the corny name, but thought better of it when he saw the man's stern gaze. "Okay."

He rubbed his forehead. This was all too much to handle, too much to process. So he decided to address things in chronological order. The first item on his mental agenda was Gnorrin's reference to himself as a gnome. Vincent looked at the man, studying his face and stature. "I'm sorry. I don't mean to stare."

Gnorrin waved him off. "I gather you've never met a gnome before."

Shaking off thoughts of ruby slippers and a yellow brick road, Vincent merely nodded. "You gather correctly." He shivered slightly.

"Are you cold?" Gnorrin asked. "Let me light a fire."

"That would be great," Vincent said as the gnome moved over to the fireplace beside Vincent's chair. He was acutely aware of Blade studying him intently. The man made him uncomfortable, so Vincent watched as Gnorrin adjusted the logs. Then, to his amazement, the gnome mumbled a few words, held out his hand, and the logs burst into flame. Vincent gasped and jumped backward.

"Gnorrin!" Blade said harshly.

"Oh, hush," said the gnome.

"How did you...?" Vincent stammered.

Gnorrin turned, blinking innocently. "I'm a mage, obviously."

"You take unnecessary risks," Blade said under his breath.

The gnome moved closer to Vincent. "You've never heard of mages either, have you?"

Vincent's mental overload was now firmly established. "Not outside of story books," he said.

Blade stroked his chin, his dark eyes drilling into Vincent. "If the truth be told, you are as strange in your appearance to us as we seem to you."

"Yes," Gnorrin agreed. "Why don't you tell us a bit about yourself?"

Vincent nodded, thinking this was probably a good idea. If he kept trying to figure things out, he was likely to go crazy. Talking would help. "Well," he began, "I'm seventeen. I'm in my first year of college, planning on becoming an astronomer." Seeing the puzzled looks this elicited, he explained. "Someone who studies the stars."

"Ah," said Blade. "An astrologer."

Vincent sighed. "No, that's someone who claims to divine different things based on the stars, like your future or something."

"And what else would you study of the stars?" Gnorrin asked.

Vincent didn't try to explain. Instead, he shook his head. The panic was rising again. "Look, I can tell you about my background any old time. Are you guys just joking with me? Because this is really freaking me out."

Blade shifted slightly in his seat. "I do not know the expression, though your meaning is clear."

"Yes," Gnorrin agreed. "And I imagine we would be equally as disturbed to find ourselves in your world."

"Gnorrin!" Blade spat. "Don't be ridiculous."

The gnome frowned and faced his friend. "Your skepticism, I'm sure, has served you well in many an instance. But for once in your life, will you accept what is obviously true?"

The words sent a chill through Vincent. There he had it—a plainly spoken confirmation of the irrational thoughts he'd been denying. He was in a different world. It was impossible. But it seemed almost to be the only possible explanation. Unless he really was just dreaming.

Now there was a thought, he had to admit. A thought that made him a bit less frightened. If he were only dreaming, it would do no harm to play things out. Soon enough, he'd wake and be in his own room back home. He'd heard of lucid dreaming, in which the dreamer is aware of his dreaming state. That would certainly explain a lot. Gnomes. Magic. He nearly chuckled. Of course he was dreaming. And that would also explain how people from different worlds could communicate and understand each other, and how he could be transported here and still have his own clothes, not to mention his cassette player, which he felt in his vest pocket. "Yes," he said, less despondently, now that he knew he wasn't going insane. "I imagine you would be disturbed by that. So tell me about where I am. What's the name of this world?"

Gnorrin looked at him, a peculiar expression on his face. "Name?"

"Yeah. You know. Like, my world is called Earth. What about this one?" He smiled. This could be a fun dream.

Gnorrin shook his head. "We give names to different lands. Different kingdoms and such. But the world is simply...the world."

"Fair enough," Vincent said. "Do you mind if I take off my shoes? My feet are killing me." When there was no opposition, he removed his sneakers and socks, all still damp from puddles on the road. He turned his feet toward the fire.

"You have been walking for some distance, judging by the blisters," said Blade.

Vincent looked at the sole of one foot and touched the blisters tenderly. "Yeah," he said quietly. Blisters didn't seem right for a dream. He wondered if he could make them disappear. He concentrated, imagined them shrinking, but nothing happened. He frowned. So maybe it wasn't a lucid dream, just a plain old dream he couldn't control. His cassette player was digging into his ribs, so he removed it from his pocket, and adjusted his vest.

"What is that?" Gnorrin asked.

"This is a tape player," he replied, pulling out the earphones as well.

"What does it do?" The gnome leaned forward.

Continuing to go along with the dream, Vincent opened the machine and pulled out the cassette. "It plays these," he said. "It has some music on it." He inserted the tape.

"How lovely!" said Gnorrin as Vincent reached over and put the headset on him, adjusting the earphones to fit properly. "And what is this?" Gnorrin fingered the earphones.

Vincent checked, then lowered, the volume setting. "This sends the sound right into your ears. Blade and I will barely hear a thing."

"How is the music made to come from such a thing?" asked Blade.

"Beats me. Something to do with magnetic encoding. I don't understand it," he said. "It's very technical."

Blade raised an eyebrow. "And you were amazed by Gnorrin's little fire spell?"

Vincent merely nodded. "Good point." He turned to Gnorrin. "Ready?" When the gnome nodded, Vincent pressed the "play" button. He smiled as Gnorrin's eyes grew wide and his mouth dropped open. After a few moments, Vincent stopped the tape. "Well?"

Gnorrin removed the earphones. "Incredible! I've never heard such sounds! You see, Blade? How would you explain this?"

"The same way I would explain any other magical device, of course."

"Oh, rubbish," said the gnome.

Vincent smiled feebly as Gnorrin described the experience to his friend, having Blade listen as well. As the two marveled and argued over the device, Vincent rose from his seat. Was this a dream or not? He wanted it to be a dream, but the sickening feeling was returning. He moved to a window, and gazed out at the setting sun. It looked like the sun he remembered, but if what he feared were true, it was a different sun than was setting on Earth. A lump formed in his throat.

"Are you hungry? I'll warm us up some dinner," Gnorrin said. "Blade, would you mind?" He turned back to Vincent. "I hope the remains of last night's stew will be acceptable."

Vincent nodded, noting Blade's frown as the man walked across the room. He obviously wasn't happy about Vincent's presence here.

"I have heard of others," Gnorrin said, "people from other worlds, so rumor holds, who find themselves here."

Vincent turned to look at him. "Really?"

The gnome nodded as Blade returned with a pot and hung it over the fire. Gnorrin began to stir the stew. "Yes. But I have never known any of them to have discovered the method of their arrival. Nor how to return."

"Wonderful," muttered Vincent.

"Tomorrow Blade will try to find some clue to your arrival."

"I'll do nothing of the sort," the taller man said gruffly.

Gnorrin ignored him and continued. "Perhaps he will learn something."

Vincent wasn't sure whether to thank Blade or not, given the man's reaction. "Okay," he said quietly.

"You will stay here with me, in the meantime." He turned to Blade. "He has been through enough, don't you think? You can sleep in front of the fire for one night, my friend."

Vincent protested. "I don't want to put anyone out," he said. "I can sleep on the floor."

Blade shook his head. "No. If that is Gnorrin's wish, I will abide by it."

"Thank you," Gnorrin said to him. Then, to Vincent, "While he goes about his quest, I will take you into town. We need to provide you with more suitable clothing, I think." He stepped over to Vincent and held open the boy's vest, studying his outfit. He indicated the breast pocket. "Of what possible use is such a tiny pouch? And in such an odd location?"

"Obviously," said Blade, "it is to keep one's gold closest to one's heart." He smiled at his wit.

Vincent drew the vest closed again. He was ashamed of his weight problem and wore vests to help conceal his body. "That's as good an explanation as any," he said.

Gnorrin shrugged and returned to the pot, announcing momentarily that the stew was ready.

Vincent wasn't sure he could eat, given the knots in his stomach. Blade carried the stew to the small kitchen and dining area, while Gnorrin laid out utensils and bowls. As he sat, Vincent noted the bowls and spoons were wooden. He picked up a mug made of very stiff leather. The seam appeared to be nailed together, with a wooden base similarly fastened. The inside was sealed with wax.

Gnorrin ladled out thick stew full of vegetables and meat unfamiliar to Vincent, though not too dissimilar to Earth counterparts. Dark bread served to sop up the gravy. Gnorrin produced a small cask of ale, which Vincent eyed dubiously.

"Does ale not appeal to you?" the gnome asked. "I have wine, if that is more to your liking."

"Actually," Vincent said, "I don't think either is quite what I had in mind. Maybe some of the water you offered before?"

Gnorrin shrugged and fetched him a pitcher.

After dinner, Vincent excused himself and put on his shoes before stepping outside to find a handy tree. He raised an eyebrow as he saw what was clearly an outhouse off behind the cottage. Resigned, he made his way toward it.

He took a tentative sniff upon entering, and was surprised to find his fears unwarranted. In fact, it wasn't any worse than some of the public restrooms he'd used. He frowned, though, when he saw what was obviously meant to be the toilet paper equivalent: large, broad leaves. Soft to the touch, he found, but still not anything he looked forward to using. "This has got to be a nightmare," he muttered.

Before entering the cottage again, he looked to the sky. The night was beautiful, clear and speckled with stars. There was no moon out, yet. He took a deep breath of the crisp air, enjoying the refreshing sensation. His pleasure was replaced by despair as he looked more carefully at the sky. There were no familiar constellations. No Big Dipper, no Cassiopeia. No Southern Cross, for that matter, which discounted the likelihood of him somehow being south of the equator. Could he truly be on a different world? He should be enthralled by the very concept, he told himself, but couldn't manage to summon that particular emotion.

Upon returning, he apologized to his hosts and voiced his desire for sleep. Gnorrin showed him to a tiny room, giving him a lit lantern, should he need light during the night. He wished Vincent a good night and left for the outer rooms.

He was pleased to see a window on the wall above the fluffy mattress. He enjoyed fresh air during the night. Vincent placed the lantern on a small table beside the bed. The tape player joined it. He removed his wristwatch, glancing at its face. Probably won't need this anymore, he thought. The watch was an old, spring-wound thing he'd owned for many years. It always stopped at a few minutes past midnight due to some kink in the spring. Absently, he tossed the watch onto the table. He pulled out his wallet. More useless junk. United States paper currency certainly wouldn't be worth anything here. He removed the rings from his fingers: his high school class ring and one of cheap silver plate and turquoise bought during a trip to the beach one summer. A plastic comb clattered to the tabletop beside his wallet. A few coins, also worthless. And last, his keys and glasses. He looked at the keys. At least he hadn't been driving when he was somehow sucked into this world. He was thankful for that. If the car had gotten wrecked, his dad would kill him.

Thoughts of possibly never seeing his father again sent a wave of grief through him, but he fought it down.

From the outer rooms, he heard Gnorrin and Blade arguing. He couldn't make out everything of what was said, but it was clear that Blade didn't put much stock in the idea of Vincent being from another world. Gnorrin wasn't able to convince the man of this, but was able to achieve a small victory. Blade agreed to retrace Vincent's path of arrival, to see if it would be possible to find where he came from.

Vincent sighed and finished undressing, dropping his clothes in a heap on the floor beside the bed. He lay down, throwing an arm across his eyes and yawning. He imagined the events of the day would not help his insomnia any. All he needed was to lie awake with his brain in overdrive all night. Then again, he thought, what was there to get up early for anyway? Only to wake from the dream. He chuckled nervously. By the time the smile left his face, he was asleep.

ॐ ॐ

Morning brought an end to Vincent's slumber. As sleep slowly faded, he yawned, adjusted his pillow, and rolled onto his side. Since he hadn't woken to an alarm, he knew he didn't have classes today. Funny how he couldn't think of what day it was. He sighed happily, content to stay snuggled in the blankets. He loved the feeling of being not-quite-awake, but aware enough to appreciate the warmth of the bed and maybe mull over some of the weirder dreams of the night. And did he have a whopper, he thought with a faint smile touching his lips.

Then his eyes snapped open. The dream! It had been so real! Absolutely unbelievable! His heart began to pound, and his eyes gradually focused on the lantern on the table beside his bed.

Vincent's stomach bunched up. Every nerve in his body was suddenly hypersensitive. He was aware that the bed he occupied was nowhere near as comfortable as the one he was used to sleeping in. And this wasn't his bedroom. He closed his eyes again, then opened them, but nothing changed. He was awake. And no matter how improbable it seemed, he knew he hadn't been dreaming at all.

Against his better judgement, he crawled out of the cot. The blisters on his feet hurt, reinforcing the idea that he hadn't been dreaming. He began to pick up his clothes from the floor, but noticed other clothing was draped across the foot of the bed for him. From the look of them, they must belong to Blade, he thought. With a sigh, he put them on, then left the room.

The cottage seemed to be empty. He spied his shoes, propped in front of the fire. Gnorrin must have put them there for him. They were quite dry now, and he put them on, frowning at their stiffness. Walking would not be pleasant, he thought. He finished just as Gnorrin entered from outdoors.

"Ah, you're awake. Did you sleep well?"

Vincent stared at him, managing to nod.

The gnome tilted his head, his face taking on a sad expression. "You had hoped to find this all a dream, hadn't you?"

Vincent let out a breath he hadn't realized he'd been holding. Gnorrin's words seemed to snap him out of his state of shock. "You can't blame me, can you?"

Gnorrin shook his head. "Not a bit. Are you hungry?"

"No," he replied. "Thanks."

Gnorrin eyed Vincent's outfit. "Blade's garments are a bit long on you."

"Not to mention snug," Vincent agreed.

"He had no spare boots, however," the gnome concluded. "If you're ready, we can walk into town. We'll go to the market and get you some things."

Vincent followed him out the door. They walked in silence for a time, Vincent trying to make sense of this strange, new reality. "Blade went looking for a clue as to how I got here, didn't he?"

"Yes. He left at first light. With luck, he'll turn up something and before long, you can be home and just pretend it all really was a dream."

Vincent tried to hang on to that possibility without getting his hopes too high. He looked down at Gnorrin. "Thanks for talking him into it."

"My pleasure."

"So where does Blade live?" Vincent asked, though he wondered why he even bothered. He didn't know anything about this world. Blade's residence would be meaningless to him.

"In fact, he has no permanent home. Blade wanders here and there, taking root nowhere. He frequently stays with me, however. We've been friends for several years." Gnorrin smiled up at him. "Would you be so kind as to tell me about your world? If it makes you uncomfortable, I understand. But I am very curious."

Vincent nodded. Why not? If he couldn't be there, he might as well talk about it. At least he'd have something familiar to think of. So he told Gnorrin of Earth, of Pennsylvania, of his small town. He spoke of his family and friends until such thoughts began to depress him. Gnorrin absorbed it all and, true to his word, didn't pry anything further from Vincent once he stopped.

Eventually, they reached the edge of town. They passed first through a residential area, and Vincent noticed hints of unpleasant smells. Naturally, he thought, spying familiar mounds in the road. Horses don't care where they do their business. For that matter, he wondered about the human waste that must accumulate. He didn't see outhouses behind every home. He was glad the town was a small one, for the stink would likely be much worse.

They reached the market after only a few blocks. It wasn't quite what Vincent had expected. He'd thought of how his social studies classes had described old European town market days, with people selling produce and other edibles from carts and baskets, all to pack up and leave when the day was done, reappearing the same day the following week. This market, however, was a permanent part of the town. The buildings, though not made of concrete and steel, were there to stay. There were a few street vendors, but not many. Most of them sold confections to people on the streets. It was not crowded at all.

"What shops would you like to visit?" Gnorrin asked.

"I don't know." Vincent felt awkward. "I figured you were just bringing me here to pass the time."

"Well, partly. But we really should get you some proper clothing."

"Why?" Vincent stopped in the middle of the street. "Blade will find a way to get me home, won't he?"

Gnorrin looked up at him, then at the dirty street. "Possibly."

"Then why would I need clothes? I have clothes."

"You certainly do." He looked up again. "Just think of them as mementos of your brief stay here."

12

Vincent tried to fight off the panic that was growing. Gnorrin obviously didn't believe Blade would find a way to get him back to Earth. "Okay," he said. "I suppose that would be all right."

"Good. Let's go, then." Gnorrin led him to a nearby shop.

Vincent looked at the sign above the door. The characters weren't those of any alphabet he knew, but somehow, he could read it. It said, *"Tarel's Apparel."*

The man behind the counter looked up as they pushed through the door. He smiled. "Gnorrin. Pleasant morning."

The gnome nodded at the man. "Yes it is, Tarel. Come to outfit my friend here in some decent garb. Thought you might be able to help us."

The man moved around the counter to face them. "Good day to you and welcome to my shop. What sort of apparel were you looking for?"

Vincent turned to Gnorrin with a shrug. The gnome smirked. "Everything. From tunics to breeches. Undergarments. The whole bundle."

Tarel looked at Vincent, then at Gnorrin. "Someone leave him naked on your doorstep, old friend?" Gnorrin smiled, but did not reply. "Well, let us take your measure." Tarel produced a cloth tape and proceeded to do just that. After a few moments, he turned to his counter and made notations on a slip of paper with a quill pen. "Now, what fabrics would you like?"

Again Vincent turned to Gnorrin. The gnome smiled and led him to a wall stacked with bolt upon bolt of cloth. Vincent chose several, all in earth tones: browns, dark greens, and gold. "I like all of these. How about you, Gnorrin?"

"You're the one to be wearing them, not me. Though I'd be choosing something a bit more colorful."

Vincent looked at the gnome's outfit: bright red trousers with a blue tunic and a purple belt. "So it seems," he said.

Tarel interrupted. "Pay him no mind. All are handsome choices." The shopkeeper went over the color schemes with Vincent, then announced they could pick up the items in two days. Gnorrin negotiated with him over a price, leaving him a portion of the agreed amount as a deposit. They left the shop and entered the streets again.

"Two days?" Vincent blurted. "Won't I be home in two days?"

"You never know," Gnorrin replied. "If so, then you have nothing to take home with you."

Their next stop was the leatherworker. Gnorrin commissioned the craftsman to make several items, including boots and a belt. Vincent paid attention as they dickered over prices, noting how Gnorrin seemed to know just when the merchant would go no lower.

In the next few hours, Gnorrin covered almost everything Vincent could think of. In two days, providing he was still here, he would be outfitted with a complete wardrobe. Then they set off for Gnorrin's home.

But just before they left the market area, Vincent caught sight of another shop. "Whoa," he said. "Can we look here for a moment?"

Gnorrin nodded and followed him to *The Nib and Quill.* It was a small shop, with the front porch of the building being the sales area. Upon arrival, they were greeted by the proprietor, a middle-aged human by the name of Mepis. Vincent looked over the wide selection of papers, bound and loose, and an assortment of pens and inkwells.

He picked up a thick book of plain pages bound by lacquered vines, with a cover made of a collage of autumn leaves preserved by a clear varnish.

"This is beautiful," he said.

"Aye," Gnorrin agreed. "You know your letters?"

"Um, I can write, if that's what you mean."

"Wonderful. Select whatever else you like, then."

Vincent smiled and added a simple quill pen and a single inkwell. Gnorrin paid for the items, and they bade farewell to the shop's owner.

"Thank you," Vincent said as they began the journey home.

"My pleasure, lad."

"Maybe, but I still feel guilty. You've given me so much, and I have no way to repay you."

"And you have no need to." He paused. "I know it isn't something you wish to think about, but if Blade is unsuccessful, you will need money to get by." Vincent certainly didn't wish to think about it, and made no comment. Gnorrin continued. "You said you know your letters. Another scribe would be more than welcome in town."

"Yes, I know my letters. But I doubt I know *your* letters. Somehow we are able to communicate verbally, but I have this feeling we're really not speaking the same language. I'm able to read what I see written here, but I don't know you'd be able to read what I write."

"How do you mean?"

"I don't know. Don't you find it odd that two people from different worlds are able to comprehend each other?"

Gnorrin thought a moment. "Lad, whatever force brought you here was a powerful magic. I don't imagine it would be beyond its power to impart the ability to comprehend, or even alter, languages. Alter them in some way as to be understood."

Vincent's brow knit. "You sound like you know something you're not telling me. Do you?"

The gnome shrugged. "There are rumors I've heard in the past. Stories of some who might know. We would need to find a druid."

"A druid? In my world, there are stories of druids. The druids and the witches were of the oldest religions, supposedly."

"And here. Ah, Vincent, our world has changed so much. The old legends tell of magic so powerful that the magic of today is pale by comparison. It used to be said one supreme mage could wield power enough to affect half the world. Dragons abounded in the old tales. There are few today, and even the most powerful mages cannot do anything like what the legends hold."

"Dragons?" Vincent breathed.

"Aye. Oh, I see. Your world has no such creature?"

"Only in mythology." He shook his head. "So do you believe the stories?"

Gnorrin raised an eyebrow. "Why shouldn't I?"

Vincent shrugged. "Well, legends sometimes grow into something bearing almost no resemblance to the truth," Vincent said. Both walked in silence for a time before Vincent spoke again. "My country is very young. Our history as a civilization reaches back only a couple hundred years. Our documents of our past are fairly intact, so our history should be very accurate." He frowned. "Yet, in our elementary schools, the children are taught lies. When I was young, I was taught the reason our country fought its civil war was because of slavery."

Gnorrin interrupted. "What is so civil about war?"

Vincent smiled. "A civil war is a war in which one nation is divided against itself."

"Ah. A revolution, then."

"Well, you'd call it a revolution if those doing the rebelling win. If they lose, it's called a civil war, I guess." He shrugged. "In our case, it was the established Union of the north against the rebel Confederacy of the south. Anyway, we were taught the North fought the South in order to free the slaves. But in truth, that was only a side issue. It was fought primarily for economic and political reasons. The children are taught, essentially, a legend. A noble one, perhaps, but still not the truth." Vincent suddenly laughed nervously. "I'm sorry. I'm rambling. I tend to do that."

Gnorrin looked up at him. "The truth is important. You should not feel ashamed to believe that." The gnome was silent a moment. "Still, I think you might enjoy having work." Gnorrin rubbed his chin. "Though you'd have to be especially careful not to let too many people know about your origins."

"Why?"

"This is a small town, Vincent. Many of the people here have never been past its borders and never will be. Their beliefs are very shallow. Talk of other worlds would most likely get you branded heretic or some such, and you'd find yourself with plenty of crazed townspeople blaming you as the cause of all their ills."

"I'm guessing you're not one of those who's never been outside the town."

Gnorrin smiled. "You've seen my magic. Displaying it in public here would alarm most people. I've learned most of my craft during travels. Blade and I have been companions on many a trip."

"Do you really think Blade can find some clue as to my arrival here?"

"I don't know. I'm sorry, but I wouldn't get my hopes up."

Vincent stared dejectedly at the dirt road as they walked along. Gnorrin remained silent, and Vincent was grateful for that.

❧ ❦

Blade returned just after sunset. All afternoon, Vincent had thought of Blade's quest, anticipation growing within him. And when the man walked through the door, Vincent's heart began to race. But when he saw the man's face, his hopes fell.

"I was unsuccessful," Blade said as he sat in front of the fire.

"I sort of guessed that from your expression," said Vincent, trying not to succumb to the sense of doom growing inside him.

"I was easily able to follow your trail on the road north for approximately two leagues. There, the road intersects another, and at the crossroads, your trail disappeared."

Vincent blinked. "What do you mean?"

"I mean I could find absolutely no trace of your passage further north on the road, nor on the road running east and west. Not even off the road anywhere surrounding the intersection."

Gnorrin spoke up. "Could the crossroads be the point of his entrance into this world?"

Blade smiled grimly. "It could easily be the spot at which his magic deposited him."

"My what?" Vincent said.

"Pay him no mind, Vincent," said Gnorrin. "He's being his normal suspicious self." He turned to his friend. "You know as well as I that this boy is no more a mage than you are."

Vincent ignored their words, too caught up in his own emotions. He'd thought he was finally heeding the oft-repeated advice of his father by not getting his hopes up. But he realized now that he'd done just that, unconsciously. He shook his head, staring at the floor. "No. No, there has to have been something." He looked up, urgency filling his voice. "Blade, you have to take me there tomorrow."

"For what purpose? I told you nothing was to be found."

"Then you missed something!" Vincent regretted the words as soon as they were uttered. Blade's eyes widened in what Vincent could only interpret as indignation. "I'm sorry," he said quickly. "I didn't mean that the way it sounded. But maybe I'd recognize the surroundings or something." Even to himself, the notion seemed improbable.

"I very much doubt it," Blade said. "There is no point in returning."

As Gnorrin cleared his throat, Vincent noticed the subtle glare the mage cast at Blade. "If you like," Gnorrin said to Vincent, "I'll go with you. Perhaps there is some residue of magic I can detect and possibly trace. It's worth a try," he said.

Vincent nodded. "Thank you. I'd really appreciate that." He rubbed his forehead, then said, "Look, I'm pretty wiped out. I think I'll just go to bed early." The others bade him good night as he rose and left the room.

In the bedroom, Vincent turned up the oil lamp and lay on the bed. He opened the notebook Gnorrin had purchased for him and uncapped the inkwell. Earlier in the day, he had written a summation of all that had happened since his arrival in this new world. He scratched his chin with the tip of the quill, dipped the nib into the inkwell, and continued where he'd left off.

As I feared, Blade returned with no results. He says he was able to follow my trail easily for two leagues, which is about six miles, if my memory serves me right. But then it disappeared, at some crossroads.

I don't know what's up with Blade. He obviously doesn't like me. First he accused me, essentially, of being a liar about being from Earth, and now he's accusing me of being a wizard or something. A mage, they call it here. I don't know if Blade really believes this, or if he's just really upset about losing my trail. He seems to be a very proud guy, very sure of his abilities as a tracker. I'm pretty upset, too. I mean, I guess I didn't really think he'd find a way for me to get home. Still, it would have been nice.

Tomorrow, Gnorrin and I will go to that intersection. I don't know why. It's not as if I expect to find anything Blade missed.

I suppose I should be thankful for one thing, anyway. If I were going to get popped to another world, I could have done much worse than to be taken in by someone like Gnorrin. I could just as easily have wandered off in the direction of someplace unpopulated. I could have starved to death or been eaten by any one of a thousand different nasties.

Still, I'm sure this calm façade of mine will crack pretty soon, especially after I see what Blade saw. Or didn't see. Right now I'm just going with the flow, trying not to go completely nuts. But I want to go home.

Vincent stopped writing, fighting down the lump in his throat. His emotions cycled through anxiety, frustration, despair, and resentment, leaving him drained. With a sigh, he set the book aside so the ink would dry. Then he capped the inkwell, undressed, and turned the wick of the lamp down to its lowest setting. Sleep was not as easy coming, this night.

❧ ❦

Darella sat thinking of the boy as she warmed herself in front of a crackling fire. The portal's luck certainly appeared to be working well for him. He'd fallen into the company of a mage and a man who was, at the very least, an accomplished tracker.

How fortuitous, she realized, that she'd maintained her watch over him. The tracker might just have been able to trace the boy's steps to the cave, had she not made certain such a trace was impossible. She rarely roamed very far from the cave, but in this instance, she'd gone forth with haste. Her magic easily swept any evidence of the boy's passing from the road. No tracker in the world could locate her cave now.

And to make doubly sure she was not discovered, she had cast a very potent spell, one which would eradicate any trace of her magic. Now, even if the tracker brought his mage friend to the intersection where the boy's tracks vanished, he would not be able to detect the magic used to erase them.

A rumble in her stomach reminded her that other things were also important to think about, and she turned her attention to feeding herself and the children in her womb. Her divinations had revealed she carried twins, a boy and a girl. They would be the latest in her line, and hopefully the last. Darella found child-rearing to be a nuisance. This time, at least, the experience should prove to be interesting.

❧ Two ❧

Vincent woke to a gentle rapping on the bedroom door. He rubbed his eyes and propped himself up on his elbows. Pale light came in through the window. Peeking outside, Vincent saw it was barely past dawn. There was another rap on the door. "I'm up," he croaked, then did his best to live up to the words.

His desperate need to see the infamous intersection in the road had faded somewhat overnight. The idea that he might learn something new was a slight one now. This time, he told himself, he'd definitely keep his hopes in check.

Vincent yawned as he sat on the edge of the cot, thinking of how desperately he needed a shower. A toothbrush would be nice, too, he thought, trying to ignore the feeling of morning mouth. The door opened and Gnorrin stepped inside with a bowl of steaming water and a rag. "You read my mind," Vincent said.

"I most certainly did not!" Gnorrin said, offended. "I'd never do so without your permission."

Vincent chose to simply wash his face rather than question the seriousness of the statement. The hot water felt wonderful, but what he really wanted was the full works, including a good shampooing.

"Breakfast is waiting, by the way," Gnorrin said.

"I'll just be a minute," Vincent replied as his friend left the room. After mopping down his face, he rubbed the wet rag through his hair, hoping it would do some good. He finished with a few swipes in the underarms. Then he put the bowl aside and dressed. He donned his own clothing, rather than Blade's uncomfortable outfit. When he was ready, he joined Gnorrin in the kitchen.

"Where's Blade?" he asked.

"He had some business to attend to. Today's exploration will be just the two of us, it seems."

Vincent nodded, silently grateful for that. He turned his attention to the breakfast Gnorrin served him. It consisted of a hot cereal similar to oatmeal, but not quite as tasty. Vincent decided the gloppy mess could use some brown sugar and cinnamon. Or fruit. Or something. Anything. Gnorrin seemed to love the stuff, which led Vincent to determine that gnomes prefer bland food to balance out their love of garish clothing.

Vincent wasted no time trying to actually taste the cereal, but gulped it down so they could be on their way. Minutes later, they were.

For some time, they walked in silence, Vincent taking in his surroundings. Some of the landscape he recognized, having seen it during the brief time span he actually recalled prior to collapsing in front of Gnorrin's cottage. Eventually they reached a point where he believed he'd first come to awareness upon his arrival in this world.

As they continued, Gnorrin asked him many questions about his life on Earth, and Vincent obligingly answered. He was thinking about home, anyway, so he figured he might as well talk about it. His own curiosity about this world could wait until the return trip, assuming their quest would be as fruitless as Blade's had been.

It took about two hours to reach the intersection Blade had mentioned. But to Vincent, it seemed like ten. His back and feet were killing him, and he was sure several blisters had popped. How had he managed to walk so far, before? Gnorrin didn't seem the least bit tired, though. Vincent looked down at his overhang of stomach and felt himself flush with shame.

"Where do these roads go?" he finally asked, looking in either direction.

Gnorrin stood at his side and nodded to the north. "Another four leagues or so in this direction would bring us to the town of Treehill. The road west skirts the edge of the marsh, then forks at the mouth of the forest, one road continuing west, the other north, then northwest along the perimeter of the woods. The road east leads to the edge of the foothills before splitting to run along the base of the mountains in either direction."

Vincent sighed and shook his head. "And there's no telling which direction I came from." He looked down the roads, not knowing what he expected to see. What he did see was a lot of nothing.

Gnorrin, however, paid no attention to the roads, but to the intersection itself. Vincent watched as his friend scooped some dirt into his hand. Waving his other hand over the dirt, Gnorrin mumbled something quietly. After a moment or two, he tossed the dirt to the ground and clapped away the excess.

"What was that all about?" Vincent asked.

With a frown, Gnorrin said, "I had hoped to determine that some magic had been used upon this area. Some sort of spell that hid or erased your trail. But I sensed nothing. It's as though you simply appeared right here, then made your way down the road until you reached my cottage." He shook his head. "But if that were true, I should definitely detect something."

Vincent nodded, and continued gazing down each road. "Should we bother to try another direction?"

Gnorrin was silent for a time, also scanning the horizon. "We could," he said. "But Blade has already done so, and at this point I wouldn't even know what to look for. We might stumble upon something completely by accident, but I'd say the chances of that are like finding spit in the sea."

Vincent's heart sank. Blade had been right. It *was* a wasted trip. Depression washed over him, and he sat in the dirt in the middle of the intersection. It wasn't fair. It just wasn't! Questions swam through the despair in his mind, but he couldn't sort them out. There were too many. Too many unanswerable questions, and certainly far too much despair.

He sat there for a long time, Gnorrin maintaining a respectful silence. Vincent felt tears sliding down his cheeks, but he didn't care. He wanted to go home. That's all. Just to go home. He sniffed, then took a deep breath. He looked up at Gnorrin, who returned his gaze with a look of compassion.

Then Vincent stood, brushing the dirt from his jeans. "Ready?" he asked.

Gnorrin nodded, and together they set off.

They walked quietly for a while, then Vincent said, "You mentioned something about druids yesterday. How would a druid be able to help me?"

The gnome shrugged. "I do not know for certain one would be able to help at all, honestly. As I told you, druids were the original users of magic. They were the first to harness its forces, the first to unlock the secrets of the elements, the first to truly learn the mysteries of the world."

"And so they are the ones with the most knowledge, the ones who might know what brought me here."

"In theory," said Gnorrin. "The problem is I don't have a clue how to find a druid. I don't even know if there are any remaining. I've certainly never known one."

Vincent's stomach knotted with each passing moment. "So I'm really stuck here. There's no evidence to give any idea of how I got here. No druids to be found. No answers at all. Does that about sum it up?"

His friend nodded. "That would be the thick and thin of it. At least, for the present. One can never tell what the future may bring."

"Super."

Vincent chose not to pick Gnorrin's brain about his new home as they traveled. Instead, he did his best to come to grips with the fact that he wasn't going home any time soon. This wasn't the easiest of tasks, but he made the attempt.

Once back, they entered the cottage. Gnorrin went straight to the kitchen. "I'll heat up some lunch."

Vincent headed straight for his room. "I'm too tired to eat. Need to lie down for a while."

In the room, Vincent collapsed on the cot. His back was a bundle of knots, and his feet were throbbing. He kicked off his shoes and stretched out, giving some ease to his aching neck and back. Throwing an arm over his eyes to block out the sunlight streaming in the window, he was soon asleep.

When he woke, the sun was lower in the sky, but there were a few hours of daylight left, he could tell. He was still stiff, but no longer in agony. Thinking the padding in his shoes would feel better than only socks, he put them back on. Then he picked up his tape player and headphones before leaving the room.

Gnorrin was asleep in his chair when Vincent reached the main room. Though he tried to walk quietly past his friend, the gnome woke with a start. "Ah. You're awake. Hungry, then?"

Vincent shook his head. "Not really. I was thinking of stepping outside for a bit."

"Fine, fine. There's a small stream out behind here, just through the brush. I've found it to be a nice place to gather one's thoughts."

"Thanks. I won't be very long," he said as he left.

Once outside, he found the stream easily. It was a lovely little brook, only a few feet wide and shallow. It was cool, though, under the trees flanking the water. Vincent shivered, wishing he at least had long sleeves. He walked along the stream for a while, enjoying the sound of the rushing water.

The water looked pure and delicious. But he had no thirst, in addition to no hunger. His stomach was a knot, and his mind was spinning again with all the unanswered questions.

With an overwhelming sense of futility, he sat on a large rock beside the stream. Absently, he reached inside his vest pocket and pulled out his headphones, placing them to his ears. He reached in again and turned on the player, leaning back against the stone, hoping to forget his situation in the music.

But it was a sad song, and only served to make him feel homesick and sorry for himself. As it faded, Vincent shut off the player and removed the headphones. He never should have turned the thing on in the first place. He stood, straightening his vest and tucking the headphones into one of its pockets.

He thrust his hands into his jeans pockets, looking at the land around him. He could see the cottage through the trees, about a quarter mile off, looking too story-bookish for its own good. The huge willow hung its sad branches over its roof, as though dusting it off. It was quaint and cozy, inviting and warm. But to Vincent, it was alien. As picturesque as it was, the cottage still represented his predicament, still reminded him he wasn't where he belonged.

With a sigh, he made his way toward it.

❧ ☙

The following day, Vincent and Gnorrin went into town again to pick up his new wardrobe. The last stop was *Tarel's Apparel*. Gnorrin paid the balance due, then Vincent stepped into the store's single fitting room to change from Blade's loaner clothes into one of his own new outfits.

The natural-hued breeches and medium brown tunic were loose, though not baggy. The sleeves of the tunic ended midway between elbow and wrist. There was no collar, just a slight V-neck. Best of all, the tunic was very roomy. Vincent had always been self-conscious about being overweight, and often wore vests and sweaters over his shirts to partially conceal his gut. Sometimes it even worked. He smiled. He was very pleased with everything, though the boots would take some getting used to. They weren't quite as comfortable as sneakers, but he'd adjust.

He thanked Tarel again as he and Gnorrin left.

"Now you look a little less conspicuous," Gnorrin said as they stepped into the street. "Except for your spectacles, but you say you need them to see."

"To see well, anyway." He was quite aware of how people looked oddly at his face. The glasses did seem to stand out.

Vincent stopped in the road, causing Gnorrin to look inquiringly at him. They stood in front of *The Nib and Quill*. The new clothing had reminded Vincent of how generous Gnorrin was being. The thought of getting a job didn't appeal to him at all, but he didn't want to be a freeloader. He looked down at his friend. "Go on ahead. I'll catch up with you."

Five minutes later, he fell into step beside the gnome. "Guess who has a job?" He smiled. "I start tomorrow."

"Very good! How much did old Mepis agree to pay you?"

Vincent's face fell. "Oops."

The next day, Vincent walked into town for his first day as clerk at *The Nib and Quill*. He joined the proprietor inside the building to discuss salary. Vincent felt like an idiot for not bringing the subject up before, but attributed his forgetfulness to the fact that his choices of occupation seemed rather limited, so it wasn't a critical factor. Fortunately, it had given him the chance for Gnorrin to tell him about the coin of the realm.

"The job pays five coppers a day," said Mepis. "And that's just for runnin' the shop. Seein' fit the customers get what they want. Now, eventually, you'll become a

21

scribe. And that's a commission kind of thing. Dependin' on what the customer needs done, that determines what you get."

Vincent nodded. That seemed fair. The commission part, anyway. He had no idea if five coppers a day would be adequate. Gnorrin really couldn't give him a basis for comparison with Earth wages. "What are the shop's hours?" he asked.

"We open a couple hours before mid-day and stay open 'til a few hours after." Mepis grunted, as if he considered the hours more than fair for anyone wanting their goods or services.

"What about days off?"

"What about 'em?"

"Well, do I work all seven days, or what?"

Mepis hesitated, hemming and hawing to himself. "Well, we're closed on Firstday of each week, but I could really use you for a bit, then. For cleaning and suchlike. After worship, of course."

Vincent frowned slightly. "Of course."

"Other than that," Mepis continued, "if you need a day off, let me know the day before. Just don't make it habit."

"Right. So, five hours a day, six days a week. Plus, what? An hour on Firstday. What do I get paid that day? One copper?" Mepis grunted an assent, which told Vincent he'd hoped the boy would do the work for nothing. "So we're talking thirty-one coppers a week."

Mepis thought for a moment. "Yes. Yes, that's right." He shook his head. "You're good with your numbers, as well, Vincent. I'm surprised you're in search of a job with such skills. You youngfolk," he muttered. "Never with your heads in the right places."

Vincent played with the buckle on his new belt as he studied Mepis. The man was middle-aged, yet spoke as though he were ancient. "You're what? Maybe forty-five?"

Mepis chuckled, running a gnarled hand through his dark, thinning hair. "Be fifty this very month. Gettin' on, Vincent." He rubbed his chin. "Old Gnorrin says you're from pretty far away. Must be. Never heard the name Vincent before. What lands you come from?"

"Um... Penn's Woods," he said, thinking quickly.

Mepis nodded wisely. "I knew it. Could tell from your accent."

Vincent smiled and stifled a laugh. "You seem to know a good many things, Mepis."

"Aye, that I do. Studied at the best schools, I did. Hobnobbed with some of the smartest folk in the land."

Vincent smiled. "Really? Did you know Sagan the Astronomer?"

Mepis blinked, his eyes raising. After a moment's hesitation, he said, "'Course I did. He and I used to hunt together years ago. Yes. Quite a shot with a bow, he was."

"Uh, huh. I'll bet. How about—"

Mepis shook his head. "Nay. No time to talk about old friends. Time to set up." Mepis rose and headed to the front area of the shop, motioning for Vincent to follow. There, they began opening procedures. The front of the building was basically an enclosed porch with wooden flaps that closed down over the sides. Mepis unlatched each of these from wooden anchors on the floor, pushing them up with a pole, which also held them in place, forming a shaded area under which patrons could stand and examine the wares on display. Vincent helped him secure the poles and uncover all the goods on several tables. The shutters weren't airtight, and the coverings prevented wind and rain that often blew through the cracks from damaging the merchandise. Mepis took the folded canvases inside.

When he returned, he pulled a stool out from under the sales desk and sat. He reached under again and pulled out a wooden box. He opened it, displaying a number of coins of various denominations, primarily copper. "You make your change out of this. Keep the money out of sight of the customers, below here." He put the box aside. "Now, let me show you the different items we have for sale." Mepis indicated each selection as he spoke of them. "First, our pens. These ones here are the most popular. They're the cheapest," he explained. "Very plain. Narrow, regular, and wide nibs. And the more fancy ones." He waved his hand over a variety of pens, including ones with feathers, others with intricate carvings in the wooden handles, and still others with handles made of semi-precious metals, rare woods, or bone.

"Next, our papers." He indicated the rows of papers held down by a variety of fancy paperweights. "Pretty simple. Low quality here, moving to high quality here." Vincent looked over the papers, at their variety of color and texture. He nodded as Mepis explained the prices of each. "The weights are for sale, too, in case I hadn't mentioned it."

Next, he showed Vincent the assortment of inkwells and bound paper books. "And last, our supply of inks. Again, lower quality to higher quality." Mepis puffed up with pride. "The good ones I make myself."

"Really?"

"Indeed. They're damned good inks, Vincent. In fact, I'm often asked by merchants from Dynsa if I'll sell my inks to them. I always say no. Why would I want another merchant to pass my wares off as his own? No, sir. I won't do it. Likely I'd sell more that way, but it's a matter of pride."

"I understand. I don't blame you. Will you show me how to make ink?"

Mepis rubbed his chin thoughtfully. "Perhaps someday, boy. We'll see how you work out here, first, yes?"

"Sure. So tell me about being a scribe. What do you do, exactly?"

"Well, quite frankly, I write a lot of messages. Folks who don't know their letters come to me and tell me what to write, so's they can send messages by courier to friends and family." He shrugged. "The rest of the time I mostly copy things. Folks'll bring in things they need copied. If you're looking for an adventuresome job, boy, this isn't it."

"So how much business do you really do here? I mean, how many customers would I expect in a normal day?"

"Oh, two or three."

"Two or three? You're kidding."

"Sometimes none, sometimes ten. Hard to tell."

"How do you stay in business?"

"Well, I'm the only scribe in town. Doesn't cost me anything to keep the place open."

"It does now that you have to pay me."

"True, but having you here will give me time to make more inks and get more paper. I get the paper from the city. Can get lots of things wholesale there. And in fact, I'm learning to make my own paper, too. So that'll be another profit-maker." Mepis shook his head. "Don't you fret about the business, boy. I might not be swimming in riches, but I'm doing all right. Now, you just carry on. Get to know the wares and their prices. You're a bright lad. You'll get to know the different qualities of goods right quickly. I'll be in the back if you need me."

Vincent sighed as Mepis entered the building. He glanced over the selection of papers, inks and pens. Mepis was right. The differences in quality weren't difficult to see. Yet he could only study them for so long. "What I wouldn't give for a book to read," he muttered.

      ❧ ❧

I never thought five hours could drag so long. I had a whopping three customers today. Actually, I had two and Mepis had one. A person had left something to be copied and just came to pick up the order. As for the other two, I sold one bottle of ink (cheap) and five sheets of paper (not-so-cheap). Mepis seemed to think this a fairly profitable day. And I guess it really was. What he took in, just with those few customers, will stock his larder for a week. There are no utility bills to pay here. No rent or mortgage payments, though there are taxes and things. I don't know much about those. Nevertheless, it's truly a simple way to live. No wonder he can survive on so few customers.

Gnorrin stopped by at the end of my shift and we stopped for a bite to eat at a nice little tavern before coming back here to his place. Naturally he asked me all about my day, and I did my best to give an accurate description of the boredom I suffered. I guess the day wouldn't have been so bad if Mepis had been out there to talk to. I mean, the man's not too well staffed in the brain department, but at least I could wheedle out of him more things I'll need to know in order to get by here. Unfortunately, he stayed inside the whole time.

Blade hasn't been around all day. Gnorrin said he was out looking for work. He didn't say of what sort, and I didn't ask, since Gnorrin's tone of voice wasn't very positive. I got the impression he wasn't too keen on the kind of work Blade was looking for. With a name like "Blade," who knows what sort of activities he'll be up to?

I shouldn't jump to conclusions, though. Blade is an imposing man, with a very powerful presence. He looks like a nasty son of a bitch, actually. Still, there's something I instinctively trust about the guy, even though he doesn't trust me. Maybe it's because he's Gnorrin's friend. I have the feeling he's a very private person, though, and I doubt I'll really know or understand him anytime soon.

      ❧ ❧

Vincent sat politely at the dinner table a few days later, watching Gnorrin ladle stew into his bowl. He frowned. "I don't want to sound disrespectful, or ungrateful, but I've been here for over a week now, and every day we've had stew for supper."

Gnorrin paused in his ladling. "You don't like stew?"

"No, I love stew. Really. But I'm kind of fond of variety, too."

"I'm sorry. I'm just so used to having stew all the time, except when I don't eat at home. I admit, I'm not much of a cook. Stew is easy, keeps well, tastes good, and you can make one big pot that'll last a good long time. It just suits my needs well."

"In other words, you're used to being a bachelor." Gnorrin grunted and continued ladling. "So how come there isn't a Mrs. Gnorrin?"

24

"I'm barely over a hundred. Don't rush me."

"Don't rush you? Geez. When do gnomes get married?"

Gnorrin sat and promptly began eating. "My parents were in their early two-hundreds when they married," he said. "I don't see why I should be any different."

"Wow. So what's the normal life span of gnomes?"

"Oh, about six hundred to seven hundred years, usually. Give or take fifty."

"Wow," Vincent repeated. He ate in silence for a bit, then said, "When do you expect Blade will be back?"

Gnorrin shrugged. "When he finds work."

"And what kind of work is he looking for, exactly?"

"Any number of things. Blade has many skills. Tracker. Hunter. Swordsman."

"Mercenary work?"

"Something like that."

"Where'd he go to look?"

"Probably Dynsa."

Vincent finished his small helping of stew, wiped his mouth, and leaned back in his chair. "You don't sound too thrilled. Why?"

Gnorrin was silent for a while, eating. Vincent knew he'd struck some sort of nerve. There was a flicker of what he thought was pain across Gnorrin's brow. Finally, the gnome spoke. "Blade and I used to be companions in this line of work. On the last job we were on, I lost a friend. The first friend I ever made after leaving home. He was a dwarf, named Blôrain. I miss him, Vincent. And I've not been too anxious to go gallivanting about. I've spent the last year mostly just sitting around here, getting used to living near the town, gaming with Blade on those occasions when he visits."

"Blade has been trying to get you to go back out again, hasn't he?"

Gnorrin nodded. "He says I waste too much time in mourning. Perhaps he is right."

"It's never easy to lose a friend."

Gnorrin looked up. "You've lost a friend, too?"

"None as close as Blôrain apparently was to you, but, yes. I've lost a friend or two." Vincent was silent, remembering friends. And family. And home. He stood and picked up his empty bowl and mug. "Excuse me," he said, and took them to the sink.

The sink was a basin in the countertop, with a wooden pipe hanging over as a faucet. The end of the faucet opened by unscrewing it, much like a garden hose. The pipe ran up the outside of the cottage to a large tub. Rainwater would roll off the roof into gutters, which funneled it around the cottage roof into the basin. Gravity pulled the water down from the basin into the faucet and down the drain through another pipe leading outside to be dumped. Since the pipe was very narrow, there wasn't much water pressure. When there was no rain to fill the basin, water could be hauled from the nearby creek. Vincent cleaned his dinnerware and set them aside to dry.

As he stood leaning against the counter, staring out the open window above the sink, Gnorrin cleared his throat. "Fancy a game?" he asked, indicating the board in the other room. Vincent shook his head. Gnorrin tried again. "Lovely day out. How about a walk?"

Vincent was quiet for a moment. "I think I just might. But if it's all the same to you, I think I'd prefer to go alone." He smiled gratefully as Gnorrin nodded in understanding. "I'll see you later," he said, and stepped outside.

Vincent didn't know his way around, other than the road to town. And he had no desire to go there. So he cut back through the small patch of woods until he came to the creek, which he proceeded to follow.

It was, indeed, a lovely spring day, Vincent thought as he followed the burbling creek. He corrected himself. "Season of Green," they called it here. That made sense, he thought, for them to call the season something else. They had different names for the months and days of the week, too. Then again, he wondered, if stew could be stew both here and on Earth, why couldn't spring be spring?

Earth. The thought struck him as amusing. He was no longer on Earth. For years, he'd dreamed of becoming an astronomer, studying the stars and planets and hoping one day to find signs of intelligent life elsewhere in the universe. And now, here he was, not even through with one semester of college as an astronomy major, and he was on another planet. Brought here by some unknown, powerful force, chatting with aliens. If gnomes weren't aliens, he didn't know what were.

The worst part about being here, he thought, was the effect it must be having on his family and friends back home. Did they think he was dead? Or abducted? Or run off to Mexico with some bimbo? He shook his head. No, they'd never think the last. On the other hand, some of his friends might applaud that one. He'd never had any luck with girls. High school had not been a wellspring of dating experiences for him. He hadn't gone to his prom, not wishing to face rejections aplenty from the girls he'd liked to have asked. He'd hoped college might prove more fruitful for him. Now, though, he'd never get the chance to find out.

"Hello." The voice startled him so much he jumped back, tripped over a root, and fell into the creek.

He looked up, his heart racing and his clothes soaking, to see a girl of perhaps fourteen laughing at his predicament. He scrambled to his feet. "Very funny," he said.

"I think so," said the girl.

"It's not nice to scare people," he said as he sloshed out onto dry land.

"It's not wise to wander around so preoccupied." The girl had stopped laughing and was sizing him up.

Vincent wrung out his clothing as best he could and was grateful he had not been carrying his cassette player. The water would've ruined it. He looked at the girl, so studiously appraising him. She was strikingly pretty, with pitch black hair and violet eyes. Quite beautiful, really, he thought, though still young. She was dressed in a dark violet cloak and plain shift, tied at the waist with a rope. A knife hung in a sheath from the rope. Even dressed so plainly, she was still gorgeous, he thought. Too bad she wasn't older.

She spoke again. "Are you done staring at me yet?"

Vincent suddenly realized he'd been gazing into her eyes for quite some time. "Sorry," he said, feeling his face flush with embarrassment. "I am, if you are." He smiled, hoping she didn't have an inclination to use the knife.

"Mm. Yes, I think so." She paused before saying thoughtfully, "I've never seen you around before."

"I'm sort of new to these parts. My name's Vincent."

"I'm Ariaziane. And I won't say anything about how odd your name is if you won't say the same about mine."

"Deal," Vincent said, not really knowing if her name was any odder than the norm.

She stared at his face. "I have never seen spectacles like those, before. You wear them all the time?"

He nodded. "My vision isn't so great."

"I would imagine not, if you wear them constantly. I tried a pair once. Everything was so big! I could hardly walk straight. Though I did not trip and fall into a creek." Vincent frowned in mock offense at her joke. "So where are you going?"

Vincent shrugged. "Nowhere in particular. Just walking."

"Obviously. Where did you start?"

Vincent laughed. "You sure ask a lot of questions." The girl smiled in response, but offered no apology. "About half a mile or so back that way. A friend's place."

"You're staying with him?"

"Until I can get my own place, yes." His answer sounded strange to him, for until that moment, the thought of obtaining his own home had not occurred to him. The idea of settling down in this world had never truly been more than a tiny voice at the back of his mind. "I'm working, in town. At The Nib and Quill."

"Really? I have to go there tomorrow to pick up some paper for the Sisters."

"Who?"

"The clerics at the town abbey. That's where I stay."

"So you're a cleric-in-training?"

"Not exactly." Her voice softened. "I'm an orphan. I've been raised by them for the past eight years."

"What about before that?" Vincent immediately regretted asking so personal a question to someone he'd just met.

Ariaziane shrugged and said, "With my parents, until they died." She was quiet a moment. "And then I was taken in by the clerics, who have brought me up ever since." She paused awkwardly. "I should really be getting back. They worry so."

"Where's the abbey from here?"

The girl pointed. "That way, through the trees."

"Can I walk you there?"

"I don't think it would be a good idea. Thank you, though. Are you working tomorrow?"

"Yes."

"Good. I'll see you there."

Vincent smiled as she moved off. He watched her disappear through the brush, shaking his head at himself. She was a girl, barely past childhood, he thought. Still, she *was* beautiful.

He turned, heading back toward the cottage. He was dripping wet, which was becoming more and more annoying. So when he came upon the large stone he'd visited before, he spread himself out upon it, taking advantage of the sun.

Some time later, he woke to a familiar voice. "Well," Gnorrin chirped. "There you are! Had a nice walk?"

Vincent yawned, turned his head, and smiled at him. "And a nice swim, though that was unplanned."

Gnorrin chuckled. "Did a tree push you in?"

Vincent began a sarcastic reply, but cut it short. Was Gnorrin kidding, or were there really trees capable of doing so on this world? He shook his head. "Just wasn't paying attention to where I was stepping." He sat up. "You up for the game you offered earlier?" He jumped down off the rock and the pair headed back to the cottage.

❧ ❦

The day had been slow thus far at *The Nib and Quill* and Vincent was glad he'd brought his journal with him.

I surprised Gnorrin by cooking dinner last night. Purchased some cubed meat from the town butcher and some fresh veggies. With the addition of some skewers from the smith, we were able to have steak kabobs over the fire pit. Nice change of pace from stew. Gnorrin seemed to appreciate it.

Every night over dinner, I question Gnorrin about this world. I learned last night that there are seven days to the week, which I'd just been assuming, before. Good thing I was right, or I would have really embarrassed myself in front of Mepis. There are also three weeks to the month, and sixteen months, plus two week-long holidays, one in summer and one in winter. Only they don't call their seasons by those names. Mid-year Week is between the Season of the Sun and the Season of the Harvest. And Celebration Week, which I'd evidently just missed when I arrived here, is between the Season of Sleep and the Season of Green. This makes the length of their year pretty similar to that of Earth. The only oddities, really, are that the beginning of their year isn't in the middle of winter, like I'm used to, but at the beginning of spring. Makes more sense, actually. I think I read somewhere we used to start the calendar year in spring, back on Earth, a long time ago. Wonder why we ever switched?

Vincent stopped in his writing and cast a glance out to the street, looking for any potential customers. He scratched his chin.

I'm not too fond of the straight razors used for shaving, here. Nasty things. Gnomes evidently don't grow facial hair, so Gnorrin doesn't even have one. Blade must, since he's clean-shaven.

I shaved my beard off a couple months before my arrival here. It's so strange. Having grown the thing when I was fifteen, I was always taken for someone older. Now without it, everyone thinks I'm younger than seventeen. Time to grow it back, I guess.

I've been hoping the girl I met yesterday will be stopping by, like she said. I mean, I like Gnorrin, but he's over a hundred. Not exactly in my age group. Blade's got to be in his thirties, which I normally wouldn't consider problematic. But he's not open at all. And there's the little issue of his distrust of me.

As for the girl, I haven't the slightest idea in the world how to spell her name. The last part is pronounced like 'Diane,' so we'll assume the spelling is similar. The first part is like 'Mariah,' though I doubt it's spelled with an 'h.' Maybe just four letters. Aria. So altogether it would be Ariaziane. Pretty. Just like she is.

Shit, what am I saying? She's still a kid, even though she seemed pretty intelligent for her age. I wonder if we could be friends. I'd really like someone closer to my own age to do things with. Not that there's anything here to do that I couldn't just as easily do with Gnorrin, but truthfully, I can't picture myself having much fun with him. He seems happiest just hanging out in his cottage and playing chess, which he doesn't call chess, naturally. As for Blade... assuming he ever decides to like me... he's just so... regimented. Strict. Intense. Almost like he doesn't permit himself to have fun, for some reason.

Ariaziane, on the other hand, seems like she'd be a lot of fun. She could be the little sister I never had.

Vincent stopped and stared at the sentence he'd just written. Sister. The word made him remember his sister on Earth, fifteen years his elder and his favorite person in the world. He had a lot of fun with her, spending summers at her home. She had been a teacher in West Virginia and he would go there for a month at a time. They'd play miniature golf, go to movies, play tennis. She'd moved to North Carolina recently, and their frequent visits with each other became much rarer. He frowned to himself. And now that he was here, wherever here was, their visits would be non-existent. He put his pen down and waited for the page to dry. Suddenly he didn't feel like writing any more.

He looked up. True to her word, Ariaziane was coming to pick up paper for the clerics at the abbey. He thought about moving the journal, not wanting her to see he'd been writing about her. But the ink was not yet dry, and besides, he told himself, she probably didn't know how to read, if the ability was as rare as Gnorrin implied. Even if she could read, she couldn't read English.

She greeted him and smiled as she stepped over to the selection of papers. She gazed at his journal. "You're writing?"

Vincent smiled and pushed it aside without closing it. "A journal of my time here."

She lifted her eyes from his journal to look at him strangely. "Doesn't sound too exciting."

"Oh, you'd be surprised."

Ariaziane chose the goods she needed and paid for them. "Thank you," she said as she placed the change in her pouch.

"So... what are you doing later?" he asked.

"Why?"

"I thought you might like to do something together. Maybe you could show me around a little."

She looked at him in a way that told him she found his suggestion amusing. "Well," she said slowly, "I have a couple more errands to do here in town, and I have to take care of the horses—"

"Horses? The abbey has horses?"

"Six of them, yes."

"Do you ride?"

"Of course. Don't you?"

"Well, no. Not really." He felt uncomfortable, knowing she found it quite unnatural for someone not to ride horses. "I'd love to learn. Can you teach me?"

"Probably. If I get permission." She paused, thinking. "Stop by after you finish here. The stables are at the rear of the abbey. You know how to get to the abbey from here?" Vincent nodded. He'd watched for the road on his way to work. "Good," she continued. "I'll make the Sisters aware you'll be coming by."

She bade him farewell and smiled as she walked away from the shop. Vincent waved as she peeked over her shoulder once, to see if he was still watching her. And he smiled to himself as he continued his usually boring shift at *The Nib and Quill.*

Finding the abbey wasn't difficult. The building sat about a hundred yards off the road to town, through a small stretch of wooded area. Woods surrounded its grounds, but the abbey itself sat on about three acres of cleared land. He could see the corral in the back and headed in that direction.

He reached the split rail fence and had started toward the stables when Ariaziane came bounding out toward him on a large brown horse. She reached the fence where he stood and pulled back on the reins. The horse slowed to a stop.

Vincent smiled up at her. "Hey."

"Yes?"

"Yes what?"

"You said 'hey.'"

"Yeah. Sorry. I meant 'hello.'"

"What does 'yeah' mean?"

Vincent frowned and stared at his boots. Communication was going to be rockier than he'd expected. Gnorrin ignored his odd phrasings, but this poor girl was truly baffled by his expressions. He looked at her again. "'Yeah' means 'yes.' And 'hey' means 'hello.' We talk a bit differently where I'm from, I guess."

Ariaziane sighed in frustration. "No guess. It's certain. Well, no matter. Come on." Vincent climbed over the fence and onto the horse's back as she beckoned him to do. He held tightly onto the saddle as they trotted around the corral. "You've never ridden before?"

Vincent firmed his grip on the bouncing saddle. "Well, I recall two horses when I was very little, when I was living with my mother out in the country, but I was no more than three or four at the time. If I rode them, I really don't remember."

Eventually, they reached the stable and dismounted, Vincent trying his best to do so in a graceful fashion. Ariaziane looked at him curiously. "You didn't live with your mother after you were four?"

"No. I lived with her parents. She moved away."

Ariaziane began removing the saddle from the animal. "Why?"

"I've never been totally clear on that, myself. We kept in touch, but I only ever saw her four times after that. She came home when her mother died, which was only a few years later. And I visited her when I was thirteen, and again when I was fifteen, and then she flew home for the holidays last year."

Ariaziane stopped her work and stared at him. "She *flew?*" she asked excitedly. "She's a mage?"

Oops, Vincent thought. "Ah, no. Can we change the subject?"

Ariaziane shrugged and put the saddle away. "If you want. What do you want to talk about?"

Vincent watched as she pulled out a currycomb and began grooming the horse. "I don't know. I guess I was just hoping to get to know you a little better."

"What do you want to know?"

"Well, what do you do with your time? I mean, when you're not running errands for the folks here, or taking care of the horses."

"I cook, occasionally. We rotate turns. And do laundry, and other such things."

"What about your free time?"

She shrugged again. "Not much. Go for walks. That's what I was doing when I met you yesterday. Go riding, if it's nice enough."

Vincent nodded. "You're bored."

The girl laughed nervously. "Why do you say so?"

"I can hear it in your voice. You're not happy here."

She stopped brushing and put the comb away. "I'm satisfied here. I'm grateful for everything they've done for me. I could have turned out a street thief. Or beggar. Or worse."

"You don't feel you're accomplishing anything. You feel trapped."

She looked him in the eye. Her voice was quiet. "Yes." She turned away. "But I shouldn't..."

"What you shouldn't do is feel guilty about feeling that way. I understand perfectly."

"Truly?"

"Yeah. I do."

"What do you think I should do?"

Vincent sighed. "I wish I could offer a suggestion. Like I said, I'm new around here. More than you know. And I know practically nothing about the customs and everything. I don't know if you're considered too young to do things you might do where I come from, or if you're considered old to do some of them."

"You sound as trapped as I am."

Now it was his turn to laugh. "That's the truth." He shook his head. "I know only five people. You, the guy I work for, Tarel at the clothing store, and Gnorrin and Blade."

"Gnorrin?"

"That's who I'm staying with."

"The gnome who lives outside of town?"

"You know him?"

"No, but..." She shook her head. "I'm sorry. It's rude."

"Go ahead."

"Well, there are things said about him. I don't know if they're true or not, but they certainly are interesting."

"Like what?"

She paused before speaking, looking around to make sure no one could hear. "They say he's a mage."

"Well, I know he knows some magic, if that's what you mean."

Ariaziane's eyes widened. "He does? Honest? How much?"

"I have no idea, really. Since I got here, the focus has really been on me more than on him."

"I'd love to meet him sometime."

"I'm sure we can arrange that. Why don't you come out for dinner tonight? Hope you like stew."

The girl turned her face away. "I don't think I'd be permitted to."

"Why not?"

"Because it's not proper."

"It's just dinner," he said, confused.

"I know, but I still don't think so."

31

Then a thought occurred to him. "Oh, right. You have clerical caretakers. That explains it."

"What do you mean?" the girl said.

Vincent frowned. "Just that religious orders have a nasty habit of trying to keep their followers from experiencing the world."

Ariaziane stared at him. "It's not like that."

"Isn't it?" he spat. "Then why would it not be 'proper' for you to have dinner with us?"

When she averted her eyes, he knew he was closer to the truth than she'd admit. "You sound so bitter," she said finally.

"Religion tends to bring it out in me." He shrugged it off. "Well, if not dinner, would you be able to go for a walk or something?"

"If I'm not gone long." She opened the gate and they walked out. "Wait here. I'll let them know I'm going. Be right back."

She was gone no more than a minute, and when she returned, they set off through the woods toward the creek. Vincent wanted to pry more information out of her, without giving out too much about himself. This wasn't the easiest of tasks.

"So where are you from?" she asked.

He shrugged. "You'd never have heard of it."

"That's okay. How far away?"

"Real far."

"Well, it can't be very far. You don't have any odd accent, so you have to be from reasonably close."

"I don't think so."

"Is there some reason you won't tell me? Are you running from the law?"

"No! Nothing like that."

"Then what? Why won't you tell me? I thought we were friends."

Vincent looked at her, struck by the sense of earnestness in her voice. "Are we?"

"Are we not?"

"No. I mean, yes! I mean, we are! I hope. I'd like very much to be your friend."

She smiled at him. "Good. If I'm going to be your 'little sister,' I should be your friend, as well."

Vincent's mouth hung open. She'd seen his journal entry. And she could read it!

Ariaziane laughed. "You're embarrassed."

He smiled at her, sheepishly. "Sorry," he said. "Look, I didn't mean to presume anything."

"I don't mind," she said. "For some reason I don't understand, I feel quite drawn to you. Like we have something extraordinary in common."

"I find that hard to believe."

"As do I, since I find nothing extraordinary about myself."

Vincent fought back the urge to say he found everything about her extraordinary. Instead, he said, "So what do friends do around here?"

Ariaziane looked at him and shrugged. "The same things friends do anywhere, I would imagine."

Vincent shook his head at himself. "Sorry. Stupid question. I'm still a bit nervous."

"It wasn't stupid at all, and what makes you nervous?"

He stammered a moment. "You do."

"Why in the world would that be?" She laughed.

"Stop it! You're amused by this, aren't you? Planning on pushing me in the creek again?"

"I didn't push you in! You fell! Your mind was off somewhere and you fell in!" She laughed. "You're absent-minded and clumsy."

Vincent pouted. "So friends insult each other. I see." He did his best to seem hurt by her words.

"No. I'm jesting. I did not mean..." She reached out and touched his shoulder. "I'm sorry."

He turned to look at her and was caught in her eyes. His pretended offense was gone and he was overwhelmed by her concern. His heart fluttered and he turned away. "Sorry. I was kidding, too."

"What's wrong, then?"

He smiled awkwardly, still not looking at her. "I'm just nervous."

"So you've said. Why?"

They stopped walking. She stood beside him, forcing him to look at her. "Because you're beautiful," he said. "And I'm always nervous around beautiful girls."

Ariaziane stared bashfully at the ground. "Is there something wrong with thinking I'm beautiful?"

"Oh, no! You are! You're also pretty young."

"I am not! I'm fourteen!"

"Yes, but where I come from, you're barely more than a child."

Before he knew what was happening, her hands were on him, her leg behind him. Then he was falling. He landed hard on his rump. Ariaziane stood over him, seeming quite satisfied with her execution of the move, a look of indignant determination on her face. She abruptly sat, facing him. "Enough. Once and for all, where are you from that a fourteen-year-old is considered a child? And if you won't tell me, you should have a very good reason not to."

As he looked into her violet eyes again, he knew he had to tell her. The prospect of spending time with her was so much more enticing than the thought of living out the rest of his days working for Mepis and living with Gnorrin.

So he did. He hesitated only a moment before telling her everything that had happened to him since arriving. He told her as much about Earth as he felt was important. She sat dumbfounded for half an hour as he talked. And when he was done, she was still speechless. Vincent waited for her to say something, but it became clear that she hadn't a clue what to say. He cleared his throat. "I warned you."

The girl cast a glance at him. "Aye. That you did. Still, for some reason, I believe you. Totally." She stared at him. "What is it about you, Vincent, that makes me want to believe anything you would say to me?"

He shrugged self-consciously. "I don't know. No one's ever said that to me, before. I feel some sort of bond with you. I don't think I could explain it, or even describe it, but there's something there."

Ariaziane stood. "I should be getting back."

"So soon?"

She nodded. "I'm afraid so. I have to be back before dark. You should get back, too. Your friend will be worried."

"You're right." They set off back toward the abbey. "Will I see you tomorrow?"

She smiled. "Would you like that?"

"Of course I would."

"I might be able to stop by your shop." She returned Vincent's smile, slapping him playfully on the arm. "Race you." She dashed off ahead and Vincent bounded after.

Gnorrin was, indeed, worried when Vincent arrived back at the cottage. He apologized and explained the reason for his delay. Gnorrin smiled. "Ah! So that's why you've been in better spirits! A romance!"

"Gnorrin! Get a grip! She's just a kid!"

Gnorrin frowned. "How old is she?"

"Fourteen."

"Fourteen? If she's human, she's not a child. Simple as that. Do the humans where you come from wait until mid-age to begin courting?"

"Mid-age? Gnorrin, a person isn't considered middle-aged on Earth until about forty years old." Vincent thought for a moment. "Though in less developed nations, it's younger." He paused. "Well, now that I think about it, I suppose the ages of dating vary, too. In my country, the average age to begin dating is probably sixteen. Though it seems to be growing younger every year. Other places allow it quite younger. And in times past, girls her age were often already married. Our society's view on that subject seems to change every hundred years or so."

"So what... How did you say it? What's your point, pinhead?"

Vincent shook his head at the words coming from his friend's mouth. He fought back a chuckle. "My point is that during the time and place I was raised, a first-year college student simply did not go out with a girl who's barely high school age."

"As you are quite aware, my friend, you are no longer in the time and place in which you were raised. You've been doing your best to become a part of this society, and that is wise, since it seems to be true that you'll be here for some time. So, why keep to your old ways on this one subject?" He paused. "Now, that's enough about it. You give it some thought." He moved to the kitchen. "Hungry?"

In truth, he was starved. But he thought of how exhausted he was after losing the footrace to Ariaziane. He looked down at his gut and felt a familiar knot of disgust. "A little," he said. "Just a small bowl, thanks."

ॐ ॐ

Vincent sat at the tiny table in the kitchen, his journal open in front of him. He wrote sporadically, occasionally looking up to watch Gnorrin as he busied himself with cleaning the main room of the cottage. *Ariaziane stopped by the shop again, today,* he wrote. *She couldn't go for a walk afterward, but she did sit and talk with me for a bit. She asked me more questions about Earth, and I answered them.*

One thing I did ask her was how she was able to read my journal. As far as I can tell, I'm writing this in English. I haven't shown it to anyone else to see if they can read it. Could my letters show on paper as whatever language passes for the English equivalent here? I've no idea. It seems a valid thought, though, since I tried a little experiment. I took a sheet of paper and wrote a few words in French. And she couldn't read them. Don't know if anyone else here could or not, though.

I have to admit that I've definitely got a crush on her. But, despite what Gnorrin says, I don't think I could bring myself to confess my feelings to her yet. I'm afraid she wouldn't feel the same way. Maybe if I lose some weight. I've tried to before, but any success has always been temporary. Then again, with a decided lack of junk food here, I could have better luck.

Gnorrin was cleaning the small shutters of the window. The shutters didn't form a very tight seal around the open hole, and Vincent wondered idly how the winter months were tolerated in such a dwelling. "Are you sure you don't need any help?" he asked.

"Not a bit, lad, but thank you again for asking," Gnorrin said without looking over at him.

Vincent sighed and scratched the stubble of his face. His beard was growing in and, as usual, it itched. He couldn't wait until the hairs were longer. With a sigh, he turned back to his journal.

I told Gnorrin that Ariaziane would like to meet him, as she has an interest in magic. He seemed hesitant to take on a pupil, but I think he'll at least talk to her, just to appease me. He's a great guy.

The front door opened and Vincent looked up to see Blade enter. He felt a twinge of concern. Despite the fact that the man was friends with Gnorrin, Vincent was afraid of him. To his shock, Blade turned directly to him.

"Good news, Vincent." Blade smiled as he spoke.

A surge of hope welled up inside him. "You found out how I got here?"

But Blade shook his head. "Not quite that good. However, I have obtained a job for you."

"I already have a job."

"You can continue working for Mepis when you return. But for a few days you can make considerably more money than that old braggart is willing to pay you."

Vincent noticed that Gnorrin had taken an interest in Blade's words and was looking at his friend with a strange expression on his face.

"What sort of job?" Gnorrin asked.

Blade turned, still smiling. "Vincent and I will be guards for the tax courier to Dynsa."

Gnorrin shook his head. "Guards? Nay. That is unsuitable for him."

Blade turned to look at Vincent again. "What say you? The job pays three silvers. That's far more than Mepis is giving you."

"I dunno," Vincent said. "It sounds dangerous. I can't defend myself, let alone guard money."

Blade dismissed the protests. "I assure you the danger is slight."

"Blade..." Gnorrin began.

"Now, Gnorrin," his friend said, turning again. "You are not the boy's father. He is old enough to make his own decisions. Besides," he said, his voice turning friendlier, "it was you who told me that I should get to know our new acquaintance better. This will afford us ample opportunity to do just that. We'll have three days and nights together. And you know very well that I shall look out for his safety." He turned once more to Vincent. "What do you say?"

For a minute, he said nothing. Was Blade being sincere? Perhaps he was simply being paranoid, or allowing his preconceived notions of the man to affect his judgement, but Vincent had the slight feeling that Blade wasn't being entirely honest with him. Some little voice at the back of his mind told him that Blade was hiding something.

The thought occurred to him that maybe Blade really did dislike him and that he'd just lied to Gnorrin about safeguarding Vincent's well-being. Maybe the job really was dangerous, and Blade hoped Vincent would get killed.

He should refuse. Obviously, that was the sane choice. He should politely thank him, but state that Mepis wouldn't allow him the time off. Or something like that.

But if he did refuse, how would Blade think of him? Or how would Gnorrin think of him? He might very well take it to be a sign that Vincent didn't trust Blade, which wasn't entirely untrue. But Gnorrin might be offended, since Blade was obviously the gnome's good friend.

He hoped his judgement of Gnorrin was as accurate as he thought it was. In the end, his decision was based on that, more than anything else. Gnorrin wouldn't have a friend who would do what Vincent feared Blade might. Or at least, he hoped not.

"Okay. Sure. I guess so."

"Excellent," Blade said. "We leave at dawn. Gnorrin will notify your employer of your brief absence." He turned to the gnome. "Yes?"

Gnorrin looked up at his friend with a look that told Vincent that he wasn't the only one wondering about Blade's motives. It was a look that didn't instill any confidence in him for his recent decision. "I'll see to it."

Blade excused himself. "I shall see you in the morning, Vincent. Sleep well." He pulled the door closed behind him as he left.

Vincent sat immobile after Blade's departure, the quill pen still in his hand. He looked at Gnorrin. "Did I just agree to something I shouldn't have?"

His friend smiled half-heartedly, then shrugged. "Blade is an excellent swordsman. If you encounter any danger, he is eminently capable of taking care of you. Under normal circumstances, that is. But I still don't like the idea."

Vincent recalled Gnorrin's story of his friend who'd died on an adventure. Likely as not, this was the cause of his concern. As the mage returned to cleaning, Vincent glanced at the journal entry he'd written before Blade's arrival, and wondered if it would be his last.

❧ Three ❧

Vincent shuffled out of the cottage just after dawn. Gnorrin had awakened him half an hour earlier and served him some hot cereal for breakfast. As tired as he was, Vincent didn't mind it being tasteless. He wouldn't want to waste something delicious on still sleeping taste buds.

Blade stood outside waiting for him, two horses with him. Vincent frowned. His brief period on horseback with Ariaziane was certainly not enough preparation for this. "Good morning," Blade said.

Vincent mumbled a polite reply, shifting the backpack Gnorrin had prepared for him from one shoulder to the other. He looked at the horses. Blade's was a handsome black steed, while the one for Vincent was a plain-looking brown mare. The animals, Blade informed him, were from the abbey. Vincent smiled at this, grateful to have a reminder of his new little sister while he was gone. Blade took Vincent's pack and strapped it to the back of Vincent's horse.

To his great relief, Vincent made it into the saddle on the first try. He beamed at Gnorrin, who stood in the cottage doorway, then waved farewell.   No sooner were they out of sight of the cottage than Blade began to ask questions of Earth. And not just general questions, either. Blade's inquiries were very specific. They didn't seem to be those of someone curious about another world or culture, but of a person trying to catch another in a lie.

"Tell me of this land of yours. Pennsylvania, you called it."

"Yes. It means 'Penn's Woods,' named after the father of the man who founded the area. It's one of the fifty states in our country, the United States of America."

"And what of the king of the United States of America?"

Vincent smiled, then explained that his country didn't have a king, but a president. "The difference is that the president is elected by the people. Elections are held every four years."

"Which people elect him?"

"Anyone who votes. Anyone over the age of eighteen is able to, though no one has to if they don't want to."

"You mean to say that even the peasants vote?"

"We have no peasants, Blade. We don't have that type of society. Certainly, we have people who are much poorer than others, but that's the result of circumstances and bad luck, rather than a birthright. We don't believe in that sort of thing."

"How big is your country? How many leagues from end to end?"

"Well, the mainland states are probably about a thousand leagues from east to west. But there are two other states. Alaska is far to the north, and the country of Canada is in between. Hawaii is a chain of islands off the southwest coast."

"Then your states aren't united at all, are they?"

Vincent laughed. "Not in that sense, no."

"What about—"

"Blade," Vincent interrupted. "This is going to be a long trip if you're going to do nothing but grill me about Earth. It's obvious that you don't believe me. I really have no problem with that. I don't care if you believe me."

Blade was silent for a time. Then he said, "I apologize if I have made you uncomfortable. And if you are telling the truth, I apologize all the more. By the end of this trip, I have no doubt that I will either believe you wholeheartedly, or expose you as a fraud. I will either call you friend or foe. If friend, I hope you will forgive my suspicious nature."

"And if foe?"

The man shrugged. "If foe, you'll be dead."

Vincent's heart skipped a beat as he heard the casual remark. His mouth went dry. What, he wondered, would be the basis for Blade's decision?

They passed the remainder of the morning mostly in silence.

At mid-day they stopped along the roadside to eat. Vincent's butt was killing him, but he didn't complain about it. He sat quietly and ate the biscuits and dried meats Blade handed him, suppressing the desire for some stew to dunk the biscuits in. Immediately after eating, they remounted and continued on.

During the afternoon, they encountered the only other travelers they saw that day. The meeting was uneventful, as the pair was headed in the other direction. Blade greeted them respectfully, and they returned greetings the same. Vincent studied them closely, noticing the two men both wore swords and knives at their belts. He noticed Blade wore a knife, but what seemed to be his sword was wrapped in cloth and strapped to his horse's back behind the saddle.

As the sunlight began to fade, Blade announced a stop for the night. He led his horse off the road toward the trees. There was a clearing Vincent hadn't seen from the road, but he had no doubt that it hadn't escaped Blade's keen eye. Blade dismounted and handed his reins to Vincent, who led the animals to the edge of the clearing and tied them to a tree. Blade then instructed him to unsaddle and unpack them, while he cleared a space and began a campfire. By the time Vincent was finished, Blade had a roaring fire going and had begun constructing a large lean-to for shelter.

Vincent recognized the structure as one he'd used when camping with friends when he was much younger. As children, he and his friends had used blankets supported by two tall sticks at one end and held in place by bricks and stones at the bottom. Blade's construct was more sophisticated than that, but the overall effect was the same. When he was finished, he moved to the pile of goods and tossed a bedroll to Vincent, taking the other for himself. He showed him how to unroll it into the lean-to quickly and efficiently, helping him pile the rest of the gear under its protection, between the two bedrolls. Then he said, "I shall return shortly with dinner."

Vincent stood next to the horses, stroking their muzzles. He spoke absently to them, looking at the stars, at the constellations that were so different than those seen from Earth. He sighed, wondering what his loved ones were doing. Were they missing him? Were they mourning him? He shook his head to rid himself of such depressing thoughts. And he wondered what Ariaziane was doing at that moment. In its own way, that thought, too, was depressing.

He gave each horse a final pat before he walked over to the provisions. He was glad to see Blade had packed some of the toilet paper substitute. He'd be needing them before the evening was out, and he certainly didn't know where to look to find them growing wild. Eventually, he crouched in front of the fire, waiting for Blade to return. The heat felt wonderful, even though the night wasn't especially cold. It was relaxing, and he definitely needed to relax.

Aside from Blade's initial interrogation, conversation had been virtually non-existent the remainder of the day. Vincent found it very stressful. He'd kept wanting to start a conversation, but had no idea what to say to the man. He hadn't wanted to risk asking too personal a question and possibly cause Blade to be even more suspicious. So he'd kept his mouth shut and allowed his thoughts to run away with him, making him worry about what he'd do if they were attacked. But now, the warmth of the fire drove such unpleasant scenarios from his mind.

Blade soon returned, carrying two rabbits. Vincent wondered briefly how he'd caught them, but figured this was better left a mystery. Blade tossed one of the dead animals to land at Vincent's feet. Vincent looked at the animal, seeing the bloodstains around the slit throat. He frowned, wondering if Blade really expected him to eat Thumper. When a knife stuck into the dirt beside him, he realized those were exactly Blade's expectations.

"You do know how to skin and gut, don't you?"

"No, not really," he mumbled. Vincent knew dieting wasn't going to be difficult. He winced as Blade chopped off head of his rabbit. Vincent tried not to watch what followed, but was drawn to it like an accident on the highway. He watched Blade hold the animal by the hind legs, then carefully slice the rabbit's hide from pelvis to headless neck, then down each limb to the foot. He then cut off the front feet. In a motion that Vincent felt was far too practiced, Blade peeled the hide off the carcass, still holding it by the rear legs. In spite of the disgust he felt, Vincent couldn't help thinking of sick humor. The terms "bunny-sicle" and "meat pop" ran through his head.

When Blade sliced into the stomach, running his knife from belly to breast, Vincent's growing smirk disappeared. He watched as the internal organs began to spill out. Blade reached inside, pulling out the lungs and remaining viscera. Vincent felt his skin go pale. Then Blade chopped off the rear legs, with the hide still flapping at the end of them, and ran a stick through the body. He held it out to Vincent, who hesitantly accepted it, then surrendered the dead rabbit at his feet to the same procedure.

Blade quickly dressed and skewered the second rabbit, then got up to wash his hands and knife as Vincent held his soon-to-be-dinner over the fire.

As they were eating, Vincent said, "If that's what's required to eat meat, I'll be becoming a vegetarian, I think."

"A what?"

"Never mind. I was joking, anyway." He continued picking meat off the bones. Finally, he turned and said, "Can I ask you a question?"

"You just have."

"Very funny. You know what I mean."

"Ask what you will, then."

Vincent wiped his lips on his sleeve, then said, "Have you ever been in love?"

Blade seemed to stiffen slightly, but it could have been Vincent's imagination. "Yes," the man said quietly.

"So was I, once." Vincent paused, remembering. "Or at least, I think I was. I guess I really don't know." He stopped eating. "How do you know when it's really love and not just a real strong friendship? Or an infatuation? Or something else entirely?"

"I'm not the one to answer these questions. Why do you ask them of me? I am hardly your confidante."

"Well, who else would I ask? Gnorrin seems to have no interest in romance at this point in his life. And I certainly don't want to get Mepis going on the subject."

Blade chuckled at that. "I see. Is there someone for whom you are feeling what could be love?"

"Yeah. There is. Her name's Ariaziane. She lives at the abbey."

"Ah. The girl who looks after the horses."

"You know her?"

"I know her to see her. She is the only girl who lives at the abbey aside from the clerics."

"Well, we've sort of become friends. And I can't get her off my mind."

"So what is your confusion?"

Vincent briefly explained his concerns: her age, the fact that they'd just met, that he was from another world, and anything else he could rationalize on the spot. Blade nodded through his speech, and Vincent finished by saying, "So what's your opinion?"

Blade shrugged. "What is yours?"

"I don't know! I'm confused!"

"You enjoy being with her?"

"Yes."

"She enjoys being with you?"

"Seems to."

"I suggest you accept your relationship for what it is. Don't try to force it into something else. If more is meant to be, it will be. In time."

Vincent frowned. "I knew you'd say something like that."

"You find fault with it?"

"Not at all. What you said is perfectly sensible, and I've told myself the same thing a dozen times. I guess I just want someone to tell me what to do." He threw the remaining scraps of rabbit onto the fire and stood.

"Bed so soon?"

"Nope," he replied as he walked toward the trees. "Gotta take a load off my mind."

When Vincent returned from his task, Blade was unwrapping his sword from its protection. As Vincent moved closer, he saw there were actually two weapons inside, both in leather scabbards.

Blade turned and handed one to him. "Do you know how to use a sword?"

Vincent took the weapon. "Yeah, you swing it."

"It is very doubtful that you will need its use this trip, but it is better to be prepared. I shall try to expand your knowledge."

"You mean you'll try to test me some more, to see if I'm lying to you."

"Perhaps. Whichever way you wish to consider it."

As they moved away from the fire, Vincent said, "Why do you say I probably won't need a sword on this trip? What makes you so sure?"

40

"We will be carrying very little money. It would hardly be worth the effort for bandits to rob us."

The words didn't comfort Vincent. He'd never known of crooks unwilling to take small purses.

"Are you ready?" Blade asked.

Vincent shrugged. "I guess."

Over the next half hour, Blade demonstrated simple attacks and defenses. By the time they finished, Vincent's arm felt ready to fall off. He handed the weapon back to Blade and sat in front of the fire, massaging his shoulder muscles. Blade put the swords away and sat beside him.

"You are a liar," he said.

"What?" Vincent asked, panic rising inside him.

"You said you've never handled a sword before."

"I haven't! I swear it!"

"Then you have the best defense I've ever seen in an untrained arm."

Vincent smiled and thanked him, feeling proud, but wondering if he should. Violence was always something he found distasteful.

"On the other hand, perhaps you are speaking the truth. You have no attack to speak of."

Vincent shrugged, immediately regretting the action as his shoulder twinged. "I didn't want to hurt you." He looked at Blade with a smile on his face, hoping the man would laugh. But he saw only suspicion in the steely eyes.

He sat in front of the fire for awhile longer, afraid of what Blade would make of his apparent skill with a sword. He half expected the man to kill him at any moment. But when the fire had burned low, and Vincent was still alive, he allowed weariness to overcome him. He wished Blade a peaceful sleep and headed for his bed.

❧　❦

There was a light rain during the night. Vincent had finally fallen asleep to its gentle patter on the lean-to. His insomnia was still strong, and he welcomed the rhythmic beating to help him drift off. The rain had stopped well before morning, leaving the grass wet, but their provisions stayed as dry as he and Blade.

They were on their way an hour after the sun rose. Vincent tried to work out some of the kinks in his back. He didn't enjoy sleeping on the ground. He shivered as they rode. The Season of the Sun had yet to arrive, and the nights were still quite chilly. The mornings weren't too warm, either.

The day passed uneventfully, though they did see more travelers on the road as they drew nearer the city. Blade told Vincent what the next several days would hold.

"The Baron lives three days ride to the southwest of our current destination," he said.

Their own trek was due east, Vincent realized, which meant they would not have to backtrack on the journey home.

Blade continued. "We will meet at the tax assessor's offices first thing tomorrow morning, where we will join the other escorts. Once the money is received, we shall depart immediately."

"How much are we being paid for this?" Vincent found himself asking.

"Three silvers apiece."

Vincent thought about this for a moment, but it was no use. Virtually all of the transactions at work involved iron and copper pieces, not silver. He couldn't remember the conversions, though. "Sorry. I'm not sure how that translates."

Blade nodded. "Quite simple, really. There are twenty irons to a copper, twenty coppers to a silver, and twenty silver to a gold. And twenty gold to a platinum, but you'll probably never see a platinum coin."

"Why not?"

"Well, platinum is valuable for more reasons than any other metal. For example, it holds magic very well. Any metal can be enchanted, but only platinum can take serious physical abuse and retain the magic. If you ever encounter magical swords or magical armor, they will be most likely be made of platinum."

"Oh." Vincent frowned. The coin ratios were, indeed, easy enough to remember. The tricky part was figuring out the relative values of these coins, judging by what he could buy with them. From working at *The Nib and Quill*, he knew the blank book Gnorrin had bought for him cost five coppers. On Earth, at least during the time he lived there, something of such quality, made by hand, would probably have run upwards of twenty-five dollars. That would make a copper equal to about five dollars. He frowned and shook his head. No, that couldn't be right. He couldn't compare the same item on two different worlds. All things were made by hand, here. Naturally they would be cheaper. Maybe if he asked Blade about something more common between the two. Though what that could be, he wasn't sure.

So he tried again. The blank book was five coppers. A bundle of fifty sheets of decent quality paper was one copper. An inkwell of average quality ink was five coppers. So he decided to give a copper the value of a dollar. An iron piece, then, would be worth a nickel. A silver coin would be worth twenty dollars, a gold would be about four hundred dollars, and a platinum coin worth a whopping eight thousand bucks. So he and Blade were being paid about sixty dollars for three days of work, or twenty dollars a day, which would equal less than two dollars an hour, considering they certainly wouldn't be adhering to the eight-hour workday. Vincent frowned. Two bucks an hour. He turned to Blade. "Three silvers."

"Aye," the man said, riding silently beside him.

Vincent frowned more. "That really sucks."

Blade cast him a bemused glance. He smiled, ever so faintly. "Aye."

❧   ❧

As Blade had said, they met in front of the taxman's office at dawn. The captain in charge of the expedition took care of matters inside, emerging with a small bag, obviously heavy with coin, which he inserted with care into one of his horse's saddlebags. With a solemn glance over the party and a nod, he mounted up and off they rode.

Aside from the captain, Vincent and Blade were accompanied by six other men. Four of them were obviously from the same military outfit as the captain. They carried both swords and bows. The other two men seemed to have been recruited as he and Blade had been. He wondered if they could be trusted.

The road they traveled was fairly well-used. It was open, Vincent noted, for quite a ways off, and the tree line was back a considerable distance. These made ambush or assault from a distance unlikely. He sighed. The next three days certainly looked to be very boring.

Conversation wasn't going to be in abundance. He would have dearly loved to talk more with Blade, but he couldn't afford the risk of others overhearing and learning of his true origins. He settled back in his saddle and enjoyed the peacefulness.

They broke for lunch when the sun was high, dining on dried meats and biscuits, drinking lukewarm water from skins. He and Blade chatted briefly as they ate, Blade mostly mouthing encouraging statements to keep Vincent's boredom in check. Vincent watched as one of the soldiers removed a feedbag from his mount, slapping the beast kindly on its neck. He'd seen Ariaziane lovingly stroke the horses after feedings, as well. He wondered if you could really feel the same way toward a horse, or any animal bigger than yourself, the same way you could toward a dog or cat. He missed his dog. A black Labrador Retriever, his pet for thirteen years, had passed away on the same day he'd taken his college entrance exams. He considered that an omen that his college career would not go well. As it turned out, he would never even complete his degree. Still, he thought he might miss Earth a little less, having an animal to spend time with and take care of.

His thoughts were disrupted by a concerned word from Blade. Vincent looked up to see a party of men approaching on horseback. He joined the rest in repacking and mounting up again. Warily, they moved back onto the road to continue their journey. Blade's eyes were squinted, studying the oncoming party. There were twelve, Vincent counted, dressed mostly in black. Aside from that, he could ascertain nothing. He saw no weapons, but he was certain the others suspected they were armed. Seemed everyone was armed in this world, he thought. And the tension among their ranks spoke of their concerns.

The men rode closer. He saw one of the soldiers begin to ready his bow, only to catch a stern glance from his captain. That made sense. They couldn't just shoot on them if they didn't provoke such an action. The man's hand reluctantly left his bow, but settled firmly on the hilt of his sword. Vincent did the same, sincerely hoping for a rapid return to the boredom he'd so recently known.

"I thought you said we wouldn't meet any bandits," Vincent whispered.

Blade shrugged. "Perhaps the taxes went up."

As the twelve drew within easy speaking range, the apparent leader of them nodded politely and bade them a good day. The captain tersely responded, though not rudely. Vincent watched them as they drew past, to just beyond peripheral vision, at which point Blade's whisper came to him. "Ready, lad."

And with that, the strangers drew bare swords out from under their cloaks, wheeled about on their horses, and attacked. Vincent's party turned, drawing their weapons, and rushed into battle.

As for himself, he was having a devil of a time unsheathing his weapon. He looked up, panic-stricken, as his comrades moved ahead of him, leaving him alone and behind with a cowardly sword. He slapped his horse onward into the fray, his weapon suddenly letting go of its home. In front of him, two men in black were approaching behind Blade, one with his sword poised to strike. Vincent let out a yell nowhere near bloodcurdling, yet sufficient enough to draw their attention. The pair turned their heads, seeing him charging. Vincent forgot every scrap of offense Blade had taught him, swinging his sword like a baseball bat. The flat of the blade caught one of the attackers in the midsection, unbalancing the man enough to fall off his horse. Vincent's eyes grew wide as he saw the other man's blade come flashing toward his neck. Without thought, his arm was up, deflecting the stroke with his own sword. And as the man prepared to follow up with another swing, the hilt of Blade's sword came down firmly atop his head. The man's eyes widened, then he, too, fell to the ground.

The rest of the battle was a blur to Vincent. He stayed close to Blade's side, doing little actual attacking, but rather guarding his companion's back, though there was little guarding really necessary, either. It was over shortly. Vincent shook his head, as though coming out of a trance. His breathing was heavy and his heart raced as never before. He quickly looked around. The would-be thieves were running off, some clasping injuries. Two still lay in the dirt, including the one Blade had conked on the noggin. And miraculously, at least to Vincent's thought, all nine of his own party were intact. Most specifically, he himself was intact. He turned to face Blade, noting the man hadn't even broken a sweat. He panted for a moment, trying to catch his breath. Then he smiled. "Wow."

They camped at nightfall. While horses were being fed, watered, and tethered, and bedding being prepared, Blade tended the few injuries gained by some of the men earlier in the day. Vincent finished preparing their bedrolls. Blade soon joined him. "None shall die this evening," he said.

Vincent smiled faintly at his joke, but he wasn't feeling much mirth. The events of the afternoon weighed heavily on his mind. Immediately after the battle, he'd felt pretty good. But now that the adrenaline had worn off, he was a bit frazzled by the experience. Footsteps made him look up.

The captain stood in front of them. After glancing oddly at Vincent's glasses, he addressed Blade. "That was some fine swordplay today, friend. Much appreciated." Blade nodded, accepting the compliment. The captain's eyes narrowed. "It speaks of military training. Have you any?"

Blade gave a small, proud smile. "My father did. He taught me as a boy."

The captain nodded approvingly, clasped Blade's hand, and wished him a good night before moving off back to his men. Once the man was some distance away, Blade made himself comfortable and bedded down.

Vincent frowned, looking at him. "That was a lie."

Blade raised an eyebrow. "Pardon?"

"I said you lied. About your father teaching you."

Blade studied him. "Why do you think so?"

Vincent shrugged. "I dunno. I just get this gut feeling you're not telling the truth."

Blade was silent for a moment. Finally, he said, "You are correct."

"What's the big deal? Do you have military training?"

Another pause. "Yes."

"Why the lie?"

"I do not welcome the questions that could come of it."

Vincent nodded. Blade's tone of voice said this included any questions from him, as well. He decided not to press the issue and bade him good night.

Earlier, after the evening meal, the captain had listed the pairs of men who would be standing guard throughout the evenings. Each pair consisted of one soldier and one hired hand, which meant Blade would not be his partner in the watch. Evenings would be split in half, with one pair standing watch for the first half, then waking the second pair. The following evening, the other two pairs would split the chore. By the third day, they would reach their destination. Blade and Vincent would both be on watch the following evening. Vincent was glad of that. After today's battle, he could use the sleep.

Unfortunately, sleep was not easy in coming. Thoughts of the battle ran amok inside his head. Oddly enough, the fear he should have felt was only now imposing itself on his mind. During the fight, things just happened too fast for his mind to give way to terror. But now that he had a chance to think about the danger he'd been in, he also had a chance to be scared.

Giving up on a simple night's rest, he contented himself with watching the stars. The campfire was down to low embers by this time, and did not obscure his watching very much. The moon was gibbous this night, and he watched its slow progression across the sky. This planet had a beautiful moon, with plenty of craters, rays, and mares. It was smaller than Earth's moon, from his perspective on the planet's surface. It was also more yellowish in color.

For perhaps the thousandth time since his arrival, Vincent found himself wondering just how he could be on another planet. He was familiar with Edgar Rice Burroughs' character of John Carter of Mars, a man who found himself somehow transported to the red planet, known as Barsoom, where he became a powerful warlord and took the beautiful princess Dejah Thoris as his queen. He sighed. This wasn't Barsoom. And he was certainly no warlord. Nor did he ever expect himself to be. Ariaziane, however, could certainly be princess material, he thought. Then he shook his head. Stop it, he scolded himself. Thinking like that was dangerous and would lead to heartbreak. He knew from experience. He'd always had the tendency to fall in love, or what he'd taken for love, from a distance. Almost like the concept of courtly love in medieval times: unrequited. And it led to more than his fair share of tears. He certainly didn't want to start a streak of heartbreaks here on this new world. Now was the time to start fresh. He nodded his head once, firmly, as if to set this solidly in his mind.

Still, he thought, she was very pretty. He closed his eyes and a vision of a violet gaze under ebony bangs filled his mind. A smile played about his lips as he thought of her, going about her business taking care of the horses. And sleep came.

Vincent and Blade talked throughout the following morning. Since they were riding at the rear of the party this day, they could easily chat quietly, without others overhearing.

Vincent told him more of life on Earth. He tried as best he could to explain the different cultures, or at least, the major ones. He gave a brief history of the United States, as he remembered from school. From the original thirteen colonies to the Revolutionary War, up through the expansion into the West, the Civil War, the Industrial Revolution, the whole way up to the latter half of the twentieth century. He was more specific when talking about this era, and was inwardly amused at Blade's confusion over all the different things he mentioned. The Civil Rights Movement, the Women's Movement, hippies, yuppies, the Space Race, the Arms Race, Watergate, Gay Pride, and so on. Vincent paused, frankly surprised he could relay so much information on topics he'd never been interested in. He'd hated history classes all throughout school. Apparently, though, some had sunken in.

"You seem to be very well educated."

Vincent shrugged. "I had some good teachers, I guess. I don't really consider myself too far ahead. I was a quick learner. I went through grade school without ever learning to study, though, and that created a problem in high school. And I'm sure it would have in college, too." He was quiet a moment. "I'm tired of talking about Earth culture. Let's change the subject."

"Very well, what would you like to discuss?"

"Well, what's *your* story? I mean, I have serious doubts about 'Blade' being your real name, for starters. And you seem to be hiding a story. I'd just like to get to know you."

Blade showed the barest of irritation. "I am not given to speak much of myself, but as you have been so open in revealing your own past, I will at least say that you are correct. 'Blade' is not my birth name. Beyond that, I do not wish to reveal more at this time."

Vincent nodded. Blade still didn't trust him. He wasn't surprised, though he was somewhat disappointed. He sighed heavily, and they rode on in silence.

The halfway point of their journey was fraught with anticipation. Blade explained to him that bandits would be most likely to strike at a point furthest from civilization, where they would have easy access to the woods in which to hide. The fact that they'd already been attacked once was no assurance that there would be no more.

But the middle of the journey came and went without incident, much to Vincent's relief, and the surprise of others. Again, though, there was no guarantee that another attack wouldn't come before they reached their destination.

The thought of another battle did not exactly thrill Vincent, but neither did it frighten him. Odd, he thought, how he hadn't been totally terrified during the previous day's fighting. He'd never been in a fight before in his entire life. Not even a simple fistfight, let alone a battle with deadly weapons. He shook his head, unable to figure it out.

He studied the land around him. This alien world was much like he imagined Earth would have been before civilization became so advanced. Could he really get to the point of being content here? He missed Earth so much. His friends. His family. He had to admit, though, he hadn't been leading the happiest of lives there. The one thing he wanted more than anything had so far eluded him—love.

True, he was only seventeen, and he had plenty of time for romance to come into his life. But for an overweight, unpopular teenager, romance was mostly the stuff of fantasy. It hurt to be alone when all his friends had dates, or worse yet, steady boyfriends and girlfriends. High school had been worse than his first term in college, simply because the atmosphere was different. Still, he had no doubt things would've gotten worse in the college setting, and no illusions that he would've found Miss Right any time in the foreseeable future.

On the other hand, there was Ariaziane. So enchanting with her youthful spirit, her sharp tongue, her warm heart. Only a few days had passed since he'd last seen her and already he missed her. He stroked the horse under him, picturing her combing the animal, carefully untangling the knots in its mane.

He could be content here, he decided, if he could be with her.

The sun eventually grew low in the sky, and the party prepared camp several yards from the road. A fire was built and dried rations unpacked for dinner. After the meal, Blade took him aside and they practiced attacks and parries with their swords.

Later, around the campfire, one of the other hired guards pulled a wooden flute out of his saddlebag and played for awhile. The music was pretty, in a haunting way. "Damn, I miss my guitar," Vincent murmured.

Blade turned to him. "Your what?"

"Guitar. It's a musical instrument, made of a hollow body with a fretted neck, and six strings stretched end to end over a sound hole."

His friend nodded. "We have similar instruments here, but to my thinking, none have six strings."

"His playing is so sad," Vincent said. "What I'd really like right now is a nice bluesy Les Paul with the sustain kicked up..." Blade's confused look made Vincent chuckle. "Sorry," he said, smiling. "I'll shut up now."

With that, he moved off toward his bedroll.

Morning came too quickly. Vincent had stood guard during the second shift, and he didn't appreciate the small amount of sleep he did manage to get. He was stiff and sore from sleeping on the bedroll, and couldn't wait to be back in his own cot. It wasn't the most comfortable sleeping surface, but it beat a bedroll any day.

The party had packed up and mounted fairly quickly once the sun was up. They were over an hour into their travel when Blade said to him, "We should reach the town of Dynsa by mid-afternoon, my friend. Once there, our captain will take the revenues to the Baron, we will be paid, and our business concluded."

"And then we return home."

"Nay. That waits until tomorrow. Dynsa will be a new experience for you. We'll stay a day or two. Tonight you can experience the night life of a bigger town than you're used to."

Vincent shook his head slightly. "I'm not exactly a party animal, Blade. I appreciate the thought, but I think I'd really rather just hit the sack. I didn't get much sleep last night."

"We'll stay at the inn, which should be a welcome change for you after sleeping on the grass."

Vincent nodded slightly, though inside he was thrilled. A real bed would be even better than the cot. He frowned, then, trying to stretch his spine. His back was a bit annoyed with him. He desperately needed to crack it, but found it wasn't the easiest thing to do on horseback. Nevertheless, he attempted to, by twisting his torso around, grasping the rear of his saddle, and further turning his spine. He was rewarded with a quick series of pops from his sacral region. He sighed happily, repeating the movement in the opposite direction. A single pop was elicited. He performed the same feat on his neck, forcing a couple snaps to erupt, and ended with a glissando on his knuckles.

Blade eyed him strangely. "Most interesting," he said. "What causes you to do that?"

"Bicycle accident a few years ago. Threw my hips out of line, pinched a nerve. Haven't known a waking moment without some kind of ache ever since."

"Even after your ritual?"

"It helped a lot, but my upper back is still screaming at me. Can't do much about it now."

"What type of accident, did you say?"

Vincent smiled and shook his head. "Bicycle. Ten-speed, to be precise." His smile broadened, seeing Blade's confusion. "Sorry. That's mean of me. A bicycle is a vehicle for transportation. Two wheels, one in front of the other, moved by a pedaling action of the feet. Very efficient."

"And very dangerous, seemingly."

"No, that's really not true. My accident was just dumb luck. The front tire hit a rock and the bike tipped over. I landed on my right hip, my head hit the road, and the next thing I knew, I was waking up with a dozen people standing around, making a fuss over the size of the bump on my skull. All I cared about was getting my legs untangled from the damn bike. I was in a lot of pain, but very little was coming from my head. I couldn't walk the rest of the day." He paused, frowning. "I guess I should've realized right away something was very wrong. Instead, it just gradually grew until I'm like I am now."

Blade shook his head. "Surely something can be done."

Vincent shrugged. "Maybe. But not now. No one here could help me."

"I would not be so certain. There are healers here who might be able to help tremendously."

"Well, that would certainly be nice. Don't worry. I've been living with it. No biggie."

Vincent smiled to himself as he saw Blade mouthing the word "biggie" to himself. Blade didn't ask what he meant, but when Vincent started to laugh for no apparent reason, he saw the curious look on the man's face.

Not long after lunch, Vincent began to grow worried. Blade had said they'd reach Dynsa by mid-afternoon, which meant if there were to be another attack, it would be very soon. He mentioned this to his companion.

Blade nodded and said, "Aye, that is true. However, I would not begin to be concerned until you actually see someone else on the road."

Vincent nodded at this. The man had a point. No sense in worrying yet. He settled back into his ride, to his daydreams, thoughts of Earth. But more often, thoughts of the girl who looked after the horse he was riding.

His thoughts were shattered by an urgent word from Blade. He shook his head roughly to bring himself back to the present. Far ahead on the road were four riders. Vincent smiled. Only four. Much better odds than last time, he thought. He turned to Blade. The big man was frowning. "What?" he asked him.

"There are only four of them," he said, his voice tinged with concern.

"Yeah! No biggie."

Blade looked at him sternly and shook his head. "Biggie." He paused, then gave a small shrug. "If they are bandits at all. They could be simple travelers."

"What do you mean, saying it could be a biggie?"

"Distance weapons, most likely. Bows. Crossbows."

"We have those, too."

"Aye. But how much damage might they do before we can strike back?"

Vincent sighed. The figures were getting closer, now. "You said distance weapons were most likely. What else could it be?"

"Almost anything. Most are far too unlikely to mention, but they could certainly have a minor mage in their midst." Before his friend could reply, Blade continued. "I doubt it, however. The spies would certainly have provided information on how much we're transporting. A mage would never settle for such a small amount."

"Why? Are they greedy?"

"Not as a rule, no. Magery is an expensive undertaking. A mage would expect to be well rewarded for his art. And we don't offer that kind of reward."

Vincent grunted. "Distance weapons, then."

"Aye. So I think."

"Mm." He paused. "Bet it hurts like hell, getting shot with an arrow."

Blade nodded. "That it does." He lifted the side of his tunic, exposing two scars, entry and exit wounds around the kidney area.

"Geez." Not what I needed to see, Vincent thought. He felt his pulse quicken as they rode forward. He wondered how close they had to be for a bow to be effective. And what sort of defense they'd use. "So why don't we just gallop on?" he asked. "A moving target's gotta be hard to hit."

"Aye. But once past, they would have clean shots at our backs, boy. And I don't fancy that idea."

Vincent nodded glumly. Should've thought of that, he told himself.

Time seemed to crawl. The suspense was eating away at him. "Isn't there something we can do?" he asked. The riders were still too far off. Nothing could be determined at this distance.

"What would you suggest?"

"I dunno. I just hate the anticipation. Can't one of the captain's goons ride on up and see what the deal is?"

"That would serve several ends. One, we would lessen our ranks, should something occur. Two, we would present them with either an easy kill or an easy hostage."

"We'd also get the ball rolling."

"True, but I doubt the captain would be in favor of such a move."

Vincent sighed. This was ridiculous. It was also, he realized, the kind of paranoid fear that caused nuclear first-strike scenarios. He shook his head. At least there was no worry of that on this world.

The waiting was driving him crazy. Finally, he frowned, clenched his teeth together, and muttered, "Screw this," before spurring his horse onward, out around his companions. He heard the captain yell at him to stop, but he ceased when Vincent didn't slow.

Vincent trotted forward, keeping his horse pacing faster than his fellow riders, but not tremendously so. He didn't want to alarm the approaching foursome. He took a shaky breath, and wondered what the hell he was doing. His hand strayed to the hilt of the sword he wore. Not that this'll do me much good, he thought. Better to rely on other defenses.

Before long, he was within easy sight of them. He smiled to himself at the way they studied him, how several looked toward one of them as if for guidance. Vincent nearly chuckled. Yes, they were bandits, all right. His smile vanished. They were *bandits!*

What to do, he wondered. The riders were growing concerned. He was within fifty yards of them and closing fairly quickly. He saw them deliberating, turning toward the lead rider, as if he would tell them. Suddenly, an idea struck him. He smiled at them, yelled "Howdy!," and spurred his horse into a gallop, hanging on for dear life as the animal surged forward.

The sudden increase in speed startled them, and they began drawing bows. As soon as Vincent was past them, he began riding in a weaving pattern, back and forth across the road. He nearly fell off every time the horse swerved.

Behind him, he heard Blade yell, "Go on, lad! Get that money through!" Vincent smiled. Good idea, Blade, he thought. He couldn't have hoped for a better ruse. If only the bandits were gullible enough to fall for it.

When the first arrow whizzed past his ear, he knew they were. He kicked his mount again, and stole a glance over his shoulder. The four riders were divided. Two pursued him, while the other two were turning to face Blade and company, now in full gallop with weapons readied.

"Far out! It worked!" Vincent faced forward again and continued his race. It had actually worked. He smiled, pleased with himself. But when an arrow took him in his left arm, his smile turned to a grimace of pain. He lost his balance and pitched off his horse.

The impact and subsequent rolling slide sent horrible screams up through his arm and into his brain. The arrow had gone through the fleshy part of his arm, missing the bone, but stayed impaled halfway through. He thought briefly that he was lucky he hadn't been killed when he fell off the horse. But his thoughts on this were torn away by the sight of two riders charging him.

Frantically, he groped for his sword, and was amazed to find he hadn't lost the thing. He pulled it quickly from its sheath, wishing like mad for a shield. A sword wouldn't stop an oncoming arrow, except by the sheerest luck. And since he hadn't the energy to stand, the weapon would be nearly useless against other swords, too.

I'm going to die, here, he thought with a sinking feeling. Before he could dwell on the concept, his mouth was moving. "The gold's in the saddlebags on my horse. Better hurry."

Perhaps it was greed; perhaps it was gullibility; perhaps it was the sight of Blade bearing down on them like a runaway bull, but the bandits tore off in pursuit of Vincent's dashing horse. He heaved a sigh of relief before a surge of panic struck him. What if they did something to Ariaziane's horse?

Blade was coming to a halt in front of him. Vincent waved him on, urgently. "Get 'em! Don't let them hurt the horse!" Blade didn't question, but did as instructed.

Vincent sighed again and slumped forward. Not a bright idea, he thought, feeling the throb in his triceps. He put the sword down beside his leg and looked at his arm. Queasiness washed over him as he saw how much blood he was losing. Suddenly, he felt faint. He knew he had to remove the arrow. And he'd rather do it himself than let anyone else do it. Even so, he didn't look forward to the experience.

He had to break off the back end of the arrow in order to pull it easily through the other side. This wouldn't be easy to do with only one hand to operate with. Attempting just to snap the end off would only cause the arrow to move around inside his arm. And it might not even break. If only he could anchor it next to something.

He let his arm lie limp at his side. The front of the bloody arrow protruded straight through, on the inside of his arm from the bone. Well, he thought, there's something to anchor it against. He pressed his arm firmly against his side, turning so the arrow was snug up against his ribcage. He gasped slightly in doing so. Then he reached out and around with his right arm and grasped the back of the shaft. He took a deep breath. And snapped.

The world spun. The sky turned orange. He closed his eyes. It was still orange. The breath he was holding exploded out, then back in. Repeatedly. "Fuck!" He ground his teeth together. "I hate pain," he groaned. "I can't deal with pain. Pain and I are not friends." He dropped the broken shaft. Without opening his eyes, he reached around to the front, quickly gripped the front of the arrow, and yanked it clean through.

This time, the world didn't spin. It toppled backward. And the orange was replaced by black.

❧ ❧

Darella raised an eyebrow as she watched the battle. This alien youth who'd unknowingly planted his seed in her womb was blessed with astounding luck, as had been all the others who'd come through the portal in the years since she'd discovered it. Good fortune seemed to reek from some. Try as she might, she'd never been able to harm any of them. Her tests had shown she could touch, but not strangle them, for example. Knives wouldn't touch them after they came through the portal. Destructive spells had no effect. They weren't invulnerable for long, though. She'd seen them hurt, even die, through her scrying orb. She determined the portal must impart a protection upon the strangers, albeit a temporary one, lasting something less than a fortnight.

All the other-worlders also seemed to age slowly, to one degree or another. Far more slowly than anyone not of the ancient races, or of the Craft, as she was. She attributed both of these traits to being some sort of residual effect of the portal. And both were crucial to her current experiment.

She shook her head as she looked into her ball. She didn't particularly care one way or another what happened to the boy. But a flesh wound! A simple flesh wound after such a foolishly daring escapade? And the riders who were running him down! Why had they not run him through? She'd seen his lips move, saw them almost immediately leave him. And his friend, who dashed off at a word from the boy. Almost as if he knew the secrets of voice, as did she, being of the Craft. She frowned even more, wishing her scrying could convey sound as well as sight. At last she turned completely away from the ball. She stood, stretching her legs, the muscles stiff from sitting on the floor of the cave. The ball went dark as she walked away.

She paced, her thoughts returning to her own situation. There was something not quite right with the offspring in her belly. She had hoped the slow aging of the sire would pass on to the children. But something had gone awry. She felt her stomach, only weeks into the pregnancy, but she was showing already, as though she were months into gestation. At this rate, she would birth in less than two months! Instead of long-lived children, she would bear twins who would mature to young adulthood in only a handful of years. This would not be a problem, though, and in fact, could be fortuitous. The children would mature more quickly, be useful more quickly. The longevity factor was only a bonus the portal could have imparted. Its absence was of little importance. A witch could slow time's aging of the body. She would teach the children this ability, though she'd hoped not to have to devote her time to that particular discipline. She sighed and hoped, at the very least, that their sire's outstanding luck would carry over. The presence of this would prove certain factors were able to be transferred from generation to generation. And that was certainly an interesting bit of information to add to her understanding of the portal.

❧ Four ❧

There were voices. And darkness. And pain. And the sensation of slow spinning. The spinning was of a local sort, centered somewhere behind his forehead. The pain, too, was fairly concentrated, centering around his upper arm. The darkness was due to the fact that he couldn't open his eyes. And the voices were from somewhere near him, but he couldn't tell where.

He was lying on something soft. A bed, he thought, but the thought wasn't very coherent. His brain was muddled and sluggish, like the borderline state between sleeping and waking. The throbbing in his arm seemed to wash slowly over him in waves. He tried to open his eyes again, failed, then his concentration faltered and all he could think about was the spinning, torpid state of his present existence.

There was a new sensation, now. He sensed someone was standing near him. And there was a tugging at his head. At his hair. He wondered how anyone could grab hold of his hair while he was spinning like this. Maybe they were spinning, too, he thought. Then whoever was holding his hair suddenly let go.

"Will such a small lock be enough?" asked a deep, familiar voice.

"Since I have the blood, yes," replied a fair, unfamiliar one. There was a long silence while he contemplated the nature of spinning before the fair voice was heard again. "Who is he?"

And the familiar voice said, "A stranger. And evidently a long way from home." Vincent tried to smile, but was unsuccessful. At least, he thought he was unsuccessful. At any rate, he knew who the familiar voice was talking about. He, himself, was a stranger, a long way from home. He smiled in his mind. Someone was talking about him. That's nice, he thought, and allowed the spinning to carry him off, away from the voices, away from the pain, into the darkness.

When he finally woke, he opened his eyes to see Blade looking down at him. The man appeared to be relieved. "Good afternoon," Blade said. "High time you joined the waking world."

Vincent took in his surroundings. Bed. Chest of drawers. Washbowl. "Where am I?"

"Dynsa. One of the local inns." Blade picked up a wooden cup from a small table near the bed. "This is an herbal mixture that should quicken your healing. It will also make you drowsy." He handed the cup to Vincent. "How do you feel?"

"Weak. And my arm hurts."

Blade smiled slightly. "Now you know how it feels firsthand."

"I could've done without that knowledge." Vincent sniffed at the beverage, then took a drink. He nearly gagged, the mixture was so foul. "Okay, now I feel worse."

Blade sat on the edge of the bed. "I have been doing some thinking, while you slept," he said soberly. "And I feel I owe you an apology."

"For what?" Vincent asked as he drained the liquid and put the cup aside.

"I did not expect anything like this to happen. I should not have put you at such risk."

Vincent nodded. "I heard the talk you had with Gnorrin the night before we left. But you didn't force me to join you, after all. I knew there would be some danger involved. You don't need to apologize."

"Aye, I do, lad. But not simply for that." Blade was silent a moment, then spoke without looking directly at Vincent. "I have never had the ability, or indeed the desire, to befriend others easily. I realize that I have not been as friendly toward you as you have been toward me, and for that, I am ashamed."

"Blade, you don't—"

"Please. Allow me to finish." He paused again, then went on. "I have allowed my own suspicions and fears to blind me to the truth. I was unwilling to believe that you are from another world, not because I am skeptical of such a likelihood, but because I would never have expected to be befriended by such a one. I am not only ashamed of my suspicions of you, but I am also stupid, for there is much you can teach me."

"There is more that you can teach me, I think."

"The point is that I had closed off to you in my mind. But that was the action of a shallow person. While you slept, I thought of our talks during the trip. I thought of your valiance in battle. And I was impressed by these things."

"Oh, stop."

"Do you know what most impressed me? When you were lying in the dirt with an arrow through your arm, you told me...nay, you *commanded* me to go after the horse."

"I'm sorry," Vincent said sheepishly.

Blade laughed. "Oh, do not be sorry. Vincent, you have a quality in you of which you are perhaps unaware. When you commanded me, I went! Without question, without any hesitation. Don't you see?"

Vincent shook his head. "See what?"

"You are a born leader."

Now it was Vincent's turn to laugh. "You're crazy. I'm a kid! And I don't *want* to be a leader. That's not my style."

"Is it not?"

Even as Blade asked the question, Vincent knew he hadn't told the truth. As a child, he'd often been the center of attention, the one to whom others turned for guidance. Only within the past half dozen years or so, after his genes had caused the weight gain he hated so much, did his role as leader disappear. His self-image had tarnished, his confidence had fallen, and almost no one came to him for guidance anymore.

"No," he said. "So what's our plan? When do we leave?"

"Tomorrow. We'll dine here tonight and tomorrow morning, then depart."

"So what happened after I passed out, anyway?"

"We captured the bandits and turned them in to the authorities. The Captain was impressed by your valor, though he did think you acted far too recklessly." Blade smiled at that. "And I've collected our pay. We received double, due to the attacks."

"Hazardous pay, huh? Great. Though twice as much is still pathetic."

Blade nodded. "Aye. You will not become wealthy by being a guard for the tax couriers. Oh, and for future reference, what you did was unwise."

"You think?" he said, indicating his wounded arm.

"I meant pulling out the arrow as you did. The arrow, when still in place, prevented much blood from escaping. Once you removed it, you lost a severe amount. Had we not been so close to Dynsa, you could easily have died there."

Vincent blinked, his heart skipping a beat. Stupid. He knew enough about injuries to know this to be true. What had he been thinking? "You're right," he said. "I don't know why I did it."

Blade smiled. "It is a natural reaction, I think. But next time, think before you pull."

"Next time? You've got to be kidding. If you think I'm going to put myself in danger of being someone's target again, you're crazy."

His friend laughed and slapped Vincent's leg as he stood. "Indeed. Now, get some rest."

Vincent nodded, his eyes already drooping. The herbs were doing their thing, he realized. And then he slept.

☙ ❧

Vincent sat behind what passed for the front counter at *The Nib and Quill*. The awning cast ample shade over him and the shop's wares on display. He paused in his writing to gaze at the sunny square, scratched at the new growth of beard on his chin, and sighed.

Bored, bored, bored. The only thing that bothered him more than the boredom was the occasional throbbing in his arm. He glanced down at the sling and the bandages. A bitter smile played about his lips as he turned back to continue his accounting of the adventure in his journal.

I've had a lot of time to think about what I've just been through. After the initial battle, I was pretty freaked out. I think, though, that I became a bit cocky after having survived it. Maybe that's why I acted so rashly during the second encounter. I thought I could do anything. I can be so stupid, sometimes.

Anyway, that room was about all I saw of Dynsa. Not that I really care. Blade treated me to dinner there, and breakfast the next morning. Not long afterward, we were on our way back home.

And now I'm back, working at The Nib and Quill, *writing this to take my mind off the boredom and the pain.*

I can't wait until my shift is over. I want to stop by the abbey and see if Ariaziane's there. Not that I expect she'd be anywhere else, but you never know. Evidently, she's been a bit busy since Blade and I went away. Gnorrin tells me she actually approached him about the possibility of becoming a pupil of his. I'm not sure how he feels about the idea, but he accepted her. I'm pretty sure he did it so as not to upset me.

And speaking of Gnorrin and being upset, what a reaction my injury got from him! He chewed Blade a new rectum, reprimanding him for allowing me to get hurt. I defended Blade, of course, advising Gnorrin that there wasn't a bloody thing he could have done to prevent it. It didn't matter, though. In Gnorrin's eyes, it was still Blade's fault for taking me on the trip in the first place. To his credit, Blade simply suggested that next time Gnorrin ought to come along as further protection for me.

Vincent chuckled and stopped writing, laying aside the book. He gazed around the square, wondering if other shops were having as slow a day as *The Nib and Quill*.

He sighed. He didn't mind his job. Not really. He had to admit, though, he was beginning to tire of the work. Or lack thereof.

The little sidetrack with Blade resulted in an injury, but at least had been something to do. What was there to do here, other than work for Mepis? Not much. There was Ariaziane, yet deep down he knew he was just fantasizing with that. Nothing was ever going to come of his relationship with her, other than friendship. And while that was wonderful, it didn't fill the void inside him that had been steadily growing over the past several years. He didn't want his new life here to be as depressing as the one he'd left behind.

What could he do? He'd need money. *The Nib and Quill* was providing some, but too slowly. Surely he could make money more quickly. Playing hired guard to tax couriers certainly wasn't the answer, but he knew that wasn't Blade's normal line of work. The problem was how to ask him. The man seemed very hesitant to talk about himself. Then again, after their shared escapade this past week, he might be more open to the idea. Vincent decided to approach him about it sometime. For now, he resigned himself to the remainder of his shift.

Business didn't pick up the rest of the day, and when closing time came, Vincent did so with enthusiasm, or at least with as much enthusiasm as he could muster with one arm in a sling. He bade Mepis a good afternoon, dropped his day's wages into his pouch, and headed toward the abbey.

He picked some wildflowers from the roadside on his way, arranging them into a lopsided but colorful bouquet. They looked like daisies of a variety of colors. He hoped Ariaziane would like them.

At the abbey, he found the horses playing in the corral. He was very glad no harm had befallen the one he'd ridden the past few days. He took a deep breath before knocking on the abbey's front door. He wasn't sure what the Sisters or the Abbess thought of him, but hoped Ariaziane wasn't getting hassled about him. The door opened, pushing the thoughts out of his head. The cleric who answered was named Haleen. He'd been introduced to her once before. She greeted him politely, but was sorry to tell him Ariaziane was not in, at the moment. Haleen wasn't sure where she'd gone. Just for a walk near the creek, she thought. She'd left some time ago. Vincent thanked her and turned away.

The flowers hung at his side as he walked along the corral fence. If she'd been out for long, why didn't she walk to the shop and see him? Probably had better things to do, he decided. Maybe there was someone else she was visiting. Someone she liked better than him. Or in a different way.

He shook his head. Thoughts like those wouldn't cheer him up, that was for sure. He made his way through the thin span of woods until he reached the creek, where he turned in the direction of Gnorrin's home.

That thought struck him, too, as he walked quietly along. *Gnorrin's* home. Not his. Since he was going to be on this world a while, he'd have to find his own place to live sometime. He'd been enough of an imposition already.

Naturally, this made him think of the money issue again. *The Nib and Quill* wasn't going to get him a house.

He glanced down at the flowers in his left hand. One of them was purple with a black center. He began plucking individual petals from the bloom. "She loves me. She loves me not. She loves me. She loves me not." The petals fell like a trail of violet snowflakes along the bank. He pulled the last one from the flower. "She loves me not." He sighed again and stopped walking, then tossed the stem into the water and watched it float away. When it was too small to be discerned, he began walking again.

He chose another flower, this one having pink petals and a white center. "She likes me. She likes me not. She likes me. She likes me not." He ended with "She likes me." He shrugged. "Well, that's something, anyway." This time he walked alongside, pacing this stem as it floated downstream. Soon he reached a familiar landmark—the large rock he'd rested upon while sunning himself dry after his initial, damp encounter with Ariaziane. He perched himself atop the stone and watched the water in silence.

"Clumsy," said the voice behind him. Vincent jumped and whirled in place, wrenching his injured arm in the process. He winced, but forgot his pain as he saw the source of the voice. Ariaziane was shaking her head.

"What?" Vincent asked.

She reached out and gingerly touched the arm in the sling. "Still, for all your clumsiness, I hear you were pretty impressive."

"Thanks," he replied. "I think." At this point, he remembered the flowers in his hand. He realized Ariaziane had been looking at them, too. He held them out to her. "For you."

Ariaziane smiled and accepted the bouquet, holding them to her nose. "Thank you. You're very sweet." She joined him on the rock. "So what have you been pondering so much that you didn't hear me approach?"

He shrugged. "Lots of things. Mostly money, I guess. Trying to figure out how to get more. And trying to figure out what to do with my new life here so I don't go crazy from boredom."

Ariaziane frowned. "You're unhappy?"

"It's not so much that, really. I mean, I'd certainly rather be back where I belong, but that's apparently not an option. Well, I'm very glad I've done so well. I've made some wonderful friends. I have a job, so I'll at least have a slow, but sure, way of paying Gnorrin back for all he's done for me. But I've never liked doing things the slow way, no matter how sure they are. I want to be able to repay him soon. I want to get my own place to live. I want to do more with my new life than work for Mepis." He stopped, not brave enough to tell her the thing he wanted most.

"I know you do. And so do your friends. Gnorrin mentioned to me how concerned he is about you."

"You've spoken to him quite a bit lately, haven't you?"

"I have. In fact, I just came from there. He and Blade both spoke freely about you with me. I'm not sure why. I mean, Gnorrin doesn't know me very well, and Blade even less. Yet they seem to trust me completely, even with things about you. I don't know if I should feel flattered, or if you should wonder why they speak so loosely of your concerns."

Vincent smiled. "Feel flattered. It's mostly because they trust me. And they know how I feel about you." As soon as the words were out of his mouth, he knew he'd made a mistake. He tried to cover as best he could. "I mean, they know I've spoken very highly of you." As his face grew warm, Ariaziane gave an awkward half-smile and pushed herself off the stone.

"I have to get back," she said.

"Why? Can't you stay a while?"

"Not today. I'm sorry. I have to start making the evening meal soon." Vincent nodded, gazing at the ground near her feet. "Are you working tomorrow?"

"If you can call it work."

"Well, whatever you want to call it, do you want some company?"

Vincent brightened. "Certainly! When should I expect you?"

She gave him a sly look. "When you least expect me." She smiled and bade him farewell, and began her trek back to the abbey. Vincent watched her depart, his heart doing tiny flip-flops for several minutes. Then he, too, abandoned his seat and headed home.

They sat outside with their supper that night. The sun was setting and the air was crisp. The birds were taking to their roosts among the trees behind the cottage. Their tweets, chirps, and whistles reminded Vincent of home, of the woods that lay in his back yard, and how the birds would gather there by the hundreds.

Gnorrin had heated the pot of stew hanging from a tripod over a small fire in a pit. The three of them ate mostly in silence, enjoying the peacefulness of the evening. Vincent finally decided to begin a conversation.

"So," he said, clearing his throat. "What's your opinion of Ariaziane as a pupil of magic?"

Gnorrin thought for a moment before replying. "She has a sharp mind. Naturally inquisitive. She seems to have grasped the basics of what I've shown her thus far quite well." He spooned another mouthful of stew. "I think she'll go far, so long as she doesn't lose herself in it."

Vincent raised an eyebrow. "What do you mean?"

Gnorrin shrugged. "I mean she must always realize that magic is a tool. Like a mallet, you use the tool to help you in your work. Unlike a mallet, this tool can use the wielder, rather than the other way around."

Blade spoke up. Vincent noticed he had already finished his bowl of stew and was reclining on the grass. "Speaking of tools and learning, lad, we need to continue with your sword training."

"Kinda tough with my arm in a sling."

"Nonsense." He sat up. "You need only one arm to handle your weapon."

"True, but using a sword would aggravate my other arm anyway. I'm not keen on self-inflicted pain. Or any other kind, for that matter."

"You seem to have handled pain quite well a few days ago."

"I passed out!" he said with a laugh.

"Nevertheless, there could most certainly be times in the future when you will need to maintain your wits and your weapon when overwhelmed with pain. Your life will depend on it."

Gnorrin shifted uneasily. "Must we discuss this?"

Vincent sighed. "He's right, Gnorrin. Pain is inevitable in life. Like your analogy with magic. Pain can either be controlled or it can control you."

The gnome grumbled. "Wise words, young one, but wiser still to avoid pain. What need have you to go traipsing around in search of adventure? You could be content here, without risking your life in some forsaken—"

"Gnorrin," Blade began.

Vincent interrupted him. "I appreciate your concern. I'm not generally a risk-taker. But I can't just live here. I'm already growing restless. I have a whole new world to explore. And maybe someday, if I search hard enough, or am lucky enough, I might just find my way back to my own world. I have to try. Surely you can understand that."

Gnorrin was silent a long while. He pushed around the small bit of stew left in his bowl, but did not eat it. Finally, he nodded his head. "I do. More than you know." He was silent a while longer. "I grew up in a family of miners. Oh, I know, I know. Gnomes aren't generally known as miners."

Vincent nodded, though he had no idea what gnomes were or were not known as, other than tasteless dressers, if Gnorrin was a normal specimen of gnomedom.

"My great grandfather, ages ago, discovered a clearstone mine."

. "A what mine?"

"Clearstone." Gnorrin held out his fist, indicating the ring Vincent had admired many times. Vincent had assumed it to be diamond. Gnorrin withdrew his hand after Vincent nodded his understanding, and continued. "I was expected to have an active role in the management of the mine, as my father and his brothers did, and my own brothers do to this day. But I couldn't. I hated the very idea." He chuckled softly to himself. "Your friend reminds me of myself, in a way. Like her, I met another practitioner of the art of magic, and became fascinated. Soon, clearstone mining sounded like the most boring thing in the world to me.

"My father was beside himself when I told him I was going to leave the business and go off on my own. He refused to accept my decision. When I went ahead with my plans, he never forgave me." Gnorrin hesitated. "We haven't spoken in fifteen years." He paused again, giving a slight smile. "So, yes. I can understand your wishes. Know this, though. It isn't all joy and sunshine. You'd best be prepared for your pain, my friend. Controlled or not." With that, Gnorrin rose and carried his bowl into the house. Vincent and Blade watched him go.

They put their own bowls aside and took up swords. Blade reviewed with him the things he'd shown Vincent on their first little adventure. After the review, he progressed on to new moves.

Vincent's wounded arm twinged with each thrust, swing, parry, and dodge. He tried to keep it close to his body, as immobile as possible, but didn't succeed very well.

He tired quickly. Blade hadn't even begun to slow, Vincent noticed with some envy. He redoubled his own efforts in an attempt to save a least a little dignity.

Blade was unquestionably, and unsurprisingly, dancing circles around him. Little jabs and slices left tiny spatters of blood on Vincent's weapon arm. And then, as if to prove some sort of point about what he'd said earlier about pain, Blade lashed out and smacked Vincent's injured arm solidly with the flat of his sword.

Vincent gasped in pain, but his sword was up in a flash, parrying his friend's follow-up swing, which he noticed was very hard and could have been deadly, had it connected.

Anger gripped him. He leaped into an all-out attack against Blade. His sword flew faster than he ever thought possible, but each attack was dodged or blocked by the more experienced fighter.

Soon, Vincent's manic energy dwindled and he staggered to his knees, his breath ragged. Blade stood over him and eventually helped him to his feet. As they made their way toward the cottage door, he nodded his head. "Very good, boy. Very good."

– –

The surprise of the morning was finding *The Nib and Quill* already set up and ready for business when he arrived. Mepis was just finishing by folding up the covering canvases and storing them inside. He bade Vincent good morning as the boy approached.

"To you, too, boss. Why didn't you wait for me to help you?"

"Wait for the help of the lame when I had two strong arms in addition to my own?"

Vincent placed his pack containing his journal atop the counter. "Whose?"

At that moment, a pair of hands bolted out and tickled his ribs. He whirled to see Ariaziane giggling behind him. "Mine, clumsy."

Vincent broke into a huge smile, then frowned. "You can stop calling me that any time, y'know."

Mepis leaned slyly over to the girl's ear. "Now, don't you let him get fresh with you, Missy. He tries anything, you let me know. We'll put his other arm in a sling."

Ariaziane blushed, and Vincent felt his cheeks grow red as well. He watched Mepis as he stepped inside the shop, closing the door behind him. He nervously cleared his throat and pulled out a second stool from under the counter. "Have a seat." She did so, and hid her eyes from his by looking over the selection of pens and inks and papers.

"So tell me about your studies with Gnorrin."

Ariaziane looked up and smiled at him. "Well, there hasn't been much studying, yet. He's just been telling me the basics. I think he's testing me, to see if I'm really interested in learning the art, or if I'm just mildly curious."

"I think he knows you're not just curious, to hear him talk. He thinks you're pretty sharp."

"Truly?"

"Yeah. And for what it's worth, so do I."

"Thank you."

"Not that I would have any idea who would or wouldn't make a good mage," he continued. "I think you've got what it takes to be anything you set your mind to."

"Again, thank you," she said. "And what of you? Will you be learning swordsmanship from Blade?"

"Mentioned that, did he? Well, yeah. I guess so." Vincent pondered the nature of that particular endeavor, glancing at the cuts on his arm. His voice grew quiet, partly because he didn't want Mepis to overhear, and partly because he wasn't sure of his words. "It's ironic, really. The sword is such a violent weapon. I mean, all weapons are inherently violent." He sighed. "I've never been a violent person. I hate guns—"

"Guns?"

"The primary weapon of choice on my world. A gun hurls a projectile, usually a small piece of metal, at incredibly great speeds. Much faster than you could comprehend." Ariaziane seemed a bit indignant at what he seemed to think she could

60

or could not comprehend, so he explained more fully. "For example. See that oak tree over there?" He pointed, and she nodded. "Its trunk is fully a foot thick, wouldn't you agree? Well, there are guns that could shoot a bullet clean through with no problem at all." He noted how her eyes widened in disbelief. "Well, most people didn't carry such weapons around on them. Still, the average small hand-held gun could probably pierce the best armor I've seen here."

He was silent for a time. "I never liked guns. But there's always been something about a sword. It's almost... I know this sounds stupid, but it's almost a romantic weapon. They're so archaic in my world. Sure, you'd see them in movies all the time, but the only time you saw them in real life was as a sport. Fencing matches and the like. People rarely thought of them as weapons to actually use, other than to hang on their walls as decorations."

"And here you are, intending to use one on a regular basis."

"Yeah. I feel really weird about it. But there are other differences, too. The sword is a much more personal weapon. If I wanted to kill someone, and he was standing out there in the square, I couldn't kill him with my sword without going up to him and engaging in battle. A gun is impersonal. I could sit here and lazily pick him off without thinking twice. I wouldn't even work up a sweat. I dunno. It just seems so cowardly."

He could have gone on. He could have told her about grenades that could be tossed through the window of a cottage and kill everyone inside. Hell, he thought, he could've told her about nuclear weapons. But even the concept of a handgun was probably more than she could be expected to assimilate in one day.

"If you have such moral problems, why are you even bothering to learn?"

Vincent looked at her for a long time before answering. When he finally spoke, it was with uncertainty. "Damned if I know. Something tells me I can find the answer to the question of how to get home, back to Earth. And I'm not going to learn it by sitting here selling stationery. I could probably learn the ways of magic, but my instincts tell me magic isn't the way to my answer. I might not have the patience for it, either. I'm a very patient person, except with regard to myself."

"So, you think the key to finding your way home lies in the sword?"

"No. That's not what I mean." He frowned in frustration. "I don't have an answer for you. I feel some sort of affinity to the weapon, somehow. Maybe it's just the romantic, swashbuckling image holding over from Earth. I dunno." He smiled awkwardly. "Then again, I spend the bulk of my life in an uncertain state, so this is nothing new." Vincent paused, before changing the focus of the conversation. "And exactly how have the Sisters at the abbey been taking your newfound interest?"

Ariaziane turned her head away slightly, embarrassed. "They don't exactly know."

"Ah."

"I've been using a variety of excuses to be away for a few hours every so often."

"Okay, so how do you think they'd react? Or is that a stupid question?"

"You have asked more sensible questions, yes."

Vincent smiled and gazed into her eyes. He knew he should look away, knew he was probably making her feel uncomfortable, but couldn't bring himself to stop.

Ariaziane met his gaze evenly. "You're staring," she said.

"I know," he replied. "Can't help myself. Does it bother you?"

The girl averted her gaze, looking absently at the pens and papers again. "A little."

Her admission snapped him out of it. "Oh. I'm sorry."

"Don't worry. I just..."

"What?"

"Nothing. Truly."

"I don't believe you," he said. When she tried to speak again, he interrupted. "But I'll let it go. I'm sorry."

Ariaziane sighed. "I cannot explain it, Vincent. You have a strange effect on me." She paused, gathering her thoughts together. "I find myself thinking things I never have before. Wanting to do things I've never done before."

"What sorts of things?" Vincent found his heart beating faster. Could she feel for him the same way he was feeling about her? That would be too good to be true.

"I agree with what you said. Remember? About feeling trapped." She shook her head, eyes turned downward. "I feel guilty, though. The Sisters have been so good to me. I owe them so much. But I have the urge to go out and experience life on my own. And I feel like a traitor."

His heart resumed its normal beating, now that he realized what she was referring to. "Listen," he said. "There's no reason you should feel guilty, or traitorous. It's a natural desire, what you're feeling. It's like any child wanting to move out from living with their parents. Everyone experiences this."

"I wouldn't know what is or isn't natural regarding children with their parents."

"I know. I'm sorry. I wasn't thinking. Let me assure you, though, it's the truth. I'm sure the Sisters would understand, too."

"I want to know what's out there, beyond this town, Vincent. I want to learn magic! I want to see distant lands and strange beasts in the wild. I want to ride a horse across open plains, without keeping track of the day, having to return him to a stable after an hour."

Vincent nodded, knowing full well how she was feeling.

She turned to him, embarrassed. "Silly of me, yes?"

Vincent shook his head. "Not at all. As I said, it's natural." He cleared his throat. "So that's why you've been learning magic? As a means to escape? To seek adventure?"

She let out a sigh. "Perhaps." Her eyes trapped his. "Is that so terrible?"

He laughed, nervous now that she was the one staring. "How many times do I have to say it? No! It's perfectly understandable. I mean, I doubt the Sisters would understand the magic part, but the rest is typical teenage wanderlust, Annie." He paused as he caught the quizzical expression on her face. "What?" he asked.

"Annie?"

Vincent felt the blood rush to his cheeks. "Shit." He laughed. "I'm sorry."

"Explain, please."

"It's a name. Annie. Sort of a short form of the last syllable of your name. See, I have this cousin. Her name's Ruth Ann. I always called her Annie." His smile lessened, but did not vanish. "I haven't seen her in years. When I was young, we used to do things together. Go to movies and things. She was one of my favorite cousins." He shrugged. "I guess the fun I have with you reminded me of the fun times I had with her. And so I sometimes think of you as Annie."

"You think of me as your cousin?"

His jaw dropped. "No! Not at all! I just... I mean..."

Ariaziane laughed at him. "I know. I'm jesting. I knew what you meant. It's very sweet." She was quiet for a moment before asking, "Will you help me?"

"Help you what?"

"Will you help me see the world?"

He smiled. "In any way I can." He reached out and squeezed her hand. And she squeezed back.

The Season of Green gradually grew into the Season of the Sun. Vincent's arm healed and his beard grew thick. Blade taught him the sword, sometimes with such intensity that Vincent thought his friend was honestly trying to kill him. He taught him how to fight with a sword and shield, with sword and knife, with two swords, but mostly, at Vincent's insistence, with just a single sword. Many times Blade pointed out to him the dangers of this. A single sword, he told him, afforded only the protection its parry provided. Any of the other three styles added additional defense and/or additional attacks. And each time, Vincent would agree. But he still preferred the single sword technique.

Gnorrin continued teaching Ariaziane the ways of magic. Of this, Vincent knew little. She was either unwilling or unable to convey to him on a daily basis the knowledge she'd gained. She did, however, share with him some of the books Gnorrin loaned her. They were not books of magic spells. Despite his ability to read whatever language existed here, as well as speak it, spells were evidently written in a language exclusive to the realm of magic. Vincent wasn't surprised. The books she brought him were of a historical nature, telling tales of ancient mages, describing powerful artifacts of old, and rare magical devices rumored still to be found in certain areas.

Vincent continued working at *The Nib and Quill*. He wrote in his journal daily and read the books Ariaziane let him borrow. He read of the beasts of this world, some familiar to him through the literature of fantasy: dragons, unicorns, pegasi, griffons, and scores of others he'd never heard of. He read of the other races: dwarves, elves, gnomes (obviously), halflings, dryads, and others. Some of the creatures he read of had a humorous effect on him. He read of brownies, and envisioned hordes of junior league Girl Scouts. He read of pixies and thought of a powdered candy you ate from a paper straw. He read of djinni, and Barbara Eden in a harem outfit blinked into his mind.

He'd lost some fat since his arrival on this world, too. One day he hoped to replace it with muscle, but so far the only muscles he'd been building were in his arms. Not that this was a bad thing, but other areas certainly needed improvement. His new life wasn't all easy. After his workouts with Blade, he was sore. His back bothered him more often than not, and he still felt like a freeloader living with Gnorrin. And the big bucks weren't rolling in.

His "romance" with Ariaziane made no progress in the following month or so, while their friendship grew by leaps and bounds. The Sisters didn't seem to mind her going to meet with him. Perhaps they simply saw the inevitability and chose not to butt their heads against that particular wall. She would meet him after his shift at work and they would go for walks and ride the horses to the edge of what was considered safe land. Vincent was becoming fairly comfortable on horseback. They had many picnic lunches out in big fields far from town. And they still enjoyed walking by the stream where they'd first met.

Blade still hadn't opened up to him about his past, and Vincent had stopped pressing him, for the most part. He knew the man would tell him when he was ready. Gnorrin's opposition to adventuring seemed to lessen. He spoke with Vincent on several occasions about his late friend, Blôrain. And the conversations invariably brought out good times as well as the sadness from his loss. Gnorrin even laughed out loud in the telling of some of their exploits. So when the day came that Blade returned from the city with news of a possible "job" for them, Gnorrin's protestations weren't very loud. Even if they had been, they'd have been totally drowned out by Ariaziane's excitement.

❧ Five ❧

The campfire crackled in the warm night, sending sparks floating to the heavens. Vincent's insomnia was in full force, and he used the sleepless time to write in his journal. He re-read his entry thus far.

South River Keep, according to Blade and Gnorrin, is located three days journey south of Gnorrin's home. In years past, it was the fortress of a great mage, now long dead. The keep had, naturally, been ransacked top to bottom long ago. But Blade's recent trip to the city yielded the information that an unknown section was rumored to have just been discovered. Evidently, it had been unearthed by a recent landslide in the hills where the keep was built. Few know of this, according to Blade's sources. And he says it is doubtful that many have attempted to breach this section, since many died during the original raid. The keep is apparently well-guarded with booby traps. Nevertheless, the four of us are marching right in.

Vincent stole a glance at the small lean-to occupied by Ariaziane, who was now fast asleep. *I'm still amazed the Sisters permitted Annie to accompany us. I know Blade spoke to the Abbess about the trip, but I don't know what was said. I think Blade offered a percentage of the booty to the abbey. Ariaziane was basically bribed away from them.*

The journey today wiped her out. She sacked out right after dinner. Blade and Gnorrin stayed up for a while, talking. I'm surprised at how tolerant Gnorrin's being about the whole affair, considering his stand against adventuring in the first place. In fact, when Blade first announced it, Gnorrin was quite adamant about not having anything to do with it. By morning, though, his tune had changed. I don't know if he just had time to reconsider, or if Blade talked him around. Guess it doesn't matter, either way.

Vincent decided he'd written enough for one evening. His eyes were getting heavy. Blowing gently on the page to dry the ink, he closed the book and tucked the journal into his pack, then sealed and stowed away his jar of ink.   Lifting his glasses, he rubbed the bridge of his nose with his thumb and forefinger. He hated wearing glasses. It had been over two years since he first got them, and certainly this new pair felt lighter and more comfortable than the first, but he'd give a lot to see clearly without them. He pulled the annoying things off, folded them up and put them aside before he curled up for slumber.

❧ ❧

Our second day's journey was equally as uneventful. The land here is beautiful... so pure and undeveloped. I'm sure I'll miss the luxury of shopping malls and pizza joints, but for peace and quiet, you can't beat this.

Vincent's writing was interrupted by Ariaziane stooping in front of his lean-to. "You write in that thing a lot."

He smiled up at her, pushing the book aside and capping the ink bottle. "Yeah, I know. I'm a bit obsessive, I guess. So what's up?"

"The opposite of 'down,'" she said with a smile. "Your expressions are really strange, in case I haven't mentioned so before."

"You have."

"I know." She sat on the ground next to the front of his shelter. "I'm not really tired. Thought I'd keep you company."

65

"Great. Come on in." Vincent moved his things aside to allow her room to lie beside him. She crawled under the lean-to and lay on her side, one hand propping up her head.

"Gnorrin and Blade certainly spend a lot of time talking."

"Yeah. I've noticed." He paused. "So. You nervous?"

The girl nodded. "Somewhat. You?"

"I guess. I really don't know what to expect."

They were silent for a time, looking at each other. Vincent was surprised she didn't look away as he gazed into her eyes. Finally, she rolled onto her back, folding her hands under her head. "Tell me about your home."

"Again?"

"Yes."

He sighed. "Well, it's small, as towns there go. About twenty-two hundred people."

"What's your idea of a big town?"

"Annie, the largest cities there have millions of people in them. The closest thing to a city near my hometown had close to ten thousand, which still wasn't much in the way of a real town."

"Fine. Go on."

"It was a factory town, with a huge glass bottle industry. One of the largest in the country, in fact. There were other industries, too, but the glass company was the main one. We had a bowling alley when I was younger, but it closed up. Really, you had to go ten miles away to do anything significant, even for decent shopping."

"Tell me about your school."

"Yuck. Why?"

"I like to hear about learning. It's wonderful! I'm learning so much from Gnorrin!"

"Yeah, well school can be like that. Or it can be awful, too. For every class you take where you're learning something you really like, there are a couple others where you're bored to death. For every really good teacher, there's a really bad one, and a bunch of mediocre ones. More than the educational standpoint, though, school was a social thing. And I think that's the aspect I disliked the most. The way the kids formed little circles of elite. There were so many different cliques, all with their own type of snobbery."

"Which one were you in?"

"None of them. A lot of people thought I was in with the brains, but I wasn't. Some thought I was a druggie, but that wasn't true, either."

"A what?"

"Someone who used illegal drugs. I have no idea what the equivalent would be, here, or if there even is one. At any rate, I wasn't one of them. I just sorta looked like one, to some people. I certainly wasn't a jock, an athlete. I played on the tennis team, which didn't mean much. I wasn't very good. Like all sports, I had the basic skills, even some talent. I was a good pitcher in baseball. I was good at shooting in basketball. I could place the ball well in tennis, but didn't have any stamina. Being overweight was always the problem. And I've told you about the problem with my back from the accident I was in. The two combined made it impossible for me to be more than moderately good at any sport that required endurance."

"You've told me about these sports before. I don't understand why your world seemed to put so much importance on them."

Vincent shrugged. "I lived there for seventeen years, dear, and I never figured it out, either." As he paused, Vincent found himself once more captivated by her eyes. Even when her gaze didn't fall on him, he still felt their attraction. He watched the starlight reflected there, and felt a flutter inside. His smile faded and he looked away.

He saw Blade checking the horses one last time before turning in. Gnorrin was fiddling around near the fire. He watched his friends and tried to take his mind off the loneliness he suddenly felt. When he turned back to Ariaziane, he saw she'd put her head down on her arm, facing him. Her eyes were closed. He smiled slightly and made himself comfortable. He stowed his glasses, then drew the blanket up, covering her as well. With a sigh, he settled in for sleep. "Good night," came a whisper in his ear. He looked to see Ariaziane's eyes closing again, a smile on her lips. He returned the wish. And mirrored the smile.

❧ ❦

South River Keep was a handsome structure, simple in its design. Certainly not built to repel more than the smallest of invading hordes, nor designed to impress architects for centuries to come. It was functional, though, and not unpleasant to the eye, even for having been abandoned for several decades.

The party reached sight of the keep late in the afternoon of the third day of travel. Vincent was relieved at the prospect of spending a night indoors for a change. At the foot of the hill, they tethered their mounts, fed and watered them, and began their trek up the slopes to the entrance.

Vincent and Ariaziane exchanged frequent, anxious glances. Blade and Gnorrin were quiet, save for the occasional remark from Blade to watch the footing on the overgrown trail they followed. Within half an hour, they were at an entrance to the living area of the keep. The door was broken in, the portcullis propped open—signs from raiding parties of the past. The sharp spikes of the portcullis gate were rusted over, as were the hinges on the door. Vincent raised an eyebrow as a rat scurried out of the shadows, then back in, once it saw them.

Blade led them through several rooms, up a flight of stairs, and through more rooms. Everything they saw was in ruins. Soon they came upon a room that was once very obviously a sleeping chamber. The remains of a destroyed bed occupied the center of the room. When Blade unshouldered his pack, the rest did the same. "So when did you say you were here last?" Vincent asked.

Blade gave a small shrug. "Perhaps five or six years ago."

"Hell of a memory you have for finding the bedroom."

"Not especially," he confessed. "Most keeps of this size are set up in standard ways. I didn't remember where this room was. I simply deduced this would be the logical place to find it."

"Thank you, Mr. Spock." Vincent stretched and cracked his back. "Well, now that we're here, what do we do?"

Gnorrin spoke first. "We eat." He broke out his rations of biscuits and jerky.

"Oh, yum," Vincent drawled. "Can't we call out for pizza?"

Blade was tidying up the room, with some help from Ariaziane. Vincent started arranging his things in one corner, and broke out his own rations. "Will we be beginning our explorations tonight, or waiting for morning?" Ariaziane asked.

Blade finished his set-up and shrugged. "Which would the two of you prefer?"

The teenagers exchanged glances. Ariaziane spoke for both, as she joined Vincent. "I see no reason we cannot begin tonight. At least a little. I'm curious about this mage, though. What do you know of him?"

The four sat near Vincent's corner of the room, nibbling their dinners and passing a waterskin around. Blade began the story. "His name was Kurean—"

Vincent snorted. "You're sure it wasn't Vietnamese?"

The trio stared at him. Ariaziane turned back to Blade. "Earth humor. Ignore him."

"Yes. Well, his name was Kurean..." Blade shook his head at Vincent's second, softer, snort. "... and he was a powerful human mage in these parts, roughly a hundred years ago."

Vincent cleared his throat. "Why do you stress he was a *human* mage?"

Ariaziane answered him. "The ancient races live much longer than humans, so it is far more common for strong mages to be other than human. They have more years to study and become stronger."

Vincent nodded and noticed Gnorrin's smile. Blade continued. "As I understand it, his specialty was in the field of elemental research."

Gnorrin continued. "Yes, this is true. Kurean was very much interested in the four elements: air, earth, fire, and water. Especially fire."

"Did you know him?" Ariaziane asked.

"Not at all. I was barely born when he was defeated. I have known those, however, who did know him. I understand he was a very intelligent and very good man. Naturally, though, he was looked upon with fear by many people, simply because he was a mage."

Vincent finished his jerky. "Who defeated him? And why?"

Blade answered. "Rumor held that Kurean had vast wealth and a number of magical artifacts in his possession. Greed defeated him. The greed of others."

Gnorrin picked up the tale. "A group of mercenaries came from the north. The exact method they used to defeat Kurean is unknown, but he was killed after a great battle. The entire western face of this hill was once dense with woods. Reports say at one point during the battle, a huge explosion of fire swept the trees totally off, and the ground has remained barren to this day."

"The mercenaries ransacked the keep," Blade continued. "After they eventually departed, Kurean's body was recovered and burned. The townspeople felt it was fitting." He paused, drinking from the waterskin. "In the ensuing years, parties of adventurers continued to come, hoping to find additional hidden troves of booty to be had. Some succeeded, I imagine. But there has always been the one secret area under the hill that remained totally hidden. Until recently."

"So how come no one else has come to raid this not-so-secret area?" Vincent asked.

Blade shrugged. "Perhaps they have. I know not. We might discover the area already cleaned of whatever goods it possessed."

Vincent absorbed this with a thoughtful nod. He noted everyone had finished eating, and said, "Well. Shall we begin?"

Ariaziane smiled in anticipation. Gnorrin rose to his feet. Blade began handing out torches to the others. Vincent looked at the two he was given. They were simply wooden branches, about a foot and a half in length, with oil-soaked rags wrapped around one end. Vincent tucked his into his pack, allowing the wet ends to protrude from the top.

"Each torch will burn for approximately an hour," Blade announced. He produced two pieces of flint and struck them together. A spark ignited the rags on one of his torches. "Ready?"

Before entering the area to be explored, Blade showed the others around the rest of the keep. Vincent was curious to see how one was set up inside. It was one thing to read of ancient castles and constructs in books, and quite another to see one in person, even totally wiped out.

At the end of the tour, they arrived in the lower sections of the keep. Here, access to Kurean's secret rooms was to be gained. Vincent and Ariaziane looked around in wonder at the devastation. Stone walls were scorched in many places. Charred stumps of wood were strewn about. Certainly the only way anything of value would be found here was if there were, indeed, newly revealed areas. The pair looked at each other and at their mentors. Blade and Gnorrin were already leading them through to another chamber.

This proved to be a closet-sized room with the remains of a single door set in its far wall. This room, too, was scorched, the door reduced to kindling. The sight revealed through the doorway was the important feature of the room: a stairwell.

The steps were carved out of stone, Vincent realized. How long it must have taken to accomplish the work! The light of Blade's torch didn't reach very far into the underground darkness, and Vincent felt Ariaziane's hand clasping onto his tunic sleeve as they descended. He looked upon her face and saw a bit of nervousness in her eyes. She was afraid of the dark, he realized. He smiled reassuringly and removed her grip on his tunic. Instead, he wrapped her fingers with his own. She seemed to appreciate the gesture.

The descent seemed to take forever, but bottom was eventually reached. The stairwell let out into a large square room in ruins, just as the upstairs had been. Blade led them out of the room and into a corridor. It was a winding passage, carved out of the hillside, and held side passages at frequent intervals. Blade bypassed them all, and Vincent assumed this was because he knew they all led to areas already thoroughly looted. When the big man spoke, he felt Ariaziane's hand jerk in surprise.

"If my sources are correct, we should soon reach our destination."

Ariaziane exhaled loudly and self-consciously removed her hand from Vincent's. She smiled in excitement.

Vincent loved her smile. He was enchanted by it, and he grew giddy just from his near proximity to her. How he wanted to know she could feel similarly around him. He wanted desperately to impress her on this venture. She was still calling him clumsy. True, she did so with a certain amount of affection, as if he were a lovable clown in the neighborhood circus. Even that was slightly humiliating. When he was a young boy, his mother had called him "Vinnie the Pooh." A cute enough nickname for a four-year-old, but when his friend Joni had discovered the cutesy name in eleventh grade, voicing it aloud in a full classroom and causing him to live with it for the rest of high school... that wasn't so pleasant. "Clumsy" could haunt him the same way "Pooh" did. So he resolved to prove himself to her.

His first act along these lines was to promptly walk smack into Blade's back, stumble backward in a vain attempt to regain his balance, and plop directly onto his butt. Ariaziane stifled a giggle as Gnorrin turned around to shush them both. Vincent felt his face grow red and he briefly contemplated ritual suicide to atone for his humiliation, then noticed why Blade had stopped walking so abruptly. He heard a noise coming from around the corner immediately in front of them. Ariaziane noticed, too, and her chuckling disappeared. Vincent rose slowly to his feet and listened intently. It was a faint scratching sound, followed by the louder sound of a rock tumbling down over what must have been a pile of rocks. He saw Blade relax and poke his head around the corner. He turned to his friends. "No matter. Only rats."

They rounded the corner. There was, indeed, a huge pile of rubble, reaching nearly to the ceiling. A few rats scurried away at the sight of the approaching light. Vincent saw Ariaziane suppress a shiver. He couldn't blame her. They were big rats.

Blade glanced at his torch. "Time for a change. Who will be the next carrier of the flame?"

Gnorrin pulled out one of his torches, lighting it from Blade's. "I will. Let the young ones have their fun."

"Very well," Blade said, "are we all ready to enter the dragon's lair?"

"Excuse you?" Vincent said.

"Just an expression," his friend replied. "You'll not be seeing any dragons this day, lad. Come." With that, Blade began to climb the rubble. The cave-in seemed awfully thorough to Vincent, but he was willing to go along if Blade seemed to think it was worthwhile. Gnorrin motioned for Ariaziane to follow behind Blade; he climbed up after her, while Vincent went last.

He hoped his lovely Annie wasn't claustrophobic as well as being afraid of rats. There was very little clearance between the top of the rubble and the ceiling. Gnorrin could walk nearly upright, given his stature, though the rest of them had to make their way in a crouched position. Vincent couldn't see where they were headed, but assumed Blade could. He had very sharp eyes, even in the dark, so the order of their procession seemed to make sense.

It was cool and damp inside, and Vincent could see his breath in front of him. More rats scurried out of their way as they sometimes walked, sometimes crawled across the top of the caved-in tunnel. Vincent realized most of the debris was from the right wall, dug out of the hillside, having collapsed inward. Some was from the ceiling, however. These were the areas that allowed Gnorrin to walk upright, and the rest of them nearly so.

They remained skirting the left wall for quite a distance, until Vincent saw Gnorrin begin moving to the right. Soon they came upon a narrow opening, as though the rubble were piled in front of a doorway. As he neared, he saw this was exactly the case. Blade was peering inside, as was Ariaziane. Gnorrin held the torch safely out of distance of them and tried to glance in as best he could.

"What can you see?" Vincent whispered.

Blade answered over his shoulder. "Others have been here," he said with a touch of surprise in his voice. "Enough rubble has been pushed in from this point to allow us to pass through comfortably. I suspect our visit here could prove fruitless."

"That's too bad," Vincent said. "I wouldn't mind a nice, crisp apple right now."

Ariaziane stared at him while the others simply shook their heads. Then she said, "Remind me again why we brought you along."

Blade sat down in the doorway, his legs hanging inside. He slid down into the room as though on a great sliding board. Gnorrin reached in, tossing the torch down to him before assisting Ariaziane and Vincent through the small opening. Then he, too, went sliding down.

The room looked to have been thoroughly searched. Tables were overturned, chairs smashed. There was one other door, on the opposite wall, which stood wide open. Vincent pondered the fact that the room was even intact. The landslide, or whatever caused all the devastation, had somehow left the room unharmed. And evidently the other room as well, assuming the door didn't lead to a dead end. How could that be, if the entire tunnel wall all around the entrance to the room had been collapsed? Magic, perhaps, he thought. But the more he thought about it, the more he realized it didn't matter. His thoughts returned to the situation at hand, and to trying to impress the girl he was falling in love with.

He joined the rest in looking about the room. It wasn't very large, perhaps twenty feet square, and seemed to have been a sort of study. A broken bookcase lay on its side near one wall. Gnorrin was busy perusing the few remaining volumes that were still intact. Blade lit his remaining torch and shoved it into a wall sconce as he searched the other side of the room. Vincent moved over to Ariaziane, who was peering over Gnorrin's shoulder.

"What do you think?" he asked.

She turned to him, the excitement showing on her face. "Incredible," she breathed. "I've never felt so... I can't describe it! So..."

"Alive?"

"Yes! Yes, exactly! It's so thrilling! Not knowing what we might find, who we might encounter."

Vincent nodded in understanding. She really had lived a sheltered life, he thought. He smiled, happy he'd been able to provide this kind of experience for her. Or at least introduce her to those who did the actual providing.

He moved away from her, over to the area Blade was searching, leaving the others to finish with the books. He wouldn't have minded looking over the tomes himself, but figured Blade would want him to tag along on his heels, not Gnorrin's.

Kurean had evidently been fond of artwork. The remains of a very nice vase were scattered about one corner. A torn tapestry lay against the wall. A small wooden rack had been knocked from a wall. Bits of glass were everywhere on the surrounding floor, as well as three bottles of varying sizes that had somehow survived the fall.

Vincent stooped and picked them up. The smallest of the three was no bigger than a two ounce vial, bluish in color, and simple in its design. A cork stopped up the opening, though the bottle was obviously empty. The largest one was pale green in color, more ornate in its styling, and had a glass plug, ringed with cork, as its stopper. It, too, was empty, but would have held about a quart, Vincent imagined. The last bottle was amber in color, with a hint of red. This one was pint sized, but empty. The design was almost boring, but the stopper was interesting, as it was attached to the bottle's neck by a heavy wire brace, operating with simple leverage to close the bottle very tightly.

The small bottle could find some use, he was sure. Perhaps to hold oil or something. The larger one was attractive simply for its own sake. Yet there was something about the middle bottle. He wasn't sure what. Certainly the stopper was nice, but there was something else.

No matter. Whatever the appeal was, he'd keep the bottle. Vincent smiled at his find and unshouldered his small pack. He tucked the two smaller bottles away, and was in the process of depositing the third, when Blade came to his side. He glanced at the prize. "Bottles, lad? Not exactly treasure."

"I know. It's kind of a sentimental thing, actually. I had a neighbor, back home. An elderly fellow who collected old bottles. He'd go out into areas where people had once dumped trash, and he'd dig. He had hundreds of them, all different shapes and colors. Glassblowing and bottle making had sort of become an obsolete art, by the time I was born. Everything became so mechanized and uniform. The bottles Mr. Douglas had in his house, though, were beautiful, like nothing I'd ever seen before. He even gave me a couple, once." He shrugged. "I'm no expert on bottles or glassware, but I always enjoyed visiting him and looking at his newest additions."

Blade nodded. "Perhaps I was wrong. Memories are dear treasures. Items that spark pleasant memories are valuable, indeed." He fingered at something just under the collar of his tunic as he spoke, his eyes distant. Suddenly he smiled and clapped his hand on his friend's shoulder. "Shall we continue?" Vincent nodded and they rejoined their friends.

Vincent stepped over to Ariaziane, impulsively stroking the back of her hair. "Find anything?"

Clearly, the girl's enthusiasm hadn't dimmed. She turned her head, causing Vincent to quickly remove his hand from her hair. "There are a few books that should prove interesting. Nothing truly valuable, but interesting nonetheless."

Vincent nodded, noticing Blade had spoken a few words to Gnorrin before moving off toward the room's remaining door. "I found some kinda nice bottles," he told her, gazing over the selection of books she and Gnorrin had chosen and put aside.

Gnorrin stood. "I think we've exhausted the possibilities here, lass. Let's pack them up." Vincent assisted as they lowered three of the volumes into Gnorrin's pack and two into Ariaziane's. "Let's see what Blade is getting into."

The trio joined Blade in the small room opposite the entrance. It was completely empty, and no more than closet-sized. Blade was standing quietly in the room, his head cocked, as if listening for something. He stood close to the far wall. When they entered, he turned and bade the younger pair to approach. "Feel the walls on either side of you," he said. Vincent and Ariaziane did so, not really knowing what they were feeling for. "Now," he continued, "feel this one." Again, they did as he said. "What difference do you detect?"

The pair glanced at each other, unsure. Vincent wondered for a moment what kind of game Blade was up to, before he realized the difference. "The temperature," he blurted. "This wall is slightly warmer than the others."

"Aye, lad. Very good. Now stand near either side wall, close to the corners up here." Once more, they obeyed. "Stand very still. What do you feel?"

After a moment, Ariaziane said, "There is a faint breeze, coming from behind us!"

"Excellent!" Gnorrin piped in. "A hidden doorway!"

"Cool!" Vincent said. "How do we open it?"

Blade frowned. "I haven't yet discovered that."

The trio joined him in a search of every nook and cranny in the carved walls, looking for some sort of trigger mechanism. When many minutes had passed without success, Gnorrin said, "Remember this was the keep of a mage. There might well be no physical way for the door to be opened."

Blade nodded. "Very well. You may proceed."

Gnorrin rubbed his chin. "Oh, I don't know, my friend. I think I'll leave that to my pupil." He turned to Ariaziane. "Do you remember?"

The girl fidgeted. "I think so." She took a deep breath while the others moved out of her way. Vincent's eyes narrowed. She hadn't told him she'd actually learned any spells. He watched as she mumbled a few words under her breath and made odd hand gestures. After this, she touched the door with the knuckles of her fist, as if to knock. To Vincent's astonishment as well as her own, the stone wall moved, recessing about two feet straight back. The sound of stone grinding on stone echoed from the revealed chamber.

Vincent's jaw dropped and he stared at Ariaziane, who had turned first to Gnorrin, brimming with pleasure, then to Vincent. "Far out!" he said. "You never told me!"

She gave a sheepish smile. "I wanted to surprise you. And impress you, I suppose."

"Yeah. Well, you certainly did both." He glanced at Gnorrin, noticing the pride in his friend's eye. He shook his head. "Well, let's make use of it."

He strode toward the opening, only to have Blade's hand clamp onto his shoulder. "Not so fast, boy. This is no place to rush in without caution." Vincent turned to him. He hated being called "boy" in front of Ariaziane. "Mages have a love for setting magical traps, you'll find. Impulsiveness is unwise."

"Haste could waste me, in other words." He shrugged. "Fine. After you."

Blade shook his head. "I think not. Gnorrin?"

The gnome nodded and stepped into the aperture. After a word or two and a gesture, he announced, "It is safe. At least here." Gnorrin motioned them to follow and led the way inside, taking the passage revealed on the right of the stone. Once inside, he noted with satisfaction, "There is but one passage. Both entrances merge inside."

Blade handed Vincent the torch before they entered. The corridor was a narrow, descending tunnel, allowing only single-file ranks. Gnorrin led, followed by Blade. Ariaziane and Vincent followed him. Vincent noted that the walls grew damp to the touch the deeper they went. Light from his torch glistened on their surfaces. He tried to look ahead, but the other three blocked his view. He sighed, resigning himself to being the one to always pull up the rear.

The corridor was dotted with deep alcoves on either side, some of which appeared to reach back many feet. Gnorrin examined the first few they encountered, reaching in with the torch and examining closely, but all were empty. They went in a few feet from the hall proper and ended. Vincent wondered idly what purpose they served, thinking perhaps they were natural occurrences, like the huge niches he'd seen in cliff faces along Arizona roads. It was possible, he supposed. He glanced into a few of them, as well, yet could see nothing in them.

The passage seemed to go on forever, though he was sure this was just his own impatience. Finally, he said, "How long is this damn tunnel?"

Blade replied, "Perhaps another hundred yards. I am sensing a change in pressure. I believe we will encounter a chamber soon."

Vincent shook his head. Blade was a piece of work, all right. He glanced again at the walls, noticing a sparkle he hadn't seen before. He slowed, examining the wall more closely. He stopped. "Son of a..." he whispered. He withdrew his dagger and picked at one of the bright veins. "Blade?"

The party stopped moving, many yards away. "Yes?"

"Look in the walls! Is it gold?"

Blade chuckled as Vincent worked at prying out a piece. "Nay. Knave's gold, only. Come, now. Don't lag too far behind."

Vincent sighed. He should have realized. Certainly no need to get excited over iron pyrite. He turned away from the wall and continued after his friends. As he went to insert the dagger back into its sheath, he fumbled it. The blade fell to the floor, where he proceeded to accidentally kick it several feet down the corridor. "Clumsy," he muttered to himself. "Annie's right."

The dagger slid to a stop in front of one of the alcoves. He bent over to pick it up. As his hand closed on the hilt, he noticed something in the alcove. A pair of feet. His stomach dropped. Oh, shit, he thought. He looked up. When the sword began its swing toward his head, instinct took over. He ducked. The attacker's blade rang off the stone floor, causing the others up ahead to turn in surprise. The brigand rushed out, raising his weapon once again. Vincent heard Ariaziane yell "No!" just as the blade began its descent. Without thinking, he raised his arms to cover his head, laying his dagger flat along his forearm. The sword impacted on the blade with a loud crack, surprising the man. Vincent swept out his leg, knocking the man's feet out from under him. He fell with a grunt onto his back. When he attempted to rise, Vincent's dagger was at his throat. He wisely chose to remain on the ground.

The others were at his back instantly, Blade rushing to Vincent's side. "Are you all right?"

"Fine," he said as his heart slowly calmed to a more reasonable speed. "You?"

Blade laughed. "You're... How did you say it? A trip. In this case, literally. I did not teach you such a move."

Vincent smiled with false bravado. "What? That? Just something I picked up from frequent visits to the land of Nintendo." He reached down and removed the man's sword from his grip, handing it to Blade. "On your feet, dipshit." Vincent grasped the front of his tunic, helping him rise. Slowly. He didn't move the dagger. "Who are you and what are you doing here?"

The man swallowed, his Adam's apple bobbing close to the dagger point. "The same as you, I imagine," he croaked.

Blade interrupted the interrogation. "How many are with you?"

The man shook his head a fraction of an inch. "None. The others have taken things out. I was left to watch and continue to gather." He paused. "I'm sorry for attacking you. Honestly."

Vincent frowned. "Right. Well, if you were left to gather more loot, why were you here in the corridor?"

The man smiled sheepishly. "Nature requires breaks. Your pardon, Miss," he said to Ariaziane.

"Think you can hold it just a bit longer?" Vincent asked, nudging the dagger slightly.

The man hesitated, his face flushing in embarrassment. "There... ah... that would no longer be necessary."

Vincent heard Gnorrin chuckle as they all noticed the wetness spreading across the front of the man's trousers. Blade said, "Join us, then. Give us the tour, if you will."

"Certainly." He swallowed hard and sweat trickled down his face. "My pleasure."

Vincent allowed Blade to take over guarding him. The man walked in front of the party, Blade's sword keeping him in line. Ariaziane turned to Vincent. "Are you sure you are well?"

"Fine," he lied. His stomach was doing somersaults.

She paused. "I thought you were going to die."

"I'm fine, Annie. Don't worry." He squeezed her hand and was pleased when she squeezed back.

Their captive led them to the end of the corridor, to a large room. The door was open and light came from within. Vincent smiled in anticipation as they neared. When the man was a few feet from the door, however, Vincent's smile disappeared. Something was wrong. He didn't know what, or how he knew it, but something was definitely wrong. "Down!" he shouted as the captive dove into the room.

Vincent tackled Ariaziane and hit the floor. Like marionettes with their wires cut, Blade and Gnorrin fell to their knees. Arrows whizzed over their heads and a handful of what Vincent swore were bottle rockets scorched by. The arrows missed. The rockets, however, zeroed in on Blade's chest like guided missiles. The man was knocked back a foot or two, and sat there stupidly for a moment. The chain mail under his tunic seemed to protect him from harm, though.

Gnorrin made a motion and instantly there was a shimmering wall of force in front of them, blocking the doorway. Vincent and Ariaziane watched as two more arrows hit the magical wall and bounced harmlessly away. Gnorrin turned to Blade. "Are you well?"

"Aye." He rose to his feet. The others did the same.

"We seem to have a minimum of two archers and a mage against us," Gnorrin said. "As well as our less-than-honest former captive." Blade and Gnorrin exchanged long looks. Vincent noticed this, and suddenly had a sick feeling of comprehension.

Blade turned toward him and Ariaziane, his face a mix of regret and surprise. "My apologies, friends. Gnorrin and I did not intend for this eventuality to occur."

"What you mean," Vincent countered, "is you had thought the entire place to have been completely wiped out by now, so we wouldn't be in any danger whatsoever, yet still think we were on a real treasure hunt."

Blade said nothing, then Gnorrin said, "This really was with the best intentions, lad."

"Sure it was. And that was why you went along with the idea, isn't it?" He sighed. "Fine. Well, I forgive you. Provided," he said firmly, "that we survive. If I get killed, I'm gonna be pissed." He paused. "How long will your invisible wall last, Gnorrin?"

"As long as I wish, but the shield is only good against things moving at high rates of speed, such as arrows. We can walk through it any time we like. However, the mage will realize that quite soon, in all likelihood."

"The archers have given up," Blade observed. He handed Vincent the sword taken from their captive. "Ready, lad?"

"You betcha. Let's go get 'em."

Leaving the torches behind in the doorway, Blade and Vincent entered first, each providing cover for Gnorrin and Ariaziane respectively. The two former archers had taken up swords and both converged on Blade. Vincent didn't think this would be a problem for the man. The mage and Vincent's former dancing partner were left for the rest. The swordsman had obtained another weapon and charged at Vincent.

Vincent parried the mad attack easily enough, which seemed to remind the man to be intimidated by him. He was very cautious in his attacks after this. Vincent found this unexpected caution gave him confidence. He drew upon every bit of training Blade had given him, and before long, the man was bleeding from half a dozen minor wounds. Vincent himself sustained a slight gash on his sword arm, but the adrenaline kept him from noticing it after the initial injury.

Out of the corner of his eye, Vincent caught a glow of green, a flash of golden light, and the unmistakable sound of Ariaziane gasping in alarm. The sound alone was enough for Vincent to want to finish his opponent immediately. Obligingly, the man gave him the opportunity. A sword slash came at his neck. Vincent ducked, then retaliated with a swing to the back of the man's head with the flat of his sword, knocking him unconscious onto his face. After picking up the fallen man's sword, just in case he resumed consciousness, Vincent scanned the room for Ariaziane.

First he noticed that Blade had defeated both of his assailants, who lay wounded but conscious on the floor. He was tying them back to back with a length of rope. Then he saw Ariaziane.

She stood rooted in fear, staring at the ground. Five trails of green dust stretched from close to her feet, across the room, ending just before the enemy mage. The mage stood still, too, but not in fear. He was frozen in place, a look of surprise on his face. Gnorrin was examining his stiffened form.

Vincent stepped over to the girl. He put his hand on her shoulder and was gratified when she clung to him. "Are you okay?" She nodded, but he could see she looked ready to throw up. They moved over to Gnorrin, Ariaziane staring at the green dust the whole way.

"Geez. What'd you do to him?" Vincent asked.

"Merely paralyzed him. I was lucky. Had his attention not been occupied by his attack on the girl, he could easily have resisted my spell. I broke his concentration with that flash of light, then paralyzed him."

"I think I'm the lucky one," Ariaziane said. "What spell was this?"

Gnorrin glanced at the dust and clucked his tongue. "I don't think you want to know," he said. He turned back to his task of relieving the mage of his possessions. Ariaziane began to help him.

Blade summoned Vincent to his side and he dashed over. Blade opened a tiny chest that sat in a corner, among other items. Inside were handfuls of coins, all of them bright and shiny. "This," he stressed, "is *real* gold."

Vincent did the mental calculations, estimating the number of coins in the chest and multiplying the figure by his idea of the value of a single gold piece. His eyes widened. "Wow!" he said. He ran his hands through the coins, enjoying the feel of them and the sound they made. His fingers came out with two silver chains wrapped around them. He also unearthed a ring. The chains held amulets at the ends. He held them up to show Blade.

As Blade took the chains to Gnorrin, Vincent looked back in the box and extracted the ring. It was dull gold, with strange carvings that appeared to be letters, but in a language he couldn't read. His first thought was to give it to Ariaziane, but the ring seemed too big for her small fingers. Besides, it wasn't really very attractive. He tried it on. At first it seemed too loose, but it must have been his imagination. After a moment, he realized he couldn't have asked for a more perfect fit. He smiled and dug around through the box again, but the coins were the only things present.

Blade returned with the chains and set them back inside. "Nice enough," he said. "A jeweler might pay a handsome price for them."

Vincent smiled and closed the lid of the coffer. "Well, let's see what other goodies we can scrounge up."

Over the next several minutes, they gathered up what they could. In addition to the coin chest and the items Gnorrin removed from the mage, there were the weapons used by the fallen attackers, a cache of potions in a rack Gnorrin discovered, and a few more books.

After packing these items away, they left the room. Whomever regained consciousness first, the mage or the swordsman, could attend the wounded fighters. Blade mentioned it would be best if they were elsewhere when this happened. There was no argument.

Leaving the underground behind, they returned to their room upstairs.

❧ Six ❧

We took turns standing guard that night, just in case our friends from the underground decided to track us down. Gnorrin magically hid us, as well as our horses, but we still didn't want to risk discovery.

Ariaziane had trouble getting to sleep. She was tossing and turning in her corner of the room. My insomnia, combined with the adrenaline rush of the evening's events, caused me to lie awake, too. At any rate, at one point, Annie crept over to my side. She still seemed a bit spooked by her close call with the mage's spell. Her mind was full of horrible thoughts of what his spell could have been. Eventually, she slept, but not soundly. She tossed and turned all throughout the night. I heard her moan in her sleep twice.

In the morning, we returned home. The trip was uneventful, except for Ariaziane throwing up not long into the journey. I'm pretty concerned about her.

Blade had evidently promised the abbey an equal share of whatever we found. The coffer held one hundred forty gold coins. At $400 per coin, we'd made quite a haul. We each kept thirty, the other twenty going to the abbey. The pendants went to them, too. Gnorrin estimated they would bring their total equal to our own.

This morning I gave two gold pieces to Gnorrin. He gave me a hard time, but I insisted on repaying him for everything he's done for me. I wanted to give some to Blade, but he wouldn't hear of it.

Vincent looked up as Gnorrin sat across the gaming table from him.

"Well, Vincent," he said gaily, "have you decided what to do with your treasure, yet?"

Vincent pushed the journal aside and capped the ink bottle. "I think I have, actually." He smiled briefly. "I think I'd like to buy a house."

Gnorrin raised an eyebrow, then chuckled. "Buy? Boy, we don't buy houses. We build them!"

Vincent frowned. "I don't know anything about building a house."

"Well, neither do I. You hire craftsmen to do the actual construction. Where would you like to build?"

"I dunno. Somewhere near here. I don't want to travel far to have to visit you."

"Or the girl," his friend said with a knowing grin.

Vincent flushed. "Well, yeah. So do you know of any nice locations around here? I'd like to keep close to the stream."

"I'm sure Blade will take you scouting today, if you like. You'll have something to do while I'm occupying your girlfriend's time."

"She's not my girlfriend. She doesn't like me that way."

Gnorrin shrugged. "Perhaps not. But be patient, lad. It will grow."

"I hope you're right."

Blade stepped out of the cottage, a large empty sack rolled up under his arm. "I'm going into town, Vincent. Would you care to join me?"

Vincent saw his journal page was dry and closed the book. "I would, thanks. Let me get ready." He turned to Gnorrin as he headed inside. "If we don't pass Annie on the road, tell her I'll see her when I get back." Gnorrin nodded, and Vincent disappeared into the cottage.

Once in town, Vincent and Blade split up. Vincent's first stop was *The Nib and Quill*. The shop was closed, this being Firstday, and Vincent had begged off several days in a row due to the trip to the old keep. He wasn't due to return to work until the following day. Mepis was sweeping the porch and greeted Vincent warmly.

"How was your adventure, lad?" he asked, and Vincent could tell he'd expected it to have gone the same way Blade and Gnorrin had.

"Quite well, thanks. So well, in fact, that I've come to tell you I won't be needing employment with you any longer."

Mepis stood in stunned silence, the broom still. "What do you mean?"

"I mean," he said, stepping onto the porch and taking over the sweeping, "I acquired enough wealth so as not to need to work for you. I'm not going to retire, mind you, but for a while, I'm just going to get comfortable."

Mepis was flustered. "That old keep couldn't have had any treasure left!"

Vincent gave Mepis the short version of his trip. Mepis listened closely, amazed at the tale. Vincent finished his story and sweeping simultaneously. Mepis took the broom back from Vincent, but was obviously uncomfortable. "Well, that's some story. I'm happy for you, but I've put a lot of time into training you! It's not right for you to just leave like this!"

"I'm sorry for the inconvenience. I think I might have something to ease the strain on you." Vincent reached for his pouch. "I remember you telling me how other merchants want to sell your wonderful inks, and how you don't want to, since the inks are a source of pride and accomplishment for you." Mepis nodded as Vincent pulled out a bottle from his pack. "There might be a way you can profit by selling your inks to other merchants, yet still keep your pride intact." He placed the bottle on the countertop. Vincent had made a label for it, a simple rectangle of white paper, glued to the glass, with the inscription "Inks by Mepis" in bold print across its face. "Simply put, you sell your inks in bottles with labels like this, instructing that they be sold as advertised. With your name on them."

Mepis examined the product, nodding. "Very handsome. But how will I know the merchants will do so? They could easily remove the labels or pour the ink into other bottles and sell them as their own."

"True. Unless you had a written agreement, a contract, stating everything clearly. Any violation, like what you just mentioned, would be cause for damages to be paid to you for breach of contract."

Mepis glowed. "Ah! I see! We would get a litigant to oversee the writing of such an agreement! Oh, this is a wonderful idea, Vincent! I'm surprised no one else has thought to do such a thing!"

Vincent smiled and nodded. He, too, had wondered the same thing. He hoped Mepis would have good luck with the idea. And he hoped he hadn't just created a marketing monster. He stuck out his hand. "Good luck. I'm sure it'll work out for you. And if there's anything else I can help you out with, just let me know."

Mepis shook Vincent's hand, and Vincent felt the man was treating him with a new respect. Treating him as an equal, not an apprenticed boy. "Certainly, my friend. Don't be a stranger, now."

"I won't. I'll still be buying my paper and things from you. And I'm looking forward to seeing your inks in other towns!"

After a few more pleasantries, they parted, Mepis to draw up labels for his bottles, and Vincent to his next stop. He stepped out into the street from *The Nib and Quill* and began walking, nodding politely to the hooded and cloaked figure who came around the corner and fell into step behind him. Vincent resisted the urge to turn around and find the face hidden under the cloak. With a shrug, he went on his way.

His next stop was another familiar one. "Good morning, Tarel," Vincent said as he entered the clothing shop.

The tailor looked up from behind his counter. "Well, look who has returned. Quite a beard you've grown since last we met."

Vincent rubbed his chin and laughed. "I suppose. I will be needing more clothing, Tarel. Thought I might give you some business."

Tarel nodded, coming forward with his tape measure. Once more, Vincent was measured for a proper fit. Then he chose fabrics and trims, and gave Tarel instructions for his needs. He was sure to pick out fabrics for all seasons. When he was done, he asked for the total price from the man. Tarel totaled the figures in his head and mentioned a sum. Vincent smiled. "This is where I'm supposed to haggle, yes?"

Tarel shrugged. "That would be expected, yes."

"Well, fortunately for you, I'm not very good at it. I'm also feeling generous. The price will be fine." Tarel beamed with pleasure. "However," he continued, "I will expect nothing less than your finest work."

"And you will have it."

"Very good." Vincent tossed a single gold piece to the man.

Tarel raised an eyebrow, and gave a tiny bow. "One moment."

Vincent smiled while accepting his change. "I'll pick them up in a week."

Tarel nodded, all smiles. "Very good. And give my regards to Gnorrin!"

He joined up again with Blade, as they'd agreed, at the small weapons shop in town. The big man clapped him on the shoulder. "Did you leave your job, as you said?"

"That I did. Then I went and spent money! Something I've always enjoyed a great deal." He eyed the selection of weapons. "So what looks good?"

Blade indicated a few swords laid out on the tables. "These three are nicely made and have good balance."

Vincent hefted all three, a shortsword, a broadsword, and a bastard sword. Vincent had to wield the last one with both hands. "No contest. I like the shortsword best. I don't think I have the muscles yet for the other two."

Blade nodded. "I suspected as much. This is a fine weapon. There is a scabbard with it, but the price is steep. I think you can talk the merchant down."

Vincent shrugged. "It's only money." He signaled for the merchant, who ambled over. He was a large, robust man, with a pot belly and three days of beard on his face. "I'll take this shortsword, sir. I'd like to see your selection of bows, as well."

The man blinked with heavy lids. "Size?" he croaked, his breath smelling strongly of wine.

Vincent turned his head and took a clean breath. "Oh, not too long, not too short. Average pull."

The man took two bows from the wall. Vincent tested both, asking Blade his opinion of them. He chose one, as well as two quivers of twenty arrows each. After paying for everything, they left for the armory.

There, Blade helped Vincent get fitted for a chain mail tunic and padded cloth for underneath. While he was being measured for these, his eyes caught sight of some leather armor on display. One piece in particular stood out. It looked like a leather trench coat, dark brown. The bulk appeared to be boiled leather: hard, but not too thick. The sleeves, however, appeared softer, not as stiff as the rest of the coat. When the measuring was done, he tried it on.

"What do you think?" he asked Blade.

His friend shook his head. "That's an archer's coat. Too awkward to fight in."

Vincent made a few lunges and other movements. "Actually, it's not too bad. Take some getting used to. Besides, I think it looks really cool." He inquired of the price, paid for the coat, as well as the cloth and chain armor. The coat he wore, the rest could be picked up in a week.

Ariaziane was still in her studies with Gnorrin when Vincent and Blade arrived, so they continued past the cottage. After about fifteen minutes, they left the road, stepping into a large field perhaps three acres in size, mostly long grasses and a few odd shrubs. Blade led him back along the edge of the woods until they were close to the stream. Hidden in the recesses of the woods, just out of sight of the main road, was a small square of land with little vegetation. Vincent looked it over, surveying the entire field from its vantage point. He smiled to himself, looking at his friend. "You'd intended to build your own place here, hadn't you?"

Blade shrugged. "Perhaps. I had not decided yet whether I am ready to settle down in one location. There are many things I have yet to do." He paused for a while, looking out on the horizon. "A beautiful location for a small home. I should hate to think of it going to waste."

Vincent nodded, wishing again for the man to open up and spill his guts. But he didn't probe. "Well, in that case, it will not. Thank you."

Blade nodded. "Tomorrow we will hire the builders."

"Sounds great." He took a deep breath. "I'm hungry. Ready to go?"

Blade nodded, and they headed back in the direction of Gnorrin's cottage.

While waiting for Gnorrin and Ariaziane to finish their lesson of the day, Blade and Vincent engaged in a game of chess. During the game, Blade noticed Vincent's ring. "Where did you buy that?" he asked.

"I didn't. I found it at the keep, in the box with the gold and the necklaces." He held it out for Blade to examine.

"You never mentioned this before." Blade frowned over the inscription on the ring.

"I'm sorry. I didn't think to. Is it valuable? I didn't mean to take more than my share."

Blade waved a hand. "The monetary value is of no consequence. I am more concerned..." He paused before saying, "May I?" Vincent nodded, and Blade slipped the ring from his finger, carrying it to Gnorrin.

Vincent sighed and looked down at the game board. He was getting trounced, as usual. A strategist, he wasn't. He heard footsteps and looked up to see all three of his friends approaching. Gnorrin now held the ring and was frowning.

"What's the matter?" Vincent asked.

Gnorrin looked up. "Well, nothing is the matter, really. I had simply assumed the mage in the keep had contained all the magic to be found there."

"Magic?" Vincent said with a small voice. "Then I shouldn't have it. I mean..."

"Oh, fiddle," said Gnorrin. "Magic is not the exclusive province of mages. This ring," he said, holding it up in front of him, "was definitely enchanted by a mage. Yet anyone could benefit from its abilities."

Vincent swallowed. "And what abilities are those?"

"I've no idea. The writing is a tongue I'm not familiar with. I could test the ring for you. It would take considerable time, but if you're interested..."

Vincent accepted the ring back, and held it for a while before slipping it back on his finger. "I'll let you know," he said. "Actually, there is one thing you can possibly help me with." He removed his glasses. "I'm getting sick of everybody always staring at me when they see these on my face. As you and Blade mentioned when I first arrived here, I don't need additional attention drawn to myself. What can we do to change this? I can't see well without them, though, so I can't just discard them."

Gnorrin frowned and rubbed his chin. Ariaziane leaned over and whispered something in his ear. The gnome lifted his eyebrows and stopped rubbing. "That could work. But I cannot make the state permanent."

"What?" Vincent asked.

"The lass has suggested making the spectacles invisible. As I said, I would be able to do this, but lack the skill to make the state permanent." Suddenly he brightened. "Just a moment!" He dashed inside his cottage and returned a few moments later with a few small bottles.

"The rack of potions at the keep, remember?" He handed a bottle to Vincent and one to Ariaziane. "This is healing potion."

Vincent eyed the clear liquid dubiously. "What exactly does it heal?"

"Injury. It is a rejuvenator. If you are hurt and weakened, drink it down. In moments you will be healthier."

"Wonderful, but that doesn't help me with my glasses."

"No, but this one will." He uncorked and handed the third bottle to Vincent. "Now," he said, "take the spectacles and dip one arm into the bottle."

Vincent did as instructed. When he removed it, the arm was half gone. "Hey!" he said, alarmed. "This stuff just ate my frames!"

"No, lad," Blade piped in. "It made them invisible." He held out a handkerchief. "Dip this into the potion, being careful not to get any on you, and wipe the spectacles."

Again, Vincent did as instructed, raising an eyebrow when the potion seemed to eat the handkerchief away. He dabbed at his glasses. When he was finished, they were totally invisible. "Far out! How long will it last?"

Gnorrin shrugged. "Quite some time. The liquid is intended to be drunk, to turn a person invisible. As such, it lasts only temporarily, because the body burns it up, as it would food. Your spectacles will do no such thing. The oil should last days. Perhaps more than a week before needing to be applied again."

Vincent smiled and lifted the invisible glasses to his face, putting them on. "Weird! But great! Thank you!"

Gnorrin corked the bottle and pushed it toward him. "My pleasure."

Ariaziane spoke up. "What about the scroll you got from the mage?"

He nodded. "I have deciphered much of the writing. There are spells, as I mentioned to you once before. They are not ones I am very familiar with, but I am trying to translate them. The mage who inscribed it must have been from far off. I am unfamiliar with the dialect used." Seeing Vincent's frown, he explained. "The language of magic is like the spoken word. There are many variations. Just as someone from the southern lands and someone from the northern lands might speak the same tongue, yet only understand each other a little, so it is with mage tongue."

"It's all Greek to me," Vincent said and cast another look at the ring on his finger. He wasn't at all sure he wanted it there. He smiled weakly at Gnorrin, thanking him for looking at the ring and for the potion.

As Gnorrin and Ariaziane finished their studies, Blade completed his devastation of Vincent in the game. Ariaziane left not long thereafter, but not before she assured Vincent she was feeling much better. The fact relieved him. A little.

The following day, Blade and Vincent sat with the man Vincent intended to hire. He explained to him what he wanted in the way of a house. Since he intended to get a horse, he included having the acreage fenced in like a corral, and a small stable in the rear. He watched as the man sketched the layout on a piece of paper, nodding in approval at his understanding of what he wanted done. As for the inside of the cottage itself, it would be very similar to Gnorrin's, with two sleeping chambers, a living area, and an eat-in kitchen area. Vincent smiled, and they shook on the final plans. Then Vincent asked the two most important questions, those of cost and of projected construction time. The man estimated one week, much to Vincent's surprise. On the other hand, he wasn't talking about building the Taj Majal. Vincent reached into his pouch, and dropped three gold coins into the man's hand. They shook hands again, and he and Blade left.

"Getting the cottage built won't be quite as expensive as I'd expected," he told Ariaziane as they walked through town later that afternoon. "And the plans look pretty nice. It's no palace, but it'll be nice enough."

"That's great," she said.

"So why don't you look into getting a place of your own?"

She gave him an odd look. "That's hardly proper."

"Oh. I'm sorry. I should've realized." They walked along in silence for a moment before Vincent said, "I can't wait to see what kind of horse this is."

"He's a fine beast," she told him. "At least, for riding. Not too fast, but sure enough. Not weak, but not suited for a heavy load, either."

Vincent had never walked to this particular section of town before. Here the congestion of the shops was gone, and residential homes were the norm. Here and there, farms were seen. Ariaziane led him to one of these.

They walked back along the edge of the corral. Vincent noted several horses in the stables. "You realize I wouldn't know a good horse from one at death's door if my life depended on it."

"I'd rather assumed so. Don't worry."

They were met outside by the owner of the farm, who immediately led them out back to view the horse. Vincent nodded approvingly at the animal, a pleasant looking beast with medium brown coloring and long mane and tail. "How old is he?" Vincent asked.

The farmer cleared his throat. "'Bout six years."

Ariaziane pried open the horse's mouth and examined the teeth. "Closer to nine, I'd say." She eyed the farmer with a look that told him not to try to pull any fast ones. She showed Vincent the inside of the animal's mouth. "See the teeth? These ones here," she said, indicating the second incisors, "don't have indentations any more. That usually happens around eight years. And these central ones are beginning to look rectangular in shape. No way is this animal six years old. Nevertheless, there's still a lot of years left to him."

The farmer cleared his throat again, nervously this time. "He's gelded. Be good for a first horse."

Vincent looked over his shoulder at the man as he said this. He nodded in agreement with him, even though he had no idea whether a gelded horse was good or not for such a purpose. As he began to turn his attention back to the horse, he felt a jolt to his shoulder. He stepped back abruptly, noticing the horse turning his head away. Vincent looked at his shoulder in puzzlement. "I think he bit me," he said to Ariaziane.

She ignored him, stepping back to inspect the animal's legs. "A bit over at the knee," she said matter-of-factly. "No scarring, though. Doesn't look to be a fighter. Slightly sickle-hocked," she said, looking at the rear legs. Then she moved to the head.

Vincent watched as she looked into the animal's eyes, ears, and nose.

"Good head, though," she said. "Nice wide nostrils. Coat looks good." She walked around the horse, picking up each foot for inspection.

He had no idea what she was looking for, but continued to watch.

Finally, she said, "Would you trot him, please?"

The man nodded and stepped over to the horse. Vincent watched, at Ariaziane's urging, as he led the horse directly away from them for a ways, then back toward them. He looked at the legs, as she told him to, but still didn't know what he was looking for. She saved him the embarrassment of looking too stupid.

"Not bad," she said as they returned. "How much are you asking?"

The man cleared his throat. "Thirty silver."

Ariaziane laughed. "You must be joking. Fifteen would be more likely."

"Young lady! That's thievery!"

"Fine. Make us a more reasonable offer."

The man frowned. "Twenty-five silver."

The horse nipped Vincent's shoulder again. He spun on the animal, which gazed at him with an innocent expression. "Knock it off," he said, then shook his head at himself for expecting the beast to understand him.

"Twenty silver," Ariaziane was saying, "and you throw in saddle, bit and bridle."

The farmer chewed his upper lip. "Agreed."

The transaction was completed, the horse saddled up. Vincent took care to not stand near the animal's front end. "That was amazing," Vincent said as they rode away. "I never could have haggled like you did."

She shrugged. "Twenty silver was a very fair price for this horse, and he knew it."

The two of them sat upon the horse, Vincent guiding him slowly along the road. They were taking a different road back to the abbey, one that ran along the perimeter of town.

The sound of barking came to their ears. They turned and saw a black puppy yipping at them as it ran along the inside of a fence. Vincent pulled the horse to a stop and the puppy squeezed under the fence, bouncing around the horse's legs, yapping away. Vincent smiled down at the animal. "Do you like dogs?"

Ariaziane smiled. "I guess so. We never had one at the abbey."

They dismounted so Vincent could play with it. As soon as he reached out, the puppy was all over him, licking his face. He giggled and fell backward onto the grass as the animal perched itself on his chest, as if it had just won a game of king of the hill. Hearing more barking, Vincent craned his head to see four more pups bounding through the grass toward them, a woman in an apron chasing after them.

By the time the woman reached the edge of the fence, all five puppies were scrabbling atop Vincent, who lay flat on the ground, hysterical with laughter. Ariaziane watched them play, laughing, too.

The woman fussed at them. "Oh, you nasty animals! Come back inside here this instant!"

Ariaziane rescued her friend, removing puppies from him and handing them over the fence to the woman.

"Thank you, miss," the woman said. "I'm sorry if they troubled you, m'lord."

Vincent sat up, the first puppy held in his arms. Ariaziane handed the last of the others over the fence. "No trouble at all, ma'am. I was in need of a bath."

"Our latest litter has proved to be a bit rowdier than most," she said, still apologetic. "I'll be glad when they're all gone."

Vincent looked down at the little one in his hands. "You're for sale, pup?"

The woman laughed. "Yes, she is. And she seems quite taken with you. Two silvers and she's yours."

"Two silvers!" Ariaziane blurted. "For a dog?"

"Pure-bred, they are, miss." The woman sounded slightly offended. "I generally ask three, if you must know, but seeing as how troublesome they just were..."

Ariaziane shook her head and smiled. She looked down at Vincent. "It's your money."

What a day! I bought a horse! And a dog! This is so great!

And I'm going to have my own house. This is a very bizarre thought, for me. I mean, I'm not even eighteen years old and I'm buying a house! Without even the intermediate step of renting an apartment, first! What would Dad think?

I miss Dad. I wish he could see me, how I'm succeeding here. I never felt like I was much of a success in his eyes. I never "applied myself" or had much direction. Don't know if I ever would have, back home. But here, it's strange. Sometimes I just get the feeling I'm really going to accomplish something. I just wish my family could see it. Whatever it proves to be.

Maybe I should write a section of this journal as a type of "letter home" or something. Like a postcard from a vacation away. "Dear Dad... Doing well. Having some adventures. Making new friends. Mosquitoes suck. Miss everyone. Wish you were here."

Or maybe not.

In other news, Annie seems to be feeling better. I'm thankful for that. I was beginning to get worried. She says she hasn't had any more pains or nausea since the trip back from the keep.

She's so much fun to be with that sometimes I forget about feeling homesick. Now there's a thought! I wonder what it would be like if I could find my way home... and take Ariaziane with me...? I wonder if she'd be able to adapt to Earth society any easier than I'm doing here.

Probably best not to fantasize about it. Home is where you hang your swordbelt, I suppose. And I guess this world is mine, now.

During the following week, Vincent watched the laborers clear the land and build his new home. He found himself engrossed in the details of building the stone and wood house, the erection of the fence surrounding the big yard. He was pleased with how everything progressed.

And at the end of the week, Vincent sat in his new front yard. Blade and Gnorrin had left not long before, after helping him get moved in and surprising him with presents. Ariaziane was still there, helping him straighten up after the housewarming party.

"It's really a nice little place," she said.

"Yeah, it is. What a day. Thanks again."

"You're welcome."

"I thought housewarming parties were just an Earth thing." He looked over at the small doghouse not far from his front door. The puppy was sleeping in front. The horse whinnied in the stable. "I named the horse 'King.'"

"An impressive name for so average a beast. And the dog?"

"Blaise."

"But she isn't even the color of fire."

"Not that kind of blaze. Short for Modesty Blaise, actually. I had a dog much like this one, growing up. On Earth, we call the breed Labrador Retrievers. She died not long ago."

"I see." There was a long pause before Ariaziane cleared her throat. "I should be getting back."

"I'll ride with you," he said as they headed for the horses.

They rode mostly in silence. The sun was beginning to set, and they gazed peacefully at the sky. Vincent's thoughts turned again to his life here. He had wonderful friends, his own place to live. A dog. A horse, too, though that was an unusual thing. And money. After all the expenses, he still had almost half his initial booty left. It certainly helped that his friends had supplied most of his home's furnishings as gifts.

His finances would be eaten away pretty quickly, he knew. Horses, he found, ate a hell of a lot. And this puppy wouldn't stay little and cute for long. He remembered well how much food his dog on Earth went through in a week's time. But even with all that, he was beginning to feel like he almost belonged here. He liked the feeling.

He also liked his new sense of patience. Especially with regard to Ariaziane. He'd always had the tendency to rush things with girls. Or to try to, anyway. They never really went anywhere. Perhaps because of all the other matters he had to deal with, he was just allowing his relationship with her to go on whatever course it wanted to take, without rushing anything. And he was enjoying it.

They arrived at the abbey and Vincent bade goodnight to the girl who was stealing his heart. She smiled as she returned the wish. He waited until she had gone out of sight before heading back to the main road. At the end of the path, he nodded to a figure in a hooded cloak.

He frowned. The figure seemed familiar. Was this the same person he'd seen the previous week? Was the guy following him or something? A knot of concern formed in his stomach. Who could be doing that, and why?

With a shake of his head, he berated himself. Paranoid, that's what he was. No one would be following him. No one had any reason to. He pushed the worries out of his mind and headed home.

Home, he thought. This world certainly could be home, if he'd only let it. Thoughts of Ariaziane entered his head and he smiled. He decided he would allow it to be.

❧ ❧

The birth, when it came, was as relatively quick as the pregnancy itself had been. And far less painful than some of her other births over the centuries. She could be thankful for that, at least.

The boy child came first, as she knew he would. He popped out with a full head of dark hair and eyes open and inquisitive. They were intense eyes, dark and forbidding. Darella smiled. This was appropriate.

The girl child followed quickly behind. Her hair was even darker, and she could tell immediately the little witch would have a beautiful countenance, much like the one she'd adopted when seducing the girl's father.

Cleaning the babies and herself after the birth was not enjoyable. Though she'd done it before, she certainly preferred the convenience of a midwife. But circumstances would not allow her such a luxury.

She nursed the hungry babes, placing them into a small double basket she'd made. Her cloak served as their blanket. She stood and stared at the infants. Though she'd given birth to many children in her life, she'd only grown attached to the first few. It was too painful when they were gone. She certainly wouldn't become overly fond of these two.

She left them to sleep, then turned her attention back to her study of the portal.

Book Two

Night Vision

❧ Seven ❧

The Season of the Sun was moving toward the Season of the Harvest. Vincent had nothing to reap, though the idea sounded pretty good to him. Next year he wanted to be able to harvest something, which was why he had ploughed out a small plot of land, about twenty feet square. He figured this was plenty of room to produce food for himself and some extra for Gnorrin's stew. And it was close enough to the stream for easy watering during dry spells. King provided more than ample fertilizer. Blade had taught him composting. By the Season of Green, his little garden spot should be quite fertile.

He straightened up from his work, leaning against the hoe, trying to wish away the throbbing pain in his back. He recalled the tiny garden his sister had started one summer when home from the school where she taught. That garden had been half this size, but produced plenty of green peppers, onions, tomatoes, radishes, lettuce and cucumbers. He hadn't cared for the peppers, onions, and radishes. The carrots and cucumbers never did too well, which were the only thing she planted that he really liked, of course. And when she returned to West Virginia in the fall, the garden had been entrusted to him to look after, at the mature age of ten or eleven. Naturally, everything had gone to seed.

He smiled to himself and looked over at Ariaziane, who was sitting with Blaise, brushing the dog's coat. He marveled again at the dog's growth. She seemed to get noticeably bigger from day to day. He'd missed that stage of her namesake's life on Earth. His brother had brought her home from college nearly fully grown. He brushed some dirt from his sleeves as he walked toward them. "So tell me what I'm in store for next week."

Ariaziane smiled without taking her eyes off the dog. "Mid-Year Week is wonderful," she said. "Activities for everyone. Speeches by the town elders. Games and shows of all sorts. And food! Since we're about to begin the Season of the Harvest, much of the remaining foods from last harvest are used. Breads and cakes are made, along with pies made from fruit preserved over the year. You'll have a fantastic time!"

Vincent dropped his hoe onto the grass beside her and moved on over to King's stall. The horse was out walking by the fence, along with the horse Ariaziane had ridden out on her visit. "And what exactly is being celebrated? You told me Celebration Week is to commemorate the ending of one year and the beginning of another. We have a similar holiday on Earth. But what's this one for?"

The girl stopped brushing and moved over to join him, giving the dog a final scratch behind the ears. "Well, there are many things, but not any one in particular. Individual towns will have different causes to celebrate. For example, one town might celebrate a record number of survived births in the latest year. Another might honor the outstanding accomplishments of a particular citizen or two. Some things are common to celebrate. Honor is often paid to the founders of the town, or the pioneers who settled into the region first. Anything that can be celebrated will be, you can be sure."

"Sounds like fun." Vincent was in the stall, a twelve by twelve square. A small wagon sat in the entrance. Ariaziane leaned against the wall, watching him muck out the manure.

He scooped up a pile with the manure fork and loaded it into the wagon. Then he plunged the fork into the straw bedding beneath and shook it out. Wet bedding fell to the floor of the stall. The dry bedding he piled against the wall. The wet bedding joined the manure in the wagon. He continued this until the wetter center portion of the stall floor was bare. Using a flat bladed shovel, he scraped the floor clean. Next he put down a layer of a powder similar to lime used for disinfecting, over which the dry straw from the pile by the wall was spread. Clean straw was applied over the top to replace what was removed.

"You're getting pretty good at that."

Vincent smiled. "Always been my dream in life," he drawled. Putting the fork and shovel away, he wheeled the wagon out to his future garden. Ariaziane tagged along, watching as he worked the straw and manure into the soil.

When he finished, he stood, removing his glasses. He gazed at them, or rather, at where they should have been. The invisibility potion Gnorrin had given him had lasted about two weeks. Reapplication was easy enough, and used little of the fluid. And no one stared at his odd spectacles anymore. He wiped sweat from his forehead with the back of his sleeve and exhaled heavily. "Whoo. I stink."

"I shouldn't wonder," she replied.

"Let me go get cleaned up."

Vincent knew Ariaziane still didn't know what to make of the odd construct behind his cottage. He stepped into a square unit, about four feet to a side, and disrobed. He stepped through a door into another unit of the same size. Mounted above this one was a large metal tank full of water. On the floor was a wooden platform with drainage holes. He threw a latch on the nozzle overhead and water came trickling out of a head like on a watering can. The water was warm, the sun having heated the metal tank. A trough below the wooden platform caught the water and sluiced it out and to the sides.

Vincent washed his body, then rinsed, watching the soapy water drain out of the shower. Then his eyes widened as he saw the toe of a boot near the drain, under the wall. Ariaziane's boot.

I'll be damned, he thought. She's spying on me!

There were plenty of cracks between the boards where a clear, if dim, view of the shower's interior could be had. He casually turned his back to her and smiled. He looked at his own body. In half a year's time, Vincent had gone from a clumsy, overweight boy to a surer, less overweight young man. He shook his head at his furriness. Nearly every inch of him was covered in hair. He knew his back was, if anything, even more lush than his chest. When he was done with his shower, he reached up and closed the nozzle, smiling as he heard Ariaziane quickly backing away.

Vincent entered the outer stall and grabbed the towel he kept there. He dried off, wishing he had a nice, thick, absorbent towel for the task. He settled for the closest equivalent this world seemed to offer. The cloth would be thoroughly damp by the time he was finished. As he dried, he wondered about Ariaziane. What was really occurring? In the time since their first adventure together, they'd become even closer. She spent a good deal of time visiting him, when she wasn't studying with Gnorrin. He frowned as he wrapped the towel around himself. As usual, he'd forgotten to bring clean clothes out. And despite the fact that Ariaziane appeared to enjoy looking at him, he was still very self-conscious about it. True, he'd lost weight, but his torso was still on the flabby side. Lifting the dirty and sweaty breeches and tunic from the hook on the wall, he balled them up in front of him, covering his midsection. Then he took his glasses from the small shelf nearby, and left the shower.

"I'll be right out," he said to Ariaziane. She smiled at him, and he could swear she was blushing a little. He shook his head. Silly girl. He didn't allow himself to think her Peeping Thomasina act was because she was honestly attracted to him. She was just at that curious stage. Any guy could've been in the shower. She'd still have looked. He wondered what she thought of what she saw. Maybe she was just morbidly curious about his hairiness. He wished he could do something about that. Shaving it off didn't appeal to him. He guessed he'd just have to deal with it. At the very least, he'd be warm in the colder months.

Inside, he withdrew a clean set of clothes from the small dresser in his room. He sat on the edge of his large bed, then lay back, enjoying the softness of the mattress. The pain in his back had faded a bit. The problem itself was lessened considerably from losing weight and firming up his muscles, but certainly hadn't disappeared completely. His back was too messed up for that to happen. If he could only do something about that and his eyesight, he'd be pretty happy. The fact that his glasses were invisible was fine, but better still not to have to wear them. Oh, well, he thought. Not much to do about it. He dressed and returned outside.

Ariaziane was sitting in a chair under a tree. Her arms were crossed over her stomach and she was doubled over, rocking. She looked up at his approach and smiled weakly. Vincent frowned as he stepped to her side. "Are you okay?"

She nodded half-heartedly. "Yes."

He knelt beside her. He'd seen her like this on numerous occasions over the past couple months. At first, he'd thought she was having her time of the month. However, unless she was on a bi-weekly cycle, it was something else. He stood and returned to the cottage, bringing out a large cup of water. Now she was holding her head, not her stomach. He wished he had some aspirin or something for her.

She accepted the water, gulped it down, and handed back the cup. "Thank you. I'm sorry. It just... hurts."

"Have you seen a doctor?"

"A what?"

"A healer."

"Oh. No. This isn't so bad. It passes quickly."

"Maybe, but it's been happening a lot. I really think you should be checked out."

"It is nothing."

Vincent sighed. "Whatever you say." He sat down beside her, picking at the grass. "I don't like seeing you in pain. It hurts me, too. How often does this happen?"

She shrugged. "Every few days."

"What! You said it was only about once a week or so!"

"Which was true, at the time."

"Damn it, Annie, why won't you see a healer?"

She smiled and sat up straight. "Because there is nothing for a healer to do. See? No more pain. The water helped." She glanced at the sky. "I must be going."

Vincent shook his head in frustration. "All right." He stood and helped her up out of the chair. "I'll join you."

"That's not necessary. I'm fine."

"I have to go into town, anyhow. I'll be ready in a minute."

Inside, he slipped on his boots and belt, filled a pouch with money, and returned outside. Ariaziane had fetched both horses and was adjusting the saddle on hers. Vincent saddled King and soon they were on their way.

Half their journey was silent, Vincent watching as his friend occasionally rubbed at her temples. When they'd passed Gnorrin's cottage, Vincent decided to talk about something to take her mind off her pain and his concern. "So why haven't you spent any of the money you got on our adventure?"

"I have."

"No, I don't mean on a few new outfits. I mean on something big."

"Like what?"

"I dunno. What do you want?"

"To learn magic. Money doesn't help with that."

He nodded. "Guess I'm just more materialistic than you." He was quiet for a moment, then said, "You know, you really mean a lot to me."

The girl smiled softly. "So you've said."

"I know, but sometimes I wonder if you know what I mean. I never would have made it here, without you."

"Nonsense. Gnorrin and Blade are the ones who helped you, not me."

"Yes, they helped in one way, but you helped in another."

"You're being silly."

This wasn't working, he thought. Best not to push it. He cleared his throat. "I've never really figured out why you like me."

She laughed. "Neither have I, to be honest. As you said once, there is some sort of bond between us. We're much alike."

"I don't know. I've always felt we were very different."

"How so?"

"I do still feel there's a bond between us, though it seems more like we're opposite sides of the same coin. You're so... so full of light. So carefree. And I'm not. I feel I have that sort of thing within me, but I can't let it out."

"I sense that." She stared at the reins in her hands atop the saddle horn. "As for myself, I sometimes feel inside me is a darkness that wants to come out. It's a part of me I try to keep hidden. I don't want anyone to see that side of me."

Vincent frowned. "Why do you think you have that inside you?"

She shrugged. "I don't know if I can explain. I'll be fifteen this season. Yet sometimes I feel so much older. I've met other people my age. And they never seem to be as..."

"Mature?"

"Yes. Exactly. So I try to act like them. To always be, as you said, full of light. To not allow things to seem so serious to me."

Vincent nodded, pondering her words. "I understand. Really, I do. I felt like that at your age, too. But I took the other road. I allowed myself to hide the light. I took things more seriously. Maybe I shouldn't have." He paused. "Still, that doesn't exactly mean you're 'dark' or anything."

"Perhaps not," she replied quietly.

"So when is your birthday?" Vincent asked, trying to lighten the mood.

"I don't know precisely. I generally celebrate it during Mid-Year Week. Since there's celebrating going on, the time seemed fitting. When is yours?"

Vincent laughed. "January twentieth. For whatever that's worth, here. Let me think. That would correspond to about four weeks after the winter solstice on Earth, which would be around the first week of the second month of the Season of Sleep, here. So the second week of the month of Snow." He smiled. "I suppose I could celebrate it during Celebration Week. Why not?"

"Yes. And you'll be eighteen this year?"

"I feel a lot older."

"Well, you shouldn't. Come on. I'll race you!"

She kicked her horse into a gallop and Vincent followed suit. Her horse was the faster of the two, not to mention that she weighed a good bit less than he did, so there was no contest. She reached the entrance road to the abbey several lengths ahead of him.

He pulled to a stop beside her. "No fair."

"How do you come to that conclusion?"

"I dunno. Just sounded good."

"You're crazy."

"Yeah. About you."

She flushed and lowered her eyes. "I must go. I'll see you tomorrow?"

"You bet." Vincent smiled as he watched her trot her horse back toward the stables. He thought he saw her holding her stomach, but wasn't sure.

In town, Vincent made his way to a small shop he'd discovered a few weeks ago, completely by accident. A luthier's shop. He'd been delighted to see the different instruments displayed, and had tinkered around with a lute-like instrument. And then an idea had struck him. He'd sketched a picture of a guitar for the luthier, specifying the open stringed notes each would sound, as well as the number of frets on the neck, with half-steps between each. Today was the day his instrument would be ready.

Tethering his horse outside, Vincent entered the shop. A bell on the door jingled, and shortly a balding little man emerged from a doorway behind a counter. Vincent greeted him warmly and said, "Is it ready?"

"Aye. A most curious instrument, young man. Where did you say you'd seen these before?" He ducked inside the back room to retrieve the instrument.

Vincent's smile froze on his face. That was a good question. Where *did* he say he'd seen them before? What the heck, it worked once before. "Penn's Woods."

"Penn's Woods," the man said from the back. "Is that in the northern provinces?"

"A very small locale in there, yes. The instrument was the invention of an old luthier there who passed on years ago. Only a few were made, apparently. Never caught on."

The man nodded as he emerged again, accepting the story. "I can understand why. Only six strings." He shook his head. "So limiting." He placed the instrument on the countertop with the greatest care. "For your inspection."

Vincent picked up the guitar. Though he was used to playing a full-bodied instrument with steel strings, this one was smaller. More like a classical or folk guitar, with gut strings. He plucked out a few notes, and strummed a chord. He smiled. "Very nice," he said.

The man smiled and gave a sort of nod that could have been a bow. "I enjoy my work. I would like very much to hear you play."

"And I would love to play for you. Another time, however. I'm dreadfully out of practice." The man nodded again. Vincent put the guitar down and pulled out his pouch. He counted out three silver pieces. "This should cover the remainder."

The man accepted the coins. "Very generous of you."

"My pleasure."

"Your next restringing free, then."

"Quite kind of you. Good day." The man nodded as Vincent departed.

A length of twine served as a temporary strap and Vincent looped the guitar around his back as he rode. He had to admit, he felt like an idiot riding through town like some troubadour. Then again, feeling like an idiot wasn't new to him.

❧ ❧

Tomorrow begins Mid-Year Week. Annie says it will be seven days of festivities, much like the Fourth of July celebrations we had back home. Without fireworks, though. Too bad.

Annie celebrates her birthday this week, too. I want to get her something really nice. I have no idea what that would be, though. I thought about jewelry, but she doesn't really seem like the jewelry type. Clothing? Well, I wouldn't know how to go about that, here. It's not like there's a department store to pop into and browse through the racks.

My guitar sounds pretty nice. Nothing like my Höfner back home, naturally. I made a wooden floor stand and keep it here in my bedroom. Reminds me of the stand I used at home.

Haven't seen much of Gnorrin and Blade lately. Blade doesn't seem like the type to go in for all the celebrating we'll evidently be having this week. For that matter, I've never been much into celebrations, myself. Perhaps I'll spend some time with him.

Most of my time these past several weeks has been spent getting into the life of a homeowner. Or rather, a horse owner, which is proving to be a lot more of a chore than having a little cottage. Horses eat a lot. A whole lot. It ain't cheap keeping him in straw and oats. He's a good horse, though. Annie has been wonderful in showing me everything on how to care for him. She enjoys grooming him on her visits, too.

Now there's a thought. I could buy her a horse of her own. She has several under her care at the abbey, but doesn't own any of them. Something worth thinking about, anyway.

I'm still worried about her health, though. She's still suffering from headaches and stomach cramps. And I think the pain has spread to nearly her entire body, now. She tries to hide it, but doesn't do a real good job. She was here yesterday, as well as three days ago. She was in pain both times. It's happening more frequently. She refuses to see a doctor. I don't know why. Kids on Earth often are afraid of doctors because of shots. Healers here don't give injections, though, so I'm clueless as to her reasons.

I just dread it's something serious. I couldn't bear to lose her. That would be worse than anything I can imagine.

❧ ❧

The town market was like a huge fairground. Vincent and Ariaziane walked through the square, Ariaziane gaily pointing out the attractions. There were wandering minstrels, jugglers, puppeteers, street theater groups, and stand after stand of food for sale. Vincent drooled over the array of sweets and breads. The first harvest of apples had been taken in and delicious cider was readily available.

There were games, many of which were familiar to him, such as dart throwing, even axe throwing. There were also some unfamiliar games, such as sword throwing. This intrigued him. To throw a sword... What a bizarre, yet interesting, idea. He tried his hand and was not surprised to find he was no good.

The prizes won at these games did not differ much from carnival games on Earth. Stuffed animals were found. Not high quality ones, merely simple animals of colored cloth stuffed with straw or rags. He won a few for her, just for fun.

He was delighted to find a merchant there who sold tea. He looked over the variety of teas and herb blends for sale, purchasing a bag of dark black tea and a concoction of herbs intended to help one sleep. He hoped they would help his insomnia.

He asked this of the merchant, a rather attractive, coppery-haired woman. She smiled and obligingly answered his questions. "My name is Rhia," she said. "If you are ever in Dynsa, please visit my shop."

"Hm," Vincent said, rubbing his chin. "My last experience in Dynsa was less than pleasant. He rubbed absently at the scar on his arm. Again, Vincent thanked her, then turned his attention back to her wares.

Since he didn't have a teapot, he purchased a beautiful set of earthenware, including a pot and four cups. The design was lovely. The bottom portions were brownish gold and the upper portions slate blue, with the middle sort of alternating between the two. A golden circle was in the center. Its overall effect was of a sunset on the ocean, as seen from the beach. Birds were represented in the sky by simple gold painted lines, like stretched-wide "V's."

They spent hours in the square, until Vincent thought he would collapse. He purchased a gallon of cider to take home, as well as a few loaves of wonderful dark bread and sweets. He'd been good since arriving on this world, where his diet was concerned. He could afford to splurge during this holiday time.

After leaving, they made a brief stop at the abbey. Ariaziane dropped off her stuffed trophies and they retrieved their horses. Vincent noticed she seemed always to choose the same horse from the several stabled there. He asked her about this.

"Ressa's a fine horse," she told him. "I've taken care of her since she was a filly. You couldn't ask for a gentler beast."

Vincent smiled to himself as they departed.

The following day, while Ariaziane was with Gnorrin for further studies, Vincent dropped in at the abbey. Haleen met him at the gate, and he explained that he wished to meet with the Abbess. Haleen frowned slightly. "And this would be concerning...?"

"I would like to purchase Ariaziane's favorite horse for her as a birthday gift."

Haleen seemed to be relieved. She smiled and led him inside. She bade him wait while she fetched the Abbess. Vincent nodded and waited just inside the door. It was the first time he'd ever been inside the abbey. He looked around, noting the very plain appearance. The Sisters obviously led a rather Spartan existence. He sighed and sat on the wooden bench against one of the walls.

Should he mention Ariaziane's illness? If he knew her, she was probably hiding it from them. Perhaps one of the Sisters knew something about healing. No, that wouldn't make sense. If one did, then surely she would have gone to her in the first place. She'd lived with them for years. That would be a natural thing for her to do.

Haleen returned before he could ponder any longer. "This way," she said, and led him to a small chamber wherein the Abbess sat behind a large desk doing paperwork of some sort. She looked up as Vincent entered. Haleen closed the door behind her as she left.

The Abbess had a stern, no-nonsense face. Vincent would have been surprised to find anything else. "I understand you wish to perform a business transaction," she said without stopping for formalities.

Vincent nodded. "Yes, I do. My name is Vincent—"

"I know who you are."

He raised an eyebrow. "Yes. Well, as Haleen might have—"

"*Sister* Haleen."

Vincent stopped, clenching his teeth. He counted to ten before continuing. "As *Sister* Haleen might have mentioned, I wish to purchase the horse Ariaziane seems so fond of. I'd like to give it to her as a birthday gift."

The Abbess stood. She was taller than she appeared when seated behind the large desk. "Our horses are very important to us, young man. We could not easily part with one."

"I'll give you four gold pieces."

The Abbess blinked. She opened her mouth, and Vincent knew she was thinking of what could be done with four gold pieces. Another horse, and a darn good one, could be purchased for half that. "Four, you said?"

Vincent nodded and drew forth his change purse. "This would also include stabling and feed for the animal for one year." He counted out four coins, each bright and shiny and gleaming in the dark room.

The woman cleared her throat. "That would be an adequate settlement," she said.

"It's more than adequate, and you know it," Vincent said, tiring of her attitude. He walked to the desk and plunked the coins down atop her paperwork. "Be so kind as to draw up a document to make the sale official, using Ariaziane's name instead of mine."

"As you wish," she said. She seated herself behind the desk once more, pointedly ignoring the coins. A fresh sheet of paper was produced, and she uncapped her inkwell.

Vincent strolled back away from the desk as she wrote, examining the room. "You don't like me much, do you?"

The Abbess spoke flatly. "No."

"And why might that be?"

"It is none of your concern."

"If not my concern, then whose could it be?"

"Young man," she said, and Vincent turned to face her, watching as she sprinkled fine sand over the wet ink. "I do not appreciate your intrusion into Ariaziane's life. You are disrupting her duties here. Filling her head with notions of another type of life. And worst of all, exposing her to that vile mage!" Vincent started to object, but she continued. "I cannot dictate what the girl may or may not do. Yet if I had my way, she would be forbidden to so much as speak to you again." She tapped the sand from the document, capped the inkwell firmly, and held out the paper to him. "Your document."

Vincent stepped over and accepted the scroll. "I'm not good enough for her, but my money is good enough for you, is that it?" The woman said nothing. Vincent rolled up the paper. "So what are you gonna do? Give her extra duties to keep her busy here? So she won't have time for me?"

The Abbess raised her head indignantly. "Certainly not. Duties are shared equally here."

"Well, that's nice to know. Because I intend to continue seeing her as much as I can." The Abbess bristled slightly, and he smiled to himself. "The idea evidently displeases you. Well, you know what? That's too damn bad." He turned abruptly and left the room.

He took his time riding to Gnorrin's, the confrontation with the Abbess still bothering him. He hadn't meant to be so rude, but the woman was just too arrogant for his liking. And despite what she said, he wouldn't be surprised if some sort of actions *were* taken against Ariaziane, just to prevent her from seeing him.

When he arrived, Gnorrin and Ariaziane were still in study together. Vincent waited, relaxing outside under the big tree. The day was pretty, and he hated having this bit of a dark cloud over his mood. He gazed down the road, remembering the first time he'd laid eyes on it. Or rather, the first time he'd seen it from this cottage. The day Gnorrin and Blade had discovered him. He frowned, wishing he could remember more than he did of his first day in this world.

Vincent's thoughts were interrupted by greetings from his friends, who had finished studying for the day and now joined him outside. Vincent smiled and presented Ariaziane with the document. She opened and read it. Then she looked at him. "You bought the horse for me?" Her voice was full of disbelief.

"Happy Birthday." He smiled.

In a second, her arms were around him in an embrace so tight he could scarcely breathe. "Thank you! I can't believe it! This is wonderful!"

"You're welcome," he choked out. He allowed himself the pleasure of enjoying her touch, despite the lack of air in his lungs. He opened his eyes to see Gnorrin smiling in approval, an "I-told-you-so" look if ever he'd seen one.

Once she'd let go, and he'd resumed breathing, they sat and talked with Gnorrin for a while before bidding farewell to him and making their way to Vincent's cottage. Vincent debated telling her of his "discussion" with the Abbess, but saw no reason to.

The pains hit her not long after dinner, starting with her head, then moving to her stomach. Vincent thought about having her drink one of the potions Gnorrin had given them, but decided this didn't really fit Gnorrin's description of what the potion could treat. Instead, he put water on over the cook fire and tossed some of the herb blend he'd purchased into the teapot.

Before the water was hot, she began vomiting. Now Vincent was truly worried. He fetched her some water, which she gratefully accepted. He helped her into a chair inside the cottage. She sat there, doubled up in pain, as he fetched the water from the fire.

He poured the water into the teapot and covered it. While the brew steeped, he returned the pot to the hook over the fire. He checked on Ariaziane to find she was rubbing at her knees, wrists, and shoulders, as if she had bad arthritis. When the tea was ready, he poured her a cup. She smelled it tentatively, and sipped. After she drank the entire cup, Vincent helped her to her feet and guided her back to the bedroom.

He tucked her into bed, turning up the oil lamp on his bedside table. Then he fetched another cup of herb tea. This one she sipped, setting it aside on the table.

He knelt on the floor beside the bed, squeezing her hand and stroking her silky black hair. He felt her tremble frequently, but soon her eyes closed and she faded into sleep.

For many minutes he sat there, watching her. The sun was setting. He hoped the Sisters at the abbey wouldn't worry if she didn't return tonight. He left the room quietly, going outside. He checked the dog and horses, extinguished the fire, and returned indoors.

He entered the bedroom again, removed his boots and belt, tossed his invisible glasses on the table, and tried to get comfortable beside her in bed, lying atop the blankets. His hand found and held hers.

He wished he could get to sleep so easily. He reached for the cup of water he always kept by the bedside, finding it empty. He frowned, then glanced at the tea. He drank some, grimacing at the taste. He never had really liked herb teas. Especially flowery ones. And this one definitely had some sort of flower in the mix. He sighed, leaning his head back into the pillow.

Many more minutes passed. He wasn't sure what the problem was. Most likely the fact that it wasn't real late, yet. The sun had set, but it was still hours before he was used to going to sleep. His mind was awhirl with worry about the girl sleeping beside him, and with the worry came all the thoughts of how much he cared for her.

He glanced at his guitar, sitting on the stand he'd made. No. He didn't want to wake her. Instead, he extracted his cassette player from the drawer in his table, fitted the earphones into place, and lay back to listen.

Mellow acoustic guitar issued forth from the tiny speakers in the headphones. Just what he needed.

Vincent's eyes roamed over the contents of the room as he listened. Finally his eyes lingered on Ariaziane. She was so full of light, he thought. And he was so full of darkness. The playfulness he exhibited around her was just an act, not the real Vincent. Wasn't it? He was so used to being the outcast, the oddball. The quiet one. The solitary one. He could never share the life of such a vibrant person as this sleeping girl. He would just darken her life. If he hadn't already.

He pondered this idea for some time before he, too, closed his eyes in slumber.

He woke with a start, wondering where he was. He was often disoriented when waking suddenly. Then he realized what had wakened him. Ariaziane was groaning and tossing in her sleep.

He turned to her, tangling himself in the cord to his earphones. He ripped them off and tossed them onto the table. He tried to comfort her without waking her up. He failed. She woke with a loud moan of pain, sitting bolt upright in bed. Vincent grabbed her hand and allowed her to squeeze. Her grip was very strong.

She finished the moan and sat panting. Her grip relaxed a bit. She opened parched lips. "Drink," she wheezed. Vincent reached for the cup. The tea would be cold now, though he doubted she'd care, as long as it was wet. She drained the cup and handed it back, then doubled over in pain. Vincent cursed to himself. Tomorrow they were going to a healer. Period. But his frustration and anger took a backseat to the immediate. Ariaziane turned over onto her stomach, buried her head in the pillow, and screamed.

When Vincent's heart started beating again, he quickly reached out for her. As soon as she'd stopped screaming, she'd stopped moving. He rolled her over and checked her breathing. He sighed in relief. She'd passed out. Fortunately, perhaps. He arranged her in a comfortable position and brought the blankets up to cover her again. He lay there, looking at her for a minute, before trying again to fall asleep.

Vincent had always been a night person, though that was in the days when he lived in a place with electric lights. After being here for a couple months, he'd become a morning person, out of necessity. This was why it wasn't too strange for him to build his cottage so the morning sun would enter the two windows of his room. The light was his alarm clock.

He woke this morning and stretched, then looked over at Ariaziane. She was lying on her side, with her back to him. She seemed to be sleeping soundly. Vincent yawned and got out of bed. He drew on his boots, glancing at the bed again as he heard her stirring.

She'd rolled over onto her other side, now, and Vincent noticed something. He shook his head and rubbed his eyes. He reached for where he thought his glasses were, found them, and put them on. Was it just a trick of the light, or... No. No tricks. Her hair was a different color. Where once was black hair, now was auburn. Dark brown, with a red sheen. No, he thought. He had to be imagining things. He stood there for a few moments, then left the room, shaking his head.

Outside, he started a cooking fire, allowing the pot of water to remain there. He could use some real tea this morning. After feeding the dog and horses, he returned inside.

He scrounged up some things for breakfast. Bread and jam purchased from the fair. Then he checked on the water outside. It was hot enough and he removed the pot from the fire. As he turned to enter the cottage, he saw Ariaziane standing in the doorway. No mistake, now. Her hair had definitely changed color during the night. "Morning," he said.

"Morning," she said. Her face was worried.

"How do you feel?"

She looked up at him. "Fine. I feel fine." She chuckled. "In fact, I feel great. Oddly enough." She frowned. "I shouldn't have stayed here last night. They'll be worried to death."

Vincent was standing next to her now and he looked into her eyes. And nearly dropped the pot of water. Her eyes. They weren't violet any more. They were indigo. Very dark, with traces of blue as well as purple. Ariaziane laughed. "What are you staring at?"

Vincent forced himself to look away. He took a deep breath. "Just a minute," he said, and took the water inside. She followed him in. He poured water into the teapot, which already held a handful of tea leaves. He lowered the blue lid onto the pot. "You're sure you feel okay?"

"I told you. I feel wonderful. Why?"

He shook his head slightly. Then he took her by the hand. "Come with me." He led her out into the sunlight and stopped. He reached behind her head and drew her long hair out from behind her back. He held a lock up for her inspection.

She stood there, her mouth hanging open, looking at her hair. She grabbed more, bringing it around, as if she thought only the one portion was a new color. When she'd searched all the hair she could, she looked up at Vincent, her indigo eyes full of panic. "What happened? What does this mean?"

"Beats me. But it's not just your hair. It's your eyes, too."

Her brows shot up at this. "My eyes?" He explained their new hue to her. This did not lessen her state of apprehension. "Gods," she whispered. "Is this what all the pain was about?"

"Could be. If you don't have any more pains, we'll know."

She let out a long breath, and followed Vincent back inside. "What do we do now?"

"Have breakfast," he replied, as she stared at him dumbly, "while we try to make sense of this."

Ariaziane nodded as she sat at the table. She nibbled on a roll with butter and sipped some strong black tea. "The mage," she said suddenly. "The mage at the keep! His spell worked! This is what it did to me!"

Vincent frowned and put down his teacup. "Pretty strange spell that just changes the hair and eye color of the victim."

"Well, who knows what it was actually meant to do? Maybe it was only a partial success. Maybe I could've been polymorphed!"

"Excuse you?" Vincent blinked.

"Sorry. It's a magic term. I mean I could have been turned into a lizard or something."

He frowned again. "Right. Well, even so. Don't you think it's unlikely? I mean, that was months ago! Why would the spell take this long to take effect?"

"Maybe because of Gnorrin's intervention?"

Vincent nodded. "Now there's certainly someone we should talk to."

They finished their breakfasts, saddled up the horses, and departed. Vincent noted Ariaziane's look of apprehension during the short ride. He was pretty sure his own face bore similar signs.

Gnorrin was outside when they arrived, relaxing in his chair. He greeted them warmly and gave Vincent a look. Vincent shook his head, knowing what the gnome was thinking.

"The pains came back again last night," he told his friend. "I thought it best for her not to try to travel back to the abbey." He proceeded to tell Gnorrin the events of the night.

All the while, the mage looked the girl over. He rubbed his chin as he stared at her new colors. "I've never seen anything like this," he said.

Ariaziane spoke up. "The mage's spell, right?"

The gnome shook his head. "I don't think so."

"Your spell caused his not to work, at least not completely. But it did this!" Gnorrin shook his head again and began to speak, but she cut him short. "It's a possibility, isn't it? You said yourself when a spell goes afoul, nearly anything can happen, right?"

The gnome sighed and nodded. "Yes, but..."

"But nothing! That's what it was!"

Clearly this was the explanation Ariaziane wanted to use. Vincent supposed he could understand. When faced with something unbelievable, people tend to grasp onto the first thing that seems to explain it. Gnorrin's glance at him told him his friend realized the same thing. He cleared his throat. "Well, now that we know, we should get you back."

Ariaziane agreed. They thanked Gnorrin and left.

As they arrived, Haleen hurried over to meet them. Her eyes widened as she saw Ariaziane. "What has happened to you?" she said. Ariaziane and Vincent dismounted. Ariaziane quickly summed up her explanation of the change. Vincent caught Haleen's eye and quickly shook his head. Haleen smiled, though concern was evident on her face. She suggested the girl make her presence known to the Abbess, so she, too, could stop worrying. As Ariaziane hurried off, she turned to Vincent. "You find fault with her explanation?"

Vincent was slow to answer. "I have reason to doubt this is true. Gnorrin does not feel it to be the case."

"Then what?"

He shook his head. "I've no idea." He told her of Ariaziane's pains and Haleen confessed she knew of them. He continued to tell her of the previous day's events. The vomiting, the scream in the middle of the night. And the waking to find her changed. "If Gnorrin doubts it was the spell of the mage, so do I. But neither of us have any other explanation."

Haleen nodded and thanked him for looking after her. Then she said, "I think you should go, now. I suspect..." She paused. "Well. I just think it would be best." Vincent nodded and remounted. Haleen began leading Ariaziane's horse away without another word. Vincent sighed, knowing full well what she meant.

Later that day, Vincent was washing his clothes and thinking about the situation. No matter how much thought he gave to it, there were still no answers. He sighed and put renewed effort into his washing, shaking his head as he did so. Of all the things he never envisioned himself doing, this was up near the top of the list. The washboard in the tub was harsh on his fingertips. He still hadn't quite gotten the hang of this business. Vincent wrung out the tunic, rinsed it in another tub of water, wrung again, and hung it over a length of twine stretched between two trees, fixing the tunic in place with clothespins at the ends. He turned back to his wash, only to find Ariaziane coming down the path toward his cottage. Her horse was loaded down with two large cloth sacks, and the girl's head was downcast.

He walked over to her, a sick feeling building in his stomach. "What's going on?" he asked.

She looked at him, and he saw her eyes were red from crying. Her voice was a whisper. "They threw me out."

"They *what?*"

She slid down off her horse and embraced him. "They said I was tainted by demons. They said they knew I would come to a bad end ever since I started speaking with the gnome."

"What a load of shit!"

"I've lived with them almost half my life! And they threw me out!" She began crying again, and Vincent pulled her head down to his shoulder.

After the worst had passed, he said, "This is all my fault."

She sniffled. "What do you mean?" Vincent sighed and told her of his confrontation with the Abbess the day before. When he finished, Ariaziane said, "I can't believe she said that about you. And Gnorrin."

"Well, she did, I'm sorry to say. Anyhow, what's done is done. This doesn't have to be all bad. You can move in with me."

She pulled away. "No. I couldn't do that."

"Why not? It'll be fun! I'll make up the spare room for you."

"I just... couldn't. I'm sorry. It wouldn't be right."

Vincent bit back his reply. Then he nodded. "Okay. What about Gnorrin? I'm sure he'd let you stay there."

"I was hoping he would. That way I can continue my studies with him." She moved a step away from him. "Could I keep Ressa here? Gnorrin doesn't have a stable."

Vincent looked at her horse. "Sure. No problem."

She smiled her thanks.

By evening, they had her settled into the room Vincent had stayed in when he lived with Gnorrin. The gnome fussed about, trying to make her as comfortable as possible with her new quarters. The emotional drain of the day had exhausted her and by nightfall, she was ready for sleep.

Gnorrin and Vincent sat talking afterward. Vincent tried not to show he was upset she hadn't chosen to stay with him, but suspected his friend knew anyway.

"It's not fair, Gnorrin. They didn't have to kick her out."

The gnome nodded. "She'll be fine, lad. Don't you worry."

"I know she'll be fine, but this just shouldn't have happened. She's gone through enough in her life. Orphaned, then orphaned again by being kicked out by a bunch of hypocritical nuns. She deserves better."

"I agree. Just as you deserved better than to be stolen away from the world of your birth. You two have much in common. I suggest you make the best of it. Both of you."

❧ Eight ❧

The nights were getting colder, Vincent thought as he lay in his small tent, looking up at the sky. This particular night was a clear one, late in the Season of the Harvest. He shivered, wishing he were warmer. His sleeping sack certainly wasn't of the quality he'd slept in on Earth, but would have to do. The crackling of the fire, though comforting, wasn't throwing enough heat to his liking.

He was on the latest of several exploratory jaunts. In the past couple months, he'd traveled out away from home, gaining a knowledge of the land for a radius of perhaps twelve miles in each direction. And a pretty unexciting twelve-mile radius it was, he thought.

Rationally, his reasons for the excursions were to learn the land and, just maybe, find some clue as to how he'd come to be here and how to get back. But there was an irrational side, too, that wasn't as easy to acknowledge. He felt as though he were running away. No, that wasn't right, either. He felt as though he were being pushed away, being shut out of Ariaziane's life. His little trips were excuses, to take his mind off that particular situation.

Ariaziane's change appeared to be merely cosmetic, but Vincent saw a psychological change, as well. She was harder to talk to. Colder. As if the dark side she'd mentioned had begun to surface. As the months passed, she spent more and more of her time studying with Gnorrin. Vincent was sure she was trying to find a way to reverse what had happened to her. He suspected this would be as hopeless a task as his own in finding a way back to Earth.

He didn't often inquire as to the nature of her studies. Such things were evidently very personal. Not like meeting a new student at college and saying, "So, what's your major?" She was, without doubt, very proud of what she was doing. Yet she wouldn't discuss it in more than the most ambiguous way.

Vincent had leafed through some of the books she and Gnorrin possessed. He skipped over much of them, but enjoyed reading of certain magical items that had existed. Some still did, he assumed. It was like looking through a book of archaeology. But instead of pictures of ancient cookware, there were drawings and descriptions of powerful artifacts capable of wondrous things. He'd found many rings mentioned, though none with a description matching the one he now wore. Maybe he should take Gnorrin up on his offer to magically test the thing. He stifled a yawn. Maybe.

Reading through the books of magic spurred him to leaf through the bestiaries again. He remembered the sense of wonder he'd felt, as a young boy, in getting books from the library about dinosaurs. To think such behemoths had walked the world, millions of years past. Reading Gnorrin's books was similar. It was amazing to think there were dragons in this world, whose heads were as tall as his own body. Beasts older than the oldest living human, and more intelligent. Vincent closed his eyes and fantasized about meeting such a creature.

With a sigh, he opened his eyes again. Unreal. The dragons, the magic rings, magic that Ariaziane was learning, and the fact that he was becoming an accomplished swordsman. In fact, everything about his life here had a bit of an unreal feel. Whenever he looked at all he'd done since arriving here, he felt detached from it all, as though everything had happened to someone else.

The adventure in the keep, for example. Had he really fought against people who were trying to kill him? He hated violence. Why was he engaging in it? Could he ever force himself to really kill someone else? During the fight in the keep, he simply wasn't thinking of such things. He'd treated it like a game. He had never given thought to the idea of himself suffering any kind of real harm. Even after getting shot with an arrow while escorting tax money, he still didn't take it seriously. Sure, he could remember the pain, both of the arrow going in and the arrow coming out, but the truth still didn't register in his head as something to be very concerned about.

The only thing he *was* truly concerned about was Ariaziane, and the reality that the closeness they'd so recently formed was beginning to deteriorate. Her self-imposed seclusion was driving a wedge between them. He was losing her, without ever having had her, really. The idea plunged him into depression. And though he knew he should do something about it, something to draw her back to him, he just couldn't manage to. Instead, he ran away. He escaped to the wilderness under the guise of exploration.

Vincent shifted in his sleeping sack, trying to get comfortable. Thoughts of Ariaziane, combined with his insomnia, were wreaking their usual havoc in his mind. He wished he could listen to some music, but his batteries had finally given the last of their juice. The fact that they were rechargeable didn't do him any good in a land without AC wall outlets. He rolled onto his side and exhaled a deep breath, welcoming the sleepy feelings washing over him.

The sound of King's nervous snort caused him to open his eyes. The horse was moving around, obviously unhappy about something. He looked out of the tent in the horse's direction and saw movement in the brush. His heart started to beat faster.

He pulled his arms free of the sleeping sack and reached for his sword, which lay in its scabbard along the side of the tent. Then he realized his sword would do him little good if he were still encased in a big muslin bag of goose feathers and straw. He frowned and began easing himself out of the sleeping sack, as quietly as possible.

As he extracted himself, he heard a loud snuffling sound. King whinnied and reared up as a large boar-like creature came bursting out of the bushes in an explosion of snorts.

"Shit!" Vincent blurted as he grabbed his sword. The scabbard went flying as he whipped out the blade. Then Vincent went flying as he leaped out of the boar's path. He was astonished by the animal's speed, especially given its size. The thing must be three feet tall at the shoulders, he thought.

As the beast came charging back for a second pass, Vincent was ready. He sidestepped and brought his sword crashing down. The boar bellowed, but went on past. To Vincent's shock, his sword had put only the shallowest of cuts in the boar's thick hide.

Once more, the animal charged him. Again, Vincent dodged at the last moment and swung. But the animal was ready for this trick and ducked inside his swing. The sword bounced harmlessly off the boar's side, while the beast's head glanced off Vincent's hip. The blow wasn't solid, but was enough to throw him off balance.

As he stumbled and tried to recover, the boar charged again. Vincent panicked and fell backward onto his rear end. He scrambled to get up, but there wasn't enough time. Lunging forward from his knees, he thrust his sword out straight in front of him. And the animal impaled itself.

But to Vincent's horror, the beast continued its charge. Flat on his stomach, being pushed backward, Vincent used all his strength to keep the blade in front of him, trying to jam the hilt against the ground. Should it slip to the side and come free of the animal's chest, he knew he'd be done for.

He kept the sword straight, though, for all the good it did. Still barreling forward, the boar forced the blade deeper into its chest with every stride, but it didn't seem to care. A crackling noise behind Vincent caused the blood to turn cold inside him. The boar was pushing him straight toward the fire!

He thought about rolling to the side, to avoid the blaze, but that would only allow the boar to trample him. Instead, he hoped the boar's velocity would propel him through the fire quickly. The flames were fairly low. They might not even ignite his clothing.

Suddenly the hilt of the sword jammed into a slight dip in the ground. The boar wailed as the point drove deep into its body. Vincent was shocked by the sudden stop. He stole a quick glance backward and saw his feet were only inches from the fire pit.

The boar, however, wasn't dead, and Vincent knew he had to finish it off. Rising to his knees, he gripped the sword tightly and gave a mighty shove. As he did so, the boar roared and, sluggish though it was, threw its body forward. Despite himself, Vincent recoiled, falling on his rump again. Then the boar gave a final lunge before falling dead across his thighs. The force knocked Vincent's torso backward into the fire.

Panic exploded inside him. He jerked his body up, but the boar's dead weight held him down. He screamed as the fire leaped up around him.

Then he stopped.

He wasn't burning!

His breath came in short, terrified puffs, and he coughed from inhaled smoke. *He wasn't burning!* Orange flames licked up past his face on either side. But he wasn't burning. Neither was his clothing. He felt heat, but not burning heat. With a great effort, he heaved the boar's carcass off himself, then stretched his legs. Thankfully, they didn't seem to be broken. He turned his attention again to the fire.

He held his hands out into the flames. They became warm, though not unbearably so. His tunic sleeve, too, was unaffected. He frowned, then took his hand from the fire. Out of curiosity, he removed the ring from his finger, then held his hand toward the blaze. This time, his hand became painfully hot before even touching the fire. He slipped the ring back on and repeated the action. His hand went into the flames without pain.

Well, he thought, that seems to solve that mystery. He rose to his feet, brushed dirt from his clothes, and returned to his tent. He hoped the boar wouldn't begin to stink before morning. After the adrenaline rush wore off, he knew he'd have no trouble falling asleep.

He was glad that he was on the return leg of this trip. He'd had enough for one outing. In the morning, he'd return home. He glanced at the boar's body again. At least he'd have a lot of meat to show for his beating.

Several hours into the following afternoon, Vincent arrived at home. Blaise barked happily, prancing in front of her house as he and King walked down the trail toward the cottage. Vincent saw her food bowl was mostly full, which told him Ariaziane had already been out today to check on the dog.

After taking care of King, he untied Blaise from her confinement, letting her run free. Though his huge yard was fenced in, he didn't want her running away while he was gone, and had left her tied in front of her small house. He was sure Ariaziane had untied her each day for exercise, though. Finally, he took a much needed and appreciated shower, then collapsed onto his bed.

No sooner had he begun to fall into a nap than Blaise began barking. Vincent roused himself, annoyed at the disturbance and the fact that he hadn't gotten much sleep the previous evening. He looked out his bedroom window, and realized he'd forgotten to unplug his windows after coming home.

The square windows were basically just holes in the walls. Fine for warm, dry weather, but when rain or cold came, there needed to be protection from the elements. Shutters wouldn't suffice for more than the gentlest of rains. For heavier rain, or for cold weather, he had the plugs. Thin sheets of animal skin were stretched across a box frame, oiled to translucency. These "windows" were shoved into the holes from the inside. Outer ledges of wood were sealed onto the wall with melted wax, to keep the cold out as much as possible. For temporary use, such as rainstorms and his trips away, he did without the wax seal. Though the oiled skins admitted light, one couldn't truly distinguish anything through them. With a sigh, Vincent rose and yanked out one of the plugs. As he glanced outside, his stomach tightened with anxiety.

The cloaked and hooded figure walking down the path to his home was the same one he'd seen on previous occasions. Were his fears justified? Was this person following him? His first thought was to grab his sword, but somehow he felt it wouldn't be needed. Curiosity kept him at the window. Blaise was jumping and yapping happily alongside the stranger. He frowned, wondering if he were about to encounter this world's equivalent to the traveling salesman. If so, he'd have to train Blaise better. He moved from the window and stepped outside.

The visitor stopped a few paces away from him, then reached up and pulled the cloak's hood back, exposing bright, orange-red hair. Then she showed a dazzling smile and said simply, "Hello, Vincent."

He stood there stupidly for a moment, then said, "I know you. I bought tea from you during Mid-Year Week, right?"

She nodded. "My name is Rhia." Moving closer, she studied him. "I trust your arm has healed," she said, standing next to him, now. Though he wore long sleeves, she reached out and touched his arm, right where the scar was. "Arrows can be such nasty things."

Her voice, he thought. It was oddly familiar. "I'm sorry," he said. "Should I know you from somewhere else?"

"You're going to know me. At least a bit. Only you can say whether you should or not." She smiled again. "I must say, you're looking in much better shape than when first I met you."

And then it came to him. "You were in the room at Dynsa! You're the herbalist! And..." He paused, odd thoughts coming to him. "And you took some of my hair!"

Rhia laughed. "Yes, I was, and am, and did." Her gaze lingered on Vincent's trimmer torso. His face flushed, and she grinned. Then she began untying a pouch from her belt. "And I've brought you some gifts in return. May we go inside?"

Vincent was too stunned by this realization to say anything, so Rhia stepped past him and entered the cottage. Vincent shook himself from his stupor and followed her inside.

He watched her exploring everything, from the kitchen sink to the furniture. By the time he finished putting away the window blocks, she had made her way back to the bedroom.

There, he found Rhia handling the pouch of herbs he had purchased from her. "Have they helped?"

Vincent shrugged. "I haven't used them much. I don't really care for things with flowery tastes. That has some sort of flower."

"Elf leaf, yes."

"Yeah, well, I don't like the taste."

"Well, it probably doesn't care much for you, either," she said. "Try this, instead." She sat on the edge of his bed and opened her pouch. She pulled out a tiny vial of liquid, holding it for him to examine. "This is the ethereal of the elf leaf flower. Very potent." She uncapped the vial for him.

Vincent sniffed, and closed his eyes, smiling his approval. "Ethereal" evidently meant the same here as "extract" meant to him.

"Nice, isn't it?" she said. "When you're having trouble sleeping, sprinkle a few drops of this onto your pillow. That should take care of your problem." She capped the vial and handed it to him.

He accepted the gift. "Why were you there?"

She shrugged. "You needed a healer."

"I've seen Blade bind wounds. He could have taken care of me."

Rhia shook her head. "You were bleeding severely. When you pulled the arrow out, you opened a major vessel in your arm. I gave you a mixture of herbs to counteract the loss of blood and fight the heat."

"Pardon?"

"The arrowhead was unclean. Your friend and I stayed with you for many hours, until the heat broke. He told you none of this?"

"No, he didn't." Vincent paused, remembering the question he wanted to ask her. "Why did you take some of my hair?"

"Your friend and I spoke at length while you slept. He spoke somewhat freely of your origins."

A brief wave of concern touched Vincent. "He did?"

"Yes," said Rhia. She idly reached up and toyed with a long, thin braid of her hair, much longer than the rest. "And an interesting story it was. He told me how he had been unable to discover how you got here, much as he'd looked."

Vincent nodded. "Gnorrin says we'd need a druid."

The woman chuckled softly. "That would be most helpful, yes. But finding one would be just as difficult as finding your way home. They are hard to come by, these days. That is why your friend enlisted my aid. A lock of your hair was needed for me to have a sample of your essence."

He tried to stifle a snort. "My what? And just why did he feel an herbalist would be able to discover anything new?"

Rhia's green eyes gleamed. "Herb lore is only one of my trades." She turned her attention back to her pouch. "I have more gifts for you." She withdrew several candles of various colors and laid them out on the bed. "The blue candles are for many things. Protection during sleep. Healing. Peace and restfulness. I have enhanced them with ethereal of garden mint for just such purpose. The yellow candles have been enhanced with devil's bit, for extra aid in clairvoyant abilities. They will assist you in remembering things about your arrival here that you had not known before. And the white candles are for nearly everything, including prosperity. I have enhanced them with ethereal of five-fingered grass."

Vincent shook his head under the barrage of information. "Wait a minute," he said. "What are you talking about? Protection from what?" And then it hit him. He looked at Rhia and finally put the pieces together. "You're a witch."

Again, the woman smiled. "I certainly can be."

"And witches and druids have a lot in common, right?"

Rhia rose and began placing the small, flat-bottomed candles at varying locations about the room. "Somewhat, yes," she said. "Both have been in this world for ages untold, though neither is in great number today, I fear." She finished displaying the candles and returned to sit near Vincent. "The druids were primarily male, allowing only exceptional females to rise in their ranks. The witches were the exact opposite. Only extremely promising males were allowed access to the knowledge held in highest regard among witches."

"Did Blade tell you where I came from?"

"Another world, he said. He did not go into specifics."

"Yes, well, on my world, we had both druids and witches. In fact, many still exist who practice Wicca, the religion or way of life exclusive to the witches. Is that what you're referring to? A religion or way of life?"

"No, it is not a religion. And the word 'Wicca' means nothing to me. But being a witch most assuredly is a way of life."

Vincent paused, the question he wanted to ask sitting on the tip of his tongue, almost afraid to be voiced. Finally, he spoke. "Can you help me get home?"

Rhia looked him in the eye. "I do not know. From the sound of things, the skills of a tracker have had no luck. You need a different sort of help. The help only a magical insight can give." As Vincent began to look hopeful, she warned him, "This will be a long process, and difficult. Had you arrived not long ago, the residue of your arrival would still be fresh. As it is, the energy has had time to dissipate. I cannot promise any kind of results."

Her host nodded slowly. "I understand. How will your search be done?"

"By communing with nature, with the world you have touched. By divination. And with a little help from you."

"From me? What kind of help?"

"I need you to try to remember. If your mind can summon up the memories of the events immediately after your arrival here, it would be of great use. Perhaps the key to unlocking the mystery."

Vincent shook his head. "I've tried. You don't know how often I've wracked my brain while trying to fall asleep at night. But nothing comes. I remember nothing before seeing Gnorrin's cottage."

"This is why I have given you the yellow candles. Burn them, inhale their scent, while trying to remember." She gathered her things and prepared to leave. "When next I visit, I shall bring more herbs and oils to assist you. For now, begin with the candles."

"Where are you going? Are you staying in town? When will you be back?" Vincent drilled her as they walked out toward the door.

Rhia laughed. "So many questions! I am going off in the direction from which you came, the day your friends found you. No, I am not staying in town. And I cannot say exactly when you will see me next. But it will not be so very long." She smiled at him, then raised her hood.

Vincent stood on his doorstep, watching her walk away, until Ariaziane entering the path on horseback drew his attention.

He smiled when she dismounted from Ressa. "Who was that?" she asked. As they walked the horse over to the stable, Vincent gave her a brief synopsis of his meeting with Rhia. When he finished, he noticed Ariaziane's perplexed look. "Sounds pretty strange to me," she said. "How was your journey?"

They went inside, and he told her, especially about his discovery concerning the ring. He even demonstrated, by lighting a candle and holding his finger in the flame. "Yes," she said. "Gnorrin has told me of such things."

Vincent frowned. "Something's bothering you," he said.

"Why do you say so?"

"Because whenever you speak formally with me, I know something's wrong. So what's up?"

The girl frowned and shook her head. "Something happened while you were gone."

Vincent raised an eyebrow. "What?"

"Just after you left, Blade came back from his latest little journey to wherever. With him was this woman named Sianon." She shook her head. "She seems nice enough. But there's something about her..."

Vincent frowned. "What sort of something?"

She sighed. "Something that makes me distrust her."

Vincent drummed his fingertips on his knee as he sat on the edge of the bed. He fingered the candle he was still holding, then extinguished it by pinching the burning wick. He placed the candle back on his nightstand. "You know, sometimes when a person says there's something they don't like or don't trust about another, it's because the other person either has or wants something the first person has or wants." He fixed his gaze on her. "Is this jealousy, Annie?"

"What? No!" she said firmly. "Don't be ridiculous."

"I dunno. Blade's a good looking guy, I'm not too blind to admit."

"So Sianon says. She's been very clear on how she feels about him. Or how she claims to feel, anyway." She sighed in frustration. "I can't explain what about her I don't trust, but I'm sure you'll agree with me."

"Why?"

"Because you and I think alike. I assume you'll feel the same way about her."

111

"I see. Well, I guess we'll find out when I meet her. Whenever that will be."

"Well, if you're at all interested in joining us for dinner, you'll meet her shortly. Blade wants to take us all to the inn."

"You never said how Blade feels about her."

"Neither has he."

"Oh. Well, then. I guess we should get going."

They walked to Gnorrin's, then the trio walked into town. The inn was located not far from *The Nib and Quill*. Vincent had been there on a few occasions. It was really just a bar and a kitchen, with a dining area and one floor of rooms for rent. Gnorrin told him Blade was meeting them there, for that's where Sianon was staying.

They entered the dining area and spotted Blade sitting with a woman at a table near the fire. They worked their way back through the other tables and joined him. Vincent was introduced to Sianon, a woman of perhaps twenty-five, with long blonde hair streaked with brown. Vincent greeted her warmly. He found her attractive, but didn't have an immediate sense of distrust, as Ariaziane seemed to feel he would.

The server arrived and began reciting the list of available dishes, then took their orders. Vincent ordered the venison steak and hot ginger tea to drink. He drank from his cup of water while Blade recounted to him how he had met Sianon while returning from Dynsa, where he'd been looking for work. They were traveling in the same direction and decided to ride the road together. Sianon interrupted his story to say, "We'd ridden no more than two leagues before I knew I wanted to stay by his side."

Blade blushed a little at this, and Vincent felt a strange twinge inside him. He glanced at Ariaziane and saw she was frowning to herself. He couldn't blame her. The story sounded a bit phony.

Their drinks arrived and Vincent sipped at the hot liquid. Very invigorating, though he was sure it wasn't an actual tea. Setting the mug down, he asked Sianon where she was from.

"A town called Port Remil," she said, smiling, "far east of here." She cast a sidelong glance at Blade. "We grew up only a league apart, seemingly."

Vincent blinked in surprise, looking at his friend. The man had never once mentioned his home. Blade's expression was difficult to read. His smile seemed forced, to Vincent, as though he didn't want to be reminded of his youth. Vincent cleared his throat. "What brings you this far from home?"

"Actually," she said, "I'm mostly just traveling for its own sake. My father passed away recently, and since he had no sons, his estate fell to me. My mother would have inherited it, had she not died a few years ago. I found myself with a considerable amount of money. I'd always wondered what inland cities were like, having known only the life of a port town. And I figured the best place to go to get the feel of an inland city would be Falconwall."

Falconwall, Vincent knew, was the largest city in this part of the continent. At least, that's what Blade and Gnorrin had once told him. "I see," he said. "When do you expect to head out? It's a good week's journey by horse."

Sianon looked at Blade. "When do you think?"

All eyes turned to Blade at her question. He lowered his mug of ale and wiped some foam from the corners of his mouth. "Soon, I would imagine."

There was a silence after his answer, broken only a minute later when the server brought their food. Vincent frowned to himself as their plates were set before them. Annie's right, he thought. Something definitely weird is going on here.

Their meal passed quickly, filled with small-talk. Sianon took over the conversation, shifting its focus from herself to the others. Vincent found himself answering far more questions than he wanted. After the meal and more conversation, Sianon excused herself and returned to her room.

Gnorrin waited until she was out of earshot. "You're going with her to Falconwall?"

Blade shrugged. "Why not? It has been quite some time since I've been there. The selection of goods is better than anything around here, or even in Dynsa. I might be able to find some bargains."

Gnorrin was silent at his answer. Ariaziane, too, was quiet. Vincent spoke up. "Well," he said. "Do you need any company?"

Blade shot him a look. "No. Thank you." Vincent nodded and then Blade, too, excused himself, thanking the group for joining them for dinner. The trio watched him head off toward the stairs.

"He's staying here, too?" Vincent asked Gnorrin.

"Aye. He's staying here, too."

Vincent sighed. "He told me he hates Falconwall."

"He hates all cities," Gnorrin said. "The bigger they are, the more he hates them."

Vincent frowned and looked at Ariaziane. "I told you so," she said.

He nodded in reply. "That you did," he said. "That you did."

❧ ❦

What a day, Vincent thought as he sat on the edge of his bed that night. Blaise snuffled at him as he unlaced his boots. He tossed them in the corner after pulling them off, massaging his feet a bit, and glanced at his bedside table, where Rhia's colored candles sat. With a yawn, he made room on the bed for the dog. He patted the mattress and she eagerly jumped up to lie beside him.

Candle magic, he thought. What's so magic about a candle? He reached out for the small bottle of oil she'd brought him. What did she call it? Elf leaf? He uncapped the vial and sniffed again. The smell was familiar. Blaise looked curiously at the bottle, sniffing the air. He held out the bottle to her nose. "What is this, pup?" The dog sniffed at the bottle, then drew back. She sneezed. "It's what?" Vincent asked. The dog sneezed again. "Snot?" Vincent shook his head. "I don't think so. Smells more like lavender."

He felt bad for the dog. The liquid was very potent, and with a dog's more sensitive nose, the oil must have been intolerable. "I know how you feel," he said to her. "I did the same thing with a vial of hydrochloric acid in high school chemistry class." He frowned in recollection of his stupidity. His eyes had watered and his sinuses had felt about to melt. He held the oil toward the dog and waved his hand like a fan over the mouth of the bottle. The dog sniffed at the flowery breeze. She panted happily. "That's what I should've done," he told her.

He turned back to the candles. Clairvoyance, he thought. He believed in such things. Or at least, he thought he did. Ever since he'd been old enough to understand what ESP meant, he'd been fascinated by the whole concept. Not many years past, he'd thought he might even have a touch of extrasensory perception himself. He remembered one incident as though it were yesterday. In the locker room, after gym class, he'd turned to ask a question of the boy next to him. And suddenly everything had gone black. It cleared after only a second or two, and he'd chalked the experience up to a round of vertigo. But the next morning he learned the boy had been killed that very night. He had been cleaning his collection of guns. A friend who was visiting was playing around with one. It was loaded. A common enough story, unfortunately, but one that had affected him greatly. Not because the boy had been a close friend. He wasn't. But because of the "vertigo." Had it meant something? He didn't know, and never would, though he always conceded the possibility.

He gathered up the pair of yellow candles and sniffed at one. What had she said they were laced with? Devil's bit. That was it. Lovely name, and so encouraging. He set one of the candles on his bedside table, the other on the windowsill above his bed. He lit a punk from the oil lamp that burned continually on his table, then carefully lit the candles. What he wouldn't give for a butane lighter, he thought for perhaps the thousandth time since arriving. He stripped and prepared to climb into bed, only to find the dog fast asleep. Her eyelids fluttered with dreaming. That was quick, he thought. He gently squeezed under the sheets, trying not to disturb her.

Vincent relaxed, allowing the rich, full-bodied scent of the candles to fill his nostrils. He'd never smelled anything quite like this before. He took a deep breath. And another. Then he allowed his thoughts to drift back. Back to his day of arrival in this world.

He remembered all he typically remembered. Seeing the cottage. The splash in the face, courtesy of Gnorrin. The sense of sudden disorientation, the inability to recognize any of the surroundings, and the odd appearance of the pair of strangers. He remembered the feeling of exhaustion that had overtaken him, finally, and collapsing to the ground. He didn't remember Blade picking him up, but suspected he was actually unconscious by that point, anyway. But there was more. Now he remembered more of his journey before the feeling of disorientation. There was no sense of clarity attached with the memory, however. The feeling associated with it was more like being almost asleep, in the borderline state where one is aware, but unable to move.

There was something else, too. No. Someone else. A girl. Who was she? He could picture her, just barely. Gorgeous, he thought. Who was she? And what connection did she have to him? He concentrated harder, trying to picture the surroundings. Dark. It was dark. And empty. Like a basement. And the girl... She was naked. She approached him. And then...

Vincent opened his eyes and bolted upright in bed. "Holy shit," he whispered. Blaise yawned and looked at him inquiringly. He absently reached out to pet her. "Sorry," he said to her. He looked at the candles again, and blew them out. Clairvoyance my ass, he thought. Hallucination, more likely. He shook his head and smiled. Damn nice hallucination. One he didn't mind having, that was certain. But it couldn't have been an actual event. No way would he have forgotten that.

❧ Nine ❧

I've been neglecting my journal, lately. My last entry was the night I met Sianon, so I'll continue from there.

She and Blade left for Falconwall a couple weeks later. I didn't see much of them during that time. When I did, I tried to speak to Blade about the trip, which only got me more harsh stares. Gnorrin seemed to resign himself to being in the dark. The explanation I got from him was, "He's a grown man and can make his own decisions." I suppose that's true, but it doesn't mean anyone has to like those decisions.

I also spoke with Sianon on one or two more occasions, but they were empty conversations. She never really seemed very interested in talking to me.

At any rate, that was about a month ago. Blade said they might be in Falconwall for a while. Possibly quite a while.

Odd... The name "Sianon" is very similar to the Earth name "Shannon." After meeting people with names like "Ariaziane," "Mepis," and "Gnorrin," I sure didn't expect to hear any names so familiar.

Celebration Week began today. Since I've chosen to celebrate my own birthday this week, I guess I'm officially eighteen. Yippee skip. Celebration Week seems to be pretty similar to Mid-Year Week, only less public. Most businesses are closed and folks stay home with their families. There hasn't been snow, yet. Otherwise, the season reminds me of Christmas.

I wonder if it's that time of year on Earth. And what my family is doing for the holiday. Without me.

Vincent stared vacantly at the notebook. After a few minutes, he shook himself back to the present and dipped his pen in the well again. As he did so, he smiled.

Evidently, old Mepis is doing quite well for himself. He carts his "Inks by Mepis" to other towns and is very happy with their popularity. Every time he sees me, he tells me how many orders he's had that week and how grateful he is to me for my genius of an idea. I think Mepis has become my first groupie.

Everything seems to be going well, here. The winter season, or the Season of Sleep, as it's called, is quite a chore to live in. And this one is pretty mild. First of all, there's the firewood. I hate to think how my muscles would be aching now if it weren't for Blade's lessons in swordplay. Chopping wood for hours on end is hard work!

The fireplace in my cottage works fairly well. Then again, it's a small cottage. What I wouldn't give for real windows, though. It's good I can get a form of filtered light in here, but it'd be nice to be able to see outside, too.

King and Blaise are both well. Blaise has taken to staying indoors, now. She's remarkably well behaved inside. But every morning, I wake to a pile of wood shavings from the sticks she's chewed throughout the night. I'd forgotten how much Labs like to chew. Oh, well. At least she hasn't gone after anything important, yet.

Warm showers aren't quite as easy to come by now. I have to boil a pot of water, carry it up the ladder, and dump it in the basin to heat up the other water in there. Not too much of an effort, though the stall is awfully cold! I suspect I'll soon just have to rely on the bathtub until the warmer weather hits. A shame, though, since showers are much more to my liking.

The best news of all is that Ariaziane has loosened up a little. I don't know what caused it—perhaps nothing but time. At any rate, she seems to have decided to make the best of her new hair and eye color. She purchased a cloak dyed the same color as her eyes and has taken to wearing it almost all the time, just like she had when her eyes were more of a violet color. She visits me every day, which I confess I enjoy tremendously. I still don't have much hope of a romance between us and am focusing instead on being the best friend I possibly can to her.

I visit Gnorrin frequently, which is nothing new. He beats me at chess. Again, nothing new. We seldom talk about Blade. None of us particularly want to.

Vincent stopped writing and frowned. Funny how the entry went full circle, he thought to himself. As he put away his pen and ink, he thought about Blade. They weren't cheery thoughts. Though Blade didn't really live here, going about normal daily routines without him around was very strange. Vincent blew on the page to quicken the drying of the ink. Then he closed the book and put it away.

That evening Gnorrin and Ariaziane took him to the inn, one of the few establishments open during Celebration Week. They had a wonderful dinner and enjoyed the festivities the inn provided. There was singing and storytelling, juggling acts and dancers. Impromptu music floated over from several of the surrounding tables.

After the meal, a server brought out a cake laden with eighteen candles. Vincent was wide-eyed. Birthday cake was not a tradition on this world. He looked at Ariaziane, who grinned with pleasure. "Surprise," she said.

He laughed. "It certainly is. Thank you."

To his amazement, Ariaziane and Gnorrin broke into song, singing "Happy Birthday" to him. Other patrons stared in puzzlement and Vincent regretted having once sung the song for Ariaziane. He had a habit of doing things that would come back to haunt him. And Gnorrin's singing wasn't something he was likely to recover from quickly.

As the pair finished the song, Vincent smiled sheepishly. He was always embarrassed when people sang the song to him. "As I understand this ritual," Gnorrin said, "you are now to make a wish and blow out the candles?"

"Right," Vincent replied. He thought for a moment. Certainly not a difficult choice of wishes. Home, he thought. Then he looked up at Ariaziane, and he felt his heart leap a little. Love, he thought. He sighed and closed his eyes. Okay, so it *was* a difficult choice of wishes. After a moment, he opened his eyes, lowered his face to the cake, and blew out the candles in one long, sweeping breath.

Ariaziane cheered. "You did it! Does this mean you get your wish?"

"Maybe," he said as the server began plucking candles from the cake.

"What did you wish for?" asked Gnorrin.

"I can't say. It won't come true if I tell anyone."

Gnorrin nodded wisely.

Vincent examined the dessert as the server sliced the cake. It was a deep tan color with a dark frosting. "Happy Birthday Vincent" was piped onto the top in cream colored frosting, and there was a sprinkling of tiny, sugared violet petals. Once all three were served, the others urged him to take the first bite. He did so, and voiced his approval. "Mmmmmmm."

"Is it good?" Ariaziane asked.

Vincent swallowed, savoring the creamy caramel frosting and moist cake, potent with warm spices. "I think this is the best cake I've ever had." He smiled as the girl beamed in satisfaction. "Thank you."

"You're welcome," she said as she dug into her own piece. Then she glanced at Gnorrin. "Let's give him his presents."

"Very well," Gnorrin said, lowering his fork. "A very nice custom you have in your world, this 'birthday cake,'" he said as he rooted through his backpack. "Perhaps we should institute it here, eh?" Gnorrin produced a small parcel, about the size of his fist, wrapped brightly in colored paper and secured with a ribbon. He pushed the package across the table to his friend. "That's one," he said, still gazing into his pack.

Vincent accepted the gift and waited for Gnorrin to finish. A moment later, the gnome looked up. "Well, go ahead."

"I was waiting for you," Vincent explained.

"I already know what's inside," he said, returning to his pack.

Vincent shook his head with a smile and unwrapped the gift. It popped open when the ribbon was untied. Inside were the batteries for his tape player. He looked at Ariaziane in puzzlement. She smiled. "You said they could be charged again," she said. "And once you explained what powered them, it was no trouble to make them work again."

Vincent looked at Gnorrin. "How...?"

"No different than enchanting a wand, boy," he said, still rooting. "I just used a mild lightning spell, is all."

Vincent closed his mouth. "Son of a gun," he said.

Gnorrin finally came up with another small package. Vincent thanked him. Again, he untied the bright ribbon and the paper popped open. Inside the small box was a round cut stone. A gem the size of the nail on his little finger, the red of dark blood. Vincent picked it up and examined it, noticing tiny engravings on the flat facet on top. "This looks like a garnet," he said. "Is it? That's my birthstone. How'd you know?"

"I am not familiar with the stone of that name," Gnorrin said. "In fact, it is not an ordinary gem. I chanced upon it during one of my adventures, years ago. The engraving is a sigil of healing."

Vincent raised his eyes. His voice was low. "Magic?"

Gnorrin nodded solemnly. "And very useful. Whenever you are injured and sustain a bleeding wound, this will stop the bleeding very quickly. I have also noticed when wearing it, healing seems to occur more rapidly."

"And you're parting with such a valuable item? Why?"

"Because such an item will be of far more use to you than to me."

Vincent looked at his friend. His eyes narrowed. "Gnorrin, what has caused you to change your tune so much? Not so long ago, you were hellfire and brimstone against adventuring as a way of life. Now you give me this. Practically an incentive for continuing."

Gnorrin looked down at his folded hands and said quietly, "It is not so much that." He looked Vincent in the eye. "Let us say I have realized how firm both of you are on continuing in this line of work. And perhaps..." He shook his head at himself. "Perhaps I even feel this is what the gods have meant for you to do." Vincent placed the gem back in the box, having no reply for his friend. Gnorrin shifted the conversation. "Go on, girl, give him your present."

Vincent turned to Ariaziane, to see her pulling a small box from her pouch. Again he untied a colored ribbon and removed the bright paper. His jaw dropped when he saw the contents.

Inside was a brooch, shaped like a stylized "V," such as he used when writing his name, looking nearly like a square root symbol, with a sweeping upper bar. The "V" was made of something similar to onyx. Underneath the horizontal bar, running parallel and stretching out from the upstroke, were seven feathers made of gold. They decreased in length from top to bottom, the top nearly reaching the end of the upper bar, the bottom only stretching perhaps half an inch. Each of the feathers was tipped with a tiny, red stone, giving the feathers the appearance of being tipped with blood. The entire brooch was about three inches at its widest point.

"Wow," he breathed.

"Do you like it?"

He looked up at Ariaziane's anxious face. "It's beautiful! Whatever gave you the idea?"

"I've always liked the way you sign your name. And I've always thought of you as being wild and free, like a bird. One day, the idea just came to me. Gnorrin helped with the design and choosing the stones."

Gnorrin frowned. "Don't let her fool you. I just gave opinions."

Vincent smiled at her. "Thank you." He fixed the pin upon his cloak. "I'll treasure it always."

As the others finished their cake and Gnorrin had seconds, Vincent gazed over the other patrons of the inn. There was quite a crowd, mostly due to Celebration Week. He recognized many people and nodded to them if they happened to catch his eye. Then he noticed someone staring directly at his table.

The man stood at the bar. He was young, probably not any older than Vincent himself. He was stocky and muscular, with short, sandy hair, and dressed in clothes that had obviously seen much wearing. He turned his gaze when Vincent noticed him staring, but not right away. Clearly, he didn't care if his attention were noted.

Vincent returned his own attention to his friends and his birthday celebration. Every once in a while, he would steal a glance over at the bar. The young man was still staring at them. Vincent spoke in low tones to Gnorrin. "There's a gentleman observing us from the bar. Rather intently. Friend of yours?"

Gnorrin stole a peek to the side. Ariaziane frowned. The bar was behind her and she couldn't look without being obvious. Gnorrin shrugged. "Not that I know of. I've never seen him before."

The young man noticed the glances his way and approached the table. "Well, we'll soon find out," Vincent said. He rested his hand under the table, atop the dagger at his belt. When the man was at their table, Vincent said, "May we help you?"

The stranger's eyes held a determined look. "I'm looking for a woman," he said.

"Aren't we all?" said Vincent.

Gnorrin added, "You might speak to the proprietor. I'm sure something can be arranged."

The humor was lost on the stranger. "I have spoken to him. He told me a woman of her description was seen here with you. She stands a few inches shorter than myself. Long hair, lighter than mine. She traveled through here, coming from the east."

Comprehension dawned on Vincent, but Gnorrin was the first to speak. "Why do you seek her?"

"That is none of your affair. Where is she? The proprietor told me she checked out some weeks ago. I must find her."

"You've been told correctly," Vincent said, "but you will not be told more until you explain your reasons."

The stranger glared at him. "It is personal," he snapped. He closed his eyes, shaking his head. Suddenly, he looked very tired. He ran a hand over his face. "Forgive me." He nodded at the remaining chair at the table. "May I?"

After a quick exchange of glances, Vincent nodded. The man pulled out the chair and sat down. The three introduced themselves, and he nodded politely at them all. His eyes lingered on Ariaziane, the last to speak. Vincent bristled and cleared his throat. "And you are...?"

"Again, my apologies. My name is D'Ty."

Ariaziane caught his attention again. "Would you like some cake?" Vincent frowned as the man eyed both his cake and his would-be girlfriend. He glanced at Gnorrin, hoping for some backup. Or at least sympathy. But the gnome was frowning, as if in thought. His hand rubbed his chin.

Vincent turned back to D'Ty, who was now enjoying a piece of birthday cake. "Will you tell us your reasons for seeking the woman?"

The man sighed and wiped crumbs from his lips. "Years ago, there was a scandal in my village. A love affair between a young man and woman, an affair not approved of. The girl's family was very well-to-do. The boy's family was poor. In addition, the boy himself was known to be troublesome. He drank too much, fought too much. Despite this, the girl loved him enough to accept his proposal of marriage."

D'Ty smiled ruefully. "Not having enough money for a formal betrothal gift, he made for her a pendant out of delicate vines. He braided them into a beautiful knot to symbolize their union. He dried and preserved it and she wore it proudly, infuriating her snobbish parents."

The man's face grew serious. "The girl became pregnant, which would have been scandalous enough. One day, though, the young man got into a drunken fight in a tavern. He stabbed and killed the eldest son of a prominent businessman. The act was in defense, though the townspeople would not believe this to be true. He was sought down for a public hanging, but escaped into the forest.

"The outcry was enormous. The boy's family was ordered to surrender him to the authorities, but they knew only that he was hiding out in the forest, nothing more. They turned to the girl and her family." D'Ty shook his head. "These proud folk were shamed to their core by this affront. They blamed the daughter, since the boy was not around to be blamed."

D'Ty closed his eyes for a moment before continuing. "The girl was shamed beyond reasoning. And in a fit of emotion, she killed herself and her unborn child. The young man never forgave himself for this. He went away and was never seen there again." His voice became more urgent. "In the years since, the girl's younger sister, who also never forgave the crime done to her family by the boy's actions, became a mage." Heads turned at this and D'Ty lowered his voice. "She intends to find the one who caused her sister's suicide and destroy him. Her goal is to make him fall in love with her, and then reveal herself to him. And when the guilt and shame and betrayal have consumed him, she will kill him. I have determined to prevent her from doing so."

Vincent and Ariaziane were speechless, staring at the young man. Gnorrin cleared his throat and spoke with a pained expression on his face. "D'Ty." He frowned. "Sianon has already found your brother."

❧ ❧

The trio did not hesitate a moment in pledging their aid to D'Ty. Blade was their friend and they would stop at nothing to ensure his safety.

While Ariaziane and Gnorrin returned to their cottage to put together their necessities, Vincent walked with D'Ty to his own home. As they made their way there, Vincent began conversation. "I knew there was some sort of secret your brother had been hiding. I must say, though, this isn't the way I wanted to learn of it." D'Ty simply nodded absently in response. "How long since you've seen him?"

D'Ty stared at the ground. "Fifteen years. I was eight when it all happened."

"How exactly did you learn of Sianon's plot?"

D'Ty stirred uncomfortably atop his horse. "It is rather embarrassing."

"I was only curious. No need to tell me if you'd rather not."

"No, I will tell you." D'Ty took a deep breath. "I suppose you could say I, too, never allowed the matter to rest, all these years. As I grew older, I began to wonder about the other family. I wondered how the events were still affecting them. My family had lost a son to exile; theirs had lost a daughter to death.

"There were many similarities between us. Each family had one other child. Myself and Sianon. Each of our fathers had served in the same war. And later, each of our mothers died the same year. I was too intrigued to resist.

"I knew of their other daughter, by word, anyway. I'd never seen her, though I wanted to. I had only a physical description and she sounded beautiful."

Vincent nodded. "So you went to find her?"

"Yes. I knew I couldn't enter the grounds of her home. It was a private estate. However, I was able to observe the school she attended. For a week, I spied on the students as they ate their lunches outdoors. By the end of the week, I had singled out the girl who most closely resembled the description I'd been given. For a month, I watched her closely, trying to discover what she was like."

"Sounds like you were pretty obsessed."

"Aye, that I was. Have you ever felt that way, Vincent?"

Vincent smiled. "Oh, yes."

D'Ty frowned. "I've been meaning to ask you, what kind of name is Vincent? I've never..."

"Some other time. Continue with your story. We're almost to my cottage."

"Yes. Well, I studied this girl for awhile and found myself entranced by her every action. The way she talked with her friends. The way she walked. Even the way she ate her food." He smiled mostly to himself. "I allowed myself to be seen watching her. She seemed flattered by the attention. We flirted, I suppose you could say. Eventually, I worked up the courage to introduce myself to her." D'Ty shook his head. "I told you it was embarrassing."

Vincent smiled. "She wasn't Sianon."

His new friend shook his head. "Nay. Apparently, Sianon was a bit on the antisocial side. She spent her lunch hour in private study, practicing the magic she had recently begun. I covered my blunder easily enough. I told her I'd asked a friend who she was, describing her to him. And the friend had told me the girl's name was Sianon. And she seemed to allow that someone could make such a mistake. This saved further embarrassment."

"Well, that's something, at least."

"Yes, but then I had to renew my original search for Sianon. Though now it wasn't difficult. I would wait for Tisen after school to walk her home. This was how I eventually met Sianon." He frowned. "I learned quite a bit about her through Tisen. Sianon was the object of considerable gossip in the school, due to her studies of magic. She made no secret of her studies, and others made their speculations about her. If Sianon had been more outgoing in nature, she would not have been so discussed. The words spoken about her ran rampant. And evidently, at some point previously, she had let slip a single fact. When pressed by a classmate on the reasons for her magical studies, she said one word. 'Revenge.'" D'Ty firmed his expression. "I didn't need more speculation to know what she meant."

They arrived at Vincent's cottage.   Inside, D'Ty concluded his story. "I convinced Tisen to be my ears inside the school. She became friendly with Sianon and eventually began to pry. Naturally, I had to tell her the entire story. And she also convinced Sianon to divulge her side of things, as well. This is how I learned her full plan."

Vincent nodded as he began laying out clothing for the journey. "Sadistic bitch, isn't she? Well, I guess that's fortunate. It requires time. Otherwise, Blade might be dead already."

D'Ty shook his head. "Strange that he should continue to hide behind that false name."

"I always got the impression it was by choice, rather than necessity. I don't know the specifics of your brother's past, but I've sensed how deeply his guilt runs. Seems to me he's tried to erase his past, to pretend his real existence began upon adoption of that name."

His guest pondered this. "Likely so, Vincent. I only hope that erasure does not include myself."

❧ Ten ❧

In the morning, D'Ty assisted Vincent in making sure the cottage was properly sealed from the elements. The plugs were inserted into the windows and wax poured around the edges.

The previous evening in the tavern, Gnorrin had explained that there was little he could do to get the four of them to Falconwall quickly. He alluded vaguely to a certain magical method of transportation, saying it would work for no more than two people. The decision was for Gnorrin and D'Ty to proceed in this fashion, while Vincent and Ariaziane followed behind on horseback.

Ariaziane and Gnorrin soon arrived. Ariaziane's mount was packed for the long journey. After making one last check to be sure everything was in order, she and Vincent were off, leaving Gnorrin to transport himself and D'Ty with whatever magic the gnome had decided to use.

Their journey was long and cold, and Vincent worried about how well Blaise would handle the journey. But he didn't want to board her at the local equivalent of a kennel. His fears proved unfounded, however. The dog kept pace with their horses and rested when they stopped for breaks.

During the day, the pair spoke of Blade's situation. They both hoped Gnorrin and D'Ty could resolve everything by the time Vincent and Ariaziane reached the city, but neither seemed very confident about this possibility. When they weren't discussing that, Vincent concentrated on making the most of his time with Ariaziane.

They ate the dried foods they'd packed, and there were plenty of grasses in the fields along the road for the horses. Vincent had packed some kibble for Blaise, which she virtually inhaled, so much energy did she need.

Their nights were spent around campfires, bundled warmly into sleeping sacks. They didn't worry about keeping watch at night, trusting Blaise to warn them of any danger. Vincent would have preferred snuggling with Ariaziane through the night, but she didn't appear interested in such closeness.

The worst part of the journey for Vincent was not the cold or the snow, but that his back wasn't exactly suited to prolonged horseback riding. Just as when he and Blade had guarded the tax money, Vincent was soon in pain. It was exacerbated by the nights sleeping on the cold, hard ground. He would enjoy nothing more than a steamy hot bath to soak in, he realized.

On the fourth day, his wishes were answered when they came to a major crossroads. There they encountered a small town. They spent the night there, restocking their provisions, taking advantage of sleeping in rooms sheltered from the weather, and soaking for an hour in the baths. Early the next morning, after a hearty breakfast, they were on their way.

Three more days and nights of travel and they reached the gates of Falconwall.

Vincent gazed admiringly at the entrance to the walled city. The stone wall itself was fully thirty feet high. The open gates were made of wood and looked sturdy enough to withstand a small army. Atop the wall, armed guards paced, and at the gateway itself were three men. Vincent noted two of them were huge, burly types with bulging biceps and imposing swords hanging by their sides. The third was a nondescript little man who sat at a table in front of him. A chest sat atop the table, as well as an open ledger.

As Vincent and Ariaziane dismounted, the little man made two ticks on the page of his book and said simply, "One copper each." Vincent obligingly dropped the coins in a slot atop the locked chest, after which they entered the city, leading their horses behind them.

Vincent looked at Ariaziane and cocked his head back toward the little man. "We get to go on the rides all day, or what?" Vincent gazed at the back of his hand. "Didn't even rubber-stamp us."

The first thing that caught Vincent's attention, once they were through the gate, was the smell. Or rather, the multitude of smells. The gate through which they'd entered was located in a merchant area of the city. A bakery was obviously nearby, for the delightful aroma of fresh bread seduced him. He looked to his left, and there it was. Next to it was a butcher shop, from where the tang of fresh entrails emanated. The combination of bread and guts made him slightly queasy. He tried to ignore the smells and concentrate on the impressive sights.

The wall was visible the entire way around the city, due to the fact that their entrance had been on a slight rise and they were now descending into the city itself. The buildings were primarily low constructs of one or two floors. There were exceptions, naturally, but none nearby. The streets were of dirt and in fairly good condition, with a minimum of stones to trip up unwary pedestrians. Still on a slight incline, he was able to pinpoint other areas of the city. There was a large, obviously residential section, yet the bulk of the area seemed to be reserved for commerce. Vincent wasn't surprised.

There were many people going about their businesses, though not quite as many as Vincent would have expected. Though Falconwall was a city, it couldn't compare to cities of his acquaintance. He turned to Ariaziane. "What's the population of Falconwall?"

She shrugged her shoulders. "Perhaps thirty-five thousand. Perhaps more."

Vincent nodded. Hardly what he'd call a city, though still impressive, all things considered.

As they walked along, looking for the inn where they'd agreed to meet the others, another odor drifted to him, an unpleasant one, but not overpowering. He tried to ignore it, but the further they walked, the stronger it became, a foul and pervasive stench. "What *is* that?" he finally croaked.

"The tanner," she said. "The smell of tanning hides isn't one you'll soon forget, I imagine."

"It's *awful!* Reminds me of paper factories back home." Vincent stuck his tongue out. "Yuck."

Several minutes passed before they were out of reach of the offensive odor. And by that time, they'd reached the inn. They stabled their mounts behind the building before going inside to reserve rooms. As Ariaziane did so, Vincent asked the innkeeper if he happened to know if Gnorrin or D'Ty were in the building. The man shook his head. Vincent thanked him, then he and Ariaziane took their baggage to the room. They left Blaise there, then entered the tavern, where they took a table and ordered meals.

"I think," said Vincent, once their beverages were served, "we should split up. We can cover different avenues of the city. We'll check out the other inns and once we have located where they are staying, we can intervene as necessary."

"If we're not too late," she replied.

Vincent shook his head. "I don't think we are. If she's as bent on torturing him as D'Ty thinks, she'll make it last. You don't plan revenge for fifteen years, then get it over and done with so quickly."

Ariaziane lifted an eyebrow. "You would know?"

"I would *imagine*," he corrected, with a smile. "We might duplicate the efforts of the others, but until we see them, we need to do something."

Ariaziane nodded her agreement as their meals were served. As they ate quietly, Vincent wondered how the others were doing. Gnorrin was probably overwhelmed by anxiety. After losing one friend to premature death, he certainly wasn't prepared to lose another so soon. D'Ty had come a long way, and now that he was close to his goal, the stress of the situation had to be incredible.

He turned his gaze to Ariaziane, only to find her staring intently at him. She smiled sheepishly and turned her eyes back to her plate. A tightness suddenly surged in his chest. He took a deep breath and tried to return to his food, but hunger had left him. He found himself pushing the remainder around his plate with his spoon. Eventually, he stopped doing even that. He pushed himself back from the table.

"I'm ready to get started. How about you?" The girl nodded impatiently and Vincent noticed she hadn't eaten much, either. He tossed a few coins on the table as they rose. In minutes, they were on their respective ways.

The better part of an hour later, Vincent was checking his third inn. The proprietor shook his head. There was no one he knew of answering the descriptions of Blade or Sianon lodging with them presently. Vincent sighed, thanked the man, and turned to leave. At the door, he paused, a thought striking him. He returned to the proprietor.

"Tell me," he said, "what would be the fanciest inn in the city?"

The man sniffed, as if his establishment had just been insulted. "Well," he drawled, "I would have to say the *fanciest* inn would be *The Old Grey Mare*. However," he hastened to add, "their service..." He shook his head.

"I know," said Vincent. "Ain't what she used to be." The man gave him a blank look, but provided directions to the inn at his request. Vincent thanked him again and departed.

As he hurried along the streets, Vincent thought about his line of reasoning. If I were trying to string someone along, he thought, I'd certainly want to go all-out. Sianon would want to stay in the nicest place. He hurried across town until he located the establishment.

He entered the inn, going directly to the front desk. He found the establishment to be very attractive, even what he'd call elegant. No one staffed the desk, though there was an ornate crystal bell. He rang, then waited. And waited. He rang the bell a second time. And waited. Finally, a carefully dressed woman appeared, a carefully dressed smile on her face. "May I help you?"

"I'm looking for some friends who are likely to be here. The gentleman is about a head taller than me, mid-thirties, very dark hair, severe grey eyes. The lady is of average height, long blonde hair, mid-twenties."

"Yes," the woman droned, her careful smile now gone. "They are in the dining area even now." She indicated a double-door leading off to one side, then turned and left.

"Thank you," Vincent muttered to the empty desk. Relief washed over him. Blade was still alive. He turned and pushed open the double doors.

Inside the dining area, the tables were mostly full. The room was lavish, with a roaring fireplace set in each of the four walls. There was a great deal of ornamentation, mostly bronze, which reflected the glow of the fires beautifully. Heavy tapestries depicting woodland scenes and royalty adorned the walls. Each table was large and sturdy, with lovely, carved chairs. Candelabras sat on each table. Service might suck, he thought to himself, but it sure is pretty.

Vincent gazed over the patrons, trying to spy Blade and Sianon. As no host or hostess met him at the door, he began a slow trek around the perimeter of the room. He had no idea what he'd do when he found them. He wished Gnorrin were here. If Sianon really were a mage, he reasoned, Gnorrin should be the one to handle her.

Out of the corner of his eye, Vincent noticed a figure approaching a table. It wasn't a waiter, however, but D'Ty. And he was holding a dagger.

"Oh, shit." Vincent hurried across the room, but he couldn't reach their table before D'Ty did. Vincent watched as his new friend jumped behind Sianon, holding his weapon to the girl's throat. Blade jumped from his seat, but paused when he saw the knife.

Vincent snaked his way between tables, jostling more than one diner's elbow in the process. Soon he was near enough to his goal. He looked at Blade and drew a sharp breath. The man's eyes, which had always been piercing, now held a look of cold death. Vincent hoped never to have such a look directed at himself. The object of the gaze was Blade's own brother, but of course, Blade probably didn't realize this, since he hadn't seen D'Ty in fifteen years. Vincent held his breath as he stepped to the side of the table.

"Fancy meeting you here," he said.

Blade cast him the merest glance, then did a double-take upon realizing who had just spoken to him. His brow knit, then he turned his stare back at D'Ty.

Vincent cleared his throat and addressed Sianon. "This would probably be the best time for you to undo whatever enchantment you've put him under."

Sianon turned a cold glare upon him. "What is the meaning of this?"

D'Ty was more than happy to answer her. "Revenge, I believe." His voice dripped with hatred.

"What do you mean?" demanded Blade.

D'Ty looked at his brother, his face softening. He didn't reply, merely shifted his dagger, dipping the point down the front of Sianon's tunic. He slowly withdrew the blade, having hooked its tip under a golden chain. Looped in the chain was a golden pendant in the shape of an acorn.

"A necklace," Blade said. "What of it?"

In reply, D'Ty reached down and grasped the acorn and squeezed. The bottom half of the pendant came off in his fingers, revealing inside a beautiful knot of lacquered vine.

Blade's face paled. Vincent watched as his friend's hand crept up toward his own neck, a movement Vincent had seen before. He withdrew and idly fingered a matching pendant. His eyes lost their intensity, being replaced by confusion. His breathing grew quicker, more shallow.

D'Ty allowed the chain to drop from the tip of his dagger and returned the blade to its original position. Sianon's head drooped, oblivious to the blade at her throat. D'Ty reflexively moved the weapon, so as not to cut her. Vincent smiled to himself. D'Ty didn't really have a murderous bone in his body. He could probably learn to like this fellow. He cleared his throat and put his hand on Blade's shoulder. The man's reverie broke and he looked at his young friend. "Blade, I believe you know this gentleman, though it's been awhile."

Blade looked at his brother, his eyes becoming clearer. D'Ty looked back at him, almost pleading for him to come to his senses. Blade's breathing slowed and he finally closed his mouth. He sat down again, slowly. "Please remove your dagger from her throat, my brother."

D'Ty did so, but kept the blade in hand. Vincent sat down, motioning for D'Ty to do the same. Patrons were beginning to become alarmed and the last thing they needed was the local constabulary coming down on them. Vincent turned to Sianon again. "As I said, the enchantment should be removed now."

Blade spoke up. "There is no need, my friend." His gaze never left Sianon's face. And he spoke, barely above a whisper, in a voice more tender than Vincent would have imagined him capable of. "I didn't remember your name." The girl looked up at him, guilt in her eyes, where Vincent would have expected something quite different. "But I remember we took you to the puppet show in town." Sianon turned her face away. "You laughed and laughed. And we bought you roasted nuts and chewy candy." Blade's eyes misted and Vincent found his own doing the same. He was almost embarrassed to be there with them. "She loved you very much."

"I know," the girl whispered.

"And so do I," Blade said.

Six eyes stared at him in surprise. Vincent raised an eyebrow. Sianon merely gaped. Only D'Ty found his voice. "She means to kill you!"

Blade looked at her. "Do you?"

Sianon turned her eyes to the tabletop. Vincent smiled again. Sianon didn't really have a murderous bone in *her* body, either. He spoke to D'Ty. "I think you can put that away, now."

D'Ty looked at him, at Sianon, then at his dagger. With a nod, he sheathed the weapon.

Vincent relaxed a little. Everything seemed to be working out just fine. Then he suddenly felt strange. His limbs felt heavy and stiff. He couldn't move his arms or legs. He turned to Sianon and saw her wave a finger in D'Ty's direction, noting his friend also seemed immobile. She stood, a flare coming into her eyes.

Sianon clenched a fist and gritted her teeth. Her fist glowed. Blade looked unflinchingly into her eyes, his face impassive. "This is for taking my sister from me," she growled. As her fist flew out, the glow brightened, then surged from her hand toward Blade's face. Vincent and D'Ty strained vainly at their magical bonds. They watched as Blade recoiled from the blow. Half his face erupted in a brief flame, which was just as soon extinguished.

Patrons were screaming as Blade fell to the floor. Vincent felt as though his heart would burst its way through his chest. D'Ty was cursing up a storm. And suddenly there were two huge men on either side of Sianon, grabbing her by the arms. At this, the pair could move again. They both rushed forward, Vincent going to aid his friend, D'Ty going for his dagger. But Blade was already rising to his feet. "*Hold,*" he said. And his voice froze them all in their tracks.

Half his face was burned red. Tiny blisters were already forming. He strode forward, brushing past D'Ty and motioning for the two guards to release the girl. They did so, but did not move away. Vincent saw Sianon look up at him, as if expecting a blow. Instead, he stood before her and spoke quietly. "Fifteen years would likely have spawned much more from most people." Sianon said nothing, just looked at him questioningly. "I thank you for sparing me that to which I've already subjected myself." He reached out and took her by the shoulders, drawing her closer to him. Then he bent and gently kissed her, eliciting noises of another sort from the patrons.

Vincent cleared his throat and moved to the guards. He slipped a coin into the hand of each of them. "I think we've got this under control, now." They glanced at the shiny metal in their palms and nodded at him as they moved away.

Sianon stepped back, nearly stumbling over her own feet. Blade gave her a weak smile and turned his back on her, facing his brother. His smile widened and soon D'Ty was caught in a bear hug. "Gods, it's good to see you! You're all grown up!"

Vincent nearly chuckled aloud, looking at D'Ty's face. The young man was torn between staring at his brother and at Sianon, who seemed all but forgotten by Blade. Vincent looked at the girl and knew any threat she might once have posed was now gone. He turned to her.

"Are you all right?" The girl looked vacantly at him. Vincent repeated the question.

This time, she answered. "I don't know." He nodded. He doubted he'd know how to feel in her position, either. She turned and quietly left the dining room.

At the door, she turned, gazing at Blade. Then she was gone.

Vincent stood by the brothers and put a hand on each one's shoulder. "I'm going to find the others. You two have a lot to catch up on." They thanked him with smiles. "You really ought to take care of that burn, too."

Blade's eyes washed with pain Vincent knew didn't come from the injury. "Why?" he asked simply.

Vincent absorbed the man's meaning, and his pain. He nodded, then turned to leave.

He walked slowly back to the inn where he and Ariaziane were staying, his mind weighing the scene he'd just witnessed. The look of pain in Blade's eyes as he asked "Why?" still haunted him. To think that this was the torture he'd been living with for so many years. Vincent couldn't imagine how his friend must feel. Certainly he had his own private pains he carried with him. Who didn't? But nothing Vincent had experienced could quite compare with Blade's story.

An interesting trio, he thought. Blade carrying that guilt with him. Sianon carrying the desire for revenge for so long. And D'Ty, who only had a curiosity over past events and had gotten drawn into the middle of everything. Fortunately, perhaps. Vincent still wasn't sure Sianon could have carried through with her plans, intervention or no intervention. Who knows? Maybe she just came to realize how decent a guy Blade was during their week-long trek to Falconwall.

He felt rather positive by the way things had ended, there in the dining room. Yet there was more to come. He could sense it. And equally, he sensed something was needed to help it come into being. It was a vague feeling, but enough to cause him to stop walking.

He stood in the middle of the street and looked around. The hour was getting late. The streets were dark and cold, and he really should be getting back to advise Ariaziane and Gnorrin of the turn of events. That could wait, though, he thought. And something else couldn't.

He turned and headed back toward *The Old Grey Mare*.

He neared the inn, his pace rapid. He paused at the door, a movement catching the corner of his eye. He turned and saw a figure about fifty yards away, lit by the light of street lanterns, moving away from the inn. And though all he could see was a dark form, he knew who it had to be.

Sianon turned at the footsteps behind her. Her eyes widened, seeing him. "What do you want?" she said with a thick voice.

Vincent stopped a few paces away. "To talk," he said simply.

"Fine. Go talk to yourself," she said, and turned to continue walking.

Vincent shrugged and fell into step close behind her. He summoned his best Groucho Marx voice. "I can do that. Do it all the time, in fact. I even talk back to myself." Sianon stopped and turned, staring at him with an incredulous expression. Vincent completed his act. "Sometimes I even argue."

"What do you *want*? Leave me alone!"

Vincent cleared his throat. "Actually, I can't."

"Why? I'm not going to kill your friend! Isn't that enough for you?" She turned again and started off rapidly.

He kept pace with her. "That's what I wanted to talk to you about. I want to know why you aren't going to kill him."

"Why? You want him dead?"

"Of course not," he said as they rushed along the street. "But I thought *you* did."

At this, Sianon seemed to lose all energy. She slowed her pace until she stopped, leaning against the stone face of a building. When her voice finally came, it was a whisper. "I do."

He leaned against the wall beside her, shaking his head. "I dunno. That's getting kind of hard to believe."

"I don't care if you believe me or not," she said, and pushed off the wall to continue walking.

Vincent kept pace beside her. "Tell me why."

"What are you? Deaf? You know exactly why I want him dead. As dead as my sister."

"Well, I've heard D'Ty's story. I'd like to hear yours. Maybe his was biased."

Sianon stopped walking and turned to face him. "Why do you care?"

He looked into her eyes. "I just do. Isn't that enough?" He looked up, seeing they were next to a tavern. "Come on. Let's go inside and talk."

Sianon looked at him for a long while. Then she turned and entered the tavern.

They took a table near a corner, away from the crowd. Sianon ordered a flagon of mulled wine, Vincent one of spiced cider. Once they'd been served and were settled comfortably in, Vincent posed his first question. "What was your sister like?"

Sianon's eyes became wistful for a moment. "Headstrong. Always got her way." She took a drink. "Mother always seemed to be yelling at her for one thing or another. But Adina never took mother's anger seriously. She was rebellious and wild and I thought that was really funny."

"Sounds as though you turned out a lot like her."

Sianon drank again and gave a slight inclination of her head. "Suppose I did." She was quiet a while before she continued. Vincent didn't prompt her. "Mother's anger took a serious tone, though, at one point. I still can hear her voice, condemning Adina for this boy she was seeing. He was no good, she said. He was poor. He was trouble. He was everything my family should have avoided at all costs." She looked up at him, almost apologetically. "My family tended to be a bit snobbish." Another drink and a shrug. Then she pulled out the lacquered vine knot she wore. "This thing," she said, "made mother absolutely crazy. Adina would wear it all the time. Proudly. Almost to push it in mother's face. And this brought on more nasty comments. At such a young age, I didn't know anything about social status, so all I knew was my sister was hurt by this constant ridicule. What I didn't know was something else was bothering her. She was pregnant. And when our parents found this out, things got really harsh."

Vincent nodded, but didn't speak. He listened as she repeated D'Ty's story of how Blade had killed a man in a bar fight and run off, leaving the pregnant girl behind. And how Adina killed herself. As he'd hoped, Sianon talked about the aftermath of this event.

"My family was devastated by Adina's death. A suicide within a family is the ultimate social embarrassment. So we lived in shame for a time. And naturally, your friend became the target of blame for the event. It was all his fault."

"Was it?"

"Wasn't it?" she countered. "He killed the man in the tavern. He ran away! He should have stayed, accepted whatever punishment was due him, and then..."

"And then what? To hear D'Ty tell the story, the only likely punishment would have been death. So he should have stayed and been put to death for accidentally killing someone?"

"How do you know the death was an accident?"

"I don't. But I don't know otherwise, either. Do you think that fact would have made a difference?"

Sianon averted her eyes. "Probably not."

"Okay. So why do you blame him for everything? I mean, the way you're talking, I don't think you really hold him guilty of any crime."

"Not guilty?" she flared. "Certainly I find him guilty! Who else could be guilty? If he really had loved her, he would have stayed. If he really loved her, he wouldn't have killed that man."

"If he really loved her, he would have been a better person? Is that what you're trying to say? Come on, Sianon. What's the real story? This isn't serious."

"Who are you to tell me it isn't serious?" she flared. "You wanted the story, and I told you the story!"

"Don't get indignant with me. You owe me the truth."

The girl gaped at him. "And how did you decide this?"

"You don't think D'Ty would have hesitated to make things a lot rougher on you if I hadn't intervened, do you? He was ready to slit your throat at the slightest provocation!"

Sianon stared at him for a long moment, then laughed. "You're a worse liar than I am, Vincent." She signaled for another round for the two of them. "Hmph. Well. So we're a pair of liars."

"Okay, so let's tell the truth."

"Agreed. You first. Why are you here?"

Vincent accepted the tankard of cider from the waitress and took a hot swallow. "I told you. I want to know the real story."

"Yes, but why? Just out of curiosity?"

"Let's just say I'm usually a pretty decent judge of character. And I want to see if my suspicions about you are correct."

"And what are they?"

Vincent smiled. "Well, when I first met you, I only sensed something was wrong. I didn't necessarily think it was anything directly concerning you, though. I think I was just picking up on Blade acting strangely, because you had him enchanted. And all I've been able to read lately is that you're in a state of extreme confusion. You seem like you've been thrown completely off track by something."

"That much is certain," she whispered to herself.

"I think, if I may be so bold, that you had painted yourself a picture of Blade as being an insensitive ogre. And you found out otherwise." He watched Sianon stare silently into her wine. "So I guess I'm here in order to prove that you are as decent a person as Blade is. As good a person as he apparently thinks you are."

"Prove it to whom?"

"Well, mostly to you."

Sianon looked up at him, but said nothing. She gave a faint smile as she turned her eyes away.

"Okay," he said. "Your turn."

Sianon took a long pull from her wine, then stared at Vincent. Finally, she leaned back in her chair, crossing her arms over her abdomen. "My life was torture, after Adina died." She spoke slowly, as though she found it hard to relate the story. "My family was terribly stigmatized by her suicide. Perhaps that means nothing to you, but to them, it was everything. Eventually, the town gossip and ridicule became so bad that we moved. But the stories caught up with us. So we moved again. We moved often." She bent forward and leaned on the table. "This wouldn't have been so bad if my family had moved into a lower status kind of society. But they refused. They were high class all the way. So the stories kept coming behind us, and they kept being embarrassed." She sighed and drained her wine. "Eventually, we moved back to Port Remil. I don't know why. I didn't question these things. I was past caring, by this time. Things became more difficult for me. My mother vented her frustrations on me."

Vincent frowned. He didn't like the sound of that.

"No, she didn't beat me, though there was emotional distress. Always being compared to Adina. Always being told, 'You'd better turn out better than her. You'd better not shame us like she did.' Those things hurt me. It hurt to know the memory of the sister I'd adored was being soiled all the time."

Vincent shook his head. "That's terrible."

"Yes. A horrible way to grow up."

"So when did you take an interest in magic?"

She laughed. "Oh, that was practically inevitable. Learning magic was the only thing I could think of that would offend my parents more than anything Adina had done when she was alive."

"I'm confused. Explain to me, if all you suffered was because of your parents, why did you want to kill Blade?"

"Because he was the instigator of everything!"

"Bullshit!" Sianon raised her eyebrows, but he didn't stop to explain the expression. "Blade instigated nothing. He was just as blameless in the entire affair as your sister was. With the exception of the knifing in the tavern, and we'll probably never know the truth to that." Sianon was shaking her head, but he continued. "You've been suffering your whole life for something that was nobody's fault, unless it was your parents' fault."

"It wasn't my parents' fault!"

"No? Sure sounds like it."

"You don't understand," she mumbled.

"No, I don't. Please explain."

She frowned, shaking her head again. "You can't. You just don't. The parents are never at fault. Not ever."

And suddenly a light went on in Vincent's head. "Ohhhh..." he moaned. "I get it. No matter what, the parents are blameless. That's how things are in the upper crust, huh?"

"Exactly."

Vincent sat dumbstruck for a moment. Then he shook his head and sighed. He rubbed a hand over his forehead and, without thinking, removed his invisible glasses and placed them on the table. He slowly rubbed his eyes while trying to think of something to say. A second or two into this, he realized what he'd just done. He snapped his eyes open and looked up.

Sianon was staring at something she was holding. Except she wasn't holding anything. At least, nothing Vincent could see. But the actions she made with her hands told him she was holding his glasses. She looked up at him. "Spectacles?" He nodded. "Invisible spectacles?" He nodded again. "Why?"

He reached out a hand, palm up. "Long story. For another time, perhaps." Sianon handed them over and he put them on. Then he frowned. "Back to the truth. Why didn't you kill him?"

"I don't know," she said flatly.

"Yes, you do."

"And evidently you do, too?" The irritation in her voice was unmistakable.

"I think so. I just want to see if you're aware of the reason yourself. I think you are."

"Enough games! If you have something to say, say it! I'm tiring of this!"

Vincent shrugged and traced with his finger some cracks in the tabletop. "I think," he said slowly, "you realize exactly how weak your arguments are about Blade being guilty. You're using him just as an excuse."

"An excuse for what?"

He shrugged. "Lots of things. An excuse to learn magic. An excuse to leave home. An excuse to get away from your family."

"My parents are dead."

"You started this whole business before they died. You knew they were wrong. You never felt comfortable within their social class, not caring for the superficiality of that kind of life. Yet you were so immersed in the ways of that class that you couldn't question them outright. You couldn't blame them for what they were doing, so you blamed Blade. Everyone else had, so joining the crowd was easy enough." Vincent paused, finished his cider, and scratched his beard before continuing. "My guess, though, is you found it more and more difficult to maintain the artificial hatred you'd built up, once you got out into the real world. And though you continued your search for him, your heart wasn't in it. So once you found him, and discovered what he's really like, you couldn't go through with your plan." He watched for some sort of sign from her. Then he prompted her. "Well?"

Sianon didn't reply for awhile. She didn't meet his gaze, but toyed with her empty tankard. Finally, she said, "Why did he say he loved me?"

Vincent nearly laughed. "Why do you think?"

"I don't *know!* Stop being an ass and tell me! You know him better than I do."

With a shrug, he did so. "I think he went through the same thing as you, only much faster. After you'd released him from the enchantment, he was free to reflect upon the time you'd shared. Blade's a smart guy. Very perceptive. He realized who you were, and knew why you were there. But when you didn't kill him, he realized you weren't evil or anything. You were just doing what you felt you had to do, but your real nature prevented you from completing the act. Blade saw you for who you really are. And he loves that person." As Sianon absorbed his explanation, Vincent decided to change the subject. "So where were you going when I stopped you in the street?"

Sianon leaned back in her chair again. "Away. Anywhere. I didn't have a destination in mind."

"Running away from what you'd been chasing so long?"

She hesitated. "Perhaps." She ran a hand through her long hair. "I think I've had enough conversation for tonight." She rose. "Thanks for the wine."

As she began to leave, Vincent jumped from his seat. "Wait!"

Sianon stopped, her head drooping. "Now what?"

Vincent tossed some coinage on the table as the waitress approached. "I'll walk you back to the hotel."

"How do you know I'm going back to the hotel?"

He smiled as he reached her. "Because I know everything."

"Oh, really?" she drawled.

"Really."

"You don't even know what your friend's real name is." She smiled as she said this, for the first time Vincent recalled all evening.

He leaned in close. "I'd tell you, but it's nasty. It means 'goat droppings' in elven-tongue."

Sianon laughed aloud at this. "You're *full* of goat droppings. It means nothing of the kind. And you're also one to talk about names. What kind of name is 'Vincent,' anyway? That's so peculiar."

"Yeah, well, so am I. I make nice with women who try to kill my friends."

The night was cold as they stepped into the street. Sianon shivered. Vincent offered her his cloak, but she declined. They walked mostly in silence back toward *The Old Grey Mare*. Once there, they stepped inside. Sianon hesitated. "I suppose I'll need to take another room. Or perhaps I should go to a different inn entirely."

"They're still in there," Vincent said, gazing through the double doors. He glanced over his shoulder and saw Sianon chewing her lip in hesitation. Then she stepped over and peeked through the door. Vincent watched the play of emotions on her face. She closed her eyes, stepping back from the door. She took a deep breath, then turned and walked over to the desk. She rang the bell. When she wasn't looking, Vincent leaned into the dining area, waving his arm to get Blade's attention.

Vincent joined her at the desk. Amazingly, someone arrived in less than a minute. "I need a room," Sianon said firmly.

The clerk cleared his throat. "I'm afraid we're full up, miss."

Sianon stared at her feet. She turned to leave, only to find Blade and D'Ty standing behind her.

Blade smiled weakly. Sianon winced at the redness of the burn. The burn she'd inflicted. "There is no need for you to take another room," he said. "There's a perfectly good one waiting."

Sianon stood there, staring at the tiny blisters around his eye. She looked at Vincent, as if pleading for help.

He gave a tiny smile and a nod. "Good night," he said simply.

"Tomorrow morning for breakfast," D'Ty added, slapping his brother on the shoulder.

Blade agreed and bade them both a good night. And then they slipped out the front door, leaving Sianon alone. With him.

⁚ ⁛

We stayed a few more days in Falconwall. I'm still trying to get over everything that happened there. All the emotions aren't spent, yet. Needless to say, we're all very pleased at the way everything turned out. Something tells me, though, it's still not complete.

Blade is back to his old self, pretty much. I think my assessment of Blade's feelings was accurate. He obviously cares deeply for Sianon, but he seems to be holding back. His brother, to his credit, has been remarkably gallant about the whole thing. It can't be easy for him to see Sianon with his brother, after having been convinced for so long that the woman was trying to kill Blade.

And as for Sianon... I really feel for her. I can't imagine being as torn up as she must be right now. Our talk might have actually done some good for her. She's trying her best to fit in. You can tell she's still uncomfortable, though. Given time, I think things will work out fine. Gnorrin and Ariaziane have accepted her as part of our little group, though Annie seemed particularly reluctant to.

I worry about Ariaziane. She seems distant and reserved. Not that I can't relate. I've certainly been accused of such things in the past. But it's not like her. She was so open and carefree when we met. And now she's... I dunno... Just a shadow of what she used to be.

It's funny, though. You really have to look to see the shadow. To most people, I imagine she seems just the same as she ever was, except for the color of her eyes and hair. But not to me.

I think she's scared. I know how painful that transition was for her. The weeks of pain she endured, and then a final night of pure torture. Can't help but be afraid she might go through the whole thing again. And I know she thinks about it a lot, trying to figure out what caused it. She can chalk it up to that mage in the old keep all she wants, yet I think she knows deep down his spell wasn't to blame. So what was? Likely as not, she'll never know that any more than I'll ever know how to get home.

❧ Eleven ❧

The Season of Sleep proved to be the mildest winter Vincent could recall. He wondered if he were residing in a more southern latitude than his home in Pennsylvania. Or possibly the planet's axis had less tilt. He didn't know. There could be many reasons for the mild weather. He didn't care about the reason. He liked the fact that there were many snowfalls, but no snow*storms*. Humidity wasn't high, either, as it was in Pennsylvania. And these things made a world of difference. As if being in a different world wasn't enough to make a world of difference.

On the other hand, the Season of Green was off to a particularly white start. The Season of Sleep seemed unwilling to depart just yet. Several inches of snow had fallen a few days after Celebration Week and hadn't melted yet.

D'Ty stayed with Vincent for several weeks, and they quickly became good friends. Vincent had never had a roommate, before. It reminded him of having friends sleep over on weekends when he was younger. They had snowball fights and hunted together. Eventually, Vincent told him of Earth and his life there. D'Ty took the news pretty calmly. He was only slack-jawed for a few minutes.

In turn, D'Ty told him about life in this world. Life as he knew it, anyway, which was quite different than the words spoken by Gnorrin and the others, for he had been raised in a different area, under different socio-political conditions. He also spoke a lot about Tisen, the girl back home. These passages gave Vincent a tight feeling in his chest.

Everyone but Gnorrin seemed to have a love in his or her life, and in Gnorrin's case, it was by preference. D'Ty had Tisen. Blade had Sianon. Vincent mentioned this to D'Ty one night as they warmed themselves in front of a crackling fire.

D'Ty frowned. "I had been under the impression you and Ariaziane..."

Vincent snorted. "I don't think so."

His friend shook his head. "I apologize, then. By all outward appearances, you seem quite taken with her. I judged wrong, apparently."

"Oh, no. You judged perfectly."

"Then why did you laugh at the notion?"

"Well, come on... She's fifteen. I'm eighteen."

"And?"

"Isn't that enough? Three years is a big difference."

D'Ty laughed aloud. "You must be jesting!"

"No, I'm not. Where I come from, it would matter."

"Three years would matter?"

Vincent shook his head. "If we were both ten years older, the difference wouldn't mean a thing. But at our present ages... On Earth, she would be considered little more than a girl, and I would be becoming a man. I don't know. I guess it shouldn't bother me."

"Perhaps I am making a hasty assumption, but it seems to me as though you're less troubled by the age difference than you are by the simple fact that you have such feelings at all. Is this the first time you've been in love?"

Vincent paused. He felt a knot in his stomach. "No," he whispered as his eyes gazed off into space. "I've been in love before. Once. I had a few infatuations I thought were love, but there's only one time I can honestly say I was in love." He watched D'Ty stroking Blaise, but didn't elaborate any further.

"And that relationship did not go well?"

Vincent looked up at him. "What relationship?"

D'Ty paused. "You never...?"

"Never."

"Well, I think you should forget your worries and tell her how you feel."

Vincent sighed. "I have. Sort of."

"Sort of?"

"She knows how I feel. I think."

D'Ty shook his head. "You don't know what you think, or what she knows." He looked down into the dog's face. "Does he? No. Tell him he's being senseless." Blaise looked from one to the other, then went over and licked Vincent's face. "That's a good girl. You tell him."

After kissing him, Blaise collapsed across Vincent's feet, happily thumping her tail on the floor as he wiped his cheeks. "Well," he said, "I don't know. Maybe." He yawned. "I'll sleep on it, okay?"

His friend nodded and moved over to add another log to the fire. "Good night, then."

Vincent returned the wish and retired to his room. He undressed slowly, mulling over what his friend had said. Was D'Ty right? Could Ariaziane really not know how he felt about her? Was he assuming too much? He frowned, knowing what was said about the practice of assuming and what it tends to make of one. He climbed into bed, pulling the heavy blankets and down-filled comforter up to his chin.

His mind was awhirl, thinking of Ariaziane and his own confusion. After many minutes of restlessness, he swore under his breath and propped himself up on an elbow. He groped around until he found the vial Rhia had given him. Following her instructions, he sprinkled a few drops on his pillow. Then he replaced the stopper and set the vial upon his bedside table. As he did so, he noticed the candles Rhia had provided. He hadn't been using them as she'd recommended. What the heck, he thought, and lit one yellow, one white, and one blue candle. Returning to his pillow, he inhaled the pleasant aroma of Rhia's concoction.

He tried to recall what each of the candles was for. The yellow was what? Clairvoyance. He distinctly remembered the dream he'd had the last time he had burned this candle. Interesting, yes. Clairvoyant, he doubted. The white candle, he thought, was a catch-all. Rhia had said it was for just about anything. And the blue was for peace, which he felt sorely in need of, and for protection during sleep. She didn't say what he was to be protected from, and he wasn't sure he wanted to know.

Soon the scent of the candles combined with that of the droplets of oil on his pillow. The combination wasn't awful, as he'd feared. Rather than a mixture of scents, one aroma would dominate, then another, alternating. The effect was quite pleasant. Before long, Vincent was asleep.

He woke early. He knew this for two reasons. One, it *felt* early. And two, he heard snoring from the outer room. D'Ty was typically up and about by the time Vincent woke. He climbed out of bed, dressed quietly, and crept into the living room to find D'Ty asleep on the sofa. His friend slept there more often than he did in the second bedroom, probably because the living room was warmer. Vincent smiled. *Living room.* Why did he insist on that name? He had no idea, but it was a hard habit to break. And *damn*, could D'Ty snore!

Blaise noticed his entrance and rose to her feet. She yawned and stretched, then did an excited little dance that indicated her need to go outdoors. Vincent quickly obliged her, pulling on his heavy fur coat. He exited as silently as he could.

The sight greeting him outside was one he would not soon forget. During the night, a heavy fog had frozen to a fine layer of ice over the naked tree branches and everything else in sight. The sun had just risen, and its glow on the ice made everything appear as though on fire. "Wow," Vincent breathed. "Talk about a Kodak moment."

There were three things in his life that Vincent considered to be the most beautiful he'd ever seen. When he was thirteen, he'd visited the Grand Canyon. When he was fourteen, he'd seen the Aurora Borealis. And when he was fifteen, he'd seen huge masses of billowing white clouds, lit by the sun and shining against the bluest of skies, while flying home after visiting his mother. This vision ranked right up there with them. And he knew he had to share it. He buttoned up his coat and set off for Gnorrin's cottage, Blaise padding along beside him.

By the time he reached the cottage, the sun was fully above the horizon. The ice now twinkled in reflection, but no longer glowed orange. Everything was quiet. Everything was beautiful. He stepped over to the corner of the cottage where he knew Ariaziane's room to be. He knocked on the wood, three raps, then paused, and repeated. This way she'd realize the noise was deliberate, not a tree branch knocking up against the wall. Soon, he heard shuffling noises inside and stepped around to the other side of the cottage just as Ariaziane opened the door. She gave him a quizzical look.

"Get dressed," he said. "We're going for a walk." He watched as she glanced around the glittering scene, and her eyes twinkled, as if in reflection of the vision. She smiled at him and ducked back inside.

A minute later, she joined him, taking in the sight. "It's so beautiful," she breathed. She greeted Blaise with a scratch behind her ears. "Where are we going?"

Vincent smiled and shrugged. "Doesn't matter, as long as you're with me." He felt his stomach flutter as he said the words. He watched her face for a reaction. He was pleased when she smiled, yet disappointed, too. He'd hoped for more.

"Wait here," she said suddenly. Then she dashed back into the cottage, returning shortly with a large, heavy blanket. "I know where to go."

They walked together back through the woods Vincent had come to know so well. Back toward the stream that ran there, the snow crunching under their feet as they walked. And they gazed in pleasure at the trees, their branches enveloped in ice, their tiny extremities sheathed in crystal gloves.

Vincent glanced at the girl beside him. She was so beautiful. She lived in that borderline state: not quite a woman, yet more than a girl. Was there any state more alluring, more enigmatic, more lovely? His heart quickening, Vincent reached down and gripped her hand in his. She seemed surprised, though pleased. She squeezed tightly and smiled.

Soon they reached their destination: the large, flat rock they'd shared on many an occasion over the past several months. The rock was as iced-over as the rest of the landscape, but there were pockets of air between the glaze and the stone. A few sharp raps of Vincent's fist broke the ice enough to be swept off. He helped Ariaziane spread the thick blanket atop its cold surface, and they perched beside each other, watching sunlight play among the trees, listening to the gurgle of the water.

"It's gorgeous," she said.

Vincent's attention was focused on Ariaziane. He allowed her presence to wash over him. The natural beauty around them was forgotten for a moment. "So are you," he whispered.

She smiled, though she did not look at him. "So you've said. Thank you."

Vincent fought down the butterflies inside him. *D'Ty is right,* he thought. *I have to tell her.* He took a deep breath. "Annie..."

She turned to look at him, peaceful inquisitiveness on her face. "Yes?"

He hesitated. He couldn't do it. He was too frightened. *No,* he thought. *I must.* He looked her in the eye. "I love you."

"I love you, too," she said, giving him a friendly hug.

"No," he said, pulling away gently. "I mean as more than a friend. I think about you all the time. I want to be with you all the time. I'm in love with you."

Ariaziane's eyes widened, and she gave a tiny, nervous laugh. "You're full of surprises this morning, aren't you?"

His stomach began to knot. "Are you upset?"

"No," she said. "That's not a word that comes to mind." She looked away. "However, I'm not quite sure how to respond. I'm stunned."

"I see." He looked down at his hands. "I'm sorry."

She laughed, sliding closer to him. "I'm not." She smiled at him when he looked in her eyes. Then she rested her head against his shoulder, and continued to admire the scenery. Vincent put his arm around her. Eventually, his heart returned to its standard pace. And even the butterflies took naps.

❧ ❦

Well, D'Ty gave me a big "I told you so" when I got home. And I deserved it, so I didn't mind.

I can't really begin to describe how I feel about this. Part of me is overjoyed. But part of me is still cautious. The fact that Annie didn't say she was in love with me, too, probably has a lot to do with it. Maybe my concerns about her age were well-founded, after all. Maybe this kind of announcement is too soon for her. Or maybe I'm just being paranoid.

Speaking of D'Ty, he's pretty anxious to go home. I think once the weather turns fair again, he'll be leaving. It's been nice having him around, though. I'll miss having someone always here to talk to.

Hard to believe I've been here nearly a year. Seems like only yesterday that I arrived. On the other hand, with everything that's happened, I'm surprised it doesn't seem like a longer span of time. This new world is so unlike Earth. And I've only seen one minuscule area. I'd like to see more. I have money. Maybe I should travel. There's something to think about, I guess.

I haven't seen much of Blade recently. He's been staying at the inn with Sianon ever since we returned from Falconwall. Another person I haven't seen recently is Rhia, but I don't know whether to expect to see her or not. For all I know, I'll never see her again. Wish I knew exactly what to make of her. Will she be able to help me or not?

138

And more importantly, at this point, do I even want her to help me? Boy, is that a stumper! I certainly miss my friends and family as much as ever. But the thought of going back to a loveless life on Earth, rather than staying here with Annie... I dunno. Tough choice.

Well... It's pointless to think about that right now, anyway, since I don't have to make the choice and possibly never will have to. For now, I'm just going to concentrate on making my life here as pleasant as possible.

❧ ❦

The next few weeks passed quickly. The snows melted, the trees budded. Vincent opened up his cottage, removing the window inserts to let the fresh air cleanse the inside.

The wintry weather had caused some damage to his cottage. Part of his roof needed to be replaced. And he found, much to his surprise, that he rather enjoyed the endeavor. There was something about working on his own cottage that felt good. He couldn't quite comprehend such a thought.

Soon he would need to plant his garden. He tilled the soil and fertilized it with the compost that had been decaying throughout the cold season, and began a mental list of what he wanted to plant.

He spent more time with Ariaziane, loving every minute they spent together. When the snows had gone, they rode their horses over the hard ground. Soon it, too, would thaw, creating a muddy mess. But before the thaw, they rode together, dashing across open fields, eating picnic lunches under big trees. They were giddy times, for the most part. Vincent fell more and more in love with Ariaziane. When he was alone, though, he wondered about her. The girl still hadn't echoed the sentiment. He knew absolutely that she enjoyed spending time with him just as much as he did with her. Still, he couldn't shake the suspicion that she loved him only as a friend. And always would.

During the second month of the Season of Green, Blade announced he was leaving. The announcement came during an outdoor feast held at Gnorrin's cottage. Vincent and Gnorrin were carving the stag Blade had provided. The beast had roasted over a fire for the better part of the day, tended by Ariaziane, who had coated the meat with honey.

As they sat around a small fire, eating, Blade raised his mug in salute. "To good friends," he said. The others echoed, hoisting their drinks. "And," he continued, once they'd swallowed, "to safe journeys." The group joined him in this toast as well, though Vincent did so with a puzzled expression. Blade sat forward on the edge of his seat and elaborated. "I understand you will be leaving soon, my brother."

D'Ty nodded and tossed a stripped rib into the fire. "Yes. I have obligations at home, as well as people I miss."

"Then I hope you would like some company." He smiled grimly as his friends looked at him. "I've decided to go home."

Gnorrin wiped his mouth on a bright orange sleeve. "Are you certain of this? Would there not still be risk?"

Blade shrugged. "Perhaps. Nevertheless, this is something I feel is long overdue." He turned to look at Vincent.

Vincent noted the apologetic look on his friend's face, and knew Blade was asking his forgiveness for leaving, since he'd promised to help Vincent try to find a way back to Earth. Vincent smiled and nodded to the man to show he understood.

Blade smiled and said to his brother, "I should think we'd be ready to leave in just a few days. Would that suit you?"

"That would be fine," D'Ty replied.

Vincent finished his meal and set the empty plate on the ground. "How will you go?"

"We will travel to Dynsa. A caravan is due to pass through there next week. We will accompany the caravan to Linnael, where we will book passage on a ship."

Ariaziane spoke up. "We shall accompany you to Dynsa! To see you off!" She turned to Vincent. "It'll be fun!" She smiled.

The others nodded. Blade clapped a hand on his thigh. "Very well. We depart in three days."

So Blade, Sianon, and D'Ty prepared for their journey home. Three days later, Vincent, Ariaziane, and Blaise met them in front of Gnorrin's cottage, their horses laden with the necessities of the journey. The other three had rented horses in town, which their friends would return after seeing them off. Vincent noticed Gnorrin's pony was not to be seen. He turned to the gnome.

"You're coming with us, aren't you?"

The mage shook his head, gazing vacantly at the ground. "No. You go on along. I've things to tend to."

Blade stepped over to his old friend. "You are certain you will not accompany us? I would enjoy having you along."

Gnorrin again shook his head. "Nay. No sense in prolonging a farewell." He pulled out a parcel wrapped in broad leaves and tied with twine. "I salted some venison for your trip." The big man graciously accepted the package, laying a hand on Gnorrin's shoulder. There were no verbal farewells. None were needed. In a few short minutes, all were ready to depart. As they rode off, Vincent turned and waved to Gnorrin, who stood in his doorway watching them go.

The first day and a half of their journey to Dynsa was without event. The time was spent in relaxed discussion and occasional laughter. They were a fine group of friends, Vincent thought. Sianon had slowly but surely opened up to them all, eventually becoming comfortable around them. Vincent felt, though, that she was still shocked to have been forgiven for her intended revenge. And maybe she was still just a little wary of D'Ty. But overall, things between them were just fine.

Vincent was looking at Sianon as he thought these things. She was riding at the head of the party, beside Blade, smiling at something he was saying. Then Vincent noticed her smile fade and her brow contract. She turned her head, glancing at the landscape around them. Slowly, she reined in her horse.

The rest of the party stopped as well, waiting for Sianon to voice her concerns. She was gazing now at an outcropping of rock among the low hills they were passing through. "What is it?" Blade finally inquired.

Sianon frowned. "I sense something," she said.

Ariaziane turned her concentration to the rocky area just as Sianon guided her horse from the road and trotted off toward the outcropping. Then she, too, headed off the road.

Vincent looked at Blade and his brother. The pair seemed as baffled as he was. With a shrug, he followed, his two friends close behind. By the time they met up with Sianon, she had dismounted, tied her horse to a small tree, and was wandering around the base of the escarpment as if looking for something. In a moment, Ariaziane joined her. Vincent scratched his beard. "Okay," he mumbled to his friends. "I don't need to be hit in the head. Guess it must be something magical in nature, huh?"

Blade was the next to dismount. By this time, Sianon had climbed to the top of the outcropping and was gingerly making her way across the boulders. Suddenly she stopped and knelt. As Vincent and D'Ty finished tying up their mounts, Sianon turned to face them. "There's an opening," she said.

Blade turned to Vincent. "We'll need torches."

Vincent nodded and unstrapped his backpack from his horse. There were several torches inside, along with other things he felt might come in handy on any given outing. He slung the pack over his shoulder, turning to Blaise. "Stay," he said firmly. The dog snorted in response and sat down. She wagged her tail expectantly as the rest of the party joined Sianon on the rocks, but didn't follow them.

The opening Sianon had discovered was small. A tight fit, Vincent thought. From first glance, the opening seemed to be just a rift between two boulders. Sianon insisted there was more, though, and Ariaziane evidently agreed. "Well, who's going in first?" In reply, Sianon began lowering herself through the opening. "Okay," Vincent said. "I'll buy that." He unshouldered his backpack as Blade sat on the edge of the rock and inserted his feet into the opening. He extracted a torch and was about to hand it to his friend when the interior of the crevasse suddenly glowed yellow.

Blade glanced down inside, then turned to Vincent and his outstretched torch. "Never mind," he smiled, and dropped down inside. Vincent sighed and stowed the torch back inside his pack. D'Ty and Ariaziane followed Blade down between the rocks, then Vincent squeezed through, dragging the pack in after him.

His feet touched a steep decline and he nearly lost his footing when his ankle twisted unexpectedly. Carefully, he half-slid down until the slope evened out. He sidestepped several large chunks of rock. Vincent assumed these were the remnants of whatever had once sealed the opening through which they'd come. He raised his eyes and looked around.

They stood now on a flat, rocky surface. A glowing ball of light floated near Sianon's head, illuminating what appeared to be a man-made corridor. Vincent frowned. "What could this be, Blade?"

The tall man was slightly stooped, inspecting the walls. The ceiling was about the same height as Blade. "Dwarven, I'd wager."

"You can tell that just by looking at the walls?"

Blade smiled faintly. "No. But most dwarven clans prefer to live in rocky terrain. And if they can't have mountains, they'll take caverns. Or make their own. Plus the low ceiling, obviously."

Vincent tried to recall the height of dwarves. Gnorrin's books said they averaged perhaps a foot taller than gnomes. So they would be somewhere between gnomes and a typical human. "So what might be in here?" None of his friends seemed to have an

141

answer to that. He frowned. "Then why are we going in?" No one offered conjecture on this point, either, so he resigned himself to following them in silence down the corridor.

Before too long, they began encountering wooden doors along the walls. Or rather, they encountered what was left of them. Most were shattered ruins. Some were intact, though wide open. Either way, the rooms behind the doors were barren but for strewn rubble. Occasionally they would encounter the carcass of a stray animal that had perished within the underground passageways.

Over the next hour, they searched the intersecting corridors, always finding more of the same. The entire area seemed to have been thoroughly looted. None of them was sure what had once occupied this place, and they could find no sign of any current residents, save for the occasional scurrying rat.

An hour spent searching through an evidently empty area can seem like an eternity, and Vincent began to grow bored. Finally, Blade announced they had covered the entire area. "Well, that's that," said Vincent. "Lead us back to the great outdoors."

"No," Sianon said flatly. "There's something here."

"There's nothing here," he said. "We looked."

She leveled her gaze on him. "We'll look further."

Vincent grimaced and turned to Blade. But his friend was staring at the length of passage down which they had just come. Suddenly, he strode down the hall to the last intersection they had encountered. The others hurried to catch up to him. Vincent opened his mouth to speak, but Blade held up a hand. He was looking down the adjacent corridor and seeming to retrace their steps in his mind. Vincent worried Blade had gotten them so turned around in all the passageways that he couldn't guide them back. Then the man turned around and began studying the empty wall behind him. Sianon maneuvered her light to better assist him. Blade turned to Ariaziane. "Would you care to do the honors?"

The girl smiled and stepped over to the wall. Just as she had done in the keep, Ariaziane mumbled a few words and reached out as if to rap on the stone with her knuckles. This time, however, the hidden door slid a few feet *toward* them, instead of away from them. She stepped aside as it opened a passage.

Sianon was the first to slip inside, followed by Ariaziane and D'Ty. Vincent addressed Blade before entering. "How did you know this would be here?"

"Dwarven construction tends to be very symmetrical," he explained. "I simply recalled the passages we'd traversed, noting which ones had branching corridors and which ones did not. Using such a system, it was a fair wager that another corridor should begin here."

Vincent nodded. "Remind me never to gamble against you."

They stepped inside and looked around. The new area seemed much more like a living area rather than the region they'd just explored. Blade seemed unsurprised. "This would explain the direction of the door," he said. "Obviously, the area we just came from was the region intended for secrecy by the builders of this warren."

"Came in the back door, did we?" Vincent said. "So now what? Still looks a mess."

They roamed the corridors of this new section for several minutes with identical results. The place was thoroughly looted, though there were signs that this section had been quite lavish at one time.

Eventually, they encountered a broad hallway. At the end of this hall was a pair of large double doors that seemed intact. As soon as she spied them, Sianon hurried forward. "In there," she said.

"Yes," Ariaziane said, following close on her heels.

The three men followed rapidly after, until they were all standing before the door. Sianon had a perplexed look on her face. She looked up at Blade. "Very unusual. I sense a strong magical force that seems somehow... I do not know. Restrained, perhaps. And yet not."

"We must be cautious."

Vincent's eyebrows shot up. "No shit," he said. His heart raced in anticipation, remembering their last adventure in a keep. Were they barging in on a mage again? Or worse? As Blade reached out to the door handle and began quietly sliding the door open, a strange sensation struck Vincent. *Worse*, he decided.

The party stood in awe of the sight before them. The room, which must have once been the underground keep's great hall, glowed a cherry red. Flames spouted up from the floor in many spots, yet nothing burned. In the center of the room, lounging on tremendous pillows and surrounded by all manner of splendor, was a sleeping giant of a creature. Someone let out an oath, and they all stared in disbelief.

Definitely worse, Vincent thought as he turned to Blade. "What in hell is a creature like that doing here?" he said, a bit louder than he'd intended. Blade shook his head, dumbfounded. Vincent noted the reactions of the rest of the party. D'Ty and Ariaziane stood gaping. Sianon stood rooted by the door, not moving.

The being opened a lazy eyelid and the five of them drew in simultaneous breaths. The creature slowly rose. It was tall, reaching close to the ceiling in the vaulted room. Very tall, Vincent noted, with skin of a deep red. The face was not attractive, with a broad nose and deep-set eyes. The eyebrows were thick, the mouth wide and toothy. Horns sprouted from the forehead, seemingly to be opposite ends of the sharp incisors protruding from its mouth. It loomed over the party, staring down at them for what seemed several minutes. The creature was completely naked, yet Vincent could make out no features to give an indication of gender. His heart skipped a beat as recognition dawned on him. He'd seen this creature illustrated in one of Gnorrin's books.

It was an efreeti, a creature from the elemental plane of fire, notorious for being unfriendly in the extreme. Among other things. Despite the heat in the room, Vincent felt a cold sweat break out. His heart was like a trip hammer. He wanted to run, but his legs wouldn't work.

The efreeti lifted an eyebrow and glanced directly at him. It yawned, and in a thunderous, though bored, voice, said, "Begone."

Vincent's nervousness got the better of him. His lips were moving before he knew what he was saying. "Who are you to tell us where to go?"

His friends all stared at him. If he'd been capable of doing so, he would have stared at himself. "By the gods, Vincent, what are you trying to do?" whispered Ariaziane.

Blade leaned toward him. "This is not a creature one should antagonize, my friend."

The efreeti leaned down, staring at the impetuous youth. "Who am I? Who am I, you ask?" The efreeti laughed, a deep, booming sound. "I am your death, human!"

Vincent stepped forward, for some reason becoming surer of himself. He thought he knew how to handle this situation. "You're one of them genies, huh?" He smiled inwardly as the efreeti scowled. The genn were the sworn enemies of the efreet, he knew from Gnorrin's books. Both were of similar physical natures, yet radically different in their philosophies. Humans tended to lump both creatures, and others as well, into the generic heading Vincent had used. And he knew the effect this would probably have on the creature. The efreeti would most likely hate it. He spoke again. "Grant us a wish."

Again the efreeti laughed. "And why should I?"

Vincent shrugged. "Generous nature?"

"I shall display my generosity by granting you quick oblivion."

"Hey, here's an idea!" Vincent clapped his hands together. "Let's have a wager."

The efreeti blinked. "A more tenacious human I doubt I have ever met," it said to itself, though Vincent thought people in the neighboring province could have heard the booming voice. Blade reached out a restraining hand as the efreeti spoke again. "And what sort of ridiculous wager do you have in your brain, human?"

Vincent shook Blade's hand off his shoulder. "Well, I picture this. You want to kill me, right? And I want you to grant us... what is it? Three wishes? I will give you your chance to kill me. If you fail, you start granting. How's that sound?"

"Like a waste of time. I think I shall kill you now."

"Wait!"

"Why?"

"Uh..." Vincent thought quickly. "Because." He thought more quickly. "What could make the wager more interesting?"

The efreeti blinked slowly. "This wager you propose. If you win, which is highly unlikely, you gain wishes. Yet if I win, I gain nothing, save the minor pleasure of having killed you. This seems most unfair."

"Ah. I see. Well, I have valuables, some of which you might find interesting. If I die, you naturally get them." He wiped sweat from his brow. This time, it wasn't cold.

As Vincent removed his pack from his back, D'Ty whispered to him. "You're mad."

Vincent smiled. "Maybe."

"Don't do this, Vincent," said Ariaziane. "If you stop now, perhaps it will let us go, unharmed. You're only making it angry."

"Then why don't you all just turn and leave?" he said sharply. He turned back to the creature. He held aloft jewels and gold chains. "How's this grab you?"

"Baubles. Though you amuse me, I think I am losing interest in this, human. Prepare to die."

"Oh, just give me a minute, will you?" Vincent proceeded to sit down on the floor and unpack his valuables. He piled them in a semicircle around him. Vincent saw the efreeti's eyes grow wide as he set a reddish amber bottle with a levered stopper among the treasures. "Ah! How about this?" He held up a napkin ring. "An object of inestimable power, I'm told. Deal now?"

The efreeti did not take its eye from the bottle on the floor. "Tell me precisely what you had in mind, human."

"Great." Vincent stood and moved a few paces away. "I'll stand here. My friends will wait outside the door. I don't want them harmed. And you can attack me. One time. Give it all you got with one shot. If I'm still conscious afterwards, I win. If not, you get the loot. Fair?"

The efreeti nodded. "Begone." The rest of the party left the room, casting worried looks at him. He winked at them in return. As he closed the door behind them, Vincent glanced down at the ring on his finger. Then he felt a knot in his stomach. The thought had never occurred to him that the ring might not be of any use against fire of a magical nature. Oh, well, Vincent thought. There's nothing to be done about that, now. He turned back to the efreeti.

"Ready when you are." Vincent stood firmly, arms folded across his chest. The efreeti gave him a smile. With a wave of its hand, a pillar of fire bolted down from the ceiling. Vincent sensed its approach and caught his breath. Fire engulfed him. He hoped it wouldn't last long.

Soon the fire died away. The efreeti turned its head to see the charred remains of the human. Vincent whistled. "I don't think I'll ever feel cold again."

The efreeti's eyes bulged. "You live! What trickery is this?"

"Oh, just calm down, Red. Shit happens, you know. Now lose like a man." He paused. "If you are one."

"I shall kill you with my bare hands!"

Vincent's sword was in his hand in a flash. "I don't think so. You'll keep your end of the bet."

The efreeti glowered at him. "A curse upon you, human. I have never been so humiliated. You'll pay."

"So will you. Let's have some wishes."

"Yes," the creature snarled. "The wager was for three wishes. Yet you have more than three people in your little company. How do you expect to settle such a difference, human? I should watch my back from now on, if I were you."

Well, Vincent thought, there was no danger of that. They were all his friends. However, three did not divide into five very fairly. "Okay. The wishes will affect everyone in the party equally."

"If this is to be the case, human, you are limited to one wish."

Vincent thought about this. "Fair enough." He moved over and began to repack his valuables, noting the efreeti's eyes again fixated on the bottle. "I admit I didn't play fair, my friend. The bet was a tiny bit fixed. I'm sure you've imagined how by now. But very well. One wish." Vincent thought long and hard. Suddenly he had an idea. "Y'know, standing there holding my breath while your fire burned all around me, I got to thinking. I thought, wouldn't it be nice if I didn't need to breathe? If I could survive without having to take air into my lungs. How about it, genie baby? Think we can pull that one off?"

The efreeti glowered again at Vincent's insulting nomenclature, then smiled. "This is your wish?"

"Yeah. For the entire party, now."

"Yes. For the entire party." The efreeti smiled again and mumbled a few syllables, then waved its arm. Vincent felt strange, suddenly. "Done," said the efreeti. "You will no longer need to breathe in order to survive. When you stop breathing, your body itself will provide the needed energy for survival. If you are quite lucky, you will last perhaps one or two minutes before you die. Painfully." The efreeti laughed mirthlessly as it turned its back on the boy. "Begone."

Vincent paused, looking at the being's back. "I guess that's what I deserve for not wording my wish more specifically." He continued repacking his goods. As he finished, he looked at the bottle in his hand, one of those he'd found at the old keep. The one that reminded him of his neighbor on Earth. The one he'd read about in Gnorrin's book. "Hey, genie." The efreeti turned to face him once more, a scowl on its broad, red face. "Catch." Vincent tossed the bottle in a high arc across the room. The startled efreeti reached out as if in supplication, and the bottle fell into its open hands.

Vincent swung his pack over his shoulder and headed for the door. "Human," came the creature's booming voice. Vincent turned. And the efreeti said, "Wait." It paused, looking at Vincent with confusion. "You know. You know what this is." Vincent nodded soberly. The efreeti stared at him. "And you give this to me? Freely?" Vincent nodded again. "Why?"

Vincent finished strapping on his pack. "It is an object of slavery, used to entrap your kind. I cannot abide that. Not out of love for the efreet, but out of a love for freedom and a hatred of slavery, in any form." The efreeti continued to look at him questioningly, so he continued. "My land, where I come from originally, has a rather disgraceful history. Slavery is one of the more repugnant of its atrocities. I kept the bottle, in all honesty, for just such an occasion as this. So call me selfish."

"Yet you could have used the bottle..."

"Don't disgust me. I'd sooner... Well, never mind. I've got to go now."

"Human."

"I've got a name, damn it!"

The efreeti nodded. "Vincent." The creature moved its eyes to the floor. "Forgive me. In my anger, I have compromised my word. Allow me to rectify this." With a few more words, and a sweep of an arm, the efreeti recast the spell. "Now your wish is more to what you really want. Your bodies will indeed feed off themselves in such a way as to provide air. This will, I'm afraid, cause some weakness after a time, yet for short durations, it will be of no noticeable discomfort. For longer durations," the efreeti said with a smile, "simply eat a lot beforehand."

Vincent smiled and nodded politely.

"I, too, have a name," the efreeti continued. Vincent blinked. In his mind, the efreeti's name formed. "You are a friend of the efreet. Use the name, if you ever have need to. All of my kind know the truenames of all others of our kind. They will treat you with the respect you deserve." The creature nodded its head. "I thank you again. You have taught me a valuable lesson today. Go now. Fortune be with you."

Vincent smiled and left, closing the door behind him. He held a finger to his lips to silence his friends, then opened the door a crack, peeking inside. He watched as the efreeti held the bottle before its eyes. Anger on its face turned slowly to disgust. Abruptly, it crushed the bottle between its palms, the resulting explosion throwing shards of glass around the room. Dusting off its hands, the efreeti returned to the cushions. But instead of returning to sleep, it lay staring at the doorway through which Vincent had exited.

In the hallway, Vincent smiled, closed the door, and allowed his heartbeat to finally return to somewhere near normal. His friends stared at him, speechless. He looked at the girls. "I hope your curiosity is satisfied. Can we leave now?"

On the way out of the underground keep, Vincent related the events to his friends, explaining to them their new non-breathing ability. Once they recovered from the shock, Ariaziane said, "I can't believe you did that." The others seemed to agree with her.

Vincent merely shrugged. "I was scared and nervous. Just like you guys were. But when I get scared and nervous, I tend to do stupid things." He glanced at Blade and saw the man smile faintly, and he knew his friend was recalling the episode that resulted in Vincent catching an arrow with his triceps.

They made their way back outside in silence. Blaise greeted them happily and Vincent embraced her, hiding his face from his friends. He was still scared, he realized. They untied their horses, mounted up and set off again for the last leg of their journey. Vincent smiled. "Hey," he said. "Let's see who can hold their breath the longest." He joined them in laughter as they traveled down the road to Dynsa.

Darella cast her hand over the crystal ball and the images inside faded away. The twins were sitting with her, and as the orb darkened, they turned their inquisitive young faces toward her. The children were less than a year old, only three seasons, in fact. But their bodies were those of three year-olds. The babes were aging at a rate four times faster than a normal human. Darella found it fascinating, though disappointing. Even after all these centuries, there were still new things to discover in this mundane world. Children under a year of age who stood nearly to her hip certainly qualified.

She smiled down at them, at their innocent faces. But her smile quickly faded.

Soon they would need an education, a thorough and quick one. And educating them in such fashion would run the risk of one or both of them questioning every action, every motive. Questioning her. And possibly turning against her. Her only hope was to start educating them as soon as possible. She had to be sure their rapidly aging bodies were matched by rapidly maturing mentalities. No easy task.

She had made her decision. Rather than waste these two specimens, she had decided to raise them. The crystal ball would be of immense assistance in this regard. It was their eye into the world. She could teach them plenty without using the orb, though this was the closest they'd get to application of her theories. She was teaching them the use of the globe. She'd shown them their father, not putting any importance on their relationship to him, merely using him as her model, her example of life outside the cave. She showed them his encounter with the efreeti. Despite herself, she found him, or at least his deeds, captivating. She would have given anything to have heard his exchange with the creature, there in the ancient dwarven home. Still, though silent, the scene taught her two things: the boy was somehow impervious to flame, and he was becoming familiar with this world enough to know what an efreeti bottle was.

And so her children were learning of magic and of the world. It was an interesting task, though often annoying. The boy child in particular seemed to have a rebellious streak in him. His favorite activity seemed to be hiding her scrying orb whenever she wanted to utilize it. The girl child was much more accommodating, though she was also nowhere near as inquisitive as her brother.

Darella was pleased at their curiosity, typical of young children. She only hoped it would improve with time.

❧ Twelve ❧

The following months passed quickly. Vincent spent most of his time tending his garden, making repairs to his home, and exploring the surrounding areas. He spoke at length with Gnorrin to learn as much as he could about the societal structure of this world. And naturally, he tried to spend as much time as possible with Ariaziane.

This wasn't always the easiest task, however, since she was so often with Gnorrin, studying magic. He wished he were privy to these activities. For all her studying, Vincent had never seen her perform more than a few rudimentary spells. He knew from experience that she could cause hidden doorways to open by themselves. And he saw her perform the glowing ball of light thing, too. On one occasion, she treated him to an impressive display of light and color. It was like watching fireworks, only on a smaller scale and without the booms. Beyond that, he was clueless to her abilities.

His feelings for her continued to deepen. Every time they were together, he found something more to love about her. He ventured, on a few occasions, to voice these feelings aloud. Each time, she would smile shyly, as if embarrassed by his attention. And each time, his heart would sink when she did not return the expression.

On these occasions, he would envy the love shared by Blade and Sianon, long since returned to their homeland. If such an unlikely relationship could develop into romance, why couldn't his relationship with Ariaziane lead to the same thing? They certainly seemed to be more likely candidates for such a relationship. After all, neither of them had ever wanted to kill the other.

Regardless of how right he felt a romantic relationship between them to be, Ariaziane didn't seem to share his feelings. And so, in an attempt at stoicism, Vincent eventually put the idea in the back of his mind. He didn't want to risk alienating her by pushing too hard for something more than friendship.

These thoughts were haunting him this day, as he worked in his garden under a scorching sun. He knelt in the dirt, trying hard not to think about them, while digging up the delicious tubers he'd recently become so fond of. They were shaped like a medium-sized potato, with deep red skin, like a beet, and a white flesh that tasted almost, but not quite, like a sweet potato. They grew quickly and proliferated well. This, combined with their delectable taste, made them a staple of his diet.

He ate less meat as time went on. Not because he didn't desire it, but because he didn't really enjoy hunting. Occasionally he would make a purchase at the town butcher shop, but since fresh meat didn't preserve well, he generally went without. Instead, he obtained his protein from the occasional fish he would catch in the stream, and from legumes reminiscent of lentils. He purchased these in large sacks in town.

His back started bothering him again, so he stopped digging, put his small hand shovel aside, and gathered up the tubers. He glanced at Blaise, snoozing in the shade, as he entered his cottage. In the kitchen, he washed the vegetables, then set all but one of them to dry on the windowsill above the sink. This one he carried with him as he returned outdoors. Drawing his dagger, he proceeded to cut off small chunks and eat them.

He'd never been able to tolerate raw potatoes back on Earth. His sister loved them, though. He'd tried them once or twice, hating the pasty, slightly bitter taste they left in his mouth. These tubers, on the other hand, were more like an apple, but not as juicy nor as sweet. He sat in a wooden *chaise longue* of his own construction and rested, allowing the sun to warm his face, chewing a piece of the vegetable every now and again. Blaise approached and nudged his arm, so he tossed a few of the chunks to her. When the tuber was gone, he stuck his dagger in the ground and settled in for a nap.

Vincent was a light sleeper. So when a shadow fell across his face, he woke. He opened his eyes, expecting to see a layer of clouds above. Instead, he saw a cloaked and hooded figure. He bolted upright in his chair, alarmed. Then the figure reached up and pulled away the hood, revealing coppery red hair, green eyes, and a smile. "Sleeping in the sun is a good way to make yourself sick," Rhia said.

Vincent rose, smiling. "Nice to see you, too. Been awhile." He led her toward the cottage. "Have you learned anything new since the last time I saw you?"

"Possibly," she replied as they stepped inside. "Have you been using the candles?"

"Not very often," Vincent said. "I'm sorry."

"I cannot do this alone, Vincent. You must put forth some effort, as well."

Rhia removed her shoulder pack and placed it on the floor, then took a seat on the sofa, curling her legs up beside her. Vincent stepped into the kitchen and opened a small door in the floor. This was his icebox, a chamber two feet to a side and two in depth, well insulated with hay. When available, he would line the walls of the chamber with ice, placing the food or drink in the center. No ice was to be gotten at this time of year, but the chamber served to keep items cooler than room temperature. So, while the beverage he served Rhia wasn't exactly "iced" tea, it was at least cool and refreshing.

"So what have you learned?" he asked as he took a seat across from her.

Rhia frowned. "I'm not certain. I've had some dreams, things that made little sense to me."

"Such as?"

The witch met his gaze. "I saw a great grey wall. And on the wall was a feature, at times a huge eye, through which I could see other lands with strange images. At other times, it was a mouth. And the mouth would spew forth babies."

"Babies?"

"Babies."

Vincent raised an eyebrow at this. "What do you think it means?"

Rhia shrugged. "As I said, I make little sense of the imagery. However, I am hoping we might shed more light on it this evening."

"How so?"

"Tonight is a witch's moon, a time when my abilities are greatly enhanced. The two of us together should be able to make some progress."

"What's a witch's moon?"

"When the crescent moon is tilted so the points are aimed upward."

Vincent nodded. "Why exactly are you doing this, Rhia? I mean, I know Blade asked you to help out, but you've been putting a lot of time into this. What are you getting out of it?"

Rhia smiled enigmatically. "At first, just money."

"What money?"

"Your friend paid me handsomely to undertake this venture."

"He did, huh?" Vincent tapped his fingers on the arm of the sofa.

"He did. Yet that is no longer my main concern. I am fascinated by the entire situation."

"Meaning...?"

"Meaning I am fascinated by the circumstances surrounding your arrival. By the prospect of other worlds. By the dreams I've had. And by you."

"By me?" he said, surprised.

"You are, essentially, a creature from another world. How could I not be fascinated by you?"

Vincent smiled politely, unsure how to react. Certainly, he felt flattered, though he couldn't shake the feeling that hers was a clinical sort of fascination. Seeing no point in dwelling on it, he decided instead to make dinner.

While Vincent built a fire and cleaned some vegetables, Rhia walked off toward the stream carrying a fishing net. By the time the fire was in full flame, and the vegetables were cleaned, cut, and beginning to cook, Rhia returned with two small fish. Vincent took them indoors, where he cleaned them. He noticed Rhia enter and retrieve her pack as he rubbed the filets with herbs and oil and placed them in a metal box affixed to a long handle. Outside again, he placed the box in the fire, allowing the handle to hang well out of the flames.

He glanced over at Rhia and saw her inserting metal objects into his yard. He walked over for a closer look and saw they were candleholders. She plunged the pointed ends of the holders into the soil, seven of them, altogether. They formed a circle about seven feet across. Into each holder, Rhia inserted a long, purple candle. From her pack, she also removed two yellow tapers, which she placed on the grass inside the circle. Vincent noticed that all these candles were fairly thick, with wide wicks. Definitely for outdoor use, he surmised.

Vincent brought a loaf of bread from indoors, as well as more tea. They ate in silence, each to their own thoughts, staring at the fire. When they'd finished, Rhia turned to him. "What we are about to do will require a good deal of concentration and, possibly, a good deal of time. You will need to have a clear head, free of distracting thoughts." He nodded in understanding. Rhia looked to the sky. The sun was beginning to set. "We shall start soon. The moon will rise shortly."

Vincent took the dirty utensils inside, rinsed them quickly, and returned outside to find Rhia pacing a circle around the ring of candles, mumbling to herself. He fished a burning branch out of the fire and carried it over to her. She thanked him, taking the brand. Then she slowly walked around the circle, lighting the seven purple candles with a quiet invocation. Vincent noticed the wide wicks were also fairly long. The resulting flames were very large, for candles. He doubted the wind would extinguish them. When Rhia was finished, she handed the brand back to him and he threw it back on the fire.

When he returned, Rhia was removing her cloak. Vincent thought little of this, assuming she would spread it inside the circle for them to sit on. She then removed her boots and motioned for him to do the same. He knelt and unlaced them, then pulled them off. When he looked up again, he was looking at Rhia's naked back as she placed the remainder of her clothing in a neat pile. Vincent felt his cheeks flush as she turned toward him. He averted his gaze.

"Remove your clothing," she said simply.

Vincent gave a nervous little laugh. "Um... I'm afraid I don't quite... um..."

"It is necessary," Rhia insisted.

"Why?"

"Vincent, the Craft is a very natural art. The flow of the magic must not be impeded by anything that doesn't belong. No clothing, no jewelry. Just you."

He still avoided looking at her body, glancing instead at the ring of candles. "Hey, my clothes are natural. No polyester!"

"And were you born into this world wearing clothing, you would be right to wear them now. Why don't you understand this?"

Vincent hazarded a look at Rhia's face, then struggled to keep it locked there. "I'm just not accustomed to removing my clothes in front of the opposite sex, okay?"

Rhia's eyes widened. "You have never...?"

"Fine, yes, I'm a virgin. Okay?" His gaze turned to the ground in embarrassment, then began, mostly against his will, to journey upward.

Rhia nodded slowly. "I imagine, then, that you would probably not couple with me this night?" Vincent's jaw dropped as he stared at her face. "The act would heighten my energies further," she said simply. "Still, we can make do without, if we must." She stepped into the circle and sat, cross-legged. "Come, Vincent. Time is passing."

"Is this really necessary?"

Rhia frowned. "You tell me. You are the one wishing to return home."

Vincent sighed, then began divesting himself of tunic and breeches, his face growing warmer by the second. Once he was in his birthday suit, he stepped into the circle. Rhia instructed him to sit facing her, cross-legged as she was. A chill breeze tickled his buttocks as he obeyed. He crossed his legs, which was not the most comfortable position he'd have liked, considering his back pain. He hoped like crazy that a certain member of his anatomy wouldn't embarrass him and, to this end, he concentrated on the blades of grass up his butt. That should ward off any titillating thoughts, he hoped.

"What we are going to do," Rhia began, absently toying with the two yellow tapers, "is focus on your arrival here. Your part will be to try to remember the event. Not necessarily through intense concentration, but by allowing your own mind to bring the memories to you. You will clear your head and allow your mind to wander. Knowing inside what you are trying to find, your mind will accommodate you."

"And what will you be doing?"

"I will be attempting to pick up on the same thoughts. Trying to push your mind in the right direction, to pull the thoughts out of you." She smiled with a hint of wickedness. "Nothing more... a combination of pushing and pulling. Pushing... and pulling..." She swayed her body forward and back, ever so slightly.

"Very funny," Vincent interrupted. "Enough with the sexual allusions."

"Sorry," she said with a chuckle.

"No, you're not."

Rhia laughed. "You're right. At any rate, we should begin." She shifted herself forward just enough so their knees touched. Then she placed her hands atop Vincent's legs. He immediately looked down in surprise, then realized the angle also allowed him to see more than just her hands. He looked back up. "Relax," Rhia said. "Close your eyes and clear your thoughts."

Vincent closed his eyes and did his best. The first step, he thought, was to clear away the thought that he was sitting naked in his front yard with an extremely attractive girl, who also happened to be in an advanced state of undress. That was the first step. And it was a doozie.

With a little help, though, he finally succeeded. The help took the form of mental recitation of the mean distances of the planets from the sun, listing names of major satellites, and so forth. However, he realized this wasn't exactly a *clearing* of his mind. More like a *cluttering*. Either way, his mind was now off his groin, thus allowing him to get to the matter at hand.

His arrival in this world. What could he recall? Being found by Blade and Gnorrin. He'd never forget that. But what came before? Obviously, he'd walked for some distance before collapsing on the road. Try as he might, though, he could remember nothing of his journey aside from a brief period of walking before seeing the cottage.

Rhia's voice broke his reverie. "The moon has risen." Vincent opened his eyes to look. What his eyes found, instead, was Rhia lighting the two yellow tapers. She held one in each hand and reclined backward, reaching behind her to light each taper from a different purple candle. Her legs were uncrossed and flanked his own. Vincent couldn't help himself. He stared. He ran his gaze from her long legs, upward... And at this point, she arched back to an upright position, legs immediately crossing again, and flung her red hair over her shoulder. The long, thin braid that lay mostly hidden in her thick tresses whipped around, finally settling over one breast. Vincent's eyes lingered. He nearly jumped when she spoke. "Take these," she said, handing him the tapers. "One in each hand. Hold them crossed over your chest." Vincent closed his mouth and did as instructed. Suddenly he noticed something else. Rhia noticed, too. His face grew hot as she smiled. "Thank you," she said. "I'm flattered."

He didn't reply, but closed his eyes again. He felt the heat of the candles near his chest and hoped his chest hair wouldn't ignite. Rhia's command of "no jewelry" unfortunately included his magical ring. He attempted to clear his mind again, finding this to be rather difficult, all things considered. Several minutes passed, and he still couldn't focus his mind on anything other than what his groin was focusing on.

Perhaps that was what caused the memory to pop into his mind. Perhaps it was the scent of the yellow candles as they burned. Possibly it was a combination of the two. But his mind started to flash images of a dream he'd had. A dream where he had made love to a stunningly beautiful girl. He shook his head. This wasn't what he needed.

Rhia gasped. "What was that?"

Vincent's eyes popped open and began scanning around. "What?" He saw no wild beasts, no strangers. He looked at Rhia, only to find her staring at him.

"What was that thought?" she whispered.

He frowned. "What thought?"

She leaned forward, placing her hands on his knees again. "There was an image. Of you and a girl."

"Oh, man," Vincent whined. "Don't start."

"No! I'm serious! What was it?"

"Just a dream I had once."

"When?" she insisted.

Vincent shrugged. "I dunno. Not long after your first visit, because..."

"Why?"

"Well, I was burning a yellow candle at the time."

Rhia's eyes widened. "I must see this dream. Run through it in your mind."

"No! Are you kidding?"

"Close your eyes and dream," she urged. Vincent knew she was serious, so he tried to comply. He closed his eyes again and inhaled a deep whiff of the candles' scent. He hoped it would help. He tried to remember the surroundings in the dream. It was dark, he remembered. Dark and barren, like a basement. Or maybe a cave. "Cave," whispered Rhia. "Yes." And then he felt Rhia's imposition on his thoughts, forcing him back, right back into the dream. He had no control over his own thoughts.

He dreamed now, as if Rhia controlled his mind. His eyes, in the dream, looked around. They saw the grey walls. And something in the back. The back of the cave. Like a great eye. "Eye," whispered Rhia. "Yes." The eye... No. Not an eye. There was a frame around it. A picture of an eye. No, not quite that, either. More like a mirror, without the reflection.

And now the girl entered the dream. She was the most beautiful girl he'd ever seen, though he knew he could never describe her appearance once he was out of the dream. "Yes," he heard Rhia whisper. And then the girl was seducing him. Now was when he could wake up. But Rhia would not allow him that courtesy. She pushed the dream. And the dream-Vincent made love to the dream-girl. The act was so real. He felt Rhia's hands move on his legs. His breath quickened, and he could hear Rhia's do the same. "Yes," she said, massaging his legs. "Yes... yes... yes..." Vincent opened his eyes abruptly, snapped out of the dream by Rhia's abrupt gasp.

She sat, eyes and mouth open. Her hands stopped their motion on his legs. She caught her breath. "Goddess," she whispered. "Darella!"

Vincent lay in his bed, the oil lamp burning brightly on the table beside him. His journal lay open, a pen in the little clay well. *Inks by Mepis.* He sighed and took a mouthful of hot tea, placing the mug back on the table. His mind was awhirl as he set pen to paper.

Darella is evidently another witch of Rhia's acquaintance. She told me very little about her, but she's evidently not a very nice lady. And my dream apparently wasn't really a dream. Those events actually happened. Rhia seems quite certain this Darella woman basically read my subconscious mind to find all the traits in a female I'd find irresistible, then changed her own appearance to match them! I suppose I should be flattered, but I'm not. I'm still trying to get over the fact that I've had sex for the first time in my life, and I don't even remember it! At least, Rhia seems sure I have.

Gotta admit, though, I came damn close to trying to have sex tonight. Rhia is not what I'd really call beautiful. At least, not in a classic sense. There is something about her, though, that is undeniably sexy. And I'm not saying so because she was nude. I noticed it about her the first time we met. Well... second time, actually. I wasn't quite conscious the first time.

Disturbing trend, that. Lots of things happening to me without me being aware of them!

Anyway, Rhia packed up her things shortly after this and took off for parts unknown again. Oh, well. I'm getting used to it.

So... Now I have even more questions than usual. The new additions are: Why was I in the cave in the first place and how did I get there? What was the big eye-thing on the wall? And most pressing to me, why in the world would a witch want to have sex with me?

Vincent stopped writing, inserting the pen back into the inkwell. He drank from his tea, reading over what he had just written. He felt a twinge between his legs as he read the paragraph concerning Rhia's sex appeal. He took a deep breath, then lifted the pen again.

This is absurd. I'm feeling guilty for finding Rhia attractive! Like I'm being unfaithful to Annie. If there were a relationship between us beyond friendship, then my guilt might be somewhat justified. But why should I feel guilty now? Annie has shown no inclination toward becoming "involved" with me. It's not wrong of me to have lustful feelings toward another woman.

But then, that's where the difference is, isn't it? I felt lust for Rhia. I've never felt lust for Annie. Different feelings altogether. I suppose that's all the more reason for me not to feel guilty, but for some reason, it doesn't help at all.

He put the journal on the floor by the bed. That was enough for the evening. This had been one long day. He finished his tea, put the inkwell and pen up out of the way, and turned the lamp's wick low. He removed his eyeglasses, folded them up, and made a mental note to wash them with the invisibility compound soon. And as he lay back on his pillow, he tried to think of things to take his mind off the day's events. If his groin would let him forget, he felt he just might get some sleep.

❧ ❧

The following day, Vincent set out on horseback for a ride. He had no destination in mind, and didn't plan on being gone long. But his unconscious mind had other ideas. Before he realized where he was going, he found himself stopping his horse near a familiar outcropping of rock.

He sat there, his pulse beginning to quicken. Against his better judgment, he walked his horse over to a tree. Before long, he was squeezing his body through the rocky crevasse, a burning torch in hand. Much to his surprise, he found his way to the secret door, still standing open from his last visit. A minute later, he stood before the great doors behind which he knew he would find the efreeti. Vincent swallowed hard, took a deep breath, and opened them.

A blast of fire shot forth and enveloped him. Vincent jumped in astonishment. The blast ceased, and a frowning efreeti stood staring at the doorway. Its countenance softened upon seeing who stood there.

"Is that any way to welcome a friend?" Vincent asked.

The giant creature laughed deeply. "I was not expecting a friend to visit. And I must say, I am surprised. Enter, *human*." The efreeti chuckled again at the last word.

Vincent smirked. "Funny." He snuffed his torch by closing it in his armpit. Then he walked into the creature's parlor. At the efreeti's prompting, he made himself comfortable amongst several huge pillows. He looked about the place as the being reclined on the pillows, too. "I'm sorry for barging in uninvited," Vincent said.

"Nonsense. You shall always be welcome here."

"Very kind of you." He hesitated, then shook his head at his own presumption. "I can't believe I'm really here, though, sitting with you."

"I am pleased you are. You intrigue me, young Vincent."

Vincent snorted. "Seems I intrigue a lot of folks around here."

"I can well imagine," said his new friend. "It is not every day that typical humans meet a being such as we two are."

"Excuse me?"

"We are much alike. We are both from other regions."

Vincent frowned. "How did you know about that?" he said, toying with the extinguished torch.

"Magic," the creature said with a smile. "Forgive me for prying, but after our first meeting, I felt I had to know more about you. About what kind of human would do what you did."

"Why do you say that? You don't think anyone else would've given you the bottle?"

The giant shook its head. "Hardly. Humans are a selfish and greedy lot."

"Some of them. Some of us. Yeah." Vincent paused, raising an eyebrow. "You know, the little information I have read about your people seems to imply that the efreet are all... well, evil."

"And some of us are." The creature nodded wisely. "We both have learned something today."

"I suppose so. I would guess the only humans that efreet generally encounter are those who are treasure seekers and such. Likewise, the only efreet that humans generally encounter are those who are defending what the humans are after."

"Exactly so." The pair sat quietly for a minute, allowing this bit of information to digest. Finally, the efreeti said, "Why *did* you come here today?"

Vincent held the torch in front of him, propped up between his two index fingers. Suddenly the torch burst into flame again, causing Vincent to drop it into his lap. He extinguished it with his hand. Then he turned to his host with a weak smile. "I guess I'm here because I hope you can help me."

"I see. In what way?"

"What do you know about witches?"

The efreeti gave a slight shrug. "What is there *to* know about witches?"

Vincent briefly told of Darella and the cave, and the mysterious object on the wall that was Rhia's primary concern.

The creature nodded throughout the telling, then said, "I can tell you nothing of the witch. However, the object you describe puts me to mind..."

"Yes?" Vincent prompted.

"I believe it to be a Seeker Portal."

Vincent frowned quizzically. The torch took advantage of the time to burst into flame again. He snuffed it again. "Any chance of lowering the heat a little? This is getting on my nerves."

"Certainly," said the efreeti. "My apologies."

Vincent thrust the torch aside. "What's a Seeker Portal?"

"The invention of the druids who lived ages and ages ago. They are amazing devices of the most powerful magic. They have one purpose only, and that is to maintain the equilibrium of the world."

"Why? Is the planet dizzy?"

The efreeti smiled, then said, "Druids believed in balance in all things. Any move away from center, in any direction, was not to be tolerated. The purpose of the portals was to bring forth influential beings from other worlds, other dimensions, to help maintain the neutrality. For example, if the world's balance shifted, allowing evil to become widespread, the portals would bring forth champions of goodness. And so on."

Vincent gaped. "These things are actually capable of scanning other worlds and bringing their inhabitants here? That's amazing!"

"Your own presence here seems to be ample evidence."

Several minutes passed while Vincent tried to fathom this. Then he frowned. "Wait a minute. You said the portal brought forth influential beings." He snorted. "I don't think the thing is working very well if it brought *me* through." He looked at the efreeti. "Why are you smiling?"

"You amuse me, Vincent. How long have you been here in this world?"

"About a year. Why?"

"And in that year, let us see what you have accomplished. You have acquired a magical ring that makes you immune to fire. You have gained the ability to survive without breathing for short durations. And you have befriended an efreeti. I should say that is quite a list of accomplishments for one year's time."

Vincent was speechless for a moment. Then he said, "Add to the list that I've finally gotten physically fit, have become an accomplished swordfighter, and have gained some wealth."

"Exactly so. So you see, you are quite a remarkable young man. And I, for one, believe you are on the road to greatness."

Vincent shrugged. "Thing is, though, none of this is really very important to me. I really don't care about the money, or the magical stuff. I am grateful for your friendship, and of the others I've met. Those are the important things." He shrugged again. He certainly didn't need to discuss his love life, or lack thereof, with the creature.

"And what else is important to you?"

"All I really want," he said, "is to find my way home."

The efreeti seemed startled at this answer and raised one great eyebrow. "Oh?"

Vincent wasn't sure if the creature were being sarcastic or not. He didn't want to find out. So he decided to change the subject. "You know, there's something I've wanted to ask you ever since I first laid eyes on you."

"And what is that?"

"I've no idea why in the world a creature such as yourself is occupying time and space in this old abandoned dwarven home, buried under the rocks in the middle of nowhere! What's the story?"

The efreeti was silent for a time, and Vincent could have sworn the being looked forlorn. Finally, it spoke. "This dwarven home was the abode of a very wealthy and powerful dwarven king. He was in the category of greedy and selfish I mentioned before. He decided it would be a novelty to have an efreeti slave. Lacking a bottle such as the one you so kindly presented to me, he hired the most powerful mage he could find to fashion an alternative form of entrapment. This room, you see, is much like a very large bottle. A very powerful magic contains me."

"You mean you're stuck here?"

"Yes. The mage hired by the king was very familiar with fire. He knew exactly how to render this room resistant to anything I might cast. There is also a sort of shield preventing me from getting back to my own dimension. I cannot leave this room by physical or magical means."

"So you were enslaved."

"Oh, no. I was trapped, but not enslaved. I killed the dwarven king the very first time he set foot into the room. The fool had made the room impervious to me, but he had never considered making himself so." The efreeti smiled. "I have not yet decided whether that rash act was a good idea."

"What about the other dwarves?"

"They were of no consequence. Once their king was reduced to ashes, they packed their things and moved away. That was, oh, perhaps a hundred and fifty years ago. Perhaps less."

Vincent began laughing quietly.

As the boy's laugh grew, the efreeti scowled. "I fail to see the humor in the situation."

"I'm sorry," Vincent said as his laughter subsided. "Kurean. He was the mage your little king hired to build this room."

"And?"

"Well, I found both the ring and the bottle in Kurean's keep! I don't know if he had them in his possession when the king hired him, but still... It's rather ironic."

"In fact, it makes perfect sense. It explains how this mage knew what to do in order to imprison me here. He used the ring and the bottle as guides."

"But he could've just used the bottle on you, or sold it to the king."

"Which would have left him without the bottle. The king was willing to pay him handsomely to fashion an alternative to the bottle. In doing so, the mage was paid well, and retained the bottle."

"Which the king probably never knew he had. Clever." He shook his head. "But that means you have no idea what could break you free from this prison?"

"None," the efreeti said. "I have tried everything I could think of."

Vincent smiled apologetically. "Well, if I'm on the road to greatness, as you say, maybe I can manage to get you out of here."

The efreeti smiled at the young man. "I would not be surprised."

Vincent retrieved his torch and stood. "Well. I should be getting back. My dog will be worried."

"Very well. Travel safely. I look forward to seeing you again." A stream of fire lanced out from the giant's finger, igniting the torch.

With a nod, Vincent departed.

⚭ ⚭

"You did *what?*" Ariaziane stopped in her tracks as they walked along.

"I went back to visit the efreeti," Vincent repeated. He bent over to extract a big stick from Blaise's mouth, then threw it for her again. The dog bounded off. "It's a prisoner there," he continued, and proceeded to tell her the creature's story. "I want to find a way to free it," he concluded.

Ariaziane let out a breath as they resumed their walk. "You would need some powerful magic to undo something of Kurean's," she said. "Especially if the efreeti has already tried."

"Do you think Gnorrin will have any suggestions?" he asked.

The girl shook her head doubtfully. "You can ask him when we get there, though I'd be very surprised. By his own admission, Kurean's magery skills far exceeded Gnorrin's abilities."

They walked in silence for a time, Blaise prancing in front of them, the massive stick clenched between her jaws. Vincent's thoughts had jumped from the efreeti to Rhia's revelation. He had not yet told Ariaziane of this. And he hesitated to do so, for a reason he couldn't quite grasp. Thinking of Rhia made him think of the way he felt about Ariaziane. And so, he decided one more time to try to gain insight to her feelings.

"Annie," he began. "I need to know something. I need to know how you feel about me."

She smiled. "What do you mean?"

He took a deep breath. "What I mean is I'm in love with you. And I'd kinda like to know if you have similar feelings toward me."

Ariaziane's smile faded. She stared at the dirt road. Finally, she said, "It's not that simple." She looked at him briefly, before turning her attention back to the road. "I don't really know if I can say I love you or not. I just don't really think in those terms. I mean, you're my favorite person, Vincent. I enjoy being with you. I can't see how I could ever not enjoy being with you. But I don't think I'm ready to feel for you what you're apparently feeling for me."

"Not *ready* to feel? What do you mean?"

"I mean that right now, I'm devoting my time to magic. Learning magic is very time-consuming and very difficult. Draining. I enjoy spending time with you because you refresh me. Lately, though... I don't know. You've been so intense. And if that's what being in love does to you, I'm just not ready for it."

Vincent absorbed her words in a way he hoped was gallant. Finally, he said, "I see. So what you're saying is...?"

"What I'm saying is there's no one I'd rather spend time with than you. And I know you feel that way, too. Yet, at least for right now, our reasons for wanting this are somewhat different."

"Right," Vincent said. "I want to be with you because I love you. And you want to be with me because I provide relief from your studies."

"No! That's not what I meant at all!" She stopped walking and forced him to face her. "You know that's not true."

Vincent sighed. "I'm sorry. I didn't mean it."

"I know you didn't." She smiled and reached out to hug him, pressing her cheek against his. "Now, can we put this subject aside for awhile?"

Vincent allowed her to withdraw from the hug. "One more question, and then we can put it aside." Ariaziane nodded. "I've always been a patient person. So I guess what

I'm mostly concerned with is, will there be a time when you'll be ready to feel for me what I feel for you?"

The girl brushed a lock of auburn hair away from her dark eyes. She smiled, and her eyes twinkled. "I think so. Just don't rush me."

Vincent smiled weakly in return. "Deal." He took the hand she held out, and they continued on their way.

❧ ☙

I suppose I should be happy to know there's at least a strong possibility of Ariaziane loving me, sometime in the future, Vincent wrote in his journal that evening, *but I really can't bring myself to feeling like I haven't just been gut-kicked.*

I can't blame Annie for her views. Far from it. In fact, were I a rational person, I'd probably applaud her wisdom. She's not even sixteen years old yet. She's too young (by the standards I'm used to) to be seriously involved with someone. She's intent on her studies, which is more than you could say about most kids her age on Earth. In fact, her argument this evening was so convincing, so logical, so... mature... I almost feel ashamed for having put her in such an awkward position to begin with.

And I'm afraid the argument affected me enough to be noticeable. We met Gnorrin at his cottage, then proceeded into town for dinner at the tavern. All throughout the meal, I was quiet. Gnorrin noticed, but didn't pry. I think he suspected the situation. Likely as not, Annie will tell him all about it. I guess she's probably closer to him now than I am.

Vincent stared at the flame in the lantern for a moment. Then he dipped his pen again and returned to writing.

Another thing I can't seem to stop thinking of is what the efreeti said. About me being destined for greatness, or some such thing. Naturally, I find this to be pretty unbelievable. The truth is, I really have accomplished a heck of a lot since arriving here. That's more than can be said for my years on Earth.

What does it mean, though? What greatness am I destined for? (I have difficulty writing that without laughing.) Maybe it's an indication that I should move on. Head for where the action is, or maybe find some on the way. I could move to Falconwall, or some other city.

Or perhaps I should just continue my explorations. Maybe I should set out for parts unknown.

Or maybe I should turn my attention to returning to Earth. Now that I know what brought me here, I should be able to make a lot more progress in figuring out how to get back.

But if that were the case, and if I really wanted to do it, why didn't I mention this new information to Annie or Gnorrin?

Sometimes I just can't figure myself out.

Book Three

Wish You Were Here

❧ Thirteen ❧

In the following months, Vincent was able to obtain several maps of the known world. By the end of the Season of the Sun, he had a more or less accurate representation of all charted regions of the planet. He had spent a considerable sum in obtaining the maps, printed as they were on thin sheets of animal hide, for durability. Typically, a map would be rolled up and stored in a wooden cylinder casing. Vincent, however, preferred the book format. Mepis proved to be an adequate bookbinder for the task. However, when they were finished, there were so many volumes that an entire new shelving unit was needed in Vincent's cottage to accommodate them.

The maps he studied most intently were those of the vicinity in which he currently lived. He was able to locate the areas that he'd explored on his many excursions into the wilderness, and added his own notes. He labeled Kurean's keep, as well as the efreeti's temporary prison. He charted the route he and Blade had taken when they'd escorted the taxes to Dynsa, as well as the trip to Falconwall. One spot he marked, *Nasty-tempered boars that don't like humans.*

There were many areas he might explore, he thought. There was a forest to the northwest, a mountain range to the east, and a really huge chain of mountains far to the west. A couple good sized rivers could be found to the east and west. He should probably just pick a place at random, he thought. Or he could go about trying to obtain more information than the maps held.

Mid-Year Week came soon thereafter, bringing Ariaziane's sixteenth birthday with it. Vincent spent a great deal of time with her at the festivities. He surprised her by getting a birthday cake at the bakery, and they shared it with Gnorrin back at his cottage, accompanied by hot tankards of some real tea that Vincent bought from one of the merchants. Vincent took the opportunity to pick Gnorrin's brain about the lay of the land.

Gnorrin, unfortunately, was not exactly a font of knowledge on the subject. "The forest is a forest, the rivers are rivers, and the mountains are mountains. What more did you want to know?"

Vincent then turned to another source of information.

The efreeti welcomed him, just as before. They exchanged pleasantries before Vincent dove into his reason for visiting. "I've been thinking about what you said," he began, "about me having this great destiny or some such silliness." He shrugged. "Well, whether it's true or not, I doubt it's going to happen by me hanging out in the middle of nowhere. I've decided to explore."

The efreeti nodded. "Where did you have in mind?"

"That's the problem," he replied. "I was hoping you might have a suggestion for me. I've got some pretty good maps, but that's only geography. I need to know more."

"I trust you are not yet prepared for an extensive journey?"

"Well, not one that would cause me to be away for more than a few months, I wouldn't think."

The efreeti nodded again. "You would be traveling alone?"

"Yes."

"And what would you like to find?"

"I... don't know. I hadn't really thought about that." Vincent sat quietly for a time. Then he said, "One thing I've been thinking of. I'd like to find another efreeti bottle."

The giant raised its ropy eyebrows, then smiled. "Quite considerate of you, but not necessary. Few of the efreet ever have the opportunity to destroy even one of those loathsome things. I do not need to enjoy that pleasure twice."

The boy shook his head. "No. I wouldn't let you destroy it. I'd put you in it."

The creature stared at him in shock for a moment, then its eyes widened. "Damn my horns! Of course!"

"Had I known you were a prisoner here, we could have used the bottle to get you out."

The efreeti was beside itself. It leaped to its feet and raged. "Damn my rashness! How could I have been so blind?" Vincent winced at the volume of the creature's voice. "Encase me in the bottle, depart this room, then let me out... Yes, yes..." It quieted down somewhat, then lapsed into despair. "Ah, but I do not know where you might find one. Those damned bottles. Even the most powerful of the efreet cannot detect the presence of one, unless it be in plain view." It frowned, then looked Vincent squarely in the eye. "Still, that is sound thinking. If you do happen to encounter one, we shall try it. But back to your original question." The efreeti collapsed again onto the massive cushions and sat deep in thought for many minutes. Vincent sat idly while waiting for a reply. It was so long that he wondered if the creature had forgotten about him entirely. Finally, the efreeti turned to face him. "I have no suggestion."

Vincent blinked. "What?"

"I am sorry, my young friend, but I cannot give you a recommendation. I can suggest many paths that would doubtless take you on the road to adventure. But, traveling alone, they would likely lead to death. Also, they are predominantly long journeys. The distances would keep you away for longer than you would like. No. I believe you will need to choose your own path in this matter."

The boy sighed. "I was afraid of that." He frowned, then his jaw firmed. "Okay. I'll travel northwest. There's a forest up there. What could I expect to find?"

"Trees," said the efreeti.

"Thank you. I'll be prepared." Vincent shifted in his mound of cushions, cracked his knuckles and repeated, "Seriously, what might I encounter? Keep in mind that this is a world totally new to me. Creatures that commonly inhabit forests here are probably pretty different than what would occupy forests on my home world."

The efreeti nodded. "Forest creatures, you will find, are varied. Wild beasts in abundance, as you'd expect. Unless you spend a great deal of time there and become attuned to the ways of the forest, it is doubtful that you will meet anything further."

"But if I did...?"

"Then the possibilities become fairly endless. Dryads, woodland elves, other faerie-folk. Treants. Dragons."

"Excuse me? Dragons?"

"Aye. There are dragons in some forests. Why do you seem surprised?"

Vincent hesitated. "I don't know. I guess I just never pictured dragons living in forests, that's all."

"Dragons live wherever they want. That's a principal law of nature." The efreeti chuckled. "But it is true that different types of dragons prefer different climates."

The information gradually registered upon Vincent's mind. He racked his brain, trying to recall anything from Gnorrin's books regarding the other creatures the efreeti had mentioned. He cleared his throat. "So. Any words of advice for me, just in case I happen to encounter any of these creatures?"

"Very well. If you meet a dryad, smile sweetly and go on your way. If you meet an elf, nod politely and go on your way. If you meet a treant, put out your fire and go on your way."

"And if I meet a dragon?"

"Go on your way. Rapidly." The efreeti chuckled again.

Vincent smiled and rose. "Well, with that, I'm going to go on my way. I thank you for your hospitality, my friend."

"I wish you well on your journey. Be careful."

"I shall." Vincent nodded and departed.

He spent the next two weeks preparing for his journey, listing everything he could imagine himself needing, then reducing it to what his horse could comfortably carry. He gave his glasses a new coat of invisibility, and made arrangements with Gnorrin and Ariaziane to look after his cottage and garden. Since Blaise would be accompanying him, there was no need for her to be looked after. The only thing left to do, he thought, was to say goodbye to his friends.

Gnorrin wished him well and gave him a packet of food similar to that which he'd given to Blade on his departure. Once he'd learned Vincent's planned itinerary, he offered some advice. "The forest is home to some unsavory types. I'd be sure to remember Blade's lessons, if I were you." He raised his eyebrows. "You have the stone?"

Vincent nodded. He'd taken the magical healing stone that Gnorrin had given him on his birthday and had it set into a necklace. He pulled the thin, silver chain from under his tunic. Gnorrin nodded, noticing the round setting that held the gem open to inspection from either side. Vincent tucked it away again when he saw his friend smile.

Ariaziane, however, was not quite as blasé about the affair. Escorting him away from Gnorrin's cottage, she led him back toward the creek. "Why are you doing this?" she asked again, as she had several times since he'd first mentioned it to her.

"Annie," he began, "I can't give you any clear reasons. I'm not entirely sure, myself. Maybe it's just wanderlust. I'm curious about this world, and want to see more of it than just this area and occasional trips to Dynsa or Falconwall. I'm easily bored, I guess."

Vincent intentionally left out one reason that was probably the most critical. He just couldn't bear to hurt her. And he knew she'd be hurt if he told her that he was going away in order to get over the pain of being near her all the time, but not being able to really be *with* her all the time. His hope was that, by the time he returned, she might realize how much she meant to her. She might be more able to return his love. If her magic allowed time for it, he thought bitterly.

As lame as the reasons sounded to him, Ariaziane accepted them. Or rather, she didn't make a fuss about them. She did, however, have something to say.

They ended up at "their" spot, the large rock by the creek. Ariaziane leaned back against it and brushed a lock of hair away from her eyes. "I'll miss you," she said simply.

Vincent felt a pain in his chest and averted his gaze. "I'll miss you, too."

The girl sighed. "Your urges for exploration aside, I get the feeling your heart isn't really in this." She waited for him to say something, but he didn't. "I'm don't like the idea of you going alone, either. It could be dangerous."

At this, he smiled, putting on mock bravado. "Hey, I hang out with an efreeti! What do I care about danger?"

Ariaziane didn't smile at his joke. "How long do you expect to be gone?"

Vincent's smile faded. "I don't know."

The girl frowned, staring at the ground. "I just don't understand this."

"Don't worry."

"How can I *not* worry?" she shot back, turning to face him. "Vincent, this is pointless!"

He watched her for a moment. "You don't want me to go," he said flatly.

With a grimace, she turned away. "It's not that. Or perhaps it is. I don't know."

"Annie," he said softly, causing her to look at him again. "I'll think of you every moment I'm gone. I can't help it. I love you. And when I come back..."

She waited for him to continue, then prompted him. "Yes?"

A soft, ironic chuckle escaped his lips. "I don't know. It's not up to me, really. I was going to say that when I return, we'll be together again. Except..."

"Except what? Stop making me drag everything from you."

He smiled sadly. "Nothing. We'll be together again. It'll just be a handful of weeks."

After a minute of silence, they walked back to Gnorrin's cottage. There, they said their last goodbyes. Vincent returned to his own home, then, for one final night's sleep before departing.

He rose early and treated himself to a hearty breakfast of pancakes. A dark flour he'd purchased in town served the purpose wonderfully. The flavor reminded him of buckwheat. And pure syrup was readily available. He cooked them over the fire on a flat iron griddle that hung atop supports he'd hammered around the interior of his firepit. It was quite similar to a huge backyard barbecue. He ate his fill, doused the fire, and made sure the cottage was properly sealed. By mid-morning, he was off.

The first leg of his day's journey was all familiar territory to him, and before long he reached the crossroads, the spot where Blade had lost Vincent's trail so long ago. He turned west, here, skirting the marsh, heading into unfamiliar lands.

After a few hours, he stopped for a rest, stretching and massaging the various body parts that ached, which seemed to be most of them. There was a small stream nearby, where he relieved his thirst, as did Blaise and King. As his horse grazed, Vincent shared a piece of jerky with the dog. Then she stretched out for a nap. Half an hour later, they were underway again.

After another few hours of travel through unfamiliar but unexciting land, Vincent decided to halt for the day. He made camp, erecting his lean-to as the fire he built got into full flame. Then he strung his bow and went looking for small game.

If anyone had ever told me, he thought, that one day I'd hunt animals with a bow and arrow, I'd have said they were crazy. But then, he realized, he was leading a rather crazy existence at the moment.

He let Blaise find the rabbits. She would sniff them out, usually alerting them in the process. If they didn't scamper completely away, Vincent was usually able to peg them where they stopped. Blaise happily fetched the carcasses.

Dinner was cooked and consumed. The sun set not long thereafter. As Vincent lay under the stars, smelling the wood smoke and watching for meteors, he realized that this life wasn't bad at all. Like a long camping vacation. He sighed. Except that he always managed to have toilet paper when he went camping.

The following day, he was able to get an earlier start, the sun having wakened him just after dawn. He repacked his lean-to and bedroll, made doubly sure the fire was out, then ate. It was a quick breakfast of moist jerky, courtesy of Gnorrin, and granola mix that Vincent had put together. Then they were off again.

By mid-afternoon, they had reached the edge of the forest. And here Vincent had a choice: to go headlong into the forest, or to skirt the perimeter. He knew there was a town on the southern edge of the woods. But towns, he was familiar with. Forests, he wasn't. This particular forest had a narrow section on its southeastern side, rather like a handle. Or an entrance hall, Vincent thought as he guided his animal companions into the forest.

Entrance hall was right, Vincent saw immediately. There was a clear trail leading into the forest. They proceeded slowly, the horse assuming a leisurely walk. The light dimmed soon after they entered. By the time they had progressed a hundred yards, the amount of light was barely sufficient for sight. Vincent certainly hoped this would change. Perhaps exploring this forest wasn't the best idea. He glanced overhead. The upper boughs of the trees formed a thick canopy. Very little sunlight could penetrate. Would it improve or worsen? If it stayed the same, it would be tolerable, but not very exciting.

A rustle in the brush drew his attention. He reined in his horse. Blaise stood alert, staring into the woods. The noise died away. "Just some little thing," he told the dog as they proceeded once again. The woods were a mixed lot of deciduous trees, he realized. It would be lovely here in a few more weeks, he thought. It was early yet in the Season of Harvest. The month of Colors would begin soon. He looked forward to seeing it.

He turned his attention to the sounds around him. Chirping insects seemed everywhere, unsurprisingly. Birds were beginning to settle in for the coming night. He looked around, but couldn't see them.

The smells of the forest were many, but mostly unidentifiable to him. Vincent hoped someday to travel through a forest of evergreens. What an olfactory feast that would be.

His stomach rumbled, so he assumed that the dog and the horse were probably hoping for dinner soon, too. He frowned. Where were they going to bed down for the night? They had yet to see a clearing. Vincent prodded his horse into a faster pace.

Foolish of him to put off making camp for so long, he thought. He looked anxiously about for a clearing, but after fifteen minutes more of travel, nothing presented itself.

He contented himself at last with an area just off the trail where a patch of sunlight made it through the canopy. It was very little light, since the sun was well on its way to the horizon. The area wasn't large enough for him to erect the lean-to. But that was okay. The bedroll would suffice.

He unloaded his horse and tied him to a tree. He unpacked the feedbag and filled it with oats. He'd brought it along for just such an emergency. There simply wasn't anywhere for the horse to graze here.

There wasn't space to build a large fire, so he'd have to be content with a small one. He cleared out a circular area about a foot and a half in diameter. He placed a ring of stones around the perimeter, then struck a torch with his flints. This he lay in the pit, with the one end of the torch upon the ring of stones. Quickly he gathered some fallen branches and broke them into the appropriately sized pieces. Once he had enough, he built up the fire, removing the torch once it was ablaze, extinguishing it for later use.

Now he had to find food. He doubted that this would prove difficult. Lots of critters in a forest, he told himself. He pulled out his bow and quiver of arrows and set out upon his hunt. Blaise began to follow him. "Stay," he commanded. The dog looked at him in a way he could have sworn was petulant. But she sat, staying near the outskirts of their tiny camp. He knew she'd be right there waiting for him when he returned.

Choosing this evening's repast would be tricky. He had no hopes of bagging a pair of rabbits like he did the previous night. In the forest, it would be far too simple for them to duck behind trees. He wasn't *that* good an archer. So he needed to set his sights on something larger and slower. Doubtless there were many deer in the forest, but he wasn't quite that hungry. Never eat anything larger than yourself, he thought. Maybe he could find a raccoon, or this world's equivalent.

After several minutes of careful walking through the woods, he stopped. Sadly, he realized that he was not the silent tracker that Blade was. Most likely, he was scaring away all the prey. So he stood, his back against a tree, an arrow nocked and ready.

He gazed at the forest floor as he waited, his mind passing the time by idly speculating. He pictured autumn, with all the leaves turning colors and eventually falling. He thought of the branches that would fall, too. Of entire trees that fell. Of the animal carcasses that must litter the forest. All that substance falling in any given year must be an incredible amount of mass, he thought. Over time, surely the forest would suffocate itself, were it not for the ground-dwelling residents. Everything from invisible microbes to insect larvae to burrowing mammals such as woodchucks. All these combined to eat the leaves and wood and aerate the soil.

His thoughts were broken by a noise. He glanced in its direction, waiting. Soon he heard the shuffling sound again and tried to pinpoint the source. Finally he saw it. Brownish-gray fur. He smiled. He'd just been thinking about woodchucks and now it seemed that one answered his call. Quietly, he raised his bow, and let fly.

Again, thanks to Blade's instruction, he and his dog would not go hungry. Vincent retrieved the animal, noting that it seemed to be similar to a woodchuck in form, but to a raccoon in coloring. Interesting, he thought, as he pulled the arrow from the corpse. He made his way back to the tiny campsite.

Sure enough, Blaise was waiting right where he'd left her. She wagged her tail happily and did a little dance. She sniffed curiously at the dead beast, then watched eagerly as Vincent quickly gutted and skinned the animal. He did it rapidly and without thinking. He didn't particularly like to think about it. When the animal was reduced to small pieces, he cooked some over the fire for himself, giving the rest raw to Blaise.

As he expected, the dinner satisfied himself as well as the dog. And there was enough left over for lunch the following day. He had shared water with the animals and expected soon to find a stream. This forest had two rivers running through, about ten leagues apart, give or take. By his estimation, he should encounter the first river in three days, at their present rate of travel. However, there must be many tributaries. Soon he should encounter one. With this pleasant thought in mind, he climbed into his sleeping sack. Blaise curled up next to him, not far from the fire. Soon, she was asleep.

Vincent wasn't so lucky. He couldn't make himself comfortable. And he would have gladly traded Gnorrin's magical wound healer for a magical insect repellent. The noises of the forest kept him awake, too. If the insects weren't biting him, they were making all sorts of racket. And he heard owls, too. Fortunately, they seemed to be the hooting type, rather than the screeching.

He had no idea how much, or little, sleep he actually got that night. But he rose early, packed quickly, and was soon back on the trail, in a miserable mood. He itched all over and frequently scratched at the bites on his face and neck. His stomach rumbled, so he chewed one of the oatcakes Gnorrin had packed for him. He tossed one to Blaise, too, for good measure. She stopped to eat it, then pranced forward to resume the lead.

Despite his discomforts, he was happy to be traveling again. The canopy overhead was thinning somewhat, and light was beginning to stream in. This might not be so bad a place after all, he thought.

Before too long, he came upon a clearing, the likes of which he would have been pleased to encounter the previous evening. It was a large, sunlit field and the trail ran right through it. Whoever blazed this trail had been no fool. It was perhaps an acre of land. Who could tell what had cleared it? Vincent didn't know and didn't care to guess. But Blaise enjoyed herself by bounding through the tall grasses, flushing out birds and bunnies, barking happily.

A stream cut its merry way through the middle of the clearing. Vincent dismounted and filled his water bottles. He'd brought four, three of which were now empty. He dumped out the fourth, filling it with a fresh supply. The horse drank his fill, and once the dog noticed the stream, she lapped some up.

Vincent admired the beauty of the forest. The sun shone on gorgeous wildflowers all along the stream, in colors too numerous to mention. Berry bushes were to be found, too. He picked handfuls of the tiny fruits. They looked too much like blueberries for him not to try them. Could be lethal as strychnine, he thought as he popped one into his mouth. But what the heck. He bit into it and chewed. "Damn," he breathed. "It is a blueberry!" He filled a small sack with them.

As he was preparing to mount up again, he heard the call of a bird. It reminded him of the noise a bird of prey would make. He turned to look, just in time to see a hawk-type creature diving for his face. He froze, too startled to do anything more. The bird soared past his head, the tips of its feathers brushing his cheek. The sensation broke him out of his paralysis, and he turned to watch the bird as it flew almost straight up, then leveled off. It gave one more call before flying out of sight over the trees.

"Ha!" Vincent touched his cheek where the bird's feathers had brushed it. Once the fright wore off, he was thrilled by the experience. "Did you see that, girl?"

Blaise let out a quiet woof, then moved off, evidently convinced the bird wasn't going to return. She went bounding off in search of more bunnies to spook. Vincent kept watching the sky where the hawk had disappeared, almost hoping for its return. His heart slowly returned to its normal pace, and finally Vincent turned back toward his horse. And nearly had a heart attack.

His mount was happily chomping away at an apple... held in Rhia's hand.

There were only a handful of times that Vincent could remember finding himself speechless. The last one was when he had turned around and found Rhia disrobing in his front yard. He closed his mouth. Well, he thought, at least she's dressed this time. "What are you doing here?" he asked, once he could remember to ask anything.

"Feeding your horse," she said. "He's hungry."

"How did you know I was here?" he stammered.

Rhia smiled in that way that Vincent found almost irresistible and pushed a lock of her red hair up under the ever-present black hood. "A little bird told me. Actually, it was a pretty big one, wasn't it?"

He raised his eyebrows. "You mean... The hawk... It..."

Before Rhia could stifle her chuckling long enough to answer, a third voice was heard. An irritated voice. "Which one of you did that? Who thinks they're being cute?" The pair looked in the direction of the voice and saw a young man striding across the field toward them. He was dressed in natural colored breeches and a red tunic with puffy sleeves. The tunic looked like silk. Over this he wore a jet black cloak with the hood thrown back. He wore black gloves and black boots that reached halfway up his calves. He was a bit shorter than Vincent, thin, with dark skin, black hair and a short, black moustache and goatee. The man quickly reached them and stood with his arms folded defiantly across his chest. "Well?" he demanded.

Just then, the hawk returned, circling around them. The newcomer held out a gloved hand and the bird alighted. Rhia's eyes widened and she held her hands out, palms up. "I'm terribly sorry," she said. "I had no idea."

"You just go about grabbing any bird you see?" the stranger shrilled. "You *should* be sorry!"

"It was only for a moment," she pleaded. "Sincerely, I meant no harm. And your friend looks none the worse for wear."

He stroked the bird's back. "He has a headache! And so do I!"

"Again, my apologies. How can I make it up to you? Let me give you something for the pain..."

The stranger waved it off. "Never mind. It will pass soon enough."

"What the hell are you two talking about?" Vincent yelled.

This caused the others to cease their discussion. The newcomer looked Vincent over, then turned back to Rhia. "Who's he?"

Rhia smiled graciously. "A friend. It was for him I was searching, and I am very grateful to your friend for his assistance."

The young man frowned slightly, then mumbled to himself, staring at the ground. "Well," he finally said aloud. "You're welcome. I'm glad we could help." He turned to the bird. "It wasn't so bad, was it?" In reply, the bird reached over and poked him in the nose with the blunt part of its beak. The man smiled and turned back to Rhia. "Well and good. No harm done. Good day, then." He nodded to both, then turned to leave.

"Wait," Rhia said.

The man turned. "Yes?"

Rhia smiled. "Would you be willing to accept some company?"

The man frowned, and Vincent did likewise. He pulled Rhia around to face him. "What are you up to?" he whispered. "We don't know anything about him! How do you know we can trust him?"

The witch whispered back. "If we couldn't, he'd already have attacked us, after what I did with his familiar."

"His who?"

"I'll tell you later. But he could be of great assistance to us."

"What's this 'us' stuff? Since when are you joining me?"

"Since right now," she said, and turned back to face the stranger.

The man approached again, a thoughtful expression on his face. "I certainly would not mind keeping company with you," he said to Rhia. "But I am not so certain of him."

"I assure you," she replied as Vincent started to bristle, "that he is completely trustworthy."

The stranger now looked Vincent over. "I do not know," he said. "I have never liked his type."

Vincent could no longer hold back his indignation. "And just what type is that?" he demanded.

"The type that tends to think with a sword," he replied. Then he turned to Rhia. "There are, admittedly, times when they are useful, but..."

"I understand," she said. "But Vincent is not typical of the breed."

The stranger looked at Vincent, then held out his hand. "Vincent. Pleased to meet you." With a frown, Vincent grasped his hand and shook. Then the stranger grasped Rhia's hand and kissed it. "And you are...?"

"Rhia," she spoke.

"Rhia," he repeated. "And you may call me Jaz." He smiled broadly.

Vincent bit back several musically sarcastic retorts, unable to decide which to use. Instead, he said, "No offense to either of you, but I had intended for my journey to be of a solo nature."

Jaz nodded. "Very well. I wish you good fortune." And he turned his attention back to Rhia, who smiled at him apologetically.

"Again, I am sorry," she said. She reached out a hand to stroke the bird's head. He warily allowed her to do so. She smiled at Jaz, who nodded politely to the pair, then turned and strode away. When he was out of earshot, Rhia turned to Vincent. "What bothers you?" she asked.

Vincent stared at the grass beneath their feet, then lifted his face. But he refused to make eye contact with her. "As I said, I'd planned on being alone for a while."

Rhia raised an eyebrow, then glanced at the provisions and equipment strapped to his horse. "How long were you planning on being gone?"

He shrugged. "I'm not sure."

"How well do you know how to live off the land?" When he hesitated, she said, "I thought so." Vincent continued to remain quiet. Finally, she hit the nail on the head. "You're upset with me."

The accusation was like a slap in the face. Vincent looked at her and realized it was true. He felt ashamed. "I suppose I am. To a degree." He paused, then dove into it. "I mean, you show up at my place one night, telling me that your powers are at a height and we might be able to divine something. Then you proceed to get naked in my front yard, have me strip, too... And then you take me through this dream that wasn't a dream, after all, and tell me that I've had sex with a witch! And I don't even remember it!"

Rhia ignored his rising voice. "You make it sound like having sex with a witch is abhorrent to you."

That took the wind out of his sails. He looked at her and felt a stirring inside, remembering all too clearly how he felt the last time they were together. "No," he sighed. "That's not a word that springs to mind." He closed his eyes for a moment. "The abhorrent part is the method in which it was done. I don't like the idea of being used that way." Then he firmed his tone. "And I don't like the fact that you just up and disappear on me for months at a time. I mean, we learned something that night. Something important. And instead of trying to learn more about it, you vanish. How is that supposed to make me feel?"

Rhia nodded in understanding. "I'm sorry. You must believe me, though, when I tell you that I left in order to learn more about it all."

"Well, that's fine. But why am I always left in the dark? Why do I never know what you've discovered?"

She smiled sadly. "I've been remiss, haven't I? To be honest, I was unable to learn much. I had hoped to be able to determine Darella's location. I was unsuccessful. Wherever she is, she is well hidden."

Blaise chose this moment to come prancing up to them, soaking wet and with something in her mouth. She bent her head and dropped the something at Vincent's feet, then looked up at him expectantly, tail wagging. It was a fish. A big one, still flopping feebly in its last minutes of life. Vincent laughed. "I've got a fisher dog!" He smirked and looked back at Rhia. "And me without any Old Bay seasoning."

Blaise then shook herself dry, showering the pair. The situation lightened Vincent's mood. He gave Rhia an apologetic look. "Can I interest you in lunch?" he asked, hefting the fish. She smiled and nodded in response.

While Vincent built a fire, Rhia prepared the meal, which consisted of the fish, some of Vincent's supply of biscuits, and the blueberries he'd picked.

"I know you said you wished to be alone on this expedition," Rhia said. "But may I accompany you for a few days?"

Vincent shrugged. "I don't suppose that's too much to ask. Why?"

"I can show you the forest. Teach you things. Help you to learn to live off the land."

He hefted a handful of berries. "I think I'm doing okay," he said.

"Did you *know* those berries were safe to eat, or did you just guess?"

"Well, they just looked like a berry from back home."

"But you're not back home, Vincent. You might find two bushes or trees within arm's reach of each other, both with tiny berries that look very much alike. One can be a tasty morsel, the other could be a mouthful of poison. You don't know the difference. But I do. And I can teach you."

Vincent nodded. His ego could be grand at times, but he never let that get in the way of the truth. "You're right. That's a good point."

"And then there are the creatures of the forest. I can teach you which snakes to ignore and which to avoid."

"I'll avoid all of them, thanks."

"Fine. But all of them may not avoid you. I'll tell you how to identify the more dangerous variety."

"Okay! I concede the advantage of all this. Teach me whatever you like. I'll be grateful."

Rhia smiled. "Good. We'll get started after we eat. We'll cover the area around the clearing."

Vincent nodded his approval, then accepted the portion of fish Rhia served him. They ate in silence, Vincent trying to ignore the way Rhia looked at him. Instead, he watched Blaise splashing in the stream.

When they were done, they cleaned their plates and utensils, then began their study of the area.

"Very good," Rhia said, as they came upon a small tree. "Notice this plant." Vincent did so. It was about eight feet tall, its branches going up from the ground as though sprayed from a fountain. There were bluish berries on some of the branches. "Note the leaves," she said. "Broad at the base, then quickly tapering to a point. Sharp edges," she pointed to the serration, "and green." Then she indicated the berries. "The fruits are on one big, flat hand."

Vincent nodded.

"Don't eat them."

"Poison?"

"No," she said. "They just taste terrible. Might upset your stomach, too." She moved on to another tree. "Now," she said, "look this one over."

This tree was about fifteen feet in height, with a noticeable trunk. The trunk split almost immediately into two, then three vertical trunks or branches, before spreading out into a fairly standard branch pattern. This tree, too, had bluish berries.

"Note the leaves on this one," she said. In addition to being red, the leaves were oval-shaped, also serrated, but not as sharply. "And the berries," she added. These were hung in smaller clusters than those on the other tree.

Rhia plucked a few and handed them to him. He popped them in his mouth and chewed. They were slightly sweet and juicy, but not particularly exciting. Rhia nodded. "They'll certainly do when you're hungry, but they're not something to go out of your way to find, otherwise."

They walked on further. Rhia pointed out different plants to him, mentioning different uses other than food. These didn't interest him as much, since they usually required processing of different parts of them to get the useful stuff out.

Suddenly, Rhia stopped. She gave him a big smile. "You're in for a treat, now," she said, and pointed up into the branches of another tree. About twenty feet off the ground, in the branches of an otherwise plain-looking tree, were oddly shaped, green fruits. They almost looked like big, green peanuts, about four to six inches in length, but smooth-skinned, not coarse like a peanut's shell. "Give me a leg up," she said.

Vincent cupped his hands and she stepped into them. He boosted her up to grab a low branch and watched her climb nimbly up to the fruits. She began plucking as many as she could reach, dropping them down to him. He caught them, piling them on the ground. Rhia descended rapidly, jumping the last few feet to land beside him.

"So what are these?"

"They're called Mina Loba. And they're delicious." Rhia pulled out a knife from a sheath on her hip, then sliced one of the fruits down the middle. She pulled it open. Inside, the pulp was soft and yellow, with several shiny brown, oblong seeds. She dug her fingers in, pulled out a wad of the flesh, and ate it. "Mmmm."

Vincent smiled at her obvious pleasure. Then she dug her fingers in again and held it out to his mouth. He hesitated only a moment, then allowed her to feed him, quickly scooping the fruit off her fingers with his lips. Then his eyes widened. It *was* delicious. "It tastes like custard!" he said, swallowing the fruit.

"You didn't get it all," Rhia said, still holding her fingers in front of his face. She poked them into his mouth again, and he sucked off the remainder. She allowed her digits to linger, smiling as he cleaned them. He felt somewhat uncomfortable, especially at the way she was smiling. He stopped sucking.

Rhia gave a quiet chuckle and withdrew her fingers. Then she removed her cloak, piled the remainder of the fruit inside, and hoisted the makeshift sack over her shoulder. Then she turned abruptly and continued onward.

They explored this way for nearly two hours before returning to the campsite. By the time they had finished, Vincent was able to recognize no fewer than ten types of edible fruits and an equal number of those to avoid. They'd seen no snakes, though. Not that he minded that a bit.

They stoked up the fire again and sat near it, talking about their exploration until long after the sun went down. "In the Season of Green," Rhia said, "you have the added benefit of being able to distinguish the plants by their flowers. We'll have to come back again for you to see that."

He agreed with her as his mind wandered away from the subject of local biology. He kept wondering what Rhia was driving at. The way she'd practically forced him to suck on her fingers. The way she'd looked at him, then. And naturally, he couldn't help but think of their last encounter.

The temperature dropped quickly. Vincent unrolled his sleeping sack, wishing once more for a nice, comfy pillow to go with it. Rhia had produced a simple bedroll from her pack. It seemed awfully thin to Vincent, and he hoped she'd be warm enough. Then he chided himself for his concern. She knew what she was doing. He couldn't argue that point.

Rhia walked over to a large bush a few yards away and pulled several leafy stalks from it. She returned to the fire and thrust the leafy ends into the flames. Then she walked around the perimeter of their little campsite, waving the smoking branches in a sweeping motion. When she had completed this, she tossed them onto the fire. "The leaves of this plant, when burned, will keep insects away for hours," she explained.

Vincent nodded. One more thing he had learned from her. He turned his attention to matters at hand. The horse had been unloaded and was tied to a tree on the other side of the fire. He had grazed to his content in the clearing. Blaise was curled up near the fire, too, perfectly happy. Nothing more to be done except go to bed. Well, one more thing, he thought, as he stepped away from the campsite to relieve his bladder.

When he returned, he saw that Rhia had stripped down to a single, knee-length tunic. She turned at his approach and gave a brief smile. "Call of nature," he said.

Rhia raised an eyebrow as she walked toward her bedroll. She stopped next to him, looking into his eyes. "Nature has many calls," she said, gliding her hand along Vincent's thigh. Then she continued to her sleeping sack.

Once he started breathing again, Vincent stripped down to breeches and tunic and climbed inside his own sleeping sack. He hunkered down inside, trying to keep as much of the forest's night chill out. He glanced over at Rhia. She sat in an upright position with her eyes closed and legs crossed, lotus-style. The glow of the fire lit her face and hair beautifully. He propped himself up on one elbow and stared at her. It was a minute before he realized that she had opened her eyes and was watching him stare at her. He looked back at the fire, embarrassed.

"Tell me about your world, Vincent," she said.

Here we go again, he thought. Between Blade, Gnorrin, Ariaziane, and D'Ty, he'd talked about as much as he wanted to of home. But she was a friend, and it was a simple enough request to grant. He gave a half-smile as he looked at her. "My home town is not far from a forest. Probably about the same distance as my home is from here." He reflected for a moment. "You know, I never once spent any time in it. I was lucky even to spend any time in the many wooded areas around my home. Not forests, but lots of woods. I regret that." He offered the half-smile again. "I wasn't really an outdoorsy type. I just wasn't physically active."

"Why is that?" she asked.

Sensing that this conversation was likely going to last a while, Vincent maneuvered himself into a sitting position, too, drawing his knees up toward his chest. "I was overweight. I had no stamina. I preferred staying indoors and reading to being outdoors."

Rhia shook her head. "I can't imagine that. Nothing can compare to being in the midst of Nature."

Vincent chuckled. "Maybe so, but when I was a kid, I couldn't tolerate even going barefoot outside."

Her eyes widened. "You must be jesting."

"Nope. Tender feet. Hated the idea of running through the yard without shoes on. Always afraid I'd step on a stone or a stick. My friends couldn't believe it, either." He smirked. "I was quite the recluse, really."

Rhia hit him with a level gaze. "And yet, here you are, forging your way through a strange forest, oblivious to the dangers."

Vincent shrugged. "Things are different now."

"How so?"

"I'm not fat anymore." And he felt a surge in his chest at that. "Yeah, I have to say the one thing I'm truly grateful for is that fact. I'm not in great shape, but I'm a damn sight better than I was."

"I find nothing wrong with the shape you're in."

Vincent looked away. "Thank you," was all he could say.

She shifted her position slightly. "I ask you again, Vincent. Why are you doing this?"

He was quiet for a long time, avoiding her gaze. He looked at the dog's sleeping form instead, then turned his attention to the fire. Anything but meet eyes with her. Finally, he said, "I just needed some time away."

"You can't get away from your own feelings," she said.

His eyes snapped to her face, astounded that she was reading him so easily. When the shock wore off, he said, "No. But I can take my mind off them for a while."

"Can you?"

He turned away again, offering no reply. Rhia stood and moved over to the fire. She poked around, stoking the blaze, and added a few more branches to it. Vincent found his eyes moving over her body. As she crouched near the fire, her tunic clung tightly to her curves.

He frowned as he thought of what he was feeling. He loved Ariaziane. He had no doubt of that. When he thought of her, he ached in his heart. She was beautiful and fun and he would rather be with her than do anything else. He did not, however, have lustful feelings about her. It was almost as though those types of thoughts were beneath him. Impure.

On the other hand, he couldn't deny that he *did* have lustful thoughts about Rhia. And he felt guilty about the fact. He had an idea of how Rhia probably felt about sex. She was a witch. Very earthy, very natural. She was probably able to separate sex from love very easily, treating sex as something for its own sake. Vincent wasn't sure he could do that. It wasn't how he was raised to think of it.

He snapped out of his reverie to find Rhia standing beside him. He looked up at her, trying not to stare at the shape beneath the tunic. Suddenly, she turned away and approached her bedroll. She gathered it up and moved it next to Vincent's. Then she crouched down, arranging it neatly. When it was to her liking, she climbed inside, lying to face him.

"Why are you doing this?" he asked.

"Doing what?"

"Rhia, you've been sort of hitting on me all day."

She shook her head in confusion. "Hitting on you? What does that mean?"

"You know. Flirting. Teasing, sort of. Sexually."

"Is there something wrong with this?"

"I just want to know why you're doing it."

Rhia stared at him. "Isn't it obvious?"

His heart skipped a beat. "Well, it does rather point in a particular direction, yes. But..."

"But what?"

Vincent struggled with several responses, then finally said, "Rhia, I can't. My heart belongs to Ariaziane."

"Ariaziane can have your heart, Vincent. I'm not interested in that part." She reached out and stroked his arm. He made a move to withdraw it, but she grasped it firmly. "I know you find me desirable," she said. "I've always known it. Even before you so blatantly displayed it, within the candle-circle."

Vincent's cheeks flushed as she stroked his arm. "Rhia... Please..."

"If nothing had come of the divination that night," she continued, "I'd planned other activities."

Vincent yanked his arm away from her. "Enough!" He calmed himself, then apologized. "I'm sorry. I didn't mean to yell. But, please stop." He sighed. "Yes, I do find you attractive. And I'm more flattered than you can imagine that you find me so. But I can't do it like you can. I love Annie. And it would be wrong to... You know... Engage in those other activities with you." He shrugged. "Maybe I'm just naïve, but I've always felt that someone's first time should be an act of love, not lust."

Rhia gazed at him for a long time, then she said, "As you wish, Vincent. I shall stop... hitting on you."

"It would make my life easier. Thank you."

"However, I think I like having my bed next to yours, if you don't mind."

Vincent hesitated, wondering if she planned to make a move on him during the night. Then he reprimanded himself for being so suspicious. Blaise chose that moment to come snuffling over. She stepped between them and stretched out. Vincent chuckled. "My guard dog," he said. "She's here to protect me from you."

Rhia smiled and stroked the animal. "Good night, Vincent."

"You never did get around to telling me why it was that you were looking for me in the first place," he said.

She shrugged. "Is it not enough that I simply wanted to see you?"

"It's not that it isn't enough. I just don't happen to believe it."

Rhia propped herself up to face him. "I had intended to help you find out more about how you came here. I'd intended to inquire if you'd had any further dreams or other visions."

"Then why haven't you?"

"Because I sense that the desire isn't as strong within you, now. It is as though something else had become more important to you."

Vincent cast his gaze to the ground and stared at nothing for a long while. When he looked up again, Rhia was lying peacefully, eyes closed. "Good night," he whispered. Then he snuggled up close to Blaise and wrapped an arm around her. She licked his face. Sleep was not soon in coming.

In the middle of the night, he woke. The hoot of an owl had roused him. Blaise was no longer beside him, he noted. And with a start, he realized his arm was now draped around Rhia. In fact, they were snuggled against each other, spoon fashion. His arm was held snugly between her arm and her body, as if she meant to keep it there. He made an attempt to remove it, but this caused Rhia to stir. She turned her head to face him, partially opened her eyes, and smiled. She twined her fingers around those of his captured hand, raised his hand to her lips, and kissed it. Then she snuggled up closer to him and returned to sleep.

For a moment, Vincent didn't know what to do. Then he realized there was little he really could do. And snuggling with her was comfortably warm and cozy. He sighed, then settled back in to sleep.

Two days later, the pair reached the first of the forest's rivers. Along the way, Rhia continued to teach Vincent of the different plants of the forest. She showed him more that were edible, more that were not, and more that had medicinal values. Along the edge of the river, she delighted in finding one particular plant. It was a couple feet high, with a hairy stem, bristly, oblong leaves, and lilac-colored flowers. "The flowers are often whitish," she said. "But they are unimportant except to aid you in identifying the plant. We call it the Healing Herb."

She pulled her knife and began digging around the base of the plant, uprooting it. "The roots are the parts you'll want to use." The roots were black-skinned, and when she cut one open, he saw it was glutinous inside. "If you chop the fresh rootstock, add a bit of hot water and wrap it in a fresh cloth, you'll have a poultice for use on sores, bug bites, and other external wounds." She began uprooting more of the plants. "Boiling a piece of root as big as your finger in a mugful of water for several minutes will give you a wash with which you can treat sore throats, bleeding around the teeth, and so on. Or, drinking it will help with stomach problems, and problems you menfolk don't have to worry about." She stashed away chunks of the roots in her pouches. "But the dried root, when powdered, is probably the most useful. A small amount, when consumed, will help soothe coughs, and dry up runny stool. And when applied directly to cuts and other external injuries, will stop the bleeding and hasten healing." She smiled as she finished packing the stuff away. "A very useful little thing, wouldn't you agree?"

"Sure sounds it," Vincent said. He was studying the river, trying to determine how to cross it. It wasn't a big creek, it was a full-blown river. Not a huge one, but plenty big. Finally, he turned to Rhia. "How do we go about crossing this thing?"

"We don't," she said. Vincent looked at her stupidly. "My path will take me south, with the river. I sense your journey will take you north, however," she said. "You will find a ferry to take you across. Another day's travel at moderate pace."

"I see. How much is the fare?"

Rhia laughed. "Oh, there is no fare. No one to pay it to. This is a small ferry you operate yourself, with ropes and pulleys attached to trees on either side. This forest does not bear enough traffic to warrant a ferryman."

Vincent nodded. He gazed longingly at the water and scratched his scalp. "I would absolutely love a bath. And I'd kill for some shampoo."

"Some what?"

"Stuff to wash my hair with."

"Oh." Vincent watched as she unshouldered her pack. She pulled out a clay bottle and handed it to him. "That should do well. And I agree, a bath sounds lovely." She began removing her clothes.

Vincent turned his back, his heart quickening. He wondered why he'd even brought it up. But the shampoo in his fist reminded him. He uncorked the bottle and looked inside. There was a white, creamy liquid with a pleasant scent. It appeared thick, too. He corked it back up and put it aside. He *did* need a bath something fierce. Let modesty be damned.

He heard a splash as Rhia entered the river. The current was slow at this point on the water. "It's very nice," she called. And that was all the enticement he needed. He threw off his clothes, placed his glasses atop the pile, grabbed the shampoo, and jumped in.

Ah, luxury! The water was like silk against his skin. It was warm enough, having had the sun beating on it all day long. He dunked his head and brought it out, shaking the water off. At this point, he heard another splash and saw Blaise paddling around, happy as could be.

Rhia was suddenly near him, her hand on his shoulder. He jumped, as much as he could jump while trying to keep his head above water. She took the shampoo from him, poured out a handful. He did likewise. And it felt wonderful.

"It has snakeroot," Rhia said a few minutes later as he finished rinsing it from his clean hair. "For my hair. It makes its color more pronounced. It might bring out the red highlights you have, too."

"I don't have red highlights," Vincent argued.

"You certainly do! Especially in your beard."

"Either way, it was wonderful to be able to wash my hair. Thank you very much. How do you make that stuff? I've just been using plain old soap to wash my hair ever since arriving here. It's just not the same."

"I'll show you another time. But you may keep the rest of that bottle, if you like. I'll make more."

"Thank you, again." He smiled. "It's been ages since I went swimming. It feels great!" He gave a kick and took a few strokes away from her.

She matched his movements and caught up. "I like to play in water," she said, and proceeded to dunk him.

He rose from the water, sputtering and wiping his eyes. "Wench," he said, smiling. "I'll get you for that."

"I'm ready for you," she said teasingly. Vincent paused, suddenly aware of her proximity, and her nudity. Very aware. Rhia smiled. "Thank you, again," she said, gazing down into the water. "Are you sure I can't interest you in another sort of play?" She reached out and stroked his chest.

Vincent tore his eyes away from her and backpedaled. He chuckled nervously. "I never said you couldn't interest me," he explained, "just that you should stop trying to convince me."

She smiled and slowly ran her fingers over her own body. "I thought I'd make one more attempt."

He took a shuddering breath and turned away. "Right. Well, I think I've had enough water." He made his way to shore, calling for Blaise, who followed. Once he was back on land, however, he realized that he had no towels. Rhia stepped out and stood next to him. "How are we to dry off?" he asked.

In response, she pointed up to the sky. "It's slow, but it works." And she proceeded to lie down in a sunny part of the grass and close her eyes.

Vincent's heart accelerated. He found himself staring at her. Again. With a sigh, he stretched out, too. The breeze was chill, but the sun was warm.

Rhia opened her eyes and turned her head to face him. "Want to snuggle?"

Vincent hesitated. "I don't think that would be the wisest idea right at the moment."

She glanced lower on his body, then smirked. "Your choice," she said. "But it appears you might find it otherwise." She closed her eyes again and took a nap.

They woke about an hour later, dry and warm. Vincent dressed quickly and made sure everything was in order. He turned to Rhia, now dressed and prepared to go on her way. "All right." He cleared his throat. "I wish you well on your journey."

"And you on yours," she replied.

"When do you think we'll meet up again?"

Rhia shrugged. "Difficult to say," she said. "But I'll try to make it soon."

He smiled. "I'd like that." He gazed upriver again, then turned to face her. "Well. I'd best be going, then."

She moved over to him and clasped his hands. "Be careful. The tribes to the north are not always hospitable. Better to move quietly and invisibly, if you know what I mean."

"Gnorrin warned me, also. Are they really that bad?"

Rhia shrugged again. "Depends what you compare them to." She let go of his hands. "Here," she said, withdrawing a small leather pouch from her cloak. "This is some of the powdered Healing Herb. I always carry some with me. I can make more, now. Remember what I said about it."

Vincent nodded and tucked it into his belt. "Thanks," he said. "For everything."

"You wouldn't accept everything," she said, watching him blush. "Will you at least accept a goodbye kiss?"

"Fair enough." He leaned over, expecting a buss on the cheek. Instead, he found himself the recipient of locked lips and probing tongue. Her teeth gnawed on his lower lip. Then her mouth slid across his cheek and neck, until her lips brushed his ear.

"Farewell," she whispered, and sucked on his earlobe briefly before disengaging. She chuckled softly as he tried to catch his breath, then hitched her pack over her shoulder. "I'll see you soon," she said. With a final scratch behind Blaise's ear, she set off, heading south with the river.

Vincent watched her go, listening to his heart pound in his ears. Blaise gave an inquiring whine as her red-haired friend moved away. "I know," Vincent said. "I feel the same way."

❧ Fourteen ❧

As Rhia had predicted, Vincent came upon the ferry toward the end of the following afternoon. It was really nothing more than a big raft located at a particularly narrow section of the river. Vincent estimated the width at this point to be no more than fifty yards.

A long rope stretched across the water, looped into pulley sets anchored to trees on each side, and attached to both ends of the ferry. He worried about how difficult it would be to pull himself and a loaded horse across the water. But after several unsuccessful attempts to coax the horse onto the raft, he decided that pulling would be the easy part.

Several minutes of cajoling later, the horse finally consented to step onto the creaky wooden structure. Once he was sure the beast wouldn't change his mind, Vincent stepped on, Blaise following. He lifted the rope and gave a test pull, but the ferry didn't budge. "Great," he muttered, then put his back into it. With a lurch, the raft slid from the shore. The pulleys were apparently well designed and in good condition. The ferry skimmed across the river with only moderate effort on his part.

The trip itself wasn't noteworthy. Vincent was concerned mostly with crossing as quickly as possible, hoping the horse wouldn't spook. His fears were unfounded, however. His mount stayed relatively still. Blaise, on the other hand, pranced about, peering over the sides at the moving water. By the time Vincent's arms began to tire, they reached the opposite shore. He gave King a slap on the flank and the horse bounded off, only to stop as soon as he was firmly aground.

A look at the sky told him it was time to find a campsite. The sun would set within two hours and he still needed to gather dinner for them all. There were three well-traveled trails leading off from the ferry "dock." One led south along the river, another north along it. The third continued to the northwest, deeper into the forest. Vincent mounted his horse and headed down the last.

To his great relief, he found a small, rocky clearing after only about a quarter mile. He unloaded his horse and left him to graze on whatever food he could find. After rapidly building a fire inside a circle of stones, he set out to find dinner. An hour later, he returned with a large sack of edible berries and fruits, as well as another of the coon-chucks. He shared the fruit with both animals, then he and Blaise polished off the roasted critter. The sun had set by the time dinner was finished. Vincent smiled, enjoying the fact that there were no dishes to wash.

As he lay in his sleeping sack that night, several thoughts drifted through his mind. The first was that he regretted Rhia having gone her own way. The nights would be colder without her to snuggle against. The second thought was how time had flown. He'd been in this world a year and a half. He couldn't believe it had gone so quickly. And the third was that he was amazingly tired.

He dozed, but not for long. A noise woke him. Opening his heavy lids, he found Blaise lying next to him, head up and alert. Then they heard it again. Voices. Vincent reached out and placed his hand on her muzzle, hoping she wouldn't growl. The last thing he wanted was for the owners of those voices to realize that he was camped here.

Though there was only a hint of flame remaining amongst the embers of his fire, Vincent knew it would be visible from the trail. There was a good deal of moonlight, though, so he might get lucky enough for it to drown out the orange glow of the coals.

The voices grew louder. Vincent eased himself out of his sack and pulled on his boots. He put on his glasses, then quietly drew his sword from its scabbard and stood, prepared for the worst. Prepared mentally, he told himself. But physically, he wasn't so sure. He looked down at Blaise and saw that her fur was ruffled over her shoulders. A low growl began to issue from her throat.

Again he reached for her muzzle. She stopped growling and cast him a concerned look. He stroked her head, then noticed that the voices had ceased. He looked up again, to the edge of the clearing, and his glance took in all necessary information in an instant.

Four men, ranging in age from mid-twenties to forty-ish. Harsh, bearded, dirty, with suspicious eyes. All carried swords, two had crossbows. None were drawn, but the distance between them was too great for him to have any advantage, even though he had sword in hand. Everything about them smelled bad.

The eldest, obviously the leader, spoke. "Well, what have we here, lads? A vicious cutthroat, weapon ready for the attack." He chuckled, and the other three echoed him.

Blaise growled loudly. One of the younger ones eyed her nervously, unslung his crossbow and cocked it, loading a bolt at the same time. "You keep that hound of yours heeled," he warned, aiming the weapon. "I don't care for dogs."

Vincent laid a restraining hand on the animal's neck, hoping she'd obey his wishes. Trouble was, he couldn't quite seem to vocalize them. His throat was frozen with fear. Why was he so afraid? He'd faced worse than this, hadn't he? He'd been caught up in a full-blown battle, had even taken an arrow in the arm, and hadn't been this afraid, then. But this was different, he told himself. Before, he'd had backup in the form of Blade and the others. Or, more accurately, they had backup in the form of him. This situation had no backup, no cavalry. And not much prospect for success, he had to admit.

Seemingly satisfied that the dog wasn't about to attack, the man turned to point his crossbow in Vincent's direction. He spoke to his fellows. "Don't seem quite friendly," he drawled, "for this boy to have a sword drawn against us, does it?"

His comrades murmured their agreement. The oldest stepped forward, coming within a few paces of Vincent. "I think it might be best for you to sheath your sword, young man," he said. "My companion tends to be a bit anxious, if you know what I mean."

Vincent took a deep breath, then stepped over to his sheath, carefully inserted the sword, and let it drop to the grass. Then he turned to face the group, stepping deliberately in front of Blaise, not wanting her to incite any unnecessary bloodshed. Notably, his own.

He looked carefully at the leader, sizing the man up. He was about Vincent's height, probably stronger, and definitely more experienced. He had a dagger tucked into the front of his belt. It was sheathed, but not strapped in. "Very well," he said, forcing the words. "What do you want?"

The leader stepped over to him and smiled through stained teeth. "What do you have?"

182

"This," Vincent said, and drove his fist into the man's nose. He ignored the man's curses of pain and anger and felt the blood splatter onto his hand as he quickly reached down to seize the man's dagger. He snatched it from its sheath, simultaneously spinning the man around. He held the blade up to the man's throat. "Drop it!" he warned the one with the crossbow. "Hands up!" he said to the others.

The crossbow had just begun to be lowered when Vincent's temporary prisoner plunged his elbow deep into Vincent's stomach. As the wind rushed out of his lungs, everything seemed to happen at once. The man ducked away, the crossbow came back up, Blaise leaped through the air, and the crossbow bolt slammed into Vincent's forearm.

He gasped in pain, dropped to his knees, and looked at the wound. The bolt was stuck in his arm, seemingly right between the bones. Not again, he thought. Then his mind swam, everything becoming a blur. He heard Blaise barking and growling, a man screaming, then a dull thud, Blaise's yelp, and silence. He gritted his teeth, shaking his head to bring himself back to awareness. In front of him, he saw Blaise sprawled on the ground, blood on her head. Rage flared up inside him and he surged to his feet, only to have the point of a sword thrust in front of his face.

He staggered, weak from his wound, and was soon surrounded by the four. One of them appeared to have bite marks on his face. Vincent realized it was the man who had shot him. He smiled, then his stomach sank. His glance flicked to the dog. She still wasn't moving. Tears stung his eyes.

The leader's face hovered into view, blood-covered and angry, his nose most definitely broken. "Right," breathed the man. "Let's see if you take as good as you give."

Before he knew what was coming, Vincent found himself flying backward, stars shooting behind his eyes. He landed hard, jarring the crossbow bolt. He felt himself slipping into shock from the combined pain, but he fought it off. His face had gone numb and tears were streaming down his cheeks. I will *not* pass out, he told himself, fighting down the waves of pain coming from his arm and his nose and trying to stand. Then a wave of pain reared up inside him. I *won't* pass out, he denied again.

So he threw up. *Then* he passed out.

Something wet was on his face. Then it was gone. Then it was back. And gone again. And back.

Vincent's head pounded madly as he stirred. What was that disgusting taste in his mouth? Oh, right. He'd tossed his cookies. His face throbbed, as did his arm. Carefully, he opened his eyes. The wet thing was hanging in front of his face. It was Blaise's tongue. She licked him again.

Despite his pain, he felt his heart leap inside him. He struggled to a sitting position and stroked her face. "Good girl," he soothed. "I thought you were dead." He closed his eyes again and let her lick his face. When her tongue flicked over a bare eyelid, he knew his glasses must have gone flying when the man decked him. He opened his eyes again and looked around.

Every movement brought some sort of pain to him. In a way, it was a relief. "I hurt. Therefore, I am," he mumbled. Then he chuckled to himself. "*Agony ergo sum.*"

He looked up at the gibbous moon, thankful for its light. He sat for a moment, reorienting himself. The bolt was still embedded in his right arm. His pulse raced, causing the arm to throb. He knew he'd have to remove the bolt, but recalled the last time he'd plucked an arrow from a body part. He didn't want to pass out again. He decided to let it wait a few minutes.

He lifted his left hand to gingerly feel his nose. To his surprise, he found it didn't hurt much. Evidently, he'd gotten lucky. It might actually not be broken. He felt dried blood in his mustache and beard. And further down, a sticky substance that was semi-dry vomit. He looked around for a pool of it, finding it a couple feet away. The nasty gentlemen must have rolled him. Since he'd been sleeping when they arrived, they weren't likely to find much on him. Then, panicked, he felt for the necklace. He sighed. It was still there, caked under a layer of drying puke. No wonder they didn't take it. He noticed, though, that his ring was gone. "Shit," he said. Then he sobered.

He realized he'd been fortunate in a far more vital way. Much to his surprise, he was alive. Why hadn't the men killed him? Possibly they wished to leave him empty-handed in the middle of a forest, assuming he'd suffer more that way. That could be true, he realized, or there could have been another reason. Most likely he'd never know.

Vincent turned his thoughts to more urgent matters. Glasses. He needed them. Carefully, he made his way over to where he'd seen the vomit. Doubtless they'd fallen off somewhere near there. After several minutes of searching, his hand found them. But as he picked them up, his heart sank. They were broken. One of the men must have stepped on them. More like *stomped* on them, he thought, since both arms were snapped from the frames. One lens was cracked. The other was intact, but that did him little good. "Damn," he whispered. "Now what am I gonna do?" In anger, he hurled the broken eyewear into the trees.

By instinct, Vincent used his right arm to throw the glasses. Unfortunately, this was the arm with a crossbow bolt stuck through it. He felt the color drain from his face as his jaw dropped. His eyes widened, but no sound came from his mouth. Two things amazed him: the amount of pain generated by the throw, and the amount of stupidity generated by his brain. He stood there, gasping, blinking tears from his eyes.

"Okay," he said to himself and the dog when he regained his senses. "Aside from my mind, let's see what else I've lost." He searched as much as possible, making a mental list. His sword and scabbard were gone. No surprise. The horse was absent, too. Again, no surprise. He went through the packs that lay on the ground. His pouch of money was gone, naturally. No biggie. He had more where that came from. The healing potion of Gnorrin's, also gone. Could have really used that right about now, he thought. On the other hand, he still had the shampoo and Healing Herb from Rhia. They'd been tucked away separately from the others, after she'd given them to him. All other weapons were gone, even the knife he kept in his boot. Going through his clothing, piled beside his sleeping sack, his heart skipped a beat. His cloak pin. The one Ariaziane had had made for him as a birthday present. It was gone.

Anger swelled in him. The money he could afford to lose. Even the ring. The horse was a major loss. But the cloak pin was far too important to him. "Damn!" he repeated, and made a silent vow to find the men. He would not allow them to take any gift of Ariaziane's from him. He turned to Blaise, summoning her to follow him, and made his way down the trail back to the river.

He was glad for the darkness at the moment. His vision wasn't very good without his glasses. The astigmatism made everything blurry, even disregarding the nearsightedness. Unless he tried to look at the stars, the effect wasn't too bad at night, everything being difficult to discern already from the darkness.

At the river, he saw the ferry was still on the near side, telling him that the thieves hadn't come this way. He stopped at the river's edge and stripped. He looked at the bolt in his arm and sighed. Not yet. He carefully tore the sleeves from his tunic, then ripped them into strips. It was a painful process, and he clenched his jaw against the pain with every rip. Finally, he set the makeshift bandages aside, and waded into the river. Blaise followed him to the edge, but did not go in. Vincent soaked his punctured arm in the cold water while rinsing himself of blood and other unpleasant substances. When he was done, he edged over to shore, where Blaise sat.

He picked up the sleeveless shirt and soaked it. Then he sponged at the back of the dog's head. The shirt came back bloody. He continued this until no more blood came. Then he opened the pouch of Healing Herb and sprinkled some into her injury. He smiled. "Good girl," he said. The dog obligingly let him perform the deed without complaint.

When he was done, he turned his attention to his arm. "Guess there's no more putting this off, is there?" he asked no one. The cold water of the river had somewhat numbed his arm. The coagulated blood was wet, now, and partially dissolved. This would make it easier to remove the bolt. By a smidgen. He was at least grateful that the bolt did not have a barbed tip, but was instead simply sharpened to a point. Vincent took a deep breath, grasped the bolt as firmly as possible with his left hand, and yanked.

Mercifully, the bolt came clear on the first pull. The pain, however, defied description. Vincent felt himself beginning to swoon, and immediately dunked his head in the cold water. The jolt kept him from passing out. His teeth were clenched as he lifted his soaking head. A growl that Blaise would have envied escaped his lips.

He allowed the cold water to soak into the wound for some time, gingerly probing it with his fingers enough to allow the water to enter. Finally, he left the river and sat on the bank. After applying the Healing Herb liberally, working it into both sides of the wound, he reached over and cupped some water into one hand, poured the powdered herb into it, and made a paste. Once both ends of the puncture were plugged with this, Vincent wrapped the strips of tunic sleeve around his forearm, tying them with his teeth and left hand. When he was done, he sat there, his knees drawn up, arms across them. He rested his head on his arms. The pain and the anger took his mind off the chill of the night wind on his already cold skin.

Back at his campsite, exhaustion won out over anger and pain. Vincent collapsed into his sack and slept until morning. When he woke, he was surprised to find himself in only a little pain. His nose felt better, though it stung to touch it. His arm was only a mild throb. His most profound complaint was how blurry the world had become.

He put the thought out of his mind and turned to matters at hand. By all rights, he should leave the forest and strike out for civilization. Without weapons, he had little faith in getting food for himself and Blaise. Then again, being without money, it might be hard to get food even if he did find civilization. Then he shook his head. Who did he think he was fooling? He had no intention of leaving the forest until he'd caught up with the four men who'd stolen Ariaziane's gift from him. Within minutes, he'd packed up his remaining belongings and headed back out to the trail.

He went immediately to the crossroads of the trails near the river and studied them. The men could have crossed the river, then sent the ferry back to the other side with the pulleys. But he didn't give them credit enough to think of that. This left three options. North or south along the river, or northwest, the direction he'd been heading, himself.

North was definitely out of the question. The men had passed by his campsite, which was off the north-south trail. If they'd come from the northwest, there would be no reason to turn back north again. South was a possibility. But from his maps, Vincent knew that the river eventually took a sharp turn to the southwest. So if the men had come from the northwest, as they seemingly had, this meant that they would go south, then bear back westwards. Like a big semicircle. Didn't make much sense. Then again, he thought, if they'd come from the south and then turned northwest, it stood to reason that they'd originally come from a southwestern direction and were making the same semicircle, but in reverse. He sighed in frustration. Either one, he thought, could be the right answer. Or neither.

"Well, what do you think, girl? Which direction did they go?" The dog looked up at him. Vincent frowned, wondering if she could detect the scents of the men. He was sure she could, but didn't know how to make her understand what he wanted her to do.

He thought for a moment, then decided to play Charades, of a sort. He kept the dog's attention, reached out and lightly touched her head wound. She pulled away, looking warily at him. He scowled at her. Then he held out his wounded arm for her to inspect, and he growled slightly. Blaise looked at him, with what he hoped was a glimmer of understanding in her eyes. Then he pointed away from them, down the south trail. "Get 'em!" he urged.

Blaise barked and jumped, then headed toward the south trail. Vincent stood in the crossroads and watched her. She sniffed the ground on the trail, headed in a few yards, sniffing all the way. She stopped. Then she came back, repeating the process on the north trail. Again she came back, turning her attention to the trail leading to the northwest. She sniffed more, here. Finally, she barked and headed off toward where they'd made camp. Vincent hoped that wasn't what she smelled, as he trotted behind. But his concerns were unfounded. Blaise ran past the site of their camp, and he increased his pace to keep up with her.

He took some pleasure in the fact that this was the direction he'd been heading in the first place. Catching up to the rogues wouldn't require him to go out of his way. Not that he had any idea what he was going to do, once he did catch up to them. But he'd think of something.

As it turned out, Vincent had plenty of time to think of something. Most of it was spent thinking about his discomfort. His arm throbbed, though not as badly as he had expected, and his lower back was rather displeased with him for some reason. Not to mention the fact that, after several hours of travel, his stomach began to growl.

Catching something to eat was virtually impossible without any weapons. Had they been traveling the trail along the river, there would have been the chance that Blaise might catch some fish. But even that slim chance was denied them. Vincent gathered what edibles he could from the plant life near the trail. It seemed precious little to feed the both of them.

The worst part of the experience was his eyesight. His head was throbbing from the strain of trying to distinguish things. He couldn't tell what kind of plant one was unless he was quite close to it. True, there were no road signs he'd have to read while driving by at high speeds, as there would have been back on Earth. But that was little comfort. They traveled all day, resting frequently, and continued into the night. He found that nighttime was when he most regretted the loss of his glasses. The stars, which should have been bright pinpoints of light, were now fuzzy, diffused things. Not stars at all. He found this more depressing than he would've imagined.

Sleep was taken in small doses, a few hours at a time. Vincent knew that his prey had many hours head start on him. Assuming they'd keep a typical sleep schedule, he hoped to gain a few hours a day on them. He relied on his body's internal clock to wake him after a few hours nap. The only thought that plagued him concerned their mode of transportation. Although he hadn't seen any horses when they'd entered his clearing, that didn't mean they didn't have them. If they'd had mounts waiting for them, in addition to his own stolen horse, then it was doubtful he'd ever catch them on foot.

On the third day of his quest, they arrived at another crossroads. The trail, still heading northwest, intersected with another trail that headed southwest and northeast. Without prompting, Blaise immediately sniffed out the two new paths. Vincent noted without surprise that she didn't pursue either of the new trails. He resumed his northwest trek. But Blaise halted on the trail a few yards past the intersection. She sniffed the ground in a circle, from side to side. She looked up at Vincent with a soft whine. Then she continued sniffing the ground. Vincent watched her, his brow furrowed with concern. They couldn't have just disappeared, he told himself. Or could they?

Just as he was about to concede the possibility, Blaise let out a low bark and wagged her tail. Vincent looked to where she stood, at the north side of the trail, near the edge. He walked closer and saw that there were, indeed, signs of passage. A bit of trampled undergrowth. Bent fronds of tall plants. "Good girl," he said. But inside, he frowned. It was one thing to travel through a forest on a trail. It was quite another to blaze the trail. He looked down at the dog. "Ready when you are, boss." At his urging, Blaise stepped off the trail, following the scent. Vincent sighed and followed.

If Vincent had asked Blade to teach him more than just swordsmanship, he might have been able to track the four men who'd wronged him. If he hadn't lost his glasses, he might even be able to track them to a small degree, even without Blade's tutelage. As it was, he was wholly reliant on his dog's keen nose. As he followed her through the trees, he hoped it would be enough.

To his best estimate, they were traveling due north. He couldn't help but be concerned that he might be walking into a nasty situation. Perhaps the four were members of some sort of larger group of mercenaries and somewhere up ahead was where their conclave was located. Great, he thought. That would be just what he needed.

A squint at the sky told him it was late afternoon. If he was going to be raiding a bad guy hideout, he thought, he needed to be well rested. Finding a relatively comfy tree to rest against, he settled in for a nap, Blaise lying alertly next to him.

He woke hours later. The forest was growing dark, the sun nearly set. The light filtering through the trees was faint and red. Vincent rubbed his eyes and stretched, massaging his stiff neck muscles. He looked around for Blaise.

"Good evening," said a voice.

Vincent started, then whirled to find the source. Blaise came prancing over to him, licking his face. Straining around her happy head, Vincent saw a figure seated up against another tree. Recognition took a moment. "Jaz," he said. "What brings you here?" he asked suspiciously. He couldn't help but wonder if the man were in cahoots with the four who'd waylaid him.

"I was about to ask you the same question. Though I think I might be able to guess." He smiled politely. "You looked much healthier when last we met. And better equipped."

Vincent sighed. "That's for sure." He briefly told him how he'd come to be in his current state. Jaz listened intently throughout the story. "And so," he concluded, "I thought I'd follow them to try to get back my stuff."

Jaz raised an eyebrow. "Your what?"

"My possessions," he explained.

"You use some unusual language, Vincent. I get a strange feeling about you. As you slept, I watched you. While getting to know your dog," he added. "And a fine and friendly animal she is." He smiled. "But something about you just seemed unusual. You seemed so out of place, sitting there under the tree. I'm not sure I know why." Vincent did not respond to the man's lead, so Jaz changed the subject. "How did the thieves manage to miss that magical necklace?"

Vincent frowned. "How did you know it was magical?"

Jaz raised an eyebrow again. "How do you think?"

"I have no idea," he replied.

The dark-skinned man eyed him strangely, the hint of a smile playing at the corners of his mouth. "You're jesting, yes?" Seeing Vincent's frustration, he frowned. "No, you are not. Did you not know I am a mage?"

The boy shook his head. "No, I guess I didn't." He paused for a moment. "Where's your bird?"

"Oh, up and about, somewhere."

"You let him fly around free? Aren't you afraid he won't come back?'

Jaz chuckled slightly. "You are on the simple side, aren't you?" As Vincent's cheeks reddened, the mage held up a hand. "I did not mean that in the way you seem to be taking it. Simply that you are unlearned in sophisticated things."

"That wasn't much of an improvement."

"I do apologize. The bird is not my pet, as you seem to be thinking. He is my familiar. What that means is that we share a bond. I can see through his eyes. I feel what he feels."

"That explains why Rhia was so apologetic." A thought struck him, then. "You see what the bird sees."

"Correct."

"Can he detect any sign of the four buttwipes who kayoed me?"

Jaz smiled. "Your words are strange, but I understand your meaning. And yes. The four have joined up with a large group of their fellows approximately twenty minutes walk from here."

Vincent sighed. "I was afraid of that. How many are there?"

"Oh, not more than thirty."

"Shit," Vincent said, smacking his hand onto the ground. He felt the blood drain from his face as the pain from his wound lanced up into his brain. He gnashed his teeth together and swore at his own idiocy.

"What were your plans?" asked Jaz.

Vincent recovered from his pain. "I didn't really have any," he confessed. "All I know is that they stole my things, and I'm going to get them back."

Jaz rubbed his chin. "That's one of the shortcomings of you warriors."

Ignoring the label, the boy replied, "What? That we don't make plans?"

"Exactly. Also, that you're unable to handle thirty antagonists."

Vincent eyed him suspiciously. "You mean to say that you can take out all thirty of them?"

"Certainly. Or, I could accomplish the deed you're intending without them being any the wiser."

Vincent was unsure if this was braggadocio or simply the truth. "How?"

The mage shrugged. "Several ways. But there is one that I rather favor."

Vincent listened closely as Jaz outlined his plan. Finally, he gave his agreement. "Sounds pretty good. You can really do all that?" Jaz nodded patiently. "Cool." Vincent hesitated. "By the way, you never did tell me what you were doing out here in the woods."

The man was silent for a moment, stroking his beard. "You might say I am on somewhat of a quest. It is rather involved, and I would prefer going into it at another time. I propose this. I shall aid you in retrieving your possessions from these thieves. In return, you will assist me in my search."

Vincent hesitated. "It doesn't involve anything... um..."

"There is nothing you need concern yourself with, aside from the slim possibility of some danger. But it seems you are quite familiar with that."

"Quite," Vincent replied. He thought about this for a few moments. He knew next-to-nothing about this mage. Yet, now that he wasn't feeling jealousy since Rhia wasn't present, he got the same kind of good feeling about him that he had about Blade and Gnorrin upon first meeting them. He felt no sense of danger or falseness from the man. He nodded his head. "Well, it sounds fair to me. I can certainly use the help."

Jaz nodded toward Vincent's injury. "That is your sword arm?" Vincent nodded affirmative. "How good are you with your left?"

He smiled sheepishly. "Doesn't matter. No sword."

The mage gave a slight nod, and looked around at the rapidly darkening forest. "Are you ready?"

They rose and Jaz immediately implemented the first stage of his plan. Vincent watched as he wove his hands in intricate gestures while mumbling incomprehensible things under his breath. Then it seemed as if his voice was just cut off, though he could see the mage's lips still moving. Without his glasses, he had to squint to see anything, including the mage's lips. It took a moment for him to realize that it wasn't only the sound of Jaz's speech that was silent. The entire forest was quiet. Every single sound he had been hearing rapidly faded away to nothingness. No birds, no bugs, no cracking of twigs or creaking of branches. Jaz had explained the zone of silence was small, extending for a radius of perhaps ten feet. They'd need to stay close together in order to remain within its effect. He glanced down at Blaise, also caught inside the zone, and chuckled at her puzzlement. Vincent could hear himself chuckle, but he knew the others couldn't.

Jaz completed his spell and they set off in the direction of the thieves' camp, the silence moving with them. They stepped off the faint path that led to the camp, making their quiet way instead through the thick trees and brush off to the side. Though a sentry would not hear them, they wished no risk of being spotted by an alert guard.

After a time, they sighted the glow of a campfire through the trees. Shortly, they were on the edge of the thieves' camp. Carefully staying beyond the border of the clearing, they circled around to the opposite side of the camp. Since beyond the camp was nothing but deeper and deeper woods, they felt this was the safest approach. Here there were no permanently stationed guards, merely a roving sentry.

They waited at the back of the camp for the sentry to make his way past them. Jaz readied a spell. Then, just as the man was in front of their hiding place, the mage stepped out. The sentry, startled, made as if to yell a warning. But the zone of silence now engulfed him and no sound came from his mouth. Then Jaz completed the spell, and the man swooned, falling face forward onto the ground.

Vincent stepped out of the woods, Blaise at his side. He cast a concerned glance at the fallen sentry, then looked at Jaz. He made a slashing motion across his throat, raising his eyebrows in question. The mage shook his head, then closed his eyes and rested his head on a pillow made by his hands. Relieved, Vincent joined the mage in moving forward.

The camp was comprised of three large buildings and two smaller shacks. Vincent surmised that the larger ones were sleeping quarters. Of the two smaller, one was most likely a multi-purpose building. The other, his instincts told him, was storage. It *looked* like a storage shed. Vincent tapped Jaz on the shoulder and pointed to this building. The mage nodded and they made their way toward it.

As they moved, Vincent noticed that the shadows seemed deeper around them. He looked behind, to see Jaz mumbling some more. Shadows seemed to follow him as he walked. They reached the building without incident.

Jaz opened the door, then cast a quick spell. Inside the empty building, a small glowing ball materialized, casting enough light by which to see, but not enough to alert people outside the structure. Then he motioned Vincent to enter.

Inside, Vincent closed the door behind him, then looked around. Everything was in sacks or boxes. This didn't surprise him, but it did make it more difficult to locate his own goods.

He had one hope, and that was that the most recent acquisitions would be nearest the door. So he began studying the sacks, hoping to find something hanging out of one that might immediately give its identity away. Unfortunately, he was not so lucky. Even more unfortunately, what luck he did have was about to change.

The first thing he noticed was noise. Specifically, he heard barking that sounded suspiciously like Blaise. Then it was Jaz's voice. "I hope you're nearly done in there. We're about to have some fun."

"Shit," Vincent muttered. And, taking one last stab in the dark, he grabbed the nearest sack to him, then bolted out the door. Jaz stood just near the doorway, cloaked in shadow, his arms and lips moving furiously. Vincent looked up. The sight that awaited him made him nearly drop the heavy sack.

Blaise ran amok within the camp, barking at the armed men as she ran. Several of them made vain attempts to catch her. Some even shot arrows at her. Every time one shot, Vincent's heart leaped to his throat. But every time, the arrows missed. Blaise seemed to just... not be there, whenever the arrow neared. He cast a sidelong glance at Jaz, and his opinion of the mage rose considerably. Jaz was casting spells to protect Blaise, making her appear to be just a little way off from where she truly was. He thought he saw another dog, too, but could have been mistaken.

The smile soon faded from his lips. Moving toward them from the side was a figure that Vincent recognized, even without his glasses. It was the leader of the gang of four that had accosted him. And, to Vincent's relief, the man carried another sack. His own belongings, if he wasn't mistaken.

As the man neared within a few yards, his eyes penetrated Jaz's shadow gloom. He stopped. "You!" he cried, looking straight at Vincent. In turn, Vincent stared at the man, and what he saw made his anger flare. Pinned to the man's cloak was Ariaziane's birthday present to him. He felt his blood grow hot.

At the man's cry, Jaz turned to look at him. He began to turn his magical attention upon the man, but Vincent shook his head. "He's mine," he growled.

The thief began to draw his sword, but Vincent leaped instantly forward. With a two-handed wind-up, he swung the bag with all his might. The man raised an arm in alarmed reaction, but it was of little use. The bulk of the sack plowed into his forearm, then into his head and shoulders. With a grunt, he was rocked back off his feet and landed harshly in the dirt.

Vincent was on top of him, now, tossing the sack aside. He pounced, knees first, onto the man's torso. The man groaned and doubled up, as much as could be done with Vincent sitting on top of him. Then the boy grabbed the cloak pin and yanked it free. He held it in front of the man's groaning face. "If you hadn't taken this," he sneered, "I might have just let you get away with it." He stuck the pin haphazardly onto his tunic. "But you really pissed me off, old man."

As Vincent attached the pin, the man recovered his wits enough to reach out and punch Vincent's wounded arm. Vincent howled in pain, tearing his arm free and rolling away from the man. Too late, he realized what a dreadful mistake this was.

The man was on his feet in a flash, his sword appearing quickly in his hand. Vincent glanced around for a weapon, but none were to be seen. He lay on his back, watching as the man raised his sword for the deathstroke. And when it came hurtling downward, the only thing Vincent could think of to do was to move out of the way. A little.

The sword missed his body by a foot and impacted on the ground. Immediately, Vincent kicked with all his might, sweeping his foot under his antagonist's legs. This had, unfortunately, no effect whatsoever. The man swung again, and again Vincent rolled away, this time scrambling to his feet. But he was too slow. As he gained his upright balance, he glanced up to see the sword beginning its deadly arc sideways toward his head.

Several thoughts went through his mind in the split-second before he was to be beheaded. The first was that he was too young to die. The second was that he didn't want to die, even if he was old. The third was how Jaz's plan had been shot to shit so quickly. And the fourth, naturally, was why didn't Jaz *do* something?

Vincent jerked his head backward and stumbled slightly. The blade, which had been heading clean and true toward his naked neck, now cut a deep gouge directly across his eyes.

As he fell, blood spurting and pain hurtling him into shock, Vincent thought he heard muffled explosions. And screaming. But, he thought, it could just as well be his own pain. And his own screams.

❧ ❧

Darella and her children watched everything transpire in Darella's crystal ball. The children, now aged to six physical years, absorbed every detail. When the sword sliced its way across Vincent's face, Darella nodded. The boy's luck had finally run out. Her son cheered, applauding the gory scene. Her daughter gasped, but didn't take her eyes from the ball.

Darella frowned at both reactions. Her son seemed enamored of violence. The way he tormented his sister was evidence of that, but his laughter after seeing his father killed certainly made it clear how he felt. As for the girl, she obviously felt empathy and concern for others. While her brother's mentality was dangerous and could lead to disaster, the girl's emotional state was certain to land her in trouble one day.

As for Darella herself, she felt nothing but inconvenience. Now that the boy was out of the picture, she would have to find some other subject to use as her living example for the children. That was annoying. On the other hand, she'd found recently that she herself was paying more and more attention to the boy. It was distracting. With him dead, she could keep her mind on other matters. She rose from the floor and bade the children to come with her. She turned and left the cave, her son following.

Darella didn't realize her daughter stayed behind. She didn't see the child cast her own feeble spell on the ball, causing it to continue holding the scene they'd just witnessed. She was unaware of the actions of the mage who had assisted the father of her children. And she certainly didn't notice her daughter smile...

❧ Fifteen ❧

Vincent stood on the balcony of his room in Jaz's mountain keep. Blaise was at his side, sniffing the breeze. He, too, smelled the clean air as the wind blew across his face. The fragrance of evergreens came to him, and the sun felt deliciously warm as it touched his cheeks. He sighed, a sigh at once holding the pleasure that these simple sensations brought him, as well as a profound loss. His hands moved across the worn stone of the balcony railing. He'd bet his left arm that the view was magnificent. No, he reminded himself. Can't afford to lose any more body parts.

He toyed with the long ends of the bandage that hung down the side of his head and draped over his shoulder. Then his hands moved up to feel, ever so gently, across his ruined eyes, hidden behind layers of poultice and cloth. He'd had a good bit of time to get used to the fact that he'd never see again. He chuckled ironically. And he'd been so upset over losing his glasses.

He owed Jaz his life. The mage had succeeded in rescuing both him and Blaise from the thieves' conclave. At first, he'd been angry that Jaz hadn't done anything to prevent his injury. But once he pieced together what had happened, he couldn't fault him.

The whole thing had gone afoul while Vincent had been inside the storage shack. Evidently, Blaise spied another dog within the camp and took off after it. Jaz couldn't stop her before she was outside the range of his spell of silence. Her barking alerted the thieves, at which point Jaz had to drop the silence to warn Vincent. He then protected Blaise as best he could from them. Finally, as Vincent was engaged in combat, Jaz was fending off a hail of arrows, much as Gnorrin had done in Kurean's keep, so long ago. That was why he could not prevent Vincent's injury.

After the injury, Vincent recalled little. He was aware of vague presences and actions, noises. Until he awoke in Jaz's keep. That was eight weeks past, and in that time Vincent and Jaz had gotten to know each other. Naturally, Vincent wound up letting Jaz in on the "secret" of his real home, Earth. To his surprise, Jaz took it in stride, as though this were not uncommon news. The mage was so easy-going. So was Gnorrin, now that he thought of it. Perhaps all mages were laid back.

His fingers moved to Ariaziane's cloak pin. He wore it always, now, except to bed. He traced the outline of the sweeping letter "V" that was cut so beautifully from the onyx-like material, and the gold feathers, tipped with ruby-like stones. For perhaps the hundredth time, he asked himself if it had been worth it. He still didn't have an answer.

He'd recklessly invaded the territory of dangerous men, in order to retrieve an expensive, though sentimentally more precious, ornament. Not only had he accomplished this, he'd recovered everything except the coins he'd carried, his magic ring, and his horse, since Jaz was alert enough to grab the bag containing his things.

The money he'd lost was nothing to him. The horse... Well, at least the thieves would treat him well enough. Horses were too valuable to abuse. But he'd miss the beast. And, damn it, he'd miss his eyes! How could this have happened? *Why* did it happen?

He raged silently, fists clenched. Simple injuries he could handle. The arrow he'd caught in his arm, on his first adventure with Blade. No big deal. Even the bolt that had lodged in his forearm was easily pushed from his mind. Simple wounds heal and life goes on. His forearm, in fact, had been nearly perfectly healed within two weeks. Rhia's powder certainly lived up to her hype.

But losing his eyes! Never to look on Ariaziane's face again, or see sunsets again. To know only darkness. How could such an existence be called "life"? He found himself wondering, not for the first time, just how high up this balcony was. But no. With his luck, a suicide dive would only succeed in breaking his neck, and then he'd be paralyzed, too. His thoughts of self-destruction these days were fleeting. Not like those first days, after he'd awakened in the keep, his eyes still screaming in pain and seeping blood and pus. In those days, the despair was heavy on him, the anguish tearing him apart.

But he'd gotten over it. He always seemed to, somehow. Whenever things were unchangeable, you just had to accept them. He was no fool

He also concluded that maybe the five stages of dying pertained equally well to blindness. He'd gone through them all: denial, anger, bargaining, grief, and acceptance. Well, he pretty much had skipped the bargaining stage. Not believing in god made it pretty difficult to do. Either way, the process hadn't been pretty. And he was quite impressed by Jaz. The mage had put up with all Vincent's whining and self-pity and tried his best to comfort him, a stranger. But circumstances being what they were, he and Jaz didn't stay strangers very long. Vincent thought back to the day they became friends, about three weeks after the raid.

The injury had left him bedridden for days. Days of darkness spent in horrendous pain, with throbbing waves crashing at the backs of his eyelids, across the severed bridge of his nose, and from the shattered outer edges of his eye sockets. He was waited on by strangers who brought him food and drink, who bathed his face in cool water and changed his dressings.

In those early days, he hadn't known he was blind. When his bandages were changed, he'd thought there was still something covering his eyes that prevented much light from entering. Eventually, though, he got the picture.

After a few days, the pain had virtually disappeared, thanks to the administration of healing salves and the consumption of an odd-tasting broth designed to promote healing. It was then that the real pain had begun... the pain of realizing he was quite blind.

At first, as expected, he'd done a lot of bumbling and fumbling about. Walking into walls, stubbing his toes on a myriad of protruding corners. And the feeling of helplessness grew.

During this time, Jaz had begun to spend large amounts of time with him. He'd lead Vincent to the gardens and let him enjoy the smells, at least, of the outdoors. They would talk a lot. But the most memorable thing about these discussions was Jaz's concern. He'd seemed honestly distraught, and Vincent had suspected that the mage might even blame himself for his condition.

"Jaz," he'd asked him one day, when the mage had been particularly ingratiating. "You don't feel that this is your fault, do you?"

After a moment of silence, Jaz had said, "If I hadn't been so sure my plan would work..."

"I'd probably be dead," Vincent had finished for him. "Losing my vision is a fair trade for keeping my life."

Those had been noble words, and like many noble words, they rang hollow, even to his own ears.

This didn't mean that he blamed Jaz for his condition. Far from it. He truly felt grateful to the mage for saving his life. It was just difficult, sometimes, to keep it all in perspective.

This difficulty continued to grow inside him. It fed upon all his frustrations, thrived on his depression. Eventually, it boiled inside him, amplified feelings of anger and remorse. It was during this time that he'd first contemplated suicide.

He'd stood on this very balcony and braced himself for the plunge. But it never came. He couldn't be sure it would be fatal, and he didn't want to do it half-heartedly.

And so, the frustration grew even more. Jaz had noticed it. It would have boiled until he'd blown up, had not Jaz opened the vent. Or rather, he'd helped Vincent to open it himself, allowing some of the steam to be purged.

They'd been eating breakfast, Vincent fumbling more than usual with his meal. After spilling juice into his lap, he'd slammed his fist down on the table, making the utensils jump and the goblets rock. He'd wanted to scream a string of profanities, but his voice failed him, all the curses getting log-jammed behind his teeth. Instead, he'd just sat there, jaw and fists clenched.

And Jaz said simply, "Let's go for a walk."

And walk they did. In the gardens, Vincent stubbed his toe on a bench. He'd fought back a cry, then felt Jaz's hand on his shoulder. He'd shaken it off, plopping himself down on the bench. Jaz sat beside him. "Vincent," he began, then faltered. "I'm sorry."

"I don't want your pity," he'd spat back. "I don't want your concern, your condolences. Or your guilt, either, for that matter. All I want," he'd said, his voice rising, "is my fucking sight back!" Tears had pressed hot behind his bandages. He remembered relishing the burn.

Jaz was silent for many moments, then he said softly, "And if I could restore it, my friend, I would."

"I know," he'd said wearily. "It's just... I can't believe..." Thoughts were not evolving properly into words. "It's just not fair! This can't have happened to me!"

The mage had listened respectfully, then ventured a thought. "What is it that you mean by 'fair,' Vincent? Nothing in life is fair. Either that, or everything is. There's no difference."

"Spare me your philosophizing. I'm not in a mood to debate."

"What *are* you in the mood for?"

Vincent had whirled in the direction of Jaz's voice. "I'm in the mood to be pissed off, that's what! I want to yell and scream and bitch someone out for this!"

"Well, here I am."

"Oh, stop it. You're not the one I'm mad at. It's not your fault."

"Then who are you mad at? The gods?"

"If I believed in a god, I'm sure I'd be pissed at him, yes. But I don't. So that leaves only two people to be mad at: me and the son of a bitch who did it." He'd paused, allowing the rage to fade a bit. "Have you ever wanted to kill someone?"

"Who hasn't?"

"I mean *really* kill someone. Not just think about it, but to do it! Have you ever?"

The mage hadn't responded immediately. Then he said, "I cannot think of a time when I truly wished to kill. This only makes it harder to bear the fact that I *have* killed."

The statement had taken Vincent by surprise. Jaz was not the type of person that he could envision actually killing anyone else. "You have?"

"When no other option presented itself."

After a moment, Vincent had said, "Did you kill anyone back at the thieves' camp, after I was hit?"

"It's possible. I'm sure I maimed a few."

"I remember what sounded like explosions. And lots of yelling. And heat. I remember heat."

"Yes. There was quite a bit of that."

"What did you do?"

The mage had nervously cleared his throat. "I cast several fire-based spells."

"Which resulted in...?"

"Most of the buildings bursting into flame. And a few individuals, too. Also a wall of fire to prevent us from being attacked while making our escape."

"Right. Our escape. Just how did we manage that?"

"Just barely," Jaz had whispered.

"Sorry?"

"There is a spell," Jaz said slowly. "A difficult and dangerous spell. It causes the caster, and possibly others, to be transported from one place to another, instantaneously."

"Teleportation," Vincent had said, impressed.

Jaz had paused, incredulous. "How do you know the term? Is this something that exists in your world?"

"Only in science fiction. So you teleported us here?"

"Yes. It was a location I knew well. But the distance..."

"Why is distance a factor if we didn't actually travel it?"

"A good question. I have no answer. But it most definitely is a factor. After the fire spells, I was not sure I had enough strength left to take both of us, our belongings, and your dog."

"But you did."

"Not quite."

Vincent had raised an eyebrow. Or, at least, he'd thought he felt it raise, underneath the bandages. "But we're here. So you must have."

"I am sorry. You do not understand how the powers of magic work."

"You're right. I don't. You make it sound like you've got batteries strapped under your clothes."

"A mage acquires power commensurate with his abilities. The more experience he has, generally, the more power. It is, as you surmise, a measured thing."

"And this power is the source of the magic?"

"Not at all. The power is merely the force behind the magic. The magic is its own source. The mage is the conduit, the focus. He determines the precision or complexity of the magic. The power is what determines the degree of the magic, how strong it is."

"So... you could have a very powerful mage who isn't particularly skilled? You'd have spells of great strength, but little control?"

"Exactly. A dangerous combination, that. But with regard to power, sometimes a mage can when drained, willingly pull more power from himself than is really there. But it is physically dangerous. It comes from the body, not the mind."

Vincent had absorbed the implications of these statements. "From the body," he echoed. "You didn't overexert yourself, did you?"

"A bit. I was pretty weak when we arrived here."

Vincent had detected a lack of honesty in Jaz's reply, but before he could challenge him, Jaz's manservant approached, clearing his throat. "Your pardon, m'lord, but there is a matter that calls for your attention."

Jaz excused himself, leaving Vincent sitting on the bench. "Hennor," Vincent said, hoping the man hadn't left yet.

"M'lord?"

"Please call me Vincent."

"As you wish. What can I do for you?"

He'd scratched his beard, waiting long enough for Jaz to be out of earshot. "I was just curious about something. When Jaz and I arrived here, I wasn't the only one injured, was I?"

Hennor clucked softly. "I should say not."

Vincent nodded. "What kind of injury had he sustained?"

He'd felt Hennor sit beside him. "You have never seen the wounds caused by over-magic?"

"No. Tell me about them."

"Ghastly, they can be. I've never witnessed it in the making, but I've seen the results. It's as if something causes the body to rend itself." His words had trailed off and he'd paused. "Master Jaz came in looking worse than you did. Bleeding from several spots, including his eyes and ears. Broken splinters of bone jutting out of his shoulder." Hennor had let the description die.

Vincent found then that he'd been clenching his jaw tightly. He relaxed it, then let out the breath he hadn't realized he'd been holding. "Thank you."

"Will there be anything else, then?"

"No. Thanks."

Vincent had remained on the bench for most of an hour after Hennor's departure, digesting all the information. The beginnings of acceptance were sown that day, as well as a reinforcement of his debt to the mage. One he hoped to repay. Someday.

Vincent had spent the following weeks frequently in meditation. He would sit, usually out on the balcony, sometimes in the garden of the keep, and just think. Much of the time, it wasn't so much thinking as non-thinking. He'd let go and just *feel* the different sensations that washed over him: the coolness of a breeze, the warmth of the sun, and that weird feeling sometimes felt when being watched. He felt that a lot. He suspected that Jaz was keeping a close eye on him.

He'd also indulge his other senses. His sense of smell had never been the most acute, even before having the top of his nose slashed through. But he found that the more he allowed himself to reach out, the more his nose and ears could discern. He didn't know whether these senses were heightened, of if he were simply paying more attention to them.

Time not spent in meditation was spent in conversation with Jaz. The mage was curious about Earth, but no more so than the others. Jaz turned out to be a really decent fellow. Vincent wasn't surprised to have his theory proven true. It was rare that he was unable to peg someone in that way. Jaz was very intelligent. Vincent guessed one had to be, to be a mage. He enjoyed simple things, mostly. And he had a great sense of humor, appreciating the absurd in much the same way that Vincent himself did. He was about ten years older than Vincent, but had been studying magic since a very young age. And he evidently felt that he'd be very powerful in his later years.

Jaz taught Vincent more about magic, too. Not how to use it, but how to understand it. And Vincent came to comprehend why it so intrigued Ariaziane. He had to admit there was something tantalizing about the ability to take nothingness (well, not really nothingness, but something intangible) and work wonders with it, to shape it, to bend it to your will. To create. Or destroy.

That, he felt, was the real difference between people. Some lived to create, some to destroy. Magic was a tool that could easily be used for either. But he wasn't fond of where that analogy led. He thought of the path he'd chosen and looked at its tool: the sword. The sword was by no means a tool for creation. What did that say about himself? He didn't like to think about it.

Jaz explained to Vincent that there were many different types of magic. It was like going to college and picking a major, perhaps a minor, and different courses under different headings. But instead of English, Math, Science, Humanities, and such, there were things like Informational, Elemental, Healing, and many others.

Naturally, when Jaz mentioned the healing spells, it raised questions in Vincent's mind. "Is there a way my eyes could be healed?" he'd asked.

"Yes," Jaz had answered cautiously. "But not by me. I do not specialize in healing. And what little healing I do know would not help you in any way. You need the abilities of a major healer, one who can repair the damage, rather than just make you feel a bit better. And I know none. However," he went on, "I have taken the liberty of sending a courier off to Falconwall, and another to Linnael. Linnael is nearly four weeks by horse, not to mention the time taken to search for a healer. Falconwall is three weeks' travel. Fortunately, or not, depending on your perspective, time is not exactly of the essence. The damage has been done. A healer two months from now would not have much more of a challenge with your eyes than he would have today."

And so, Vincent waited. At the earliest, he would have six weeks of waiting. Likely it would be closer to double that. And even if a major healer was found, would he be able to heal his eyes?

The keep had many employees. Vincent had heard Jaz refer to them as servants, but admitted that he paid them for their services. "Servant" sounded too much like "slave" for Vincent. He referred to them as assistants. There were those who performed maid and butler services, including Hennor. There was a gardener, a stablehand, and a cook. Her meals were delicious. He hadn't tasted her stew, yet, but he was sure Gnorrin would approve of it. The keep had everything Vincent would have expected to be present in a large mansion. Except a chauffeur.

He certainly had no want for anything. Jaz assigned Hennor to be Vincent's shadow. He was a polite enough gentleman. Very butler-like. He drove Vincent up the wall. After two weeks of his "assistance," Vincent asked Jaz to allow the fellow to go back to his normal duties. He'd manage all right by himself.

And, much to his amazement, he did. After a surprisingly short time, he could find his way around the most necessary parts of the keep. He could find his way from his room to the dining area, to the door to the garden, to the baths, and to the toilet equivalent. It wasn't that difficult, really, since the routes were so easy to memorize by touch, along the walls.

He also learned to identify the occupants of the keep. The sounds of their footsteps were different, for example. Their scents, too, were unique. Jaz had a decidedly spicy aroma. Hennor smelled crisply clean. If he smelled cooking odors, it would be Silga. If he smelled horse, it would be Brunik the stablehand. If he smelled grass and flowers, it would be Neela, the gardener.

He spent much of his time perfecting these abilities. He allowed his sense of hearing to overwhelm him. In time, he learned to turn it inward, sitting for hours listening to his heartbeat, to his breathing, to the sound of the blood flowing through his veins. He would turn it outward, shutting out everything save, for example, the sound of birds. He learned to hear nothing but bird calls. Or the wind. He would smell only roses. Or lilacs.

Before he knew it, he'd been in Jaz's keep for seven weeks. The Season of the Harvest was nearly over and the Season of Sleep would soon come. His hopes for the arrival of a healer were diminishing. One half of his mind kept saying, "Any day now," while the other half said, "Forget about it."

His talks with Jaz grew more infrequent. The mage seemed to have much on his own mind and spent days at a time holed up in his study. Vincent spent his time enjoying the last days of the Season of the Harvest.

Since his experiments in sensory expansion were his best weapon against despair, he next focused his will on that mysterious "sixth sense" that had always intrigued him. So, over the next week, again having nothing better to do with his time, he learned to shut out all other sensations, except for something he couldn't explain. A type of energy, obviously, said the rational side of his brain. *The Force*, said the romantic side. He kept waiting for Alec Guinness' voice to come filtering to him, explaining to him how to see without eyes, how they could deceive him. If he'd had them.

After a time, he'd enrolled the assistance of his very butler-ish friend. They'd stood in the garden, Hennor holding several pieces of fruit. Vincent instructed him to toss the fruit to him and he'd try to catch it. Ludicrous though it was, the man obeyed.

It had been a terrible waste of good fruit.

&ear; &ear;

He'd try it again, today, Vincent thought as he turned away from the fresh air, stepping from the balcony back into his room. He moved with no hesitation, knowing the locations of all objects in his room. He'd had over two months in which to memorize them, after all. His nose told him that breakfast was being prepared. Straightening his tunic from habit, he checked to make sure Ariaziane's pin was safely in place, and headed down to the dining area.

He walked with one hand brushing the wall, after turning right immediately outside his bedroom door. After twenty-three paces, feeling for the three doorways he'd pass, just to be sure, he slowed, turned directly left, and walked forward, hand outstretched in front of him. A few paces and his hand encountered the opposite wall. He turned left again, retracing his steps, feeling for the wall to end. When it did, he cautiously stepped out onto the first stair leading downward.

One day, he expected, he'd misjudge his pacing, turn left to meet the opposite wall, and go headlong down the stone staircase. But it hadn't happened yet. Twenty-six steps and he was on the ground level of the keep. From there it was a simple task to find the dining room.

"Ah, good morning, Vincent," came Jaz's voice from off to the right. Vincent paused and turned in the voice's direction. He sniffed. Medicinal herbs. He entered the room and allowed Jaz to guide him to a chair. "Let's have a look," he said.

Vincent allowed him to remove the bandages and little poultice sacks that lay over each eye. The poultices were filled with a salve made from several different herbs. Jaz finished removing the cloth and the sacks. He gently dabbed away excess muck from the corners of Vincent's ruined eyes and sighed.

Vincent knew that sigh. "They're drying, aren't they?" he asked.

The mage hesitated long enough for Vincent to realize that he'd hit the nail of truth on the head. "Not so bad," Jaz said. "But it's time for fresh poultices." He began applying the new wrappings to Vincent's head. Eight weeks had passed without the return of either of Jaz's couriers. Eight weeks of darkness and attempts to keep his eyes in as healthy a state of death as possible, just in case a healer could be located.

Jaz finished the bindings, then clapped Vincent on the shoulder, as might a father who'd just helped his adolescent son put on a necktie. Vincent wasn't sure he liked the action. They rose and entered the dining area.

"I have a favor to ask," Vincent said as they were seated and served. The meal was a mix of fresh baked goods and butter, with a variety of jams. Also, fresh meat of a ham-like flavor.

"What is it?"

Vincent took a swallow of hot tea. It made him think of Rhia, causing another wave of depression. "I was hoping to send a message to my friends."

"I had only the two couriers," Jaz said apologetically.

"Yes, so you've said. But I was thinking that a written message could be attached to the leg of your bird. He could then fly to my friends and perhaps bring back a reply." The mage was silent for a time. Vincent's hearing told him that his new friend had stopped eating and was, most likely, staring at him. Then it occurred to him what he was asking. The bird wasn't a carrier pigeon, after all. It was Jaz's familiar. He recalled his first meeting with the mage, after Rhia had "borrowed" the use of the animal briefly. "I'm sorry," he added. "I know your familiar isn't meant for delivering messages. It's just that the season is nearly over, and I have friends expecting me back. It doesn't look as though I'll be able to return on schedule."

"I understand," Jaz said. There was another brief silence as he sliced into his meat. "After we've eaten, I'll help you compose the message. You can direct me as to the destination?"

"Certainly. The forest in which we met... You know the handle-like section to the southeast?"

"Yes."

"My friends live, as do I, about twenty-five leagues due east from the tip of that section of the forest."

"That should be a good start." Jaz paused, tapping his fingers on the tabletop. "Without pushing, your message should be delivered in about fifteen hours, once it is on its way."

"That quickly? Oh, right," he said. "As the crow flies."

"Crow?" Jaz replied indignantly.

Vincent chuckled. "Sorry."

Jaz's serving crew knew what to do for Vincent. So that he wouldn't be helpless while dining, they always placed everything perfectly for him. He knew that if he extended his left hand a certain distance and direction, he would find a glass of water there. His pot of breakfast tea was always in the same spot. When food was served to him on a plate, it was always served with the main item closest to him, vegetable to the upper right, and other edible in the upper left. Vincent made sure they knew how much he appreciated their efforts.

After breakfast, the pair seated themselves in Jaz's study. The mage withdrew a small piece of fine paper, as well as pen and ink. He sat at a desk, ready for the dictation. Vincent frowned, cracked his knuckles nervously, then said, "'Dear Gnorrin and Annie.'" He paused to spell the names for his friend. "'I'm sorry to inform you that I will not be home before the Season of Green. I have been detained by a matter of some urgency. For the time being, I am staying with a friend. Please don't worry; everything is fine.' Jaz, can the bird bring a return message?"

"Certainly."

"Okay, then. 'Would love to hear from you. Feel free to attach a reply. By the way, my friend is writing this note for me. I smashed my thumb in a door and am unable to write. Clumsy of me, Annie. Take care. I miss you both.' And just sign it Vincent, if you would. Thanks." He spelled his own name for the mage, too.

Jaz put the note aside to dry. "I'll take care of it. Is there anything else you'd like to do today?"

Vincent smiled. "Wanna play catch?"

They moved outside into the gardens, Jaz carrying a basket full of fruit. "This is very strange, Vincent."

"What's strange is that you don't have one single ball in your keep. So we've got to waste all this good fruit." Vincent moved into position, about thirty feet from Jaz. "Just humor the cripple, okay?"

"I've seen you out here with Hennor, doing this. What is the point?"

Vincent shared his thoughts concerning the heightened state of his remaining senses. "Eventually, I should be able to sense the fruit coming toward me, enabling me to catch it."

"I see," said Jaz. "If you'll excuse the expression. Are you ready?"

"Go for it." He waited for Jaz to throw a fruit, then jumped as one struck him in the chest. "Shit!"

"Sorry," said the mage.

"Don't be. Try again."

Piece after piece came to him, all of them going untouched by his hands. He imagined the ground must have looked like a supermarket rack by this point. He heard Blaise running after the fruits, sometimes eating them, sometimes carrying them back to Jaz. Vincent felt, though, as if he were actually tracking some of the pieces. He took a deep, calming breath, waiting for Jaz to toss the next one.

He heard the sound of the mage's arm as it threw the next piece. A strange feeling overtook him, almost as if he could feel the fruit as it sailed far up into the air. Then something else, something more urgent, tugged at his awareness. His attention distracted from the fruit in the air, his hand snapped up, effortlessly catching a pear-like fruit that Jaz had thrown directly at his chest. The action shocked Vincent. His mouth gaped and he closed both hands around the fruit. The skyborne piece chose this moment to plummet onto the top of his head, sending broken bits of juicy melon cascading down his face and shoulders. Vincent took only a moment's notice.

"I did it," he whispered. Then to Jaz, "I did it!"

Then he felt another piece of fruit coming at him. Again, Vincent raised a hand, this time slapping the fruit away. Two more pieces were hurled at him. Each time, Vincent reacted automatically, deflecting both. Then, when he sensed no more coming, he stopped. Breathing hard, he staggered backward, slipped on some melon, and fell to the grass, still holding the fruit he'd caught. He heard Jaz's laughter, but he didn't care how silly he looked. He moved his hands around the fruit, a smile breaking out across his face. Soon, he began to laugh, too.

Early the next morning, a knock on the door woke him. He stirred, moving slowly back into the state of wakefulness that had become so burdensome, especially in the mornings. He cleared his throat. "Yes?"

Hennor's voice came back to him. "Master Jaz would like to see you in his study."

The message, Vincent thought. The bird had arrived! "I'll be down shortly. Thank you."

"Do you need assistance, m'lord?"

"I'm fine, thanks." Vincent heard Hennor move away down the hall. "And quit calling me that," he mumbled. With a yawn, he rose from bed and began his morning ritual. He moved over to a table set with water basin and cloths. First, he removed the bandage from around his eyes. The poultice sacks he removed next, pulling them gently away from his eyes. He could picture what his eyes must look like. The actual wound had healed. The scar must be impressive, he thought. He could feel it, running from temple to temple, right across the bridge of his nose. As for the eyes themselves, there probably wasn't much left of them. He imagined the lids were white from being in darkness for so long.

As a test, he consciously tried to open them. It was not a pleasant sensation. He knew the eyes were drying out. It felt as though the lids were lined with sandpaper. They did work, though, moving up and down normally. Since his eyes had been open when the sword hit, the lids themselves weren't damaged.

In point of fact, he wasn't totally blind. Since the sword hadn't penetrated the whole way to the optic nerve, it was still possible for him to detect light, for example. But the lens of the cornea and the iris were both virtually destroyed, so it didn't matter. Unfortunately, it prevented his eyelids from holding their close contact with the orbs, thus properly distributing the secretions of his tear glands. His only hope now was that he could keep the eyes from drying out too much. If they did, then even a great healer might be of no use.

Gently, he irrigated the eyes with a soaked cloth, cleaning away the accumulated muck of the evening's sleep. He was at least pleased that there was no pain associated with this ritual any longer. The nerves had healed over the past couple months. At first, it had been awful, this simple act.

After cleaning, he patted away excess moisture, then replaced the poultices. Then he wound the bandage back into place. Soon, he was dressed and on his way downstairs, Blaise bounding down before him.

He made his way to Jaz's study with no trouble. The mage greeted him. "Good morning. Did you rest well?"

Vincent smiled. "Well enough, thanks. I assume our messenger has arrived?"

"Even now, he is perched in a tree in the center of the town you described to me. I need your assistance in directing him further. Let me send him aloft." There was a moment's silence, then Jaz said, "He is above the town square."

Vincent gave Jaz several landmarks to guide the bird in the proper direction to Gnorrin's house. Soon the bird was perched on a branch in the willow tree. Jaz took a seat. "I am having the bird swoop down to land atop the gaming table under the tree, and once there, screech repeated calls." After a few moments, he said, "I believe this has worked. A gnome and a girl have come out of the cottage."

Vincent felt his heart swell, picturing the scene in his mind. How he longed to see Ariaziane again. "What are they doing?"

"Examining the bird. The gnome has just discovered the message." Jaz paused. "They are reading it. The girl is smiling. The gnome is nodding his head," he narrated. "Now he is going back inside."

"Probably for writing materials," Vincent interjected.

"Yes, he's coming back out now, and sitting at the table with pen and ink. He's writing a reply." A minute or two passed. "Now the girl is adding something to the note." Another minute. "She is attaching the message to the bird's leg, now." Jaz waited a bit, then said, "Very good. Your reply is on its way back to us."

After their morning meal, Vincent went outside, taking with him a single piece of banana-like fruit. He walked a short way, then sat on a bench on one of the many paths throughout the gardens. He relaxed, clearing his mind. Then he began to toss the fruit from hand to hand. At first, he kept his hands close together, separated by only a few inches. Gradually, however, he moved them apart, until there existed a gap of two feet between them. He continued to toss the fruit back and forth, always catching it.

After several minutes, he stopped. He took a deep breath, slowly let it out, then threw the fruit upward. Only a little, to start. But, like before, the longer he kept at it, the higher he threw the fruit. Eventually, he missed, and the fruit fell to the ground. Vincent sat back on the bench, his mind suddenly exhausted from the concentration.

He sat there, relaxing, urging the feeling to drift away. He visualized his fatigue as a layer of fog that draped around his head. He took deep, relaxing breaths, picturing his exhalation blowing away the fog.

As the last of the cloud left him, he sensed someone watching him. Jaz, most likely, he thought, keeping an eye on his progress. That was okay. He didn't mind. He liked the mage, and considered him a good friend. Not for the first time, Vincent marveled at his luck in finding so many good people since his arrival here in this world.

Refreshed, he stood. He reached out with his newfound sense. He put out feelers, knowing that his body and mind were perfectly capable of telling him where the fruit had fallen. His body/mind knew the trajectory of the fruit when he'd missed it. It wasn't likely to have rolled very far, given its shape. After a few seconds, he stooped and reached out with his hand. The tips of his fingers brushed the fruit. He smiled and lifted it.

As he was about to begin tossing it again, the idea struck him that he shouldn't limit his search. Why not stretch out his senses as far as they could go? He walked a few steps, to where he knew a grassy spot was, and sat down. He placed the fruit in the grass beside him, then took a few more relaxing breaths.

Then he allowed his mind to send out its feelers again. He thought he would try to confirm the presence of the mage. Whatever the cause, he seemed to be in the right frame of mind to do it. His senses broke forth in waves, like radar looking for blips.

And he got one. He estimated that the mage was observing him from a distance of about thirty feet. Vincent opened his mouth to speak, then stopped, deciding instead to have some fun. He retrieved the fruit, then threw it to where he felt Jaz to be. He heard the mage utter a word of astonishment. Then Vincent rose and walked toward him.

"Incredible," said Jaz as Vincent reached his side. "You really are able to see without your eyes, aren't you?"

Vincent shrugged. "I don't know that I'd say it like that."

"How did you do that with the fruit? You plucked it up from where it had fallen without any effort!"

He shrugged again. "I knew it had to be in that general area."

Jaz ushered him inside. "We must talk of this," he said. "I had thought the first time was mere luck. But you prove me wrong! I would like to study this."

A surge of resentment washed up inside Vincent. He had no desire to be a guinea pig for Jaz's curiosity. He started to voice his feelings, then stopped. He did owe the mage his life, he reminded himself. After a brief pause, he nodded. "Certainly. But not right now. I'm a bit tired. I'd like to go lie down."

Vincent wasn't just making excuses to avoid the discussion with Jaz. In truth, the exercise had taken a lot out of him. He made his way up the stone staircase and into his room. Blaise met him at the doorway. He heard her yawn and knew she'd been sleeping on his bed again. The idea sounded pretty good to him right now.

He sat on the bed and rubbed his forehead. Then he gently removed the bandages and poultice bags that he'd so carefully donned such a short time before. Moving to his wash basin again, he wiped away the poultice residue, rinsed, then dried his eyes. Then he sat on the bed again, relishing the feeling of merely rubbing his eyes. He blinked several times, as if hoping this simple act would restore his vision. He sighed. No such luck. Only a haze of light, dimmer than it had been previously.

He sat cross-legged on the bed, his back against the wall. His arms rested lightly on his knees. He focused on his breathing, calmly and deeply, pushing for a relaxed state. But the wall was cold and distracted him. So he stretched himself out on the bed and tried again. This time, it worked. In minutes, he was asleep.

The dreams that came to him were dark dreams. Dark forest dreams. He walked alone through the darkness. Feelings of helplessness washed over him. He was lost. Then a vague sense tickled inside him. A warmth. A light. He searched for it. He knew it had to be Ariaziane. He dream-smiled and hurried his search. And then he saw the glow that he knew would be his love. He hurried forward, entering a clearing filled with white light. A dreamy haze lay on the land, surrounding the female figure that stood there, alone. She turned and smiled at him. But it wasn't Ariaziane. Nor was it Rhia. It was a stranger, yet someone he felt he knew. She was shorter than Rhia or Ariaziane, her complexion darker. Her eyes were green and her black hair hung long down her back. Her features were sharp, yet somehow delicate. As she smiled at him, Vincent was reminded of a cat. Then he felt a presence behind him. He turned, and saw a real cat. A real big cat. A black panther. It stared at him. And growled.

Vincent woke with a start. He knew from the silence that it was late. The typical sounds of business as usual in the keep were absent, and the noise of night insects came loudly through his open balcony doorway, not to mention a rather chill breeze.

He rose and moved carefully to close the door against the draft. Then he sat on the edge of his bed, surprised at himself for having slept so long. At most, he'd expected an hour or two of napping. The fruit toss must have taken more out of him than he'd thought.

As he was thinking of this, he suddenly remembered what had caused him to wake suddenly. The dream with the girl. Who was she? He'd expected, he recalled, to see Ariaziane in the clearing. And then, what else? Yes. He'd expected it could possibly have been Rhia.

Rhia.

As if the thought of her was enough to blow away the cobwebs, Vincent's mind grasped upon a strange thought. Strange, but somehow clear. He chided himself for not having thought of it earlier.

Rhia had healed him once. In Dynsa, after he'd been shot with the arrow. She'd pulled him through the fever caused by the infection from the wound. She had supplied him with healing herb that healed the bolt wound very quickly. Maybe she could do something for his eyes!

A shame that Jaz had no more couriers. Well, he thought, perhaps when the first courier returned, they could send him out again in search of Rhia. But where would they direct him? Rhia could be anywhere. When last he'd seen her, she was heading south along the river in the forest.

What a fateful parting that had been. It was mere days from their parting to his blindness. If they'd stayed together, what might have happened? Rhia could be dead, he told himself. Or worse. No telling what the brigands might have done with her.

He sighed and dropped his head into his hands. Okay. Sending someone to find her obviously won't work, he said to himself. So how could he find her?

At that moment, there was a shuffling at his doorway. "Ah. You're awake." Jaz's voice. "May I come in?"

"Certainly." Vincent turned his head in the mage's direction. His eyes detected a faint glow against the darkness. Jaz must be carrying a candle, he thought. "What's on your mind?"

His friend pulled a chair from against the wall and sat. "First of all, Silga prepared this tray of food for you." Vincent heard the plate being set upon his nightstand. "You need to eat."

"Thank you."

"Also, the courier from Falconwall has just returned. I'm afraid there was no luck there."

Vincent felt a sinking feeling in his heart, even though he'd expected to hear that announcement. Funny, too, he thought, how he had just been thinking of the return of the courier in order to search for Rhia. Didn't matter, he thought. There was no way to find her, anyway. He shrugged and turned his attention back to Jaz. "Well, thank him for trying, for me. It's not really..." His voice trailed off.

Jaz waited for Vincent to finish, then said, "What?"

"Candle," he said, staring at the faint glow in the room. "That's a candle."

"Yes. Can you see it?" the mage asked excitedly.

Vincent shook his head. "No more than I could have yesterday or last week, my friend. That is not the point. I must think." He rubbed his forehead, as if to stimulate the firing of neurons in his brain. "What did she say it was?" he whispered to himself. After a long moment, he snapped his fingers. "I've got it! Jaz! You must find me some devil's bit!"

"Devil's bit," he repeated blankly.

"Yes, it's a plant. Are you familiar with it?"

"Vaguely. But I know of no uses of it for blindness."

"Nor do I. But I have something else in mind. Can you get me some, as soon as possible?"

"Well, I don't really know if it is to be found in this area. I'll ask my staff first thing in the morning."

"Thank you."

"How much will you need?"

"I have no idea. Better get an armful of the stuff."

"Very well," the mage said doubtfully. "I'll see to it. May I ask your purpose?"

Vincent gave a half-grin. "Not yet. Just humor me."

Jaz stood. "Whatever you say. Sleep well," he said, pushing the chair back to its position by the wall. "Good night."

Since he'd just woken, sleep was not in his plans for the immediate future. Thoughts of Ariaziane, Rhia, and this mystery woman from his dream occupied his thoughts. Who could the woman be? Normally, he would just disregard it, chalk it up to his subconscious mind. But Rhia had convinced him that this wasn't always the best thing to do. His previous mystery dream woman turned out to be a witch that he'd evidently been intimate with, though he couldn't consciously recall it. Could this black-haired beauty also be someone he'd already met?

He fluffed up his pillow some more and turned his thoughts to his plans for the herb. He hoped some could be found. It might be his only hope for reaching Rhia. Or, more likely, it could be a total waste of time.

☞ ☜

Vincent woke to a knock at his bedroom door. He yawned. "Come in."

"Good morning," said Jaz.

"Is it? Too early to tell."

The mage entered the room and sat on the edge of the bed. He rustled a piece of paper. "Your letter has been answered."

Vincent struggled to a semi-upright position in bed. "Isn't air mail wonderful? What did they write?"

Jaz cleared his throat. "The first section is from Gnorrin," he said. "And he wrote, 'A very interesting method of contacting us, Vincent. It is good to know you are well. We look forward to seeing you upon your return.'" Vincent nodded. "The other section is from... How do you pronounce her name?"

"Ariaziane," he replied, her name catching in his throat. His chest throbbed as he thought about her.

"She writes, 'Hurry home, Clumsy. I miss you.' That's all it says." Jaz folded up the note and stood. "Are you ready for breakfast?"

Vincent shook his head from his thoughts. He took a deep breath. "I think so. I'll be down shortly."

"Very good," Jaz said and departed.

He dressed quickly, and just as quickly, performed his morning eye wash ritual. Then he hurried downstairs. He found Jaz already in the dining area. "Were we able to locate any devil's bit?" Vincent asked as he seated himself.

"Yes," Jaz said. "Hennor is in the kitchen with the plants even now."

Breakfast was hurried, at least on Vincent's part. After wolfing it down, he made his way to the kitchen, where he found Hennor fussing with the plants.

"Thank you, Hennor."

"You're quite welcome. Plenty more where this came from, I might add. Should you need it. And what form will you be needing?"

"Pardon?"

"Did you wish to use the juice? Or should I dry them so you can make an infusion or decoction?"

Vincent hesitated, not knowing how to reply. When in doubt, he thought... "I'll be needing both forms, actually."

Hennor assured him that he would take care of everything. Vincent thanked him and rejoined Jaz.

"I was thinking we might go for a ride today," the mage said.

"Oh?"

"Yes. Does that appeal to you?"

Vincent shrugged. "I guess. You got a horse big enough to comfortably hold both of us?"

"Oh, you'll have your own mount."

He chuckled. "That would assume an ability on my part to be able to guide it."

"That's right," Jaz said. "I do think you have that ability." Vincent began to argue the point, but Jaz continued. "Nevertheless, we shall not be going far, and my horses will practically guide themselves. You don't need to worry."

Not an hour later, they were mounted and journeying through the countryside near Jaz's keep. The mage was right. The horse needed no help from him to stay on the path. He just hoped Jaz didn't decide to go cross-country.

As they rode, Vincent allowed the sounds and smells to register fully on his mind. And he wondered, yet again, at the fact that sighted people overlooked so much. He took a deep breath through his nose. All these smells, he mused, of trees, and horses, and rotting vegetation somewhere nearby... All these smells would impart only the slightest information to the average person. But they were wondrous to Vincent.

And the sounds, of horses, of insects, of wind... They were so much more interesting, now. As was the sound... What was that sound? He frowned, then recoiled as the small branch of a tree struck him in the forehead. He fought back a momentary fright, then continued on, his head ducked. That's what the sound was: a tree creaking in the wind. He tuned in to that sound, and in doing so, was able to avoid further branches, ducking every one of them.

A short distance later, he frowned. Something didn't sound right. A sound was missing. He reined in his horse, bringing it to a stop. He cocked his head, listening. Then, satisfied, he turned his head in a semi-circle, left to right. Then, as this rotation took his head past the direction where Jaz stood, he stopped. He cocked his head again, and sniffed. Then suddenly, he guided his horse off the path, directly toward Jaz.

"This is your idea of testing me, huh?" he said, pulling up to a stop beside Jaz's horse.

"It certainly is," he answered, and Vincent could hear the smile in his voice.

"Yes. Well." Vincent cleared his throat. "Did I pass?"

The mage laughed. "Remarkably so. Tell me how you did it."

Vincent shrugged. "First, I realized I couldn't hear your horse's hoof beats on the path. So I stopped. Then I located you by smell."

"By *smell?*"

"Well, by your horse's smell, actually. Fortunately, the breeze was coming from your direction."

"Mm," said Jaz.

"Now what?" Vincent asked, stroking his horse's neck.

"I want to see how far this can go," Jaz replied suddenly.

"What do you mean?"

The mage snorted, as if the answer were obvious. "I have watched you catch a thrown object! I have seen you reach to an object on the ground and find it without groping! I have seen you identify people by their scents! Now you track a horse that has left the path!" He laughed with excitement. "Why believe it must stop there? Let us push your abilities. Let us see just what limitations blindness truly imposes!"

Vincent was silent a moment. His jaw clenched and his eyes burned. When he spoke, his voice was husky. "Limitations?" he asked. "You want to know what the limitations are? I'll tell you. Never being able to appreciate the color of a flower, only its scent. Never being able to see the sun rising, only to feel its warmth. Never being able to see the face of a loved one..." He stopped, his voice failing him. Tears came, but were caught in the bandages. "The limitation," he choked, "is never being able to *see* anything! Ever!"

And with that, he wheeled his horse around, heading quickly back along the path to the keep.

❧ Sixteen ❧

The flame shrank as Hennor lowered the wick in the oil lamp, the vague glow that Vincent could discern lessening to nearly nothing. "I hope this is to your liking."

Vincent smiled and thanked him. "I'm sure it will be fine." He listened to Hennor's footsteps as the man left the room and returned downstairs. Then he adjusted himself in his bed and drew up the blankets. The oil in the lamp was heavily laced with extract of devil's bit. Since Vincent didn't know how much to use, he'd advised Hennor to mix in as much as he thought was safe, and unlikely to interfere with the proper burning of the oil. Several more plants were drying on a line outside. Vincent wished again that he really knew what he was doing.

He took a tentative sniff. Yes, he thought. That smelled like his yellow candles, but stronger. He assumed this was because he was so much more aware of his sense of smell. Blaise let out a small whine and sniffed the air loudly. She sneezed, then left the room. Vincent chuckled and lay back on his pillow, unsure of how to proceed. Relaxing as much as possible, he folded his hands across his chest and let his mind wander back through the recent past. Memories of his time with Rhia came to him—days spent wandering the forest with her. He remembered the botanical tour, the swim in the river, and nights spent cuddling for warmth. And the flirting. He ignored the stirring in his groin at these thoughts.

Focusing on Rhia, Vincent whispered her name over and over, attempting to propel the thoughts outward. He envisioned them soaring out through the sky, over the hills and forests. In his mind, Rhia was out in the wilderness, and he directed the summons to her, willing her to come to him.

Vincent maintained a steady, deep breathing, in through his nose, out through his mouth, utilizing as much of the scent of devil's bit as he could. Eventually, he fell asleep, still mentally calling to the new friend he needed so much.

Every night, he repeated the ritual. During the day, he wore a sachet of dried devil's bit pinned to his tunic. He kept the oil lamp in his room burning constantly, saturating the area with its essence. If he could have been sure of the safety of eating the herb, he would have.

Meanwhile, Jaz continued to prod Vincent into different tests of his sensory abilities. One day, he suggested that Vincent should try his swordsmanship skills. "We'll go out into the garden to practice," he said. "We'll use sticks as our weapons."

Vincent reflected thoughtfully on this, then said, "Jaz, I have to hand it to you. That's the most ludicrous thing I've heard in quite a while."

"What is so ludicrous? How is this any different than your fruit tossing?"

"It just is, okay?"

But the mage was insistent and, remembering how much he owed the man, Vincent consented.

In the gardens, they stood with sticks in hand, facing each other. "I must beg you," Jaz said, "to be lenient with me. I am less than mediocre at this."

"Certainly," Vincent replied, and wondered how much of a beating he'd have to take before Jaz would realize the futility of the enterprise and take pity on him.

"Ready?" Vincent nodded and raised his stick half-heartedly. "Begin," said Jaz, and immediately struck with his weapon.

The blow stung Vincent in the ribs. "Ow!" he blurted, and immediately swung aimlessly with his stick. He connected only with air.

"You're not trying," chided his friend.

Vincent gritted his teeth. Debt or not, the man had no right to tease him. In his anger, he swung in the direction of the voice. Again, he met no resistance.

"That's it," goaded Jaz. "Keep it up!"

Again and again Vincent swung, missing each time, receiving a few small blows here and there. When he heard Jaz snicker, he allowed the fury to overtake him. All the frustration he'd been bottling up inside came welling forth. He thrust and slashed, but Jaz evaded him at every swing. Before long, he was sweating from the exertion. His heart raced until finally, the anger had spent itself. The frustration remained, but now it was from the fact that he couldn't hit Jaz with his stick.

Reason began to reassert itself once the haze of anger thinned. He began to hear what Jaz had said earlier, and found himself repeating the same question. How *was* this different than the fruit toss? It wasn't, really.

With that thought, he stopped. He relaxed his body and his mind, stretching out his awareness. It wasn't difficult, once he set his mind to it. He could imagine a day when such a deliberate act would become almost automatic. His hearing immediately targeted his friend moving up on him from the ten o'clock position. Vincent allowed his body and mind to become one. It was their natural state, after all. And his ears instantly told his brain what Jaz was doing. The telltale whisper of the stick being drawn back to strike threw Vincent into action.

As Jaz launched his attack, Vincent's stick bolted out from the other side. The upswing connected with Jaz's weapon, deflecting the blow. In the same instant, Vincent stepped and turned a full pivot, and with a great wind-up, brought his stick down solidly against Jaz's left thigh. The mage's squeal of pain brought a satisfied smile to Vincent's lips.

He lowered his stick, having heard Jaz drop his. Jaz's stream of expletives faded away, and Vincent knew the man was observing the smile on his lips. Then the mage let out a brief chuckle, which quickly grew to a full-fledged laugh. He stepped over and clapped Vincent's shoulder. "You see?" he said. "I told you so."

Vincent laughed. "Fine. I was wrong. But you deserved that."

"Aye," said the mage, rubbing his thigh tenderly. "Next time I'll send Brunik out with you. He's had training with a sword."

"What next time? You've made your point. Why bother to do this again?"

"Why, to hone your skills! Is that not why you would normally practice your swordsmanship?"

The young man shook his head. "Jaz, I'm *blind*. I can't be a swordsman, no matter how well I can hear. Why can't you get that through your head?"

"My obstinate nature, I suppose." The pair began walking back toward the keep. "In all truth, Vincent, I don't think you appreciate the gift you have. You must admit that there is more than hearing in operation here."

"Jaz," Vincent replied firmly, stopping in his tracks and putting his hand unerringly on the mage's shoulder. "I don't have a 'gift.' Not any more than you do. What I'm doing is something anyone can do, with enough patience and practice. I just happened to be struck blind, which sort of forced me to make the time to develop the patience and engage in the practice. But you could do it, too, if you put your mind to it."

"No," the mage answered slowly. "I don't believe so. Despite your words, it is a unique gift."

"Oh, bullshit. Look, Jaz, you must understand that the mind is incredibly complex, capable of things we cannot comprehend."

"Then, my friend, I would have to say that you possess a truly amazing mind."

"I'm beginning to agree with that," came a voice from behind them.

Vincent turned, startled, his heart leaping to his throat.

"Well, hello," said Jaz.

The footsteps neared and stopped in front of Vincent. He smiled at the familiar scent. Then he felt his bandages being touched, and a familiar sigh. "What have you done to yourself?"

Vincent's smile turned sheepish. "Got careless," he said. Then he beamed. "Rhia... I can't believe you're here!"

"Your voice came to me so loudly, as though you were standing right beside me. How did you do it?" she asked. Briefly, Vincent told her of his use of devil's bit. He fingered the sachet pinned to his tunic.

"We were about to have a bite to eat," Jaz interrupted. "Are you hungry?"

"I am," she said. "Thank you."

As Jaz led them to the doors, Vincent found it difficult to restrain his excitement. He smiled to himself, feeling that everything was now going to be all right.

They talked over tea and sweetcakes, and Vincent concluded that Rhia had heard his summons on the first day he'd attempted it. Unfortunately, she had no idea where he was, and had to wait for him to repeat the call every night. Then she would mentally home in on the call. Each night she had made more progress in the direction of Jaz's keep until last night, when she ended her journey within sight of it.

"Where were you when you heard me?" Vincent asked.

"In Dynsa."

"Mm," Vincent said, feeding pieces of biscuit to Blaise.

Finally, she said, "How bad is the injury? Let me see it."

Vincent hesitated, then untied the bandage. Rhia moved over to him as he removed the poultices. Carefully, she dabbed away the leakage from the small bags. Then she gently pulled up on one of his eyelids.

"I assume you wanted me here in order to suggest some cure for you." Vincent smiled hopefully, but knew what she was going to say. "I am sorry, but I am afraid it is far too severe for my talents. You need a healer, and a good one."

The boy nodded, dabbing further at the poultice leakage with his napkin. "I know," he said hollowly. "But I still hoped..." He let the thought trail off.

"I know. Once a healer is found to treat you, I can recommend certain herbs that will aid in the healing, but beyond that, I'm afraid I can't help you."

"It's helping me just having you here."

Rhia squeezed his arm. "I'm happy to hear that."

The pair spent the rest of the day together, wandering through the gardens, or just sitting on the balcony of his room. He told her of the events that transpired after they had parted in the woods—the attack of the rogues, his tracking of them, the meeting with Jaz, the thieves' camp, and the fight that resulted in his blindness. Then he described his time with Jaz in the keep, and the growth of his abilities, a test of which she'd seen the tail end when she arrived in the garden.

After the evening meal, they sat in the garden again. For the longest time they were quiet, breathing in the crisp air and listening to the insects. Then Vincent said, "I miss looking at the stars. Tell me how the sky looks."

"Cloudy," she said.

"Oh," he replied. After a moment, he said, "You're staring at me."

"Am I? I thought I was studying."

"Studying what?"

"I'm trying to read how you feel. Your face reflects what's going on inside you."

"Not if you're a good poker player."

"I expected to see many negative things in your face, but I do not. You appear to be comfortable with your situation."

Vincent's brow knit. "Believe me, there's a great deal of negativity inside. And sometimes I give in. I can't help it." He paused. "But I also realize that giving in to these feelings doesn't help anything. I'm trying to maintain an optimistic outlook. And I'm sure the fact that I'm thrilled you're here helps cover it up." He smiled broadly.

"Thank you." Vincent heard the smile in her voice, followed by a yawn.

"I'm sorry," he said. "You've had a long day. Let's go in."

Jaz had instructed Hennor to make up the room next to Vincent's for Rhia. Vincent stopped in front of it. "Your room is further on," said Rhia.

"I realize that. But yours is here."

The witch was silent for several moments. Then she said, "Yes. So it is." She squeezed Vincent's hand. "Goodnight, then."

"Goodnight." Vincent returned the squeeze, then moved on to his own room.

He heard Blaise yawn, then jump down off his bed. He smiled and sat on the bed, reaching out a hand to her. She licked it and he scratched her ears lovingly. But Rhia's words were heavy in his mind. The despair welled up inside him, and he found himself wishing to see his dog's happy expression instead of just imagining it. He wanted to look upon Rhia's face. And more than anything, he wanted to return home and see Ariaziane.

He sighed heavily and rose. He undressed, throwing his clothes in a heap at the foot of the bed, then climbed in and pulled the blankets up. He heard Blaise curl up on the floor. Then a thought struck him. The room was mostly devoid of the devil's bit aroma, due to the fact that the lamp had run out of the laced oil sometime during the day. So Vincent groped about in the pile of clothing until he found his tunic. He unpinned the sachet from it and brought it up to his pillow. He gave it a good squeeze, to crush more of the dried herb inside, releasing its volatile oils. The scent washed over him as he lay back down and tucked the sachet into the pillowcase.

He turned his thoughts to Ariaziane. If he'd reached Rhia, perhaps he could reach her. He wouldn't try to summon her to him, but he would like to communicate with her. Even if it were a one-sided communication.

Weariness overtook him rapidly. He slept, but not well. Tossing and turning, his blankets were soon a tangle. And his dreams were disturbed.

He dreamed of a girl again. Not Ariaziane, not Rhia, not even the exotic dark-haired girl from his earlier dream. This dream held a disturbingly familiar female of singular beauty. Brown-haired and fair complected, about his own age, he guessed. And in the dream she slapped him, then kissed him deeply. And while they kissed, she gasped. They separated and then she turned white, her flesh becoming corpse-cold in his embrace. Vincent screamed.

A hand was on his head, and soothing noises fell on his ears. He roused himself from the dream. "There, now," said the voice. Rhia's voice. Vincent returned to consciousness and touched the hand that was stroking his long hair.

"You had a bad dream," Rhia said. "You were making some unpleasant sounds."

Vincent nodded, holding her hand firmly in his own. "Yeah. I'll bet I was."

"Tell me about it."

He drew a shaky breath. "Later," he said, letting go of her hand and settling back in for sleep. Dreams didn't necessarily mean anything; he hoped this was one that didn't.

Rhia remained sitting on the edge of his bed, stroking his hair again. He smiled at the sensation. "That's nice," he said.

So she continued for a minute, then rose, pulled back the blankets, and slipped into bed beside him.

"What are you doing?" he asked, startled.

"I'm spending the night in the arms of a friend, to ease his troubled sleep."

"That's all?"

"That's up to you."

He was quiet a moment. Then he moved over so that she could share the bed. When she was settled in, he reached out and put an arm around her, snuggling up next to her. "Thank you," he whispered.

❧ ❧

During the following week, Rhia explored the area around Jaz's keep, gathering as many herbs as she could before the snows were due. Vincent and Brunik practiced at wooden stick swordplay in the gardens. It was becoming easier and easier for Vincent.

One day, after a grueling session, they walked out of the gardens. The sound of falling leaves made Vincent pause. "Damn," he said.

"What is it?" asked the stablehand.

"The leaves are falling. I missed it completely. I love seeing the leaves turn."

"Aye, that's a shame. The view is stunning from here."

Vincent frowned. "Pass the salt when you're done rubbing it in," he said dryly. Brunik laughed, clapped him on the shoulder, and wished him a good day before turning toward the stables.

Inside, Hennor greeted Vincent. "I'll prepare the baths. You look as though you need a soak." Vincent thanked him and headed straight for his room, where he stripped off his sweaty clothes and sat on the edge of his bed. Wincing, he rubbed at his neck and shoulders. Out of practice, he thought. Not surprisingly, his body felt like one big ache. Hennor was right. He needed a good, hot, relaxing bath.

He lay back on the bed, allowing the cool breeze from the open balcony door to refresh him. How many minutes passed, he wasn't sure. But soon Hennor's voice came from the doorway. "The baths are ready."

"Thank you," he said, and heard Hennor move off. There had been a slight quaver in Hennor's voice. He wondered what could have caused it, then realized that the man had just peeked in to see him lying stark naked on his bed. Probably just surprised him, he thought. No big deal.

With a sigh, he sat up, then stretched. He stood, removing his eye bandage and poultice pads. He placed them on the bureau, then reached for the robe hanging on a wall hook. He paused. And sniffed. On the bed, the only fragrance he'd detected was his own ripeness. But now another scent teased him. It smelled like the shampoo that...

"Rhia!" he said, throwing the robe on. "How long have you been standing there?"

"Plenty long, hairy one." Vincent's face grew red. "No need to be embarrassed. It isn't the first time I've seen your body, you know."

"I know. But it's the first time you've studied it."

"Perhaps," Rhia said quietly. "Perhaps not."

He heard her following him down the hall toward the baths. Inside, he felt the hot steam radiating from the tub. Rhia closed the door after him. Vincent shrugged off his robe. "Guess you're keeping me company, huh?"

"Do you mind?"

"Would it matter?"

"Certainly it would matter. You're a bit touchy today, aren't you?"

He tested the water with his hand and sighed. "Sorry. Just my frustration coming through again." He stepped into the tub. "Ooh. That's warm." He gently lowered himself into the huge tub, lying back so the water came up to his neck. If he'd had a tub like this back home, he mused, he'd have taken a lot fewer showers. "Mmmm... I needed this."

Rhia moved behind him and began to massage his shoulders. "I should say so. You're a bundle of knots."

Vincent allowed her to work on him. It felt wonderful. After several minutes, she stopped and picked up a bar of soap. She began lathering his chest. Under her gentle prodding, he leaned forward, allowing her to soap his back.

"I don't suppose you have any of that shampoo."

"I brought it in while you napped. Soak your head," she instructed.

"Y'know, where I come from, that's an insult." But he did it anyway, allowing her to lather his hair with the fragrant shampoo. "Boy, I'm getting the full treatment today. I should be blinded more often."

"Not funny," she said, and pushed him under the water.

Vincent rinsed his hair, dunking himself a few more times. Just as he was thinking that the tub was beginning to cool, Rhia poured more hot water in from a pitcher Hennor had placed on the floor. He smiled his thanks, but the smile froze as he heard the sound of Rhia stepping into the tub with him.

"Um..." he began. Then he sighed. Why try to protest? He should be used to this behavior from Rhia by now. He felt her legs slide in past his own, then her hand clasped his.

"This is lovely. Thanks for inviting me in," she said with a smile in her voice. He heard her retrieve the soap and begin lathering herself. When she was done, she soaped up Vincent's legs, running the bar of soap over them under the water. She moved further and further up his legs.

"I think that's far enough," he whispered as she soaped the inside of his thigh. He was becoming aroused, which was the last thing he wanted right now.

"Are you sure?" she replied. And she moved the soap to his pelvis. "Your body seems to think otherwise."

Vincent plunged his hands in and grasped hers, stopping them short. Barely. "Rhia, stop. I can't have a relationship with you. Much as my body might be inclined to."

"Who said anything about a relationship? I don't want a handfasting." She slid her fingers over him.

"Please stop that," he begged. In response, she gently dug her fingers into his thigh muscles and dragged them slowly down. He let go of her hands and leaned back. "Thank you," he said.

"You're welcome," she said, and swiftly slid over and on top of him, sending cascades of water over the edge of the tub and onto the stone floor. Before he could react, she was kissing him deeply, one hand behind his head, the other reaching the underwater target it had been seeking.

He gasped, not knowing what to do. Despite the protests of his mind, his body reacted. He returned her kiss passionately and allowed her hand to explore.

"Vincent!" came Jaz's excited voice, accompanied by rapid footfalls up the stairs and toward the baths.

Rhia returned to the other end of the tub, muttering something that Vincent didn't quite hear, but he echoed the sentiment nonetheless.

The mage burst in, full of excitement. "Vincent! You must... Oh!" he said. "I'm terribly sorry. I didn't realize..."

"Quite all right," Vincent managed to croak out between heavy breaths. "What's all the fuss?"

"The courier to Linnael has returned," the mage said, causing Vincent's heavy breaths to be held. "We could very well have a solution to your problem."

Time stood still for a moment. Vincent was vaguely aware that Rhia had stepped out of the bath and was toweling herself off. Finally, he let out his breath. "What? I mean... Really?"

"Really. Hurry down."

"Right," he whispered as Jaz departed. He sat in the tub, dazed. Should he get his hopes up? He doubted it. Such was always his way, though, and it so often met with disappointment.

He heard Rhia throw the towel aside and begin to dress. When she finished, Vincent was still in the tub. "You going down or not?" she said.

He shook his head, as if coming out of a daydream. "What? Oh. Yeah." He eased himself out of the tub.

He dressed quickly, throwing on trousers and tunic, then pulled his wet hair back and tied it in a pony-tail. In the time he'd been in this world, his hair had grown to quite a length. He didn't mind. He hated haircuts, anyway.

After dressing, he and Rhia descended the stairs and entered the greatroom where Jaz was speaking with their new arrival. The man's voice was deep and, to Vincent's ear, slightly pretentious.

"Ah, here he is, now," said Jaz. Vincent moved toward his voice. "Vincent, allow me to present his Lordship, the Baron Aedriun of Linnael. Lord Aedriun, this is Vincent, the young man you've come to meet."

Aedriun stepped over to Vincent's side and placed a hand atop his shoulder. His other hand clapped his opposite arm. "A pleasure to finally meet you, Vincent. It has been a long journey here to assist you."

Vincent mentally thanked Jaz for having just given him a nutshell primer on titles and honorifics in his introduction. "Your lordship," he said. "The pleasure is all mine. May I introduce my friend, Rhia?" The baron greeted her. She returned in kind. "I trust your trip was comfortable and uneventful," Vincent said.

"Uneventful, yes," the man replied, stepping back. He took a seat. "Comfortable is not a term I would apply to it. It is a long journey."

Rhia gently guided Vincent to a chair, since all were sitting. "I understand," Vincent went on, "that you might be able to help restore my sight. How, exactly, will this be done?"

The baron cleared his throat, quietly, but with unmistakable uneasiness. "Before we discuss the method of its execution, we should discuss the likelihood of the event."

Vincent paused. "What exactly do you mean by that?"

"In addition to being a baron, I am a Knight of the Realm of Linnae. I am sworn to give aid to those in need. But first, I must deem them worthy of the assistance."

Vincent allowed this to sink in. "And," he said slowly, "just how do you go about making this judgment?"

Aedriun clapped his hands together and rubbed them. "I will stay here for a bit, spending time with you and your friends, until I have judged that you are worthy. I will be examining your character, you could say."

"Ah. Well, I'm certainly a character, I've been told." As the baron did not do so much as chuckle, Vincent hurriedly continued. "It sounds fair enough, your Lordship. When do you plan on starting the examination?"

"After a hot meal and some rest, young man. Please be patient enough to allow me that much, at least."

"Certainly," Vincent said, standing. "I will leave you to your relaxation, then." And with a sudden remembrance of Hollywood medieval courtesy, he bowed slightly and said, "By your leave..."

Aedriun chuckled. "My, you're a formal one. Carry on, Vincent. We shall speak at length, later."

Vincent and Rhia headed out of the room toward the rear exit into the gardens. "Well, he's a bit of a pompous butthead, don't you think?" Vincent said, as soon as they were out of earshot.

"Perhaps," Rhia replied. "But he's going to cure your blindness, so I wouldn't worry about it."

"That's the only reason I didn't tell him off, right there! *But first I must deem them worthy of the assistance.*' You think he performs this little character examination whenever he sees a starving child? Does the kid have to pass a purity test before he can have food?"

"You're not really in a position to criticize his methods, Vincent."

"Yeah, I know. Beggars can't be choosers. But I still don't like it."

"Do you dislike it enough to decline his aid?"

He let out a sigh. "No. My conscience tells me I should, but I don't. And I feel guilty about that."

"Don't be silly," she said as she guided him to a bench and sat. She kept her hand on his arm as they relaxed in the garden. "There's no reason for you to feel bad about this." She was quiet for a time, then said, "Vincent, I must be leaving soon."

He turned his face toward her. "What? Why?"

"I have things to do. Important things that cannot wait."

Behind his bandage, Vincent's brow furrowed. The little tickle that sometimes existed in his head was telling him that she was lying. He tried to fathom why she would lie about having to leave. He explored several possibilities, then settled on the only one that made any kind of sense to him—she was upset that he wouldn't get involved with her.

He cleared his throat. "I see. You have some progress on your search for my way home?"

"Some," she said, and Vincent believed her. "That's the reason I have to go. Certain elements of my search cannot be delayed."

Vincent felt the lie in those words, too, but said nothing about it. "How soon?" he asked.

Her hesitation was brief. "I think tomorrow morning."

"I'm sorry you have to go. But I understand."

Rhia squeezed his arm. "I'm glad."

Back inside the keep, Vincent cornered Jaz alone. "How much should I tell him?" he asked the mage. "If he's set on getting to know me, how can I keep the truth from him? And what harm could there be in telling him?"

Jaz sighed. "I have been debating that very question, myself." He drummed his fingers on the arm of his chair. "It is difficult to tell, since we know so little about him. And I'm afraid I know nothing about his knightly order, either. On the one hand, he could be very receptive to the truth, and all the more willing to help you. On the other hand, some of these knightly orders are very superstitious. The truth could completely alienate him."

"Wonderful," Vincent drawled.

"As for what harm could come of the knowledge, that could be very great, potentially. If he were to react negatively, he could report this knowledge to powerful authorities who could imprison you, perhaps interrogate you." Vincent let out an exasperated sigh. "I'm afraid," Jaz continued, "that you'll just have to make the decision based on what you can learn of him. Examine him even as he's examining you. That might be the only way you'll ever guess how he'll react."

Vincent toyed with the tail of his bandage. "I have to tell you, I'm not real thrilled about this whole scenario. The man is so sanctimonious, he makes me want to retch."

Jaz cleared his throat. "I can understand why you say that. I have never felt very comfortable around his sort, either. But sometimes we must put up with minor offenses in order to reap the greater reward. You, especially, should appreciate that fact right now."

"Oh, I do," he replied. "But, damn it, I don't have to like it."

At that moment, Hennor announced that the meal was to be served shortly. At Jaz's request, Hennor ascended the stairs to summon the baron. "Where is Rhia?" Jaz asked.

"Gathering herbs, I believe," Vincent replied. "I'll call her." Vincent put his nose to the sachet of devil's bit that was attached to his tunic. He inhaled deeply while summoning Rhia in his mind. Then he moved toward the dining room.

Rhia arrived after the others had been seated. She sat across from Vincent and pulled her chair in. "Thanks," she said in a voice pitched for his ears alone. He smiled in return. Lord Aedriun said a short prayer aloud before they began eating.

Talk was subdued during the meal. Rhia announced her impending departure, thanking Jaz for his hospitality during her stay. Vincent could feel the baron's eyes on him as he ate, and he could understand why. Vincent ate effortlessly, thanks to all items being placed exactly so at his setting. To him, it was nothing, since he'd been doing it for so long. He was used to it. But to Aedriun, he knew it must be an amazing sight.

A thought occurred to him, then. Ever since losing his sight, he had begun to think more seriously about the body's different senses. He realized that he was now, for the first time in his life, truly paying attention to his senses of smell and touch, as well as his hearing. Paying attention to everything that was there, not just the most obvious things. But the feeling of someone staring at him... That was something he'd been familiar with almost all his life. He took it for granted that everyone knew that odd sensation. How was it explained, he wondered. What sense accounted for this? Or was it a form of extra-sensory perception? Or was there even such a thing as ESP? Wouldn't everything be a form of sensory perception, just of senses not yet understood? He sighed and shook his head before he resumed eating. He had enough on his mind as it was without engaging in such speculation.

The meal was soon over and Vincent excused himself. "Lord Aedriun, I look forward to spending time with you. However, I hope you will understand if I prefer to spend the evening in the company of my friend, since she will be departing tomorrow."

"Certainly, young man. I fully understand." Vincent could tell from his voice that the man did not understand and was reading more into his words than was really there. "It was a pleasure to meet you, Rhia. If I do not see you before you depart, have a safe journey."

"Thank you," she replied flatly. Vincent smiled to himself. Rhia was on his side in thinking this guy was a jerk after all, he thought.

Leaving the baron and the mage to continue their talk, Vincent and Rhia departed, heading again for the gardens. The evening was cool and crisp. Just as autumn is supposed to be, Vincent thought. "This is my favorite time of year," he said quietly. Rhia remained silent as they walked toward a bench set along the path. She held Vincent's hand. When they were seated, he suddenly turned to her. "Okay," he said. "Give me an update. Where does your investigation stand?"

"Well," she began, "I still have not been able to locate Darella."

"How would you succeed in doing that?"

"Mostly by coincidence," she said bitterly. "I have the ability to locate her. I know her magic."

"What do you mean?"

"I mean that if I were to encounter something of her magic, I would recognize it as being hers. A witch's magic has its own identifying characteristics."

"Its own signature, so to speak?" Vincent offered.

"That is one way to put it, yes. So, if I were to be actively searching in an area where Darella was utilizing the Craft, I could locate her."

"Seems to be a long stretch, though. Not easy."

"That's true. The area that I can search at any given time is small..."

"And she could be anywhere," he finished.

"Well, no. I don't think she would be more than a dozen leagues from where you live."

"But it could be in any direction," he said flatly.

"Doubtful. You were found by your friends as you walked down one particular road. That road came from the north. So any direction south of there would be unlikely. But it could have been north, north-east, or north-west. And there are many places throughout that region that she could be."

"The forest," Vincent offered.

"Yes, possibly. And there are mountains to the north-east, as well. Either location would offer her countless places to hide."

"The mountains," Vincent said faintly, as a ripple went down his spine. Then, more firmly, "Forget the forest. She's in the mountains."

"How do you know? What have you remembered?"

He shook his head. "Nothing. It's just a feeling."

"Very well. I'll search the mountains. Also, I have been attempting research into the nature of the aperture you saw in the vision."

"The Seeker Portal?"

Rhia spun him around by his shoulder. "How did you know what it was called?" she demanded.

Vincent shook his head. "What do you mean? The efreeti told me about it."

The witch's tone was incredulous. "Efreeti? What efreeti? You're conversing with an efreeti about Seeker Portals? By the moon's horns, Vincent!"

"Wait, wait, wait," he said, raising a hand. He thought for a moment. "Shit. I never told you. I'm sorry! I can't believe I never told you about this!" Briefly, Vincent related the story of his first meeting with the creature, and his subsequent visits, including the one in which the subject of the Seeker Portal had come up. "So that's how I know. I'm really sorry I didn't tell you about it. You did all that work for nothing." Rhia was silent for a long time, and Vincent felt her gaze boring into him. "I'm sorry," he offered again, sheepishly.

"You... knew... all along..." she began. "I can't believe you!" she laughed, slapping his arm.

Relieved, Vincent smiled. "Must've slipped my mind."

"Indeed! Well, I can understand how it might. It's such an inconsequential little thing."

"Okay!" he laughed. "Enough! I'm sorry! I'm an idiot, okay?"

Rhia sighed in exasperation. Then she said under her breath, "He's good looking and bright, but his mind..."

Vincent smiled. "Yeah. I'm sure your mother would never approve."

"You might be surprised," she chuckled.

"You know," Vincent said, "I really hate for you to leave. After we parted ways in the forest, I really missed you. And I will, again."

"Be careful, Vincent. Your words have a flavor of caring to them."

"So?"

"Your heart belongs to another, remember?"

He cleared his throat. "Hmm. I might not be able to see, but I'm not blind to the jealousy in your words."

Rhia snorted. "I don't think so. As I said, I don't want a handfasting."

"No, you just want to jump my bones."

"Interesting expression."

"Rhia, I'm not used to being on the receiving end of such desires. I don't know how to react."

"You certainly seemed to know how to react when we were in the bath."

"No, I mean emotionally. I won't lie and say I'm not attracted to you. You're very attractive, in a mysterious kinda way. I guess I just don't understand why you find *me* attractive. I mean, I'm nothing great to look at. I don't have an athletic body or a movie star face. My teeth aren't even straight, let alone pearly white."

"What is a 'movie star'?"

"Forget it. Just explain to me why you're so attracted to me. Why me instead of other guys who are better looking? Surely you can't have any difficulty in finding someone willing to... Well, you know."

"For the same reasons. I find you attractive in a mysterious way." She took a deep breath. "And that's all I'm going to say about that."

Vincent opened his mouth to protest, thought better of it, and closed it again. He was quiet for a time. Then he said, "When will I see you again?"

"That depends on Lord Aedriun, I would imagine."

"You know what I mean."

"I do not know, Vincent. From here, I must return to Dynsa. Then I will set out for the mountains in my search for Darella. But our paths are destined to cross a few more times."

Vincent shifted uncomfortably on the bench. He reached out, placing his arm around her, and felt her turn to face him. "I'm glad to hear that," he said.

Their kiss was tender, yet intense. Vincent felt as though it would last forever, until they finally broke from it. And as they moved apart, he heard her slight gasp for breath, echoing his own.

Neither said a word as they rose from the bench and walked hand-in-hand back to the keep. Inside, Rhia turned toward the stairs. "I realize it is still early, but I will need rest for tomorrow."

"I understand. Sleep well. And wake me in the morning?"

"Thank you, and I will." She kissed him quickly and ascended the stairs. Vincent listened to her footsteps until she was inside her room. Then he turned and made his way toward the voices of Jaz and Aedriun in a neighboring room.

It was late in the evening before Vincent finally excused himself from the company of his friend and the baron. Despite the long journey he'd just completed, Aedriun seemed perfectly awake enough to talk until dawn. He had done the most talking of the three of them, and he talked mostly about himself.

Vincent had tried not to look bored as he listened to the baron. He kept himself awake by noshing on the baked goods that Hennor had set out with the evening tea. They were quite good enough to occupy his mind for most of the baron's talk.

A few things did manage to slip into his ears and lodge somewhere inside, however. Vincent learned a little about the Order of Linnae. They were an order dedicated to protecting the Barony of Linnael from any incoming threats. Originally, this meant threats from the sea. Linnael was a port town and, in its early years, was prone to attack by roving bands of pirates from islands off the coast. That danger had mostly disappeared, and what little threat remained was very minor. Linnael's physical fortifications had grown over the years, making a sea-spawned attack far too difficult for mere pirates.

As this fact became well-known, the Order of Linnae had to come up with some way to justify its existence. Rather than face obsolescence, they found more and more things for them to do. The Order of Linnae became somewhat of a group of knightly social workers. Aedriun, being baron, was naturally also Knight Commander of the order.

Vincent had to admit that when he got people to help him, he certainly attracted those able to do so. He trudged up the stairs to the second floor. Making his way down the hall to his room, he paused briefly in front of Rhia's door. He listened for the sound of her sleeping breath, but couldn't hear it. No surprise, he thought. He was so exhausted that he couldn't seem to focus his thoughts, let alone his senses. He sighed and continued to his room.

Blaise yawned as he entered and got down off his bed. "Thanks for warming it up for me," he told her. The nights were getting to be more than just chilly. He hated the idea of the approaching winter. Although, he had to admit, winter on this world held much more charm for him than it had on Earth. Here, there were no cars and trucks to dirty the snow with their exhaust and high speed splashes. The snow's pure whiteness continued throughout the season, except for when muddied between thaws.

This season, however, he might not be able to appreciate it. That would depend on whether he scored well on Aedriun's little personality profile, as well as on how long the healing process would take, should it come to that. He fought down the distaste that continued to well up when he thought of Aedriun's test. For that matter, the distaste welled up whenever he thought of Aedriun at all.

The dog nuzzled up to him as he sat on the corner of the bed, removing his boots. He petted her fondly, scratching behind her ears. "You know how it is, don't you, girl?" he said to her quietly. "Some people you just don't like, soon as you meet them." Blaise licked his hand, as if to show her agreement. A smile crossed his face. Perhaps he wasn't as tired as he'd thought. He could still smell Rhia's scent in the room from the last time she'd been there.

Rising, he moved over to the washbowl and removed the eye bandage and poultice pads. He wondered why he bothered anymore. If Aedriun could and would heal them, then the pads weren't necessary. And if the man couldn't or wouldn't, then they were a waste of time. Either way, he figured their usefulness had expired. After rinsing and drying his face, he disrobed and climbed into bed.

"About time," Rhia said.

With a cry, he flew from the bed and stood next to it, his heart beating like a jackhammer. "Shit!" he breathed. Then he collapsed onto the bed again, his legs weak from the shock.

Rhia was chuckling as he made his way under the blankets. "Sorry," she said.

"No, you're not," he laughed.

"So," she said, "Did your chat with the baron do anything to endear him to you?"

Vincent yawned and shook his head, weariness quickly seeping back in. "Full of himself. Imagine most knights are."

She moved closer to him, wrapping her arm around his chest, and toying with the curls of hair that thickly covered it. Her hand moved lower.

Vincent clasped it tenderly, halting its downward movement. Smiling, he turned onto his side to face her. "Might surprise you," he mumbled, "but I'd probably enjoy that. If," he continued, "I weren't so tired."

"You might be surprised yourself to find how quickly weariness can leave you," she replied.

"For tonight, we'll never know." He brought her hand up to his lips and kissed it. Then he snuggled up next to her, putting her arm around himself again. "Good night."

Rhia sighed and squeezed him in a hug. "Good night."

❧ Seventeen ❧

In the morning, Vincent said farewell to Rhia as they stood at the far end of the gardens. He was quiet during the conversation, and she didn't pressure him. They held hands, embraced, and Vincent squeezed her close, not wanting to let go. Since her arrival, things hadn't seemed quite so dismal. But now...

Finally, she kissed him, a peck, before setting off through the long grass. Vincent stood listening to the swishing of her robe as she walked along. Fallen leaves crunched as she passed. When the noise faded, he sighed, then made his way back to the keep, where Aedriun waited.

Vincent heard the baron step outside as he approached. Aedriun cleared his throat and said, "Your friend has left, has she?"

Vincent nodded.

"Well, then," Aedriun continued, brushing the matter aside. "Let us walk to the stables." He took Vincent's arm to guide him in the proper direction.

Vincent firmly, but politely, removed his arm from the baron's hand. "That's not necessary."

"Forgive me," the baron replied. "It is a natural assumption."

"The path to the stables is clear of obstacles and easy to follow. I'll be fine, if not especially speedy."

"Remarkable," Aedriun said, and Vincent could hear the approval in his voice. Perhaps passing his little test wouldn't be as difficult as he'd feared.

"So we're going riding?"

"Yes, I thought we might. It is a pleasant day, and likely we'll not have many of those left before the snows come."

Vincent nodded. "Fine. I enjoy riding," he said, in the hopes that Aedriun would approve of that, too.

When they reached the stables, Aedriun asked him, "Which horse is yours?"

"I'm afraid they took my horse as well as my eyes."

Aedriun summoned the stablehand and had him prepare his horse and one other for Vincent. Then he said, "Your mage friend has told me of that battle. Tell me, how do you feel about it?"

"I'm sorry?"

"I mean, do you wish for revenge?"

Vincent was silent for a moment. How should he answer that? The thought hit him suddenly that perhaps Aedriun might be able to tell if he was lying. That wouldn't score him any points. "I can't say the idea hasn't crossed my mind. But all I really want is my sight back. I lost nothing of real value, other than that. I got back what I'd gone after."

"And what was that?"

Vincent's fingers brushed Ariaziane's gift, pinned to his cloak. "This has a lot of sentimental value to me," he said as Aedriun leaned over for a closer look.

"And, I should say, quite a lot of monetary value," the baron said. "That is a beautiful piece of work."

"Thank you. So's the person who gave it to me," he said with a smile.

"Ah. Your friend, Rhia?"

"Oh, no. Rhia and I aren't that close." Vincent said the words easily enough, but his heart twinged inside, as if in protest.

The stablehand approached, leading the horses. Aedriun and Vincent mounted up and were soon headed for open ground. Aedriun led the way at first, then held back once in the open area so they could ride abreast. "Tell me of the one who gave it to you, then."

"Well, her name is Ariaziane," he began.

"What an unusual name!" said Aedriun. "What does it mean?"

Vincent raised an eyebrow behind his bandage. "Mean? I have no idea."

"I wonder what tongue that is. It sounds vaguely elvish, you know. Except..."

"Except what?"

"I know of no elven tongue that contains the 'z' sound in personal names." He added, "You are unfamiliar with their language, I see."

"Completely. You're saying that elves have a 'z' sound, but not in names?"

"Yes. Well, more specifically, they don't have it in the names of elves. In the names of places, however, they do. Hm. Ariaziane. Very pretty. Is the girl pretty, too?"

Vincent smiled. "Beautiful. She is a few years younger than I am. Her hair is reddish-brown and her eyes are deep blue, almost purple." He decided not to mention her previous coloration. Who knew how he might interpret that? "And she's smart, funny, just a really great person to be around."

"You seem to care for her very much."

"I love her," he said.

"I see," Aedriun replied.

And Vincent read something after those two words. "There's nothing going on between Rhia and myself, if that's what you're thinking."

Aedriun was silent a bit. Then he said, "Tell me about Rhia."

Vincent chuckled. "Well, Rhia's different." Suddenly, he laughed.

"What humors you?"

Vincent shrugged. "Oh, every once in a while, I just picture her riding a broom." He laughed again and shook his head.

"A broom?"

"Yes. Flying on one," he replied.

"Ah. She, too, is a mage? You seem to have many of those as your friends."

"Well, yeah, I guess I do. Jaz. My friend Gnorrin is, too. And he's training Ariaziane to be one."

"My word! So many!"

"Yes. But Rhia's not a mage. She's a witch."

There was a silence, and Vincent noticed the sound of the horses' steps had suddenly lessened. Aedriun had stopped. Vincent reined in his mount, then turned in his saddle to face behind him. "What's wrong?"

Aedriun walked his horse up beside him. "Rhia is a what?"

Oops, Vincent thought. "Well, a witch. Why?"

The baron's voice was subdued. "You consort with a witch! Are you so naïve that you do not understand what that means?"

Vincent felt indignation boiling up inside. He couldn't believe it. Witches and witchcraft seemed to hold some sort of negative stigma here, just as on Earth. It was all he could do to resist telling Aedriun off. Instead, he calmly said, "Evidently, I am. Would you please enlighten me?" He hoped his sarcasm was hidden.

"Vincent," he said reprovingly, "witchcraft is evil. It is a foul magic!"

With a sigh and a shake of his head, Vincent replied, "I'm fuzzy on this whole magic thing. How is the magic that Rhia uses any different than that used by Jaz?"

Aedriun set his horse to walking again, and Vincent did the same. Then he explained. "Keep in mind that I am no mage," he began, "but the magic used by your friend Jaz, and, I assume, by Ariaziane and her mentor, is a magic based in the world around us. The magic used by witches, on the other hand, comes from the world *under* us. It is dark and foul. They engage in strange rituals involving lewd behavior. And witches have knowledge that humans were not meant to know."

"Like what?" Vincent almost laughed.

"Such as their lore of plants. Herbs and berries. Their knowledge goes far, far beyond those of healers, for example."

"Why is that a bad thing?"

"Some say that type of knowledge can only be demon-spawned," Aedriun replied.

Vincent began a retort, then paused. It suddenly struck him that he knew nothing about the religious system or systems on this world. Subconsciously, he'd assumed it would be the standard God versus Devil, divine benevolence versus ultimate evil kind of scenario. But he realized he had no reason to assume such a thing. Then again, a "demon" might just be the name of a particular creature on this world, like the efreeti. Best not to comment on it until he learned more. "Is that what you believe?" he asked.

Aedriun was quiet a moment. "I do not wish to offend you, young man. But I must say in all honesty that it does not speak well of you, in my eyes, that you count a witch among your circle of friends."

"And I have no wish to offend you," Vincent replied hotly, then quickly cooled his tone, "but I do not understand the views that you and others seem to hold toward witches. I had never known a witch before I met Rhia. But on our first meeting, she saved my life when no healer could be found. I had been shot with an arrow that was unclean. It caused..." He was about to say that it caused an infection, but realized the word would be meaningless. "It caused the inner sickness," he said. "And I lay fevered and delirious, until she cured me. That, my lord baron, is what I used to form my opinion of witches. Or, at the very least, of this particular witch. And if you don't mind, I'd like to change the subject."

Aedriun seemed more than happy to comply. They rode on, Vincent telling him about Gnorrin, Blade, and more about Ariaziane. He found himself telling stories of his adventures, taking care to avoid any mention of the efreeti, since he suspected it would elicit a similar reaction to his mention of witchcraft.

It was well into the afternoon when they returned to the keep. They had lunched on some late-season fruit that Aedriun picked from a tree. But they were now hungry again and ready for dinner. They left the horses in the stable and retraced their path back to the garden entrance.

"Before we go in," Aedriun said, "would you mind showing me something?"

"What?"

"Jaz has mentioned to me your ability to do certain things, even though you lack your eyesight. He claims you can catch items thrown to you. That you can even engage in some swordplay. I must admit, I find these claims to be very difficult to believe. Are they true?"

Vincent had known this was coming. Not only was he expected to justify himself to this pompous baron, but he was apparently expected to jump through hoops as well. With a sigh, he said, "Yes, I can do these things. And yes, I will demonstrate. Briefly."

He moved away from the baron, clearing his mind of distractions. At Vincent's urging, Aedriun picked up a rock from the ground. "Are you ready?"

Vincent took one last deep breath and exhaled. He reached out with all his senses, then nodded. He heard the subtle scrape of flesh on stone as the rock left Aedriun's hand. His ears focused on its faint whistle through the air, a sound he normally never would have even heard. Vincent took one step to the right, held out his hand, and the rock fell into his palm.

"My word!" Aedriun gasped. "How in the heavens' names did you do that?"

Vincent carried the rock back to him. He frowned. Something was different. He toyed with the stone in his hands, about to say it was just senses. It was simply that he was paying much more attention to his hearing, for example, than sighted people did. But he suddenly felt that this wasn't really accurate. Certainly this was true for his ability to tell who was walking down the hall, or how close someone was standing to him. But catching the rock... There was more to it. It was almost that he could *feel* the stone coming toward him. He handed the stone back to Aedriun, who took it. "You know," he replied, "I honestly have no idea."

After dinner, Aedriun and Jaz sequestered themselves away in the den and talked. That was fine with Vincent. He'd had about enough of Aedriun for one day. He spent some time in the garden, romping with Blaise. She never seemed to tire of playing fetch. But once the big stick was thoroughly soaked with dog slobber, Vincent decided he'd had enough.

That evening, he had Hennor refill his lamp with more of the oil laced with devil's bit. His talk of his friends earlier reminded him of how much he missed Ariaziane. Since the devil's bit had worked so well in drawing Rhia to him, perhaps it would work for him to somehow communicate with the others. Of course, being a witch, it was very likely that Rhia was simply more sensitive to that type of communication. Nevertheless, he had to try.

The lamp burned as he lay on the bed, focusing his thoughts out to Ariaziane once again. He pictured her in his mind and broadcast his thoughts and emotions to her, all the longing he felt to be with her. The love. The pain at being separated from her. And the lamp burned long into the night after he fell asleep.

The following week dragged intolerably for Vincent. His mornings were spent, usually, alone. He would breakfast with the others, then retire to one of the many quiet rooms in the keep. Sometimes, if it were warm enough, he and Blaise would play together in the garden. But the weather was turning chill, and he stayed indoors more often.

His evenings, too, were spent alone, often in front of the fireplace in the keep's greatroom. Aedriun and Jaz would frequently sit in the den and talk. Sometimes their voices would carry down the hall to him. Vincent didn't care to listen. He was tired of Aedriun's voice.

He spent every day between afternoon and evening meals with the baron. They would mount up and ride, weather permitting. One day during the middle of the week, it rained. On this day, they stayed indoors and talked.

Aedriun wasn't a complete ogre, Vincent decided. He wasn't rude or nasty. On the contrary, he was polite and courteous. But he was rather pompous. And obviously, he held some attitudes that Vincent felt were closed-minded and bigoted.

Heeding Jaz's advice, Vincent tried to get to know the man. He learned about the region around Linnael. He recalled that this was where Blade and Sianon said they would depart from, to journey home. Aedriun described it to him and he thought it sounded quite nice.

Aedriun made many references to the sea. But Vincent wasn't sure whether he meant an ocean, a small sea, or a really big lake. Not that it mattered. He'd never seen any of them.

Vincent had been born within sight of Lake Erie, but never lived in that location. He'd never been to the ocean, or lived remotely close to anything called a sea. He often wondered about it, though. His senior class trip in high school had been to Virginia Beach, but he hadn't gone. That sort of ocean experience was one he'd known he could live without. He imagined hot, bright beaches, packed with noisy tourists, most of whose bodies would make his look like a Neanderthal's. Self-consciousness was really the deciding factor in his choice not to go. His friends tried to talk him into going, but he refused. He knew he wouldn't have enjoyed it, anyway.

Linnael would have no obnoxious tourism, though. More likely, Linnael would have the kind of shore that he'd seen in books and fallen in love with. Rocky, secluded shores, with lots of seagulls and crashing waves. That kind of experience he could enjoy. Aedriun had urged Vincent to visit there someday. Perhaps he would.

Vincent learned about Aedriun's knightly order, also. He found it to be almost comically cliché. It sounded like a bunch of medieval Boy Scouts. He wondered if they got merit badges for the good deeds they performed. But Vincent couldn't help thinking of Aedriun's arrogant, judgmental air. It took the humor from the situation.

The knights were in service to some duke or other. Vincent couldn't recall his name five minutes after Aedriun mentioned it. The duke lived several leagues from Linnael. Being a baron, Aedriun owned a large portion of land outside of Linnael. All in all, it seemed that Aedriun was somewhat of a bigwig. Vincent supposed he should feel honored, but couldn't quite manage it.

Aedriun, for his part, continued in his desire to see Vincent perform. They'd taken to engaging in stick battles in the garden, as he'd done with Brunik. Aedriun was no slouch with a stick. It was almost like his training with Blade, so long ago.

The baron also asked more questions, and Vincent was growing tired of avoiding totally truthful answers about his past. He thought briefly about making up a history for himself, but didn't want to get involved in such an elaborate lie. Especially since he wasn't sure, yet, whether Aedriun could tell if he were lying or not. Best not to risk it. So he became skilled at giving non-answers. Eventually, Aedriun would get the hint that he didn't want to talk about certain things.

One morning, during Aedriun's second week at Jaz's keep, Vincent woke with a start, breathing heavily. He sat up in bed, the dream-thoughts still fresh in his mind, and a sense of alarm ringing in his head.

He'd dreamed of a woman being gang raped. It was horrible, seeing the woman struggling against the men who held her down, how they held her mouth shut so she couldn't scream. But the terror in her eyes spoke more than her scream ever could have. Most disturbing was that he'd felt the woman was Ariaziane. But her hair was red, not auburn. But it wasn't the orange-red of Rhia's hair. He had no idea who could it be. But whoever she was, she was somewhere unfamiliar to him. Somewhere dirty and seedy. Was it a dream? It didn't have a dreamlike feel to it. Nor did it have any sense of urgency to it.

Vincent climbed out of bed and tried to put the horrid thoughts out of his head. He washed his face, then quickly dressed. He wrapped the bandage around his eyes, a practice he still maintained, not wanting to gross people out with the scars. He opened the door of his room quietly and listened. No sounds from below. That meant he was up before the kitchen staff. It was earlier than he thought.

He made his way to the greatroom, where Blaise greeted him. She spent most nights either with him or, on nights when he hogged the bed, in front of the fire. Hearing no crackling from the fireplace, but still feeling some heat, Vincent knew the fire was down to embers. He made his way to the hearth, where a large supply of firewood was stacked on either side of the fireplace. Carefully, he added pieces to the pile of coals. He sincerely regretted the loss of his ring. It would be much easier if he didn't have to worry about being burned while building the fire. Then again, he sincerely regretted the loss of his sight, too, which made the loss of his ring trivial by comparison.

Building the fire was difficult, but he enjoyed the challenge. He stacked the pieces of wood carefully, leaning forward to blow the embers into flame again. It took a lot of patience.

Once the fire caught, he took Blaise outside to do her morning business. It was cold, but not breezy. Snow would be coming soon, he thought. And the thought brought back memories of the previous Season of Sleep, when he and Ariaziane had walked through a crystal wonderland.

What a strange time that had been, with the whole business of Sianon and D'Ty and Blade. He sighed. He missed them, too. He desperately wanted to go home. Why couldn't Aedriun fix his damn eyes and be done with it?

Blaise finished up and came in from the cold. Back in the greatroom, Vincent settled into the big armchair in front of the now crackling fire. His frustration of a moment ago had faded, leaving reason in its place. The truth was, he knew it wouldn't be able to work that way. Even if Aedriun healed his eyes today, he couldn't just pack up and leave tomorrow. No, he'd need to repay debts, first. He owed Jaz for saving his life and for his graciousness in allowing him to stay here for so long. And, much to his chagrin, he'd probably feel obliged to repay Aedriun, too.

Not that he had any concept of how he'd do these things. Neither of them would probably accept money, and offering payment for such things seemed rather crass, anyhow. He yawned and settled back deeper into the chair, Blaise at his feet. Soon, they were both asleep.

The smell of breakfast woke him. He sat up in the chair, stretching the kink out of his neck, then rose and made his way to the dining room.

He heard Aedriun and Jaz talking. "Good morning," he said as he entered and moved toward his seat.

"Good morning," they repeated.

"Did you sleep well?" asked Aedriun.

Vincent hesitated only a moment. "Fine, thanks. You?"

"Very well, thank you."

"I didn't hear you come down, just now," said Jaz.

"I've been dozing in front of the fire." After a pause, he said, "So, what's the plan today, your lordship? Another horseback ride? More stick fights? What?" As soon as the words were out of his mouth, Vincent realized they were laced with more rancor than he'd truly intended.

Aedriun cleared his throat. To Vincent, it seemed he did so with some awkwardness. "I haven't quite decided."

"Yes, well, please let me know as soon as you do." Vincent sighed and drank some of the apple-like juice that was already poured and waiting for him. He could almost feel the tension at the table. Why was he being so nasty toward Aedriun? Sure, the guy had annoying attitudes, but that wasn't it. He'd always been able to get along with nearly everyone, including people he found more distasteful than the baron.

He thought about it while breakfast was served. The cooks had whipped up some French Toast. It was Vincent's favorite, and Jaz was fond of it, too, once Vincent had taught them how to make it. He should have been smiling in anticipation, but his mind was too bogged down by his emotional state.

Jaz was explaining French Toast to Aedriun. "My word!" the baron said. "Such a simple dish!" Aedriun sampled a bite of the thick slab of bread, laced with warm spices and hot syrup. "Delightful!" he said with his mouth full. "And this was *your* recipe, Vincent? What does it mean? *French* Toast?"

Vincent opened his mouth to explain, then stopped. How to explain the concept of France without mentioning Earth? He decided against it. "Actually, it's *French's* Toast. French was the name of one of our servants when I was a child. I assume the recipe was common to her people, whoever they were." The lie came far too easily for him.

"A well-fed people, I should say!" If Aedriun could tell when he was lying, he gave no indication.

The remainder of the meal passed quietly. Vincent could feel Aedriun watching him eat, still seemingly fascinated despite having seen him eat many times by now. He knew Aedriun's eyes followed his fork as it quickly felt out the boundaries of the remaining slice of toast on his plate, cut carefully, and unerringly stabbed the bite. He knew Aedriun found it amazing, and likely as not, Vincent would, too, were their situations reversed. But Vincent was growing weary of the attention.

And suddenly it was as though a fog cleared in his mind. That's why he was uncomfortable with Rhia's flirtations. That's why Aedriun was getting on his last nerve. It was the fact that he was the center of attention. He had been more of a sideline observer most of his life. As a child, he'd enjoyed being in the public eye just as much as the next kid. But he had outgrown that rather quickly, thanks primarily to his size. Being fat made him want to avoid the spotlight.

But now... The blindness was bad enough. It would draw people's attention to begin with. But add in his ability to function as though he were sighted, and that drew more. Toss in his extra abilities, whatever their nature, to fully utilize his remaining senses, and that made him an anomaly. Major league attention. And he didn't really care for it.

He finished the last of his breakfast, draining his juice glass. He wiped his mouth with a napkin and stood. "If you'll both excuse me...?" The baron and the mage murmured their assents, and Vincent made his way upstairs.

He headed to the bathroom first. Not bathroom, he corrected himself. Garderobe. What a silly name, he thought. Sounds more like an article of clothing. Still, it was a lot more convenient than an outhouse. The garderobe was, essentially, an *inhouse*. The stall was enclosed in a tiny space at the end of the hall. The seat was mounted atop a deep shaft that led down the outer wall of the keep. The several garderobes in the keep all had shafts into a huge pit underground. It was simple, efficient, and remarkably enough, didn't stink. But he still would've preferred a flush toilet. And a sink with running water. And a big, fat roll of soft white toilet paper. And a bunch of other things, too, now that he thought about it.

He washed his hands back in his room, then sighed and sat on the edge of his bed. It was cold in his room. Maybe Hennor could put something around the balcony door to prevent drafts.

A chill ran through him. It was too cold to remain, so he left the room and headed back downstairs. Aedriun met him at the bottom.

"I have decided that we should practice swordplay today," the baron announced.

Vincent frowned. "Again?" he drawled. "Haven't you seen enough of it from me?"

"On the contrary," he replied. "I've seen none. What I have seen is stickplay. Today we use real swords. I've sent Jaz to fetch yours. As well as your armor."

Something about the way Aedriun stated that he'd *sent* Jaz to get the sword made Vincent uneasy. He shook his head. "Why? What purpose can this serve?"

Vincent could almost feel Aedriun's patronizing smile. "Please humor me, young man. It is something I wish to do."

It was difficult to bite back the smart retort, and Vincent felt sure that Aedriun could tell. But he was beginning not to care about offending the man. He was beginning to think he might be being played for a fool.

After Jaz returned, Aedriun helped Vincent into his armor. For his part, Vincent stood still and refused to say a word. This was getting to be too much. As soon as the armor was secure on him, he marched outside to the gardens. He was limbering up, getting used to being in chain mail again. At least, that was his pretext. All he really wanted to do was let off some steam.

Aedriun joined him. "Where are your gauntlets?"

Vincent turned to face him. "Never got into the habit of wearing them."

The baron made a disgusted noise. "It is a habit you *should* get into. One blow of a sword to your hand can sever your fingers. And if that isn't enough for you to be run through, then you'll be fingerless for the rest of your life. You think you miss your eyesight, boy, think how you'd feel to never use your hand again."

231

While Vincent was working up some indignation to being called "boy," Jaz was speaking. "I'll fetch him a pair." As the mage did so, Vincent listened to Aedriun draw his sword and begin to loosen up. Before long, Jaz returned and brought the gauntlets to him.

"Whose are they?" Vincent asked as he pulled them on. They were soft and comfortable and seemed to fit perfectly. As he gripped his sword, he felt none of the awkwardness he'd expected.

"Well, they're yours, I suppose. They were in the other bag that you took from the thieves. I picked up both, since I didn't know which was yours. I looked through it some time ago. They've been sitting there ever since."

"Thank you," Vincent said. "They feel fine."

"Are we ready, then?" Aedriun chimed in. "Time to see if your abilities are just as useful when you're under a real threat, instead of only the danger of a stick welting."

Vincent felt his annoyance with the man rising up inside. "My lord baron," Vincent said crisply as they walked to an open space, "one way or another, this is the last time I jump through hoops for you. I will entertain you this one last time. Is that understood?"

"I hear your words," Aedriun said, annoying Vincent even further. "Ready? Begin."

Aedriun began with a simple feint that Vincent easily parried. He smiled inside. It had been some time since he'd wielded a real sword. To his surprise, it seemed like a part of his arm, even more comfortable than it had been before. He countered with a lunge that Aedriun sidestepped.

They continued for many minutes, circling each other, thrusting, swinging, ducking, parrying. At last, Aedriun said, "You amaze me, Vincent. I admit it freely. I have never seen anything like this."

"And I haven't seen *anything* in far too long," Vincent replied angrily. "I'm tired of your games, Aedriun," he said, parrying with such strength that Aedriun stepped backwards. "When are you going to conclude this test?" Aedriun said nothing, merely redoubled his efforts, hacking viciously at Vincent's blind, but lightning-fast, defense. "When, Aedriun?" Vincent yelled.

"When I am satisfied! No sooner!" He attacked again.

"Wrong answer!" Vincent growled. He felt something snap inside, and he whirled the sword like a fly swatter. "It ends now! I am sick of your pompous attitude," he said, and his parry struck Aedriun's sword like a hammer blow. "Of your judgmental attitude!" The next swing struck Aedriun's blade dead center, producing a frightening crack as the baron's sword broke in half. "In short," Vincent said, drawing back once more, "I am sick of *you!*"

A flash of reason invaded his rage, and he pulled his swing ever so slightly. He paused then, shocked at realizing how he'd lost control of himself. He stood there, panting, a thought pressing at the back of his mind. Had he felt the sword connect with something? He brought the tip of it to his nose and smelled the unmistakable scent of blood. "Shit," he gasped. "Aedriun? Say something!" He rushed toward the man. He hadn't heard him fall. How bad was the injury?

Aedriun placed his arm on Vincent's shoulder. "I am unharmed," he said. But Vincent could hear the tinge of nervousness and shock in his voice. Obviously, he wasn't completely unharmed. And then, from deep down inside, a laugh began.

Vincent thought he was hearing things. Aedriun chuckled loudly, slapping the boy on the arm. "You're sick of me, eh? You dislike my attitudes and manner? Is that right?" Confused, Vincent only nodded. "Speak up," Aedriun said. "Tell me what you think!"

"I thought I just had."

"Tell me again."

"Very well," Vincent said firmly, thinking that Aedriun was leading him into another little test. "From the moment I met you, I disliked your demeanor."

"Yes," Aedriun prompted, squeezing his arm.

"Your overbearing, pompous, condescending attitude really makes me want to throw up. And your entire little testing process of me, or of anyone, is appalling!"

"Yes!" said Aedriun. "Good! And you wanted to cut me in half, didn't you?"

"No, I just wanted to punch you in the nose."

Aedriun laughed loudly. "Wonderful! But take those gauntlets off before you do. I don't want to be unconscious for the rest of the day. Or worse." He slapped Vincent's arm playfully, then turned aside. "Rather upset about the sword, though. It was one of my favorites."

"What are you talking about?" Vincent demanded.

Aedriun laughed again. "You passed the test, you ninny. What do you think I'm talking about?"

Jaz was beside them now. Vincent heard him shake out a piece of cloth. Aedriun thanked him. Then Jaz lifted one of Vincent's arms and examined the gauntlets. He mumbled something under his breath, then said, "You are right, Aedriun. Vincent, it seems you've inherited something quite valuable. These are Gauntlets of Strength."

"Huh?"

Aedriun explained. "Magically fortified gauntlets. I can attest to their effectiveness." He laughed again. "Thank you, Jaz," he then said. "Sorry about the blood."

Vincent heard Jaz say, "Ahhh. My lord baron is not without his own resources, I see."

"Resources are wonderful things," Aedriun said with a chuckle.

"Would someone please clue me in?" Vincent barked. "I have no idea what's going on. I've got magic gauntlets, okay, I've absorbed that much. But what else am I missing? Aedriun, do you mean to tell me that the entire thing was a test? Your attitude, too, was a part of the test?"

"Certainly! Do you really think someone with that kind of personality would come all this way to cure your eyesight?" Vincent only stammered in reply to that. He didn't really know. "Oh, and Vincent, I do apologize for upsetting you with my comments about Rhia. I personally have nothing against witches. Never met one before, actually. If they all look like her, I think I could be willing to meet many of them, though! But bear in mind that others in this world certainly do hold that attitude."

Vincent's heart skipped a beat. "Why did you say it like that? 'Others in this world,' you said."

Aedriun's voice grew serious. "Am I wrong in my assumption that you are not of this world?"

"No," Vincent replied after a brief pause. "No, you're not. How did you know?"

"Just a number of little things, my friend. Little things you've said, that Jaz has said. Your mannerisms, your speech. It all added up to something very odd. And Vincent, you're associating with some major people. It seems as if the gods are watching out for your welfare. You have Jaz, Rhia, your friends Ariaziane and Gnorrin. Me, if I might be so bold. I'm not a mage, but I'm not without my resources." He chuckled as he finished. "How does it look, Jaz?"

"Nearly fully healed," said the mage.

"I thought it might. It was just a scratch. Thank you, Vincent, for pulling that swing."

The young man was shaking his head. "*Now* what are we talking about? What is healed? Your wound?"

"Yes. Give me your hand."

Vincent did so. Aedriun removed one of Vincent's gauntlets, then guided the young man's fingers to his own chin. Vincent felt the fine stubble. Aedriun obviously didn't wear a beard. And running diagonally across the front of his chin was what felt like a scar. "This is what I did to you?"

"No, it's what's left of what you did to me. Jaz's handkerchief has ample evidence that you did more than this. But it is healed now, and so shall your eyes be healed."

Vincent felt a ring being slipped onto his hand. "What is it?"

"Magic," the baron replied. "The ring heals injury. It rejuvenates. It even, as you've just discovered, grows new tissue."

"Regeneration," Vincent breathed. "This ring is going to grow new eyes for me?"

"In a manner of speaking, yes. It will renew them. Any dead tissue will be restored. However," Aedriun warned, "since your injury is grievous and is now quite old, it will take many days for it to be healed. My injury was slight and recent. That is why it was healed so quickly."

Vincent wondered briefly about the process, from a technical sense. Then he wondered if it would hurt. He took a deep breath and exhaled. "I think I need to sit down."

He followed the others inside and to the greatroom. Jaz pulled chairs over to the fire while Aedriun tossed on more firewood.

"I'm very relieved," Vincent said, "that you're not as much of a jerk as I thought you were."

"Your meaning seems clear, though the word is not. Regardless, I am pleased that you find I'm *not* a jerk. Whatever one is."

"Your performance was quite believable," said Jaz.

"Tell me about these gauntlets," Vincent said.

Jaz fielded the question as he sat. "As mentioned, the strength of your arms and hands is increased, so you can grip the sword tighter, therefore having more control over it. Did it feel any different to you?"

"Yes. It felt like it had no extra weight at all. Like it was just an extension of my own arm."

"Exactly," said Aedriun as he finished with the fire. "But you know the sword still does have all the heft you'd want it to have. The fact that you wield it like part of your own body makes it just that much more effective."

Vincent took all this in. Truthfully, the idea rather frightened him. He'd nearly killed Aedriun. Were these gauntlets really a good thing to have? Another thought struck him, then. He frowned, then said, "Aedriun, I guess there's one thing I'm still puzzled about. If your attitudes were all an act, was the test an act, too? Or was it real? And if it was real, why?"

"No," Aedriun replied. "The test was real enough. But it was not for the purpose that I claimed. Vincent, all I wanted to learn was what kind of man you are. Had I decided you were a complete villain, then I would not have allowed you the use of the ring. Anything short of that and I would have, even if I found that I did not like you."

"If that's the case, why does it matter whether you like me or not? I mean, you could have concluded very quickly whether or not I was, as you said, a complete villain. Why bother with two weeks of testing?"

"Because I wanted to know your mettle. To see if you might be the kind of man I would want with me."

"With you? What do you mean?"

"As a knight, eventually. In the service of the duke. You'd begin as my squire, and eventually become a knight in your own right."

Vincent's jaw dropped as he took this in. "I don't know what to say."

"You don't need to say anything. It's just something for you to think about."

And think about it, he did. For the remainder of the afternoon, he sat in front of the fire in the greatroom. Long after Aedriun and Jaz had gone on to talk of other things, he stayed there, stroking Blaise and wondering how long it would be before he'd be able to see again.

Aedriun agreed that it had been beneficial, using the poultices for as long as he had. It might well have reduced the healing time by nearly half. Still, it could be a week or more. Vincent didn't mind that. He'd been sightless this long. Another week wasn't going to kill him.

After dinner, he went straight to his room. The day's events had taken a lot out of him. As he reclined on his bed, inhaling the burning essence of devil's bit and thinking of Ariaziane, he felt his eyes begin to faintly tingle. He smiled, then changed the thoughts he was trying to broadcast to the girl.

See you soon.

❧ Eighteen ❧

Vincent woke late on the morning of the seventh day since donning the ring. Sunlight streamed in through the small window set in the room's balcony door. He smiled as he rose from bed, wrapping his robe around him. Then he opened the door and stood on the balcony.

He breathed the chill air deep into his lungs. And he looked... He looked out over the expanse of tree-covered hills, to the craggy mountains in the distance. The range practically began in Jaz's back yard and seemed to stretch forever on either side in the front of the keep. He wasn't sure, but it seemed as though his vision might actually be better than before the fight that took away his sight. The trees would have appeared more fuzzy, he thought. But that could be his imagination, he realized. It didn't matter. He could see! It didn't matter whether his vision was twenty-twenty or not, as long as he could see *something*.

His sight had begun returning the day after Aedriun had placed the ring on his finger. That vision had only consisted of a dim haze of light, and then only when he looked directly at the sun, but it had been a start. Over the ensuing days, his sight had gradually grown clearer. There was some discomfort in the regrowth of his eyes, bordering on pain at times. But that didn't matter, either. It was nothing compared to the pain of the injury.

By the fourth day, he could discern facial features. The first of the faces he encountered was Blaise's. She'd licked him awake that morning, and he'd nearly cried when he opened his eyes to see her black snout pushing up against his cheek. He thanked Aedriun again that day.

Aedriun didn't look like Vincent had pictured. The man was in his early forties, he estimated. He was, indeed, beardless, but had a tremendous mustache with huge handlebars swooping down the sides of his chin. Both his mustache and his hair were black with generous dashes of grey. There was a kindly crinkle in the corner of each eye, but Vincent didn't notice that until the fifth day.

That fifth day was spent with people. Everyone in the keep whom he'd previously only known by voice or scent now had faces. He was mildly amused to find that Hennor looked exactly as he'd pictured him. Medium height and build, balding a little, with a kindly but proper-looking face.

The sixth day was spent riding with Jaz and Aedriun. The countryside around Jaz's keep was spectacular. He knew then that he'd want to settle down in the mountains when the time came. He hoped Ariaziane liked mountains.

Jaz's keep turned out to be much larger than he'd thought. There were wings he'd never set foot in, and several floors above his, not just the one he knew about. Jaz must also be quite a bit wealthier than he'd anticipated, which meant that he certainly couldn't offer him money to repay his generosity. He'd have to think of something else.

Vincent took one more look at the expanse before him. All the leaves were off the deciduous trees, but the hills had plenty of evergreens. There was snow on the mountain peaks, but none at lower elevations, yet. He hoped to be home before that occurred. Aedriun, too, would want to be home before the snows, and had a longer trek than Vincent.

Stepping back inside, he closed the door and then dressed. One of his bandages lay atop the dressing table. He lifted it, running his fingers over the cloth. After a moment, he tied it snugly around his forehead, tying the knot over his right ear. He'd worn a headband in high school, always wanting to be a hippie, despite being born a couple decades too late. This headband would symbolize something far different, though. He looked into the mirror above the washbasin, toying with the twin streamers of extra cloth that hung down from the knot. Yes, he thought. This would be a fitting reminder.

After breakfast, Vincent asked Jaz for some writing supplies. Then he sequestered himself in the greatroom, recounting the events thus far on his adventure. He'd previously regretted his decision to leave his journal at home. But if he had brought the book along, who knows whether he'd still have it or not? The thieves could have taken it, too. His comments could be transferred easily enough into the journal when he got home.

Vincent spent the entire afternoon transcribing all the recent happenings to paper. There were more than twenty pages, when all was finally written. So much had happened, and so many emotions needed to be captured. When he finished, he read over the summary. It didn't really convey everything he'd felt. But then, he thought, how could it?

After dinner, Vincent, Jaz, and Aedriun sat around the table, sipping hot drinks and nibbling on dessert cakes. Jaz leaned back in his chair and turned to Aedriun. "Will you be leaving when Vincent's eyes are fully healed? You're welcome to stay."

The baron smiled. Vincent couldn't get over the difference between the reality of the man and the image he'd constructed of him. "I should return as soon as possible. I appreciate your generosity, however." Then he turned to Vincent. "I imagine perhaps two more days should complete the rejuvenation."

"Two more days," Vincent repeated. "Honestly, I feel as though my eyes are as good now as they were before the incident. But if two more days will make them even better, I won't argue!"

"Then shall I assume your departure will be in three days, Aedriun?" Jaz asked, and the baron nodded his confirmation.

Vincent felt a knot in his stomach. "Aedriun," he began. "Something has been on my mind. I've been trying to think of a way that I can repay you..."

But Aedriun waved his hand. "It is not necessary. Simply promise to visit. I lead such a busy existence, generally, that it will be nice to see a friend."

Vincent smiled at being acknowledged as the baron's friend. "All the more reason I feel in your debt. You've spent nearly two weeks here, plus the travel time. If your schedule is so busy..."

"I left matters in competent hands. And though those hands will be more than willing to relinquish the reins, I have no worries that all has not gone well. Trouble yourself no longer."

Vincent sighed and allowed the matter to drop. Then he turned to Jaz. "And what about you, my generous friend and host? I am incredibly in your debt. You have saved my life, nursed me through a miserable time, and arranged for my sight to be restored.

I owe you more than I can ever hope to repay. Yet I must make the attempt. Tell me how."

The mage stroked his dark, thin beard as he pondered the question. "It has been my pleasure to assist you, Vincent. You know that. There is, however, a matter that could benefit from your aid."

"Name it."

The mage leaned forward, resting his elbows on the table. "As you may recall, when you and I first met, I was engaged in a bit of a quest. Due to the turn of events that led us to be sitting here right now, the quest remains unfulfilled. I would like your help in its completion, if you're still willing."

"Absolutely. Happy to. What were you looking for?"

Jaz cleared his throat. "Something that I'm not sure can even be found, with or without your assistance. Rumors say that, ages ago, the great mage Kurean traveled these lands in search of a place to dwell."

"That guy got around. I sure hear his name a lot."

"He was, I would say, the most talented mage in this part of the world in the past five hundred years," Jaz said. Vincent nodded. "At any rate, as the story goes, he set up a secret manufactory in the region, where he designed many wondrous magical items. No one has, to my knowledge, ever located this workshop.

"I settled in this valley about ten years ago and began looking in earnest. All my searching has concluded that he did not dwell in this valley, nor in the immediately surrounding mountains. The forest in which we met, however, seems to beckon me. But no spells of divination reveal anything. Lately, I have taken to wandering through the wood in the hopes that some forgotten echo of his magic might still remain to be detected. But nothing, so far, has called to me.

"This search could go on for quite some time. Naturally, I don't expect you to assist me for an unreasonable period. What I propose is that we strike out after our friend Aedriun's departure and search until weather forbids it."

Vincent pondered this. "I'll help in any way I can, though I don't see right now how I can do so. I'm no mage, Jaz, able to detect magic as you can." He cast a look at Aedriun, as if expecting the baron to back up his claims.

Jaz merely nodded. "I realize that, but you never know when a good sword arm will come in handy. Besides, I can certainly use the company. Talking to oneself becomes a trifle boring after a while."

The young man echoed Jaz's chuckle. "I know that from experience. Well, however I can help, I will. Even if it's only as comic relief."

The following days passed quickly, and by the time Vincent returned the ring to Aedriun, his sight was as clear as he could have hoped for it to be. He couldn't imagine how the ring had restored his sight to such a state. The only explanation he could think of would've required the ring to actually read his DNA and understand exactly how an eyeball was supposed to be shaped, then building from that blueprint. Since such a concept simply blew his mind, he tried not to think about it.

Before he and Jaz bade the baron a fond farewell, Aedriun made Vincent promise to visit, come the Season of Green. It was strange, Vincent thought, how saddened he was by Aedriun's departure. Had he grown so fond of the man in such a short time, or was it simply his gratitude for the restoration of his sight? He didn't know. Nor was it important. Either way, he'd keep his promise.

Jaz began preparations for their impending excursion almost immediately. He packed warm clothing for the two of them, plenty of dried meats and biscuits, a small barrel of water for those times when they were not near a stream. Vincent looked over the array and said, "How long do you expect this to take?"

The mage smiled apologetically. "That depends on how our fortune runs. There is no way we can scour the entire woods before the weather forces us to return. But we should be able to cover a good portion."

The boy frowned. "But what exactly are we looking for? You said you'd cast spells in order to locate where Kurean had been, but found nothing. What is our plan, here?"

Jaz folded his arms across his chest and looked his friend in the eye. "My suspicion is that he has cloaked the entrance to his lab with an intricate illusion, causing it to blend into the surrounding forest. And, he has in turn cloaked the illusion, making it undetectable by magical means. This is strong stuff, Vincent. Kurean was a great one."

"Your plan, then, is to hopefully stumble upon it?"

The mage shrugged. "I wish I could determine another way."

"Then Kurean, in his effort to keep the location secret, would have tucked it away in a place least likely to be stumbled upon."

"Yes, but the shape and location of the forest make that almost impossible to determine."

"What do you mean?"

Jaz moved to a desk and dug out some paper and a quill pen. Vincent followed and watched him sketch. "This is the valley we're in right now." He drew a long rectangular region, running diagonally on the page. "We are at the southwestern end," he said. Mountains surrounded the entire valley, except for an opening facing southeast, at the northernmost end. "The forest," he continued, drawing to reflect his words, "comes nearly to the mouth, here, stretching in each direction away from it so that only about half a league of somewhat open land lies between the mountains and the forest. These are well traveled, as you would expect." Jaz quickly completed the sketch of the forest's boundaries, a squat oval with the familiar panhandle to the southeast, where he'd entered the forest so long ago. To the south, Jaz now drew a smaller wooded area. "This gap in between, here, is likewise well-traveled. Two rivers," he said as he drew, "extend up through the forest, one of which has its origin in the mountains just north of here."

Vincent completed his thought. "Kurean wouldn't build near the rivers, either, since they'd be used for travel." He looked over the sketch. "Somewhere between the rivers, then? Deep in the forest where travel would be lightest."

"Possibly. Or would he have gone the simpler route, and put it on the very edge of the forest somewhere? From what I know of him, he would not have chosen the most obvious location."

"Then again, the most obvious location, in this case, covers an impressive area. He could have chosen that because it's harder to search. It's easy enough, though time consuming, to search the perimeter of a forest. But to go deep within..."

"Yes," he said, putting the pen and ink away. "Therein lies our dilemma."

Vincent toyed with his mustache, tugging on it just above his lip, a habit he had whenever he was deep in thought. "Tell me about the nature of the illusion he might have cast."

The mage shrugged. "Obviously he would have the area look just like the rest of the forest. As I said."

"The whole way up? Complete trees?"

"Of course. It would not be convincing, otherwise."

"Right," Vincent murmured, deep in thought. "What about wind?" he asked suddenly.

Jaz nodded. "Yes, the illusion could simulate wind."

"I don't mean imaginary wind. I mean real wind," he said, growing excited. "The winds during the warm months are predominantly from the southeast, coming off the warmer sea down by Linnael. But what about during the colder months?"

"In colder months, we often have winds coming down from the north," Jaz said.

"Yes. Now, if Kurean had set up his illusion to imitate the majority of the winds, those coming from the southeast, then what happens when we get northern winds during the Season of Sleep?"

"It's unlikely," Jaz said slowly, "that anyone would have the inclination to watch the entire roof of the forest during the coldest time of year." Vincent nodded his agreement. Jaz chuckled to himself. A slow smile grew across his face. Then he clapped Vincent on the arm. "I shall have to re-evaluate my opinion of you warriors."

☙ ❧

They considered simply sending the mage's familiar aloft and allowing him to do the aerial surveying of the forest. However, the fact that two pairs of eyes are better than one, even if that one pair is very acute, caused them to undertake the venture personally.

They floated above the forest, while the hawk did lazy circles high above them. Jaz had cast a spell of levitation on the pair. It took some getting used to, but Vincent gradually became comfortable with the sensation. He knew it took a lot out of Jaz to maintain the levitation on both of them for the entire daylight hours, with only minimal breaks. At night, they would lower themselves to the ground within the forest, resuming their observations the following morning.

Vincent scanned the roof of the forest carefully. It was difficult work, maintaining vigilance over a large area of tree branches, studying the way the breezes tossed them. After a while, his eyes would play tricks on him. The branches would seem to all blend together. He grew tired more quickly every day. And with no protection from the wind, the chill seemed to drill right through to the bone.

On the fourth day, it snowed. There was no accumulation on the ground, but it was an early snow, nonetheless. Vincent marveled at the sight of snow falling all around him, and below him, watching the flakes spiral down on their journey to the trees. It was an experience he never expected to repeat. And for the hundredth time, he silently thanked Aedriun for giving him back his eyesight.

Late on the seventh day, with little daylight remaining, Vincent thought his eyes were playing tricks on him again. A section of the roof of the forest didn't blow in the same direction as the surrounding branches. He'd gotten used to seeing sections that didn't move at all, despite branches nearby being tossed as he would expect. It took him several seconds to realize that this was exactly what he was looking for.

He turned to his friend. The mage and he faced in opposite directions to cover as much area as possible. "Jaz," he said, drawing his attention. And he pointed. "I think we might have struck paydirt."

Jaz gazed at the trees. "Yes," he said softly. "Yes!"

The mage maneuvered the pair of them over the contrary area, then slowly lowered them, treating Vincent to a second astounding sensation on this venture: that of his body passing through a seemingly solid object without touching anything. He watched the illusory tree branches go through his own limbs. He tried to grab one with his hand, only to have it also pass harmlessly through. It gave him the willies, but made him laugh just the same.

Soon they reached the ground. Vincent looked around, expecting to see some sort of building. But all he saw were trees and a tiny stream. He turned to Jaz. "So. Where is it?"

The mage frowned. "Underground, most likely."

"Oh, swell." Vincent sat down on a fallen tree trunk, thinking only after he was seated that it could've been an illusion, too. That was an embarrassment he was thankful not to have encountered. With a sigh, he rubbed his tired eyes. "I hope you won't think I'm a party-pooper, but I'm really beat. I suggest we make camp and just start searching in the morning."

Jaz stood with his hands on his hips, surveying the immediate area. His red cape flapped in the very real breeze. Finally, he turned to Vincent and nodded. "Though I positively ache with anticipation, I agree. We will do better tomorrow after some rest." He unslung his pack from his back and began clearing a smooth area on which to place their bedrolls.

Vincent put his pack down. He chuckled, looking at the fallen trunk. "At least I won't have to go far in search of firewood," he said. He dug in his pack and removed the magical gauntlets. Donning them, he began to break smaller branches off the dead tree. By the time he had enough for a long fire, Jaz had cleared the space for the firepit, surrounding it with stones.

He piled some wood into the small circle, then began stacking the rest nearby for refueling throughout the night. Jaz had finished setting up his bedroll and now joined Vincent at the firepit. "Ready?" he asked, preparing to ignite the logs magically. Vincent opened his mouth to agree, but stopped. He held up a hand and stood upright. He sniffed. Jaz immediately grew concerned. "What is it?"

Vincent began to pivot, scanning in all directions. He stopped, then pointed through the trees. "There," he said.

Jaz frowned as he saw the flicker of a campfire, perhaps a hundred and fifty yards away. "This does not bode well."

"No shit," Vincent replied. He had a bad feeling about this. He wondered what could possibly cause others to be in the exact same part of the forest. Wildest coincidence, perhaps, but Vincent didn't think so. "What do you want to do?"

"First of all," Jaz said, "I think some aerial reconnaissance is in order." At this point, the mage's familiar came swooping down to land on his outstretched hand. He watched as the bird looked in the direction of the campfire. Then it took off again, flitting through the trees. Less than a minute later, the mage closed his eyes and stood entranced. "I count six men at the campsite. Three are near the fire, the others nearby."

"What are they doing?"

"Nothing so much as preparing for the night, just as we are. They do not, however, seem to be aware of our presence, which is the most important thing." He opened his eyes and faced Vincent. "Now we must make certain it remains that way."

Vincent frowned. "Can't really make a fire, I guess."

"No, but we can still have heat." Jaz mumbled under his breath and made some gestures. He stood with his back toward the other camp's fire, and Vincent saw the tiniest of flames hovering in the air between Jaz's hands. The flame grew and grew as Jaz continued the spell, and Vincent felt the ambient temperature of the forest rising around him. Finally, the mage stopped. The flame disappeared. "That should be sufficient," he said.

Vincent nodded. The area around them was now comfortable for sleeping. "How long will this last?"

"I'm sure it will last until sunrise. We'll have no light, but this should prevent our neighbors from paying any visits this evening."

Vincent nodded. "Is there anything to prevent us from paying *them* a visit this evening?"

"Nothing at all," the mage smiled.

When it was fully dark, they made their move. Jaz instructed Vincent to keep close to him at all times. The mage was casting his spell of silence, just as he'd done when the two of them attempted to infiltrate the thieves' encampment. Vincent hoped this foray didn't have as poor a result.

Moving through the woods, making no sound at all, was again unnerving to Vincent. He only wished it were possible for them to communicate within their circle of the spell. They made their way quickly to the other campsite, gazing around the trees at the layout.

The light of the moon allowed them to count the men with little difficulty. There were ten in the campsite. Vincent frowned and looked at Jaz, who wore an expression of consternation. What were these men doing here, if not the same thing as he and Jaz? He sighed, flexing his fingers inside the gauntlets' soft leather. The situation had his nerves on edge. His natural impulsiveness urged him to just stride right into the midst of them, but his common sense won out. He folded his arms across his chest and leaned against a tree, hoping Jaz had a better idea about things than he did.

Suddenly, there was a strange sensation at the back of his head, sort of like the feeling he got when someone was staring at him. He frowned. As he began to turn his head, he felt a tap on his shoulder. He whirled, only to find himself with the point of a sword aimed at his midsection. He froze, staring at the man who held him at his mercy.

But Jaz noticed the action and before Vincent knew it, the swordsman was falling to the ground, unconscious. And then, Vincent could hear again. He looked to see Jaz move quickly to the side of the fallen man. He knelt down along with the mage.

"Not a good development," whispered Jaz.

"Nope." Vincent studied the man's face. There was something familiar about it. Then he stood and scanned the crowd in the camp again.

After making sure the fallen man was solidly asleep, Jaz joined Vincent. "What is it?"

"There are more," he replied quietly. "That man is one of the party that attacked me. But I don't see the rest of his group, which means they must be elsewhere."

Jaz nodded. "I'm not surprised. I see no one in the group that seems to be a mage, though they must certainly have one with them."

"Possibly already inside Kurean's hidden laboratory?"

"Very likely," Jaz whispered.

Vincent glanced at the fallen man. A slow smile spread across his face. "Feel up to some 'good cop, bad cop' routine?"

Jaz raised an eyebrow. "Some what?"

"Never mind," he said. "Just get that circle of silence running again."

The mage did so and Vincent hefted the swordsman, swinging him up over his shoulder. Then they made their way back to their own campsite.

Once there, Vincent dumped the prisoner on the ground, bound his hands and feet, and put a cloth gag in his mouth. Then he explained his plan to Jaz. Once the mage understood, he removed his spell from the man, then backed off to the edge of the campsite, allowing Vincent to run the show.

Vincent crouched near the man and waited for him to rouse. "Ah," he said in a low voice, once he saw movement return to the man, "you're awake." The man's eyes widened as he realized his captive state. He turned angry eyes on Vincent and began to struggle. "Don't!" Vincent hissed, restraining him with a hand. "Don't let him hear you!" The man paused, the anger turning to suspicion as he stared. Vincent nodded his head in Jaz's direction. "Look," he said conspiratorially. "The one thing you don't want to do is get him mad. You know how mages can get."

This struck home with the man. All struggling ceased as he looked at Jaz's back. "Mmph?" he asked.

"Yes, he's a mage. How else do you think we captured you? You had me cold, friend, but you never had a chance. You're lucky he didn't kill you."

"Mph mrf?"

"Certainly. He's mighty angry, let me tell you. Your friends over there would all be dead now if I hadn't talked him out of it. You see, I don't like killing people if I don't have to. You know what I mean?" The man nodded, his eyes darting back and forth between Vincent and Jaz. "Well, I told him that if we took you prisoner, we'd likely be able to get the information he wants out of you, rather than having to force it out of your friends."

The prisoner's eyes narrowed. "Mphl mbr wk."

"Oh, I know they'd never talk. But you know mages. You don't *have* to talk for them to find out what they want to know. You know what I mean?" Vincent shook his head sadly. "It's not pretty when they rip someone's mind apart." The man simply stared at him. Vincent was pleased to see beads of sweat forming on his forehead. "Now, listen, friend. I suggest you tell him what he wants to know." When the man hesitated, Vincent went on. "I'd hate to see your mind turned to pudding." With that, he turned around and motioned to Jaz. "He's awake."

The mage strode across the campsite, then crouched beside the man and stared at him for a moment. He reached out and harshly ripped the gag from his mouth. For a long moment, the two stared at each other. Finally, Jaz inched his face closer and said simply, "Well?"

At that, the man began babbling. "I know nothing! What do you want? I'm nobody. I can't... I don't... Don't kill me. Don't rip my mind!"

Vincent saw Jaz bite down on his lip to stifle the laugh. "I will, if you don't tell me what I want to know." The man's eyes widened even further and his mouth worked, but no words issued forth, merely a squeaky whine.

Jaz frowned in disgust. "He will not cooperate," he said to Vincent. "I'm going to have to pull it from him." And he reached out toward the man's face with his hand.

Vincent gently grabbed him by the wrist. "Now, wait. I'm sure he's willing to be helpful." He turned to the man, placing his other hand on the man's shoulder. "Right?" The man nodded hysterically. "See? He wants to be helpful."

Jaz smiled wickedly. "Perhaps I don't want him to be helpful." The prisoner's face blanched. Then Jaz shrugged. "All right. Have it your way."

Vincent patted the man's shoulder. "Good. That's great. Now," he said, looking at the man, "tell him what he wants to know."

The prisoner looked at Vincent, eyes wide. "But he... I don't know... He hasn't asked me..."

"Hmm," Vincent said. "I see what you mean, Jaz. He's not cooperating at all. Look, friend, you'd better tell him what he wants to hear. I can't stress that enough. Don't you understand what he might do to you?"

"But he hasn't..." The man sputtered. "I don't..."

"I do believe the man has a death wish, Jaz. Pity. I guess you'll just have to take it from him."

At this, the man sucked in a gasping breath and Vincent thought he might go into coronary arrest. "No! I'll tell you anything! Just ask me a question!" His voice began to rise, so Vincent quickly leaned in and clamped a hand over his mouth. The man froze in terror.

"You'll keep your voice down, understand?" The man nodded. "Okay. First question. How many in your party, total? And no lies. The mage will know if you're lying."

The man sucked his lower lip after Vincent removed his hand, having evidently smacked it on his teeth. "Sixteen."

"Including the mage?" Jaz put in, taking over the questioning.

The man nodded. "Aye."

"What is the mage's name?"

"Beltun Sagasht."

After a pause, Jaz continued. "And he is in the laboratory already?"

Again he nodded. "Along with five others, yes."

"What have they found?"

"I don't know. I mean, nothing, the last I'd heard. Honest."

"Where is the entrance to the laboratory?"

The man hesitated. "In the tent."

"In the tent?" Vincent asked.

"Aye. The entrance was hidden in a hollow tree stump. We put up the tent around it. The big one, in the center of camp."

Vincent looked up at Jaz. The mage shook his head slightly, then walked away, deep in thought. Vincent turned back to the man, all traces of joking gone from him. "Another question, my friend. Is your boss down in the laboratory right now?"

"My boss?"

"A traveling companion of yours. Older, perhaps in his forties. Muscular. Arrogant bastard. And, if I'm not mistaken, with a recently broken nose."

The man froze, then, straining in the darkness to make out Vincent's facial features. "How did you know that?" he whispered.

"Because I'm the one who broke it," he hissed. "You and he and two others attacked me in the forest southeast of here, some time ago. You stole my money, my horse, my sword, and a piece of jewelry that is of immense sentimental value to me. One of you hurt my dog, damn it, and put a crossbow bolt in my arm! You left me for dead."

"I remember," the man said weakly. "Then it was you and this mage who tracked us down later and destroyed our camp?"

"You're damn right it was."

"But you should be dead. They told me your head was cut off!"

"I grew another one, moron. Now you listen to me. Where can I find that old bastard? I'm going to beat the shit out of him."

"No," the man whined. "Please. Don't kill me. I never hurt you."

"Oh, shut up! I'm not going to kill you. Your friend, on the other hand..."

"He is my brother and please do not kill him. I will do anything. I will serve you."

"I don't want you to serve me, you idiot. You think I want any further reminder of what I went through for the past months? Your dear brother didn't take my head off. But he did take my eyes, damn him! He took my eyes!"

The prisoner was breathing heavily, frightened by Vincent's rage. "You do not seem to be without them."

"No. Not any longer. But I was, thief. I was. And let me tell you something else that should be no surprise to you. Having your eyes turned to pulp by a sword *hurts!*" Even in the dark, Vincent could see the man cringe. He imagined that his newly regrown eyes probably afforded him better nocturnal vision than most people. He stood up. "Brother or no, he is going to feel some pain, too."

He walked off, leaving the man to dwell on that one. Jaz was still deep in thought when Vincent approached. "So what do you think?"

The mage looked up at him. "I thought I was being the bad cop."

"Alternate scenario. Bad cop, worse cop. Not as common, but quite effective. Anyway, what should our next step be?"

Jaz frowned. "Unfortunately, I think we'll need to wait until morning for the next step. I am quite exhausted. If I'm going up against Beltun Sagasht, I'd best be well rested."

"Okay."

"I will wake you before dawn. That is when we will move."

Vincent nodded. "What are we going to do with our guest?"

His friend shrugged. "Kill him?"

Vincent shook his head. "No. I don't think that's necessary."

Jaz looked at him strangely, then said quietly, "You have never killed a man."

Vincent snorted. "Of course not!"

The mage frowned. "This world you come from... It must be wondrous to live in a land where you don't have to worry about strangers you pass by. To have no fear of being attacked for your coin."

Thoughts of drive-by shootings, carjackings, and other daily American atrocities brought a pained expression to Vincent's face as he said, "Yes. Yes, that must be wondrous."

"Ours is a violent culture, Vincent. I'm afraid that you will have to kill, before your time here is done. You might have to kill before tomorrow is done, for that matter."

After a long pause, Vincent sighed and shook his head. "You know, I feel like a total idiot."

"Why?"

Suddenly, he sobered. "Because, despite everything I've gone through since arriving here, I never came to that conclusion on my own. I've been shot twice, once in each arm. I've been attacked by men with swords on a couple occasions. Yet, the most I've done to anyone is break a nose." He spoke softly. "I guess I've been living in a fantasy."

Jaz's voice was full of concern. "I am sorry that you have found yourself in a world so much more violent than your own."

Vincent laughed. "It's not. It's just more homogenous here." He waved that tangent aside. "Jaz, I've been a fool. I know that. But, despite my somewhat romantic interest in swordplay, I'm not a violent person. I don't really know if I *could* take a man's life." He looked sharply at his friend. "What exactly is your plan for tomorrow? We're not going to kill them all, are we?"

Jaz shook his head. "No, certainly not. But it might not be possible to completely avoid inflicting any death, before we're done. I do not enjoy killing, Vincent. But it is sometimes necessary."

"Yes, I've heard that said. But can you say it's necessary in this situation? I mean, you're effectively engaging in theft. Sure, it's theft from a guy who's been dead for a long time, so I don't have a problem with it. But these other people beat you to it. Seems only fair that they should have first rights."

"It isn't that simple, Vincent," Jaz said. "Beltun Sagasht is an evil man. He would use Kurean's legacy to inflict pain and suffering on others. Do you want that on your conscience?"

"Look, I'm here to help you because I owe you a debt."

"You owe me nothing, Vincent. You are here out of friendship. If you wish to back out, now, go right ahead. I will not fault you. But I am staying. I will not let any of Kurean's artifacts fall into the hands of someone like Sagasht."

Vincent hesitated, staring at the ground. Then he turned to look at his friend. "This dude's really that bad?"

Jaz absently stroked his thin beard. "If stories can be believed, yes. It is said that a man in a tavern once insulted him. The man was drunk and said something about Sagasht's personal hygiene. The mage responded by causing the man to pour his ale over his own head. The man, however, sitting near to Sagasht, retaliated by smashing his mug into the mage's face. Then, realizing what he had just done, and that he'd done it to a mage, he ran from the tavern. The story goes on to say that Sagasht then tidied himself up, left the tavern, then incinerated it, locking the door magically so that all inside perished. He then calmly walked into the town itself, doing the same to every building he came upon. When he was finally accosted by the locals, who naturally could not harm him, he demanded that he be taken to the offender's house. He promised to stop destroying the town if they would deliver the man to him. The townspeople did so, leading him to the man's house. Once there, he summoned the occupants outside. When the man, his wife, and two young children were out, he incinerated their home as they watched. Then he killed the wife and children as the man stood helplessly by."

"And then he killed the man," Vincent finished.

"No, I told you he was cruel. He let the man live. Though he did burn off the hand that held the mug used to strike the mage."

After a long silence, Vincent said, "You intend to kill Sagasht?"

Jaz tilted his head, as if just struck with the thought. "I think it would make the world a slightly better place, don't you?"

Vincent didn't answer. Instead, he said, "Sagasht is after these artifacts because he likes fire so much, right? I mean, Kurean was evidently a master of fire-based spells."

"That's exactly right. I'm sure that Sagasht has been looking for this hidden laboratory at least as long as I have."

"And why, exactly, have you been looking for it? Are you as much of a fire freak as Sagasht?"

Jaz smiled. "I appreciate the college of fire spells as much as any mage. But I am not entirely devoted to it, as Sagasht is. No, I am more in awe of Kurean's mastery of magery as a whole. Anything I can glean from his works will be an honor."

"Okay. So, do you have a plan, yet?"

"I have a few different ideas in mind. I'd like to sleep on it. I'll let you know in the morning."

Vincent nodded. "Fine. You go ahead and get to sleep. I'm not tired, yet."

"Very well. But you should make sure you're well rested for tomorrow."

As Jaz moved off toward his bedroll, Vincent approached the prisoner. The man was eyeing him apprehensively. Vincent stopped next to him and looked down. "Are you warm enough?" The man blinked, then nodded. Vincent grunted in response, then heaved a sigh. Jaz was settling into his bedroll, on the other side of the firepit. He knew from experience that the mage would be out like a light quite rapidly. He envied that ability.

He turned his attention back to the prisoner, pulling out his dagger as he did so. "Hands," he said. The man looked at him in brief alarm, then held up his bound wrists. Vincent calmly severed the ropes. The prisoner shook off the loose strands, then rubbed his wrists. Vincent sat down next to him, pulling out a whetstone and absently sharpening the dagger as he spoke. "So what's your name?" The man ignored him. "Come on. Tell me about yourself."

The man hesitated, then said, "Why?"

Vincent shrugged. "I've been thinking about our first encounter, replaying it over and over in my mind. And if memory serves me correctly, I don't believe that you ever took an active part in anything. Is that right?"

Again, the man was slow to answer. "That is true."

"Why not?" The man did not answer this time. Vincent watched him out of the corner of his eye. The man's face held an unmistakable look. Shame. But shame of what? Shame that he had been a part of it at all, or shame for not participating? Vincent cleared his throat. "There is much written on your face that should be vocalized."

"Why are you asking me to speak of this?"

"Because I want to know what kind of person you are. I have a pretty good idea what kind of a person your brother is. Are you like him?" The sudden flash in the prisoner's eye told Vincent that he wasn't. "No, you're not. So why are you with him?"

"That's none of your business."

Amused by the man's sudden show of fearlessness, Vincent replied, "You're right. It isn't. But consider that I do have you at my mercy and the mage isn't the only one who has ways of getting information out of you." He clacked the blade against the whetstone for emphasis.

"You're planning on killing me, anyway. Why should I tell you anything?"

"Why do you think we're planning to kill you?"

"What else would you do with me? You're going to attack the rest of them in the morning. Probably to butcher them like you did to our other campsite."

"What are you talking about?"

"What do you think I'm talking about? I'm talking about when you and the mage attacked us. It was terrible. Fire everywhere. Six of us dead."

"Excuse me, friend, but please don't expect me to have pity on a gang of thieves. How many people have you and your brother, or the rest of you, terrorized for no reason other than to line your own pockets?" The man remained silent and Vincent saw him squeeze his eyes closed. "I thought so," Vincent said smugly.

"No!" the man flared. "It's not what you think!"

"Keep your voice down. The mage is sleeping."

The man paused, swallowing hard. "I'm not like that," he said softly.

"Then what are you doing with people who *are* like that? You think it was a friendly thing, the four of you accosting me in the forest and stealing my belongings? Where I come from, there's a thing called 'guilt by association.' You were with them. And since you did nothing to stop them, you're guilty of helping them." The man said nothing, merely stared at Vincent. "Let me ask you this, then. If I were to cut you loose completely, what would you do?"

The man snorted. "You'd never do it."

"Never say 'never.' Answer the question." He stopped sharpening the knife and focused intently on the man's face, listening carefully for the response.

He didn't have long to wait. "I'd go and warn my brother of your intentions."

"Good. You didn't lie. But I can't have that. Your brother would warn all the others and we'd be in big trouble. That would guarantee people dying."

"I knew you'd never do it."

Vincent put away the whetstone. Then he looked at the man intently. "What if I gave you my promise not to kill your brother?"

"I wouldn't believe you."

"Well. There you have it, then. We seem to be at a stalemate. You won't trust my word, and I can't trust your actions. So what would you expect us to do?"

"Kill me." He spoke with resignation, accepting his fate.

Vincent paused, then put his dagger away. Then he rose and fetched a blanket from his bedroll. He carried it back to the prisoner and dropped it in his lap. "Nope. Don't think so." He returned to his bedroll. "Sleep well."

He felt like he'd just dropped off to sleep when he was suddenly jostled awake. He woke slowly, dragging his eyelids open. He expected to see some sort of glow indicating that dawn wasn't far off. Instead, all he saw were a few stars still shining brightly between the overhead branches. "Shit," he muttered. "Let me explain the concept of dawn to you, Jaz." But when he looked toward the owner of the leg that had kicked him, he saw the prisoner, not the mage.

The man stood next to him, the blanket wrapped around his shoulders. His feet were free, so he'd obviously untied himself. A moment of panic struck Vincent, until he noticed the man wasn't armed. And then the prisoner sat down beside him, cross-legged, in the dirt. "Leeden," he said.

"What?" Vincent croaked.

"My name is Leeden." The man gave a weak smile. "You asked, before."

Vincent nodded. "So I did."

"Why did you do it?" Leeden asked.

"Do what?" Vincent croaked, dragging himself upright and taking deep breaths to clear his head enough to converse.

"You went to sleep. Left me with my hands free. Thought you were faking it, but you really were asleep."

Vincent yawned. "I really was, and I'd really like to be, again."

"But I could have run off. I could have killed you."

"So why didn't you?"

Leeden simply stared at Vincent, then turned his gaze away. For a long moment, he didn't reply, then he turned to face him again. "You really won't kill my brother?"

Vincent sighed. "You have my word."

"I mean, the gods know he probably deserves it, but..."

"I won't kill him." His eyes were beginning to droop. He wished the man would go to sleep.

Instead, he renewed the conversation. "I don't know why I'm with him," he said quietly. "He's ruthless and has no morals to speak of. He lies, he steals. He doesn't generally kill without cause, but there's no denying he's scum." He looked into Vincent's eyes suddenly. "But he's my brother, and the only family I've got left. You understand?"

Vincent nodded. "I have an older brother, too."

"Is he scum, as well?"

"Not at all," he laughed.

"Oh."

"But even if he were, I'd probably be as loyal a brother as you are. However, I don't think I'd accompany him on raiding parties."

With a nod, Leeden said, "I guess that would make sense."

"So what are you going to do? You're free, it seems."

He was quiet for a long moment before responding. "I'm going to get some sleep."

Vincent watched the man trudge back to the tree that he'd been sitting against and draw the blanket up over himself. With a sigh, Vincent rolled back over, wondering what the morning would bring. A shuffling noise from the other direction drew his attention, and he turned to see Jaz rolling over to face him.

"Do you have any clue what you're doing?" the mage said softly.

Vincent smiled. "Do I ever?"

"I'm beginning to wonder."

"Go back to sleep."

Jaz chuckled softly and rolled back over. Vincent, despite his weariness, did not find it easy to return to sleep. He stared at the stars blinking behind the leaves far above his head and thought of the coming day's events. Would he have to kill someone? Would he be able to handle that? Or would he *be* killed? He was pretty sure he couldn't handle *that*.

He was struck suddenly with a sharp stab of longing to see Ariaziane again. It had been seven months or more since he'd last seen her. He couldn't believe that much time had passed, but it had. He'd left home about a month before Mid-Year Week. And now it was well into the month of Frost, if it hadn't entered the month of Snow already. He'd lost track. With any luck he'd be with her again soon, in time for Celebration Week.

And he wondered what Rhia was doing. He missed her, too, he realized. In a different kind of way, he had to admit that he loved her, too. But was it a friendship kind of love, or what? He couldn't place it. It was so odd, and he was much too tired to analyze it.

Finally, his eyelids began to feel heavy again. Gratefully, he closed them.

❧ Nineteen ❧

Morning came all too soon. At least, one had to technically call it morning. It was still dark. Birds hadn't even started chirping, yet. But since Jaz was nudging him with his foot, Vincent had to assume that dawn wasn't far off. He sat up, yawned, and sucked in some cold morning air, trying to get rid of pasty mouth syndrome. It didn't work.

"Morning," he mumbled. He shivered, and realized Jaz's spell must have ended some time ago.

"If you'll turn your attention to the orphaned blanket over there, you'll note your new friend seems to have deserted us."

Vincent glanced over to the tree. "Maybe he's just gone to take a leak," he suggested. "That's certainly on *my* mind right now."

Jaz shook his head. "I've been up for nearly an hour. He was gone then. But since we've not been attacked yet, I'm at a loss to guess where he is."

"Is his sword gone?"

"Yes."

Vincent sighed and crawled out of his bedroll. He stood and stretched, popping his neck loudly. "Don't suppose you've whipped up some buckwheat pancakes since you've been up so long?"

"You're still dreaming."

"Mm. Too bad. I'll be right back."

The fact that Leeden had left upset Vincent more than he wanted Jaz to see. But what could he expect? What had he been thinking last night? He frowned as he made his way to the edge of the campsite and a convenient latrine location. He wondered whether the man had gone off on his own, leaving his brother behind, but realized this was doubtful. They were deep within the forest. He had no provisions with him. He'd die if he tried to make it out on his own. He could have crept into his comrades' camp and made off with things he would need, but Vincent didn't think so. He had to assume the man had gone back to his brother. But, as Jaz pointed out, since they'd not been attacked, perhaps he was going to keep quiet about it. Vincent thought this was fairly unlikely, too. He also thought, as he made his way back, that perhaps he should invent the zipper soon. He was tired of dropping his drawers every time he needed to pee.

Jaz was sitting near the firepit. He'd heated some water and poured it into two metal cups. He held one out to Vincent, who took it and sniffed. "What is it?" he asked, wrinkling his nose at the pungent odor.

"A mixture of roots that will provide you with energy. It's somewhat bitter, I'm afraid. Usually, I put some honey in it, but I'm afraid we have none."

Vincent shrugged and took a tentative sip. He swallowed. It wasn't bitter at all, he thought. Almost sweet, in fact. Like sarsaparilla root tea, which he loved. Then another flavor hit him. One he didn't like. Licorice. He hated licorice. And then a taste like stale coffee grounds hit him. He made a face. "If I hadn't already swallowed that, I'd spit it on you."

"Yes, it does taste pretty vile sometimes. But at least that sensation comes after you swallow."

Vincent thought about chugging it, but it was still too hot for that. He decided to nurse it, instead. "So," he said, sitting beside the mage, "you've settled on a plan?"

"I believe I have, yes."

"Care to clue me in?"

Jaz shook his head. "What? And ruin the surprise?"

Vincent smiled and rubbed his palms together. "Ooh, I like surprises!"

"Well, then you'll just love what we're going to do."

After Jaz outlined the plan to him, and they finished their beverages and some hard biscuits, the pair departed for the enemy campsite, cloaked once again in Jaz's circle of silence. They reached the campsite and took a long look around. Vincent counted ten men. Eight of them appeared to be asleep, the other two sat near the campfire, which meant the other six, including the mage, were probably down in the lab.

They maneuvered around so they were as close to the campfire as they dared without risking detection. Then Jaz made subtle hand motions and appeared to be mumbling. Vincent watched as the two men at the fire suddenly slumped, falling backward onto the ground.

They quickly made their way to the men, where Vincent bound their hands and feet with the laces from their own boots. Then they circled the camp, Jaz casting his spell of sleep on the already sleeping men and Vincent tying them up.

When this was complete, Jaz dropped the silence. "Well, that was fortuitous," he said.

"How so?"

"I was afraid that the first two men might waken the others when they collapsed. Also, there is always a slight chance that a spell might not work on someone. If that had happened, you'd have awakened the person when you tried to take his laces."

"That would have been fun."

"Exactly." Jaz turned his attention to the large tent in the center. "Now for the real challenge."

As they approached the tent, Vincent drew his sword. The door flap of the tent was closed. Jaz reached it first. As he lifted the flap, Vincent felt a wash of dread sweep over him. "Wait!"

But it was too late. An arm flashed out from inside the tent and yanked Jaz inside. A moment later, he was ushered back out, a dagger at his throat. Leeden held the dagger. And, unsurprisingly, his older brother came out of the tent right behind him.

"Well, well, well," the man said. "I guess my weasel brother's story was true, after all. You are alive. And still with your sword drawn. How impolite."

Vincent cast a look at Leeden. His face was a mix of emotions, but his hand was steady at Jaz's throat. He looked as if he wanted to say something, possibly to apologize, but Vincent didn't want to hear what he had to say. It was all quite clear to him, anyway.

"You know, when we first met," Vincent said calmly, "I thought you were merely an asshole. But you're worse than that. You're a bully."

The man laughed heartily. "Ooh, a bully am I? Goodness, that's the worst insult anyone has ever thrown at me."

"A bully who bullies his own brother, no less. You make me sick. Draw your sword. I'm going to enjoy this."

"Not as much as I," he replied, drawing his weapon.

"You promised!" Leeden wailed. "You promised not to kill him!"

Both men glanced at him. Vincent said, "Yes, I did. But I never promised not to hurt him."

The older brother laughed. "Yes, I promised that, too, you imbecile. But that was before I believed your story. Now that I know this pup is alive, I'm going to gut him."

"But you promised!"

"Oh, grow up, you nit," the older brother replied.

The man closed on Vincent, offering a few probing swings and thrusts of the sword. Vincent parried them easily, but made no counter-attacks. The man increased his attacks, and still Vincent parried. A thrust to the midsection, deflected. A swing at the head, blocked. A slice, sidestepped, but still no offensive moves.

"Ha! You really do mean to keep your promise! Well! So much the better for me!" With that, the man drew out a dagger and resumed his attack now with both weapons.

Vincent frowned. This is new, he thought. He now had to parry the sword thrusts and sidestep or block the dagger attacks. For a time, he succeeded. But then, a dagger swipe nicked him on the cheek. He danced backward, fear pulsing through him even as he felt the wound begin to close, thanks to Gnorrin's magical gift.

"Eh? What's the matter, pup?" The man laughed grotesquely.

"Just trying to keep that promise in mind," Vincent replied.

"Glad to hear it," the man drawled, and stepped in to attack once more.

The attack was one that Vincent couldn't have choreographed more beautifully. For himself, that is. The sword attack was a backhanded swing, coming from Vincent's right, a sweeping arc aimed at his neck. The dagger followed in a similar arc at ribcage level, also from the right. Vincent's sword clanged loudly as it stopped the beheading swing. Then, he twisted and caught the man's left hand as it attempted to plunge the dagger into his torso. The magical gauntlets made it easy to keep his grip on the man's wrist. Then, shifting his weight onto his left leg, he lashed out with a kick that centered directly over his enemy's left kidney.

The man would have staggered back, but Vincent had him firmly by the wrist. Instead, the man buckled somewhat, his face a mask of alarm, evidently expecting a killing sword blow to follow. But there was none. The man gritted his teeth and raised his sword to attack again, only to receive another kick to the kidney.

He let out a gasp and his knees collapsed. Off balance from the kick, Vincent couldn't prevent being toppled, also. His enemy still had wits enough about him to realize his advantage. As he fell backward, he pulled on Vincent, who still had a strong grip on his wrist. He tried pointing the dagger at Vincent's abdomen, but couldn't overpower the magical gauntlet..

Just before they hit the ground, Vincent twisted his wrist. There was a loud snap, followed by his adversary's gasp of pain. Vincent landed on top of the man, the dagger between them.

Both of them dropped their swords as they fell. Vincent rolled off the man, onto his back, then sat up and looked at his fallen foe. The dagger protruded from the belly of the man. The wound might or might not be fatal, he realized. It was hard to tell.

The man made no effort to rise. Instead, he groped for his sword, but it was just out of reach.

The man's other hand lay at a crooked angle on his stomach, the wrist clearly broken. Vincent felt it hard to have any sympathy. Then something caught his attention. He reached over and lifted the man's hand, unconcerned of the pain it caused him, and plucked a golden ring from his finger. "Is this mine?" he asked. In response, the man spat on him. Vincent slipped the ring onto his own finger, then casually wiped the spittle off his tunic. "You took quite a lot of my belongings, you know. This ring might have been helpful to you. But you overlooked something that would be assisting you a lot more right now."

Leeden had released Jaz from captivity, and both now knelt at the man's side. Vincent turned to the brother. "Do you have any healing herb?" Leeden looked at him stupidly. "Look, I promised not to kill your brother. And while it could certainly be argued that he killed himself with his actions, I'll even try to prevent that."

Jaz looked at his friend. "Healing herb is well and good, but this wound will not close well enough for it to work."

"Mm," was the only reply Vincent offered. He then tore the fabric of the tunic away from the dagger. Then he handed the younger brother his own pouch of healing herb that Rhia had given him. Vincent then withdrew the dagger and pressed on both sides of the wound to hold it open. The injured man groaned and struggled, but Jaz restrained him. "Go ahead," Vincent said, and watched as Leeden sprinkled a liberal amount of the powder into the open wound. Then Vincent let go, allowing the wound to close. He removed his necklace and placed it around the fallen man's neck. "I expect this back when we're through," he said to Leeden. "I also expect you both to be here."

The man looked into Vincent's eyes for a moment, then turned his gaze away. "You have my word," he said.

Leaving him to watch over his brother, Vincent and Jaz stood and looked at the tent again. "Well, Jaz, only four more thieves and one mage. You up for it?"

His friend looked at him and smiled. "If you are, you lunatic."

Vincent laughed, picked up his sword, then led the way into the tent. In the middle was a huge tree stump, just as they'd been told. Vincent frowned. It looked solid enough. He ran his hands over the sides and the jagged surface. "How do we get in?"

Jaz rested his hand on the top of the stump. "Like this," he said, and pushed his hand seemingly through the wood.

"Shit!"

"Another illusion, my friend."

"But I felt it! It's solid!"

"The better illusions imitate solidity, to a degree." Jaz then withdrew his hand. "Once you know it's an illusion, it isn't difficult to dispel it." He waved his hands over the stump, mumbled a few words, and suddenly the stump was gone. In its place was a hole in the ground, about three feet wide, with rungs planted in the wall like a ladder. "However, determining that it is an illusion isn't the easiest thing. Illusions like this one would be nearly impossible to detect. Had I not expected one, likely I wouldn't have realized its presence."

Vincent shook his head in wonder, then followed Jaz down the ladder. It was about forty feet, from his best estimate, much of it in darkness. But as they neared the bottom, a faint glow met them. Eventually, Vincent's feet encountered no more rungs, so he carefully lowered himself by hand to the bottom rung, from which there was a drop of about five feet to the floor of a short hall with a wall right behind them and a door at the opposite end.

"Geez, Kurean was either very tall or a good jumper," Vincent said softly. Jaz looked oddly at him, then moved under the ladder. A moment later, he was levitating up to the lower rung. "Duh," Vincent said. "But then, why have the rungs at all?"

Jaz lowered himself back to the ground. "Who says it was Kurean who put the rungs there?"

Vincent nodded. "Good point." He looked down the hall, then drew his sword. "Ready?"

"Not quite," Jaz whispered. "I'm going to put up some defensive spells. I want us to get in and incapacitate the others as quickly as possible. Most of the spells will be centered on me, since it will take less effort to maintain them that way. If you stay close, they will cover you, too, just like the circle of silence."

"I assume you're casting that, too?"

"Yes, but as soon as we're detected, I'll drop it."

Vincent nodded.

"I'm tempted to render us invisible," Jaz continued, "but that will likely not prevent Sagasht from detecting us. And it would be quite draining on me, as well."

"Don't worry about it. The silence ought to be enough."

"Let's hope so." With that, Jaz began casting the spells. A few minutes later, they were ready to proceed.

Vincent wondered how big a radius the circle of silence had. The door at the end of the hall opened at their touch. He sincerely hoped the radius encompassed any squeaky hinges it might have. On the other side of the doorway was a large room, lit by several torches in wall sconces. It was lavishly decorated, with beautiful, upholstered furniture, ornately carved tables, and a few intricate tapestries.

The room's other three walls each held a doorway. Only the one opposite the hallway held a door; the other two were just neatly cut arches in the walls. The pair headed to the one on their left first. Here they encountered a fancy but small dining area. A door off that room held a pantry.

The door directly across from the entrance hall led into a similarly elaborate boudoir. Vincent was surprised that all the furniture appeared in good shape. The upholstery was not threadbare, the linens not rotted with age. But then, Kurean had been a very powerful mage. From what he'd been led to believe, very powerful mages tended to live a long time. And any mage that could put off death for centuries could certainly find a way to preserve material things against the ravages of time, too.

The final doorway led into another hallway, this one about ten feet wide. Vincent found his heartbeat increasing in anticipation. How powerful was this Beltun Sagasht? He certainly wouldn't want to come up against someone of Jaz's caliber in a fight. And from what Jaz implied, Sagasht was even stronger. Well, if he were lucky, Jaz would take care of him, leaving only the four thieves for Vincent. Then he laughed. Now that he thought about it, that wasn't a great definition of lucky.

The floor inside this hallway was different, Vincent noticed. Instead of being firmly packed dirt, this hallway was of cut stones. It was smooth enough, though there was no mortar in the cracks between the stones. He thought nothing of this, until he stepped on a stone that felt like it gave way slightly under his foot. Instantly, a stab of dread hit him, and at the same time, gouts of flame shot out from the ceiling. Both cringed, but the flames seemed to strike an invisible bubble around the men and did not touch them. The blast lasted for several seconds. Long enough, Vincent realized, to fry anyone not magically shielded. Jaz's protection saved them, but it was nice to know that he had his ring back. Assuming, of course, that it was his ring that had been on the man's finger.

When the flames at last died away, Jaz turned in alarm to look at Vincent, who pointed to the stones in the floor to indicate the trap. Jaz frowned, and Vincent knew his friend was wondering whether the spell of silence had covered the noise of the booby trap, or if it had drawn the attention of the thieves or Sagasht. He looked down the length of the hall to the door at the far end. No one was bursting through with sword in hand. So far, so good.

Vincent felt a few more stones give way underfoot, but no traps were sprung. They did, however, come upon a place in the hall where dozens of crossbow bolts littered the floor. And there were stains on the stones that looked like blood.

Finally, they reached the door at the end of the hall. It was metal, highly tarnished, with no handle. Vincent looked for hinges on the wall, but it appeared as though the door was actually built into the surrounding stone, including the ceiling and floor. At least, that's how it appeared from this side. It could be quite normal looking from the other, he realized. Either way, he could detect no way at all to open it.

He saw that Jaz was also sizing up the door, looking at how it was set into the surrounding earth. Vincent watched him place his hand against the door and push. Nothing happened. Jaz shrugged and looked at Vincent. He waved his hand and the circle of silence disappeared. "It's no illusion," Jaz said.

"Worth a try," Vincent said. Then Jaz tried something that Vincent recognized, having seen Ariaziane do it on more than one occasion. He performed some hand rituals, then made a fist and lightly knocked on the door. Again, nothing happened.

As Jaz crossed his arms and frowned at the door, Vincent rubbed at the tarnish on an area of the door, revealing a gleaming, silvery shine underneath. He removed one gauntlet and ran his bare fingers over the surface. It was smooth and almost silky to the touch. "What kind of metal is this? It seems familiar, somehow."

His friend ignored the question. "Maybe a hidden lever..." Jaz began feeling along the wall near the door, starting at the floor and working upward.

Vincent put his gauntlet back on and copied Jaz's actions on the other side. The mage continued around the entire door, levitating to where he couldn't reach.

When he reached the center of the top of the door, he stopped. "Ah ha!" He smiled down at Vincent, pushed something, and the door began to lower into the floor. "Be ready," he warned as he returned to ground level.

Vincent quickly drew his sword, expecting to find four thieves on the other side waiting for him. He wasn't disappointed. As the door lowered enough for him to see over it, he spied all five of their quarry. Far at the back of the laboratory, a man who must have been Beltun Sagasht was staring directly at them, yelling to the four thieves who were even now jumping up from their positions of rest on some chairs in a nearby corner.

Vincent and Jaz both hurdled the last of the door as it reached knee level and went toward their respective targets. Vincent knew instantly that this was going to be nasty. Four against one was not something he felt anywhere near ready for. His only hope was that these four were not great swordsmen. Or even mediocre ones, for that matter. With luck, they'd be nothing more than ordinary thieves, used to stealing from the unaware, and not accustomed to those who put up a fight.

To his surprise, one of the men did not join in the attack, but held back, watching. This was fine with him, since three to one odds were significantly better than four to one. He quickly established his defense, working his way backward into the opposite corner. With some dismay, he noted that the door had now begun to rise. No matter, he thought. He had more important things to worry about.

Being cornered wasn't his favorite tactic, but it prevented his opponents from surrounding him. Still, he thought as he parried viciously, he couldn't keep this up for long. Eventually, his opponents would be able to synchronize their attacks so that his parry of one would leave him open to another. He had to take advantage of their initial zeal before it was too late.

Finally, he saw his opening. The man on his far left reached in with a long swipe that passed in front of Vincent. Quickly, he stepped to the left, grabbing the man's sword arm with his left hand. Once again, the magical gauntlets aided him. He yanked the man in front of him as a shield, just in time for him to intercept a sword thrust in his side. The man dropped his weapon and fell, clasping the injury.

One down, Vincent thought as he allowed the man to drop to the floor. He expected the fourth man to take the fallen thief's place, but he didn't, still keeping to the rear.

Now Vincent took the offensive, hacking madly while still keeping up his defense. His opponents were wary, though, having seen Vincent's rather unorthodox method of fighting. He hoped their wariness could be pushed into outright fear.

To test this theory, he waited for the next long reach by one of the men. Vincent lunged out with his left hand and was delighted to see the man recoil in terror. Then Vincent's foot slipped in the blood of the fallen man. His legs flew out from under him and he fell in a heap.

Reflexes took over and he rolled toward the two thieves, allowing the downward strokes they'd initiated to impact on the stones just behind his body. Terror wracked his chest, but he freed his sword and swung viciously at the legs of his assailants. He was thrilled when he felt the sword connect and heard one man scream before falling to the ground, his sword flying away.

But this victory was short-lived. The third man had him at his mercy. As powerful a defense as he had, Vincent knew he couldn't hold out for long. The man swung incessantly, causing Vincent to either parry or roll out of the way. He had no time to attack.

He was beginning to panic, he knew. His heart raced and skipped a beat every time the man's sword impacted on his own, or hit the stones nearby. What could he do? The sword struck stone near his head. Then it was aimed at his legs. He shifted to avoid it. Then at his neck, and his own sword stopped the blow.

He supposed he could hope that the man would have a sudden heart attack or something, but didn't feel he should count on it. Likewise, it would be too much to hope that Jaz had finished off Sagasht and would dash in to his rescue. He went through a long list of things he couldn't rely on, including the idea that his opponent would tire out before he himself did. And he was tiring awfully quickly.

Another blow to his neck intercepted by a parry from his sword. And then the idea hit him. It was outrageous, he thought, but it was better than decapitation.

He studied the man's movements carefully, while trying to stay alive. He could tell when he was going for another throat strike. And when Vincent saw blow begin to fall, he brought his own sword up, laid its blade diagonally across his throat, and let go.

As the sword fell, Vincent's hands were on their way up. The sword struck Vincent's blade solidly, and before it could be drawn back up again, Vincent grabbed it in two locations, one hand above the other. The man tried to yank the weapon free, but the magical gauntlets' grip was too strong to break. Vincent gritted his teeth and pushed with both hands, using all his strength.

To his amazement, the sword's blade snapped in half, and the thief staggered back from the sudden release. Vincent used that moment to snatch up his own sword and jump to his feet.

But his opponent didn't remain weaponless for long. His backward stagger had taken him to where the second man's sword had landed, and he quickly picked it up. Vincent was exhausted, but he couldn't allow the man to see that. He calmly inched forward, sword at the ready.

It was then that he recognized the man. His resolve hardened. "So," he managed to say through heaving breaths, "still afraid of dogs?" The man frowned and looked more closely at Vincent's face. "Recognize me?" he continued. "In the forest... months ago. You shot me in the arm. And hit my dog."

"Shut up!" he yelled as he backed across the floor.

"Your companions are dead," Vincent panted. "Now it's your turn." He attacked viciously. To his disappointment, the man did not simply throw down his sword in abject terror and surrender.

Vincent swung harder and harder, and the man's parries were knocked farther and farther away. There were a number of openings where he could easily have impaled the man, but did not. Finally, one of his swings sent the man's sword flying from his hand. And now he stood there, obviously horrified. He hung his head. Whether he was praying, or just hoping not to see the killing blow, Vincent didn't know. Nor did he care. "Thank you," he said, and swung his sword at the man's unprotected skull. He hit it with the flat of the blade, knocking him unconscious.

He let out a long breath as he watched the man sprawl on the stones, then spared a glance to the far end of the room, where he expected to see the mages engaged in mortal combat. Instead, he saw them engaged in... Well, not much of anything, he had to admit. They circled each other, but there were no bursts of flame flying back and forth, no explosions. Probably too worried about harming anything in Kurean's precious laboratory, he thought. They did look kind of tired, though, especially Jaz.

Behind him, he heard the sound of a clearing throat. He turned to see the one remaining man who had not chosen to fight earlier. He'd forgotten all about him. The man was standing in the open, now, legs spread wide, and holding the biggest hammer that Vincent had ever seen in his life. The shaft must have been five feet long. The head looked to be a foot long, carved of solid rock.

The man himself was short, standing only about five feet tall. But he was positively covered with muscles. His arms looked to be as big as Vincent's thighs. He had a narrow waist, which told Vincent that he was probably fairly agile. Vincent frowned. This was a time for one thing. Bravado.

He smiled as he slowly approached the man. "Look," he said calmly. "I've just bested three men who attacked me at once. I don't even have a scratch on me. What makes you think you'll fare any better?"

The man merely smiled and hefted his hammer, wielding it with the ease that Vincent might swing a tennis racquet. This did not please him. Then he thought about his own weapon. There was no way he could deflect that hammer with his sword. With a shrug and a resuming panic, he sheathed it. "Fine," he said. "Let's go."

The way he figured it, he only had one real chance to beat this one. If he could grab the hammer the same way he'd grabbed the other guy's sword, he might be able to yank it free. Or something.

When the first swing audibly whooshed past his face, it was clear to Vincent that his plan was not going to work. The attacks were so lightning fast that it was all Vincent could do to dodge them. And if he'd tried to grab the hammer at the speed it was flying, he figured he'd probably break every bone in his hand, gauntlet or no gauntlet.

Once again, he found himself studying the pattern of attack. Once from the left, then back to the right. Sometimes he altered the height of the swings. Then, seemingly on every third repetition, he'd put in a downward stroke to either the left or right.

The man had started out using only one hand for his swings, but after several unsuccessful attempts, he began using both hands. Vincent was glad of that, for he hoped to be able to do one thing without any hope of a blocking move. He waited, dodging, until the next downstroke came. As before, Vincent avoided this one, and as the man began his powerful upswing, Vincent jumped in and planted a roundhouse punch directly in the man's nose.

The hammer flew from the man's grasp, and the man himself dropped like a felled tree. A short one, anyway.

Vincent waited to see if he would get up again, but instead saw the man shudder and lie still. He moved closer, then saw the blood beginning to pool out from the man's ears. A chill washed over him. He knelt down and looked at his face. The nose was smashed nearly flat. He looked at the gauntlets and realized what he'd done. He'd always heard that you could kill a man by driving bone fragments up into the brain. He just never thought it would be that easy. Then again, he never thought he'd own magic gloves of strength. But the man's glassy stare told him that he was, in fact, dead. Vincent felt sick.

Behind him, the man with the wounded leg gasped. "Gods below!"

Vincent whirled on him, startled to hear him speak. His mind was awhirl with anguish. But the man recoiled as he spun around, misunderstanding the twisted expression on Vincent's face.

He'd killed a man. With one punch. He hadn't meant to. Yes, the guy was trying to kill him, but he didn't mean to kill him like that. It was just a punch in the nose, he didn't mean to kill him like that, didn't meant to kill, didn't mean...

Before he knew what was happening, he was heaving up the sour contents of his stomach. He felt about to pass out, and fell to a sitting position as the last convulsions shook him. His eyes burned. Then he panicked again.

The one he'd hit with the flat of his sword... Had he killed him, too? He scrambled over on hands and knees to the wall where the man had fallen, seizing the man by the tunic and pulling him upright. He ripped off a gauntlet and felt for a pulse, and nearly cried in relief when one was located. Then he looked down at his hand, ripped off the other gauntlet, and stuffed them both into his belt. He let the man fall back down to a prone position, his arms flopping on the stones.

No more, he thought. No more killing. Especially no more killing because of those damn gauntlets. No, that wasn't fair, he thought. Those damn gauntlets had saved his life. He couldn't blame them. It was his own fault, not the gauntlets' fault.

He waited for his panic to pass as he stood there looking down at his hands. Then he remembered Jaz and Sagasht. He looked over to the far end of the room, and felt the bottom drop from what was left of his stomach.

Sagasht held something out in front of him. Something like a stick, about a foot and a half long. He was pointing it at Jaz, who floated near the ceiling. His friend was writhing in agony, his body surrounded by a sickly green glowing halo. Vincent saw the concentration on Sagasht's face and knew that Jaz must be putting up a terrible struggle. His friend's face was a mask of tensed muscles and sweat. But as valiantly as he fought, Vincent knew Sagasht was stronger.

Distress over his unintentional killing fled from him, replaced by sharp concern for his friend. He had to do something, but what? Instinct took over and he jumped to his feet. He drew his sword and sprinted forward. Reaching Sagasht, he roared a challenge and swung with all his might.

His sword bounced harmlessly off some unseen field surrounding the mage. Sagasht glanced at Vincent, then spared a moment to gesture with his free hand in his direction. A blast of wind came from nowhere and hurled the young man across the room. Vincent landed roughly, sliding into the unconscious body of the dog hater, the force pushing both of them backward toward the wall.

He shook his head and gathered his wits. Well, he thought. That worked real good. A direct attack on the mage apparently would accomplish nothing. His protections were too strong. But he had to do something before Jaz was killed. He looked around the lab. Perhaps there was something else he could use.

Try as he might, he could make no sense out of the things he saw. The room didn't even really look like a laboratory. He didn't know what he expected, but when he thought of laboratories, he thought of tables filled with complex equipment, vials of combustible liquids, and so on. This room looked more like a library than anything. Sure, there were tables that held unusual things. But they were things like shiny rocks, piles of dirt, and sticks.

Wait, he thought. Not sticks. Wands. Magic wands. Sagasht was using one against Jaz right now. He got to his feet and made his way to a table that held a stick. He picked it up, looking it over. No buttons or switches, he thought dejectedly. So what do I do? Aim it and *think* it into action?

With a frown he pointed the thing at the mage. "Sagasht!" he yelled. To his amazement, the mage actually took the time to glance in his direction. "Let him go! I'm warning you!"

An expression of concern flickered across the man's face. Surely he didn't think Vincent had any idea how to operate the thing, did he? And then the mage spoke. "Put that down before you hurt yourself." Then he turned his attention back to Jaz.

Vincent tried to activate the wand. He concentrated on it, willing it to do something. Anything. But nothing happened. Then, feeling like an idiot, he talked to it. "Abracadabra," he said. "Alakazam!" He frowned, feeling at least some gratitude in the fact that no one in this room had ever heard those terms before. "Shazam!" he tried. "Open sesame?" Still nothing. "Shit," he muttered, and slammed the wand down on the tabletop.

At this, Sagasht spun his gaze back to him. He looked at the wand, then at Vincent. Then he frowned at him and raised his hand. Vincent expected to be blown across the room again. But instead, the wand levitated up and began floating toward the mage.

"Oh, no you don't," Vincent said, and leaped forward to snatch it out of the air. Then a thought struck him. The mage wasn't worried that Vincent could operate the wand. He was afraid he would harm it, the wand being one of Kurean's precious relics and all. Vincent smiled nastily and gripped the wand in both hands, as if to snap it like a pencil. "Let him go, or I break it! And I can break it before you do anything to me!" He added this last not knowing if it were true, but it sounded good and made him feel a bit better.

The mage stared at him. Vincent took the moment to study him. He was tall, probably six-four, with jet black hair and eyes. The hair was long, tied back in a pony tail. His face was clean shaven and lined with small creases. He looked exhausted, but still much better than Jaz, who was positively haggard. Sagasht wore what seemed to Vincent to be a swashbuckler's outfit. Trousers and a tunic that had a deep "V" neck, with laces to bind it up. The trousers and tunic were both of a burgundy shade. Over top of this was a grey cloak that now hung down his back.

Vincent looked at the man's face. Those black eyes were staring right back at him. "Give me the wand, boy."

"Up yours."

"Give me the wand and I shall let you live."

"Screw that. I'm gonna break it. You wouldn't like that, would you?"

The mage tilted his head a fraction of an inch. "Not at all. Nor would you, since it would undoubtedly kill you."

Vincent blinked. "How's that?"

"The energy stored within that wand would, if broken, explode with such force to reduce this entire laboratory to rubble. Including you, me, and your friend here. That isn't how I would want to end this day." Vincent hesitated, knowing deep down that the mage wasn't lying. And he had to agree, he certainly didn't feel like dying today. "Give me the wand, boy."

Vincent lowered the wand somewhat, but did not let go of it. He shook his head in confusion. What was he to do? He looked at the powders and chunks of shiny rock on the table. Nothing he could identify, much less use. Then he looked again. A glimmer of a thought struck him. He looked back at Sagasht, letting go of the wand with his right hand and resting it atop the table. "This would really blow up?"

The mage nodded. "Boom."

"Okay," he said. "Catch." And he tossed the wand in the mage's direction, in a slow, high arc. The mage smiled, reaching out a hand to catch it. With his right hand, Vincent grabbed a large chunk of metallic looking mineral from the table. When the wand was about to land in Sagasht's outstretched hand, Vincent hurled the rock with all his might.

It caught Sagasht directly in the forehead, sending him stumbling backward. Vincent lost no time, drawing his sword and leaping forward instantly. Sagasht fell to his knees, his concentration broken. Jaz fell from the air, the green glow now gone.

And then Vincent was upon the mage. He didn't hesitate, but swung down toward the man. But the sword again bounced harmlessly away from the mage. "Uh, oh," Vincent muttered.

Sagasht rose to his feet, Jaz all but forgotten. The mage's face was the embodiment of rage. His eyes, dark as they were, held a fire that burned white hot. "You... little... *maggot!*" Every word hit Vincent like a blow. "You dare to strike me... Beltun Sagasht! I will fry you! I will roast you alive!" The next thing Vincent knew, fire was shooting from the mage's hands. It struck him, enveloped him.

And did no harm at all.

Vincent gave an inward sigh of relief. Now he knew the retrieved ring was his, and he'd found out in the most fortunate way imaginable.

Naturally, Sagasht was enraged even further by this. Vincent decided to exacerbate the situation by smiling in his most sinister fashion at the mage. "Give it up, dragon breath."

Suddenly, the mage grew calm. "Insolent child," he said quietly. "Why waste such theatrics on you?" The mage waved his hand, and Vincent felt a constriction at his throat. Not a great pressure, as if he were being strangled. Just a mild pressure. He also noticed that sound seemed slightly deadened. Out of curiosity, he raised a hand to his head. As he suspected, he found a globe of invisible force around his skull, like an inverted goldfish bowl. Sagasht meant to suffocate him. Vincent nearly laughed.

The mage smiled smugly while waiting for Vincent to start gasping for air. Instead, Vincent glanced down, seeing the hammer that had flown from the dead man's hands. It had made it the whole way across the room when it sailed from the man's hands. Vincent put away his sword, donned the gauntlets again, and hefted the hammer. Sagasht showed mild bemusement at this.

The blow bounced off the mage's defenses, but Vincent was pleased to see the faintest wince from the man. He swung again, smiling all the while. After a few more powerful blows, he could see the mage's face begin to show alarm. Wondering why I'm not gasping on the floor, you son of a bitch? Vincent laughed to himself and continued raining blow after blow upon the mage's invisible shield. But soon, Sagasht's anxiety turned to anger again. He rose up to his full height.

Another blow struck the shield and Sagasht staggered back a step, breaking his concentration. He gestured and a spark flew out from the mage's fingertip. It was followed by several more. They all headed in a line for Vincent. One after the other, they pummeled into him, knocking him backward. He gasped in pain. Ten of the glowing sparks plowed into his chest. By the time they were done, Vincent was on his back on the floor.

His chest felt like it was on fire. But he rose, using the upturned hammer to assist him. He felt weak, but had to go on. Sagasht had turned back to his primary foe, and

Vincent knew he had to keep him from killing Jaz. He staggered forward, then ran at the mage. He wound up for a haymaker swing as he ran. He saw Sagasht turn, his eyes widening in alarm.

There was a loud clap of inrushing air as Sagasht's shield imploded under the terrific blow. The effort wiped Vincent out. The hammer's head was on the ground and he leaned against the handle, exhausted. Sagasht, breathing heavily, hit him with another gale-force wind, blowing him back until he crashed into the wall, halfway to the ceiling. Vincent collapsed to the ground, feeling like he'd just been hit by a truck. He looked dazedly at Sagasht.

The mage was standing, now, and a web of lightning was building around his fist. Vincent knew he didn't have the strength to stand, let alone try to avoid the upcoming bolt. Instead, he smiled, flipped Sagasht the middle finger, and mentally said goodbye to Ariaziane. He closed his eyes.

The crack of thunder was earsplitting. He winced, prepared for the jolt that would send him to oblivion. He smelled ozone. But he felt nothing. He opened one eye.

Smoke filled the area where Sagasht had been standing. Vincent stumbled to his feet, leaning against the wall, and staggered toward the spot. The smoke slowly cleared, revealing the figure of Jaz, slumping against the nearest table.

On the ground, lying on his back, was Sagasht. Three black splotches on his chest, each the size of a baseball, still smoked. The mage's eyes were wide open, the expression on his face one of complete surprise.

Vincent made his way to Jaz's side. He looked at his friend, whose face still showed the anguish he'd gone through. Blood had dried where it had run from his nose. His hair was matted with sweat. "Boy, do *you* look like shit," Vincent said.

Jaz turned a weary eye on his friend. He put an arm on Vincent's shoulder. "Thank you."

They rested for several minutes, then Vincent heard someone groan. He rose and shuffled over to where his former adversaries lay, doing his best to avoid looking at the dead one. The dog hater was stirring. Vincent suppressed the urge to kick him in the groin. Then he frowned. There was something wrong with the man's hand. His arm lay flung back over his head, his hand resting up against the wall. But his fingers seemed stubby.

The man stirred again, his arm moving. And the fingers shortened. Vincent smiled. Then he reached down and helped the man to wake up fully. He dragged him to his feet. The man moaned and held a hand to his head. Then he opened his eyes and looked at Vincent's stern face.

"Look around you, friend." The man did so, noting his comrades, injured and dead. He then saw the body of Sagasht on the floor across the room, still smoking. He turned terrified eyes back to Vincent's face. "I think you grasp your situation, yes?" The man nodded. "Good." He carried him over to the metal door. "Tell me how to open this door from here." The man stepped to one side of the door and pressed a stone in the wall. The door lowered into the floor. "Now, you're going to do me a favor," Vincent said.

"Anything." The man was practically cowering in fear.

"Go up top. Find the younger of the two brothers you traveled with. Send him down with my necklace. And you'll need to figure out how to get your other friend out of here." He indicated the one with the crippled leg. "Likely you can haul him up the passage with ropes."

"You said they were all dead."

"I lied. But unless you do as I say, there'll be one more dead one. Now, get going."

The man hurried off, just as the door began to rise again.

As Vincent turned to join Jaz, the man who'd caught the sword in his ribs said, "You're letting us go?"

He frowned at the man. "I'm not *letting* you go, I'm *making* you go. And I want you to know how easy it would have been for us to kill all of you, instead of just him and the mage."

The man nodded, still holding a hand to his injury, and said no more. Vincent frowned, looking at the blood soaked into the man's tunic. The fellow's face was pale. He'd lost quite a bit of blood. But there was nothing Vincent could do about that right now.

Several minutes later, the door lowered as the two arrived. The younger brother looked around at the devastation, his eyes lingering on the body of Sagasht. "Gods have mercy," he said.

"Evidently they will on most of you. My necklace, please." The man obediently turned it over to him. He took it and put it around the neck of the bleeding man. He knelt next to the man, tearing open his tunic to see if the wound would heal. "Did you work out a way to remove the one with the injured leg?" he asked, glancing up at Leeden, who nodded. "Then I suggest you get to it." Leeden snapped out of his stupor and began to assist the fallen man. "By the way, how's your brother?"

"He'll live."

"I gave you my word."

"And I thank you. Though I wonder if I should have asked it of you." With that, he turned his attention to the lame man, helping him to limp away.

A few minutes later, Leeden returned, as Vincent was removing his necklace from the other man. The wound had closed. No more blood would be lost, but it would be some time before the fellow would be well enough to swing a sword again. Leeden helped his companion to his feet, and similarly assisted him toward the exit.

"We'll be coming up within two hours," Vincent called after them. "I expect you all to be gone by that time. And leave me my horse!"

Vincent returned to Jaz, who was still leaning against a table, regaining energy. "Come on," he said to him. "Let's get you some rest."

"Good idea," the mage agreed. "Have to thank Sagasht for giving me the lightning bolt inspiration."

"I think you've thanked him enough."

Vincent guided Jaz down the hallway and to the boudoir they'd found. There he closed the door. "Not that I don't trust our friends, Jaz, but I don't trust our friends. Can you seal this door against them?"

The mage nodded, then made a gesture. The door stayed shut against Vincent's tugs.

Vincent wasn't sure how long they slept, but he woke refreshed, though sore. Jaz woke not long afterward. He unlocked the door and they stepped outside. "I hope they all left," Vincent muttered.

"They did," Jaz replied.

"How do you know?"

"I contacted my little winged friend when I woke. The camp is deserted."

"Did they leave my horse?"

"Afraid not."

"Pricks."

They returned to the laboratory, where Jaz looked over all the items on the tables. He nodded a lot and hmm'ed a lot. Vincent heaved himself up to sit on one of the empty tables. Jaz eventually turned his attention to Sagasht and began rifling through the mage's clothing. He removed some things from pockets in the cloak, took a couple rings off the man's fingers. "Ghoul," Vincent offered. Jaz chuckled.

After an hour, Jaz had piled up a fair amount of booty atop one table. He frowned. "I have to confess I expected more than this to be found here."

Vincent nodded. "Well, perhaps you'd like to see the real laboratory, then?"

Jaz looked at him curiously. "Excuse me?"

Vincent smiled and hopped down from the table, then motioned for Jaz to follow him over to the other wall, where the dog hater had fallen. He reached out, touched the wall, and pushed. He heard Jaz gasp as his hand went through it.

"Ha haaa! Excellent!"

The pair entered the hidden room. Jaz cast a spell to light the area, then whistled. The room was, again, like a library. Books were everywhere. But there were also tables holding things that *looked* like magical items, items that sparkled or glowed. Vincent browsed around, careful not to touch anything. Jaz looked like a kid in a candy store. Letting the mage have his fun, Vincent located a chair in a corner and made himself comfortable.

He awoke with a start some time later. He'd dreamed of the fight that ended with the death of the man with the hammer. But in the dream, it hadn't been an accidental killing, but a brutal murder, with Vincent pummeling the man's face to pulp. He breathed deeply, trying to shake it off, before rising to find his friend.

He found Jaz in the process of gathering things together in a large crate he'd located somewhere. "You gonna be a while, yet?" he asked the mage.

Jaz looked at him and smiled. "Yes. Why?"

"No reason. I think I'm going to go stretch my legs. Mind?"

"Not at all. I'll be right here."

"Have fun."

He left the hidden room and headed for the door into the stone hall. He pushed the stone, and was about to cross over into the hall, but stopped. He waited, and the door rose again.

For some reason, he felt he should know what kind of metal it was, but he couldn't put his finger on it. So he thought, what kind of metal would a mage use as a door? He'd want something strong. Something that wouldn't bend easily. This door was several inches thick. Bending wasn't going to be a concern, no matter what metal it was. So what else? High melting point, obviously. Hmph. Mages. Magic. He'd want something that was resistant to magic, naturally.

That was it! Vincent smacked the palm of his hand onto the door. Magic! This was a door that could hold a magic spell despite being beaten upon. Blade had told him about it. He began rubbing furiously at the tarnish, revealing a large swath of gleaming metal. He nodded, knowing his suspicion was correct. This was a door of solid platinum.

"Holy shit," he breathed. He turned and headed back to the laboratory.

Jaz looked up when Vincent returned. "That was brief," he said.

Vincent merely nodded. "So are you finding what you expected?"

"Oh, yes! Some of the items here are just wonderful. The books alone are the envy of any mage. Some of these artifacts are totally unknown to me. They could take years of study for me to fathom their secrets."

"Good. Come with me, if you would."

Jaz frowned. "What is it?"

Vincent led him to the metal door, indicating the section he'd rubbed free of tarnish. "Did you realize this door is made of platinum?"

"Ah, yes. So it is."

"Could we, um..." Vincent scratched his beard. "Could we take this door?"

The mage looked at him in surprise. Then he raised an eyebrow, giving clinical thought to the question. He made a few gestures at the door, mumbled a few syllables. "Hmm. If I can disenchant it... Yes. Possibly. It would be worth quite a sum, wouldn't it?"

"Actually, I've been thinking it would make quite a few swords. The door is about ten feet tall by ten feet wide, and about four inches thick. A sword takes approximately two square inches by four feet in length. That's being generous, actually, but I'm allowing for waste. So, this block of metal could yield us close to three hundred swords, if it were cut carefully."

"Or a couple hundred thousand coins, were it to be melted and minted."

Vincent's heart skipped a beat. He hadn't thought of it in terms of coinage. A platinum coin, if he remembered correctly, he'd estimated at about eight thousand dollars. Calculating quickly in his head, if they could get two hundred thousand coins out of this door, that would be... A colossal amount of money. He shook his head. No, there was no way they could get that much money out of a door. He didn't care what it was made of. He must've estimated the value of platinum wrong. Still, even if he'd over-estimated by a hundred percent, this door was still worth a fortune.

Jaz thought about this for a while, then said, "Stand back." Vincent obliged, and watched while Jaz cast spells at the areas around the door. He disintegrated the earth around the door on all sides, then levitated it to the ground. Then, after a minute of intense concentration, he made a gesture and the door disappeared.

"Where...?" Vincent began.

Jaz merely smiled. "Hennor will simply not know what to make of that," he laughed.

Vincent assisted Jaz for a few more hours of searching through the laboratory. His goal was to locate another efreeti bottle. Jaz assisted him in this, after Vincent explained the reason for his search. But there were none to be found. Vincent wasn't surprised, though he was disappointed. He'd vowed to free his elemental friend, and he took that vow seriously. But neither he nor Jaz had any further ideas on how to undo a magic as powerful as Kurean's. Someday, he'd figure it out. But until then, it served no purpose to dwell on it.

By the time they were ready to leave, Jaz had filled the large crate and hinted that he might come back for more one day soon. He concentrated, then teleported the crate to join the metal door, back at his keep. Then he and Vincent took their leave of Kurean's underground laboratory to begin their aerial journey back to Jaz's home.

❧ Twenty ❧

Teleporting really takes a lot out of Jaz. Otherwise, I'm sure he would have teleported us back to his keep, too. But we returned the same way we'd gone out, arriving back a couple weeks ago. Blaise was thrilled to see me, as I expected. And I missed her, too. I told her I beat up the guy who hit her. She seemed to like that.

This is the first I've had time to write in my journal since returning. It's been busy and exciting. Jaz was able to successfully disenchant the door, which will allow it to be melted down for swords. He sent out couriers to the best swordmakers in the nearby lands, bringing three of them back here. They each examined the metal and then put in bids on it.

I don't know exactly how that went. I'm no haggler, as anyone can tell you. But one of the smiths outbid the others. I've never seen such greed. Evidently, once the swords are made, they're going to be able to make a hefty profit. Anyway, the highest bidder sent a courier who arrived just yesterday with a wagon and the money to pay for the metal. Using some sort of spell, Jaz had split the huge door to manageable blocks. We loaded up his wagon, accepted the payment, which was a combination of gemstones, gold coins, pieces of jewelry, and other small but valuable items, and then he left.

Jaz gave me the names of some jewelers who would be able to appraise the stones, but he felt sure that we'd gotten a fair trade. Me? I haven't a clue. I don't even know what the final figure was that they agreed upon. All I know is that I've got this chest full of pretty rocks.

Anyway, it's now well into the Season of Sleep. Snow has fallen and is pretty deep up here in the mountains. I'd like to get home, soon, but am not keen on traveling in this weather. But then, I might not have to worry about the travel part.

I asked Jaz something that had me curious. Why would someone as powerful as Sagasht have to use a magic wand? The answer, evidently, is that wands and other talismans hold spells like a gun holds bullets. Some, like my ring, seem inexhaustible. Wands hold a certain number of charges, so to speak, and the advantage is that the time to cast a spell is considerably reduced by using such an item. I'd been wondering, and now I know.

Jaz spends almost all day and night locked away on one of the upper floors, studying his new toys. So his keep is not exactly the most exciting place to be hanging around. But I'll say one thing... I love it up here. The mountains are beautiful, and it's so peaceful and majestic. I'd love to have a place like this.

I've been doing a lot of thinking about my return home, now that my business helping Jaz is complete. And it's a strange mix of feelings I have. Naturally, I miss Annie desperately. But I have to wonder, does she really want to see me?

I mean, the reason I went off in the first place is because I couldn't handle her not being ready or willing to think of me the way I've been thinking of her. And I've been gone for a lot longer than I anticipated. Half a year. That's a long time, from certain perspectives.

But I want to be home for Celebration Week. We'll see how things are.

It would be too much to hope for that Annie will have had a total change of heart, and feels for me the same way as I do for her. If she does, that's wonderful. But if things are unchanged...

What do I do next? Being around her was becoming pure torture. Being away from her has been pure torture. This isn't my idea of a fun relationship.

Maybe I'd be better off by just giving in to Rhia's advances. Except that she doesn't seem to want a relationship beyond the physical part of things. At least, that's the impression I get. And I want more than that. Guess I'm just too much of a romantic.

Or maybe the ache in my chest is still the result of those little blasts from Sagasht. When I finally stripped off my tunic, I was treated to seeing these black, puckered scars all over my chest. I expected them to hurt a lot more than they did. I hesitate to think about how worse things could have been if Jaz hadn't weakened him so badly.

Then again, now that time has passed, I find it very hard to believe it all actually happened. It was purest luck that I defeated those thieves without getting hurt or killed in the process. And I still have nightmares regularly about killing that one guy.

I can't really put into words how that unintentional murder has affected me. I try to rationalize it by telling myself that it was in self-defense, but that doesn't make me feel any better. I still killed him. If I was able to defeat all the others without killing them, I should have been able to do the same with him.

❧ ❦

"I'm thinking it's time to get on my way," Vincent said to Jaz during dinner.

The mage looked up. "Oh?"

"Yeah. I've been away far longer than I expected."

"Due to unforeseen circumstances," Jaz offered.

Vincent poked food around his plate. "True. But it's time, Jaz. I miss Ariaziane and Gnorrin. And frankly, you've got lots of things now to occupy your time. It's best for me to go."

Jaz nodded. "Very well. I'll have one of my horses prepared for you."

"Actually, I'd rather not take a horse through this weather."

"Surely you're not planning on making the journey on foot?"

Vincent cleared his throat and smiled sheepishly. "Well, in fact, I was rather hoping you could provide an alternate form of transportation."

Jaz smiled as he speared another bit of meat with his fork. "You were, were you?"

"Well, I figured it was the least you could do for the guy who saved your life."

The mage chuckled. "Saved *my* life? Who was about to be reduced to cinders before I saved *him*?"

"Well, who was about to be turned to green goo before I saved *him*?"

"I give up. Who?" Jaz smirked. Vincent pelted him with diced vegetables. The pair laughed together, then Jaz said, "I'm going to miss having you here."

Vincent smiled as his laughter subsided. "Thanks. It's been great. I appreciate everything you've done for me."

Jaz waved it off. "No big one."

Vincent chuckled and returned to his dinner.

❧ ❦

The following day, Vincent packed up his possessions for the trip home. It didn't amount to much. The chest of gems was really the bulkiest part of his belongings. Then he bade emotional farewells to Hennor and the others who had helped him during his blindness. Blaise seemed to understand that they were going home. She bounded around in excitement, jumping on everyone and licking faces.

Finally, he and Jaz made their way outside, where Vincent was surprised to see a large rug, about eight feet by twelve, spread out on top of the snow. "Hmm," he said. "Interesting. I like how the red contrasts to the white. What plans do you have regarding furniture?"

Jaz gave an artificial laugh and slapped Vincent on the back. "You're so funny," he mocked.

Blaise sniffed around the edges of the rug, while Vincent eyed the chest that was already sitting on it. "What's that?" he asked.

Jaz took the chest from Vincent's hands and placed it alongside his own. "My half of the payment for the door. I figured since I was flying you home, we could stop and have them appraised. Come on, put the rest of your things here and sit down."

"Sit down? Wait. That's a flying carpet?"

"I suppose you could call it that," Jaz said as he sat down at one end of it. "But it's more of a rug than a carpet, don't you think?"

Vincent stowed his gear and sat down behind Jaz. "Any particular reason we didn't take this when we went scouting for Kurean's hideaway?"

"It's easier to just levitate and look down than it is to be peering over the edge of the rug the whole time."

Vincent sighed. "Whatever. Come on, girl," he said to Blaise, who gingerly stepped in between the two of them and sat down, leaning heavily into Vincent.

"She'd better not wet on it," the mage warned.

"Oh, what's the big deal? You can just cast a pee-sucker spell and dry it up."

Jaz sighed. "Warriors," he muttered. Then, with a word, the rug lifted gently from the snow.

Blaise whined and began to squirm. Vincent wrapped his arms around her. "It's okay, girl." She looked up at him, licked his cheek, then looked over the side. Vincent did the same, watching as the ground fell away beneath them.

Vincent then told him about his desire to have a keep in the mountains, too. "Maybe a bit further south, though."

"Have you seen the mountains to the south? There's a lovely area that I nearly settled in, before I discovered this valley. Let's go take a look."

"Uh... Sure," said Vincent. "Why not?"

The rug accelerated, but Vincent felt no terrific gusts of wind, as he would have expected. "One of the added attractions to flying on a rug," Jaz said. "It's part of the over-all spell that controls it. No mussed hair."

They flew southward, over the mountains. Vincent was too awestruck to speak. Over the next hour, the only conversation was about the beauty they saw around them. Even the dog seemed impressed. Eventually, they slowed and Jaz gestured widely with his arm. "What do you think?"

Vincent looked down as the rug lowered. Below was a huge triangular valley, nestled between two arms of the mountain range. A river ran through, bisecting the valley, with its origin at the meeting of the two arms. As they sailed toward this point, he could see villages scattered throughout the valley, and asked Jaz about them.

"Yes. This entire region holds some two thousand people, spread amongst perhaps a dozen villages. Most of them are along the river. If I'm not mistaken, the area is under the protection of Duke Ghanol, who serves King Breigar." Jaz shook his head. "Can't see how he can manage it, though, since the Duke's realm is already so large."

"I've never heard you talk about the political aspect of the land before," Vincent said. "I didn't know you were into that."

"Well, I've taken a mild interest in it. I met the Duke not too long ago. He seems a good man."

"What about the King?"

"From what I've heard, he's an excellent fellow. Unlike some others I could mention. How much politics have you learned since your arrival here?"

"I think what you've just told me doubles my previous knowledge." He shrugged. "I really don't care for politics. On my world, it's a disgusting field to be in. It's rare for a political figure to be widely respected, let alone to be held in high honor." He shook his head. "I don't pay any attention to it."

They were near the source of the river, now. Vincent admired the sharp peaks of the mountains, covered with snow. Some were dotted with conifers, but most of the trees he saw were deciduous. "This is gorgeous," he said. He pointed to a plateau on one small mountain that faced northeast, out over the expanse of the valley. "Can you take us down there?" he asked.

Jaz obliged, swooping the rug in low over the plateau for a look around before finally landing. The plateau was probably three hundred feet across, and perhaps two hundred from mountain face to cliff. It was, like everything else, snow-covered. But Vincent could tell that it was normally ripe with vegetation during the warmer months. There were some trees toward the outer part of the plateau, near the cliff that formed the face of the mountain.

When they landed, Vincent stood and stretched. Blaise scampered off through the snow. Moving to the cliff, Vincent looked out over the valley, admiring its beauty. Then he walked around the perimeter of the plateau. He liked what he saw. "This isn't bad," he said over his shoulder.

Jaz stepped over to his side. "What?"

Vincent pointed down the southeastern side of the plateau. "That slope there. Do you think it extends the whole way down to ground level?"

"I have no idea. Why?"

"Because it strikes me that this would be a nice location for a keep."

They explored for an hour, climbing over the rocks that lay at the back of the plateau, up against the face of the mountain itself. They used the rug to search higher, finding a second plateau about a hundred feet above the larger one. This plateau was huge, with what looked like a stream, some ways back. There were trees, now dormant, and lots of open space.

Vincent frowned. "Building a keep must cost quite a lot of money."

"You *have* quite a lot of money."

"What? The gems we got? I know that's a lot of money, but I can't imagine it being enough to finance something of this size. If I were to have a keep of the sort I'd want, we'd need to tunnel out part of the mountain itself." He shook his head. "I doubt I could afford the kind of labor that would require."

"Whatever you say. Are you ready to move on?"

"I suppose. How far to our next stop?"

The mage pointed over the southern arm of the mountain range. "Just over the mountains is the city."

"What city?"

"Falconwall."

"*Falconwall?* How fast were we flying?"

Jaz laughed. "Pretty fast. Let's go."

Vincent called Blaise and in a few moments, they were airborne again.

Falconwall was, as Jaz said, just over the mountains. From the air, Vincent was able to get a look at the true size of the place. "Imposing," he said. "I had no idea it was that big. My few days here didn't show me much of it at all."

"You enjoy cities, then?"

"Well, sort of. I like the ready availability of so many different things. But I don't like the crowds. I don't like the smells."

"Can't blame you," Jaz said. They landed a short distance outside the city gates, where Jaz rolled up the carpet. Then he picked up the sack that held Vincent's belongings. "Mind if I stash this in here?"

"Jaz, if you can fit an eight foot rug into a three foot bag, you're certainly welcome to do so."

"Thank you. Could you hold it open?"

Vincent shook his head in amusement, obligingly holding the mouth of the sack open. Then he watched as Jaz slipped the rolled-up rug into the bag with ease. Vincent's eyes bugged out. "How did you do that?"

"It's a magic bag," Jaz said as they began walking toward the gates.

Vincent grabbed the plain-looking sack and hefted it. "It doesn't weigh any more than it did before! And I don't even *feel* the thing in there!" he said as he kneaded the bag all over with his hands.

"That's a strange property of the bag. You can put quite a lot into it, but it always weighs the same. The items seem to go into another plane of existence, where—"

"Another plane of existence? You mean, like, another dimension?"

Jaz pondered the word. "Dimension?" he repeated. "You mean such as height, width, length...?"

"Yeah. I guess. Some of the theories I've read add time as another dimension. But there are a lot of theories. For example, we live in a world of three dimensions, right?" Jaz nodded his head. "Well, we also see things in three dimensions. As well as two dimensional things. A shadow, for example, is two-dimensional. But if, say, you and I were two-dimensional creatures instead of three-dimensional, then we'd only be able to see two-dimensional and one-dimensional things. A three-dimensional object would be out of our ability to see. What we would see would be only two dimensions of its three-dimensionality. Its shadow, so to speak. Do you follow?"

"Yes," Jaz said, stroking his beard.

"Well, what that means is that you and I cannot see something that is four-dimensional. But we could see its shadow, which would, in theory, be three-dimensional."

The mage furrowed his brow in concentration. "So what you're saying is that the three-dimensional things that we see around us could in reality be only the shadows of something four-dimensional?"

Vincent paused. "I've never looked at it that way, before."

"That's all very interesting, but what has it to do with this bag?"

"Probably nothing."

"Ah."

"What I was getting at is that the bag could be a gateway to the fourth dimension. So that objects placed inside it are, possibly, converted to four dimensions. Maybe." He frowned. "How do you get them back?"

"I reach in, think about what item I want, and then it's in my hand."

Vincent hesitated, staring at Jaz as they walked. "You *think* about it. And it comes to your hand."

"Right."

The young man shook his head. "Well, hand me a horn and call me Dizzy. That makes my head spin." He frowned, looking into the bag. He could clearly see the bottom of it, which looked no different than the bottom of any other sack. "You ever considered... I dunno... just diving in?"

Jaz smiled. "Once. I put the bag over my head far enough that it should've poked through the bottom."

"And...?"

"And I nearly vomited. I was overcome with a feeling of disorientation, stronger than I could ever imagine. I was barely able to remove the bag before falling over."

"Ah. Guess I won't do it, then."

Soon they entered the city, by the same gate through which Vincent had entered before. It seemed like a lifetime ago, so much had happened since then. But he remembered it clearly. The smell of human waste, the nostril-numbing odor of the tannery, and other smells not so unpleasant.

They made their way to a section of the city that Vincent did not see during his previous visit. Eventually, they came upon the jeweler's shop that Jaz had mentioned to him. *Berel's Baubles* was, Vincent decided, named with tongue firmly planted in cheek. Inside, he gazed upon showcases full of fancy jewelry and brilliantly cut gemstones. The shop was beautifully, tastefully, decorated. Berel herself seemed to be a walking advertisement for her business, bedecked as she was with prominent, yet tasteful, jewelry.

Berel seemed to be in late middle age, still attractive in a regal fashion. And her smile was warm and sincere. "Jaz! How good to see you. What have you been up to, lately?"

"More trouble, as usual. Meet my friend, Vincent. He has some things to show you."

"How delightful. Pleased to meet you," she said. "And you, too," she said to Blaise, who was prancing around excitedly. Berel obliged her by petting her and scratching her ears. Then, turning back to Jaz, "You're in luck, too. I happen to have a little extra lying around that I was hoping to invest." Jaz merely smiled as they joined her at a table behind the counter and placed their goods in front of her. Berel paused in the act of sitting. "Are these both *full?*" she asked.

Jaz smiled again. "To the rim."

"Oh, my."

"Exactly," said the mage. "So how much extra did you say you had lying around?"

Berel sat and pushed back the lid on one of the chests. She blinked. "Not that much," she said. "Gods on toast, Jaz, how did you and your friend come into such a trove?"

"Long, boring story, I'm afraid," said the mage.

"You don't have any boring stories."

"What we need, Berel, is your best appraisal. Of everything. Naturally, anything you wish to purchase is your exclusive domain. As always, I've come to you, first."

The woman sighed. "Hope you're in no hurry."

"Not at all. Just do your best. We have some other errands to run. Could we leave the dog with you?"

"Surely. She's a lovely animal, Vincent."

"Thanks."

Jaz fished some of the gold coins out of the open chest and handed them to Vincent. "We'll be back later this evening."

"Very good, then. I'll give this my undivided attention. Could you turn the sign to 'closed' on your way out? Thank you." She picked up her magnifying glass and set to work as they left.

"You must really trust her," Vincent said, once they were outside again.

"I've done business with her for over ten years. She's always given me the fairest appraisals. Though that fortune we've left in her possession would be the kind of temptation for anyone to close up shop and run off."

"You don't think she'll do that, though?"

"No. She's aware that I'm a mage. It's one of the advantages to the mystique we have. People don't generally try to steal from us. Now... That bakery we passed made me hungry. How about lunch?"

"Why, thank you, Rabbit! Have you got any honey?" Jaz looked at him oddly. "No? Oh, bother," Vincent said, trying his best to sound like Pooh.

"You are so odd," said Jaz, as they entered a tavern.

After a quick meal of hearty soup and freshly baked bread, Jaz took Vincent to other parts of the city. They watched a short play in a theater. Vincent felt Shakespeare might do well amongst these folks. Perhaps one day, he'd try to draft a script of *A Midsummer Night's Dream*, if he could remember enough of it. They did some shopping, too. Vincent purchased some scented oils for Ariaziane and some winter vegetables for Gnorrin to use in his next batch of stew. He also purchased an expensive vial of flower extract for Rhia, to give her whenever their paths crossed again. By the time all this was done, it was time to eat again. They returned to the tavern and had a large meal.

When they finally returned to the shop, Blaise jumped all over them as soon as they were in the door. Berel greeted them with a smile as they entered. She was still seated at her little table, which was now covered with piles of cut gemstones, as was the counter behind her.

"What I've done," she explained to them, "is divide these stones into piles according to their relative worth."

"'Relative' worth?" Vincent asked.

Jaz elucidated. "Meaning that you could perhaps get slightly more, or slightly less, depending on the decision of whoever is doing the appraisal when you attempt to convert the gem to coin."

"Appraisals are never exact, my young friend," Berel said. "But I think you'll find mine to be accurate as to what you can expect elsewhere. I try to be conservative with my estimates so you'll know if someone is trying to cheat you."

"How will I know what's too little?"

"My estimates are good to ten percent. If someone offers less than ninety percent of what I've appraised this stone for, you tell him you'll take your business elsewhere. Likewise, I doubt you'll find anyone willing to give you more than ten percent above what I've appraised."

"I see. So what are the values?"

Berel pointed to different piles as she rattled off numbers. "One... Two... Five..."

Vincent interrupted by plucking one of the stones from the "five" pile. He held up the large, green gem and said, "Five? I'm sorry, but this is a beautiful stone. I'm no jeweler, but even I can see that it's worth more than five gold pieces."

Berel raised an eyebrow as Jaz choked back a laugh. "Hundred," the mage said. "She means five hundred, not five."

"All these are in hundreds," Berel said with a smile.

Vincent gaped. He looked at the piles, tried to do some quick tallying in his head. He failed. His mouth moved, but he couldn't form words. "Five... Hundred? You mean for the pile, right?"

Berel chuckled and shook her head. "For each stone in the pile."

Vincent felt faint. "Oh, man," he muttered.

Jaz put his hand on the boy's shoulder. "Now. About that keep that you couldn't afford...?"

He looked stupidly at the mage. "I'm... I'm, uh..."

"Rich," Jaz supplied.

"Filthy," Vincent added.

"Exactly."

Vincent shook his head. "But... But..."

Jaz just smiled at him.

The pair stayed in the shop with Berel for two more hours. Jaz stepped out for a few minutes, returning with a large quantity of small pouches. He and Vincent placed the stones into separate pouches as Berel appraised them, allowing Vincent to keep track of which stones were worth what amounts. Similarly, the coins all transferred to their own pouches. Finally, Berel finished with the stones.

"Would it be acceptable to put off the jewelry until tomorrow? My eyes need rest."

"Certainly," said Jaz.

"Actually," Vincent said. "There's no need for you to do my jewelry at all. I'll just keep it." Jaz agreed that it could wait for another time.

"Some of those pieces are worth quite a lot," Berel warned.

"I'm sure they are. But that's okay. How much do I owe you for doing this?"

Berel hesitated. "Well, my normal fee for appraisal work is one silver piece per hour. I do, however, offer a discount for the opportunity to purchase from your supply."

"Oh! I'm sorry. Yes, of course. You did mention that before. What would you like?"

The woman smiled wickedly. "There is one particular item that struck my fancy. I took the liberty of looking at it quite closely while you were gone." She picked up an ornate necklace from the box, a beautiful silver chain with a small but brilliant red stone, surrounded by smaller diamond-like stones, all set in a fancy filigreed oval. "I have one customer who's been looking for something like this for some time. I'm sure she'd love it, and pay handsomely for it. I'd like to offer you... oh, six hundred gold pieces. I don't have *quite* that much on hand, however..."

"It's yours," Vincent said.

Berel blinked. "I beg your pardon?"

"I said it's yours. That necklace is your payment for your services."

"Oh, you're jesting, now. Don't be ridiculous."

"For your services today," he continued, "and any appraisals for myself or Jaz in the future. How's that?"

The woman hesitated, looking at the necklace, then at Jaz. "Is he serious?"

Jaz nodded. "Most likely. I suggest you accept."

Berel let out a breath. "My goodness. I don't know what to say!"

Vincent laughed. "Say 'yes.' I'm tired, too, and want to get some sleep. I've got a busy day tomorrow."

"In that case... Yes! I accept! But you're much too kind. You'd better come to have me do an awful lot of appraisals if you want to get your money's worth!"

Vincent looked at the pouches of costly gems. "To be honest, I don't think I need to worry about that very much."

They packed up the valuables, thanked Berel for her time, and departed.

They spent the night at a nearby inn, Vincent insisting on paying for both rooms. In the morning, they had breakfast in the inn's tavern. An hour later, they were sailing through the skies to the north-east, toward Vincent's home.

Throughout the journey, Vincent pondered his newfound wealth. He had to laugh. Back on Earth, money was always a concern. He hadn't yet reached the stage where it was a full-blown concern. He'd been attending the local university, living at home with his father. He hadn't needed to worry about rent, or car payments, or insurance, or anything like that.

Here, those worries were nowhere near as great as they were on Earth. Here, he'd been living a fairly modest existence and been perfectly content. Sure, he'd acquired enough wealth in Kurean's keep to allow him to quit working at *the Nib and Quill*. Now, though, he had enough money to live anywhere he wanted, and to live fairly well, too.

What he found funny was that here, money was rather superfluous. On Earth, it would've been the answer to his dreams. But here it was just a pleasant turn of events. He smiled, looking forward to lavishing his friends with gifts.

The thought nagged at him that he didn't really deserve the wealth. It wasn't like he'd earned it. He'd stolen a door, of all things. Just a door.

A door that was worth millions.

"You've been awfully quiet," Jaz said at one point, as he absently stroked the dog, lying asleep by his side.

"Yeah. Sorry I haven't been better company. Got things on my mind."

The mage chuckled. "I'd say you do. Two chests of things."

"Yeah." Vincent frowned. "Um... *One* chest of things. The other chest is yours."

Jaz shook his head. "You need it more than I do."

"I don't *need* it at all. And we both did the work, you should take half of it!"

"The door was your discovery, your plan entirely. All I did was disenchant it and split it into pieces able to be carried. A simple enough matter. Besides, the items I took from Kurean's laboratory are what I was after. I got what I wanted. Actually, I got more than I expected. Which reminds me..." He reached into a pocket in his cloak and withdrew a ring. "I got this from Sagasht's body. Since you were so helpful in defeating him, it's only fair that you share in what I got from him."

He handed the ring to Vincent, who slipped it on. "What's it do?"

Jaz smiled, then leaned over and shoved him roughly. Vincent toppled over the edge of the rug and plummeted toward the ground.

Before he could build up a really good scream, his descent abruptly slowed, so that his fall was no faster than a child's balloon being dropped.

As he slowly began to realize that the ring was the reason he wasn't becoming pasture pizza, he had to laugh. "Very funny!" he yelled up at the mage. He smiled and waited while his friend maneuvered the rug in a long, slow arc, finally hovering directly below Vincent's slowly descending form. Vincent crossed his legs and rested his elbows on his knees, yoga style, and landed softly on the rug. Blaise whined and licked him.

Jaz was laughing. "You should have seen your face!"

Vincent smiled. "Now I won't feel guilty about taking all the gems."

After what seemed an eternity, Vincent started recognizing familiar territory. He watched the snow-covered hills beneath him until he spied a familiar grove of trees. Then a familiar road. "This is it," he said to Jaz. He pointed to a cottage, snow-covered, with a large, fenced-in yard.

They landed, and Blaise bounded off, plunging through the snow. Vincent followed, a warmth growing inside him. Knowing that Ariaziane was just up the road with Gnorrin filled him with an anticipation that almost overwhelmed him.

Jaz stepped up behind him. "Looks as though you'll need to get a new horse to fill that stable over there."

"Yeah," he replied, opening his door and stepping inside. He frowned. "Nuts."

Jaz looked around, stepping in behind him. "Where?"

"I didn't expect to be gone as long as I was, so I don't have any wood for the fire. Definitely not how I wanted to spend the afternoon."

The mage cleared his throat, then pulled the magical gauntlets from the bag. He held them out to Vincent. "I don't think it will take all that long."

One hour later, the pair arrived at Gnorrin's cottage. Blaise had preceded them, hurrying ahead and barking up a storm when she neared the dwelling. Gnorrin leaned his head out the door, looking up at the road when he saw Blaise. His eyes widened and he smiled. Vincent saw him say something over his shoulder before he stepped outside to greet them.

"Vincent, lad!" he laughed. "Welcome home!" He rushed over to his side and began slapping his friend on the back. At least, as high as he could reach.

"Thanks, Gnorrin," he said, hugging the gnome. "Good to be back. Great to see you! This is my new friend Jaz. I think you two will find much to talk about."

At that moment, Ariaziane stepped through the door. Vincent's breath caught in his throat. He waited, not moving, to see what her reaction would be. For a moment, she just stood outside the door, looking at him, ignoring Blaise, who was jumping up on her, trying to lick her face. Then she walked slowly forward, never taking her eyes from him.

A pit formed in Vincent's stomach. She wasn't smiling. She wasn't hurrying to meet him. His mouth went dry as he thought that she might be angry with him. That she might not forgive him for going away in the first place.

Finally, she reached him and stood staring at him. It wasn't an angry stare or an accusing stare. In fact, her face seemed to be devoid of any expression. Then her eyes seemed to waver somewhat. Her eyebrows arched ever so slightly. And then she threw her arms around him, pressing her face against his shoulder.

"You really *are* home," she whispered in a choked voice.

He returned the hug, a tightness in his chest replacing the pit in his stomach. And when he felt her hot tears on his neck, he cried, too.

Darella's daughter watched the reunion in her mother's crystal ball. She frowned, not knowing why.

She and her brother were now just a few months shy of being two years old. But the rapid aging made them equivalent to normal seven-year olds. The incessant "education" of their mother made them mentally even older than seven.

The girl had successfully hidden from her mother and brother the fact that her father was still alive. She didn't exactly know why she felt it necessary to keep it a secret, but she did.

Perhaps it had something to do with the fact that she felt different than her brother and mother. She felt like an outsider. Though she had nothing to compare them against, she thought of them as mean. Her mother talked about magic and knowledge. She didn't seem to care about people, only about knowledge, for its own sake. She didn't even seem to care about her or her brother.

And her brother... He seemed to enjoy nothing more than inflicting pain. He would sometimes catch the little tree rodents and torture them. He liked to torture her, too, though he did it with words. He'd make fun of her. He was better at learning the things their mother planted in their minds and he knew it. He liked to remind her of this at any given opportunity. She was starting to hate him for it.

Maybe that was why she felt such a tenderness for this man who was her father, this man who seemed to care so much for those around him. If her cold mother and nasty brother didn't care for him, then there was probably good reason for her to like him. That's why she had vowed to keep his survival a secret from them.

Maybe, she thought, she'd one day be able to meet him. Maybe, if she explained to him how she'd kept that secret, he'd like that.

And maybe he'd be her friend.

❧ Twenty-One ❧

Jaz remained Vincent's guest through Celebration Week and spent a good deal of time in conversation with Gnorrin and Ariaziane, discussing things of a magical nature. Vincent felt slightly left out, but certainly couldn't be upset with his three friends for it.

Jaz did his best, however, to include Vincent in the conversation. He spoke highly of his participation in the vanquishing of Beltun Sagasht. Gnorrin, especially, was quite impressed, having heard much of Sagasht and his abilities.

Vincent spent as much time with Ariaziane as he could. He told her about most of his half-year adventure, including the injury that stole his sight. She'd berated him, of course. "I can't believe you went after them," she said. "It was only a cloak pin! That's not worth your life!" And he had to agree with her. But at the time, it seemed the most important thing to him, he explained. Perhaps it was because he'd just gone through a traumatic event and wasn't thinking very clearly, but the idea of losing something that she had given him was just too much to bear. When he explained this, Ariaziane had nothing to say.

Celebration Week proved to be great fun. The four of them spent long nights in town, watching the festival shows, singing songs and dining out. They celebrated Vincent's nineteenth birthday with cake and presents. Gnorrin gave him a selection of fancy Inks by Mepis and another journal to match the one he was rapidly filling up. Ariaziane gave him a new cloak of dark brown leather lined with fur.

Vincent purchased a new horse, at Ariaziane's insistence. There were few things she enjoyed more than riding, and she wanted him to join her. His new horse was fairly young, only four years old. A good-spirited, gray and black mare. She was spunkier than Vincent's previous mount, and he rather liked that.

They spent hours going for long rides during the afternoons. And they talked. Ariaziane told him of her studies with Gnorrin, and for the first time, Vincent could relate to what she was saying. His time with Jaz, and especially the encounter with Sagasht, had opened his eyes to the seriousness of the art. He had new respect for what she was doing. Compared to her studies, his ability to catch a piece of fruit with his eyes shut seemed pretty trivial.

Finally, the day came when Jaz announced his departure. Vincent was sorry to see him go, but certainly understood the mage's desire to get back to the study of Kurean's artifacts. Ariaziane extracted a promise from Jaz that he'd allow her to study with him in the future. He also promised to keep in touch with Gnorrin, to share any interesting insights to Kurean's art that he might find. To Vincent, he promised an open door whenever he wanted to visit. And then he took off, sailing back to his mountain keep.

Vincent and Ariaziane spent more time together than they had before Vincent's time away. This was certainly an improvement, but Vincent still wasn't sure exactly where he stood with her. She seemed to go out of her way to be with him, but never engaged in any behavior that he could quite call romantic. She would hold his hand when they went for walks, greet him with a hug and give another when leaving. But she seemed awkward if he tried to prolong their embraces.

Once, he'd kissed her. After a dinner he'd prepared for them, they sat in front of the fireplace and talked. Earlier, he'd gone through his new horde of jewelry, trying to choose something nice to give her. Most of the items were just too ornate, in his opinion. Ariaziane was not a fancy person. She was still a girl, and anything very elaborate seemed to him to look out of place on her. Finally, he decided on one particular ring. It was silver, with a bright blue stone. Some carved knotwork adorned the sides. Sitting there in front of the fire, he presented it to her.

She lit up, as he hoped she would. "It's beautiful," she said. "I love it."

"I'm glad," he replied. "Because I love you."

Her eyes had met his as she looked up from the ring. Her mouth opened, but no words came forth. Fighting back the nerves that threatened to return his dinner, he leaned forward and planted a quick but serious kiss on her soft lips.

As his heart beat frantically, he'd waited for some sort of reaction. Unfortunately, the reaction received was the one he expected, rather than the one he'd hoped for. She'd smiled shyly, then turned away, asking him questions for the fiftieth time about Beltun Sagasht.

Vincent knew he couldn't complain. He was home, safe and sound, not to mention filthy rich. He was able to spend lots of time with Ariaziane, and even though she seemed not to have a romantic interest in him, she did love him as a friend. And that was very important.

Soon, the Season of Green began to warm up. It felt good to open his windows, sealed for many months, and let the fresh air in. Vincent plowed and planted his garden and enjoyed the mild weather. Before too long, he found himself wanting to travel again. But this time, not alone. Remembering a promise he'd made, he started planning a trip to Linnael to visit Aedriun. He asked Ariaziane to accompany him. To his pleasant surprise, she agreed. To his even greater surprise, Gnorrin expressed a desire to go along.

So it was that, one week later, Vincent sealed up his windows again and they departed on the journey. Even Blaise seemed excited to be hitting the road again.

The trip itself was uneventful. The worst encounters they had were miles and miles of muddy road. Vincent had a lot of time to think on the road, and found his thoughts turning frequently to his family. He felt guilty that he'd not thought of them much since returning home from Jaz's keep. That wasn't right, he told himself. Just because my fortunes have changed for the better is no reason for me to stop thinking about home.

They reached Linnael during the mid-morning hours, several days after their departure. The first thing they did was find an inn. There, they acquired three of the best rooms available, stabled their horses, and had them washed and groomed. A few pieces of small coinage got the same treatment for Blaise. Then they availed themselves of the baths provided for the inn's guests. Afterward, Vincent wrote a note announcing his arrival and sent it by courier to Aedriun.

After lunch in the inn's tavern, they went down to the docks. There they marveled over the great sailing ships. A fishing vessel had just pulled into port and was unloading her catch of the day. The smell made Gnorrin's nose wrinkle.

Ariaziane led them on a walk down the shoreline, away from the docks. They were all impressed by the huge expanse of water before them, but it seemed to Vincent that

Ariaziane was the most profoundly affected. He saw the sense of awe on her face, in her eyes. And he knew then that the girl had found something she could love. She'd fallen in love with the sea.

They found an expanse of sandy beach. So lovely, Vincent thought. No crowds of sun-worshipers turning the virgin beauty of it into a whore of a tourist attraction. He heaved a deep sigh. He could certainly enjoy being near such an untouched beach, too, though it couldn't compare to the inspiring majesty of the mountains he'd recently left behind.

After a couple hours of resting on the sand and throwing sticks for Blaise, Vincent announced that he was going to head back to the inn to see if Aedriun had answered his message, yet. Gnorrin brushed off his breeches and joined him. Ariaziane stayed with Blaise on the shore, promising to follow along later.

"I do believe she likes it here," said Gnorrin as they made their way back.

"Looks that way," Vincent agreed.

They walked in silence for a while, then Gnorrin said, "You've changed."

"Oh? How do you mean?"

The gnome shrugged. "You seem a bit more withdrawn. More thoughtful, perhaps."

"Well, I went through some shit," Vincent said bluntly. "I guess that has a way of maturing you."

"Yes. But I get the feeling that you haven't told me everything about what kind of... um, *shit*... you went through. Your injury and recovery certainly seem to have had a profound effect on you. But I think you're keeping something else to yourself."

"Why do you think that?"

"I sense a darkness about you. Like you've shut a door inside yourself."

Vincent shook his head. "I've always been like that. You've just never noticed before."

"Not true. I have noticed it before. But this is different. This is something painful."

Vincent was quiet for a while, staring at the ground as he walked. "I killed a man, Gnorrin."

His friend nodded in understanding. "I thought that might have been it. I have been concerned about this eventuality ever since Blade began teaching you the ways of the sword."

Vincent frowned. "I always thought you were upset because you didn't want me getting hurt."

"And isn't that what has occurred?" Vincent didn't respond verbally, but he knew Gnorrin didn't miss the pain in his eyes. "Tell me how it happened."

Vincent shrugged. "I punched him in the nose."

His friend raised his eyebrows. "You punched him in the nose?"

"While wearing the magic gauntlets I showed you."

"Ah. Hmm. Yes, I could see how that could do it. But he was trying to kill you, I assume?"

"Yes," Vincent said with a nod. "But that doesn't change how I feel about it. I mean, if I knew the guy was a total scum, I wouldn't be so upset. Like Beltun Sagasht. I might not have laid the killing blow, but I certainly was part of his death. But I don't regret that, because the man was contemptible. This guy I killed, though... I didn't

281

know anything about him. For all I know, he could have been a decent fellow who only happened to be working with Sagasht. And likely as not, he had friends and family who loved him." Vincent shook his head. "All I can think about is what I've stolen from them."

Gnorrin was silent for a time. "I understand your pain. Still, you cannot expect to be able to merely incapacitate all those who fight you. That is pure fantasy."

"Well, it'll never have to happen again," Vincent said with relief. "I've got lots of money, now. I can just settle down and mind my own business for the rest of my life."

"Oh? No longer trying to find your way home?"

Another jab of guilt hit him. "Well, yes. Of course."

"You don't sound very convincing."

"Don't be ridiculous. You know I want to go home."

"Mm. Yes. So long as you could take the girl with you."

Vincent avoided Gnorrin's gaze. That *was* what he wanted. He'd thought about it before. "Somehow, I doubt I'll ever make it home, let alone be able to take her with me." He gazed at the land around him. "I guess I've accepted that. I sort of feel bad, like I'm giving up hope. But it's been two years, Gnorrin. I'm sure my family has given me up for dead, anyway."

"I hope you're right. About never having to kill again."

"Why wouldn't I be?"

Gnorrin smiled ruefully. "Life is rarely so predictable."

Vincent chuckled. "Nonsense. My life is nothing if not predictable."

Gnorrin laughed. "Whatever you say."

A message was waiting for them when they returned to the inn. A clerk produced it for them, then returned to his bookkeeping duties.

"'Vincent and friends,'" Vincent read aloud. "'Welcome to Linnael! I regret that I am unable to meet with you this evening, but please join me for dinner tomorrow. I shall expect you by mid-afternoon and insist that you stay as my guests for the rest of your time here. Enjoy your stay at *The Yellow Beard*. It is a fine establishment. Yours sincerely, Aedriun.'" He folded up the note. "That's all well and good," he said to Gnorrin, "but I haven't a clue how to find his place."

"Excuse me," said the clerk. "Baron Aedriun is easy to find. Take the road from here toward the docks. At the intersection where the fishmongers do business, turn left. Continue for about half a league. His is the large estate with the iron gates. You will have no trouble recognizing it."

"Thank you," Vincent said. Then, handing him a coin, he said, "We are expecting a young lady to be joining us." The clerk gave a leering little smile and nodded. "She'll have a big, black dog with her." The clerk's smile faded and he raised an eyebrow.

"A dog?"

"Yes, a dog. Is that a problem?" Vincent asked, concerned about the inn's regulations.

"Not for me, m'lord." He forced a smile and laughed weakly. "Whatever is your fancy," he said.

"Very well, then. My friend and I are going out for a bit. If she arrives before our return, please have her wait in the tavern for us. We will be back by sunset." The clerk looked strangely at him, but nodded. Then Vincent and Gnorrin entered the street again.

They browsed the small shops along the avenue. In one store, he found a beautiful hair brush. It was of polished oilnut wood, inlaid with strips and whorls of a darker wood that Vincent didn't recognize. Intricate designs were carved into the back of the brush. He showed it to Gnorrin. "Don't you think Annie would like this? I think I'll buy it for her. Kind of expensive for a hairbrush, but she's worth it. What do you think of it?"

Gnorrin shook his head sadly. "You cannot buy her love, my friend."

Vincent's jaw dropped. "Is that what you think I'm trying to do?"

"Isn't it?"

"No! I just like to give things to people. What's wrong with that?"

"Nothing. It just seems, sometimes, that you have this desperation about giving things to her. As though it will make her notice you."

Vincent looked at the brush in his hand, then put it back on the shelf. Then he turned and headed out of the shop, Gnorrin following. "I don't know what else to do, Gnorrin. I love her so much. And I think she feels pretty strongly about me, too. But she won't let it show."

The gnome toyed with the bright green collar of his yellow tunic. He cleared his throat. "Yes. Well. I might be able to shed some light on that."

Vincent stopped walking and turned to look at his friend. "Oh?"

Gnorrin shrugged. "Possibly. She does live in my home, you know. We do talk about things other than magic." He paused, then continued. "You are correct. She does feel very strongly about you, and without question loves you as a friend. I suspect she loves you further, but..."

"But what?"

"Well, to be honest, she's frightened."

"Frightened? Of *me*?"

"After a fashion, yes."

"That's ridiculous!"

"The girl is extremely perceptive. She sees things in you that perhaps you do not see yourself."

"What are you talking about? What is there to see in me that could possibly frighten her? Gnorrin, this is absurd! What has she said to you?"

Gnorrin was quiet for a moment, then turned and began walking back toward the inn. Vincent fell in step beside him. "Then there is the possibility of you leaving. Going back to Earth. She does not look forward to that eventuality. She knows she will lose a friend. She doesn't want to lose her heart at the same time."

"Okay," Vincent said. "I can understand that. But as I said, I really don't think I'm ever going to find my way home. Even if we do locate the device that brought me here, how will we figure out how to make it send me back?"

"True. It would be difficult."

"Yeah. So I can't really accept that as being a real problem, here. What did you mean before? About her seeing things about me that I'm unaware of?"

Gnorrin was silent, and Vincent could see on his friend's face that he was trying to formulate a way to express his thoughts. Despite his anxiety, Vincent didn't press him.

They reached the inn, entered, and headed straight for the tavern, making their way to an empty table toward the back, near the fireplace. A cheery blaze was crackling away, making it uncomfortably warm in Vincent's opinion. Come nightfall, he was sure he'd welcome it. They ordered beverages, then Vincent said, "I'm still waiting."

"Tell me," Gnorrin said, leaning back in his chair, "why you took up the sword."

Vincent blinked. "What does that have to do with anything? Don't change the subject."

"This concerns the subject at hand, in a way. Why did you do so?"

"I don't know," he said in exasperation. "Because Blade wanted to teach me. Because... I don't know. I guess because I've always thought of swordplay as being... well, romantic, I guess."

"*Romantic?* You have an odd idea of romance on your world."

"Well, no. Not romantic in that sense." He tried to explain, telling Gnorrin of the human sense of romantic periods of history. Telling him of the Hollywood versions of swordplay. Robin Hood, King Arthur, the Three Musketeers, Zorro, and others.

Gnorrin listened to his explanation, then said, "And how do you compare those imitations of reality with the experiences you've now had?"

The serving maid brought their beverages as Vincent pondered the question. As she left, he said, "I'm not sure. Oh, I realize this is reality and Hollywood is fiction. But to be honest, so far, it's been pretty much what I expected."

"Truly? What about your fight with Beltun Sagasht? What about your first kill?"

"Don't say it that way!" Vincent snapped. "It was an accident! I didn't mean to kill him. And the fight with Sagasht was Jaz's fight, not mine. I just helped out."

"And got terribly lucky, as well. Vincent, there is an old expression that we have. 'He who lives by the sword, dies by the sword.'"

He couldn't help laughing. "We have the same expression on Earth, though it's more of a metaphor than anything."

"Here it is reality."

"I wish you'd quit worrying about my safety. *I'm* not that worried about it, so why should you be?"

The gnome ran his finger through the perspiration on his tankard, then took a quaff of the ale. He tapped his fingers idly on the table top. "The girl says you have an angry streak inside you."

Vincent's eyes widened. "That's crazy! Gnorrin, you've known me ever since I arrived here. Have you ever seen me get angry?"

"Never. But Ariaziane feels that is the problem."

"Pardon me?"

"She believes you keep your anger inside. And she's afraid of what will happen when it comes out."

Vincent sighed, shaking his head. "I don't get it. Where is she getting this? It makes no sense to me. Did she offer any evidence to this?"

Gnorrin nodded. "I felt similarly, too. So I asked her for examples."

"And?"

"She gave some, yes. For instance, when she was turned out of the abbey."

Vincent recalled that incident clearly. "Yeah, that ticked me off pretty good."

"Mm. And what did you do?"

"Do? Well, nothing. What *could* I do? I couldn't change their minds, could I?"

Gnorrin shrugged. "How did you feel after that, when you asked her to move in with you and she moved in with me, instead?"

Vincent sipped at his spiced cider. "Disappointed. Not angry, if that's what you want to hear."

"No? She thinks you never understood her reasoning."

"She wanted to be with you so she could study magic with you."

"But you think she could have done so while still living with you."

Vincent traced a line in the grain of the wood on the table. "Yeah."

"And you harbor some resentment. Some anger."

He frowned. "Maybe! So what?"

"And what about your presence here at all? Aren't you angry that you were plucked away from your world, your family, and brought here against your will?"

Vincent's jaw tightened. "Wouldn't you be?" he said quietly.

"Absolutely. That's exactly my point. Or rather, Ariaziane's point." He leaned forward. "Vincent, she is worried about you. And scared for you. And a little scared *of* you. She feels that you are holding all that anger inside and..."

"Yeah," he interrupted. "One day I'll just explode. So you said. But I don't see any real evidence to that fact. Okay, so she's astute enough to see that there are things that get me mad. And it's true that I don't generally give vent to that anger. But what harm is there in that? Would she rather that I yelled and hit things every time something bothered me? I mean, that doesn't help any!"

The gnome finished his drink. "Perhaps it does, perhaps it does not."

Vincent shook his head in disbelief. "I don't understand."

"How long do you think that you can keep ignoring anger?"

"Well, I've done it for nineteen years, so far. Gnorrin, what's the big deal? I don't understand why this bothers her so much! Does she think I'm going to snap one day and take out two decades of anger on *her?*"

His friend frowned. "I don't believe that is her fear. Rather, I think it is simply the idea of you... *snapping...* that concerns her. She does love you, Vincent. In her own way."

"But not the way I love her."

Again, Gnorrin shrugged. "I don't know. I suspect she might, to be truthful with you."

Vincent tried to ignore the sudden tightness in his chest. "But she's holding back because she thinks I'm gonna go postal?"

"Eh?"

Vincent waved the question aside and raked his fingers through his long hair. "Okay. So, how do I convince her that I'm not going to snap? How can I make her see that she has nothing to worry about?"

Gnorrin looked him in the eye. "Doesn't she?"

"No! Gnorrin, I'm not the kind of person who gets violent. I've known violent people. They're the kind who punch walls when they get pissed. They're the ones who throw things at the television when their hockey team loses. I'm not like that! I *can't* be like that!"

The mage nodded quietly, looking absently into his empty tankard. "And if you... what did you call it? 'Go postal?' Is that when you punch walls?"

The simple question stopped his tirade short. He grimaced, then sighed. "No," he said softly. "Not exactly." Then he gave a short chuckle. "'He was such a nice man,' the neighbors all said. 'Kept to himself. We couldn't believe he could do such a thing.'" He rubbed his eyes with the heels of his hands. "So," he said. "That's what she sees in me?" He didn't wait for his friend to reply. "Do you think she's right, or is she exaggerating?" He removed his hands from his face and looked at Gnorrin.

"I feel she is exaggerating." Vincent felt himself relax. "But I also think her fears have some root in truth." The relaxed feeling vanished. "What I mean is that I feel that you could easily become what she fears, unless you are careful to stay clear of situations that could cause such a change in you."

Vincent put two and two together. "Which is why you want me to put aside the sword. What do you want me to do? Learn magic instead? Your friend Beltun Sagasht is ample proof that magic isn't any safer a practice than swordsmanship. And Annie is learning magic herself!"

"There are vast differences, and I know you're not blind to them. The study of magic is a study of knowledge itself. Only a small percentage of magic is of a martial nature. You cannot say the same thing of swordsmanship."

Vincent frowned, fidgeting from the heat of the fireplace. "So what's your point?"

Gnorrin looked intently at his friend. "How serious were you when you talked about settling down? Are you willing to put your quest for glory aside?"

"What quest for glory? Who's putting these ideas in your head? Yes, I'm willing to settle down. If I never have to swing a sword again, it wouldn't bother me." He frowned. "Why are you looking at me like I'm a raving lunatic?"

"Because I find it difficult to believe that you can so easily put such things aside. You're young. You've had a taste of adventure, and I think you like it enough that you'll continue to pursue it."

"Oh, great. First I'm a repressed psycho, now I'm a closet thrill-seeker." He gulped the rest of his cider, then wiped sweat from the back of his neck. "It's too hot here. I'm going out for a breath of fresh air."

He stood and headed out, knowing Gnorrin would leave him to his time alone. And right now, he certainly needed some. The cool air outside was a welcome relief. He looked at the sky. The sun was low on the horizon. He was surprised that Ariaziane hadn't returned yet. For a moment, he worried that something had happened to her, but then decided that she was probably still on the beach. It was too bad, he thought, that the beach faced east instead of west. An ocean sunset would have been something to see.

He walked, not caring where his feet led him. His thoughts raced, filled with Gnorrin's words. Before he knew it, he was at the docks. The last of the fishing boats were being unloaded. Vincent stopped and watched the stevedores working. Then he located an empty pier and seated himself at the end of it, looking out to sea.

He looked down the beach on the off chance that he might spot Ariaziane or Blaise. No such luck, though. With a sigh, he turned back to watch the darkening waters. He closed his eyes, trying to blot out everything but his thoughts. Trying to make sense of them. Trying to discover if any truth could be found in Ariaziane's ideas.

His body relaxed. He could feel the weight of it slipping away. Unconsciously, he found his senses focusing. He felt the proximity of the gulls as they swooped in for food. The sharp smell of the sea hit him. The sound of the surf grew louder. Not wanting any distraction, he concentrated on closing them off. The gulls' presence became tolerable. The smell of the saltwater faded away to an acceptable level. The surf quieted, but then the voices of the dock workers increased. Snatches of conversation pelted him.

"... right here. Good. Thanks."

"... so many times. But then, don't we all?"

"... you're full of dung, Rabu, you know that?"

"... we kill him. At the presentation. Justice will be..."

"... birds! Gods! Right in the..."

Vincent's eyes snapped open. What was that? He focused his hearing again, trying to find that voice. It was like surfing the stations on the radio dial. Suddenly, he found it.

"... cannot wait that long! It is unacceptable!"

"You fool. It is perfect! What better time to kill him than during the presentation? Think how symbolic it will be, how much it will make our cause memorable!"

"Ahh... You're right, of course. But I am impatient."

"Understandable. You will be contacted again as the time approaches. Until then..."

"May the sun always shine on you."

"And on you."

The voices stopped, then. Vincent blinked, his heart racing. What had he just heard? It sure sounded like a conspiracy to him. Thankfully, it didn't sound imminent. He'd talk to Aedriun about it tomorrow. Not that he had much information to give him.

A dog's bark roused him from his thoughts. He turned to see Blaise trotting across the sand toward his dock. Ariaziane was further behind, not even trying to keep up with the animal. Vincent felt a knot form in his stomach. He hadn't had time to fully think over Gnorrin's statements. Should he address them with Ariaziane, or just let them pass?

Moments later, Blaise was dashing down the dock toward him, tail wagging and tongue flapping. He smiled, accepting the dog's kisses. She pranced around him for a minute, then sat at his side, staring at the swooping birds out over the waves. He stroked Blaise's black coat, wondering if Ariaziane had voiced her thoughts to the dog, much as he sometimes did.

He watched her approach. Her gaze frequently went out to the gray horizon, then back to him. He turned his attention to the dog until she had joined him on the dock. He hated not knowing what to say to her.

"Enjoy yourself?"

"Yes," she said. "I had no idea the sea was this beautiful."

"Yeah, I can tell you're pretty taken with it." She smiled at him and he smiled back. He studied her face. So young, he thought. At sixteen, he would have expected her face to have taken on some adult characteristics. But he detected no changes at all over the past year, ever since her bizarre color transformation. She did look different, though. That transformation had brought on an emotional disruption that had shown itself on her face for some time. It seemed, though, that she had accepted it all now. No longer did she look perpetually worried.

He cleared his throat, then said, "Gnorrin's waiting for us in the tavern. I think he's hungry, so let's not keep him from his dinner."

She took his hand as they walked back to the inn. It made him uncomfortable, but he tried his best not to show it. They didn't speak during the walk, either, which only added to his discomfort. It was with relief that he led her into the tavern and seated her at the table by the fire.

Gnorrin was perusing a menu. "I was beginning to think the pair of you had gone on home."

"I'm sorry," Ariaziane said. "It was just so relaxing on the beach. I didn't realize time had gone by so quickly."

Vincent picked up the other two menus, handed one to Ariaziane, and looked over the other one. There was an unusually broad variety, compared to the other taverns he'd seen. "What looks good?" he asked his friends.

Gnorrin rubbed his chin. "I think I'll try the stew."

Vincent smacked him with the menu.

They arrived at Aedriun's expansive residence during the mid-afternoon of the following day. A squire was waiting with the gate sentry, having been told to expect the visitors. Their horses were taken by another, who guaranteed their well-being. He led them inside the two-story, stone and mortar building. Their luggage was taken from them and they were led to a small audience chamber, where they were asked to wait. The room was pleasantly ornamented, with tapestries on the walls, plush furniture, and fancy rugs. Elegant, but not gaudy, Vincent noted.

Aedriun joined them in only a few minutes. He strode into the room, hand extended to shake Vincent's. "Good to see you, my friend! Welcome!"

Vincent shook his hand and clapped the older man on the arm. "Thank you. May I introduce my friends? This is Gnorrin, whom I mentioned to you."

Aedriun greeted the mage. "A pleasure. Glad you could come."

"And this," Vincent said, "is Ariaziane."

Aedriun turned to greet the girl, then stopped, his eyes widening. "A *great* pleasure," he said, bowing over her hand. Then, looking at her once again, "I'm afraid I owe Vincent an apology."

"Why would that be?" Ariaziane asked.

The baron smiled. "I was certain he had exaggerated your beauty." Ariaziane blushed at this, causing a twinge of jealousy in Vincent's stomach. Aedriun continued. "He talked of you so often that I felt he must have been painting a fairer picture in his mind than reality granted."

Vincent looked to the girl again, expecting another blush on his own behalf. But none was forthcoming, merely a polite smile.

A whine for attention came from Blaise, who was prancing at Aedriun's feet. He turned to the dog. "Yes, girl, it is good to see you again, too," he said, kneeling down and scratching the animal's head and neck. Then he stood and addressed the group. "We have some time before the evening meal will be served. I'm afraid it will be a somewhat formal affair. Prince Kale is visiting from a neighboring kingdom, and I am expected to be the dignified host."

Vincent's heart skipped a beat. "Is the prince to attend any sort of presentation while he is here?"

Aedriun frowned. "No. Why do you ask?"

"Later," Vincent said, deferring the conversation.

"Yes. Well, as it happens, the prince is currently on a hunt and will not be back until after sunset, I imagine. Dinner will be fairly late. I hope none of you are starving."

Gnorrin shook his head. "No, but wouldn't you be expected to accompany him on the hunt?"

"I begged off, advising him that I had another important visitor to greet."

Vincent chuckled. "Yeah, right."

Aedriun scolded him. "Do not think I was jesting, my friend. Kale is simply a prince of the realm. You, on the other hand, are an emissary from another world. I consider that to be quite important."

"Aedriun, I'm here against my will and without my understanding. That doesn't exactly make me an ambassador."

The baron waved it off. "Nevertheless, I am free of that boring man for the rest of the afternoon and I plan on enjoying myself."

Ariaziane spoke up. "Pardon me, but you said the dinner would be formal. We did not bring any formal attire."

"No matter. We can certainly find something suitable for you here."

"Or would you care to take us shopping?" Vincent asked.

The baron stroked his mustache. "It is unlikely that you could have garb made in such a short time."

"Oh, I don't know about that. I've seen a well placed coin work wonders with efficiency. Not to mention the presence of Baron Aedriun himself!"

Aedriun laughed. "Very good! Off we go. But only on the condition that we stop for an ale before we return. Dealing with dignitaries makes me parched."

"Why is that?" Gnorrin asked.

"I'm not certain. Perhaps it has something to do with the dry nature of the conversation."

Gnorrin smiled. "Well said!" He laughed. "Vincent told me you had a good head."

"Is the prince a pain in the butt, or what?" Vincent asked.

"Not exactly," the baron replied. "He is, however, a bit simple. Not a bad man, but not suited for the crown, if it comes to that. And I hope it doesn't."

"Yeah," Vincent said. "King Kale. Ugh."

Aedriun led them out of the audience chamber, dispatched a passing servant to have his carriage prepared, and then showed them the location of their rooms on the upper floor, where their belongings had already been placed. Once they were familiar with the layout of the important parts of the keep, they went outside and into the waiting vehicle.

They rode directly to the most lavish dress shop in the city. Aedriun made their needs known to the proprietor, who immediately pulled all his workers off their current tasks in order to complete the baron's work quickly. The baron then commandeered Ariaziane, guiding her to a selection of fancy fabrics. Vincent eyed the pair while going through his own selections, berating himself for the pangs of jealousy. He hurriedly selected some pre-made blue breeches and a fancy tunic of white with blue trim that matched the pants. He waited impatiently as the tailor marked the clothing for hemming and tucking. Then he joined Aedriun and Ariaziane.

"That's pretty," Vincent said, eyeing the fabric that she'd chosen. It was a soft goldenrod hue, which brought out the red highlights in her hair and made her indigo eyes seem more blue than usual.

She smiled briefly at him. Then Aedriun said, "Now, let's choose a style." He took her by the elbow and led her to the seamstress behind the counter. The woman opened a large book filled with sketches of different styles. Vincent peered in for a closer look.

Ariaziane turned to him. "You can't look. I want to surprise you." Vincent was hurt, at first, but when he saw the twinkle in her eyes, he smiled, nodded, and left.

He joined Gnorrin, who was seated in a chair near the wall, waiting for his clothes to be completed. He sat in a chair beside him. "She wants to surprise me," he said.

"Mm," replied Gnorrin. Then, after a moment, he said, "Are you trying to buy her love again?"

Vincent frowned. "Aedriun will pay for it."

"Yes, but the idea was yours. And you'd no doubt buy her everything in this shop." Vincent did not reply. Gnorrin chuckled softly. "You really are smitten, boy."

"You find it funny?"

"No," said his friend in a quiet voice. "If truth be told, I find it charming. But, Vincent, do not frighten her. You must keep in mind her upbringing. She was raised by the clerics in the abbey. A somewhat austere setting, I can assure you. Your lavish gifts take her by surprise, and she does not know how to accept them. You must have noticed that she has purchased very little with the money she acquired in Kurean's old keep. She is used to a simple life, free of most personal possessions. You, it seems, are not."

Vincent smirked. "That's for sure. The society I grew up in was very consumer-oriented."

"And by trying to push that sort of behavior onto her, you're confusing her."

"But Gnorrin," Vincent said, his voice urgent but low, "why should someone continue to lead an austere existence if they have the funds to support a more comfortable life?"

"If someone wants to lead an austere existence, why should they not do so simply because they have money? Vincent, your girlfriend simply might not be ready to change the way she lives."

"She's not my girlfriend. Sorry to say."

"Nevertheless, give her time to adjust to the idea of living more extravagantly. She's getting to the age where she will begin to appreciate nicer clothes and sparkly things to wear around her throat. Be patient. You'll be able to spoil her in due time."

Vincent blinked. "And she *should* have a sparkly thing to wear around her throat tonight, don't you think?"

Gnorrin dropped his face into his hand, shaking his head. "I'm talking to an anvil."

"No," Vincent said. "I understand what you're saying, but this is a formal occasion. Aedriun said so. A young lady can't go without jewelry, can she?"

Gnorrin looked up at him, frowning. "Aedriun will surely find something she can borrow."

"Not good enough. She's not borrowing the dress, is she? She'll need something to go with it, whenever she wears it in the future, right?"

The gnome sighed. "Aye."

"Well, then."

"I surrender. No more trying to talk sense to you. It's hopeless."

"We'll see, won't we?"

Gnorrin's response was interrupted by Aedriun and Ariaziane walking over to them. "The garments will be delivered to us before dinner," Aedriun said. "I'm ready for that ale, now."

"How much will this cost?" Vincent asked.

Aedriun waved it off. "It's taken care of."

"But..."

"Not another word, my friend. Consider the payment for the clothing to be my apology for making you attend the affair in the first place." He smiled, and Vincent couldn't help but accept it.

The tavern Aedriun took them to was quite a step up from any Vincent had previously set foot in. The furniture was all of polished and carved wood, some with upholstered seat cushions and backrests. The wall sconces, as well as the tabletop candelabras, were all of ornate bronze and crystal. There were few patrons at this hour. Aedriun led them to a table near a window. He ordered ale for himself, mead for Gnorrin, spiced cider for Vincent, and something Vincent had never heard of for Ariaziane.

"What's that?" Vincent and Ariaziane both asked.

"Something I think you'll enjoy," the baron said to her. The drinks arrived quickly and Vincent peered at her beverage. It was a thick, yellow-orange liquid with specks of black or dark brown throughout. A sprinkling of a brown powder lay on top.

Vincent raised an eyebrow as Ariaziane took a tentative sip. She swallowed, then licked the froth off her upper lip. Her eyes lit up. "How is it?" he asked.

"Delicious!" she said. "Try some!"

She pushed the drink across the table. He accepted it, then took a small mouthful. He recognized the warm flavor of the brown powder as being the local cinnamon equivalent. The specks must be similar to vanilla bean, he realized, recognizing the flavor. As for the golden liquid itself, he recognized that, too. The custard-like flavor brought memories rushing back to him. Memories of Rhia, and her lessons in plant identification. Of sucking fingers...

"It's Mina Loba," he said quickly, pushing the beverage back to her just as he pushed the memories away.

Aedriun nodded. "Very good," the baron said. "The fruit grows in abundance not far from here. One of our innkeepers concocted the drink some years ago. The mashed fruit pulp, when heated, breaks down to a thick, but drinkable, consistency. Additional spices and a little whipping make it a popular beverage. Too sweet for my tastes, though," he concluded.

"Well, I think it's wonderful," Ariaziane said as she took another drink. "Thank you."

"Vincent," Aedriun began in a serious tone, "I have a question to ask you. I know it is sudden, and I know that I am asking quickly for an answer, but I would like to know your reply, in case something is to be said regarding it at the dinner this evening."

"Okay. What?"

Aedriun looked him in the eye. "When we were together last, I mentioned that I had hopes for you. I'd like you for a squire. Would you accept?"

Vincent blinked. His image of a squire was that of a glorified gopher for a knight. That was probably wrong, though, he realized. He looked at his friends. Gnorrin's expression was one of complete surprise. Ariaziane, on the other hand, wore a concerned look on her face. Her brow was knit and a faint frown creased her face.

"What exactly would that entail?" he asked.

"Many things," Aedriun answered. "You would be an assistant to me. You would take care of trivial things. A sort of menial labor required of squires. I think it's supposed to teach them humility or something. But the important aspect, Vincent, is that you would learn much about the political realm. And eventually, you would almost certainly become a knight."

The thought struck Vincent at once as being appealing and ludicrous. Try as he might, he couldn't envision himself as a knight. He smiled slightly at his inner amusement.

Then his eyes met Ariaziane's. She didn't look amused at all. In fact, she looked rather upset. Then she turned her eyes back to her drink.

Vincent sobered, cleared his throat, then said, "Much as I am honored by your suggestion, I'm afraid I must decline." He was happy to see a faint smile cross Gnorrin's face, and even happier to see Ariaziane's head jerk up to look at him again. "You see," he continued, "despite what you saw back at Jaz's keep, I do not enjoy the role of warrior. I took up the sword upon the recommendation of a friend. And I am glad I did, for it allowed me to become more physically fit than I've ever been in my life. But I do not plan on making the sword my lifelong companion. I have tasted battle and found that I do not like it. Doubtless there are those who thrive on the excitement, the bloodlust. I am not one of them. I intend to settle down and lead a peaceful life, Aedriun. My only fighting will be the constant battle of understanding, trying to discover how I was brought to your world, and how I can return home. I hold little hope that I will win that battle, but it is the only one I plan on fighting from now on."

Vincent took a breath to still his racing heart. That was some speech, he thought. It made his nerves jumpy, though he didn't know why. Quickly, he glanced at his friends. Gnorrin's attention was on his mead, but the smile was still on his face. And Ariaziane... His heart skipped a beat when he saw the expression on her face. He let out the breath, relieved. Ariaziane was looking at him with an expression he could only interpret as admiration.

Content that he'd done right by her, he looked back at Aedriun, who stared oddly back at him. Vincent knew the man had caught his glances at the others. He wondered what Aedriun thought it was all about. The man held his gaze for what seemed a full minute. Then he gave the slightest of shrugs. "Very well," he said pleasantly. "I wish you luck, my friend. And should you change your mind..."

Vincent nodded. "I'll let you know." He drank some of his cider. He didn't like the way Aedriun had wished him luck, as though he didn't believe his words. Or didn't believe that Vincent would easily be able to stay out of trouble.

They stayed in the tavern for about half an hour, Aedriun talking mostly with Gnorrin and Ariaziane. Then they returned to his keep, where they were given a full tour of the area and introduced to various members of the staff. About two hours later, just before sunset, the hunting party returned. Aedriun explained that the prince would most likely bathe before descending to the dining hall. At least, he hoped he would.

Their clothing arrived shortly thereafter. Vincent went to his room and dressed quickly, donning the new garments and polishing up his boots as best he could. He dug out a pouch he'd tucked away in his bundle. He opened it, then dumped the contents onto his bed. In addition to several of the smaller gemstones from his horde, he'd brought some items of jewelry, just in case he encountered a jeweler. Or, just in case of an event like this.

He picked up the necklace from the pile. It was a gold chain with a pendant. Vincent hadn't thought much of it when he'd first seen it. It seemed gaudy, not to his tastes at all. But it occurred to him that this might be the perfect time for it to be worn. He held it up. The pendant was a setting with a large oval stone, deep blue in color, with strands of white running diagonally, like marble veins. The stone was not cut in facets, but ground to a smooth finish and polished brightly. Around the stone were a dozen tiny red stones, similarly polished. Vincent tried to imagine it against the golden fabric of Ariaziane's new dress. He thought it might look quite nice.

Putting away the rest of his jewelry and gems, he palmed the necklace and walked across the hall to Ariaziane's room. He knocked.

"Yes?" came her voice from inside.

"It's me," he said. "May I come in?"

In response, the door was opened. One of Aedriun's female staff curtsied lightly, then turned away from the door. Vincent stepped inside to find another woman assisting Ariaziane with the final touches in dressing. The woman who answered the door returned to her task of doing the girl's hair.

Vincent came to a stop just inside the door. And stared. His mouth hung open, but no words came forth. Finally, he whispered, "Wow."

"And what do you mean by that?" she teased.

"Annie, you look amazing."

She beamed. "Thank you. You look nice, too."

Vincent stared at the gown. That's what he had to call it. "Dress" didn't do it justice. The goldenrod fabric lay in billowy folds across her shoulders and her chest, dipping down in the front to expose a few inches below her throat. Below the breast, the fabric was gathered together snugly, allowing only a few folds for accent. At the hips it again flowed lavishly. The assistant was pinning one side of the dress up to expose a generous amount of leg on the left. Vincent swallowed in his dry throat.

Her hair was shiny and full. And, as if to contrast with her gown, the left side hung down, while the right side was pulled back behind the ear. A corsage of fresh yellow flowers hid the barrette. Both assistants stepped back to look over their handiwork.

Ariaziane did a slow turn. "What do you think?"

Both assistants nodded, then curtsied before leaving the room. Vincent stood gaping as they left. Finally, he said, "I um... I brought you a necklace. But..."

"But what?"

"I don't know if it's suitable," he mumbled.

"Well, let's see it."

Vincent cleared his throat, tearing his eyes from her exposed leg. He shuffled forward, revealing the necklace. She looked at it, running her fingers over the blue stone. "It's lovely," she said. She turned her back. "Go ahead."

He clumsily placed it around her neck and clasped it. Then she turned back around. The pendant lay on her pale skin, just above the folds of her dress. Vincent smiled. "What do you think?"

"It's beautiful. Is it from Aedriun? I'll have to thank him."

"No!" he blurted, more forcefully than he intended. "It's from me. A gift."

"Oh, Vincent, I couldn't! You already gave me a ring from your treasure. I couldn't accept this, too."

"Yes, you could. And yes, you will. I'm not giving you a choice in the matter." He smiled, and was grateful that she smiled back and put up no further argument.

Gnorrin appeared in the doorway, then. "We've been summoned to the dinner," he said. Then, taking note of Ariaziane, "My, don't we look elegant! Aedriun won't be able to keep his eyes off you! Nor will Vincent, but that goes without saying."

Vincent felt like he blushed even more than Ariaziane did.

They were met at the doorway to the dining hall by Aedriun himself, though a servant was positioned nearby for the obvious purpose of meeting and announcing the guests. Aedriun greeted his friends and guided them inside. Vincent surveyed the setting. It was a beautifully arranged room, with bright linens on the tables and lots of candles throughout the room. A group of musicians occupied one corner, playing quietly.

There were, he counted, seven tables. Six of them would seat ten people, four to a side and one on either end. The seventh table was against one wall, facing the rest like the table for the bridal party at a wedding reception. There were also ten chairs at this long table. The two in the center were larger and more ornate than the ones flanking them.

"You will be joining us at the master table," Aedriun said. "The prince and I will be in the center seats. The three of you will be joined on my side by my nephew Darvas, a lieutenant of my guard. He is about your age, Vincent. I think you'll like him."

"And the chairs on the prince's side will be for members of his entourage?" Vincent asked.

Aedriun eyed him with a humorous expression. "An odd word, but I understand your meaning. Yes, they will be. He will, I'm sure, arrive fashionably late. Until that time, I'm afraid we must mingle. I hope you do not mind."

In fact, Vincent did mind, but he smiled and shook his head. And for the next half hour or more, the three of them were introduced by Aedriun to a variety of local dignitaries. All smiled politely and bowed or shook hands or curtsied, as custom dictated.

Vincent made it a point to check out the musicians. He and his friends wandered over. There were a variety of stringed instruments: a lute, a harp, a hammer dulcimer. Or at least, these were the instruments they brought to Vincent's mind, though they were not exactly like their Earth counterparts. And there were wind instruments, too. A variety of flute-like things. The music they played was quite pleasant.

Darvas arrived and was introduced to the group. "Vincent, a pleasure to meet you. My uncle has told me much about you."

Vincent shook his hand. Darvas looked just like Vincent anticipated, being on the guard. Short-haired, well-groomed. Very proper looking. But he had a friendly demeanor and pleasant smile, so it was hard to think of him as a stereotype. "Nice to meet you, too," he said. "I don't know what your uncle has told you of me, but be aware that I've found him to be prone to exaggeration."

"Mm. So I've heard from his lady friends."

Vincent laughed. Aedriun pretended not to hear the comment. At that moment, Prince Kale's arrival was announced. The group turned to look, and through the doorway stepped a man of about Aedriun's age. He was dressed in dark blue silk, trimmed with red and gold. His face was clean shaven and his features were sharp. His eyes, however, seemed rather vacant to Vincent, as if his thoughts were anywhere other than in the present. Aedriun excused himself and went over to greet the man.

Shortly, he led the prince back to meet them. Introductions were made all around, except for Darvas, who already had not only met the prince, but had gone on hunt with him. Empty conversation followed for a few minutes, then the prince excused himself to mingle with other guests.

When he was out of earshot, Vincent said, "Lovely man. You have my sympathy, Aedriun. What kingdom is graced with his existence?"

"Fortunately not our own," Aedriun replied. "He is from a kingdom far east of here. Well. Let us be seated." He signaled to a servant, who then hurried off in the direction of the kitchen.

Aedriun led them to the long table, where he took one of the large chairs. Darvas sat next to him. After Darvas sat Vincent, Ariaziane, and Gnorrin. Before long, Prince Kale and his four selected guests joined him. Vincent didn't ask who they were. He simply wasn't interested.

Dinner was a lavish affair, and without doubt the most impressive meal Vincent had seen since his arrival in this world. Seafood was plentiful, naturally. Fish and shellfish seemed limitless. There were three types of meat: roast poultry of some sort, venison steaks, and what tasted like hare cooked in a brown sauce. There were vegetables aplenty. Freshly baked breads of different grains. Fruits and nuts. And for dessert, a variety of pies, tarts, cakes, and puddings.

Vincent spoke with Darvas during dinner, finding him to be pleasant company. Less boisterous than his uncle, though Vincent could see honorable traits that were common to both. He realized that Darvas reminded him of D'Ty. And that thought made him think of Blade. He missed Blade. And D'Ty, and even Sianon, he realized.

And Gnorrin had been correct. It was very hard for Vincent to keep his eyes off Ariaziane. He was thankful, though, that both he and Darvas were between her and Aedriun. Not that he was jealous or anything, he told himself. Just cautious.

After the meal, servants removed the tables and chairs, except for the master table. The guests didn't seem to find this unusual, so Vincent kept his curiosity in check. Then the musicians increased their volume and played a sprightly tune. Some of the guests began to dance in the center of the now cleared floor.

He glanced at Ariaziane, who wore a delighted expression on her face. "Oh, shit," he muttered to himself.

"Oh, let's dance, Vincent," she said, squeezing his arm.

Ignoring the flush that washed over his face, Vincent smiled sheepishly. "I don't think so. I'm really full."

The girl pouted. "You never want to dance. Never have you danced during Celebration Week or Mid-Year Week. Why not?"

"I've told you," he said under his breath. "I don't know *how*."

She frowned, narrowing her eyes. She leaned in close. "I'll bet Aedriun would dance with me," she murmured. "Or Darvas."

Vincent's throat went suddenly dry. He rubbed his temple, then cast a look out at the floor. It looked hard, but if he made himself look like an idiot, it didn't matter. He didn't know these people and would probably never see any of them again, except for Aedriun.

"Oh, okay," he heard his mouth saying. And then Ariaziane was pulling him out to the dance floor.

As they reached the edge of the dancing crowd, he said, "Um, this song is a little fast for me. Do you think we could wait for the next one?"

The girl frowned, but just then the song ended and the next began. "Fine," she said with a smile and hauled him onto the dance floor.

The song was a piece for the hammer dulcimer, which pleased Vincent. It was one of his favorite instruments. He raised an eyebrow, feeling for the beat. "A waltz," he said.

"What?" she said, but didn't wait for an elaboration. "Let's go."

And he danced. Or at least, he moved his body around in a fashion that mimicked as best he could the actions of those around him. He tried to remember how the waltz was danced. He'd never danced it, but he'd seen it in movies and on TV often enough. How hard could it be?

He tried a few experimental steps with Ariaziane. Falteringly, at first, then more confidently. Turn, turn again. He smiled down into her face. She beamed back at him.

They spiraled around the room. Despite himself, Vincent was having fun. But soon enough, the song slowed and finally stopped. Ariaziane threw her arms around him and gave him a hug. And then he noticed the applause. He looked around, to find the guests had cleared space in the center for their dancing. His face flushed again, but he smiled and accepted their acknowledgments. Then he escorted Ariaziane off the dance floor.

"Very interesting," the prince said as they made their way back to the table. "What do you call that dance?"

Vincent hesitated. "Well, you might as well call it a waltz. It's close, I suppose."

"*Waltz*," the prince repeated. "Delightful."

The pair smiled, then found their chairs. "Well, done," said Darvas. "Scored a point there, you did."

"Yippee," said Vincent.

The dancing and mingling lasted for another two hours or more, and Vincent was itching to leave long before that point. Even Ariaziane, after having dragged him onto the dance floor three subsequent times, was ready to depart. Finally, mercifully, the ordeal ended. Guests began leaving in small clusters. When half of them were gone, Vincent said goodnight to Aedriun and the prince, and the trio went to their rooms.

"Remind me not to go through something like that again," Vincent said as they climbed the stairs.

Gnorrin chuckled. "Then it is a good thing you declined Aedriun's offer of making you his squire."

"Vincent!" came Darvas's voice from the bottom of the stairs.

The group turned. "Yes?" Vincent said.

"My uncle wishes for the three of you to join him for breakfast in the morning. Shall I tell him to expect you?"

"Will there be dancing?"

"I think not," Darvas replied, chuckling.

"Then, yes. Tell him to expect us."

"Very good. The morning steward will have you all awakened. Rest well!" And he turned and re-entered the dining hall.

Reaching the top of the stairs, Vincent and Ariaziane wished Gnorrin a good night, then continued down the hall toward their own rooms. Stopping outside their doors, facing each other across the hall, Ariaziane said, "Thank you for dancing with me. It was fun."

Vincent smiled faintly. "You know I wouldn't dance with anyone other than you."

She nodded. "I know," she said seriously. She paused, then said tentatively, "Do you like it here?"

"What? You mean the keep? It's nice, but..."

"No, I don't mean the keep. I mean this area. The ocean."

"You really like the sea, don't you?"

Her face lit up. "It's like nothing I ever imagined. So beautiful."

"Annie, are you tired?"

"A little. Why?"

"I thought you might enjoy a walk on the beach under the moonlight."

"Oh! That sounds wonderful! Let me just change clothes quickly."

"Why bother? Just grab your cloak and we'll go."

She smiled, then stepped into her room. Vincent hurried into his own room to fetch his cloak. Blaise raised her head from the bed, yawned, and wagged her tail. "Come on, girl," he said. "Let's go for a walk."

Soon they were on the beach, quiet now of the sounds of fishing boats and dock workers. The only sounds were the surf and the calls of night birds.

The moon was high, casting silver puddles out over the sea, splintering into sparkling ripples as the waves came in to shore. They stood, watching the splendor, breathing deeply of the nippy air. Blaise ran off down the beach, sniffing at the shells and the stranded sea life.

Vincent felt Ariaziane squeeze his hand, and he squeezed back. He gazed at her. She was so beautiful, he thought. His chest tightened as he allowed himself to feel the full impact of the love he held for her. She was so unlike him, in many ways. She was so full of light. He, so filled with shadows. He had always considered himself to be a creature of the night, preferring the darkness to the light. He was, for the most part, prone to keeping things to himself. Not everything, but most things. He liked his privacy.

Ariaziane was generally of a pleasant nature. He, on the other hand, was often moody and depressed. He realized he'd actually been pretty good since arriving here. But the main factor in that, he knew, was Ariaziane.

She brought out the bright side of him, and he liked that. He had to make her aware of how much she meant to him, but he couldn't see how to do so. He gave her gifts. He told her that he loved her. But none of it seemed to strike home with her. Nothing he said or did seemed to make her react the way he needed her to.

Perhaps his refusal of Aedriun's offer would help. If Gnorrin were correct in that she was afraid of what he might become, then he'd certainly done the right thing. He had to assuage whatever fears she had.

And there was something else he needed to do, too, he realized as he studied the rapt expression on her face. A surprise that would top anything he'd ever done for her.

Suddenly, a feeling of anxiety washed over him. He turned around, to find the point of a very long knife under his breastbone.

"All right, then," said the gravel-voiced owner of the blade. "Let's have your purses, young ones. And that necklace, too, missy."

Fury welled up inside Vincent as he stared in astonishment at this scraggly, middle-aged brigand. How *dare* he interrupt his walk with Ariaziane? He heard Ariaziane mumble something under her breath, but paid no attention to it. The man had turned to stare at her, and that was all the opening he needed.

He spun, sidestepping the knife's point and knocking the blade away with his fist. Then he set upon the man, knocking him backward onto the sand. He raised his arm and began pummeling him.

"Stop it!" Ariaziane yelled as Vincent suddenly realized the thief wasn't fighting back. In fact, he seemed to be unconscious. And then Ariaziane was pulling him off the man. "Enough," she said.

Vincent crouched on one knee and looked at the figure. His face was a bloody mess. His eyes stared vacantly, though pain registered clearly in them. "But he..." Vincent began.

"He's no threat," Ariaziane said. "I'm not defenseless, you know. There was no need for you to attack him like that." She mumbled a few syllables and Vincent saw the man stir, then look up at both of them in fear. "Go!" she commanded. "Leave us, and never let us see you again, or we will turn you over to the authorities."

The man seemed to attempt simultaneously to back away from them and get to his feet. The result would have been comical, were the circumstances not so serious. But he finally succeeded in standing, then promptly ran away.

Vincent stayed on the sand, falling into a seated position. He'd just blown it, he thought. All his talk about wanting to live a peaceful life was just contradicted by his sudden violence. The idea of how she must feel about it hit him like a brick. He drew his legs up and wrapped his arms around them. He felt a tear well up in his eye. Ariaziane knelt down beside him. She put a hand on his shoulder.

"I can't help it," he choked out. "I thought you were in danger, and I just reacted."

"I know. But I'm not a defenseless little girl. I might not be a mage, yet, but I know enough to protect myself against some vagrant ruffian."

Vincent nodded. "I'm just not used to that, yet. I'm sorry."

In response, she sat down beside him, leaning her body against his. "No need to apologize."

He turned to look into her eyes, and the tenderness in them forced the tear to overflow and slide down his cheek. She gently wiped it away. "You have no idea how much you mean to me," he said. "I just want to be with you."

"You *are* with me."

He forced a smile. "You know what I mean." But he wasn't sure that she really did. How she could be blind to it, he couldn't guess. But something made him think that she was, perhaps, not allowing herself to be fully aware of his feelings. He swallowed hard. "Annie, I love you."

She hesitated when he said this. When she spoke, her voice was soft. "I know." Then she said more brightly, "I love you, too, silly. Now let's get off the sand before the tide soaks us." She rose and offered him a hand up. As he stood, he studied her face. She'd said she loved him. But the way she said it certainly wasn't the same way he'd said it to her. An ironic laugh echoed in the back of his mind. Love comes in many forms, he told himself. And it was obvious to him that they both were feeling different types for one another.

They brushed the sand from their new clothes. Vincent called loudly for Blaise, who shortly came trotting over. Then, hand in hand, they made their way back to the keep.

☙ ❧

We stayed with Aedriun for three more days before returning home. It was a very nice visit, all things considered. Wasn't thrilled about the dinner with the prince, but that's another matter.

Darvas and I talked quite a lot. I do like him. Seems pretty cool. I could see us easily becoming friends.

I spoke with Aedriun about the conversation I overheard that first night. But it meant nothing to him, either. Oh, well. That's life, I guess.

It doesn't appear that my display of violence that night on the beach has ruined me in Annie's eyes. And I'm certainly glad of that. It might just be wishful thinking on my part, but she seems to be opening up to me a little more. Like the shell she was in ever since I returned from my travels has finally cracked. She seems more like the Annie I remember from a year ago.

I hope my surprise goes over well with her. Aedriun is taking care of all the details for me. I left a large sum of money in gems there with him before returning home. I'm sure it'll be enough, but told him to contact me if he needs more.

In the meantime, I'm actually giving thought to having my own keep built. That location Jaz showed me was really nice. I've looked on my maps, here. Falconwall would lie directly southeast of that spot, perhaps sixty leagues as the crow flies. Of course, the crow would have to fly over sixty leagues of mountains to get there. We lowly humans would have to go out and around a big stretch of the mountains. There are probably some trails through passes, but they're not on my maps. Either way, it would be a heck of a trek.

I guess this is what Jaz meant by it being a surprise that it was under Duke Ghanol's influence. The duke's realm includes the entire section containing Falconwall, plus a huge expanse south of here. The large valley where my keep would be is secluded from the rest of the area. Effective maintenance of it wouldn't be easy.

Anyway, I think I'll at least look into it. It could prove to be more expensive than I've anticipated, or more difficult than expected, or any number of things. But it's worth checking out. Not that I don't enjoy living next to Gnorrin, but this area is no more exciting than my home town.

And as for Ariaziane... Well, naturally my hope is that she would move into the keep with me. But that's probably just a pleasant fantasy.

❧ Twenty-Two ❧

The first thing Vincent did upon returning home was hire a courier to deliver a message to Jaz. He knew his friend would be helpful in advising him of how to proceed in building a keep.

He shared his intentions with Gnorrin. To his surprise, Gnorrin had some assistance of his own to offer. Hiring another courier, Gnorrin sent a letter to an acquaintance named Feletain, the brother of his late friend Blôrain.

Feletain was a respected stonecutter and builder. Gnorrin felt that he would be quite an asset, and Vincent agreed.

Ariaziane seemed concerned when she heard of his plans, but relaxed somewhat when it was explained to her that the building of the keep would take years.

"You have given up your search for a way home, then?" she had asked.

"Not at all," he'd assured her. "But if I'm unable to get home, it would be nice to have the keep. If I do get home, I'm sure someone else can make use of it."

Over the next few weeks, Vincent did little more than tend his growing garden and go for rides with Ariaziane. The Season of Green passed and the Season of the Sun began.

One day, the courier from Jaz returned. The message said:

"I would be happy to assist you. But communicating by courier will never do. Expect me within a week of your receipt of this. We will discuss everything at that time."

Gnorrin, too, received a reply to his message. He brought the scroll to Vincent's cottage a few days later. "Feletain has agreed to accept the job of heading the mining and excavation crew," he said. "He insists on putting the team together himself."

"I wasn't aware that you'd offered him such a position," Vincent said.

The gnome laughed. "I did not. But it is most like him to assume the role for himself." He shrugged. "I would not worry about it. He is a good man, if a bit presumptuous." Gnorrin rolled up the scroll and tucked it into his belt. "Tell me, have you thought of how you'd like the keep to be designed?"

Vincent smiled. "Actually, yes. Let me show you my sketches." He quickly fetched some loose papers from a desk, then returned to the living room. He put the first one down on the small table between their seats. "This is how the mountain looks. As you can see, there are two plateaus, one about eighty to a hundred feet above the other. The lower one will be the main entrance to the keep." He put down the second sheet, which showed the face of the mountain at the back of the first plateau having walls erected, complete with two spires that rose up the sides, ending slightly above the second plateau.

"You intend to build directly into the mountainside?"

"Exactly. I figure we can do three floors." He produced the next sheet. "The ground floor will have everything you'd expect there. Reception halls, kitchen, dining areas, and so forth. Library, maybe. The next floor," he said, showing another sheet, "will have the sleeping quarters and assorted private chambers. Maybe a second, smaller kitchen and dining area." Another sheet. "I haven't really decided what's to go on the third floor. Storage, maybe. Now here's something I'm pretty excited about," he said, producing still another sheet. "That second plateau will be the real top floor. The two towers open onto a garden, here. The land was covered with snow when I saw it, but I think there was a stream up there. A tiny one. And that leaves this big, open area where we can plant trees and bushes. I figure it can be a nice little spot to relax, let Blaise run around, and so on. So what do you think?"

Gnorrin rubbed his chin. "Quite an undertaking. It would be most impressive if you could accomplish it."

"Yeah," Vincent said, arranging the papers again. "Impressively expensive. But hey, what else have I got to do with my money, right?"

"Exactly. Now, we need to notify Feletain concerning your plans and when he is to start. Let me warn you, too, that he will attempt to obtain a salary from you that is outrageously high. Do not be afraid to talk him down. He will expect that."

"You know I'm no good at haggling."

"I'll teach you. One question," he said, motioning toward the sketches. "What about lighting? Your keep, being half buried in the mountain, will have little area for sunlight to enter."

"Well, I was rather hoping I might get some assistance from some of my magically oriented friends."

"Oh, really?" Gnorrin drawled. "And what sort of assistance would that be?"

Vincent smiled. "I've seen those spells you cast that light up things. You yourself told me it is possible to cast it in such a way as to be permanent. And you said you could cast it on a particular object, effectively turning it into a source of eternal light. I figure some of those, strategically placed throughout, will be quite sufficient."

"Oh, you do, do you? And do you know how many you would need to light a keep of that size? And do you know how draining it is to a mage to cast such a spell? And so many of them? Just so you can light your keep?" He snorted. "I think you do not take magic near seriously enough."

Vincent laughed. "Yes, I know it would require a lot of them. And yes, in fact, I *do* know how draining it will be on you. Or whomever. Not very draining at all, unless Annie lied to me. I'm not expecting them to be done all at once, mind you. So don't pretend to get indignant with me, my friend."

Gnorrin chuckled. "Very well. We'll light your little castle for you." He smiled. "Now where's that dinner you promised me?"

➤ ➥

Vincent was practicing his sword throwing when Jaz arrived a few days later. He had set up a large target, a thick slab of tree trunk with a bullseye painted on it. He propped this up against a rock, supporting the back so that it wouldn't wobble when struck. Then he stood anywhere from twenty to forty feet away and hurled the sword at the target. He had first seen this done early in his days in this world, back when he was living with Gnorrin. He'd found it odd, then. He still did, to a degree. But it was fun, in a barbaric sort of way.

He had just thrown his latest round of three swords from forty feet out, striking the target's outer rings each time, when the mage sailed in on his carpet, just as Vincent expected he would do. After the final sword struck the target, Vincent heard clapping from overhead. He looked up to see Jaz sitting atop his carpet, watching.

Seeing the mage was a happy experience for him. It seemed as though so much time had passed since he'd seen him, when it really hadn't been long at all. He chalked it up to the fact that the months they'd spent together were highly emotional ones for Vincent, which made those memories all the more potent.

Vincent told him all about his trip to visit Aedriun, including the declined offer of becoming a squire. And when Jaz asked him, he told him why he'd turned it down. Jaz frowned. "You turned it down for the girl?"

"Mostly," he replied. "But I really don't think I'd want to be his squire, anyway. And I don't think he was surprised by my refusal."

Jaz smiled. "Nor am I. Now, then. Let me hear about your plans for the keep."

Vincent took him inside and, after pouring him a glass of cool tea from his in-floor icebox, showed him the plans. Jaz seemed to like them, and suggested that he could contact members of the crew who'd helped build his own keep, in order to give Feletain a head start.

Feletain himself arrived a week later. Vincent looked forward to meeting him, never having seen a dwarf. He was surprised at the similarities between dwarves and gnomes. Feletain stood perhaps a foot taller than Gnorrin. He had a thick beard and was a good bit stockier than the gnome. He dressed much more tastefully, which wasn't difficult. But aside from that, the features were fairly similar. Vincent suspected that the two might have been the same race, once upon a time.

Feletain was, however, pure business through and through. Not that he was rude, but he wanted to get right to work. He looked over Vincent's plans, scratched his beard a lot, and frequently voiced guttural noises that must have indicated that he was pondering the plans. To Vincent, however, the noises sounded like a cross between belches and growls.

"Yes," he finally rumbled. "Yes, these plans are interesting. I must see the site before I can tell if they are at all achievable." He looked at Vincent. "We will leave in the morning."

Vincent glanced across the table at Jaz, who shrugged and nodded.

The following morning, the three of them piled onto Jaz's carpet and took off for the mountains. The flight took a few hours, during which Vincent got to know the self-appointed chief of operations.

"I appreciate you taking the job," Vincent said at one point.

"I haven't taken the job, yet," Feletain corrected. "And until we discuss salary, I will *not* take the job."

Vincent nodded. "Certainly. We will discuss that after you see the site. You can tell me what will be required to get the job done in a timely manner. How many workers you'll need, what supplies, and so on. If I find your assessment to be reasonable, then we'll talk money."

The dwarf sized him up with a glance. "Aye. Fair enough." Then he turned to Jaz. "Tell me about the dwarves who worked on your keep."

"I never said they were dwarves," the mage replied.

"Your keep is in the mountains?"

"Yes."

"It is well built?"

"Yes."

"Then they were dwarves."

Jaz chuckled. "That they were. I had a crew of fifty. They completed the keep in three years."

"And what is the size?"

"Four levels. Forty-eight rooms."

"And who was in charge?"

"Jhartous, of Falconwall."

"Jhartous!" the dwarf gasped. "That pup? You trusted him with a job of such size?"

"I did," said Jaz. "And haven't regretted it at all."

Feletain scowled and seemed to withdraw into himself for some time. Vincent was content to allow the conversation to die. He relaxed and enjoyed the scenery for the rest of the flight.

Eventually, they approached the mountain Vincent had chosen for his keep. He watched Feletain appraising the valley as they flew in. The river below looked like a splinter of mirror as it wound its way out from the mountains through the valley. When Feletain studied the mountain itself, Vincent was pleased.

"A handsome stone, that is," Feletain said. Looking at the base, he said, "And treacherous, too. You've picked a fine home to stand against your enemies, Vincent."

Vincent snorted. "Thank you, but that's not a prime concern. I have no enemies."

The dwarf peeled his eyes from the mountain long enough to cast a disbelieving look at Vincent. "Is that so?" He thrust out his arm. "Then let me shake your hand, boy, because I've never met the man yet who had none who wished him harm."

Vincent smiled cautiously as he shook the dwarf's hand. A minute later, Jaz brought them in to a landing on the main plateau.

Feletain gave only a cursory look to the plateau itself. He seemed more interested in the face of the mountain into which he would be tunneling. He ran his hands over it, as if testing it, and nodded to himself frequently. Vincent and Jaz stood back and watched him as he pulled a small pickax from his belt, then chipped away at a portion of the stone.

When he seemed satisfied with his assessment, he strode over to the edge of the plateau, examining the descent. He squinted as he moved around the perimeter. The others followed, trying to ascertain what he was looking for. Finally, Feletain stopped, folding his arms across his chest. He shook his head sadly. "Hmph," he said.

"What?" Vincent and Jaz said together.

The dwarf faced them, but pointed his arm down the cliff face. "No access. If we will need to construct passable trails..." He shook his head. "Much time. Much more money."

Jaz and Vincent exchanged glances. Then Jaz said, "I don't recall Jhartous saying anything about that. Do you?"

Vincent shook his head. "He said nothing of the sort to me."

Feletain's eyebrows shot up. "You've spoken with that imbecile? I cannot believe it! He said nothing about that?"

Vincent ignored the question and began walking slowly toward the mountain face, away from the cliff. "So what is your estimate, Feletain? Assuming we can round up fifty to work under you."

"Seven years," he shot back. "And five silver pieces per day per worker. For burrowing out the mountain, building your keep, landscaping the upper plateau, not to mention plowing out a passage down to the valley."

Jaz chuckled loudly, shaking his head. Vincent merely smiled faintly.

Feletain grew enraged. "What has that upstart offered? Damn his hands!"

Vincent cleared his throat, smiling more. "My friend," he said to the dwarf, "seven years is unacceptable. I want it done in five."

"Five! You're jesting."

"I'm not."

"Ten silver pieces per day per worker, then. Plus tools and supplies."

Vincent folded his arms across his chest. "Five per day."

"Preposterous," said Feletain, and turned his back.

Jaz strolled over to Vincent's side. "Shall I contact Jhartous?" he asked.

"Go right ahead," said Feletain.

"It seems that greed is too much in our friend's mind, Jaz. Let us go." The pair walked past Feletain, heading back to the carpet.

Feletain stood resolutely for a moment, then frowned. "Jhartous is incompetent," he said flatly.

Vincent shrugged as he stepped onto the carpet, facing the dwarf. "I have seen his handiwork. I like it." Feletain frowned, but Vincent could see that he was itching to get the job. He stepped off the carpet and approached him. "Final offer. Five years. Fifty workers. Five silver pieces per day, including days off. Bonuses to be given twice yearly, assuming my satisfaction with progress and quality."

Feletain continued to frown, but Vincent saw the hint of a twinkle in his eye. "And my rate would be?"

"Six per day."

"Six?" he roared. "But I am to supervise their work!"

"Exactly. Why should you be paid much more? I'll match the bonuses for you, too." Before Feletain could protest again, he said, "This is not open for further debate. Take it or leave it. If you take it, we can journey from here to Falconwall, where I can front you the funds for tools and supplies, plus wages for the first month. If not, then we fly you back and you can return home." He turned and strode to the carpet, where Jaz waited.

Feletain hesitated for some time, staring at him. Then he walked forward, joining them on the carpet. Jaz immediately raised it into the air. "And where should I point us?" he asked.

Feletain sighed. "Falconwall."

❧ ❧

In the city, Vincent and Jaz paid another visit to Berel's jewelry shop, where Vincent sold a small bag of gems he'd brought with him. A small chest held the six hundred gold coins the gems brought in. Feletain took possession of this, after insisting on a written contract, which Vincent signed. Afterward, Feletain parted company with them, saying that he would begin putting his team together. He promised that construction would begin the first day after Mid-Year Week.

Vincent and Jaz decided to stay in the city for the night. Vincent wanted to see more of the city than he had on previous visits, so they made their way through the streets. They took rooms in a nice inn, then went in search of some enjoyable way to pass the evening.

They passed by an armory, where the shining suits of mail caught Vincent's eye. They stopped to look. "Planning on buying some armor?" Jaz asked him.

Vincent admired a shirt of chain mail, testing its weight with his hand. "I guess not. I'm turning away from a life of violence, remember?" He smiled wistfully. "Then again, it never hurts to be prepared *against* violence, does it?"

"I thought you had no enemies," Jaz teased.

After another cursory glance at the wares, they moved on, Vincent suggesting that perhaps he'd stop by again the following morning. After debating for a while on how to pass their evening, they decided to see a play.

Jaz led them through the streets until the theater was in sight. It appeared to be an open-air affair. Tickets were sold in the front, and patrons then went through doors that led around to the back, where there were rows of benches that faced the stage.

As they approached, Vincent caught a whiff of a familiar scent. "Mmm," he said. "Roasted nuts." He spied the vendor. "Jaz, you go get tickets for us. I'm going to get some of those for a snack." Jaz nodded and went to stand in line while Vincent approached the vendor.

The man had a wooden pushcart from which he sold the goods. He seemed to have found a prime location near the theater. Several patrons were gathered around to buy from him.

Vincent joined the crowd and waited his turn. As he waited, he glanced around, looking over to see Jaz's progress. As he neared the vendor, he heard a customer thank the man. In leaving, he said, "May the sun always shine on you."

He stepped up to the vendor, looking at the retreating back of the man who had spoken the words. "Two bags, please," he said to the vendor. Vincent paid the man, a strange feeling tickling faintly at the back of his mind. He accepted his change and headed to the theater.

Jaz had obtained the tickets and was waiting for him. He handed Vincent a ticket and accepted a bag of nuts. "What's wrong?" he asked.

His friend shook his head as they went through the doors and proceeded down the short passage. "Just something odd I heard."

They came out behind the building, passed the stage, and headed toward the benches that sat in rows in the outdoor arena. "Whoa. Quite a crowd," Vincent said, looking around at the packed seats. "Must be a good show."

"Not so much that," Jaz said. "I heard that Duke Ghanol is in attendance tonight. Many of these folks are probably here to catch a glimpse of him."

"Ghanol's that much of a celebrity?"

"To some."

As they threaded their way through the crowd toward two empty spaces, Vincent spied the man who'd spoken to the nut vendor. "Jaz," he said, "is the expression 'may the sun always shine on you' significant to you?"

"It seems a pleasant wish," the mage said as they sat down, "but not particularly significant. Why?"

Vincent continued to watch the stranger. "I'm not sure," he said. "Just a weird feeling." He scratched his beard.

Jaz cracked open a nut. "Oh," he said. "I nearly forgot." He handed Vincent a program for the show.

"Thanks." Vincent opened it and flipped absently through the pages. It was a simple affair, hand-written, and tied together with twine. It was only four small pages. Sure enough, there was a notice on the first page stating that Duke Ghanol would be in attendance for tonight's show. Vincent browsed the program, reading the brief summation of the story. He frowned. There was no title of the show listed. He flipped to the cover of the program, which he'd not looked at before. His heart stuttered as he saw the large block letters. *The Presentation.* "Oh, shit," he whispered.

"What is it?" Jaz said.

"Where is Ghanol sitting?" he snapped.

The mage pointed off to their right. "When he arrives, he'll be seated there on the raised platform."

Vincent followed Jaz's finger. The customer from the nut vendor's cart was heading in that direction. "He's in danger," Vincent said simply. He rose from his seat, and began making his way through the crowd, stepping over and sometimes on the feet and legs of the audience members, Jaz following closely behind.

He glanced around for someone who looked like a duke, while keeping his eye on the stranger, too. He had no idea what to expect, but knew this was the event he'd overheard being discussed that night in Linnael. But he'd also gotten the impression there would be more than one person involved. He quickly scanned the crowd around the area where the duke's seats would be. But who else could it be? He had no way to tell, and he already knew that Jaz's magic skills didn't extend into the realm of mind-reading.

Since he was making his way urgently, he was gaining on the stranger, who was fairly nonchalant about approaching the duke's seats. When he was about twenty feet behind the man, Vincent slowed to match his pace. He couldn't very well accost the man for no reason other than his own hunch.

Heads began to turn toward the stage. Vincent stole a glance and saw a figure that had to be the duke. The tall, handsome, blond-haired man made his way in front of the audience, then began to walk up the side at Vincent's left toward the seats reserved for him and his small entourage. He smiled and waved politely at the crowd, many of whom were cheering him.

Vincent's quarry now reached the end of the row and turned right, toward the rear of the seating area. Several paces away from the duke's reserved seats, the man stopped, turning to face the stage and standing with his back against a tree. Vincent didn't know what to do other than follow him. He excused himself to the onlookers as he continued stepping over their feet.

The duke's party had reached the platform. Vincent saw there were four, including the duke and his lady. The other two seemed to be bodyguard types. By the time Vincent and Jaz reached the end of the row, they were all seated. The duke continued to smile and wave to members of the audience who cheered him.

"Roasted nuts! Fresh, roasted nuts!" Vincent glanced to his left to see the nut vendor from the street entering from behind the stage. The man wheeled his cart up the side of the audience, in the direction of the platform. When he saw the duke, he stopped. "Why, Duke Ghanol!" the man exclaimed. His demeanor was such that the audience thought he was comic relief. Evidently, Vincent realized, so did the duke's party. The vendor reached into his cart. Vincent's hand flew to the hilt of his sword. He drew it, stepping out of the row, as the vendor pulled his hands out. Vincent tensed. "Have some nuts!" the vendor cried, and began lobbing wrapped packets of them toward the duke and his companions. The audience roared with laughter. The duke's lady clapped her hands and reached out to catch the falling gifts.

This world didn't have grenades, to his knowledge, but Vincent's heart still pounded in anxiety. He gripped his sword more firmly in his hand. Everyone was so absorbed in the flying nuts that they didn't take any notice of him, or his drawn sword.

Vincent suddenly realized that no one was taking notice of the man by the tree, either. He quickly turned his attention back to him, and saw the tiny crossbow pistol the man had unfolded and was raising in the duke's direction. Before he knew what he was doing, Vincent hurled his sword. This drew some attention. There were gasps from the audience and a scream or two from the ladies as the sword struck home, plunging through the assassin's torso just below the sternum and burying itself in the tree trunk.

"Get the vendor," Vincent hissed to Jaz. The vendor's face had fallen and he looked ready to run. Vincent smiled as the man looked down in confusion at his feet, which refused to move.

The duke's two bodyguards had drawn their swords and flanked Ghanol by this point. But the danger was over and they seemed to realize that. The crowd had begun to retreat from the scene, with the exception of the few inevitable curious ones. Duke Ghanol stepped out from between the two guards. He looked at the skewered man on the tree, crossbow dangling in full view from a lifeless finger, then at the nut vendor. No one else was paying any attention to the vendor until Ghanol's gaze fell upon him. Then all eyes turned in his direction. The man was struggling to break free of Jaz's spell.

The duke stepped down from the raised platform of seats and headed straight for Vincent. The once friendly eyes were now ice cold. His handsome, mustached face was hardened. But as he reached Vincent, he glanced once more at the assassin at the tree. When he looked at Vincent again, the eyes had softened. Without a word, he held out his hand. And Vincent took it.

The Duke insisted that Jaz and I be his guests for the show. We sat in his box with the two guards, Ghanol, and the Lady Brinda. Ghanol is really a decent chap. We had several minutes to talk with him while the audience recovered from the scene and the mess was cleared up. Needless to say, the duke was exceedingly grateful. He offered a reward, which I declined, naturally. I'm glad the guy didn't turn out to be an asshole, anyway. I'd have felt like shit for saving his life.

I do feel like shit for having killed again. Oh, no doubt the guy deserved death. But I don't like the fact that I'm the one who had to play judge, jury, and executioner, all in the blink of an eye. I now have two deaths on my conscience. And they weigh heavily, believe me.

At any rate, as near as we could figure things out, the two were part of a local assassins' *guild. Organized crime apparently exists here, too. Ghanol's only theory on why they wanted him* *dead is that he has put together an investigative team that has been causing the guild some* *trouble. He wouldn't go into specifics, and that was fine with me.*

Anyway, that's how that evening went. Oh, yes... I don't remember a damn thing about the *play.*

❧ ☙

Jaz returned to his keep not long after their adventure in Falconwall, promising to keep in touch and to pay a visit to the site of Vincent's keep every now and again to see how Feletain was progressing.

Mid-Year Week arrived. Ariaziane's seventeenth birthday was celebrated. Vincent gave her a present of some scented soaps and hair dressings that he'd picked up in Falconwall. He kept the gift-giving simple, taking Gnorrin's advice to heart. Sort of.

"I have another present for you," he told her.

Ariaziane put down the gift she'd just received, as they sat outside in Gnorrin's yard. "What?" she said eagerly, causing Vincent to question Gnorrin's wisdom regarding gift-giving.

"Well, I don't want to tell you before you see it. But you can't see it, because I don't have it. It was being made just for you. I received word last week that it was finished. I was wondering if you'd care to join me when I go. I'd like the company."

"Go? Where?"

"Linnael."

"Well, I suppose so."

"Good. Then we'll leave at the beginning of next week."

And they did. As soon as the celebrations of Mid-Year Week were over, Vincent and Ariaziane packed their things. In front of Gnorrin's cottage, Vincent said to the gnome, "Thanks for looking after Blaise for me. You have everything under control?"

Gnorrin smiled. "Everything." And then in a soft voice, for Vincent's ears only, "Good luck."

Vincent smiled back. Then they were off.

The journey to Linnael was uneventful. Vincent took them directly to Aedriun's keep, where they spent the remainder of the day. After a night's rest, they breakfasted with the baron and his nephew Darvas, then Vincent announced that it was time to be on their way.

"And just where are we going?" Ariaziane asked. "You said my present was in Linnael."

"Well, no. I never said exactly that."

She frowned at him. "You're being difficult, again."

"Yup."

She shook her head and smiled. "This must be some present," she teased.

Linnael sat on a small spur of land that pointed south. The shoreline they now followed led to the northeast. After about half an hour of travel, they encountered hilly terrain. It took them another half hour to traverse this region. They passed the time in silence. Ariaziane rode with her gaze usually out to sea. Vincent was glad to see that her fascination with it was undimmed. As they broke onto level ground again, they saw an expanse of beautiful land and pristine beach. There were stands of trees scattered here and there, as well as streams that had obviously originated in the hilly country they'd just passed through. In the middle of this beauty sat two houses facing south, to the sea.

"You hired someone who lives out here to make a gift for me? You couldn't have found someone closer to home?"

"Trust me."

She frowned. "And they couldn't have delivered it to your door?"

He snorted. "Not very easily."

From a distance, they could see that there was a large cart in front of the nearer house. And a small figure was carrying something from the cart into one of the houses, followed by a black dog. A pony roamed around out back. Vincent smiled to himself.

Finally, they arrived in front of the houses. The dog heard them approach and ran outside, barking. It pranced around the legs of their horses as they came to a stop. "Looks a lot like Blaise," Ariaziane said. She looked over the house and its grounds. "Very pretty," she said, admiring the attractive facade and careful landscaping. "Who lives here?"

Vincent smiled as he dismounted. "You do."

The girl shot him a look. "What?"

"Happy Birthday," he said, leaning down to play with the dog. "C'mere, girl! Oooh, yes, I missed you, too." Blaise licked his face, then returned to prancing and barking.

At that moment, Gnorrin stepped out of the front door. "Welcome!" he said to Ariaziane.

She slowly slid off her horse, looking dumbfounded at both of them. "What are you doing here?" she said to Gnorrin. "What are you two talking about? Are you saying that you had a house built for me?"

"Not exactly. I had two houses built. The one over there is mine." He grinned as she looked at the other house, just a stone's throw away, then at Gnorrin. "Gnorrin left a few hours after we did, having gathered all your belongings. All mine, too, since I'd packed everything the night before we left."

Gnorrin nodded. "Everything is in the front room." He looked at the still dumbstruck girl. "Would you like to see your new home?" Vincent took her by the arm and they followed Gnorrin inside. "They did a lovely job," the gnome continued, once in the living room.

He gave them the tour. The house was fully furnished and decorated to a minimal degree. The main room had a huge window with an excellent view of the sea. There was a pleasant kitchen, complete with dining area. One bedroom, already fitted with bed and bureau. Another room that was evidently to be her study. Bookshelves lined the walls, and a large desk sat in the middle.

The construction was of highest quality, well insulated with packed earth inside the thick walls. In the rear was a stable for her horse, complete with water trough. A stream passed within short walking distance behind both houses. Garden areas had been sectioned off, and the ground was well tilled.

Returning to the front of the house, Ariaziane leaned up against her horse. "I don't know what to say."

"Do you like it?" Vincent asked tentatively.

She raised her eyebrows, as though it were a stupid question. "It's beautiful. Of course I like it." Then she frowned in puzzlement. "I just don't understand…"

Gnorrin stepped in to explain. "You have learned from me the basic knowledge that will serve you well as you proceed with your studies on your own." The girl continued to appear confused, so he continued. "Yes, there is much more I could teach you. But it is time for you to find your own path. Pursue what you find yourself drawn to, rather than me teaching you my own personal preferences. What you now know is fairly common knowledge for all mages. Plus a few things that I'm fond of. But you need to search yourself. Find you own passions. And then go after them."

Ariaziane frowned in exasperation. "But how? Where do I find the sources?"

The gnome shrugged. "Well, Jaz was kind enough to offer to show you a few things. Likely as not, you'll discover your own sources. Things have a way of presenting themselves. Do not worry."

She smiled doubtfully. "Thanks."

"You are quite welcome," he replied. "It was a new experience for me to teach you. You're my first apprentice. Thank you for the opportunity." He gave a sharp whistle, then turned to Vincent. "Well, I think I shall be going, now."

"So soon?" Vincent said as the pony trotted around the corner of the house.

Gnorrin smiled. "You cannot persuade me to help arrange your house that easily. You're on your own."

"Whatever you say." Vincent helped Gnorrin hitch up his pony to the small cart. "Thanks for your help with all this." He clapped his friend on the shoulder. "I'll see you soon."

Ariaziane hugged Gnorrin before he mounted the pony. "Thanks for everything, Gnorrin. Please come visit us sometime."

"I'll do that," he replied, then hopped up on the pony. The pair watched him as he drove off.

After a moment, Vincent turned and said, "I imagine this is a little hard to absorb."

"That's for certain," she said, and looked him in the eye. "What possessed you to do such a thing?"

"Are you kidding?" he laughed, placing his hands atop her shoulders. "I saw how much you love the sea. And I felt it was time for you to move out on your own."

"*You* felt it was time?"

"Well, yeah. I mean, I talked it over with Gnorrin, obviously. He agreed that you were ready."

"I see," she said sweetly. "And you had to come with me?"

"Absolutely. Because…"

"I know," she interrupted. "Because you love me."

He smiled. "Yes. I do."

She returned the smile. "I know." And she moved closer to him, wrapping her arms around him. She squeezed him tight. "Thank you. It's the most amazing birthday present ever." And then she kissed him lightly on the lips. Vincent found himself stunned by even so brief a kiss. But before he could respond, she broke from the embrace. "Let's go see your house, now," she said. Grabbing his hand, she set off across the field.

❧ ❧

What a week! I probably should have written in my journal earlier than this, in order to capture all the feelings when they were fresh. But better late than never.

Annie and I moved into our new homes about a week ago. I was pretty concerned about how she'd react, but after getting over the initial shock, she's really become quite happy. She spends hours every day just walking along the shore, staring out to sea.

Aedriun followed my instructions to the letter. And even some instructions I didn't give. Back when I built my cottage down the road from Gnorrin's, I just went ahead and built the thing. After all, that's pretty much what I was told to do by Gnorrin and Blade. But here, it seems, the realty industry has a foothold. Aedriun provided me with the deed to the property surrounding both houses. Effectively, I own both houses, all the land in between, and an area stretching from the beach to about a mile into the woods, and the same distance on either side. This was all news to me, and frankly, was more than I really wanted. But what the heck.

It just strikes me as weird that someone already had laid claim to the land. I asked Aedriun about my cottage. He explained that the law varied from region to region regarding land ownership. Evidently in Gnorrin's area, I would have needed to buy the property if I'd been closer to town, or if I'd built a larger place. Why the size of the building makes any difference is totally beyond me. But then, when it comes to legalities, I'm frequently lost.

Anyway, the area that Aedriun's people chose for us is absolutely gorgeous. It's about an hour or so outside of Linnael. We get to see a lot of ships passing by as they head in to port. Some ships actually sail out at night, and we can see the fires of the torches twinkling across the water. One night we even heard the singing of the sailors.

It is so peaceful, here. We are out of the way of trade routes. I made sure to let Aedriun know we wanted solitude. He sure came through for us.

The day after we arrived here, I rode into Linnael and purchased a small cart for the transportation of goods. Since we're no longer walking distance from the market, we'll need to lay in supplies. Aedriun assures me that heavy snow is uncommon here, so I'm hoping we have no blizzards to contend with.

Aedriun's people really went all out in furnishing us. Both of our houses are filled with beautiful furniture, far more extravagant than I expected. I didn't think I'd given him a fortune. But then, he probably gets good prices on things because of his rank.

We even have outdoor furniture. At night, we sit outside together and watch the moonlight on the waves. We count the stars. It's amazingly serene. I haven't slept this well in years.

And I am thrilled to report that things on the romantic front seem to be improving. We hold hands all the time, it seems. When we sit together, it's always closely. She leans her head on my shoulder as we walk the beach. Lots of closeness of that nature. We haven't progressed to the serious kissing stage, yet. But you know what? I don't mind. What we've got is beautiful enough for now.

❧ ❧

The Season of the Harvest flew past for Vincent. Much time was spent in Linnael, with Aedriun and Darvas. Ariaziane took advantage of her new independence to take a vacation from the study of magic. She and Vincent spent most of their time together.

They tended their homes, adding personal touches that Aedriun's people couldn't have done. They took turns cooking for each other, trying all sorts of exotic fare available in Linnael. Seafood became a staple of their diets. And they swam often and for hours.

They sailed, too. Although no cruise industry existed, many a captain was willing to charter his craft for a pleasure cruise if the price was right and no other business was pending. They went on trips along the coast and to a few of the tiny islands that lay within a league of the shore.

The Season of Sleep, too, passed quickly. Vincent was pleased that Aedriun's assessment of the weather was correct. No blizzards or ice storms kept them from their travels to Linnael. In fact, the wonderfully light snows came late and went early. Just the way Vincent liked it.

And before Vincent knew it, Celebration Week was upon them.

Aedriun threw Vincent a big birthday party, after Ariaziane explained the custom to him. Gnorrin arrived for the celebration, as did Jaz. Duke Ghanol even arrived to pay his respects to Vincent. There was a huge dinner, followed by dancing. People waltzed.

Toward the end of the evening, Vincent sat at a table with Aedriun, Ghanol, Gnorrin, Jaz, and Ariaziane. Gnorrin clapped his friend on the back. "So. Twenty years old. And to me, you look barely older than when you arrived here."

"What can I say?" he asked. "I'm young at heart."

"Time for you to open your presents," Ariaziane said.

"Oh, you guys are too much," Vincent said. "Aedriun, you better not have gotten me anything else. This party was more than gift enough."

"That is what I was told," the baron said, casting a glance at Ariaziane. "And such is the case. I hope you enjoyed yourself."

"I did," he replied. "Thank you."

"Well, let us get this over with," Gnorrin said, and produced a wrapped parcel from under his chair. He slid it across the table to Vincent, who opened it carefully. Inside were clothes. Breeches and tunic of a dark brown. "I had Tarel put that together for you, in one of those disgustingly drab colors that you are so fond of. They should fit well enough."

Vincent nodded. "It's very nice, thank you. I like the cut of the collar."

Jaz spoke up next. "You recall our business venture, my friend?" Vincent nodded. "I thought you'd like to benefit from the result of it." The mage pulled out a sword and scabbard.

Vincent rose from his seat and accepted them. He stepped away from the table and yanked out the sword. It flew from the scabbard, feeling incredibly light in his hand. He couldn't imagine ever holding a sword that felt more *right* in his hand. It seemed like a part of his arm. "Amazing," he said, looking at Jaz. "You've enchanted this?"

"Yes. Do you like it?"

"I love it!"

"Good. Then don't lose it. But in case you do, here's another one just like it." He pulled out its twin, this one bound in cloth and tied closed.

"Wow. Thanks, Jaz." He took the wrapped parcel. Then he noticed Ariaziane's frown and the look in her eye. He realized she disapproved of his fascination with the weapons and his obvious delight in having them. He decided to try to lighten her mood a bit. He swung both of the swords around, one in each hand. "Hey, I can get into some Florentine action, here."

Aedriun raised an eyebrow. "Florentine? I take it that is your term for fighting with two swords?"

"Actually, it's my term for cooking something with spinach and a cream sauce." He put the swords away and returned to his seat. Ariaziane tried to hold back a chuckle, but failed. He smiled.

"My turn," she said with a grin. From inside her cloak, she pulled out a small, brightly wrapped package. She slid it across the table toward him.

Vincent accepted the parcel, unwrapped it, and pulled out a small box. Inside was a necklace, a simple gold chain with a pendant attached. The pendant was an exact replica of the cloak pin she'd previously given him, but much smaller. The pendant was perhaps an inch across. "It's beautiful," he said. "What's next? Earrings?" He slipped the chain over his neck.

She laughed. "I've been working on that for the past three months."

Vincent stared at her. "What do you mean? I didn't know you'd learned how to make jewelry. And this is incredibly detailed!"

"That's not what I meant," she said.

"She's been working on it in another way," Gnorrin said.

"Evidently the same way I worked on those swords," put in Jaz.

Vincent blinked. "Really? It's magical?" She nodded. "And you did it?" She nodded again. "Far out! What's it do?"

The other eyes at the table turned to Duke Ghanol. Vincent looked inquiringly at him, too. The duke smiled, then raised his hand from beneath the table. In his fist was a very familiar little crossbow pistol. It was cocked and loaded. Vincent felt his heart skip a beat, then the duke fired.

Vincent jumped as the bolt hurtled toward his chest. Then it slowed rapidly before sailing away from him, bouncing harmlessly into the middle of the table. Ariaziane smiled with what Vincent thought was relief. The others laughed or applauded. "Given your past experiences with projectiles, I thought this might prove useful," she said.

Vincent waited until his heartbeat returned to normal, then smiled. "Geez. Can't anyone just answer a question without a demonstration?" He stared pointedly at Jaz. He wondered briefly why Ariaziane would make such a thing for him if she didn't think he'd be engaging in that sort of activity any longer. But he'd ask her that another time. "Thank you," he said to her. "It could very well come in handy, with friends like you guys around."

"Now be warned," Ariaziane said. "The item will not work indefinitely. It will deflect no more than a dozen arrows or bolts. Well, eleven, now."

Vincent nodded. "I'll have more lives than a cat."

The duke cleared his throat, disturbing the laughter that followed. "It was not made known to me that this occasion would warrant gift-giving," he said, his rich voice washing over them. "The gods know that I have tried to reward Vincent for his bravery when he saved my life. It seems to me that such a feat is deserving of some remuneration, whereas the simple act of growing older should not particularly require any." He folded up the tiny crossbow and slid it over to Vincent. "That, too, might come in handy one day. It is fitting that you own it, my friend. It is too much a reminder to me of how close to death I came."

Vincent accepted the weapon. "Thank you," he said, though he didn't particularly want the item, either.

The duke brushed it off. "That is not your present, however." He stroked his thick mustache. "It has been made known to me, Vincent, that you are building a keep."

"Yes, that's right."

"Your friend Jaz has told me of it. And it seems that the keep lies within my jurisdiction."

"I believe it does, yes."

"You do realize, do you not, that the property you are building on is owned by my brother, the king?"

Vincent sighed. "Not again," he mumbled. "Well, now that you mention it... No. I mean, I'm building into a mountain! The king owns the mountains?"

"He owns *that* mountain," Ghanol said. "And that is what matters."

"I see," Vincent said. "So. What does this mean?"

The duke shrugged. "It would mean that your construction would be without permission. Unless I arrange to have the mountain made available to you." He smiled. "Which I will."

Vincent shook his head. "Go ahead, make me think I'm in trouble." He chuckled. "If I'd known you were like that, I'd have let the guy shoot you."

The duke laughed with him, then raised his glass. "To Vincent! Happy Birthday!"

The others raised their drinks and shared the salute.

☙ ❧

When the Season of Green began to warm, Vincent attacked his gardening with vigor. He tilled and planted. He threw together a new compost heap. And when the ground was dry again, he was able to exercise Blaise properly. Not to mention being able to go for long rides with Ariaziane.

It was after returning from one of these rides that Vincent found a courier waiting for him, relaxing in one of the chairs in front of his house. He rose as the pair stopped and dismounted. The man straightened his blue breeches and handsome red tunic with fancy blue embroidery around the neck and cuffs. "Are you the gentleman known as Vincent?" he asked.

"Yes," Vincent answered, switching his gaze back from the man's equally decorated horse. "What can I do for you?"

"I have a message for you from the king." He withdrew a scroll and handed it to Vincent.

For a moment, Vincent was startled. Then it dawned on him. He gave a brief smile and said to Ariaziane, "Must be that permission to build that Ghanol said he'd arrange." He turned back to the courier and accepted the scroll that the man held out to him. "Thank you." He broke the wax seal on the roll, opened it, and read. Then he frowned.

"What is wrong?" Ariaziane asked.

Vincent rolled up the message. "It is a summons to court," he said. "Maybe the permission has to be granted in person, or there's some sort of ceremony. I don't know. It says I have to appear in court on the first day of Mid-Year Week." He said to the courier, "Do you need my reply in writing, or just verbally?"

"It is not necessary to give a written response."

"Very well. Please convey to His Majesty that I will certainly attend." The courier gave a polite nod. "Now," Vincent said, "I can offer you a cool drink, if you like. There is a trough of water in the rear by the stable, if your horse is thirsty."

"You are most kind," said the man. "But we both relieved our thirst at the stream before you returned. I must be on my way."

After the messenger had gone, Ariaziane said, "I've never heard of a royal summons being issued for something like this. I'm curious to learn what it's all about."

"Well, you'll know when I do. You're coming with me, aren't you?"

"The summons was for you, not for both of us."

"Well, where I come from, invitations are usually assumed to include a guest."

"But we're not where you come from."

Vincent shrugged. "If the king has a problem with it, I'm sure he'll let us know."

My life continues to be a happy one. The time I spend with Annie is the happiest time I've ever experienced. I've learned more about her life prior to my arrival here. Not that she knows a great deal about her life before she was taken into the abbey, but what little she knows, she's shared with me. I'm glad she has.

It's really weird. I feel so close to her. We're very intimate in a non-sexual way. I mean, we cuddle a lot. We'll lie in the yard and look at the stars or the sea, and often, she'll fall asleep in my arms. I like that. Oddly enough, I don't have any great desire to push her into something more physical. For now, it's enough to just be with her. To hold her hand, to feel her lying next to me.

Sometimes we kiss. Nothing real passionate, but always nice. She doesn't seem totally comfortable with that, and I haven't pushed her. It sounds sappy, but one of the things I enjoy most is just lying with her while she sleeps. I look into her face, stroke her hair... I love her so much.

And she loves me, too. She's never actually come out and said it. But she does say that I'm her favorite person. And her actions speak of love. I think she's holding a lot back, repressing it for some reason. But it'll come out sooner or later. And I'll be waiting.

The first day of Mid-Year Week found Vincent and Ariaziane arriving in the city of Goldenbrook. The city was smaller than Linnael, and was quiet and clean, too. Its only industry seemed to be politics. Royalty and other dignitaries were everywhere. It made Vincent queasy.

Goldenbrook lay about two and a half days journey west of Linnael. The trip wouldn't have been so bad if it hadn't rained for most of it, Vincent thought. His thoughts turned frequently to Blaise, but he knew she'd be fine under Darvas' care.

When they arrived, they checked in at *The Gilded Bough*, an inn recommended to them by Aedriun. The desk clerk signed them in, gave them keys to their rooms, and advised them of the location of the baths. The pair thanked him, then headed for their rooms.

After a luxuriously hot soak, Vincent returned to his room. To his surprise, Aedriun was waiting for him. "I've been here for several days," his friend told him. "I'd left word with the staff here that I was to be notified upon your arrival. Ariaziane is still bathing?"

"I assume so," Vincent said. "Why? Are we rushed?"

"No, we have plenty of time. The ceremony will not begin until nightfall. But I will be entertaining you both until then. Goldenbrook has some delightful shops that I think you both will enjoy. And I imagine you are hungry, also. I know I am."

Vincent agreed. "We didn't have breakfast this morning before getting on our way. Let me go see if she's back in her room, yet."

He stepped out of the room and went down the hall to Ariaziane's door. The door was part way open and he looked inside as he raised his hand to knock. But his hand stopped, just as his breath did. Ariaziane was inside, standing near her bed, evidently deciding which outfit to wear. The clothes were spread out on the bed. None of them were on her body.

Her back was to the door, and Vincent found himself both grateful and disappointed that this was the case. He stared at her naked back as she picked up one outfit after another, holding them up in front of her for examination. He felt his heart throb as she turned around to face the closet that he knew was behind her. And therefore, faced him.

He told himself he shouldn't be doing this. But he couldn't turn away. She was so beautiful. Her body so... He groped for the right word. "Perfect," he whispered.

Ariaziane looked up as he spoke the word, and his panic caused him to jerk back out of the sliver of open doorway, desperately hoping that she hadn't seen him. He began to tip-toe toward his room when suddenly he felt his body stiffen. He couldn't move. And then he heard her step out into the hallway. "Coming to see me?" she asked, moving to stand in front of him and tightening the sash of her robe.

His body now under his own control again, he nodded. "Um, yeah."

"Did you see enough?" she teased.

Oh, shit, Vincent thought. He tried to stammer out an apology. "I didn't mean... I just..."

"You were there for a while, weren't you? Staring."

He thought about denying it. But he couldn't lie to her. "Yes. I'm sorry."

Her smile broadened a little, and took on a mischievous tone. "It's all right," she said. Then she cleared her throat. "I used to stare at you, too." Vincent raised an eyebrow, surprised at her confession. "When you'd shower. If I was there, I'd peek in through the cracks in the boards."

Vincent smiled faintly. "I know," he said. When she seemed surprised, he continued. "I could see your toes under the boards." He shrugged at her embarrassment. "I just figured it was because you were curious. You were at that age. I guess this makes us even," he said.

She laughed. "Hardly. I think I peeked a lot more than you, unless this wasn't your first."

"Hmm. Well, it *was* my first. But I'd still say we're even. I made up in quality what you had in quantity."

Ariaziane blushed and turned her face to the floor. "Why were you coming to see me?"

"Oh," Vincent said, seeing the color in her cheeks despite her turning away. "Aedriun's taking us to lunch."

"I'll be there shortly." She looked up at him again. "Now go away," she said, smiling and moving back to her door. "Unless you're planning on watching me dress."

Unsure whether she was actually offering or not, Vincent simply smiled and returned to his room.

After lunch at an outdoor eatery, Aedriun took Vincent and Ariaziane on a brief tour of the city. The shops that he wanted them to see were, to Vincent's delight, bookstores. Goldenbrook, it seemed, was filled with literate people. No surprise, Vincent thought, since it was filled almost exclusively with the upper crust of society.

He browsed through the shelves, finding several tomes of interest. Then, with a shrug, he started pulling them from the shelves. "What good is being rich if I can't buy things I want?" he said to his friends.

Ariaziane, for her part, found many books relating to different arts that she felt she could draw upon as a mage. She, too, made several purchases.

Eventually, they made their way to the castle. Aedriun was recognized by the outer gatesman, who dispatched a messenger to precede them. By the time they reached the inner gate, an escort was waiting for them.

Vincent and Ariaziane gazed in awe at the castle and its grounds. "This is huge," Vincent murmured. Ariaziane could only nod her head in agreement. "And I thought your place was big," he said to Aedriun. It was like pictures he'd seen in books back on Earth. Tremendous towers, thick walls, portcullises, arrow slits, and a drawbridge over a moat. "Unbelievable," he whispered.

Once inside, they were taken directly to the king's private reception hall. This room was the size of Aedriun's ballroom. Vincent wasn't impressed until Aedriun whispered to him that this hall was only about a quarter the size of the king's main ballroom. They were advised that King Breigar would be with them shortly.

While they waited, Aedriun refreshed them on proper etiquette when dealing with royalty. Vincent took it in, frowning inwardly at the whole thing. He had little use for etiquette. As Aedriun finished, Duke Ghanol entered. He strode over to the group and greeted them happily.

"This is all your doing, isn't it?" Vincent accused.

Ghanol smiled. "I promised you I'd make the mountain available to you, didn't I?"

"Yes, but is all this necessary? You couldn't have just popped by for tea one day and said, 'Oh, by the way, you can build your keep in the mountain. My brother says it's okay,' or something like that?"

"I'm afraid not," Ghanol laughed.

At that moment, a page announced the king. All stood and watched as a tall, stately man entered the room. The first thing that occurred to Vincent was that he wasn't wearing robes or a crown. In fact, the man looked like... Well, he looked like Ghanol, he thought. Older, certainly. With dark hair. But they shared the same sharp nose and deep eyes. He was dressed in very fine, but otherwise normal-looking, clothes. He strolled casually toward them.

"Hello, little brother," he said to Ghanol. "These are your friends?"

"Aye. The Lord Baron Aedriun you know already."

"Aedriun," said the king. "Good to see you again." He shook Aedriun's hand.

Ghanol continued. "This young lady is named Ariaziane."

The king appraised her. "Enchanting. Such a lovely name. For a lovely lady." He bent over her hand and kissed it. Ariaziane looked in shock at Aedriun, who merely smiled at her confusion.

King Breigar stood up straight again and leveled his gaze on Vincent. "That leaves this gentleman. It was you who saved the life of my dear brother?"

Vincent fidgeted. So much for Aedriun's lessons in etiquette, he thought. "Well, I guess so."

"You guess so?" the king laughed. "Ghan tells me that you skewered him from fifty feet away. Stuck him to a tree!"

"Your Majesty's brother exaggerates," Vincent offered. "It was no more than thirty."

At this, the king's demeanor turned to a scowl. "Now you listen, boy. I am the king. And if I say you killed him from fifty feet away, then you killed him from fifty feet away." Vincent stood stock still, not knowing how to reply. Fortunately, he was saved the effort. The king clapped him on the shoulder and laughed loudly. "Come. I must sit."

They followed the king to the side of the room where a great chair sat facing several rows of smaller chairs. Vincent noticed for the first time that the king walked with a limp. As they seated themselves, the king addressed them. "Vincent. It is to my understanding that you wish to construct a keep on my property. Is this so?"

"Yes, Your Majesty."

"My brother has advised me of all the details as to location. It seems the only thing preventing you from doing this is my permission."

"So it seems," Vincent agreed.

The king smiled at that. Vincent didn't know why. He didn't see anything funny about it. "Well, it so happens that I'm rather fond of little Ghan. I'm very grateful to you for preventing me from losing him. To show my gratitude, I have something here for you." He reached to his belt and withdrew a scroll tube, uncapped it, and pulled out a sheet of rolled-up vellum. He held it out and a page accepted it, delivering it to Vincent. "I think you'll find it all in order," the king concluded.

Vincent broke the seal and unrolled it. He scanned the document quickly, looking for something resembling a transfer of property.

"Please read it aloud," the king urged.

Vincent shrugged, cleared his throat, and returned to the top of the sheet. "Declaration of Ascension," he read. "It is hereby announced that on this first day of Mid-Year Week in the year 1147, I, King Breigar, do grant Vincent of Penn's Woods the title of Baron, complete with all rights, honors, and privileges so accorded." Vincent stopped reading and stared first at the scroll, then at the king. "Excuse me?" he said.

"I'm sorry," the king said. "Was it unclear?" He turned to the page. "Who wrote that? Off with his head."

"You wrote it, Your Majesty."

"I did? Well, then. Remind me to have myself executed later." He turned his attention back to Vincent. "It is a common reward for an action such as yours, Vincent. You saved the life of a duke. It is only fitting that his king should grant you a title. If baron is not significant enough for you, just say as much."

"No!" Vincent blurted. "It's not that at all! Far from it, in fact. Just the opposite. I don't deserve this!"

"Rubbish!" the king replied. "You are more deserving of it than many who hold the title. Present company excluded, Aedriun. Personally," the king said, "I will be offended if you do not accept."

"In other words, I have no choice," Vincent spat out before he could stop himself. He saw Aedriun flinch. Ghanol tried to hide an amused smile.

The king mellowed. "Of course you do. I was jesting. But please do accept, Vincent."

He shook his head. "But I know nothing about being a baron! You refer to 'all rights, honors, and privileges' in this declaration. But surely a baron must do something in return. I don't know what that would be, or if I'm capable of giving it."

"Ah," the king said. "Well, in point of fact, being a baron does not require you to do anything, really. In and of itself. On the other hand, being a land baron would have some duties attached, yes. Collecting tax revenue and providing protection for the population. That sort of thing."

"But you're not making me a land baron," Vincent said. "Right?"

"Well, now that you mention it..." The king coughed slightly. "Here's the situation. The land on which you intend to build is under Ghanol's protection right now. However, due to the death of our cousin, Ghanol has taken over a larger territory. Your area, near the mountains, is not very populated. It is not a tremendous burden on Ghanol, but the fact is that he could use his time more effectively by divesting himself of it. My proposal is to grant you the land, on the condition that you assume responsibility for it."

Vincent sighed, feeling like he was being railroaded into this. "And as I said, I know nothing about all that. I'm only twenty years old. I have a whole life ahead of me, and frankly, I'm not sure I want that responsibility."

The king rubbed his chin. "I see. When will the keep be completed?"

"Four years," Vincent said. "Give or take."

"Four years. Very good. How about this, then? Build your keep. At the time of completion, we will discuss this again. Either way, you may build. I would not withhold that from you. But if Ghanol's situation does not improve, I would ask you to consider the offer again, as a favor to me."

Vincent mulled this over briefly. "That seems fair. I accept."

"Splendid!" the king said. "Congratulations, then, Lord Vincent." The king stood.

Aedriun motioned for Vincent to meet him halfway and he did so. Another hand signal from Aedriun and Vincent knelt in front of the king.

"Aedriun, stop prompting him," the king snapped. "You're the one who said that this other-worlder was not one for formalities." He turned his attention to Vincent again. "It's nice to have a break from being kingly."

Vincent smiled, clasping the king's outstretched hand.

Then Breigar placed his other hand on Vincent's right shoulder. "Welcome, Vincent. You're now a peer of the realm."

Vincent smiled nervously as his friends applauded.

❧ ❧

Darella's daughter watched the entire affair in her mother's crystal ball. She didn't know what had just occurred, but it made her feel angry. Her father had knelt in front of this other man. That was wrong. Others should be kneeling in front of her father, not the other way around.

But the annoyance soon passed, to be replaced with the ever-present longing she felt for him. She so desperately wanted to meet him, wanted him to like her.

A shadow fell across the ball. She looked up in shock to find her brother staring down at her. A chill washed over her. Her secret was out, now. Her brother knew their father still lived. She trembled to think of what he'd do with the information.

She waved a hand over the ball and it went dark. She stood, intending to face up to her brother. But before she was even totally upright, he struck her with a powerful blow across the face. She recoiled and sat down hard on the stone floor of the cave. She held a hand to her cheek.

His blows were becoming harder. They were only three years old, but their bodies were those of four times that age. And her brother wasn't anywhere near as awkward in his body as she was in hers. He seemed to enjoy using his body. And he enjoyed hurting her.

She couldn't stand up to him, she knew. There was just no way. He was too strong, too quick. Too mean. Her only hope was that he would keep the information to himself and not tell their mother. But that wasn't something she felt was at all likely.

❧ Twenty-Three ❧

Rhia appeared unexpectedly one morning a few weeks later. She arrived at Vincent's door as he was preparing breakfast, a mixture of cereal grain, nuts, and fruit cooked in goat's milk. He stood over his wood-burning stove, stirring the saucepan. It was nearly ready, and the aroma of the fruit wafted throughout his home.

He heard Blaise barking outside in the yard. Probably chasing birds again, he thought. He smiled at the image and continued stirring.

"Mmm. Smells wonderful," came a voice from behind him.

Startled, he turned. "Rhia!" She stepped inside and greeted him with a hug. Vincent returned the embrace, but felt slightly uncomfortable about it. "How are you?" he said, stepping back. "It's been a while."

"And I do regret that," she said. "Forgive me?"

Vincent shrugged. "Nothing to forgive." He moved to the stove, turning his attention back to the pan. "Almost done," he said. "Like some?"

"Yes, thank you."

He smiled at her. "It's really good to see you."

"I imagine it's great to be seeing anything, isn't it?"

Vincent paused, then realized the last time he'd been with her was back at Jaz's keep, before his eyes were healed by Aedriun's ring. "Yes," he said soberly. "That's very true." He removed the pan from the heat, then placed the cast iron cover over the grate in the top of the stove. He carried the pan into the kitchen and ladled the cereal into bowls from his cupboard. Then he supplied two spoons from a drawer nearby. "You know, Aedriun lives just down the shore in Linnael."

"I recall him mentioning that's where he was from. But I thought you disliked him. You had some rather choice words to describe his behavior." Rhia tasted some of the cereal as they returned to the living room to sit.

"Oh, that was all an act. Trying to get to me."

"I see."

"How do you like it?" he asked. Vincent looked up at her, to see her sucking provocatively on the spoon. His cheeks flushed.

"Oh, any number of ways," she said.

"I meant the cereal, and you know it," he said. "You never change, do you?"

"It's delicious, and why should I?"

Vincent shrugged, his feeling of discomfort growing. Seeing Rhia brought back to conscious thought all the memories he had of her, and the feelings he'd been beginning to develop for her. But things were going so well with Ariaziane these days. He frankly didn't want to think of his feelings for Rhia.

They ate in silence for a minute, then Vincent said, "So how goes the eternal search?"

Rhia swallowed, then dabbed at the corner of her mouth with a finger. "I have good news and bad news with regard to that. Which would you like to hear first?"

He shrugged. "How about the good news?"

"The good news is that I have effectively located Darella's location to within a league."

"And the bad news?"

"She knows I have."

Vincent stopped his spoon inches from his mouth and slowly lowered it back to the bowl. "Just how bad is this bad news?"

Rhia pushed her spoon idly through the cereal. "I'm not certain. It will depend on whether she decides I am a threat or not."

"Okay, so what's she likely to do if she considers you a threat?"

"If she considers me to be a great enough threat, she could come after me. I tend to doubt that, however. If she's found a Seeker Portal, I don't think she's going to leave it unattended for a minute. My opinion is that she will use whatever magic is necessary to prevent me from finding her exact location."

"In other words, you think her knowledge of your search will only make your search harder?" Rhia nodded, and Vincent paused, frowning. "But if you continue, and are successful, it could turn out to be pretty dangerous for you. Is that right?"

"Yes."

"Well, then. I don't want you to continue."

"What?"

"I'm not putting you in danger because of this. That's out of the question."

"But, Vincent, how else will you find your way home?"

He sighed, then put aside his unfinished breakfast. "Rhia, I don't think I've seriously believed in the possibility of returning home since my first year here. And the longer I stay, the more I wonder if returning home is a great idea, anyway. I've been away for years. My family has most likely given me up for dead and gone on with their lives. Well, so be it. I've made a good home for myself here. I'm pretty happy. I have great friends, including you. And I'm very much in love with the girl next-door, so to speak." Vincent felt a pang in his chest as he spoke. The words were true, but he couldn't deny his fondness for Rhia. He firmed his resolution. He *had* to deny it.

"So you are content to make this world your home?"

"I believe I am, yes. So, I think we can consider your job complete. Blade hired you to help me. I'm canceling the contract."

"I see," she said softly.

Vincent frowned. "Is there a problem with that?"

"No. No problem. I've just invested a lot of time into it. That's all."

"Oh. I'm sorry. Well, what figure did Blade quote you? I'll double it. How's that?"

Rhia glared at him. "I don't need or want your money, Vincent," she said coldly.

"Okay," he said cautiously. "What do you want, then?" In reply, she merely looked at him. A hint of sadness was in her eyes, but Vincent didn't know what to make of it. "I'm sorry, Rhia. I am grateful for all you've done. You must know that."

She nodded, averting her gaze. "Yes, I know you are. Are you not aware, though, that what I did, I did for you? Not for money. For you."

Vincent smiled. "That's sweet. Thank you."

Rhia sighed, then picked up her bowl and carried it to the kitchen area. She emptied the remaining cereal into a trash bin, then rinsed the bowl in the sink. Vincent followed her and placed his hand on her shoulder. She stiffened. "I'm not blind, anymore," he said. "Something's wrong. What is it?"

She turned, then, and he saw the dampness in her eyes. He began to say something, only to have her grasp his face in her hands and kiss him deeply. He was too shocked to pull away quickly. But shortly, his brain reminded him of Ariaziane, and he broke from the kiss, angry with himself for having enjoyed it so much. His lips were tingling as he tried to speak.

"Rhia," he began. "I can't."

"I know," she said flatly. "You don't have to say it. You've said it often enough in the past."

"I'm sorry."

"So am I." She headed for the door. "I wish you the best, but I must be going, now."

"Wait," he said, hurrying behind her. "Please stay." The request came without conscious thought. And he regretted it as soon as he'd said it. It would be best if she left.

"I can't," she said. "I have pressing business elsewhere. This was just a stop along the way." She opened the door. "Take care of yourself."

"When will I see you again?" he asked, somewhat guilty to be happy she was leaving.

Rhia looked at him, a shadow falling across her face. "Hard to say," she said. And then she was out the door and walking across the lawn.

Sometimes I think I must be an idiot. It's obvious, now that I sit down and think about it, that Rhia has some sort of crush on me. And that's very flattering. I'd thought she only wanted sex. It never occurred to me that she could have been after something more serious than that. She certainly never implied anything of the sort.

I feel terrible about the whole thing, naturally. But it's a bit late to change anything, unless she should happen to show up again in the immediate future.

Things have been slow, but enjoyable, lately. I'm still trying to get over my new title. Baron Vincent. Unreal. At least I don't have to hear it much, living out in the boonies like this. Except from Aedriun, who constantly uses it, to annoy me.

We've had a lot of rain this month. Annie and I have gotten caught in more than a couple showers while out riding. Unfortunately, this has resulted in me getting a nice case of the sniffles, and her getting downright sick. She's been pretty miserable the past few days. I'll be heading over to visit her shortly. I made her some soup. She'll be better in a few days.

I wish I could feel that were true about Rhia.

Vincent carried a bowl of hot soup to Ariaziane, who was lying on the sofa, a wet rag over her forehead. Vincent frowned, wishing he could remember more herbs Rhia had told him were useful in reducing fever. He'd gathered some withy, the one he did recall, but it hadn't been helping. And it wasn't useful in easing the body aches and pains that she was going through. He sat beside her and handed her the bowl and spoon. What he wouldn't give for some good old twentieth century, over-the-counter, cold medication to give her.

Ariaziane thanked him, and sipped at some of the broth. She ate for a few minutes in silence, then stopped. She thrust the bowl at Vincent, leaped off the sofa, and rushed outside. Vincent heard the unmistakable retching of regurgitation.

When she returned, still holding a hand over her stomach, he wrapped his arms around her and held her close. She leaned into his embrace and nuzzled her face against his chest. "Guess we shouldn't go riding in the rain like that, huh?"

In response, she looked up at him, her brow knit. "You think that is what made me sick?" she said incredulously.

"I think it's what made *me* a little ill. I just assumed it hit you worse."

She opened her mouth to reply, then her eyes widened and she gasped. Vincent could almost feel the pain as it shot through her. She turned and ran outside again.

Vincent decided to summon a healer. He'd head into town right away and be back inside of three hours. When she returned, he told her this.

"No," she said.

"Annie," he pleaded. "You're sick and you need a healer!"

The girl flinched, raising a hand to her head. "Not so loud," she whispered. She returned to the sofa and sat. "Please. No healer."

Vincent frowned. Yes, she was sick. But since it didn't seem life-threatening, he nodded. He didn't like it, but he agreed. "No healer."

"Thank you." She leaned back into the upholstery. "If you don't mind, I'd like to be alone."

The request took him by surprise. But after getting over the shock, he agreed. "All right," he said. "But I'm going to check on you again before the end of the day."

The girl nodded weakly, her eyes closed. She curled up on the sofa and fell asleep before Vincent was out the door.

She was still asleep on the sofa when Vincent returned, shortly before nightfall. He imagined how stiff her neck was likely to be in the morning if she stayed there all night. He quietly moved to her side and worked his arms under her body. Carefully, he lifted her.

He expected her to waken, but she merely rolled her body closer to his chest. Vincent carried her to her bedroom and tucked her in. She groaned a little as he did so.

He went to the kitchen and returned with a cup of water. He placed it on the stand beside her bed. He lit the small oil lamp that sat there. Then he pulled over the small chair from her vanity table and sat. What a way to spend a night, he thought. It reminded him of another night that he'd sat with Ariaziane. The night that she'd gone through her transformation of hair and eye color.

What a night that had been, he thought. He was glad she wasn't in as much agony now as she was then. He thought back to that night, remembered her tossing and turning in bed. Screaming. He shook his head to break away from the thoughts. It had been awful. He'd been frightened for her, having never seen someone in so much obvious pain.

Ariaziane groaned again in her sleep and rolled over. Vincent sighed. Then he took the lamp and left the room. He deposited it just inside the front door and walked outside. The sun was setting, now. He reclined in one of the wooden chairs in front of her house and waited for the stars to begin appearing.

Hours later, he woke. The crescent moon was low over the water. Vincent frowned, annoyed that he'd nodded off. He went indoors, retrieving the lamp, and stepped quietly into the bedroom.

Ariaziane was still asleep, still in the same position as when he'd left. He placed the lamp back on the stand and returned to the small chair. And he watched her, feeling his heart throb with caring for her. He listened to her breathing. It was steady and rhythmic. She seemed to be sleeping comfortably. Perhaps she'd been right. There was no need for a healer.

After some time with no change, Vincent retired to the front room, where he made his bed on the sofa.

He awoke in the middle of the night from the touch of a hand in his hair. He dragged his eyelids open, but they didn't want to stay that way. As they drooped again, he realized Ariaziane was kneeling beside the sofa. She was running her hand through his long hair. It felt nice. "How you feel?" he whispered.

"Better," she whispered back. "Go back to sleep."

He had no problem with that idea. He smiled at her touch and settled in again. He thought he felt the caress of her lips on his cheek as he spiraled back into sleep.

In the morning, he woke to the light of the sun striking him in the face. He immediately regretted having windows in the eastern walls of the house. Blinking against the glare, he saw Ariaziane sitting in the armchair by the door. He smiled, sitting up and wiping the sleep from his eyes. "Morning," he yawned.

"Aye," she said slowly. "It is."

Vincent raised an eyebrow at the strange tone in her voice. He blinked the last of the weariness away and looked at her. And felt his heart sink. "Annie," he began.

"I know," she said.

Vincent moved to her, kneeling in front of her. He reached a hand toward her face. She gritted her teeth and let him proceed.

Her hair was red. Not the orange-red of Rhia's, but a deep, intense red. And her eyes were a deep, intense blue, like sapphires. He studied her face, but saw no emotions to speak of. "I feel quite well, if that's what you were about to ask."

"Just like last time," he whispered.

"Yes."

He frowned. "You knew, didn't you? You knew this was the cause of the sickness all along."

She turned her gaze downward. "I suspected. I suppose I did know all along, but kept hoping I was wrong." She laughed humorlessly. "No such luck."

Vincent squeezed her hand in his, and then suddenly she was crying. Tears dripped from her blue eyes and fell on his hand as she rocked forward. "What is happening to me?" she moaned. Then she was in Vincent's arms, squeezing him tightly.

They spent the rest of the day together. When they talked at all, their topic never varied. They tried to think of different things that could cause such a transformation in her. But all their ideas sounded ridiculous to their ears.

They talked in her house, in her front yard, on the beach, and at Vincent's house. Vincent continually assured her that everything would be fine. The changes did not seem to do her any harm. But that didn't seem to make her feel any better. And he couldn't blame her for that. He wouldn't have felt any better, either.

When they weren't talking, Vincent was usually staring at Ariaziane, who would be so wrapped up in her own thoughts that she paid little attention to him. Or to anything.

They stayed up very late that night, sitting on the beach and watching the waves in silence. It seemed to Vincent that she didn't want to go to sleep again. As if she expected something else, something more terrible, to happen should she do so.

But finally, exhaustion overtook both of them. "Do you want me to stay with you tonight?" Vincent asked as they walked back in from the beach.

She shook her head. "No. Thank you, but no."

Vincent walked her to her door and stood with her outside. "Well. Goodnight, then." She smiled in response. He held her close, his lips close to her ears. He inhaled the scent of her hair. Then he kissed her on the forehead and headed toward his own home.

❧ ❦

It was early morning when Vincent heard the light rapping on his door. He sat up in bed, wiping sleep from his eyes, and glanced out the window at the sky. *Very* early, he thought, with a hint of distaste. He threw back the blankets and rose, grabbing his robe from a hook on the wall. He shrugged into it as he approached his front door.

Ariaziane stood on his doorstep. The sight of her shocked him awake, remembering that she'd undergone another transformation. He wasn't yet used to her new appearance, though she was still lovely as ever. Vincent noticed a troubled look in her eyes. He also noticed her horse tied to the tree out front. It was loaded as though for a journey. A knot grew in his stomach. She smiled politely as she stepped inside.

"I'm sorry for the early hour."

Vincent cleared his throat. "No problem. I was awake, anyway."

"Liar." She smiled faintly.

"Sometimes," he said as they both sat. "So," he said, the knot growing harder and forming a twin at the back of his throat. "What's up?"

Ariaziane averted her gaze, a furrow between her brows. Her words came slowly, as though each were chosen carefully before being uttered. "I've been doing a lot of thinking. In fact, I was up all night. And I've decided I need to find out some things. Things about myself." She didn't have to explain. Vincent knew full well how disturbed she was. Her red hair hid her deep blue eyes from his view. But he knew the questions they were asking. The knots quickly faded.

"Say no more. You're right. There are a lot of unanswered questions about you. I'd want to know, myself, if I were in your position. It'll take a lot of work, but..."

She finished the sentence for him, looking him in the eye. "But I can't choose not to do it."

"Exactly. And you needn't be shy in asking my help. I'll be glad to."

"I'm sorry." Her voice froze him. He looked to see her hiding her eyes again. And the knots exploded back into existence. "I knew I wouldn't be able to say it right."

His voice was a whisper. "You're going alone." Ariaziane paused for a moment, then nodded her head, still avoiding his gaze. "Annie, this could take, I don't know, months!"

She looked at him now, her bright blue eyes shiny with tears. "Or years."

The words hit him like an ogre's hammer. *Years.* The concept was too overwhelming to fathom. Years without his love. Without the most beautiful girl in existence. Without the one thing that made his life on this alien world at all acceptable, even desirable. Without the object of all his purpose. Without his hope. Without his Annie.

The only word he could manage to squeeze out was, "Why?"

"It's something I have to do."

"I know, but why alone? Why for so long, alone?"

"I asked you a similar question once. You went traipsing off on some ill-defined quest without companionship, without even knowing what you were after. At least I have a clear goal."

"So that's what this is all about? You're getting back at me for that?"

"No! That's not what I meant!"

"Then why did you bring it up?"

The girl sighed. "I didn't think you'd understand. I'm sorry."

"I understand the purpose, but not the method! Annie, come on! You're talking about a hell of a long time, here! And it could be dangerous! You'll need me!"

"I do need you. But not in the sense of protecting me. I can take care of myself. I need to do this alone, face it alone. Your presence could easily be a distraction."

He collapsed back on the sofa, eyes shut. "Distraction." He shook his head. "I thought I'd grown to be more than that."

"I'm sorry."

"Annie, I *love* you!"

"I know!" She turned her head away, hiding the tears. "I know. You don't think this is easy for me, do you? You think I want to be doing this to you?"

"Then why are you?"

"I have to! You don't understand."

"Where are you going to start? I mean, what do you know? Nothing! This is so aimless!"

Ariaziane shook her head. "Not entirely. There are some things I do know. Things that Sister Haleen told me about my parents."

Vincent waited for her to volunteer the information. When she didn't, he sighed. "And you're not going to tell me, because you don't want me coming after you." Her silence told him he was right. He rubbed his forehead and sighed again. "Couldn't you have at least discussed it with me beforehand?"

She ran her hand through her hair. "I'm sorry. It didn't really occur to me."

Vincent gave a pained little chuckle. "Distraction. Didn't occur to you. Next you'll be telling me that I'm not that important to you. Or maybe that's what you've been saying all along and I just haven't picked up on it."

Her voice was quiet in its pain. "That's not fair."

"Isn't it? Well, neither is what you're doing."

"How could you not think you are important to me? You're my best friend. You've given me so much of yourself, shown me so many things that were always there in front of me, and I couldn't see them. I don't know if it's because you're from another world, or just because you're an incredibly special person, or both, but I can never hope to repay all that you've done for me. I love being with you. I love doing things with you. But I can't do this with you. I'm sorry, Vincent. I just can't. Please try to understand."

Vincent stood and walked slowly to the window, tightening the belt of his robe. He stared outside for a moment. "In all that you said just now, I didn't really hear you say, or even imply, that you loved me. Just what I've done for you."

"Do you really need to question that?"

"I dunno. I mean, I don't really recall you ever having said it. Not as anything more than a friend, anyway. Not one time in over three years of knowing you. So I don't really know what to think. In fact, at this point, I'm not sure I really want to know, considering I might never see you again."

"Of course you'll see me again!"

"Really? I didn't know Gnorrin taught you how to see the future."

"You know what I mean. Someday we'll be together."

"Thank you, Diana Ross," Vincent muttered.

"What?"

He didn't explain, merely stared outside again, his eyes wandering over the packs mounted on her horse. He couldn't think of anything else to say. And he knew it wouldn't matter what he did say. "I want to go with you."

"I know. But you can't."

"You mean, you don't want me to."

She sighed. And Vincent didn't know whether it was frustration, guilt, sadness, or some of each. "What I do want, right now," she said, "is for you to try to understand. I don't want you to resent me. I want to spend the remainder of the morning with you. I'd like you to take me to the docks. Because I'd like yours to be the last face I see before I'm on my way."

"Why, so you can see me cry?"

"No." She paused. "So I can have an image of you in my mind to carry with me. To give me strength to continue. Knowing you love me gives me that strength."

Vincent shook his head and chuckled again. "My weakness gives you strength. That's a good one." He was quiet for a long time, the knot in his throat threatening to burst it open. Finally, he turned and said, "You're *my* strength, Annie. You're the only reason I'm still here."

She shook her head bewilderingly. "What do you mean? You found a way back to Earth? And you didn't tell me?"

He turned his gaze to the floor. "That's not exactly what I meant."

She stared at him, then her eyes slowly widened. "No. You wouldn't do that. You're not a quitter."

"No, not anymore. But I was a big time quitter on Earth. If things weren't going my way, I'd quit. It was easy. No harm was done. Quit Cub Scouts because it was boring. Quit Little League because they wouldn't let me pitch. My first semester at college was going pretty shitty. I planned on quitting that, too." He shrugged. "I never had drive, Annie. I never had something there to propel me forward, not until I met you. Not until I realized that the one thing I wanted more than anything else was to be with you for the rest of my life, loving you, being loved by you. Being married to you."

Ariaziane's jaw dropped slightly at that. Vincent wasn't surprised. He'd never felt she really believed him when he said he loved her. And now he'd said it in a way she couldn't possibly misunderstand. And she was shocked. He watched as she turned her gaze to stare, unfocused, at the floor. He wanted to hold her, to beg her to marry him, to take him with her on her quest. But he didn't. For he saw the change in her expression. Her eyes closed and her lips pursed, as if she were trying to contain an outburst. Then she said simply, "Don't do this to me."

And Vincent, too, turned his eyes to the floor. He knew it was useless. Nothing he could say would help, if that last statement didn't. The silence that followed was long. Vincent felt the burning behind his eyelids, but he held back the flow. The knot in his stomach made him want to throw up, but he wouldn't allow that, either. He avoided looking at Ariaziane. Instead, he stood staring out the window, not really looking at anything. He had no idea how much time had passed before he felt her hand on his shoulder.

It startled him, but he turned slowly. The pain in her eyes didn't help any. Before he knew it, they were embracing, her face buried in his neck. Her words were soft, spoken hoarsely. "I love you."

And then the tears came, trickling from his closed eyes and down his cheeks, finally soaking into his beard. He held her tightly, as if the contact would change her mind and she would feel bound to him, unable to leave. But after a few minutes, she looked up at him, sniffling, and said, "Will you?"

Vincent took a deep breath. "Will I what?"

"Take me to the docks? Spend a few hours with me before I sail?"

He fought back the urge to decline. He knew he would agree, no matter how much it hurt. Slowly, he nodded his head. Then he gently disengaged. "Let me go get presentable." He turned away, wiping the tears from his face, and moved off toward his room.

During the first half of their journey, Vincent was sullen and Ariaziane didn't pressure him to open up. He knew it was obvious to her what was going through his mind. But eventually, when his silence did not cease, she broke it.

She cleared her throat, casting a sidelong smile at him as he glanced in her direction. She brushed a lock of red hair from her eye, smoothing it behind her ear. "Do you remember the first day we met?"

Vincent snorted. "As if I could forget it."

"You were really a clumsy one."

He shook his head. "I know you're trying to take my mind off all this. But I don't think this is the proper way to do it."

Ariaziane frowned. "Then what is? I didn't ask you along to see me off because I wanted to watch you be depressed."

"Sorry. Can't help it."

"I do not want your last memories of me until my return to be morose."

"What do want me to do? Cartwheels? I can't pretend this doesn't feel like you're ripping my heart out." Vincent stopped, his voice catching in his throat. He turned away from her, trying to hide the tears that threatened to fall.

Ariaziane let out a long breath. "I should have known you'd be like this," she said. She glanced at him again, then kicked her horse to a gallop and took off across the open meadow that bordered the road. "Ride with me, Vincent!" she yelled behind her.

Vincent blinked his eyes against the tears. Ride with her, he thought. Why was she tormenting him? He loved to ride with her. Doing so now was only going to make him miss her more. He shook his head in reply to her request, even though he knew she wasn't looking, and kept up his deliberate pace on the road.

He watched her, though, as she galloped across the field. Her red hair flew in waves behind her. How he wanted to run his fingers through that mane. How he wanted to hold her to him so tightly that she'd never even want to go.

He wasn't sure how long his reverie lasted, but when his eyes unglazed from their faraway stare, Ariaziane was no longer flying across the grasses. Instead, her horse was tied to one of the huge trees in the middle of the meadow. She had made herself comfortable underneath, munching on a piece of fruit from the tree.

As he neared the point on the road closest to the tree, Vincent slowed, then came to a halt. He sat there, absently stroking his horse's neck, staring at her. Then he sighed and moved his mount off the road and toward the tree. He dismounted in silence, tying his horse beside hers. Then he rubbed his rear end to relieve the soreness from riding, and sat down beside her.

She smiled at him, reaching over with the fruit for him to take a bite. He politely nibbled, chewing thoughtfully as she took another bite. He noticed her staring at him as he swallowed. "What?" he asked.

She moved closer to him. "You have some juice on your mustache." Before he could react, her mouth was on him, her warm lips pressing against his, her tongue seeking entrance. He allowed its passage, leaning into her kiss as if his life depended on it. And perhaps, he thought, it did.

It was a kiss right out of a romance novel. At least, a kiss like Vincent would have expected to be in one. It left him gasping for breath, happily so. When he finally caught it, he said, "You don't have any idea how long I've waited for that."

Ariaziane simply pulled him closer. "Love me," she said.

He froze. Ariaziane looked at him with a puzzled expression. His words were slow and quiet. "And you don't have any idea how much I've longed to hear you say that." He paused, looking at her with pain in his eyes. "But I can't. Not now. Not under these circumstances."

"Why?"

"Because it's not how it should be. I don't want you doing it out of pity for me. Because you know how I feel and you don't want me to. That's not the way to make me feel better. Neither was that kiss, now that I think about it."

Ariaziane pulled her legs up, folding her arms around her knees, burying her face against them. Her voice was pained. "What do you want from me?" she whispered.

He looked at her for a long moment, thinking that it should be obvious what he wanted. Slowly, he told her. "Everything," he said. "I want your life, shared with mine. I want your soul to be a reflection of my own. I want all you have to offer, and I will give you nothing less in return." He watched as his words hit her, and she flinched with each image. He stopped, chastising himself. It was a moment before he continued. "But," he began, "you're not ready to give me that, yet. So for now, what I want is to lie here under this beautiful tree, holding you in my arms, just feeling you next to me. One last time."

This time it was her turn to try to hold back a tear. She gave up, and it trickled down a cheek. Her arms extended, and Vincent accepted the invitation.

The ride to Linnael from that point on was mostly spent in silence, their horses walking beside each other, closely enough for Vincent and Ariaziane to hold hands. What little talk they shared was mostly of an apologetic nature. On both their parts.

When they finally reached the port town, Vincent felt the knot renew in his stomach. But he tried to ignore it. He knew she needed him to be strong right now. Or at least appear so. So he went along with her as she went to the inn where the departures of ships could be learned. And when he heard that she could be on a ship heading north within the hour, he felt his teeth grind together, his eyes burn.

The time until her boarding was spent walking together along the beach not far from the docks. The moist air smelled of fish and rotting seaweed. It didn't help his stomach any. They held hands the entire time, and Vincent knew how hard it was going to be to let go.

But the time came all too soon. Standing before the boarding plank, they embraced. He couldn't help it; he squeezed her with all his strength. The knot was in his throat now, and around it he croaked, "I love you."

He felt her own hug tighten on him. Then she drew back a bit, so as to look into his eyes. "I know you do. And I'll be thinking of that a lot. Believe me. I will come back to you. I love you, too." She took a deep breath. "How could I not?"

The embrace lasted another minute, then the final call came from the ship and she had to go. He knew it. But the ending of the hug left him standing weak on the dock. She squeezed his hand and smiled before leading her horse up the plank to board the ship.

And he stood there for many minutes, watching as the ship pulled out from the dock. Ariaziane stood on the deck, and he stared at her. He stared until her form was too small to distinguish. And kept staring even after that.

☜ ☞

Darella knew she shouldn't have been surprised by the turn of events. But then, this was the first time she'd raised two children in such a closed environment.

The children weren't yet four years old, but their bodies were those of fifteen year-olds. It was only natural that their libidos would assert their dominance over their brains.

But still... It could be inconvenient, the daughter being pregnant. She thought briefly about aborting the child. Easy enough to do with the right herbs. But there were other factors to think about.

Her daughter would likely become attached to the child she was carrying. Darella herself had become attached to her first few. And if she would rob her daughter of that bond, it could only serve to drive a further wedge between the two of them.

This was something she wished to avoid. Already, she detected the signs of discontent in the girl. Aborting the baby would most likely fill the daughter with hatred, and that hatred would be aimed at Darella herself. And that was not what she wanted.

332

Then there was the possibility that the child of her own two offspring could turn out to be an even more interesting experiment, but aging was an issue. Would the child age as a normal human, or would it age at quadruple the normal rate, as her children were doing? Or would it go to extremes? Age more slowly than the alien sire of the twins, or age even more rapidly than the twins themselves? It was difficult enough educating the two of them right now. A third would be a burden.

Only time would tell. And then she would decide what to do with it.

❧ Twenty-Four ❧

Vincent sat under a large oak-like tree atop a knoll not far from his home. With him were his guitar and his tape player. And his depression. He sat with his back to the sea. It was too much of a reminder of where his love had gone. It had been three months since Ariaziane had sailed out of his life. Three months of wallowing in his heartache.

He picked idly at the strings of his guitar, not really intent on playing anything. Random chords issued forth, all sounding minor to his ear.

He had stumbled into this world and fallen into the company of a group of people as good as he could have hoped for. Blade had departed a year later. Then he and Ariaziane had moved, leaving Gnorrin. And now she was gone. Naturally, he'd thought about rejoining Gnorrin, but sensed it wasn't the right thing to do.

Aedriun had been a great support. Vincent spent a lot of time with him in Linnael. But those times were, at best, only temporary distractions. Everything, really, seemed to be only a temporary distraction. Whether it was visiting Aedriun and Darvas, or traveling to see Gnorrin, or going for hikes in the woods with Blaise, all were somewhat empty.

With a sigh, he slipped his headphones on and hit the 'play' button on the tape deck. He cradled the guitar in his arms like the friend it was, listening to the beginning of the next song on the cassette. Then he settled his guitar and began to play along with the music.

His fingers slid with practiced ease up and down the neck. He played along with intimate familiarity, but his heart just wasn't in it. After a minute or so, he stopped, lowering the guitar gently to the ground. After another few minutes, he turned off the music entirely and removed the headphones.

Vincent shifted around the tree, turning his gaze to the sea. He replayed for the hundredth time the last day he'd spent with Ariaziane, the conversation they'd had. He remembered her confusion, laced with the conviction that this was something she simply had to do. He wondered exactly what she hoped to find on this trip of hers.

What did she really think she was going to get out of it? Would it turn out to be worth all the sacrifices she was bound to be making? He shook his head, then strapped his guitar over his shoulder and began walking home. A whistle brought Blaise from her foray into the brush and she fell into step beside him.

Maybe the limited information she had about her heritage really did bother her enough to go off as she did, but he couldn't picture someone being that driven by such a simple thing. Then again, he wasn't the one who had his hair and eyes turn different colors.

As he walked, he looked down at Blaise. Must be nice, he thought, to live a dog's life. All the human worries would be meaningless. Yes, the rational part of his brain said, but all the glories of human life would be meaningless, too.

He sighed as he made his way down the hill toward his home. It was getting late, he realized. How much time had he spent under the tree? Too much, he thought. Too much time spent doing nothing. But then, he really had no desire to do anything.

Progress on his keep was going well, according to Feletain's report, received a week ago by courier. But he felt no pleasure in that. No excitement. He frowned, berating himself. She'll come back, he told himself. Someday.

He saw his house now, in the distance, and the smoke rising from the chimney. It was early in the Season of Sleep now. Though there was no snow, the nights got pretty chilly. For that matter, the days had been none too warm, either. He pulled his cloak tighter around himself.

The cloak had been a gift from Ariaziane. The stylized "V" cloak pin was in place, too. More reminders of her. He wore another decoration on the cloak. This one reminded him of Rhia, however. It was a sachet of devil's bit. A leftover from his time spent with Jaz. He pressed the small bag to his nose and took a deep breath. The pungent odor had lessened with age, but was still unmistakable. He'd taken to sleeping with one tucked inside his pillow case, too. He hoped to be able to contact Ariaziane, but had yet to get the feeling that he'd succeeded.

Rhia was present at the back of his mind more often than not, lately. And, as he had before, he felt guilty about thinking of her rather than Ariaziane. She was a mystery. Distant, yet approachable. Intimate, yet alien. There was a time when he would have found this dichotomy to be irresistible. But not now. His mind was in too much turmoil, his heart in too much agony.

Even his dreams, lately, had become haunted with images of Rhia. This had begun weeks ago. He wished he could stop dreaming of her. It only increased his feelings of guilt. Especially since some of the dreams were rather vivid. Replays of their encounters together. Encounters with a decided lack of clothing. And in the dreams, things seemed to go somewhat differently.

He frowned, remembering their last encounter, just before Ariaziane's departure. He shook his head. It was bizarre, he thought with little amusement, how time could fly and drag at the same time. The time since seeing Rhia seemed short, while the time since seeing Ariaziane seemed an eternity.

Similarities between the two last encounters occurred to him. He'd thought a lot about Rhia's last visit afterwards. He felt so stupid. Rhia obviously cared for him a lot. And he'd shunned her. He probably would never see her again, either.

Nearing his house, he glanced again at the smoke that curled skyward from his chimney. It reminded him that he needed more wood. He'd used all but a few logs last night, and...

He stopped in his tracks.

He hadn't *built* a fire before going out today!

Blaise turned to look at him, stopping her progression to wait for him. Hope pushed aside the anxiety in his mind. "Annie?" he whispered. Swinging the guitar around to firmly grasp it by the neck, he ran toward his house.

Blaise kept pace, barking and wagging her tail. They reached the house, and while the dog went to the front yard to begin sniffing around, Vincent headed straight for the door. He stopped short, trying to slow his racing heart. He gently opened the door and stepped inside. Lying on his sofa, bare feet pointed toward the fireplace, was Rhia.

Stunned, he stood there in the open doorway, staring at her. She was asleep. Propping his guitar against the wall, he quietly closed the door. A riot of emotions tore at him. He was pleased, naturally, to see her, but curious to know why she'd come. He felt terrible about the way they'd parted the last time. And yet, there was the confusion still about how he felt toward her.

He moved slowly to her side and knelt by the sofa. He stroked her hair, remembering the good times they'd shared, and hoping that her presence here meant that she didn't hold his callousness against him.

She woke, then, opening her eyes slowly. She smiled and stifled a yawn. "Sorry," she said. "I needed a nap."

Vincent smiled back. "What are you doing here?" he whispered.

She sat up slowly. "Well," she drawled, "it might have something to do with you summoning me."

"What do you mean? I haven't summoned you."

"No? Then what would you call it? I have been receiving thought-images from you for weeks, now. Rather graphic ones, I must say." She smiled playfully and lightly traced a finger over his thigh. "Changed your mind?"

He felt the blood rush hotly to his cheeks. He turned his gaze away. "I didn't mean for you to get that. They're just dreams I've had."

She chuckled. "I like your dreams."

"I'm sorry," he said. "I didn't summon you. I didn't do anything." His voice sounded hollow even to his own ears. "I'm sorry if you've come a long way, but it wasn't necessary."

Rhia frowned, leaning back into the sofa. "So what is bothering you?"

Vincent took a deep breath, rubbing at his forehead. He sat down at the other end of the couch, turning to face her. And then he told her everything. He told her about Ariaziane's bizarre transformation three years ago. And of the second one that caused her to make the decision to leave.

Throughout it all, Rhia listened intently, with what Vincent knew to be genuine sympathy. This impressed him, since he knew she was a little jealous of Ariaziane. That Rhia could be so understanding made him all the more fond of her.

"So are you going to go after her?" Rhia asked when he finished.

"No. She doesn't want me to, and I respect her wishes. I don't like them, but I'll abide by them."

"That has to be difficult."

Vincent said nothing, merely stared into her sympathetic eyes. The caring he saw there felt like a kick in the gut. He looked away and quickly changed the subject. "So what have you been up to since I saw you last?"

Now it was Rhia's turn to avert her gaze. "Oh, a little of this, a little of that. Traveling. Visiting some friends here and there."

Vincent pondered that. "You know, I'd like to see Blade again. It's been ages."

Rhia nodded slowly. "Friends are good things to have. And travel might do you some good. Help you to get your mind off the situation."

"Maybe," he said. "The thing is... I'm not entirely sure I *want* to get my mind off the situation."

There was a long silence, broken finally by Rhia. "The last time we spoke, you told me you thought it was highly unlikely that you'd ever find your way home again." Vincent nodded his agreement. "I'm curious as to what you think the likelihood is that you'll see her again."

Vincent fought a growing tightness in his throat. "I've been thinking about that a lot, lately."

"And?"

He looked her in the eye again. "Probably not much more likely than me getting home."

Rhia absorbed this. "Then, does that mean that you've changed your mind about wanting to stay here? Do you want to go home?" Vincent stared at her without responding. "I told you before that I was closing in on Darella, and therefore on the Seeker Portal. Do you want me to resume the search?"

Vincent raised an eyebrow. Strange, he thought, how that idea had never really struck him in the months since Ariaziane's departure. He thought about it now, mulling it over in his mind. And then he looked at Rhia. She was avoiding his gaze. He saw a strange sort of anxiety on her face. And the answer that he'd been ready to give suddenly became less of a certainty. He swallowed past the lump in his throat, reaching out to grasp her hand. "No," he whispered.

She looked up into his eyes, relief and hopefulness showing clearly to Vincent. "No?"

He shook his head. "No. I still don't want you to put yourself at risk."

Rhia shrugged slightly. "I don't mind. If it's what you want, I'd do it."

Vincent looked at her, sighing. He had to address the issue before she made it into more than it could be. "Rhia," he began slowly, "I'm really flattered that you seem to have a crush on me."

"A what?"

"A crush. An infatuation."

"Oh."

He paused, waiting for her to deny it. She didn't. "Is that what you're feeling?"

She smiled faintly, still not meeting his eyes. "I suppose you could call it that."

Vincent cleared his throat nervously. "I see. Well, as I said, it's flattering. But I can't reciprocate it. I'm just not ready. Can you understand that?"

Rhia was silent for a time, then she said, "I hear you." She squeezed his hand. "Would you mind if I stayed here tonight? I'll be on my way first thing in the morning."

"Do you really have to be going tomorrow?"

"Why?"

"Because it would be nice to have someone with me. I enjoy spending time with you, and it would make me feel better if I had some company for a while. Can you stay for a while?"

Rhia smiled quickly, then gave a pretend sulk. "Let me guess. Separate beds?" Vincent merely raised an eyebrow at her question, causing Rhia to laugh. "How long did you have in mind?" she asked.

"How long can you stay?"

She smiled again and stretched, catlike. Then she cuddled up next to him. "Until you're tired of me."

❦ ❦

For the life of me, I'm still not sure why I asked Rhia to stay with me. I guess I'm lonelier than I thought. Or maybe I missed her more than I thought. Or maybe I'm looking for a substitute for Annie.

Or maybe a little of each. I haven't a clue.

At any rate, now I can make use of my spare bedroom. I'd had Aedriun set up the spare for those times when Gnorrin comes to visit. Glad I thought to do that. Of course, Gnorrin hasn't come visiting yet.

Anyway, we had a nice day together. She made dinner for the two of us. She's amazing at finding delicious herbs anywhere she goes, it seems. We had fish seasoned with something that looked like little red threads. It was spicy and sweet at the same time.

Later, we went on a moonlit stroll down the beach. Barefoot. I thought for sure we'd get frostbite walking in wet sand for a couple miles. When we got back, we sat in front of the fire and warmed our toes.

We didn't talk much, really. Funny thing is, we didn't mind. It was like the togetherness itself was enough. We didn't need dialogue. Not that I've never experienced friendship like this before, but I wasn't expecting this kind of a turn in our relationship to happen so quickly.

I've been thinking a lot about it. It's like I've shared something very personal with her, meaning the whole situation with Ariaziane, and it has led to a deeper connection between us. She hasn't shared anything like that with me, so it surprises me that this sort of empathy has developed.

Not that I'm complaining. It's nice to have her around. I've always liked being with her. And I think her presence here might be just the ticket I need to get me out of my depression.

She tried again to seduce me before going to bed tonight, but didn't put much effort into it. She knows how I feel about it and that I'd turn her down again. She'd expect that, I'm sure. It's likely to become a game between us. And that's okay. I honestly don't mind. Because as long as she knows I'm not going to take it seriously, that takes the pressure off me.

Now, let's hope she continues to view it that way.

The birth, when it came, was more than Darella's daughter could take. Darella wasn't surprised. The girl looked sixteen, but she was only four. When the baby slipped out of the girl, the new mother promptly passed out from the exertion.

Time was of the essence, now. Darella hurriedly severed the umbilical cord, then carried the dripping infant to another chamber in the cave, where her son waited.

The infant had come to term in roughly the same amount of time as the twins themselves had. This told Darella that the child would be no different than her children, not likely to be of additional interest to her. Indeed, it would pose a tremendous problem from an education standpoint. However, the infant could still serve good purpose. Though not a magick traditionally used by witches, there were certain rites that could increase her abilities. Darella had never been one for tradition. This had, she recalled with some amusement, created many uncomfortable situations for her in the past, to say the least.

She handed the baby to her son, who caught the child in a clean piece of cloth. As he wiped the birth liquids from the baby's body, Darella prepared the table and thought of other times.

There was a time, many decades ago, when she was cast out of a coven for engaging in certain rites that most witches found abhorrent. Rhia had been there. Rhia, who had evidently become friends with the alien father of her current offspring. Rhia, who was, even now, probing to find Darella's own whereabouts.

Darella quickly spread a black cloth over a small wooden table that her son had made. In the center of the table, she placed a silver bowl. Her son joined her, then, with the infant now much more presentable. The boy held the baby upside down over the bowl, causing the infant to cry.

She held the top of the baby's head in her left palm, cradling it. Tilting its tiny head backward, she mumbled a few phrases under her breath, then drew her knife. Quickly, Darella sliced the baby's throat. The infant's scream quickly faded.

Her son held the baby so the blood flowed into the bowl. It took many minutes before the last of it had dripped out. Then Darella removed the bowl, setting it aside. She wrapped the corpse in the black cloth from the table, then her son took it outside for a quick burial.

The blood would be used later, in rituals that would have revolted virtually every fellow witch she'd known over the years. She smiled, feeling the energy stored in the bowl of blood. It would be very, very useful.

In the other chamber, her daughter lay sucking in deep gulps of air. She had awakened when the baby started crying, and had forced herself to move when she heard the child scream. She'd staggered to the entrance to the other chamber in time to see the blood dripping. Then she'd fallen back to her fur on the floor, stunned.

When her mother returned several minutes later, she'd pretended to still be unconscious. And when she'd come to, a few minutes later, she'd inquired of the baby. And when her mother told her that the child had not survived the birth, and that she and her brother had buried it quickly so as to save the poor girl any extra heartache, she'd pretended to believe her.

For now.

Book Four

Land Ho

❧ Twenty-Five ❧

The Season of Green grew greener and Vincent's spirits grew brighter. Rhia's presence prevented him from maintaining a steady state of depression. She just made him feel too good for that. She would never let him be morose for long, encouraging him to enjoy what was, rather than what wasn't. And he appreciated that. He reflected often on the history the two of them had shared, on and off, since his arrival in this world, and concluded easily that Rhia was a very special person. He cared for her more than he'd realized.

It wasn't always easy, however. There were times when his chest would ache with sudden stabs of longing. Rhia took his horse for a ride down the beach once. And the sight reminded him so much of watching Ariaziane do the same that he nearly wept.

The nights were lonely, too. Not that Ariaziane had ever kept him company throughout the night. Not in that sense, at any rate. She had, on several occasions, spent the night with him. But they were nights when they'd talked until dawn, or fallen asleep on the sofa, or some other innocent situation.

Rhia, as he'd expected, continued to flirt with him. He didn't encourage it, but didn't exactly discourage it, either. In fact, lately he'd come to find it fun. And sometimes, tempting. He wasn't happy about that, but the fact remained that he was twenty-one years old and still a virgin. No, he corrected himself. He'd lost it to Darella, but didn't remember it.

Still, he was older than most people are when they have sex for the first time. He felt sometimes that he was being woefully unrealistic in his desire to save himself for Ariaziane, since it was quite possible that he might never see her again. Or, worse, that she might meet someone else in her travels who was more her type than he. That would be too much to bear, he thought. If she were to return with a lover, he just couldn't picture how he'd react.

News from the mountains was encouraging. The crew had made good progress so far and was actually ahead of schedule. Feletain had sent a courier, urging him to visit and check up on the progress, and reminded him that more wages were needed soon. He thanked Vincent again for the generous bonuses he'd given during Celebration Week, and noted that they were sure to merit a similar bonus when Mid-Year Week rolled around, all things considered.

Vincent sent a bonded courier with wages and a letter. The letter thanked Feletain and his crew for their hard work, but regretted that Vincent could not visit soon. In truth, there was nothing preventing him from going. But the distance was great. Vincent had figured the distance between Linnael and his new mountain keep to be nearly two hundred miles, as the crow flies. But the journey, if done in a straight line, would take them through part of a forest, and over a range of hills and a very large section of mountains. The more practical path would be to skirt the forest and swing up around the arm of the mountain range. Considerably longer, but less treacherous. Either way, it was still a longer journey than Vincent wanted to make right now.

In fact, Vincent's thoughts were on another journey altogether. Rhia had continued to urge him to travel again, to get his mind off his worries by having some fun. And if he wouldn't have fun with her between the sheets, perhaps he'd have fun with her between the waves. Rhia wanted to sail across the sea.

The idea held some appeal to Vincent. Gnorrin had told him where Blade lived. He really wanted to see his friend, and so he began making plans for the journey.

He'd invited Gnorrin to go along, but the gnome declined. He did offer, however, to maintain Vincent's business arrangements with Feletain while he and Rhia were gone. This removed Vincent's last concern about the trip, since Darvas was more than happy to watch after Blaise again.

As the Season of Green drew to a close, Vincent and Rhia took passage on a ship headed east across the sea. It was, according to the captain, to be a long journey. From Linnael to Port Remil was a trip of about three months, considering all the stops they were to make along the way. The trip would be mostly along coastlines, save for a gap between landmasses that would comprise more than a week of their journey.

The ship was medium sized, with a crew of fifteen. There were no other passengers. It had three masts holding triangular sails. Though it could handle the open sea, it was designed primarily for coastline travel. The ship's route took a total of seven months or more, round trip. Port Remil, therefore, was nearly halfway through the circuit.

Their cargo at departure from Linnael consisted mostly of spices found in the southern latitudes. These would be sold in the more northern towns, Port Remil among them. There, goods of various sorts would be purchased, to be sold in the southern port towns.

Vincent had never been on the open sea before, and was concerned with the prospect of seasickness. His fears were groundless, however, and he developed his sea legs very quickly. Rhia seemed to be perfectly at ease aboard the ship, too. She confessed to being a frequent traveler by water.

Owing to Rhia's preference to avoid sunlight, they spent most of their days below deck, going topside primarily at night. Oddly enough, Vincent found himself being more sensitive to daylight. He developed headaches quickly if he was in direct sun. He told Rhia about this, thinking that she might be able to suggest something for him to do to rectify that situation.

"You've been using the devil's bit, haven't you?"

Vincent hesitated. "Well, yeah," he confessed. "Why?"

Rhia regarded him with a gentle smile. "I warned you once before about prolonged use of it. Devil's bit is a powerful herb. In limited use, it has no harmful effects, but after prolonged use, it brings on a sensitivity to sunlight."

"Oh. So, if I stop using it, it'll go away?"

"No. If you stop using it, it will not become worse, but it will not go away."

Vincent blinked, absorbing this. "Bummer." He frowned. "Are there other long-term effects?"

"The devil's bit enhances your natural abilities of the mind."

"I don't feel any smarter."

"Not those abilities. The deeper abilities. Mental contact."

"The visions," he said.

"To name but one part of it, yes."

"You suffer from the same thing, don't you? Your aversion to daylight isn't due to your pale complexion."

Rhia smiled, then nodded and turned her attention once more to the waves.

They spent much of their time in such conversation. Rhia asked him about sea travel on Earth and he described for her everything from nuclear submarines to jet skis. Her questions made him realize that there were a lot of things about Rhia that he didn't know. One night, while standing at the prow, watching the moon glitter off the waves, he asked her, "What exactly does it mean to be a witch?"

She looked at him oddly. "What do you mean?"

"You've told me only a little," he said. "In my world, we have several definitions of what a witch is, depending on whom you ask."

"And do I seem to fit any of those definitions?" she asked.

"Sort of. You seem to me to be many things. You're a healer—"

"Not true," she interrupted.

"Okay," he conceded. "You don't actually do the healing, but you can locate and provide the herbs that help in healing. So, you're what we would call an herbalist. And you have a wide knowledge of things other than just herbs, so I would categorize you as what we'd call a naturalist."

"The name would seen to fit, yes."

"The magic you engage in seems to be of a very different sort than the magic used by mages like Gnorrin, though."

"In truth, it is not. The application of the magic tends to be different for witches, but the origin of it is identical."

"And that origin is...?"

"The world itself. It is the life force of our world that we channel through ourselves, bending it to our wills. The difference, though, is that mages tend to bend that force nearly to the breaking point, whereas witches bend it only a little bit. We prefer to use the world's energy in ways that the world would want it to be used."

Vincent rolled that over in his mind. "You make it sound as though the world is a conscious being," he said. "Do you really believe the world is alive?"

"I look around me and see life everywhere. Why would I conclude differently? How do you see the world, Vincent, if not as a living being?"

"Well, okay. But that also makes it sound as though it has a consciousness."

"Does not every living thing have a consciousness of some sort?"

Vincent chewed on that for a moment, turning around to rest his back against the rail. "I suppose so, though I don't generally ponder the conscious nature of an amoeba, for example."

"A what?"

"Sorry. It's a really tiny organism. So small you can't see it with your eyes, only with powerful magnifiers. It's definitely a living creature, and I guess it could have some sort of consciousness, even if it's utterly alien to what you and I know as consciousness. But do you think that grass is conscious? And if so, doesn't it make you feel bad to walk on it?"

"You ask silly questions, Vincent. Certainly the grass is conscious, but why should I feel bad to walk on it? Is that not part of its nature? To hold the soil in place so that it is not washed away by wind or rain or foot?"

Vincent chuckled. "Can't argue with that, I guess. But tell me, what more is there to being a witch? Is there some sort of worship involved?"

"That would depend on how you define the word 'worship.' If you mean that I would bow down in front of an idol, as some do, then no. Absolutely not. But I worship the world in a sense. I respect it. I am grateful for the gifts it provides every day. And I express this by honoring it in every way I can."

Vincent smiled. "That does sound like one of the definitions we have on our world. But tell me more about the magic aspect of it. You said that you use the world's magic the way the world would want you to use it. What does that mean?"

"Well, for example, the world provides us with these wonderful gifts such as the herbs you mentioned. I use the world's magic to find them, to know them, to nurture them. The more you are attuned to the world's life force, the better you can understand the world. And the better you understand it, the easier it is to persuade the world to assist you."

"And you say mages like Gnorrin or Jaz or Ariaziane are doing the same thing?"

"Yes, but in a different way. The world has many aspects, Vincent. Some are harsher than others, as I'm sure you know. The magic of mages tends to focus more on these aspects than the magic of witches."

"For example?"

"Say a mage casts a spell that causes a wave of icy cold to issue forth. Where do you think that coldness is coming from? The mage is harnessing the life force of the world to bend one of its harsher aspects to the will of the mage. That aspect, in this case, being of weather."

"I see," said Vincent. "And witches don't do that? Or can't do that?"

"Oh, we most certainly can. And some do. Most choose not to, however. Witches are still people, Vincent. Some are good, some are not. They have a certain basis of knowledge in common, but some choose to use that knowledge in different ways."

"But wouldn't mages share the same basis of knowledge, if all the power comes from the same place?"

"Not necessarily. You see, although the power is basically the same, it can be taught in different ways. I would venture to say that the way Gnorrin or Jaz learned about magic is very different than the way I learned about it. And to many of us, that difference in the method of learning is very important."

"How so?"

Rhia hesitated. "I do not wish to offend you by saying something negative about your friends, but..." She frowned. "Look at it this way. You and I have spoken about different fruits and plants in the wilderness. I have shown you some that are wonderfully delicious, and others that look the same but are poisonous. Many witches feel that mages are like the uneducated, eating wild fruit randomly, without a real education. They know enough to spit out the bitter and only eat the sweet, but sooner or later, their ignorance will be their downfall."

Vincent took this in. Finally, he said, "And how do most mages look at witches?"

Rhia laughed. "They try not to."

He smiled. "No, really. What's their perspective on this?"

The mirth faded and Rhia said, "It has been my experience that most mages think of witches as being little more than excellent gardeners. Very few mages ever take the time to look closely at us, to take us seriously. You now know more about the nature of witches than the vast majority of mages. Or non-mages, for that matter."

Vincent nodded understandingly, allowing that line of questioning to drop. "Do you consider your craft to be a religion?"

She raised an eyebrow. "Again, that depends on your definition. I've answered your question about worship. Isn't this just an extension of that?"

"Well, sort of," he said. "I guess I'm just ignorant of the religions in this world. And to be honest, I've never had much inclination to research them. I'm not a religious person."

"So what are you asking?"

He heaved a sigh and shrugged. "I don't know. See, on Earth, some view witchcraft as a religion. I told you before about the old Earth religion called Wicca. It sounds, in fact, very similar to what you've described as your views. It was kind of a nature worshipping religion, wherein nature was sometimes personified as a god or goddess. It was once very widely practiced, until it was all but fully supplanted by other faiths. In recent years, though, it has been gaining in popularity again."

"As I've said, it would not be unrealistic to refer to me as a nature worshiper. I do not, however, attach a personality to that which I worship. Again, my worship is of an honoring and respectful sort."

"Right." He smirked. "So why is it that you always have this need to get naked when you're doing magic?"

Rhia stared at him. "I should think that the answer to that would be obvious to you, given all I've said."

Vincent's smile faded and he thought about it. "You're right," he said shortly. "It is obvious. If you are channeling nature itself, it only makes sense that you, as the conduit, should be in the most natural form."

"Exactly. And I believe I explained this quite a long time ago."

"I vaguely recall you saying something to that effect as you sat in my front yard without a stitch of clothes on. You'll forgive me if my brain has difficulty in remembering anything specific about what was said, given the circumstances."

Rhia smiled mischievously. "Yes. I recall what your mind was on."

Vincent blushed, remembering his unwelcome erection during the proceedings. "Don't start," he said.

"Me?" Rhia exclaimed. "You're the one who brought it up! And frankly, I think that's a good sign." She pivoted around to straddle him, leaning him back further against the rail. She reached around and rested her hands on his buttocks. "I'll have you, yet, Vincent."

Vincent gently removed her hands from his butt. He shook his head in disbelief. "You're something else. Why are you so set on getting me between the sheets?"

"Who needs sheets? I just want you between my legs."

He felt the blood rush to his cheeks. "Geez." He shook his head. "Rhia..."

"Don't say it," she warned.

He bit back his words. They'd made an agreement that he'd not bring up Ariaziane. He was taking this trip to get his mind off her, after all. "I just don't understand why you're so set on *me!*"

Rhia laughed, falling against Vincent's body. "You *are* blind!"

"No!" he insisted, trying to disengage their bodies without seeming like he was pushing her away. He failed. "I really don't understand it. I'm not much to look at.

I've obviously got fertilizer in my testosterone, given the amount of hair on my body. I'm overweight..."

"Where?" Rhia demanded.

She had him, there. He looked down at his body. It was so difficult for him not to think of himself as still being fat, when in fact he wasn't in bad shape at all. He was no bodybuilder, and had no desire to be. But he no longer had a body that would repulse women. Except for the hair. He felt like Sasquatch.

"Well, okay," he said. "But doesn't all this fur turn you off?"

"What am I, a faucet?" she asked.

"Sorry. Doesn't it bother you, I mean?"

Rhia smiled and toyed with the curls of chest hair that flowed over the top of his tunic. "Not at all. It's very soft, you know. Most men have coarse chest hair. Yours is quite pleasant."

"You're crazy."

"Possibly. So?"

He smiled. "Good answer." Then he gently disengaged from her and wished her a good evening, stating that he was tired and wanted to sleep. It was a lie and he knew that Rhia knew it. But he didn't care much.

Despite the playful nature of her advances, Vincent knew there was real emotion underneath. And he found himself beginning to feel the same for her. Their conversations stimulated him, made her even more attractive to him. It was hard, sometimes, to keep in mind that he was "saving himself" for Ariaziane. Especially when he didn't know if he'd see her again. Rhia, on the other hand, was right there with him.

Such moral dilemmas didn't make sleeping any easier.

Their first port of call came the next day. It was a small town, and Vincent and Rhia spent the afternoon strolling through its streets. Not much was of interest to them, however. The ship stayed overnight and set sail again the following morning.

The following weeks were similar. Days of sailing, interrupted periodically by stopovers in small port towns. There were two days of dreary weather with some light rain, but otherwise the weather was pleasant. Not that the pair experienced much of it, having become exceedingly nocturnal during the trip.

Finally, they reached the point where they left the coast and set out to cross the strait between two peninsulas. Vincent knew this to be the part of the journey that marked the halfway point.

It was quite an experience for Vincent, being totally surrounded by sea, with no land in sight. He could well imagine how some people could go a little nuts from prolonged trips on the open sea. But he knew this was only temporary. Soon, they'd be in sight of land again and he'd feel better.

One day, as their trip through the strait neared an end, they were awakened by some sort of activity up on deck. Vincent dragged himself out of bed and dressed. Rhia was already topside when he arrived. She stood with the first mate, looking over the starboard bow. The mate held a small telescope to his eye. Vincent stepped over to them. "What is it?" he asked.

The first mate looked at him, then handed him the scope. His simple reply sent a chill down Vincent's back. "Pirates."

Vincent looked through the telescope. In the distance, he located a ship. It flew a square flag of green with no emblems. Pity, he thought. A Jolly Roger flying atop a ship's mast was something he'd always wanted to see. "They're not using their sails," he said in surprise.

"No," the mate said. "The wind is against them. They're using rowers."

Vincent looked again and then noticed the long oars sticking out like skinny legs, dipping into the water on both sides. He frowned. The ships were on intersecting courses. "Okay," he said to the mate. "So what do we do?"

"Pray," he replied.

Vincent raised the glass to his eye again. "How about something that'll work?"

"Is it really that bad?" Rhia asked.

"Aye," the mate replied. "Ship that size can hold fifty, sixty men, plus cargo. No way we can stand up to them. Only hope is to outmaneuver them, try to slip past. If we can do that, we might be able to get a good lead on them before they catch us. But even that's unlikely. Once they get their sails up, they can catch us, using the rowers in addition to the sails."

After a stressful pause, Rhia said, "The rowers are probably slaves, aren't they?"

The mate shrugged. "Probably. Why?"

Rhia's reply was flat. "Because I would hate to have to kill slaves." The man looked at her, as did Vincent. When Vincent saw the steely expression in her eyes, he didn't blame the mate for keeping quiet. Finally, she sighed and said under her breath, "But we do what we have to do."

Vincent took her by the elbow. "Can I talk to you privately, please?" He handed the telescope back to the first mate, then led her to a secluded part of the deck. "Listen," he said, "just what are you thinking of doing?"

"Sinking their ship."

Vincent blinked. "I see." He could easily think of ways she could do so, if her ability to persuade nature were as strong as she implied. "Planning on a big wave to capsize it?"

"Nothing quite so dramatic as that," she said.

"But you don't want to kill the slaves. I don't blame you."

"No, I don't. But if I have to, I will. And I don't see many other choices. We cannot fight sixty men."

"What if there were some way to free the slaves before you sank the ship?"

"What a wonderful idea," she mocked. "That would be lovely. Why didn't I think of it? Let's hail them and see how they feel about it. Please be serious."

"I *am* serious. Is it so impossible?"

"Yes."

"Why?"

Exasperated, Rhia frowned at him. "How would you suggest accomplishing this?"

Vincent stroked his beard. "Could you manage to get us over to their ship without being seen?"

Rhia stared at him suspiciously. "I believe so. Why?"

In response, he merely smiled. "You'll see when we get there." Vincent walked over to the first mate again. "Any problem with taking on some newly freed slaves?"

The mate was looking at the ship through the glass again. He answered as if he were responding to a child. "If you can prevent that ship from meeting us, we'll take on whatever you like."

Vincent smiled and clapped the man on the shoulder. He quickly dashed below to his cabin and extracted his magical gauntlets and both of the swords Jaz had given him. Then he grabbed a length of heavy rope and returned to the deck.

"Ready?" he asked.

"Whenever you are," Rhia replied.

Vincent took her hand and they stepped over the edge. Rhia gently levitated them down until they were a few feet above the surface. Then she coaxed their bodies into a horizontal position, and suddenly they were skimming across the waves, shooting toward the pirate ship.

As they sailed across the water, thin waves shot up and over then, hiding them from the sight of onlookers. Vincent felt as though they were passing through a tunnel made of water.

He kept looking up toward the ship, expecting to see a pirate pointing at them as they approached. But it never happened. Instead, they reached the hull of the ship, where Rhia levitated them up toward the deck. They stopped at one of the few oar holes not being used.

The holes were large, but not big enough to accommodate a human form. They levitated in place in front of the hole, peering in. Rhia located, then magically silenced and immobilized the two slave drivers before they could yell for help. She then took the rope and continued upward.

About ten feet below the deck, lifeboats were tied to the side of the ship. She tied her rope to the bar that secured the boats, letting the length of it fall past Vincent.

Vincent watched as the rope uncoiled within arm's reach from him. He nodded. Perfect. Then, gripping his sword with a gauntleted fist, he plunged the blade through the hull of the ship about a foot from the oar hole. Then he yanked it out. He sighed, relieved that his idea had worked. He'd had his doubts about the sword's ability to pierce the wood, despite its magical nature and the assistance of the gauntlets. He repeated this action, perforating the hull in a circle big enough for him to squeeze through. Then he sheathed his sword and drove his fist into the wood, punching out the perforated sections, then hauled himself through.

Once inside, he secured the hatches so the pirates could not open them from above. Then he proceeded around to each bench, freeing the slaves of their shackles with keys taken from the slave drivers. He determined from the slaves that there were no others hidden away elsewhere. Then he left the way he entered, after instructing the men in what to do next. He climbed up the rope until he reached the row of lifeboats. There were four on each side of the ship. Each was designed to hold six people, it seemed to Vincent. In this case, they'd each have to hold ten. But hopefully not for long.

Vincent knew he had to get the lifeboats in the water quickly. He climbed into the first boat, standing with his legs on either side of the middle bench. He tried his best to grip the boat between his calves. Then he withdrew the second sword. Holding one in each hand, he was able to simultaneously sever both ropes securing the fore and aft ends of the boat. As he and the boat plunged toward the water, the magic of Vincent's ring kicked in, slowing their descent to a more acceptable rate. Since the ship itself wasn't moving much, the little lifeboat descended to a point only a few feet from the rope. Vincent quickly grabbed it and began hauling himself upward. When he reached the oar hole, he yelled for the first ten slaves to get out.

The slaves deserted the ship and boarded the lifeboat, then began rowing. Vincent saw them leaving as he climbed into the second lifeboat. He repeated the action of releasing the boat, yelling for the next ten to go when he passed the hole again on his return climb.

He had just climbed into the third boat when six pirates appeared above him, looking over the side. "Hello," he said. Then he slashed the securing ropes. "Goodbye." All well and good, he thought, as he floated downward. But I could have some trouble with the last one.

And he did. Moments after he passed the oar hole and summoned the third contingent of slaves, the pirates acquired reinforcements. Arrows began whizzing past him. Reaching the boat, he grabbed the edge and hauled himself up and in, then looked up to see a pirate with a crossbow aimed right at his head.

Vincent gasped as he saw the bolt hurtle toward his face, then slow as it neared to a foot, then bounce away. His subconscious mind knew this would happen, thanks to his magical pendant from Ariaziane. But it was another thing altogether to experience it in that way. "Shit," he breathed. Then he turned his attention back to the matter at hand.

But before he could loose the final lifeboat, one of the pirates leaped over the side and landed beside him in the small craft, a dagger in each hand. A swipe of Vincent's sword kept him at bay, but then another pirate landed behind him. The new arrival laughed menacingly.

Vincent knew he couldn't hold them at bay for long, two swords notwithstanding. "Well, this sucks," he said.

As the pirates advanced on him, Vincent hopped to the middle of the boat, toward the ship's hull. He leaped in the air as high as possible, landing with all his weight on the edge of the lifeboat closest to the ship. He landed with his legs bent, then kicked downward with all his might. The little boat rocked to nearly a forty-five degree angle. The pirates lost their balance and tumbled headlong between the boat and the ship, then into the sea. Vincent lost his balance, too, falling into the boat. Then he quickly dispatched it, and fell with it to the water.

He climbed up to the oar hole again and climbed inside, urging the remaining slaves to depart. He warned them about the two soaking pirates they might encounter, but suspected neither of them would have any ability to fight remaining.

When all the slaves were safely on their way, Vincent stole a glance toward the deck. To his surprise, no pirates were looking down at him, so he sheathed his swords and decided to go up for a look. As he climbed, he saw Rhia soaring straight up into the sky. He followed her with his eyes, until she was little more than a speck in the air. Then she turned and dove straight at the ship.

Vincent paused in his climbing. What was she doing? He frowned quizzically as he saw something appear in front of Rhia's tiny form. Something that seemed to grow in size, and not just from its closing proximity. She'd thrown something, he knew, and whatever it might have been was literally expanding in dimension. He watched as it expanded and plummeted toward the deck of the ship. It looked like a big rock. A *really* big rock.

Vincent blanched. A boulder, he thought, at near terminal velocity. "Awww, shit."

There was no time to think, let alone take action. The whole ship shuddered as the boulder slammed into the wooden deck with an explosion of sound that nearly deafened Vincent. His head slammed into the hull, sending stars shooting in front of his eyes. He heard screaming and cursing and felt water striking him from all sides. He tried to shake his head, but couldn't seem to do so. The taste of blood was in his mouth and he seemed to fade in and out of reality. Water was everywhere. And then everything went black.

He came to with his head screaming in pain. Vaguely, he realized he was under water, his arms and legs tangled in the rigging of the sunken pirate ship. He strained to open his eyes, and the effort nearly drained him. He felt heavy, despite being under water. Further movement was impossible.

Out of the corner of his eye, he saw something. A mermaid! How amazing, he thought. Funny, too, he thought as the creature approached, that it looked an awful lot like Rhia. Inside, he laughed. It *was* Rhia, he realized, not a mermaid at all. How silly of me, he thought. He tried to signal to her somehow, but his body wouldn't cooperate. He realized, too, that he probably looked quite dead to her, tangled and motionless as he was.

Rhia swam around behind him and he felt some tugging through the ropes. There were some bright flashes, then her arms were around him, pulling him free. But somewhere along the way on their voyage to the surface, he passed out again.

An eon seemed to pass. Then, through the darkness came a deep voice. "How long was he under?"

Vincent slowly became aware that he was lying on the deck of a ship. His head throbbed and his chest felt very heavy.

"The whole time," came a flat voice that sounded like Rhia.

"Oh," said the first voice. "I'm sorry." Then, after a pause, it said, "Notify the captain that we'll have a burial."

Suddenly, Vincent's body convulsed. Water spewed from his mouth and nose. He coughed for what seemed an eternity, while ignoring the gasps from those around him. Then he groaned and struggled to a sitting position. He raised his hand slowly to his forehead, where a gash lay just below his hairline. He could feel that it was closed, thanks to Gnorrin's magical gift. But closed or not, it still hurt like the blazes. "Whoa," he said. "There's a pain that's gonna linger."

Rhia rushed forward and embraced him, pulling him tightly to her. Vincent's eyes bulged from the pressure, but he clung to her just as tightly. He gazed over her shoulder at the first mate and other crew members, who stared, stunned, at him. After a moment, Rhia whispered in his ear, "You have some explaining to do."

"Yeah?" he whispered back. "Well, I thought you said you weren't going to do anything dramatic."

He rested in his room afterward. He stripped off his soaked garments and hung them on pegs in the wall of his cabin. Then he crawled into bed, cold and shivering. Rhia joined him, but she was oddly silent as she lay by his side, holding him. He wasn't sure whether this bothered or pleased him. He certainly wasn't up for the barrage of questions she was sure to ask. But he also felt slightly worried over her silence. Eventually, he slept.

The galley served up hot meals for all of them, some of which was still left when Vincent rose, hours later. He and Rhia entered the galley and ate, surrounded by crew and former slaves, most of whom had finished eating and were relaxing and talking. The freed men were effusive in their thanking of Vincent. Several of them wanted to swear fealty to him on the spot, but he refused that.

"Go home," he told them. "Go back to your families. They surely miss you terribly. Home is where you belong. Not with me."

One middle-aged man with a scarred face stood up from the meal table. "Some of us have no families to return to, m'lord. Mine was killed when I was took." Others around the galley voiced their agreement. "If it's all the same, I'd like to show my appreciation by swearin' my service to ye. If ye'll have me." Again, others joined in support of the idea.

"Look," Vincent shouted above the noise. "I am sorry that some of you have little to return to. But that is not the end of the world. You are free, now. Free to start over, begin fresh. Start a new family, if it suits you. You certainly don't need to swear the rest of your lives in service to me. And frankly, I don't need you to do it."

The captain and first mate both looked sharply at him. Vincent realized he'd just offended some of these men. He held up his hand. "What I mean is," he said, "I don't need anyone in my service at this time. I am going to visit friends. I will be with them for some time before I return." He studied the roomful of faces and realized many were still waiting for something from him. "But," he continued, floundering, "I can offer you this. I am building a keep. It is far from here, to the west, in the mountains. It will not be finished for a few years, yet. But if you have not, by that point, built new lives for yourselves, you are free to find me. I will take you on at that point, but no sooner." He waited for a reaction. There were pensive looks and nods in a few places. Finally, the consensus seemed to be that it was a fair offer. The scarred man rose to his feet again, lifting his mug above his head. And they toasted their rescuers, Vincent and Rhia.

☙ ❧

Things changed for the pair on the ship after this, and Vincent wasn't sure he liked it. The freed slaves kept fawning over them. The crew of the ship treated them like royalty. Even the captain's demeanor had changed, becoming not quite ingratiating, but nearly so. It was getting on Vincent's nerves.

He wondered why the slaves didn't wish to swear fealty to Rhia as well. He knew women ruled some lands, so it didn't seem to be a sexist thing. Eventually, he learned that word had spread of Rhia being a witch. So while they certainly felt indebted to her, they still obviously feared her. It upset Vincent. He hated any kind of xenophobia.

Rhia ignored the reactions of others, keeping to herself as she always did. She even seemed to be avoiding Vincent. He'd explained to her how he was able to survive under water, thanks to the wager he'd won against the efreeti. Rhia seemed to accept his explanation, and it was then that she seemed to begin avoiding him.

For some reason, the ex-slaves and crew wouldn't allow Vincent that luxury. Fortunately, he spent little time out of his cabin during the daylight hours. At night, he and Rhia had the deck virtually to themselves. Though lately it seemed she didn't even go on deck then. Rhia was more than just a friend and her avoidance of him made Vincent feel terrible. Just how much more than a friend she was to him was beginning to become clear, and the realization made him uncomfortable.

The captain discharged the freed men at the next port-of-call. Vincent gave each of the forty astounded ex-slaves a gold piece to help them get their lives back in order. From there, he knew they'd be okay.

When they boarded ship again to depart, the captain notified Vincent and Rhia that their next stop would be an island. "What goods will you pick up or deliver there?" Vincent asked.

"None," the captain replied. "The stop is for rest and relaxation for my crew. We always stop there, weather permitting. We'll arrive tomorrow, early."

"Sounds great." He thanked the captain, and he and Rhia walked up the gangplank.

"Sounds *sunny*," Rhia said under her breath. Then she glanced at the sky. "Maybe these clouds will stay, though."

"Maybe," Vincent echoed. They walked in silence, finally ending on the deck. They stood watching the crew load crates of goods on board. "So why have you been so distant lately?"

"Have I been?" she said.

"Don't play dumb. Ever since you pulled me out of the wreckage, you've been virtually avoiding me. Why?"

"I don't want to talk about this right now," she said. Then she smiled apologetically and went below deck.

Vincent watched her go, confusion and disappointment wracking him. Eventually he gave up trying to figure it out, and went to his cabin to lie down.

True to the captain's word, they reached a small island early the following morning. Vincent and Rhia were on deck to see it before they anchored and went ashore in rowboats. It was a pretty thing, surrounded by a beautiful beach and covered with lush vegetation. It was perhaps twenty acres or so, roughly circular in shape. Nothing much, but for the crew of the ship, it was plenty of space.

It seemed that the island was often a haven for sea-goers. There were a few constructs built upon the land—small huts scattered about, to house the sailors when they stayed there. But the vast majority of the island was untouched by the hammer of man.

Vincent and Rhia rowed ashore with the first mate and the captain. "Traditionally, we have a bit of a festival at night when we stay here," said the captain. "Our men have brought ashore some fine spirits, as well as some meat purchased at our last docking. We'll have a roast, just after sunset. Will you join us?"

Vincent cast a glance at Rhia, but saw no flicker of interest. "We'll see," he said. "Don't wait on our account."

Upon arrival, the pair began to walk the beach. They were quiet for a time, but Vincent had too much on his mind to let it stay that way. "So are you ready to talk about it yet?"

"About what?"

"About why you've been so distant since the pirate attack."

"You mean to say 'ever since we attacked the pirates,' don't you?"

"Is that what's bothering you? The fact that we attacked first? You don't think they were coming at us just to say hello, do you?"

Rhia shook her head, staring at the sand. "No."

"Besides, you were the one who first talked of sinking their ship."

"I know."

"So what is it? It's something I did, isn't it?"

"In a manner of speaking."

"Well, I'm sorry! What was it?"

She laughed softly. "Vincent, when I first met you, you were a bumbling youth who had gotten shot through the arm. You were about as accomplished a fighter as a newly hatched bird. You knew nearly nothing about this world or the people in it. And now, four short years later, you are a legend."

"What? Who's a legend? I'm no legend!"

"Not yet, perhaps. But I can't help but think you will be, especially after the stories to be told by those slaves begin to circulate. And why shouldn't they speak of you in awe? Look at yourself. You have acquired magical items that prevent you from being hit by missile weapons, from being burned, from falling, from bleeding to death. You have a powerful sword."

"Two," he corrected.

"Two," she amended. "Gauntlets that bestow incredible strength. You do not require air to survive, even while unconscious," she said incredulously. "You have amassed a tremendous fortune, and carry foolish amounts of it around with you, apparently. You have developed the ability to know your surroundings without sight. You have won the favor of those you meet by chance, including a mage, a baron, a duke, and a king!"

"And a witch." He smiled.

She shook her head and returned the smile. "Perhaps especially a witch," she said. "The point is, you have accomplished so much in so little time! It's nothing short of legendary."

Vincent nodded as he kicked his way through the sand. "Yeah. The efreeti said something pretty similar."

"You see! There is another example! You have befriended a creature from one of the elemental planes!" She looked up at him. "I just feel a bit overwhelmed, Vincent. What kind of creature are you that can do so much in so little time, and with such ease?"

He shrugged. "A lucky one?"

"Aye, I should say so."

"Yeah. And to think all I had to do to achieve all this was get whisked away from my home, lose all my friends and family, be ripped away from everything I'd ever known..." He stopped, noticing Rhia's pained expression. He took a deep breath. "Rhia, I'm nothing spectacular. I just got lucky. I made some excellent friends since arriving here, and without them, I'd be nothing. Everything I am, I owe to my friends. I owe quite a lot to you. I'm very grateful." He paused, seeing that this had little effect on her. "Look. I'm no different now than I was a week ago. I don't like this rift that's formed between us. I want us to be close again."

Rhia let out a deep breath. "I do, too. I'm just unsure whether I can see you in the same light again."

"Hm," Vincent muttered. "I guess that means that you don't want to jump my bones anymore."

The witch allowed a hint of a smile to play about her lips. She cleared her throat. "Actually, no. If anything, it makes you all the more desirable of being jumped." She looked away as she said this.

"You know what I'd like?" Vincent said abruptly. "I'd like to take a swim. Think it's safe?"

Rhia nodded. "I imagine so."

They were a good distance away from the ship's crew by this point. Vincent began disrobing. "Come on!"

He saw her hesitate for a moment, then undo her clothing. He was already naked and splashing into the surf by the time the last of her clothes lay in a pile on the sand.

They swam a while, playfully splashing each other and enjoying the feel of the warm water until they were tired. Then they made their way to shore and lay on the warm sand. The sky was overcast enough to keep the sun from annoying them, but it was still warm and pleasant.

Vincent stared at Rhia's body, glistening with water. "So tell me about love." he asked suddenly.

She rolled onto her side, facing him. "Excuse me?"

"I've been thinking a lot about love, lately. I thought perhaps witches had more insight on this subject than others do."

She chuckled. "You accused me of being infatuated with you, and you ask me about love?"

Vincent blushed. "Right. Sorry."

"Why has love been on your mind so much?"

He shrugged, as much as possible while lying with one hand propping up his head. "Well, I love Ariaziane. That's no secret. But I sometimes wonder if it's not possible to love more than one person at a time."

Rhia snorted with laughter at this. "Possible? Certainly it's possible! Why would it not be?"

"Okay, see? You do have more of an insight."

"Oh, rubbish! You told me that you have three siblings. A sister and two brothers, yes?"

"Yeah."

"You love them all, don't you?"

"Well, yes, but—"

"And when the younger brother came along, you didn't love your older siblings any less just so that you could love the new arrival, did you?"

"Well, no, but—"

"What is your confusion, then?"

"I'm not talking about love of family. I'm talking about, you know, romantic love. There's a difference."

"Is there?"

"Of course there's a difference!"

"Explain it, then."

Vincent stared at her as if she were a lunatic. "Well, it's pretty simple," he began. "Love of family is... Well, it's not as intense as the other kind."

"Oh, isn't it?"

"No! I mean... Well, okay, it's as intense, just not in the same way."

"What you're stumbling over is sexual attraction. Romantic love includes it, familial love doesn't."

Vincent hesitated. "Well, yeah. I guess that's it."

"Then let me ask you this. Can you feel sexual attraction for more than one person at a time?"

"Well, obviously. I'm not dead."

Rhia smiled. "And you can feel non-sexual love for more than one person at a time?"

"Of course," he agreed.

"Then why can you not feel romantic love for more than one person at the same time, if romantic love is just a combination of the two?"

He lay there with his jaw hanging open for a moment. Then he closed it. What she said made sense, but there was still something that bothered him about the argument. He shook his head. "I understand your logic, but there's more to it than that."

"Vincent, if you and I were to make love right now, would it lessen the intensity of your love for Ariaziane in the slightest?"

"No!" he replied. "Of course not! But it wouldn't be fair to her."

Rhia nodded. "You're referring to exclusivity, which you humans seem to think is so wonderful."

Vincent sighed. "It's about peoples' feelings, Rhia. I mean, I realize Annie and I don't have a relationship. We're not lovers. But I do want that, someday. I want to spend the rest of my life with her. If she were to come back and want to be with me, do you think she'd be happy to know that I'd had a lover while she was gone? That I just couldn't wait for her?"

"I cannot say. I don't know her. It could be that she would understand completely."

"Well, I know how I'd feel if she came back with a lover. It would tear me apart."

"Because you would feel excluded?"

"Yes."

"Yet you said that if you and I were to make love right now, she would not be excluded from your heart. Could not the same be true for her?"

Vincent hesitated, realizing he was treading the fine line of hypocrisy. "Okay, point taken. But see, the problem is that I don't want to have to make that choice."

"What choice?"

His heart beat faster in anticipation of what he was about to say. "You know, the last few times we've been together, I've missed you terribly after we parted. I kept telling myself this was because you're my friend. But that's not really it. When I think of you, I get a warm feeling inside that stays with me for a long time. A feeling that goes beyond friendship." He took a deep breath. "And ever since this whole rift grew between us, I've felt awful. Like a part of my heart had been ripped out. And I knew that it was more than the feeling you get when a friend is upset with you. A lot more." Again he paused, then shook his head. "I have very strong feelings for you. I might

357

even be falling in love with you." He saw her smile at his words, but it gave him no comfort. "But this isn't a good thing."

"Why not?"

"Because! If you and I were to become lovers, and Ariaziane did come back, I'd be torn between you two. I do love her, Rhia. And I wouldn't want to have to choose between you."

Rhia shook her head with a smile. "You have such a noble streak, you know that? Always, you try to please everyone, even to the extent of worrying about a situation that might never come to pass." Vincent frowned, but she continued. "I certainly hope Ariaziane returns. I hope the two of you have a wonderful and happy life. That would make me very happy for you. But I have no way of knowing if that will ever happen, and neither do you."

"I know, but—"

"But nothing," she interrupted. "Vincent, the only choice you have to make is how you want to live your life. Do you want to live for today, or for a tomorrow that might never exist? None of us know what the future will bring. We can hope for the best, but hopes are flimsy things, and the world doesn't often pay attention to them."

She had him, there. And with a sinking feeling, he realized this was what he'd been doing ever since arriving on this world. He thought always of the future—of the possibility of returning to Earth, and the possibility of sharing an intimate life with Ariaziane. But the truth was that perhaps neither of these things would come to pass. Was he wasting his life, or at the very least missing out on happiness, by paying less attention to the present than to the future?

He looked over at Rhia and felt his chest tighten. He had already learned so much about the world from this woman, and now she was teaching him about himself, too.

"What are you thinking?" she asked.

Today or tomorrow, he told himself. Which is it? He cleared his throat. "I'll never stop loving her," he said flatly.

"I don't want you to," she replied.

"Really?" he said, reaching out and stroking her cheek with the backs of his fingers.

"Really," she said as she leaned into his hand. Then she bent forward and kissed him.

He surrendered to the feeling, losing himself in the kiss. And then their hands were everywhere, stroking and fondling. He felt his excitement growing. Then she raised her hands to his shoulders and pushed him roughly back into the sand. Before he knew it, she was on top of him. And then, he was inside her.

Some instinct he never knew he had took over, then, and he made love to her there on the beach. And he didn't regret it one bit.

❧ Twenty-Six ❧

The remainder of their voyage was spent primarily below deck. They moved their belongings all into Vincent's cabin, it being the larger of the two. Being a baron had its advantages, he had come to realize. The arrangement suited him just fine, and Rhia seemed to take as much delight in their new relationship as Vincent did.

She taught him to do more than just appreciate physical intimacy. She taught him how to appreciate every aspect of living. And he realized this was what she'd been doing ever since he'd known her. He looked back on their days spent in the forest, before the attack that had led to his blindness. In retrospect, he understood the joy she displayed in everything. She was more in tune with the world than he himself had ever felt. Her comprehension of nature was truly staggering. He could see how some uneducated and ignorant people would view it as somehow arcane. This was undoubtedly what caused the persecution of witches, just as Gnorrin had once told him that the small-minded did not tolerate magery. Vincent wondered if all the persecution of witches on Earth had something to do with this. Possibly some of it, he concluded. But he knew that most of it was due to a code of ridiculous beliefs, fueled by paranoia.

When he wasn't making love to Rhia, Vincent was thinking about it. Not about the act itself, but about the ramifications of what he and Rhia were doing. He loved Rhia. There was no question in his mind of that. And it filled him with a good feeling, just as loving is supposed to. And he had to agree that she'd been right. His feelings for Ariaziane hadn't diminished a bit. He still missed her terribly. But Rhia's companionship made that ache a little less pronounced. He was very grateful for that.

It was interesting, he thought. His love for Rhia was different than his love for Ariaziane. Nothing else, just different. It wasn't better or worse. It wasn't stronger or weaker. It was simply that Rhia and Ariaziane were two different people. And the love was different, accordingly.

So it was that as the Season of the Sun advanced, they arrived in Port Remil. Vincent and Rhia disembarked and, after pleasant farewells to the captain and crew of the ship, they checked in at the nicest inn they could find. It was late afternoon when they arrived, and their goals for the night included only a decent meal, a cold drink, and a warm bed.

The drink and the meal were found in the inn's tavern. The quiet atmosphere of the tavern seemed odd to Vincent, after the long time aboard a creaking wooden ship. But he welcomed it. It relaxed him. He finished his meal, then took a long pull from his cider. He leaned back in his chair and regarded Rhia. He smiled at her. "I love you," he said.

She smiled in return, spearing another forkful of her dinner. "I know," she teased. "What's your point?"

He chuckled. "That *was* the point."

"Ah," she said. "So when do we find your friends?"

"Tomorrow, I guess."

"After we've visited your friends, would you join me in visiting one of mine?"

"I didn't know you had friends in this area. Sure, that would be fine."

"Not exactly in this area. North of here, several days journey."

"Oh. Well, that's no problem. I'm on vacation, right?" He smiled, then drank from his tankard again. His eyes scanned the room for perhaps the fiftieth time. Vincent was a compulsive people watcher. He liked studying others, analyzing their habits and gestures. A woman was sitting across the room with her back to him. He saw her run a hand through her hair. He'd been watching her for a while. There was something familiar about the movement. He'd seen someone do that before, in just that fashion, but couldn't quite recall... Suddenly, it hit him. "Excuse me," he said to Rhia.

He rose and walked across the room, approaching her table from behind. The place opposite her seat was empty, but the remains of a meal were present. Quietly, Vincent unsheathed his dagger. He bent over the woman from behind, placing the cold steel against her neck. "Answer one question, and you won't get hurt," he whispered into her ear. The woman froze, but Vincent saw her fist clenching atop the table. He smiled. "Good," he said. "The question is..." He pulled the dagger away and spun her around to face him. "Miss me?" he said with a big smile.

Sianon's eyes widened. Her hand raised to strike, then paused. "Vincent? You son of a... I could have killed you!" She laughed, then slapped his arm. "What are you doing here?"

Vincent sheathed his dagger and sat in an empty chair beside hers. "We came to see you guys," he said. "Guess we succeeded."

Sianon looked around. "We? Who is with you?"

"Her name is Rhia," he said, turning and signaling for the witch to join them. "She's a very dear friend. But it's good to see you! How have you been?"

"Quite well, thank you. Both of us." Blade entered the room then, and stopped. He stared at Vincent. "Yes, it's him," Sianon said to Blade. "Now close your mouth."

Vincent stood up as his friend approached. He smiled as Blade wrapped him in a bear hug. "Gods, it is good to see you, Vincent!" He released his hold on him and stood back. "You look well, my friend. I hope that is the case."

"Yes," Vincent said, clapping his friend on the shoulder. "I'm just fine."

Rhia stepped up to them. "Nice to see you again," she said to Blade.

Blade cast a perplexed look between Rhia and Vincent. "And you," he replied, then introduced her to Sianon. "Wait," he said. "You two are together? You have found how to get Vincent home?"

Rhia raised an eyebrow, turning to Vincent to field the question.

"Ah, no," he said quietly. "That quest has pretty much been discarded."

"Discarded?" said Blade. "But why?"

"Look, can we discuss that later? I'm on vacation. I came to visit you guys to have a good time, okay?"

Blade smiled and indicated the vacant chairs.

"So what's happened with you over the past two years?" Vincent asked Blade.

The tall man smiled warmly. "I finished a great quest," he said simply. And to Vincent's raised eyebrows, he responded, "I have found peace."

Vincent nodded. Blade's gray eyes, which had always seemed so cold to Vincent, were softer now. They lacked the edge that had always made his friend seem tightly strung. "I can sense that," he told him. "I'm very happy for you." He found his eyes drawn to Blade's cheek, where the faint darkness of a scar showed. Vincent wondered if Sianon ached inside whenever she looked upon it.

"Do you have any children?" asked Rhia.

"No," Blade answered. "But my brother's wife has just birthed their first."

"A little girl," Sianon elaborated. "She looks like Tisen."

"What have they named her?" Rhia asked.

"Nilka," said Sianon. "After Tisen's mother."

"D'Ty is well, then?" asked Vincent.

Blade nodded. "He is. We shall visit them tomorrow, if you like. How is Gnorrin?"

"Quite well," Vincent said. "He sends his regards and hopes you will manage to visit soon."

"Aye," said Blade. "I have been hoping to do so, as I've mentioned in my letters to him. I find myself growing restless, sometimes."

Vincent smiled. "I can relate." He looked at Blade, waiting for the man to ask after Ariaziane's welfare. But Blade just looked back at him. A spark of understanding passed between them, it seemed to Vincent. And Blade did not voice the question.

"Well," he said instead, "I have told you, effectively, that for the past two years, I have led a very uneventful life. Sianon and I have been content to settle comfortably into each other's lives, and I have begun to feel at home here. That has been enough for me. But what about you? You look well, Vincent. But there's something about you that seems odd to me."

"Well, I'm an odd guy," he replied with a smile.

"Aye, this is true," said Blade. "But I mean something deeper. You seem changed from within. These two years have not been peaceful for you, have they?"

It wasn't a question, Vincent realized. It was a simple statement, as if the events of the past two years were written across his face. Then again, he thought, perhaps they were. Not the actual events, but some little trace of them. Some reminder. "You could say that," he said softly. Again, he looked to Blade, willing the man not to ask about Ariaziane. To his relief, the question remained unasked, though it was clearly on his friend's mind.

He knew Blade was concerned for him, though, and deserved more than such an ambiguous answer. So he told him about his ordeal with blindness. He told him about Jaz and the fight with Beltun Sagasht. He told him about Baron Aedriun, Duke Ghanol, and King Breigar. Rhia tossed in the fact that Vincent was now a baron, much to his embarrassment. Vincent spoke of the fortunes made and the move to the coast with Ariaziane. Immediately, he regretted mentioning her. And he knew that Blade saw the self-recrimination written on Vincent's face. Quickly he changed the subject.

"Anyway, after all of that, I felt like I needed a break, to get away and relax. And I've been wondering how you've fared for some time. So here I am."

Blade nodded, his eyes betraying the fact that he knew Vincent was withholding a good amount of the story. "Well," he said, his tone brightening with a smile. "Shall I call you Lord Vincent, now?"

"Don't you dare!" Vincent laughed.

Sianon addressed Rhia. "So how did you and Vincent meet?"

Blade laughed at this, while Rhia smiled gently and Vincent grimaced.

"It was a matter of coincidence," she said to Sianon. "He had caught an arrow in his arm. The arrow was unclean and produced the inner fire. Blade summoned me to treat him."

"You are a healer, then?"

"I am a witch," Rhia said.

Sianon's eyes widened slightly. "Oh."

"No healer was available," Vincent explained.

Rhia cast him a strange look. "What do you mean? There are healers in Dynsa."

Vincent turned his perplexed gaze from Rhia to Blade. "You told me none were available."

Blade smiled faintly and shrugged. "Did I? Perhaps I exaggerated." Vincent continued to stare at him, so he elaborated. "I have known Rhia for some time. I trust her. I do not know the healers of Dynsa. It is that simple."

Vincent felt an annoying tickle somewhere at the back of his mind. "Right," he said. "And your father was in the military."

His friend blinked, then laughed. He shook his head in amazement. "That is very annoying," he chuckled. "Very well. The truth is that I wanted a witch for the healing."

"Why?" Vincent asked.

"Because a witch uses the gifts of the land to heal. Not magic."

Vincent cast a glance at Rhia. "Isn't that a form of magic?" he asked, turning back to Blade.

His friend nodded. "You do not need to use a sword to cut flowers," he said simply.

Vincent blinked, staring at Blade. Then he smiled. Then he laughed. "And you don't need a gun to blow your mind." He smiled wider and laughed again.

Blade and the women exchanged glances. "I do not understand," Blade said simply.

"I know. But I do. And so did John Lennon, evidently. Whatever gets you through the night." He laughed again.

Sianon turned to Rhia. "Are you certain you cured him?"

They talked for another hour or more in the tavern. Then Blade and Sianon wished them well and promised to join them for breakfast in the morning. Vincent and Rhia went to their room at the inn. "Why did you not explain to them what happened with Ariaziane?" she asked him as they climbed the stairs.

Vincent felt his heart sink. "I don't know."

They reached their door and entered.

"They are your friends," she said to him.

He closed the door and stood with his back leaning against it as Rhia proceeded into the room. "I know," he sighed, staring at the floor. "It's just that it still hurts, when I think about it. When I think about her."

"Of course it does. You love her."

"Yes, I do. And I can't help but wonder what she's doing. Where she is."

"And if she's thinking of you. Missing you."

Vincent swallowed hard. "Yeah."

"Do you think she is?"

"I hope she is."

"Yes, but that does not answer my question."

He looked up to see her lying on the bed, one hand propping up her head. Her other hand was playing with the long, thin braid that had fallen over her shoulder to lie across her breast. He felt his chest tighten. "Yes," he said quietly. "I think she does."

Rhia smiled. "Good. You're not as hopeless as you seem, then."

"What do you mean?" he asked, watching as her fingers alternated between playing with the braid and brushing over her breast through the thin tunic she wore.

She smiled and laughed quietly, deep in her throat. "You have so little opinion of yourself. But it's getting better." Seeing the expression on his face, she continued. "You really don't have any concept of how captivating you can be, do you?"

Vincent pushed himself off the door and walked slowly to the bed. "No," he said simply, sitting next to her. "But I do have a good concept of how captivating *you* can be."

Rhia pushed herself up onto her elbow, bringing her face closer to his. Her hand still toyed with the braid, and Vincent watched it do so. "I thought about you often while I was away, after leaving you so abruptly last year," she said.

"Where did you go?"

Rhia smiled faintly. "To the arms of another."

"Oh?" Vincent looked into her face.

"Yes," she said. "It was something I needed."

"But you didn't stay. Why?"

"Because you called me."

He smiled, caressing her face. "Yeah, I guess I did, didn't I? I thought about you a lot, too. I always have. You're so mysterious, yet so open. It's very strange."

Rhia uttered a little gasp as his fingers traced their way from her face to her throat. "I feel the same of you."

"Me?" he said. "Nothing mysterious about me."

Rhia laughed aloud. "Everything about you is mysterious, in one way or another."

Vincent snorted. "If you say so."

"I say so."

"I love you," he said.

"Of course you do," she smiled, and pulled his face to hers.

The following day, after breakfast with Blade and Sianon, they were treated to a tour of Port Remil. Vincent found it to be similar to Linnael. One port city seemed much like the next. After they'd seen the limited sights, Blade and Sianon took them to the home of D'Ty and Tisen.

Their home was small, but very picturesque, Vincent thought as they approached. A thatch-roofed cottage with a cheery garden of flowers in the front and a stream in the back. Blade knocked on the door. Tisen answered, an infant cradled against her breast, its tiny head on her shoulder and a fist clutching a lock of her golden hair. She smiled when she saw Blade and Sianon. "Is that worthless rodent of a husband of yours home?" Blade said with a smile. "Tell him a friend has come to visit."

"I'll send him right out," she said in a melodic voice.

Blade led them to the other side of the house, to a round table surrounded by several chairs. The table was shaded by a large tree, much to the relief of Vincent and

Rhia. Vincent could feel the sunburn starting. "So where's the gaming board?" Vincent said. "This reminds me of Gnorrin's place."

"I agree," said Blade. "That is why I spend so much time here, rather than at our own home."

"Your home is not nice?" asked Rhia.

"It is very nice," Blade said, catching a glare from Sianon. "But as Vincent has said, this has a familiarity to it that appeals to me."

"What he means," Sianon said, "is that our house makes him feel uncomfortable."

Vincent raised an eyebrow at that, but before he could inquire, he heard the door to the house open. Turning, he saw D'Ty striding out to meet them, a pitcher of liquid in one hand and a basket of food in the other. "Hello, brother, you mongrel," he said loudly. "Who'd you bring with you?" He stopped in his tracks. "Well, well! Vincent! How are you?" D'Ty put the refreshments down on the table and clasped Vincent's hand.

"He's a baron, that's how he is," said his brother.

"Pardon?" said D'Ty, letting go of Vincent's hand and stepping back to look him over. "Bull chips!"

"I'm well, D'Ty," said Vincent. "As are you, I can tell. It's great to see you!"

D'Ty continued to size him up. "You don't *look* like a baron."

"You don't look like a pain in my behind, either," Vincent said, smacking him on the shoulder, then turning to the table. "What do we do, pass the pitcher around?"

As if in answer, Tisen stepped out of the house carrying a tray of goblets. "I put Nilka down for sleep," she said as she set the goblets up on the table. Then she filled them as Vincent made the introductions.

Conversation followed. D'Ty and Tisen talked about their wedding and the birth of their daughter. Vincent found himself sharing very watered-down versions of his own exploits.

They talked for hours, until the sun was high. They finished one pitcher of the sweetly tart fruit beverage and Tisen quickly fetched more. D'Ty happily carved off chunks of smoked meats and delicious cheese, which were passed out with accompanying biscuits.

During a lull in the laughter, Vincent said, "Well, I'm glad things are so good for all of you. Especially you, Blade. Ever since I met you, I always felt there was something inside you that you needed to make peace with. I'm glad that you have."

Blade smiled politely at his friend. Then Vincent heard Tisen say very faintly, under her breath, "Mostly, anyway."

He turned his attention to her. "What do you mean?" Tisen looked up, surprise on her face. It was obvious she hadn't expected anyone but her husband to hear her words. "You said, 'mostly, anyway.' What did that mean?"

D'Ty frowned at his wife, but Tisen firmed her jaw. "Glare all you want," she said to him, "but the fact remains that your brother could be in danger!"

Vincent looked over at Blade, who was frowning and shaking his head. "Danger from what?" he asked him.

Blade looked up at Vincent. "She is exaggerating."

"Exaggerating?" Tisen exclaimed. "They have threatened your life!"

"Whoa, hold on," Vincent said, raising a hand. "Who are we talking about?"

D'Ty provided the answer. "You recall the reason for my brother's departure from this town." Vincent nodded. "It seems the brothers of the young man that was accidentally killed in the tavern have returned home after being away for many years. They learned of my brother's presence and are not at all happy about it."

"Okay," Vincent said. "And they've threatened your life?" he said to Blade.

Blade merely nodded, while D'Ty continued. "They have. But they are empty threats." Tisen let out a derisive snort at this, which her husband ignored. "There are three brothers. They returned to Port Remil when their father passed away. Evidently, the old man left something to the boys and they have returned to claim it."

Vincent frowned. "How long ago was this?"

Blade took over the conversation. "They returned at the beginning of the Season of the Sun."

"Then they have returned to stay?"

Blade shrugged. "Difficult to say. They have not acquired homes for themselves. They remain living together in their parents' house."

"Odd," Vincent said. "That's a long time to stick around for just claiming something left them in a will. Do you know what the item was?"

"What difference does that make?" Tisen said.

"None," Vincent said. "I'm just curious."

There followed an awkward silence. Vincent studied the expressions on the faces of his friends. Blade's was mostly unreadable. Sianon appeared genuinely unconcerned, to no surprise of Vincent's. D'Ty was not as adept at concealing. It was clear that he was worried to a degree. And Tisen's outright concern and frustration were unmistakable.

The silence hung between them like a wall. Vincent nodded to himself, smiling faintly. Then, D'Ty cleared his throat, changing the subject, and the wall crumbled.

"Speaking of curiosities," D'Ty said, "how is Ariaziane? And why did she not come with you?"

The words were the wall's bricks, falling onto Vincent's stomach. He clenched his jaw briefly, noticing the glance that Blade sent to his brother. He frowned. "In fact, she has been better," he began. "I have not seen her in several months. She has gone on a quest of her own, it seems."

"A quest?" D'Ty asked, and Vincent noticed that Blade had stopped staring at his brother and was now looking to Vincent for answers.

Heaving a sigh, Vincent proceeded to tell his friends the full story of Ariaziane's second transformation and subsequent departure, and naturally, the events that led up to it. He found himself relating practically everything that had happened to him since the three of them had sailed from Linnael, what seemed like ages ago. The pirate story caused some astonishment around the table, as he'd expected.

When he was finished, he studied faces again. Tisen appeared somewhat stunned. Sianon wore an expression that reminded Vincent of Mr. Spock, with one eyebrow raised. He half expected her to say, "Fascinating." D'Ty stared openly at Vincent, making him feel uneasy. And Blade... Blade was smiling in that enigmatic way of his, much to Vincent's consternation.

He turned to Rhia, who smirked at him. "I told you so," she said.

"What?" he demanded. "Why are you staring at me like that?" he said to D'Ty.

As D'Ty shook his head, his wife spoke up. "You truly rescued all the slaves from the pirates?"

Vincent stared at her. He'd said they had, hadn't he? He was about to say as much when Rhia intercepted. "Aye, they were rescued. And wanted to swear fealty to him on the spot."

Vincent waved off the subject and addressed Blade. "What are you smiling about?" he demanded. "Why does everyone seem to think this is such a big deal?" Rhia put a hand on his shoulder, but he shook it off. "No," he told her. "I don't like this a bit. First you, now these guys."

Rhia just shook her head and laughed. "I think you had best grow accustomed to this sort of reaction."

"Why? I am *not* legend material! These Seeker Portal thingies must be screwed up to have brought me here. They could have sucked in someone much better than me. I mean, why take me when they could have pulled in, I dunno, Arnold Schwarzenegger?"

Blade laughed suddenly, causing all eyes to focus on him. "Vincent, my dear friend, how do you know they haven't?" Vincent paused at that, casting his friend a befuddled look while mulling over the thought. He blinked. Blade continued. "If I were you, lad, I would accept whatever role the gods have chosen for you. If you are destined to be a legend, then *be* a legend! Do not fight it."

Vincent frowned, shaking his head. "Blade, I don't believe in 'destiny.' I don't believe in any gods who dictate the events of our lives."

"What, then, *do* you believe in?" Blade asked.

"I believe in myself," he answered proudly. "Nothing more, nothing less."

Blade nodded. "Then I suggest, my friend, that you start believing yourself to be what your actions speak you to be."

Vincent had no words to reply. He could feel the headache forming, right between his eyes where the brows were pushing together. He was relieved to hear little Nilka's cry coming from the window nearest them. Tisen rose to check on the infant, and the disturbance was enough to allow the subject to die. Vincent polished off the last of his drink.

"More meat or cheese, anyone?" D'Ty asked, carving off more for himself.

Vincent tapped his goblet with his finger, the ring on his hand clacking loudly against it. "No, thank you. Rhia and I are going to be leaving shortly. Exploring this lovely little town. But I would very much like to take you all to dinner tonight. Is the inn the dining establishment of choice around here?"

"It is, if you wish to have good food at fair prices and a friendly setting in which to talk," D'Ty said. "If, however, you want fancy food at fancy prices and a fancy setting in which to sit prettily while talking little, there is another establishment we could venture into."

Vincent laughed. "Again, no, thank you. The inn will be quite appropriate, I think. Shall we all meet there at sundown?"

They all agreed, once Tisen returned with baby Nilka. They said their farewells, then Vincent and Rhia departed, leaving the others to continue their visiting.

When they were well out of earshot, Rhia said, "I am sorry the conversation so upset you."

Vincent shrugged. "Ariaziane was bound to come up in conversation sooner or later. Might as well get it over and done with quickly."

"That is not the part of the conversation I was meaning."

He smiled without pleasure. "I know."

The inn was crowded with patrons that evening. They sat at a table farther from the fire than Vincent would have liked. He enjoyed sitting near fires and expressed his disappointment in their seating, despite D'Ty's joking that Vincent's body hair would ignite if they sat any closer.

Their conversation was full of merriment. Vincent was surprised that Tisen had brought along the baby, but little Nilka seemed perfectly content. She lay quietly in her basket with her blankets, sucking her fingers most of the night.

Vincent found himself watching the baby frequently. It reminded him of when his older brother's children were babies. He had never considered the idea of fatherhood for himself, having decided that he just wouldn't have the kind of patience that babies demanded. But looking at Nilka made him wonder if his assessment might not be off target. She seemed like such a quiet, well-behaved child.

"Little demon is being good for a change," D'Ty remarked with fatherly humor. Vincent cast him a perplexed look. "Oh, she is usually like one possessed whenever we take her anywhere. Do not let her behavior fool you." He smiled.

Their dinners were quite appealing, Vincent thought. Not the best food he'd ever eaten, but far from the worst. And it was served promptly and in good portions. Fish was, understandably, quite popular on the menu. But fresh game was also to be found. He eyed Sianon's hart steak, reminding himself to try that on his next visit. As for his own dinner, he chose a mixture of fish and shellfish served with a sauce that tasted of mustard and vinegar, and enjoyed it immensely. Until their table received some unexpected visitors.

When Vincent saw the three men, he knew instantly who they were. He felt a tingle run down his spine. The men stood behind Blade's chair, surrounding him.

"Do my eyes deceive me," taunted the eldest, "or is this not the dog who *murdered* our brother?" He dragged out the word "murdered" far longer than necessary.

As the other two men murmured their agreement, Vincent looked at his friends. Blade was frowning, but made no move to do anything other than put a restraining hand on Sianon's arm. Vincent realized Sianon was having a difficult time holding back. Doubtless she wanted to do some murdering of her own, judging by the look in her eyes. D'Ty, too, seemed to want to pulverize the men. But he did nothing. Blade seemed to be content to allow the men to have their little fun and then leave them in peace.

"Do you think it is right," continued the eldest brother, "that a *murderer* should be permitted to go about freely, eat in public, do whatever his evil little heart desires?"

Again the others voiced their agreement. Vincent looked at Blade, who stoically ignored them. But Vincent could tell it wasn't easy for him.

Screw this, he thought, then put down his utensils and stood. "Gentlemen," he said. "I don't believe I've had the honor of your acquaintance. I am Baron Vincent of Penn's Woods," he said. He mentally chided himself for not even knowing the name of the region he was to be baron of. "You seem to be disturbing the dinner of not only myself," he continued, "but of these fine people here. Is there some way in which we can assist you?"

The brothers fell silent, appraising him. The youngest swallowed and turned his gaze to the floor. The other two shifted uncomfortably. Finally, the middle brother said, "Your pardon, Lord. We did not realize..."

"My presence here was not made public knowledge. Nevertheless, I *am* here, and you *are* disturbing us."

"Let's go," whispered the youngest of the brothers to his siblings. The middle brother nodded his agreement.

The eldest brother frowned, staring Vincent in the eye. "Forgive our intrusion. We meant no harm. Enjoy your meals." Then the trio made their way toward the exit. Vincent remained standing. The eldest brother made frequent glances back, always to find Vincent staring after them. Only when they were out the door did Vincent take his seat again.

All were silent at the table. Only Blade continued to eat. But he looked up at Vincent at one point, and Vincent saw in his friend's eye that which he would not vocalize. The men frightened him.

Tisen was the first to speak. "Now you have been added to the list of those they count as enemies."

Vincent raised an eyebrow. "I don't think I'll lose any sleep over that." Despite this insistence, the rest of his dinner lacked the flavor it once possessed, and the remaining conversation for the course of the evening was tainted by the unpleasant event.

The following morning, Vincent realized he had, in fact, lost sleep over it. The look in the eldest brother's eye had kept haunting him. And he knew Tisen was right. Blade *was* in danger. Vincent had tossed and turned in bed, probably keeping Rhia from a restful sleep.

He rose early, allowing her to continue slumbering, and quietly slipped downstairs to the inn for some breakfast. He sat in the deserted dining area, toying with his eggs and biscuits without really eating much of them.

He was certainly in favor of Blade's new philosophy of peace. His friend was a troubled man, and if he had found his own peace, that was wonderful. Taking up arms against these men was not what Vincent wanted to see Blade do. The man had turned his sword into the proverbial plough. And he applauded that action.

Still, he also didn't want to see Blade suffer any harm at the hands of these imbeciles. He needed to prevent that at any cost. Reaching this decision, he finished his meal, then sought out the innkeeper.

The man was only too happy to provide answers for a visiting baron. Yes, he knew the three men in question. Yes, he knew where they lived. Vincent obtained directions to their home, thanked the innkeeper, and went back upstairs to dress accordingly.

He scrawled a quick note for Rhia before he left. "Went visiting. Back by midday." He left the message by the wash basin in their room, buckled a sword around his waist, and left.

He thought about how he would confront the men. He certainly wanted to avoid violence if at all possible. He just wasn't sure it was going to *be* at all possible. He sighed as he walked along, wondering not for the first time just what kind of person he was turning into.

Before long, he reached the house in which the brothers had grown up and now shared again. It was a large affair, expensive looking. Vincent took a deep breath as he strode up the walk. He knocked loudly on the front door. And waited.

When no answer was forthcoming, he knocked again. Time passed. Still no reply. He wondered if they had seen him approach and were just not answering the door. With a frown, he walked around the side of the house toward the back.

The back yard was empty. Knocks on the back door yielded identical results. But his presence had not gone entirely unnoticed. A neighbor cleared his throat loudly. Vincent turned. "Good morning," he said to the man.

"They're not in," said the elderly fellow.

"I'd come to that conclusion, yes," said Vincent. "Any idea where I might find them?"

"Why, down at the mine, of course."

Vincent smiled wider as he slowly approached the man. "Mine? You'll have to forgive me, friend, but I am not familiar with the mine you speak of. I am a visitor to these parts."

The old man nodded and took on a conversational tone. "Their father's father discovered gem ore there. He mined quite a bit, gained a fortune, built this house. His son, the boys' father, closed the mine after his father died. Now he's dead. I expect his sons are planning on reopening it. Don't know why, though."

Vincent nodded. "And can you point me in the direction of this mine? It is really quite important that I speak with the gentlemen at once."

"Surely," said the neighbor. "Follow the main road out of town to the south for about a league. You'll come to a crossroads, there. Turn to the east. Go for a ways until you see a large, dead tree on your left. Tree was struck by lightning back when I was your age. Killed the tree, but didn't split it or anything. Anyways, near that tree, you'll see a road going back through some wooded spots. Take that road. That's where the mine is."

"You're most kind," said Vincent. "Thank you for the information."

"My pleasure," said the man. "You look like you aim to give those boys some bad news. Wouldn't mind that a bit, myself."

"Oh? How's that?" Vincent asked.

The old man snorted. "You don't know them very well, do you? Rotten to the core, they are. Just like their father before them."

"I understand they had another brother, who was killed some years ago. Did you know him, as well?"

"Sure did. Been living here most of my life."

"What was he like?"

"Not much different than these three. Always getting himself into trouble. Was no surprise that he got hisself killed."

Vincent decided to push the questioning. "And did you know anything about the person who killed him?"

The man shook his head. "Just hearsay. Came from a poor family, I heard. Also heard he's back, just like these three. Pretty strange, I say."

"Yes. Very strange," Vincent agreed. "I thank you again for the information. Have a pleasant day."

The old man nodded, then disappeared back into his own dwelling.

This trip was going to require a horse, he realized. But that was easily accomplished. During the brief tour he and Rhia had taken the day before, he had seen a stable that rented horses. He returned to the stable and picked out a decent looking animal, paid for the day's rental, and embarked on his journey.

All during the ride out of town, he mulled over exactly what he was going to say to the brothers. He hoped he'd be able to intimidate them with his position and an unspoken threat of repercussions against them. The encounter with them last night told him this tactic would undoubtedly be effective against the youngest brother, and probably the middle one, as well. But the eldest might not be so easily swayed. The man had a fire in his eye.

This didn't surprise Vincent. Being the oldest, he was closest in age to the brother Blade had killed. Likely they were close. By contrast, the youngest of them probably barely remembered their late sibling.

Before long, he spied the large, dead tree the old man had spoken of. He turned onto the narrow road there, noticing that the ground was in good shape. No carts full of ore had been through this way any time recently.

It was another few minutes before Vincent saw the mine. He brought his horse around a turn, and there ahead lay the opening, gaping like a black mouth into the side of a small hill. There were three horses tied to trees, and no sign of the brothers.

He frowned as he dismounted and tied his horse apart from the others. He didn't relish the idea of descending into a mine shaft. Stupid, he said to himself. What did you expect? That they'd be lounging around outside? With a sigh, he made his way to the entrance. Peering inside, he saw torchlight. This is good, he told himself as he ducked his head and stepped through.

There were two torches in sconces just inside. The ceiling was low and he had to crouch in order to pass through. He grabbed one of the torches and did so, finding another chamber just inside the first. But from there, the mine branched into three corridors.

"Figures," he muttered. He stepped inside the first corridor, began to walk down the incline. He stopped after about a dozen paces. He cleared his mind, closed his eyes, and listened, stretching out his sense of hearing, trying to pick up any noises from deeper within this corridor. Nothing.

He repeated the process within the second corridor. Still nothing. But in the third, he heard voices. With a satisfied nod, he proceeded down into the mine.

Once the voices could be heard without straining, he decided to announce his presence. "Hello?" he called. "Anyone home?" The voices, unsurprisingly, fell silent. Vincent stopped in his tracks and listened again. After a pause, he heard shuffling footsteps approaching. Satisfied, he turned and headed out.

He replaced the torch in the entrance chamber, then stepped outside. He stood several feet from the opening, putting on his best imposing look, legs apart and arms folded across his chest, awaiting their arrival. It didn't take long.

As expected, the eldest was the first to come out. He strode out with a severely annoyed look on his face. Vincent studied that face, looking for tell-tale changes in expression once the man recognized him. He was not disappointed. The man's look of annoyance went first to surprise, then to suspicion, then to an icy cold gaze that worried Vincent. The sense of malice that hit him was almost physical.

"You," was the only word the man spoke. His brothers now flanked him, the youngest looking concerned, the other seeming unsure what to feel.

"Me," Vincent said. "Please pardon the interruption. I trust I am not keeping you from something vital."

"It is none of your business what you are or are not keeping us from," said the middle brother.

"Quite correct," admitted Vincent. "It is also of very little interest to me. What brings me here is another business of yours." He gave a tiny, calculated smile, mixed with a slight narrowing of his eyes. "This grudge you carry against my friend. It concerns me."

"Your *friend* is a known *murderer*," said the eldest.

"So you implied last evening," Vincent said. "But tell me, was he ever put on trial? Found guilty?"

"Trial?" the man spat. "He fled from justice immediately after cutting our brother down in cold blood! I should say this is indication enough of his guilt!"

"Why, then, has he not been tried since his return?"

Anger clouded the eldest brother's face. The youngest now spoke. "With our parents now dead, no one was left to formally accuse him of the crime."

"And yet, you three are here now. Why do you not accuse him?"

At this, the two younger brothers glanced at their older sibling. The man scowled, then said through clenched teeth, "Because no one now even remembers the incident clearly enough to find him guilty. A trial would be a waste of time."

"Then challenge him to a duel," suggested Vincent.

"I did!" shouted the man. "But the bastard has sworn off violence and refuses to accept the challenge!"

Vincent nodded, stroking his beard thoughtfully. "And what does that tell you?"

"That he is a coward!"

"Might it not also tell you that this man is very different than the man who killed your brother? Do we not all change, to one degree or another, from our younger years?"

"Ha! You are one to speak of younger years, *Baron*," the man said, sneering at the title.

Vincent ignored the remark. "Do you know who the woman is who lives with him?" The question took the brothers off guard. It was clear that they did not. "She is the younger sister of the girl he loved as a youth. That girl killed herself after his departure. And the younger sister found herself consumed with a desire for revenge not unlike your own. For years, she plotted against him, even going so far as to track him down across the sea, intending to kill him. But not until after she had broken his heart, the same way he'd broken hers by being responsible, in her eyes, for the death of her beloved sister." He waited for the effect of these words to sink in on the men. "As you can see," he concluded quietly, "he still lives."

The three were silent for a moment, then the oldest said, "Rubbish. You tell fanciful tales to soften our hearts."

"I tell truth, friends. Sianon did not kill him. Instead, she fell in love with him. She found him to be, as I have said, much changed since the troubled days of his youth. His remorse over the events that took place here so long ago were carried with him over the years. You and Sianon both lost siblings. He lost his love. And his family. That sort of event cannot help but affect a man. I have known him for four years. And he is one of the most honorable men I know."

He ended his argument and studied their faces. The middle brother did nothing but turn his gaze to the ground, his brow knit. The youngest brother nodded at Vincent, as if he agreed with him and always had. He turned his gaze up to his eldest brother, whose expression held a trace of indecisiveness, but otherwise remained grim. He stared Vincent in the eye, then spat in the dirt. "Now that you have said your piece, *Baron*, I would request that you leave. This mine is not open to guests, and we have work to do."

"Well, as it happens, I am not quite finished." Vincent relaxed his pose somewhat, kicking at the dirt distractedly. He adopted a conversational tone, and made only casual eye contact with the brothers. "As I've said, the man is my friend. A very dear friend. I would hate to see or hear of anything happening to him. If you understand me." He smiled in what he hoped was a friendly, yet intimidating fashion.

The youngest brother frowned, obviously understanding him perfectly. The middle brother looked up at him, raised an eyebrow, and glanced at the eldest brother, whose eyes flared in anger, jaw tightening.

"You are threatening me?" he grated, taking steps forward.

Vincent remained calm, ignoring the quickstep his heart was doing. The man did, in fact, outsize him by several inches of height and probably seventy-five pounds of weight. Mostly muscle. He smiled at them again. "I am just stating that I would be most distressed if he should come to any harm. If you wish to interpret that as a threat, well, so be it."

The man was weaponless, other than a dagger tucked into his belt, Vincent noticed. He did, however, have fists the size of small stereo speakers. Vincent took a deep breath as the man stopped directly in front of him. It was one of the hardest things he'd ever done, maintaining his casual pose.

"I don't think I like your attitude," the man said.

Vincent nodded. "Understandable."

"Do you know what I do to people with attitudes I don't like?" Vincent shrugged amiably and shook his head. The big man smiled. "I hit them," he said simply.

The swing was not especially fast, to Vincent's relief. He knew what it lacked in speed, however, it more than made up in mass. But Vincent didn't plan on proving that theory. Raising his left hand, he caught the swinging fist. He gave the man an instant to show some shock and to see the nasty smile on Vincent's face. Then he plowed his own gauntleted fist into the man's cheekbone.

He pulled the punch. A little. Instead of breaking the man's cheek, the force merely knocked him back five feet, to lie unconscious in the dirt. Vincent heaved a sigh that was a mixture of relief and pity. He hoped the other brothers only caught the pity part of it. He looked up at them with an apologetic look on his face. "I really didn't want to do that," he offered.

The youngest brother was gaping wide-eyed at his fallen sibling and at Vincent. The other brother seemed only slightly impressed. "Yes, you did," he said. Vincent felt a stab of concern. Then the man said, "Not that I blame you."

Vincent nodded. "Well, then. Do you think I have any worries concerning my friend?"

The man shrugged. "Personally, I tend to believe your words. I have studied your friend ever since we returned. I see the honor you mention, whenever I look in his eyes. I am willing to believe the killing was not intentional." He looked at his fallen brother. "But I do not think you have convinced Pehr. We will do our best to convince him of your words." The younger brother nodded his agreement at this. "But we cannot promise anything."

"I understand," Vincent said. "And I thank you." He nodded a farewell to them, then untied his horse. As they tended to their fallen brother, Vincent mounted up and left.

His heart was heavy as he rode back toward the main road. Had he really accomplished anything? The younger brothers already seemed to be of a mind to let bygones be bygones. Perhaps he had cemented that idea in their heads, but that was about all. He certainly didn't score any points with the eldest. Pehr was his name. No, Pehr was, if anything, merely adding Vincent to his shit list along with Blade. Ah, well, he thought. He'd tried.

He broke from his thoughts and looked ahead on the road, surprised to see two pedestrians walking down the narrow path toward him. As he got closer, he saw they were a boy and a girl, perhaps in their mid-teens. They both had dark hair and wore simple clothing. The boy wore a medallion, a simple gold circle inset with a huge blue stone. He slowed his horse's pace to look at them.

They were obviously brother and sister, given the strong mutual resemblance. Possibly twins. The boy's face was passionate, his eyes dark and brooding. The girl... Vincent felt a flutter in his heart. The girl was stunningly pretty. And she reminded him of someone, too. But he couldn't place who.

She was looking right at him, a tentative smile on her face. Vincent smiled back, nearing to within several yards. "Good morning," he said to them both, but his eyes stuck on the girl.

She smiled more. "Good morning," she said in return. Her brother then cleared his throat loudly, and Vincent saw a look of distress flash across her face. She hid it promptly, however.

They all stopped, now, a few yards apart. "There is nothing down this road," he told them, assuming they were lost. They had no packs and no horses. Odd, he thought.

"What a *beautiful* animal," said the brother, stepping closer to the horse.

Vincent frowned and looked down at him and the horse. Nothing special about the mount, he thought. Just a rather average...

And then he couldn't move. His body seemed frozen. He saw the boy look up at him with a nasty smile. Then he grasped Vincent's foot and heaved, unseating him. Vincent hit the ground hard, feeling every bit of the pain. But still he couldn't move. His eyes now faced the girl, who wore an expression of concern and frustration.

Then the boy was at his side, kneeling next to him. "How about the gauntlets, sister dear?" he said in an unctuous tone. Vincent felt them being pulled from his hands. Panic ran through him. He remembered feeling this way once before, when

373

Sianon had rendered him immobile and then fried Blade's face. What was this vicious little punk planning for him? "What else should we take, sister? Perhaps his jewelry?"

"No!" the girl said. "Those are enough! Leave him alone!"

"No, I don't think it's quite enough." Vincent felt his sword being unbuckled from his waist. "This could be useful. In fact," he said, "it could be used to just kill him now and get it over with."

"No!" she yelled. "You promised!"

The boy chuckled. "And you believed me?" He stepped into Vincent's line of sight now, and he could see the boy had strapped on the sword, and was holding the gauntlets carefully with only finger and thumb, as if he didn't want to be touching them. His sister now produced a sack, into which the boy dropped the gauntlets.

"You promised," she said flatly. In response, he just laughed, then pulled the sword from the scabbard. A noise made him pause, then. They both looked up, staring down the road to the mine. Vincent saw the boy frown. Not in concern, but in annoyance. "Let us go," urged the girl.

The boy sighed, glancing at his sister. He smiled again. Vincent's heart raced as he saw the boy raise the sword. He brought it swinging down toward Vincent's head.

There was an instant of pain.

And then darkness.

❧ Twenty-Seven ❧

He woke in total darkness, as well as extreme pain. His head throbbed as though it were one giant toothache. He carefully sat up, wiped dirt from his hands, then gingerly felt his head. At the back of his skull, he felt dried blood. And then he remembered.

The boy. His sword. He suddenly realized that he was lucky to be alive, rather than decapitated. Briefly, he wondered why he wasn't. Then he wondered where he was, and how long he'd been there.

It was pitch black. Eyesight wasn't going to help him, here. But that wasn't exactly an unusual state of existence for him. He sighed, then took inventory of his person. Nothing felt broken. In fact, the only pain he felt was due to his head injury. He remembered the boy taking his gauntlets and sword. He felt around his neck. Both of his necklaces were still present. And a good thing, too, he thought. Gnorrin's magic gem probably saved him from bleeding to death. Both magical rings were still in place, too. Again, this was fortunate, otherwise he'd be dead now, if he'd ended up where he thought he had.

He suspected that he was in the bottom of the mine. He doubted he'd been carried down, so he must have been thrown down a shaft somewhere. Vincent pieced together the events as he imagined they'd occurred. The eldest brother, Pehr, probably regained consciousness and took off after him with the intention of killing him. His approach was probably what attracted the attention of the teenagers, causing them to look down the road. Finding him already unconscious from the blow of a sword, the man took him and tossed him down a mine shaft. Why he didn't steal his jewelry was something Vincent couldn't quite figure out. If a man thought little enough of you to commit murder, what's a little thievery on top of it?

At any rate, he couldn't have known that Vincent would fall gently to the bottom instead of plummeting like a rock. Perhaps Pehr didn't even realize that this is what had happened. The ring didn't kick in immediately. Vincent would have fallen normally for a second or so before his descent would have been checked. It was possible that by the time the ring took effect, Vincent's body was already out of sight in the darkness of the shaft.

He hoped so. It would make his return all the more startling. He smiled, then stood up carefully. Vertigo struck and he extended a hand for support from whatever wall might be nearby, but found none.

Okay, he told himself, time to get out of this hole. He tried to put the pain out of his mind, to relax and let his senses flow outward, while his mind raced.

He was at the bottom of a mine shaft. Theoretically, there should be some kind of pressure difference when standing directly under the shaft, as opposed to standing under the mine's ceiling. Possibly even a hint of fresher air.

Turning his face upwards, he began moving slowly in a circle, arms outstretched. Come on, he mentally urged. Give me something. He continued for many minutes. Finally, he stopped. And there it was. The faintest of breezes. And then, a sound. A sort of chittering. And flapping.

I know that sound, he thought. "Bats," he whispered. Returning from an evening of dining on insects, he thought, with full bellies and needing sleep. He envied them.

375

Instinctively, he crouched. The sound grew louder, and then he felt the animals swoop down over his head to disappear behind him. This went on for quite some time. Not a steady stream of them, but a group, then just a few, then another group.

If the bats were returning to their lair, then he'd been unconscious for quite a long time. It must be close to dawn the following day. Hopefully not more than one day had passed. His friends would be worried enough as it was. At any rate, he was now certain that he stood directly under the opening of the shaft. When the bats had passed, he stood and reached up, hoping to find some sort of ladder to climb. But nothing met his fingertips. Frowning, he explored in each direction for a few feet, hoping to encounter an incline. After several minutes of fruitless searching, he stopped. He put his hands on his hips. "Well, shit." He gave an exasperated sigh and tried not to think about the panic threatening to surge up inside him. Instead, he focused on the growling in his stomach.

Food could wait, but water could not. He was quite thirsty. In all his intent listening, he'd heard not a trickle of water. Didn't mean there was none to be found, he told himself, but there certainly wasn't any right nearby. Which meant that he had to go in search of it. He frowned. "Bloody inconvenient," he muttered. He decided that his best bet would be to go in the direction the bats had flown. The only problem was that he'd gotten turned around while searching for some method of climbing the shaft. He didn't know which direction the bats had gone.

He remembered reading something about the sonar of bats, once. Or something he'd heard. He wasn't sure now if he'd read it or not. Something about the pineal gland in humans being capable of producing the same kind of perceptions a bat has. The pineal gland, he recalled, was located in the front of the brain. Some referred to it as the "third eye." Now where would he have read that? He shook his head. And winced. Bad move. The throbbing increased. He firmed his jaw and took a deep breath, then stretched out his hearing, listening carefully for the distinctive sound of roosting bats. And he heard them. Turning in that direction, he began walking slowly, careful of his footing in the underground chamber and keeping his ears tuned at all times for the sound of water.

To his satisfaction, the sound of the bats grew louder as he walked along. The floor, which sloped downward a slight bit, was mostly smooth. He pondered this fact, wondering if it was hewn from the rock by someone, or the remnant of some underground stream from ages gone by. Either way, he was happy he didn't have to stumble. Much.

He walked slowly, and for some distance. After what seemed an hour, he noted a peculiar scent. He wrinkled his nose. What could it be? The sound of the bats was louder, now. And then it struck him. Bat droppings. He frowned at the smell, but at least he knew he was headed in the right direction.

A few minutes later, he felt the change in air pressure around him. The sound of the roosting bats was loud in his ears. And there were echoes. He knew he was within a large cavern deep underground, now. His head throbbed, preventing him from being happier about it. His mouth was dry, and on top of that, his bladder was urging him to relieve himself. He didn't want to do so right here, in the chosen quarters of these bats. That would be rude. So he held it. He walked into the cavern, wondering how many bats were there. Thousands, probably. He wondered what kind of bats they were. He wondered at how ironic it was that you could be very thirsty and have to pee at the same time. And then he started wondering if he were hallucinating, for it seemed as though he could see a glow of light in the distance.

He closed his eyes tightly, rubbing them. But when he opened them, the glow was still there. It was faint, but unmistakable. Could it be possible, he wondered, that he was closer to the surface than he had any right to believe? Hope rising inside him, he hurried forward.

A few strides later, he stumbled on some loose gravel and fell to the ground. He gritted his teeth in pain as his head glanced off the stone floor of the cavern. He felt around him, his hands coming to rest on the small stones that had caused his fall. He scooped up a handful of them, intending to hurl them angrily into the distance. Then he stopped. He brought the stones around in front of him and felt them carefully. Picking out a small stone with a round, smooth surface, he wiped it thoroughly in a fold of his tunic, then popped it into his mouth. He smiled as the stone caused his saliva to collect around it. He swallowed the moisture with great relief, easing his thirst. Now if he could only find a porta-pottie.

The glow beckoned him and he resumed his trek. There was no mistaking it. The light was not some hallucination on his part. But as he drew closer, he realized it was not light from the surface. The glow was an odd greenish-yellow and did not seem to have one specific source. It was, as he soon discovered, light generated by bio-luminescence. The walls on either side of him displayed the growth of some sort of lichen or moss, from which emanated the eerie glow.

Eventually, the glow was strong enough for him to discern some detail in his surroundings. At this point, the walls were fairly covered with the lichen. He studied the chamber, realizing as he did so that there was no noise of bats here. Possibly the animals did not like the glow. That being the case, he decided to empty his bladder. He did so, off the path. He knew he probably shouldn't be doing so. Urine was sterile and he could drink it to re-hydrate, in a pinch. But he wasn't quite desperate enough to do so. He fought off a wave of dizziness brought on by urinating, then he returned to his journey.

Vincent stood in a long, straight stretch of cavern. He looked at the floor and became increasingly of the opinion that it had once been the bed of an underground stream. Possibly altered at some point by the hand of man, but originally a stream bed.

He shook his head. Lost in an abandoned mine's caverns, seriously dehydrated, growing hungrier by the minute, and he was happy over the discovery that he was walking an ancient stream bed. What an idiot, he thought. He rolled the stone around in his mouth to generate more saliva. Then again, he mused, perhaps he was focusing on mundane things like stream beds, bats, and glowing lichen rather than thinking about truly perplexing questions. Like, who were the two teenagers? Why did they attack him? What did their snippet of conversation mean? It sounded as though they knew who he was and had been planning on attacking him for some time. And why did they steal his gauntlets? How did they know they were magical? Like his rings, they were designed to appear quite ordinary.

His head pounded and he put a hand to his temple. Now he remembered why he wasn't thinking about the kids. His head hurt enough as it was. Still, it was a mystery. And he hated mysteries. A dizzy spell hit him and he paused. He took a deep breath, hoping it would clear his head. It didn't. There were plenty of large rocks around.

Shortly, he found one with a flat top and sat down to rest, looking around as he did so.

Despite the glowing plant life on the walls, he'd have been much happier with a torch. Though his eyes were growing used to the limited light, he wanted to see more. The thought that he might be missing some darkened exit was nagging at him. Rhia and the others would be worried sick about him, he knew. He thought briefly about trying to contact Rhia by thought. The devil's bit he'd been continually using, according to Rhia, might have heightened the latent psychic abilities he suspected lay dormant in all people. That was, he assumed, how Rhia had been able to "hear" his dreams and subconscious thoughts about her.

What the hell, he thought. It was worth a shot. Closing his eyes and concentrating, he focused on the thought of Rhia. He willed his plea to fly out to her, beyond the confines of the cavern, into town, and straight to her mind. He tried to convey to her that he was not only alive, but relatively unhurt, though a timely rescue would not be unwelcome.

He maintained this for several minutes, then exhaustion overtook him. His wound had weakened him more than he'd originally thought, and he needed some serious rest. He looked around for a flat place to lie down, then decided that the middle of the path he'd been walking was about as flat as he could hope to find. It made him feel as if he were lying down in the middle of the road, but he fought that with the logic that it was highly improbable that he was going to be run over in his sleep.

He woke to a noise. Sluggishly, he opened his eyes and blinked, taking a moment to recollect his predicament. The permanent night-light glow on the walls around him served as ample reminder. Then he caught the sound again. A deep rumbling. But not steady, like great peals of distant thunder. More like intermittent grindings within the earth.

Or maybe it was grindings within his head. The wound was throbbing again. He hoped it wasn't infected. Sitting up was an effort. He wondered how long he'd been asleep. His stomach growled for food. And water. He fumbled around for the small stone he'd sucked on earlier, wiped it off, and popped it in his mouth. Then he sat and stared at the walls for a bit. He rubbed at his eyes and put his face in his hands. The grinding noise filtered to him again and he frowned. What could be making it? He looked around, but didn't expect to see anything. The noise didn't sound like something he could see. It sounded like it came from beneath him.

But as he looked around, a thought struck him. He stood, straightening his tunic. His head swam as he stood, but he ignored it. Slowly, he made his way off the stream bed and into the rocky areas beside it. Finally, he reached one of the lichen covered walls and studied the substance up close. It was, in fact, a mossy type of plant life. But its glow was much brighter than any type of plant or animal life he'd ever seen or heard of on Earth. He reached down into his boot and withdrew the dagger he kept there. Brat kid hadn't taken that, at least. Carefully, he cut away a section of the stuff— just a small piece, no bigger than his hand—and looked at it on both sides.

The back was just as he'd expected it to be, like the underside of moss. The area of exposed wall proved to be earthy, not rocky. It was slightly damp, but nothing he felt he could extract serious moisture from. He looked at the moss in his hand again.

Up close, it gave off enough light to read by. He rather liked that. Tossing down the small fragment, he attacked the wall again with his dagger. He tore off a single strip, about six inches wide and four feet long. Shaking excess dirt from the back of it, he draped it behind his neck so that it hung down like a vest in front of him. He sincerely hoped it wasn't infested with maggots or other icky things. That would just kill him.

The thought occurred to him that he might want to return to where he initially had fallen. Perhaps with the light he now had, he could find a way back. He hesitated. Normally, he would be intensely curious to find what other things might be waiting to be discovered down here. But he was hurt, hungry, and dehydrated. In the end, common sense won out, and he turned back the way he had come. If the light still didn't show an exit, he thought as he walked along, well... He didn't really want to think about that.

After a time, he came to the place where the bright lichen had first appeared. He looked down at his vest and happily noted that it hadn't decreased its luminosity at all. Eventually, he encountered the vast chamber where the bats lived. He listened. No bat sounds. It must be night, he thought, and they're all out feeding. Or perhaps it was day and they were all asleep. Either way, he envied them.

The chamber was large, but otherwise unremarkable. Or so he thought, until he saw the three skeletons lying beside the stream bed. Remains of clothing clung in tatters to the bones. Mining tools lay strewn about. Two of them were obviously human, he saw as he examined them. The third was something smaller, but still humanoid. Too big to be a gnome. A dwarf, perhaps, he thought. He wondered what had killed them. With a shrug, he rose again and continued.

But when he reached the other side of the chamber, he paused, a frown growing on his face. The stream bed evidently had been produced by the merging of four smaller streams. The end of the cavern had not one, but four separate exits. Which one had he entered through? It could have been any of them. They were very close together. And very small. Odd. He hadn't had any sensation of being in such an enclosed space when he'd walked through before. Then again, he hadn't exactly been in his most perceptive state. With a sigh, he entered the tunnel to his far left.

His glowing vest lit his way as he entered the passage, making the walls loom beside him. He found more skeletal remains inside the passage, but no whole skeletons, only individual bones scattered around. Many of them were broken, as if crushed. He slowed his pace, examining some of the bones more closely. And he heard the grinding noise again, louder than before. He frowned and dropped the bone he'd been looking at, then proceeded down the passage. It still resembled a stream bed, he thought, but narrower. And here and there, among the rocks lining either side of the passage, were what looked like holes. He stepped off the path to examine one, letting the lichen hang down into the hole for about a foot. It appeared to be perfectly round, perhaps two feet in diameter. Debris lay in a circle around the mouth of the hole. It did not seem especially deep. The lichen's light showed bottom. However, it appeared to slope off to one side, rather than just dropping straight down. After a few minutes, he moved on. Along the way, he saw several more such holes. And periodically, the sound of the grinding rumble would erupt, lasting a few seconds, then fading. Very strange, he thought. But he was far more concerned with finding his way out of the mine than with any kind of mysterious noises.

At some point during his trek, he began to pay attention to the rocks along the sides of the path. He thought it quite odd that so many of them seemed to be the same size and shape—about a foot and a half in height, and taller than they were wide. Like eggs sitting on end.

He stopped. Like eggs.

He stood looking at the stones. His mind summoned up an image from the movie, *Alien*, wherein John Hurt's character discovers a subterranean area filled with alien eggs. He examines one and a spider-like thing shoots out and wraps itself around his head.

Vincent shuddered and shook the image from his head. That wasn't going to happen here, he told himself. Fighting off a wave of panic, he stepped off the path and made his way to the rocks. He stopped in front of one and knelt. The lichen illuminated it clearly. Vincent smiled to himself in relief. This was just a rock. Not an egg. It looked like a rock, felt like a rock. It had no seams or anything that might indicate a means of escape from its confines. And the thing was solid, he realized, as he rapped on it with his knuckles. No way was this thing an egg.

He stood, wiping dirt from his trousers, and stepped back to the path. No sooner had he gone twenty steps, however, than he heard the grinding noise again. This time, it built in intensity until it seemed to be on top of him. Or rather, under him. He felt the vibrations under his boots. And then it slowly faded.

He blinked. "Okay," he mumbled, "so there's a subway."

He frowned. What could it be? He cast a glance again at the egg-like rocks, and as he did so, one of them moved. Vincent stood motionless, staring as the rock wobbled slightly. There was a cracking sound, then the grinding noise. Faintly, however. Nothing like the noise that had just passed underneath him. And then, nothing. The noise rapidly disappeared. The rock stood still again.

Eventually, curiosity won out. He stepped off the path again and went to the rock. Tentatively, he touched it. Nope. Still felt like a rock. He didn't know what the cracking sound was, but it had nothing to do with this thing. He began to rise, then paused. On a hunch, he grasped the rock with both hands and pushed.

The stone fell over easily, where it lay rocking on its side. Vincent's heart stuttered as he saw the hole. Two holes, in fact. One lay directly underneath where the stone had stood. No, not stone, he corrected himself. Egg. For the other hole was in the bottom of the toppled shell. The rock was hollow. The shell was thick enough to sound and feel solid to his hands, but it was, nevertheless, a shell. His mind raced with thoughts on what type of creature this must be. A rock for an egg. And obviously, upon hatching, it burrows into the earth. The grinding noise, then, was from the hatchlings making their way from egg to... wherever. No, he thought. The noise he heard was much louder than that. Adults, perhaps? Traveling to and fro? This seemed the most likely scenario. He shook his head. Any creature that could hatch itself from seemingly solid stone and burrow its way through rocky earth was not one he had much desire to confront.

He continued on for a few minutes, pondering these things, and grew increasingly concerned when he saw that the quantity of eggs seemed to be growing. Then he came to a point on the path that had one of the large holes in it. He determined now that this must be a point where an adult creature had exited the earth. And this was a good enough indication to him that it was time to return and try one of the other paths.

His retreat was hurried. He didn't mind admitting to himself that he wanted to be as far away from these hypothetical creatures as possible, as quickly as possible. It was not, however, quite quickly enough. Twenty yards before reaching the entrance to the large chamber, Vincent heard the grinding again. He froze. Then he stood in shock as the ground halfway between himself and the exit began to move. Without thinking, he stepped off the path and crouched down behind a rock. Then he made sure it really was a rock.

He watched as the earth swelled and parted. A quantity of earth fell down, then a small shower of rubble came spewing gently forth as something large emerged. Vincent's jaw dropped. The creature, too, was vaguely egg-shaped, and not much larger than the eggs themselves. He saw two sets of three short, powerful limbs, spaced evenly around the torso, each with three digits ending in heavy, sharp claws similarly spaced. The creature looked like it, too, was made of rock. And perhaps it was. Vincent had no intention of finding out.

The creature stood upon the path beside the hole and slowly rotated. Vincent got the uneasy feeling that the thing was looking for him. An invader in the nursery, so to speak. He stayed as motionless as possible, not wanting to alert the creature. He stopped breathing, for the same reason. He regretted having the pebble in his mouth. Saliva built up and had to be swallowed. He did so, then cupped his palm over his mouth to remove the pebble. The action produced a slight sucking noise. And the creature turned what Vincent had to assume was its face in his direction. Then it started moving slowly toward him.

Shit, Vincent thought. No weapons, nowhere to run. And a creature that would most likely be able to rip him apart like tissue paper was walking toward him. He gritted his teeth. At least he could stand up and take it. So he did. To his surprise, the creature stopped moving. It even retreated a step. Vincent frowned. Then it occurred to him. The light from his makeshift vest. This was an underground creature. Light wasn't something it was used to. He studied the creature from his full height. The top of the creature's body seemed to be a sort of mouth. It had four teeth, very similar in structure to the claws on its feet, but bigger. These looked perfectly capable of carving a swath through earth and rock. And people.

The legs themselves were situated in such a way that the creature could walk upright or prone, depending upon its orientation and/or whim. Vincent hoped its whim was not to charge him. He stepped out a little further. The creature retreated again. This was a good sign. A quick step forward elicited an equally quick step backward by the creature. To Vincent's relief, it seemed very unwilling to cross paths with someone who glowed. Vincent could understand that. He'd have the same hesitation. With a smile, he made his way around the creature, skirting the path until he was past, then onto it and to the exit. The creature watched him go. Or rather, Vincent assumed it watched him. He didn't study it enough to see anything on the creature that resembled eyes.

In the bat chamber again, he breathed a sigh of relief, his heart pounding. "Well, that was fun," he whispered to himself, and popped the pebble back into his mouth. After a moment's rest, he headed down corridor number two.

His shining vest lit the way as he walked down the uneventful path. And before too long, he found himself looking at a small slope that led up to the shaft through which he'd undoubtedly descended. He anxiously stepped underneath the mouth of the shaft. He looked up, desperately seeking some way of ascending. But there was nothing. No handholds. No rope. Certainly no ladder. He looked straight up the shaft. But try as he might, there was no telling how far he would have to climb. If he still had the gauntlets, he thought, he could probably do it. The strength that they gave him would have made it easy to dig his own handholds and pull himself out. Without them, there was no way, even if he weren't weak from hunger and dehydration, with a still unhealed head wound.

"Damn," he mumbled around the pebble. He turned away from the opening and looked back down the corridor. This left two remaining paths and a slim hope that one of them led to an alternate exit. His head was throbbing again and he felt woozier than ever. He needed to rest before continuing. He sat with his back against a wall of the corridor and closed his eyes.

He woke later, feeling little better. His head still hurt, and now his behind did, too, from sitting in gravel. He rose, grateful that he didn't feel like he was going to pass out. Then he made his way out of the corridor. He could hear the bats chittering again, somewhere in the darkness up above. He wished he knew what time of day it was. He now had to assume it was early evening and the animals were just waking. He felt sure he would have heard them come in if they were returning to roost.

He turned and entered the third corridor. For some distance, it was straight and uneventful. Soon, however, it began to twist and turn. It also began to slope downward. This fact dismayed Vincent, but he continued on. The tunnel showed some signs of traffic. There were no large stones to trip over, for example. He hoped this meant there was an exit to be found. Perhaps it would begin to slope upward, eventually.

He continued for a while, until he started to smell something odd. He took a whiff. It reminded him of the smell of natural gas, but with an unidentifiable undertone to it. It was vaguely annoying, so he dealt with it by ceasing to breathe. No breathing meant no smelling. His head was messed up enough without inhaling unknown fumes. His mind flashed back to his initial encounter with the efreeti, when he had gained this ability. He had promised to find some way to free the creature from his prison. Not only had he not found such a method, he hadn't even really been thinking about it much.

Ariaziane had been with him on that adventure. And the thought of her sent a pang of loss through him. He missed her. How desperately he wanted to see her. He might never see her again, he thought, whether or not he was able to find his way out of this mine.

Ariaziane reminded him of Rhia. He sometimes felt it was strange that he was so attracted to two very different women. But when he thought about it more intently, it seemed to make perfect sense. It was similar to being able to enjoy two very different kinds of music. Classical and rock 'n' roll, for example. He smiled at this little analogy. It made it easier for his tired mind to accept.

His smile soon turned to a frown, however, when he saw the bones. A complete skeleton, human in appearance, lay in the corridor. Vincent puzzled over this for only a moment before moving on, his attention now returned to the prospect of his own possible demise if he did not find his way out.

Soon he encountered more bones. Again, complete human skeletons, with shreds of clothing, lying in the corridor. He thought again of the nasty fumes he had smelled some ways back. It seemed probable that they were toxic and responsible for the deaths of these men. He rounded another curve in the tunnel and suddenly found himself within a chamber approximately thirty feet wide and forty feet deep. Three more skeletons lay within, one of which he nearly tripped over upon entering. The others lay near the walls.

Vincent looked at the walls, moving closer. As he did so, he confirmed what he thought he had seen. The walls held veins of some sort of gemstone. Fairly rich veins, from what he could determine. No wonder the brothers had such an interest in it.

He was not, however, able to discern what sort of stones they were. The glow given by his vest was distinctly yellowish. It was impossible to tell what color the stones were.

What about the gas? What caused it to appear suddenly? Vincent turned from the wall and rubbed his face. He was so tired. Why did he even care about these questions? All he should be thinking about was getting out of this place.

He was about to leave when his eye caught something else. On the ground near the wall farthest from him lay a dark object. As he approached it, Vincent saw it was an open chest, about a foot in length. He crouched next to it and looked inside. He dug his hand into the chest, letting the tiny gemstones trickle from his fingers.

Depending on the quality of these stones, the chest had to contain a small fortune, he realized. This must be what the brothers were after. But the gas was preventing them from gaining access to it. He chuckled. Such a simple thing. But so impossible without a gas mask. Or magical enhancement, as the case may be.

Vincent closed the chest and lifted it. Good thing these are gemstones and not gold coins, he thought. Hoisting the case onto a shoulder, he left the chamber and returned down the curving tunnel, back to what he now thought of as the batcave.

The trip seemed long, undoubtedly due to the chest he carried, which he switched from shoulder to shoulder as he tired. He thought more than once that this was a stupid endeavor. He wasn't even taking the treasure for himself, but for the brothers. A peace offering, as it were. Probably a futile effort.

As he neared the end of the tunnel, he heard the calls of the bats. They were quite loud. Probably preparing to head out for the evening, he thought. Great. He really wanted to go out there with winged rats wheeling around his head. He reached the mouth of the tunnel and paused at the entrance. Even in the dim glow offered by the lichen, he could see them flitting about. He put down the chest and sat on top of it, just inside the tunnel, and waited for them to exit the chamber.

Several minutes later, most of the bats were gone and Vincent decided it was safe enough to venture around to the next corridor. He rose, stretching his sore limbs. Then he hoisted the chest of gems again and stepped out into the open.

No sooner had he done so than a handful of the bats careened down toward him, perhaps attracted by the light of the lichen, he realized. This played havoc with his earlier theory about the bats not liking the light, but he simply didn't care at this point. He stepped briskly toward the opening of the final corridor. He wasn't frightened, knowing that bats wouldn't attack him. But still, there was no sense in dawdling.

When he was struck from behind, he nearly choked on his pebble.

The force of the blow sent him stumbling forward, the chest flying from his hands to land with a crack on the stone floor. And then Vincent felt the pain as something was plunged into him, where the neck and shoulder met on his left side. It felt like someone had just skewered him with a knitting needle.

He gasped and turned to see what had hit him. Attached to his shoulder was one of the bats. Except, his pain-addled brain now realized, it wasn't a bat. It had leathery wings like a bat, and a body like a really fat bat, but its head had a long, needle-sharp proboscis, through which it seemed to be sucking Vincent's blood.

He swatted at it with his hand, but hitting the animal only succeeded in sending another stab of pain through his body. And then he was hit by another one, directly in the neck. The pain sent him to his knees, the pebble in his mouth flying out as he screamed.

He could feel the blood being sucked from his neck. He grabbed frantically at the creature, but try as he might, he could not pull it off. If he only had his gauntlets, he moaned to himself.

A third beast hit him, at another point on his neck. And this time, he sprawled completely on the floor. This was it, he knew. He couldn't pull the animals off himself, and they were killing him. He was growing weaker by the second. Maybe one day, someone would see his skeleton lying in the open by a chest of gems and have a serious mystery on their hands.

He chuckled mentally at the image as he closed his eyes. He felt tears burning at his eyelids. He wasn't ready to die, yet. There was so much he hadn't done. So much still to enjoy from life. Most of all, he didn't want to die alone, in some abandoned mine, while his friends puzzled over his disappearance. He thought of them, trying to find him. He thought of Ariaziane, whom he'd now never see again. He thought of his family on Earth, who no doubt had long ago given him up for dead, anyway.

Anger flared inside him, then. Damn it, if he couldn't pull the little bastards off him, he'd just squeeze them to death! He made to grab one, but suddenly found his arms to be dreadfully heavy. He could barely move them. And his heart sank as he realized that these creatures were injecting some form of paralyzing venom into him, like a spider. Perhaps it was going to liquefy his body, allowing the creatures to suck not just his blood, but his entire liquid self into their hairy little tummies.

He tried again to move his hands, to clench them. He was rewarded with the sound of something scraping on the stone floor. He blinked, knocking tears to the ground. His fingers couldn't have made a noise like that. And then he heard it again. Like rock scraping against rock. This time, he knew for certain that it wasn't his doing, since he hadn't moved.

But this was a puzzle he was in no condition to worry about. His pain was intense, but fading. Now he was going numb. And that was okay with him. Numb is better than pain any day, he told himself. He squeezed his eyes closed. So this is what dying feels like, he thought.

And then he heard a nasty squawk, very loud, and there was a sharp tug at his neck, as if one of the creatures had just pulled its siphon out of him. Then there was a splat, and something warm and wet hit his face. He opened his eyes to see one of the creatures lying mangled in front of him. Another squawk and tug, another splat. Then a third sequence.

Unless he was mistaken, that would cover all the little beasties that had pounced on him, he thought with hope rising in his chest. He lay there, willing the paralyzing poison to dissipate so he could move. But he was virtually immobile and could do nothing to change the direction in which his head was pointing. He had a splendid view of the floor of the cavern, but that was about it.

Then he heard the scraping again, followed by a bizarre, guttural noise. He had no idea what it was, nor did he waste much time or energy thinking about it. He was too busy contemplating the idea that he might not die just yet.

The scraping noise returned, but faded, moving farther away. Vincent was growing cold, his body covered in a sheen of sweat in the chilly cavern. Blood ran down his neck from the wounds made by the creatures. It soon stopped, thanks to Gnorrin's gift. But he'd lost a lot of blood. The fact that he wouldn't lose more could be irrelevant.

It rather annoyed him that he was being so analytical while lying at death's door. But it beat thinking about crossing over that threshold, he had to admit.

Shortly, the scraping noise stopped. There was a moment or two of silence, then another strange noise echoed in his ears. It sounded like... Vincent blinked. It sounded like crunching. Like the sound glass makes when it's crushed under foot, or like someone chewing ice cubes.

For some reason, this puzzled him enough for him to make a concentrated effort to discover its source. The paralysis was, slowly, lessening. Focusing all his strength, he managed to flop his head over onto the other side.

What he saw should have shocked him, he knew. But he was beyond that. He wasn't sure what to feel about anything at this point. A few feet away, the chest of gems had fallen. The impact with the floor had caused the lid to pop open and the gems lay spilled on the ground around it. Standing beside the chest was one of the rock creatures. And, much to Vincent's amazement, the creature was snacking on the stones!

He watched as it gently reached down and picked up one of the gemstones between its sharp claws and lifted it, not to the top of its body, where the four-toothed maw was, but to the level he would expect it to, had the creature possessed a face and mouth. There followed the crunching noise he'd heard before, then the creature seemed to shudder, as with pleasure, and the empty claw descended again, picking up another stone.

Vincent knew he must have uttered some noise then, for the creature turned, hobbling around on its three stout legs, to face him. And then Vincent could see that the creature did possess something of a face. It had no eyes, but there were three depressions in the rocky exterior of the part of the creature that he hadn't noticed on the one he'd seen earlier. Two were situated beside each other, as Vincent would have expected. The third was above and between the two. There was nothing that resembled a nose or ears. And instead of a mouth, there was the finest of cracks, extending across the entire body of the creature.

It apparently then remembered the gem in its claws. As the arm lifted again, Vincent watched as the mouth crack split open and the claw dropped the gemstone inside. The crack then sealed itself, after which the crunching was heard.

Odd, Vincent thought. The orifice atop the creatures head looked like a mouth, but maybe its only purpose was to chew the earth as the creatures made their way through the ground. He watched as the creature finished its morsel, then stood there. Vincent swore it was studying him, but had no facial features to judge by. After a moment or two of this, the creature hobbled toward him.

A surge of panic shot through him. Now that he felt he was going to live, he damned well didn't want to be ripped to shreds by this thing. He tried to move, but still could manage only slight floppings of his limbs. He watched the creature's heavy legs approach nearer and nearer.

The next thing he knew, a clawed limb reached down and grasped him by the chain mail under his tunic. Then his torso was lifted off the ground and he was dragged across the floor by the powerful creature.

There was nothing he could do to stop it. He wasn't facing in the direction he was being taken, but he judged it to be toward the fourth corridor. The creature must have lifted him with its third arm, which he now knew to be located in its back. He couldn't help but wonder at the power this small creature had within its body. And at what intentions might be within its mind.

The creature paused by the spilled chest of gems and scooped it up with another arm. And then they were within the corridor. They traveled some ways, which caused Vincent some concern. But throughout the trek, he continued to test his limbs. He was relieved to discover that sensation was returning well enough. He could make a fist and flex his elbows. But he knew this would do him little good. He was terribly weak. The blood he'd lost, mixed with the residue of poison the creatures had put in him, all of this on top of an unknown number of days without food and water. Even before the mosquito bats had attacked, he'd felt like he'd been hit by a truck.

Suddenly, Vincent was released. He fell to the ground in a heap, cracking his head on the hard floor of the corridor. He slammed his eyes shut against a new pain that was, in fact, just a reminder of an old pain. He could almost feel the wound from the sword blow opening up again.

A minute passed as he dealt with his agony. Then, breathing heavily, he opened his eyes again. The first thing that caught his attention was the rock creature. It stood only a few feet away, watching him. Actually, he supposed it was sitting. The legs were bent outward and the rounded bottom of the creature was on the floor. It was eating while it watched him. Every few seconds it would reach down and grab one of the gems from the chest and munch down on it. This was often followed by the action Vincent interpreted as a happy shudder.

The next thing that caught his attention was the skeleton beside him. He found the energy to sit up, propping his back against the corridor wall. There were several skeletons, he saw. Where was he? In some sort of ritualistic killing field for the rock creature's victims? He glanced at the thing again. It sure didn't look like killing was on its agenda. He relaxed somewhat, looking at it.

Then a wave of pain hit him again. He winced. He had to gain strength if he had any hope of making it out, he knew. And suddenly Rhia popped into his mind. Healing. Rhia. He reached for the leather pouch that he always wore strapped to his belt. He must have some healing herb left.

He opened the pouch, but found it empty. He'd used the last of it at some point, but didn't recall when. In desperation, he rooted around in his other pouch. He knew nothing was likely to be found, but he had to look. When his fingers closed around something hard, he was surprised. He pulled it out.

It was a small bottle with a stopper in it. He frowned. What was this? Where had it come from? Wait! He remembered! Gnorrin had given this to him, and one to Ariaziane. Such a long time ago. He'd said it was a healing potion of sorts. A rejuvenator. Well, he thought, if ever there was a time when he needed such a thing, it was now.

He shakily brought the bottle toward his face. He struggled with the stopper, but finally got it out. He looked at the rock creature, who remained motionless, and nodded toward the creature. "Cheers," he croaked, then closed his eyes and brought the liquid to his lips.

It tasted of fire going down. He felt it make its way down his throat and into his stomach. There, it seemed to spread out over his entire body like an explosion, until it had reached the tips of his fingers and toes. As it did so, it did everything Gnorrin claimed it would. He could feel the wash of warmth turning into energy.

In his present state, it was probably enough to enable him to stand. It certainly wouldn't do much more than that. But he was grateful for that much. He sat there, enjoying the fact that his head hurt a little less. Then his eyes snapped open as he heard the rock creature approaching.

He sat there, knowing that anything he tried to do would likely be futile. He kept reminding himself that this creature had saved his life for some unknown reason. It would be rude to run away from it. The creature stopped in front of him. Vincent could not tell at all where the thing's eyes were aimed, but it seemed to him that it was looking at Vincent's hands. He looked down at them, too, at the bottle he held.

He slowly held out the empty bottle to the creature. Gently, it took it from Vincent's fingers. It seemed to be examining the bottle carefully. Then, as Vincent watched, the mouth split open and the bottle was dropped in. A popping and crunching noise followed. The creature made no motions after this, but Vincent would have sworn he felt a wash of satisfaction emanating from it.

Then it backed up to its previous position, grabbed another gem, and ate it. Then, as if an idea had just struck it, it returned to Vincent, holding a gem in its claws. Vincent blinked. Then, catching on, he held out his hand and the creature dropped the gem into it. Then it stood there, watching and, evidently, waiting.

Vincent smiled tentatively. The being was sharing with him. The least he could do was play along. He popped the gem into his mouth. He worked his jaw and made chomping noises, then pretended to swallow it. Then he smiled and nodded his head. This seemed to satisfy the creature. It settled back into its resting position.

Having lost his pebble earlier, he took advantage of the gem in his mouth. It was sharp, but served the purpose to a degree. The potion he'd swallowed did little more than wet his mouth. He needed water desperately.

Vincent shifted uncomfortably against the wall, wondering what to do now. Why had the creature brought him here? The skeletons around him made him feel decidedly uneasy. Even though the creature had shown no ill will toward him, he still didn't feel real happy about his predicament.

He wondered how the creature would react if he stood up. He was looking at the creature, wondering whether to risk it or not, idly watching the thing continue to munch on gemstones, when something behind the creature caught his attention. Off the path, something was rising from the floor. Vincent blinked. It was another of the rock creatures. But this one was about triple the size of his new friend.

Panic rose in his chest. Now would be a very good time to learn if he could stand up, he thought. He struggled to rise, using the wall behind him for assistance. The smaller creature had turned, by the time Vincent was on his feet and swaying. The larger creature now loomed over the smaller one. An arm swung out, cracking sharply against the smaller creature's fist, which held a gemstone. The stone clattered to the floor. Vincent raised an eyebrow, then stifled a chuckle. Just like a kid with his hand caught in the cookie jar, he thought. Then the larger creature grabbed the smaller one's arm firmly in its claws and pulled the young one behind itself. Then it turned to look at Vincent.

This was all the incentive he needed. Vincent's legs began pumping, propelling him deeper into the corridor. He glanced over his shoulder during his flight, to see if the thing was following him. He didn't think so, but couldn't tell for sure, since the glow from the vest wasn't strong enough to illuminate very far away.

A minute later, his legs buckled and he sprawled to the ground.

He woke later to a noise. It was faint, but unmistakable. It was the sound of dripping. The noise roused him like an alarm clock. His eyes snapped open and he fairly leaped to his hands and knees. He instantly regretted the action as his head began pounding. And in that instant, he felt the energy from the adrenaline rush taper off, leaving him weak and ready to collapse again.

But he dragged himself to his feet, struggling against what seemed to be a million pounds of pressure. His lichen vest, he noted, seemed noticeably duller than before. The stuff must finally be dying, he thought, and hoped he wasn't going to join it. And with incredible effort, he began to trudge forward.

The noise became steadily, though slowly, louder. Vincent's heartbeat joined it in its swelling. It seemed an eternity before he found the source of the dripping, by having a drop of water hit him in the head. He stopped then, startled and expectant. He turned his face upward and was rewarded momentarily by having another drop smack him in the forehead.

He dropped to the ground, rolling onto his back, and positioned his head to where he thought the next drop would land. He plucked the gemstone from his mouth, tucking it absently into his pouch, and lay there, waiting. A few wet splats later, he had his head positioned correctly. And slowly, drop by drop, Vincent began quenching his thirst.

It took quite a long time, but he was patient. As the drops moistened his parched lips and mouth, he relaxed, giving himself up to it. He had never wanted anything so badly in his life as he wanted this water right now. And even if it took all day or night, he would lie here and drink.

When he had finally given his body some liquid satisfaction, he rolled aside and slept. After some time, he woke again, rolled back over and enjoyed more water. Finally, he rose to his feet.

This was it, he told himself. He had to find his way out now, or he never would. He decided to continue on in the direction he was heading. This was, after all, the only corridor he had not explored. He walked slowly, noting for the first time that he was traveling up a slight incline. He wondered how much of the corridor had been on the incline. He'd paid no attention during his desperate flight from the rock creature.

He increased his pace, stepping quickly down the path that soon began to lose its straight course, to begin curving this way and that. And, to Vincent's great satisfaction, began to rise more and more steeply.

For what seemed an hour, he walked. The slope carried him higher and higher, but the winding passageway only decreased the relative distance. He stopped to rest several times, waiting long enough for his head to stop throbbing. During these rests, he stretched his hearing to its limits. He heard no sound of animal life in the vicinity. Or, for that matter, mineral life. And the only vegetable life was the dying vest he wore. Its light was less than half its original luminosity. He hoped it would last until he found a way out.

He heard more dropping liquid on several occasions. He had to surmise that it was raining up above and was soaking through, possibly dripping from unseen stalactites. The walls he touched now were damp in spots.

His stomach was making very rude noises and gestures, too. How many days had he gone without food? He had no idea. He wasn't even sure he wanted to know. He did know, however, that he'd kill for some of Gnorrin's stew right now.

Further and further he made his way up toward the surface. At least, he hoped it was toward the surface. For all he knew, he could be tunneling up inside a small mountain. But he shook his head at the thought. There were no mountains in the vicinity, small or otherwise.

Finally, rounding yet another curve in the passageway, he saw light. His heart swelled within him when he saw it. For a moment, he stood immobile, staring at what seemed to be a glaring beacon, but was in fact only a small, pale shaft of light coming from high above.

The light, he saw, was coming through an opening of unknown size. Since he could not tell how high up the opening was, he could not judge its diameter. Below the opening, however, was what caught his attention. A huge pile of rubble, rocks and dirt extending, seemingly, to the opening above. Was it a landslide? A cave-in of some sort? How could that be? The pile was huge! Such a cave-in would have left a much bigger hole than the one he saw. He frowned. It doesn't matter what caused it, he told himself. Just make use of it!

And he began to climb. Easily, at first, but growing more and more difficult. The higher he climbed, the looser the rocks seemed to be. Gaining sure footing was tricky. He slipped and slid a number of times, but finally reached the top.

What he found was quite a shock. A huge tract of a plateau had evidently collapsed to form a deep depression. Tons of rock and earth had fallen into this passageway. The opening he now came upon was fairly huge, perhaps thirty feet in diameter on its longest side, ten on its shortest.

It could have been a mile and Vincent wouldn't have been any happier to see it. He climbed out of the passage and onto the sloping, barren ground. The sky above was overcast after the storm. And he lay there in the mud, staring at the sky, feeling the tears of joy welling in his eyes.

෨ ෬

Relief rushed forth as she saw her father climb out onto the plateau. Her tears were a joy to her. Ever since her brother had struck him with the sword, she had lived in utter anxiety. She had no way of knowing whether he lived or not.

They'd teleported back to the cave, where she utilized every spare moment to use the crystal ball to learn her father's fate. She was careful not to do this under the attention of her brother or mother. Though her mother wouldn't have cared, she had to prevent her brother from discovering that his blow had not been fatal. If, in fact, it hadn't been.

She'd done all she could have done. She wasn't sure if the quick spell she'd cast at the last moment had disrupted her brother enough to save her father. And when she looked in the crystal ball for him, she could not find him. Only now, as he crawled out of the underground mine, did she know she'd succeeded.

Now, more than ever, she knew she had to go to him. But how could she do that without being followed by her brother? If he learned that their father still lived, he'd go mad.

Then again, she thought, as her tears slowly subsided and she darkened the magic orb, perhaps her brother should be made aware of his failed assassination attempt. Playing along with him could be the only way she could save her father from his psychopathic son.

It would require a lot of planning on her part. Much preparation, especially in the realm of learning certain spells that would be needed, some of which would be used only if things went disastrously wrong. And such learning would be in direct opposition to her mother's teachings.

But that was fine. She was resourceful. She'd manage.

❧ Twenty-Eight ❧

After a time, he sat up. He removed his lichen vest and placed it flat on the mud. Maybe someday he'd return to this spot and find the plateau covered with the glowing plant. Probably not, but it was an interesting thought.

The first thing he had to do, he realized, was figure out where he was. Healing potion or no healing potion, he was still very weak and needed food, water, and rest, though not necessarily in that order. Until these things were accomplished, he couldn't even think of anything else.

He entertained the notion of resting right where he was. But not only was the ground muddy, it was cold, too. He'd wake up with pneumonia and in his state, it would probably kill him. He had to move on, to find shelter and nourishment.

Vincent stood slowly, trying to avoid any dizziness. The effort it had taken to climb the pile of rocks and earth to escape had really wiped him out. He walked to the edge of the plateau and looked out over the drop. It was about twenty feet, he estimated, to solid footing. Without hesitation, he stepped off, fell a short distance, then his magical ring lowered him gently the rest of the way to the ground.

He carefully walked around the perimeter of the plateau's base. Nothing looked familiar, but he did find what appeared to be an old pathway through the brush, overgrown from years of abandonment. His footing on the steep slope was not the surest, and he slowed his descent by grasping the trunks of scrub trees along the way. His head throbbed and he felt woozy. He knew his wound was infected. Who could imagine what sort of nasties he might have picked up in the mine?

Eventually, he made it to level ground. And it was then that a smell struck him. He stopped, cleared his head, and focused on the odor. It was not exactly pleasant, but not entirely unpleasant, either. His heart leaped inside him. Apples! Rotting apples!

It was the Season of the Harvest. Apples would be falling from the trees. His mouth watered at the thought, and he rushed headlong toward the smell.

Before long, he was standing among several trees laden with the fruit. Hundreds of small, red globes lay scattered on the ground. Many were bruised and rotting. Others, he was delighted to find, were not. Still, he thought, the ones on the ground might not be safe to eat, whether they looked rotten or not.

He picked up a decent looking piece, then moved underneath a branch heavy with the fruit. Remembering identical times as a youth, when he and his friends would play among the few apple trees in their backyard, he threw the fruit straight up, where it collided with the bunches of red prizes on the branch. Half a dozen flew off. He caught one, then picked up the others. He took his treasure to a spot of grass away from the tree and sat down to feast. And when he had finished his repast, he slept.

He woke feeling weak and dizzy, and he felt a chill he hadn't noticed earlier, but he was no longer hungry. His mind seemed clearer, at any rate. He stuffed a couple more pieces of fruit inside his tunic for later, then took stock of his surroundings.

He studied the lay of the hills around him, trying to recall how they had looked upon his approach to the mine. After a moment, he chose a direction and set off. The way was heavily wooded, and he tripped often on exposed roots. At one point, he nearly passed out, so great had his dizziness become.

As he leaned against a tree for support, he glanced about him. There were many fallen branches on the ground. Possibly the rainstorm that had gone through recently had blown them down. His gaze stopped on one branch in particular. It was long and thin and quite straight. He pushed himself from the tree and shuffled over to the branch.

Snapping several twigs off the side, he examined it, nodding. It would make a fine walking stick. It was sturdy and comfortable in his hand. Yes, he thought. This could be most useful. And again, he set off.

He walked for quite a while, though his brain was incapable of estimating the time. He didn't even bother trying. He had no idea how long he'd been underground. He fully intended to refer to this period as his "lost weekend," if he didn't die of infection first.

His walking stick did, indeed, prove useful on several occasions. The further he walked, the more he seemed to need it. His head was pounding and spinning. This was how a hangover was once described to him. He wondered what the appeal could possibly be.

Finally, after what seemed like twelve hours, but what was probably closer to two, he came upon a familiar sight. It was the road to the mine. He'd come out from behind the mine in an arc and was now intersecting with the road.

He stopped, leaning on his stick, looking up and down the road. Which way to go? Should he head out to the main road and journey back into town? This would be the best idea, he felt sure. He needed medical attention and probably about a week of sleep. Or, he could turn and go back to the mining site, confronting the brothers. This was, he decided, undeniably stupid. Naturally, this was the option he chose.

None of the brothers were in evidence when he arrived. There was, however, a fire going in a pit, with a lidded pot over it. Either they had already eaten, or soon would. Vincent decided to make sure their dinner was of good quality.

He propped his walking stick against a nearby rock. Picking up one of the wooden bowls that lay on the ground, he dished out some of the stew in the pot, then sat on the rock and ate. Not as good as Gnorrin's, he thought, but it would do.

As he finished the stew, he noticed something lying on another rock nearby. It looked like a book. He retrieved it, returned to his seat, and opened it. It was a leather-bound volume, with a page marker. Vincent turned to the page it held, and shortly determined the book to be the journal of the brothers' grandfather, detailing the mining operation. The page marked was very interesting. It was a listing of the hazards of the mine. Vincent scanned it eagerly, reading about the rock creatures, the blood-sucking bat-things, and the mysterious gas. Okay, he thought, so the brothers are aware of them.

The middle brother came out of the mine entrance as Vincent was reading. He stood there, shocked, staring at him. "Good day," said Vincent. "And good stew. Hit the spot," he said. Then he reached into his tunic, pulling out the two apples. "Fruit?" he offered.

At this, the man snapped out of his shock. He glanced over his shoulder, into the mine entrance, then turned and stepped quietly toward Vincent. He stopped a few feet in front of him. "I confess to some amazement," he said simply. Vincent did not reply, merely bit into his apple. "And to some relief. I am glad you are alive. My brother..."

"Yes," said Vincent. "I understand. You seem a decent fellow. Your younger brother, too. Pehr, on the other hand..."

The man nodded. "He is hot-tempered and unforgiving, yes."

Vincent watched the man's gaze as he tried to examine the back of Vincent's head and its injury. He said nothing verbally, but the knit brow spoke volumes to Vincent.

"How did you escape the mine?" he asked.

"I found the back door, you might say."

"There is another entrance? An easier entrance?"

"It is easier, yes, but I would not recommend it. Why was I in the mine in the first place?"

With an embarrassed cough, the man explained. "For all his nasty and brutish ways, Pehr is a bit of a coward. When he brought you back, he looked at the wound on your head and presumed that you were dead, or soon would be. He also feared that others would search for you, knowing you came out here. He was afraid of being blamed."

"So he tossed me down the mine shaft, figuring that without a corpse, he couldn't be blamed."

"Exactly."

"And he didn't bother to steal my jewelry because it would be damning evidence."

"Yes."

Vincent nodded. "How fortunate for me that your brother is paranoid."

"You said you would not recommend the other entrance. Why?"

Vincent tapped the journal in his hands. "You'd have to pass through an area full of these rock creatures."

"You have seen them?"

Vincent nodded. "I've seen everything described in here. I have to wonder, how did you three plan on retrieving the treasure when so many others had failed?"

"We had hoped that the poison gas had dissipated by now."

"You've not been down inside to find out?"

The man shook his head. "No. We have been searching through the upper levels, hoping to find other means of access."

Vincent nodded. "Well, I'm afraid your gas is still there."

"You encountered it, as well?" he said, his amazement returning.

"Yes." He didn't elaborate. Some things just didn't need to be shared. "Tell me," he said. "Since I have not read this entire journal, how did the gas originate?"

"It is evidently contained within the walls of the caverns below. A miner opened a pocket of the gas during excavation."

Vincent nodded. "That had been one of my theories." He stroked his beard. "Can you prevent Pehr from flipping out on me long enough for me to talk to him?"

The man frowned. "Prevent him from what?"

Vincent sighed. "Sorry. Can you just keep him calm for a bit?"

He considered this. "I imagine he will be just as shocked as I was to see you. Quite possibly, yes."

"Very well. Please summon him." The man hesitated, casting Vincent a concerned look. "Yes, I am sure," Vincent smiled. "Trust me." The man nodded, then stepped back inside the mine.

Vincent took a deep breath, hoping that he knew what he was doing. He finished his apple, then tossed the core into the fire. He reached for his walking stick and toyed with it for several minutes, until all three brothers returned.

As they stepped into the open, Vincent kept his eyes on Pehr. He had no concerns for the other two, only the oldest. Pehr stood immobile for a moment, then finally spoke. "So. You *are* alive. My brother did not lie."

Vincent laughed. "That's what I like about you, Pehr. Always thinking highly of others." Immediately, he regretted the words, as he saw the anger flare in the man's face.

But Pehr swallowed the anger. "Then am I to believe Maeglin's other words? That you have seen the rock creatures? And the gas?"

"And the bloodsucking things I'd mistaken for bats, yes." Vincent turned his head, lifting his hair out of the way. His fingers indicated the wounds left in his neck by the creatures.

Pehr frowned, ignoring them. "You'll forgive me, *dear baron*, if I find this hard to believe."

Vincent shrugged, then opened the pouch at his belt. He reached in and pulled out the gemstone he'd sucked on in the mine. "Perhaps this will lessen your need for sarcasm." And he tossed the gem in a high arc toward Pehr.

The man caught the stone and examined it. He frowned. "This could have been lying about anywhere."

Vincent frowned, toying with his stick in front of him. What a bonehead, he thought. "Aye, it could have been. But it was not. And I can tell you precisely where a chest full of the stones can be found. Assuming the rock creatures haven't eaten them all by now."

"Eaten them?" the youngest brother asked, incredulous.

Vincent smiled at him and nodded. "And I shall give you that information," he continued, "for a very small price."

Pehr threw the stone into the dirt. "And why should we believe you, you young pup?"

Vincent gritted his teeth. "Because some people happen to be honest, Pehr. Not everyone is as much of a horse's ass as you."

At this, the man let out a roar and charged at Vincent.   With a sigh, Vincent brought the walking stick up abruptly, connecting solidly with Pehr's onrushing groin. The man doubled over, pitching forward and slamming hard into the rock underneath Vincent. He bounced off, rolled onto his side, and clutched at his groin, moaning in pain. Vincent shook his head. "You really do make such things far too easy," he said.

He looked up to see Maeglin shaking his head in embarrassment and the youngest brother dropping his head into his hand. When Pehr showed no inclination to rise quickly, Maeglin spoke up. "You will truly tell us the location of the gems?"

"Certainly. But as I said, there is a small price."

"What is it?"

Vincent looked down at Pehr. He rapped the man on the leg with his stick. "You listening?" The glare the man gave him was all the confirmation Vincent needed.

"There are two things. I require an answer to a question, and a promise from all three of you. Especially you," he said to Pehr.

"What is the promise?" asked the youngest.

Vincent smiled. "I think you can probably guess. I would require that all harassment of my friend cease. No more threats. No more accusations. You will stay clear of him."

"Pah!" spat Pehr, struggling now to rise to his feet. "He is a murderer!"

Vincent turned an icy stare at the man. "That will never be determined and you know it. Whether it is true or not, such determination would not return your brother to you. It would only succeed in ruining the new life of a man who is truly noble."

"Says you," Pehr mumbled.

"Yes. Says me," Vincent grated. "And I suggest you accept my word as golden."

"If the stones are where you say," Maeglin interjected, "you will have our word and it will be kept." Pehr scowled at his brother. "I guarantee it," he concluded, returning his brother's glare.

"What is the question that you require to be answered?" asked the youngest.

"It is a question I believe only Pehr can answer."

The eldest brother turned back to Vincent. "I? And what would you ask of me?"

"I am assuming it was due to you that I found myself in the mine in the first place. You pursued me after I left here. And you saw me attacked in the road by two youths, a boy and a girl."

"Aye," said Pehr. "This is all true. What, then, is your question?"

"After I was struck, what happened?"

To Vincent's surprise, Pehr's demeanor changed. "They disappeared."

"Obviously, but which direction did they go?"

The man shook his head. "No. They vanished. Into thin air. The boy grabbed the girl's arm, raised his hand to his chest, and they were gone."

Vincent rolled Pehr's words over in his aching head. He knew the man was telling the truth. He frowned. "A mage," he muttered.

"So it would seem," Pehr agreed. "I don't mind telling you that I was very relieved when they were gone, after I realized that."

Vincent stroked his beard again. "A mage. Why would a mage steal my sword and gauntlets?"

"I neither know nor care," Pehr replied angrily. "Now are you going to keep your word or not?"

"Patience is a virtue, they say." Vincent sighed. "All right. Let me tell you where the gems are to be found."

"Our grandfather's journal," said Pehr, finally rising to his feet, "says the chest is still well within the cavern. If you found it, then the poison gas has dissipated and we do not need your directions."

"The gas has not dissipated. And the chest is no longer within the cavern."

"You lie!"

Vincent glared at Pehr. In an even tone, he said, "Is it worth a fortune to you to assume that to be the case? Or would you rather see if I just might be telling the truth?"

The man returned Vincent's glare. The youngest brother interrupted. "I am willing to go into the caverns, Pehr. I will determine whether he speaks true or not."

Vincent spoke quietly. "The chest holds raw stone enough to allow you three to live more than comfortably for the rest of your lives, Pehr."

The man said nothing, merely continued staring at him. Finally, he turned his gaze to the youngest brother. "All right, Tyn. If you're volunteering, get the ropes," he said.

The young man hurried to do so, and the others tied them around his waist. Pehr and Maeglin played out the length, allowing Tyn to slowly descend the shaft. Vincent gave him exact instructions. The afternoon was getting late and he urged the youth to turn back if he heard the noises of the bat-like things. Tyn carried an oil lantern tied to his belt. He would have no difficulty in finding his way.

Vincent sat on the rock, eating his remaining fruit, while the brothers went about their business. The crunchy chewing hurt his head, however, and he could not finish. He tossed it on the fire, then put his head in his hands.

His thoughts turned to Rhia. Would she be able to heal him of the infection he knew he had? He wished she were with him. Or better yet, that he were with her, back at the inn.

He was startled by Maeglin's voice. "Who is Rhia?"

Vincent jumped, jerking his gaze up to see the man standing in front of him. The action hurt his head even worse. He winced. "Why do you ask?"

"You were repeating her name as you sat there, rocking back and forth."

"Oh. Well, let's just say she is someone I'd very much like to see right now."

Maeglin shuffled in the dirt. "Is she the red-haired one?"

"Yes. You saw her at the tavern."

"She also came here, two days ago."

Vincent blinked. "She did?"

Maeglin nodded. "Looking for you, she was. She said she knew you were here. Pehr did all the talking and said that you had been here, but had left. Not exactly a lie..." He shrugged. "She did not believe him. But she had no way to prove him wrong. You'd already been thrown down the shaft." He frowned. "How did you survive that?"

Vincent smiled very slightly. "My secret, I'm afraid."

"Maeglin!" came Pehr's voice from inside the mine. Vincent rubbed his temples as the man headed back inside.

Several minutes later, he heard Pehr's voice again, echoing within, along with Maeglin's and Tyn's. Their shouts and gleeful noises told Vincent that he'd not been named a liar this day.

"*There* you are!" came a voice behind him. He whirled, bringing on a stabbing pain and a dizzy spell, but he ignored them.

"Rhia!" Vincent jumped off the rock and ran to her as she walked into the site. They embraced, and Vincent felt layers of anxiety slip away that he hadn't been consciously aware of. "You have no idea how happy I am to see you," he said softly.

She disengaged, a look of concern on her face. "You jest, as usual. Goddess!" she exclaimed, looking at his head wound. "If not for your thick skull..."

"Har de har har," Vincent groaned. "You're almost funny," he said just before he kissed her.

The joyous noises of the brothers grew louder, then, as they stepped out into the compound. Vincent turned to see Pehr carrying the box of gemstones. Their faces froze as they saw Rhia, however.

"Well," said Vincent. "I trust my directions were accurate?"

Tyn nodded, the smile returning to his face. "Indeed! Perfectly so!"

Vincent looked at Pehr. "I have kept my end of the bargain. Do I have your word, as agreed?"

Maeglin stared at his brother. "You do, Baron. Is that not right, my brothers?"

Tyn readily agreed. Pehr was silent for the longest time, then gave a terse nod.

"Very well," Vincent said. "In that case, I think I shall be going, now." He retrieved his walking stick and bade farewell to the brothers.

As he turned to leave, Pehr said, "Baron..."

Vincent turned, surprised to hear Pehr use the title without sarcasm. "Yes?"

To his surprise, the man dropped his eyes to the ground briefly, then shuffled awkwardly. When he looked up, he spoke quietly. "Please accept my apologies."

Vincent raised an eyebrow, then nodded. "Done," he said. Then he departed with Rhia.

As they left the compound, Vincent relied on the stick far more than he would have liked. Halfway down the road from the mine, he stopped. "Oh, shit," he whispered, then pitched forward into the dirt.

❧ ❦

I woke with an incredible sensation of déja vu. I was in a strange bed and Blade was nearby, seeming relieved to see me awake. My head was bandaged and still in pain, though not as much as I remembered. At least I was alert. And hungry.

It seems the infection was worse than I thought. That, coupled with my dehydration, sent me over the edge. Rhia got me back here to the inn, with the assistance of Pehr, oddly enough.

Pehr must have had a serious change of heart. He also told Rhia that the horse I'd rented was stabled back at the house he and his brothers share. He even retrieved it and paid the extra money due at the stable.

Anyway, I was unconscious for two days, and apparently gone for three. I've had a lot of time to think, while lying here in bed. So many unanswered, possibly unanswerable, questions. Who were those kids? Why did the girl look so familiar? Why did they attack me? Why take my gauntlets and sword? Why only the injury instead of killing me? That sword, I know from experience, can cut through damn near anything. I don't know if it's just my memory playing tricks on me, but the boy seemed very ill at ease handling the sword. He wasn't wearing one of his own when I first saw him. Unusual, in this culture. Was he really as clumsy with it as I recall? Is that why I'm able to write in this journal, instead of being worm food?

Other questions... Why did the rock creature pull the mosquito bats off me? It didn't eat them or anything, just plopped them on the ground. And it didn't pay any real attention to me right away, either. And when I did attract its attention, why did it drag me down the corridor like that?

On this, anyway, I have a theory. I think the creature was very young. It was being inquisitive. It pulled off the bats out of curiosity, killing them in the process. When they wouldn't play with him, he lost interest. When I showed signs of life, he got interested in playing with me. I think he dragged me to his home. Perhaps in the hopes of keeping me, like a pet or something.

Listen to me. I'm giving it a gender. Well, so be it.

I wonder, though, if that's what the skeletons signified. Were they other explorers attacked by the bats, then dragged to the rock creature's home, only to die there on the doorstep? If I hadn't had Gnorrin's healing potion, I have no doubt I'd be rotting there beside them.

I just wish I had theories about those two kids. My thoughts are preoccupied with them. I guess that's not too surprising. He did try to kill me, after all. And damn near succeeded.

I owe my life, however, to that rock creature. Oh, I know it didn't intentionally save my life. But if it hadn't pulled those sucking things off me... I still get the chills thinking about it. I was ready to pack it in, right there. I felt like one foot was already in the grave.

I don't ever want to feel that way again. I don't want to die slowly like that. Let it be quick, when it comes.

≈ ≈

The Season of the Harvest passed into the Season of Sleep as Vincent recuperated from his injury. Rhia treated him with herbal concoctions and intimate attentions. His head wound was deep and took quite some time to heal fully.

He got to know Tisen and became better friends with Sianon and D'Ty. He and Blade got on as well as though they'd not been separated for two years.

Being a coastal town, Port Remil did not suffer much in the way of snow and ice. Vincent was grateful for that. The Season of Sleep passed quietly.

During Celebration Week, Vincent observed his birthday. He was twenty-two years old, now, and had been in this world for nearly five years. He spent time thinking of those years, of what he'd done, what he hadn't done. It was difficult to believe the time had flown so quickly.

Sianon had a tall mirror in her home, and one day, Vincent observed his reflection. Ignoring the beard, he studied his face. He didn't feel twenty-two. And he didn't really look it, either. Oh, he looked older than when he'd arrived. Losing some pudginess in his face had something to do with that, he realized. But he still looked only slightly older. He wasn't a good judge of age, but he'd have guessed his age, on looks, to be about nineteen at most.

He didn't really care, though. Age just didn't seem that important to him. Being alive was what he relished. Young or old, it didn't matter. As long as the heart still beat and the mind still functioned.

There was one event during the colder months that troubled him. It was a dream. A dream he'd had before, but with more detail than before.

In the dream, Ariaziane walked through the streets of a town. It was a coastal town, for he saw the ocean in some scenes, with moonlight glinting off the water. And she was attacked. Four men accosted her, pinning her arms behind her, gagging her mouth. In the dream, she struggled, panic showing on her face. Panic turned to terror. And in the dream, the men took her into an alley. And they raped her, one after the other. The dream showed only bits and pieces, always focusing on her face. He didn't see the clothes ripped from her body, didn't see them pounding inside her. All he saw was her face. One of the men kept slapping her face, as if this were his particular fetish. And in the dream, he saw, but did not hear, Ariaziane scream against her gag. The scream he heard was his own, as he sprang awake in bed.

He told Rhia about it, then, as he'd just startled her awake. As sweat cooled on his forehead, he related the entire scene to her. Anxiety filled him as he noted the concern on Rhia's face. He was scared to death that she was going to say it was a real event, not a dream, as she'd done so long ago, when he'd related to her the dream that was not a dream, but the reality of his sexual encounter with Darella.

But when he finished, her face softened. It was okay, she assured him. He breathed a sigh of relief, and when sleep soon overtook him again, he rested well for the remainder of the night.

As the Season of Green returned to the land, Vincent decided it was time to move on. They would now visit Rhia's friend, as he'd promised.

And so, after some emotional farewells, Vincent and Rhia boarded ship once again and headed northwest across the bay. The sea journey itself would take a week, after which was another few days on foot to the forest where Rhia's friend lived.

"So tell me who this is that we're going to see," he asked one day on the ship as they lay in their bunk.

Rhia toyed with her braid and smiled. "Her name is Felina."

"Is she also a witch?"

She shook her head. "In fact, she is a mage."

Vincent laughed. "I can't get away from them, can I?"

Rhia smiled. "Well, Felina is one that I can't seem to get away from, either. We often go years without seeing each other, but our paths always seem to cross."

He reached over and stroked her face. "That's nice. It's good to have friends like that. In fact, it seems to me that you and I have had just such a relationship."

She tilted her head. "That's truer than you know," she whispered.

Vincent raised an eyebrow. "What do you mean?"

Rhia shrugged, looking him in the eye. "I mean that you and Felina have more in common than you might guess." She smiled mischievously. "Felina is the lover I went to after leaving you the last time."

Vincent blinked and was quiet. Words failed him. He cleared his throat and struggled for the right way to respond. Finally, he had it. "Oh," he said.

❧ Twenty-Nine ❧

The journey was uneventful. Vincent enjoyed the trip, but regretted his departure from the home of his friends. Though he had spent months with them, it seemed such a short period of time. Then again, he found himself missing other friends. Gnorrin and Jaz. Aedriun, Darvas, and Ghanol. He definitely missed Blaise. And, ever since the dream he'd had, his thoughts had been turning more and more to Ariaziane. His intentions were to spend a few weeks with this friend of Rhia's, then return home.

Eventually, they arrived at some port town that Vincent didn't catch the name of, where they spent the evening at a small inn. In the morning they bought provisions and set off on their trek north toward the forest.

It would be several days of hiking, Rhia had told him. For two of those days, they paced along the eastern bank of a river. On the morning of the third day, they crossed the river by ferry and continued on their way.

They reached the edge of the forest during late afternoon. It was a pleasant forest, from what Vincent could gather. Being early in the Season of Green, the trees were barely past the budding stage. Plenty of sunlight came through to illuminate their way. Rhia urged him on, wanting to reach Felina's home before nightfall.

Just before sunset, as Vincent was thinking they weren't going to make Rhia's deadline, the scent of burning wood drifted to him. And then he saw the flicker of torchlight in the distance. Vincent strained his eyes and, as they approached, was able to make out the form of a single level structure. It appeared to be constructed primarily of thatch, and dried mud or clay. Several torches illuminated the entrance path, as well as parts of the perimeter and some sort of large area behind the domicile.

An expanse of trees had evidently been cleared for this to be built. And it struck Vincent that it was an odd location for such a home. They were probably an hour into the forest. Not the easiest place to find, if that was her wish. Probably it wasn't, though.

As they reached the building, Rhia said, "By the way, don't be alarmed by what you'll see."

Vincent stretched his aching back. "Why? What am I going to see?"

"Lots of cats."

They began walking toward the rear of the building. "Cool. I like cats."

Rhia merely smiled. Then she caught sight of her friend exiting the house's back door, and rushed forward to greet her.

Vincent watched as Felina turned, smiling. There was no sense of surprise on her face, just a reserved sort of pleasure. He studied her as the friends embraced. Felina was slightly shorter than Rhia, perhaps five-four or five-five, he estimated. Her build was slight and sleek, dressed as she was in tight, fur-trimmed leathers. She had long, straight hair that appeared to be completely black. Her face was quite attractive, in a strangely exotic way. She had almond-shaped eyes, slightly slanted, but not Oriental in appearance. Even in the dim light, Vincent could tell they were very green. She had delicate, yet noticeable cheekbones, a smallish mouth and nose, and flaring, sharp eyebrows. He frowned, frustrated that he could not place what her features reminded him of, or why she looked so hauntingly familiar.

The pair broke their embrace and turned to face Vincent.

Felina spoke, and her voice was quiet and captivating. "This must be your friend Vincent."

Rhia nodded. "This is he."

Felina appraised him as he stood before her. "Hi," he said. "Nice to meet you."

There was a glint of humor in her eyes and her smile. She spoke to Rhia, keeping her eyes on him. "You did not tell me that he was such a furry beast." Felina stepped forward and ran her hand through the exposed hair on Vincent's chest, which was displayed prominently by the V-necked tunic he wore. Felina smiled as she did this, emitting a noise that sounded almost like a purr.

He felt his cheeks flushing. This was not the kind of behavior he expected in new acquaintances. He raised his hands, intending to remove hers from his body, when he heard a deep growl behind him. He looked quickly over his shoulder to see a massive panther padding toward him, its eyes locked with his own.

Heart suddenly pounding, he spun to face the creature. His immediate instinct was to draw his sword, but it was propped against a tree beside his pack, several feet away. He was about to pluck the dagger from his boot sheath when he was overwhelmed by a sense of *déja vu*. And then he realized why Felina looked so familiar. He'd had a dream, long ago. A dream of someone who looked like her, and of this rather huge black creature bearing down on him.

"Kita!" The panther stopped in its tracks at Felina's admonition, turning its large, yellow eyes to her. "Be polite. This is a guest." The panther looked from Felina to Vincent, then growled in its throat again. "Now, now," said Felina. "Jcalousy will not be tolerated, as you well know." At this, the panther looked sharply at Felina, then turned and padded away.

Vincent swallowed in a dry mouth. "Nice cat," he said quietly, staring with renewed interest at Felina.

"Kita is the jealous type," Felina explained. "But he knows better." She then returned to studying him.

He cleared his throat, looking to Rhia for some sort of rescue. She seemed almost amused by the events.

"Would you like a drink, Vincent?" Felina asked. "You look parched."

As he nodded, Felina ran a hand over his chest again. "I'll fetch some water. Make yourselves comfortable," she said, sweeping her arm in the direction of the rear of her home.

As she moved off, Vincent breathed a sigh of relief, smiling his thanks to Rhia, who chuckled and took him by the hand.

The rear of the home was cleared of trees and brush. A perimeter of torches in tall stands marked the boundaries. And, Vincent now saw, several normal-sized cats lounging or playing in the area. Comfortable chairs circled a round, wooden table. He and Rhia seated themselves. Immediately, they were set upon by attention-seeking cats. One orange and white animal jumped up into Vincent's lap and began purring loudly. He smiled and began stroking the cat, scratching it behind the ears. "Hiya, puss," he said. Felina returned with a pitcher of water and goblets for all. "Must be a good sign," he said to her. "This one likes me."

"Trisket likes everyone," she said nonchalantly, then sat next to Rhia.

As Felina and Rhia chatted and caught up on events in their lives, Vincent tried to recall everything that Rhia had told him of this woman during their journey. He stroked Trisket's body as he did so, eliciting purrs of contentment from the cat. Rhia had said that Felina was a mage and that they'd known each other for many years. Vincent looked at the two women. Couldn't have been too many, he thought to himself. He placed Rhia's age at no more than thirty. And Felina couldn't be more than a few years older than Rhia.

The sun was setting now, and darkness descended rather quickly. He glanced again at the women, who were caught up in conversation. He didn't pay any attention. In truth, he was exhausted. It had been a long time since he'd walked for such lengths of time. His back was killing him. He really wanted a hot soak and a warm bed. Inn life had spoiled him, he realized.

He sighed, looking around the area. She certainly liked cats, he thought. Not surprising, considering her name. He peered around for a sign of Kita. He'd thought he was going to wet himself for a moment, there. Though he had often fantasized about having a big cat as a pet, he wasn't fond of being surprised by one from behind.

Relaxing into the comfy chair, he leaned his head back and closed his eyes for a moment. The sounds of evening insects and birds were audible over the quiet talk of the women. He consciously blocked out their voices and focused on the voice of the forest.

It had been a while since he'd really practiced using his heightened senses. But it came back to him effortlessly. Soon, the ladies' conversation was a mere buzz at the back of his head. He alternated listening intently to the insects, the birds, the wind in the branches, the play of the cats, even the sound of the oil burning in the torches. It was very relaxing, almost like meditation.

And then he felt a chill. He opened his eyes a crack, suddenly realizing that he'd fallen asleep. Trisket lay in his lap, curled up and snoring quietly. The torches still burned. The women were gone. He looked up at the sky, discerning the position of the moon through the trees. He'd been asleep for at least an hour, he realized.

He sat upright in the chair, which annoyed Trisket. "Sorry, puss," he whispered, and hoisted the cat off himself. He stood, stretching. The women were probably inside, he thought. Without quite realizing it, he focused his hearing on the house, searching for their voices. He walked toward the building as he did this. And then he stopped.

They were inside. Toward the west end of the domicile. He'd heard Rhia. He knew her sound. And he knew what caused her to make that particular sound. He flushed, then, emotions washing over him.

Rhia had said that Felina was also her lover. But he'd assumed she'd meant that Felina was a *former* lover. Obviously, he shouldn't have assumed such a thing. He felt hurt. Jealous. But he shook those off, angrily. There was no reason for him to feel that way, he told himself. Just as his own love for Ariaziane had not faded, he could not expect Rhia's love for Felina to have faded, either. Nothing had ever been said about exclusivity. He had no right to be jealous over this. But that didn't change the fact that he was.

He turned away from the house and slowly paced the perimeter of the clearing, his heart heavy. For the jealousy would not leave completely. It was an insidious thing, he realized. He leaned against a thick tree just outside the line of torches and looked deeply into the forest. Or tried to. It was quite dark now. The moonlight didn't help much. He sat, leaning against the trunk.

Vincent brought his knees up to his chest and wrapped his arms around them. No need to be jealous, he kept telling himself. It doesn't change how she feels about you. He heaved a deep sigh, then sensed someone approaching from behind. He lifted his head and peered over his shoulder, surprised that the ladies had finished so soon. Then his heart skipped a beat as he saw that it was the panther coming toward him, not Rhia.

The jealousy was replaced instantly with alarm, but he did not move. He knew it would matter little if he were to leap to his feet. He'd stand no chance against the animal if it had malevolent intent. But much to his amazement, the beast stopped next to him. It looked out into the forest, as Vincent had been doing. Then it swung its heavy head toward him and cast him a lingering look. Then it gracefully lowered itself to lie at his side.

Vincent blinked. How odd, he thought. The feeling he got was that the animal wanted company. Unlike little cats such as Trisket, Kita was not overly friendly. No nudge of the head to attract petting. But the look the animal had given him was disconcerting. He couldn't put his finger on the nature of it, but it seemed something was there. He smiled, laughing at himself. Silliness, he thought. To think the cat had given him some sort of understanding look.

He tried his best to put the notion out of his mind. The jealous twinge returned and he shook that off, too. Unfortunately, what replaced it were thoughts of Ariaziane.

He really hoped the dream had been nothing more than a dream. Rhia had assured him it was. But still, he had this nagging doubt. He'd give anything to know. And, he realized, he'd also give anything *not* to know.

Mostly, he just wanted to see her, to know that she was okay. To maybe know how often she thought of him. To know if she missed him. If she loved him.

Kita let out a low, short growl. He glanced over at the animal, to see it looking back at the house. Then the cat turned to look at him again. Once more, Vincent thought he felt some sort of connection there. Then Kita huffed and put his head down between his paws, closing his eyes.

"Well," came Rhia's voice behind him. "I see you've made friends with Kita."

Vincent glanced up at her momentarily as she leaned against the tree. "I guess. His idea, though."

There was a moment's silence, then Rhia said softly, "You're angry."

The accusation only made him feel guilty. "I'm sorry. I just..."

"You know better than that," she said.

Again, there was silence. Rhia crouched beside him, a hand on his shoulder. Vincent closed his eyes. "I've just been thinking a lot about things." Rhia said nothing, didn't prompt. So he took a deep breath and spit it all out. "I know you know how I feel about Annie. I love her very much. And I think she loves me, too. But she would never say it. It was all I could do to get her to say it before she left, and even then, I wasn't entirely sure she didn't just mean as a friend." He paused, plucking at some weeds. "Rhia, is there something wrong with me that doesn't allow women to love me?"

She laughed. "Why would you ask such a thing? That's ridiculous!"

"Is it?"

"Yes!"

"Then why would she never say it?"

"Vincent, I have no idea. I do not know the girl, let alone her heart."

He nodded. "Okay." Then he looked her in the eye. "So why haven't *you* ever said it?"

Her eyes widened. "By the moon's horns, Vincent! You know how I feel about you."

He shrugged, averting his gaze. "I thought I did, until tonight."

"Oh, Goddess... I *told* you Felina and I were lovers!"

He nodded again. "True. And I do realize, intellectually, that it changes nothing about how you feel for me. I just have to convince my heart of that. But I will. Don't worry." Again he met her gaze. "But do you love me?" His heart grew cold when he saw the hesitation in her face. A tiny crease appeared between her eyes, and a hint of sadness in them. He clenched his jaw and looked away. "I see." He rose to his feet.

"No, you do not," she said, reaching out to him.

He shook off her hand, firmly but without anger. "I think I do. And I'd like to be alone for a while, if you don't mind." He walked off toward the front of the house, leaving Rhia and Kita behind.

He felt deceived, angry, hurt, and a riot of other emotions. Tears threatened to fall. One or two succeeded.

Only when he heard Rhia enter the house did he return to the rear of the building. Taking a blanket from their supplies, he walked back to the chair he'd previously napped in. He felt drained. And since he certainly didn't want to go inside, he decided to sleep in the chair.

He made himself comfortable, spreading the blanket over his body. He tried to ignore the burning in his eyes as he attempted to sleep. Naturally, his mind would not allow sleep to come. It kept taunting him with Rhia's face and the expression she'd worn rather than confessing that she didn't love him.

How could she pretend to love him so well that he believed she did? It was like a blow to the stomach. He loved her so much. How could she not love him in return?

A creaking noise startled him into full awareness. He opened his eyes to see Felina sitting in the chair across from him. A black cloak accentuated her pale skin. Vincent felt a moment of resentment boil up inside him. It must have shown on his face, for Felina said, "I understand how you must feel."

"I'd prefer to be alone."

"And I'd prefer you not be."

Vincent raised an eyebrow at this, but said nothing.

"I will admit that Rhia and I were inconsiderate, leaving you alone while you slept. But surely you must realize no offense was meant."

Vincent gave a brief nod. That much he was sure of. She might not love him, but Rhia would never intentionally hurt him. "It's not even that event that's bothering me, to be honest," he managed to blurt out.

Felina nodded. "Rhia told me about your conversation." She frowned. "There are some things you should know to help you understand Rhia better."

Resigning himself to the fact that Felina wasn't going to leave him alone, Vincent adjusted himself in the chair, rubbed his face, and said, "Yes? And what things are those?"

Felina paused, obviously choosing her words carefully. "When it comes to love, in the sense you were doubtless referring to, a certain degree of caution is often called for. Especially when it comes to the realm of self-preservation."

"I have no idea what you're talking about."

"I'm talking about not wanting to be hurt, Vincent."

"Well, I'm already hurt!"

"I didn't mean you. I meant Rhia."

Vincent frowned. "As if she has any more at risk than I do? Come on, I love her. I thought she loved me, too. That sort of give and take routine, you know?"

Felina shook her head. "It isn't the same."

"The hell it isn't!"

"It isn't," she said firmly. "There is one particular difference that is quite significant. Age."

Vincent snorted. "Look, I know I'm not that old, but it's not like she could be my mother or anything."

Felina laughed. "In fact, she could be your great-grandmother, boy."

"Excuse me?"

"Vincent, Rhia is over one hundred years old."

He blinked. "Bullshit."

"Rhia is a witch. Witches can alter their physical appearance, stave off the ravages of age. Likely Rhia will have a witch's life expectancy of a millennium."

"Oh, give me a break," he said. But the little lie detector in his head was silent.

"It is that fact, Vincent," she continued, "which makes it hard for her. She wants very much to love you the way you want to be loved. But she's afraid to. It's painful for a long-lived one to grow attached to someone who will wither and die before their eyes."

Vincent looked at her skeptically. "So that means she doesn't really love you, either?"

Felina raised an eyebrow. "Me? I'm not exactly in the same category."

"Why? Because you're a woman?"

"No. Because I'm an elf."

Vincent raised *his* eyebrow. "Pardon?"

Felina smiled faintly. "You have never met an elf before, have you?"

Vincent dumbly shook his head.

"Not surprising," Felina said. "And you probably wouldn't recognize one if you had. We've become quite adept at blending in when we want to."

He'd read of elves in Gnorrin's books. They were evidently the most long-lived of the races in this world. "I thought you had pointy ears."

Felina smiled and pulled the hair back away from her head, revealing distinctly pointed tops to her ears. "Satisfied?"

"Wow." Vincent smiled sheepishly. "So," he said, "just how old are you?"

"I am not much older than Rhia. One hundred thirty-seven. In elven perspective, I'm about as far along my lifespan as you are in yours."

Vincent heaved a deep breath. "As if I didn't feel enough like a child."

Felina smirked. "Do not let that trouble you. If it means anything, most elves tend to think of all humans as children, despite their age."

With a sigh, Vincent closed his eyes and pulled the blanket up under his chin. He simply didn't know how to feel regarding this new information. What would it be like, from now on, with Rhia? Could he ever think of her in the same fashion? Could he ever make love to her again? It would be like making love to someone's grandmother. He frowned. No, it wouldn't. Not with a body like hers. He shook his head. How could he have even thought that for a second? He remembered the first time he'd seen her nude, in his front yard so long ago. He thought of sitting in the pentagram she'd drawn and how he'd been unable to take his eyes from her. No. No way would it be like doing it with a grandmother.

"Felina," he said, switching to another thought in his head, "does it bother you that she and I are involved?"

The elf smiled. "Not at all. Whatever makes Rhia happy makes me happy."

"Doesn't it make you feel like your relationship with her is lessened somehow?"

She shook her head. "Why should it? You have enriched her life in a way only you can. And because of the relationship she and I share, I am enriched, too."

He carried that statement to its logical conclusion. "Which means, obviously, that the aspects of Rhia I love are in part because of her relationship with you."

"I'd like to think so. When you look at our lives, Vincent, you have to see that we are who we are because of everything we experience. And the others in our lives are part of those experiences. For good or bad. Another person can enrich your life, or poison it."

Vincent nodded slowly, staring off into space. He knew she was right. But this whole situation was so bizarre to him. He'd never in his life expected to be involved with someone who was in turn involved simultaneously with someone else. Nor to actually be okay with the arrangement. And he was, he realized. He still wasn't totally comfortable with it, but he knew he eventually would be.

"It is likely to get very cold out here, Vincent," Felina said. "There is a warm bed for you, as well as a warm heart that is hurting over you. Please come inside." She stood, waiting for him to rise. And he did. Throwing the blanket over his shoulder, he took her outstretched hand.

Once indoors, he looked at the living area. It was not large, but had lots of open space. There was little furniture, but many large pillows tastefully arranged. Rhia was seated on one in front of the fireplace. She turned when they entered, and Vincent could see the relief on her face when she saw that Felina wasn't alone. Immediately, he felt terrible for his words to her. At the time, they'd seemed so justified. But now he knew how deeply she was hurting, too. He dropped the blanket and went directly to her. Felina, he noticed, continued past, into another area of the house so as to give them some privacy.

On the floor, he sat next to Rhia and gave her a hug. She squeezed back. "I'm sorry," she whispered. "I thought you knew, thought you understood. But then I realized there was no reason you should have known."

"It's okay," he said softly.

She withdrew from the hug, holding him in front of her and staring into his face. "Is it? Is it truly? I hope so. The last thing I ever wanted to do was hurt you."

"Don't worry about it. I'm okay." And a thought suddenly struck him. He frowned. "All those times that you came into my life for brief periods, then went away for long stretches..."

With a nod, she said, "I left partly because of how I was beginning to feel for you. I didn't want to get involved in that way with you. I was afraid."

"Felina explained to me that witches can deliberately slow down the aging process." Rhia nodded her confirmation. "Well, wouldn't it be possible, then, to deliberately *not* slow it down?"

Rhia averted her gaze, focusing on the fire for a moment. "Yes," she said finally. "But that hardly solves the real problem. I could certainly stop slowing my aging. I could grow old with you. You would eventually die. And then I could choose to die, too, or gradually reverse my age. I tell you now—I would not choose to die."

"I don't blame you."

"But I could not easily bear the pain of losing you. How easy would that be for you, if you were in my position?"

Vincent nodded in understanding. They sat together, watching the fire. Felina joined them a few minutes later. She pulled more pillows around them, and they all reclined quietly in front of the fireplace, Rhia between her two lovers. Vincent put his arm around her and held her. The warmth of her body and the crackling fire eased away his earlier sadness. And soon he was asleep.

❧ ❦

"So is Felina only attracted to women, or men, too?" Vincent asked one night, as he lay in bed with Rhia.

"Why?" Rhia smiled. "Ready to branch out already?"

He laughed. "No. Just some things she's said. Yesterday we were working in her garden while you were off collecting herbs, and she made a comment to the effect that most men are... let me see if I can quote her... 'nasty, brutish, insensitive pigs.' I assume she was excepting present company, of course."

"Of course," Rhia laughed.

"So what's her story?"

But Rhia shook her head. "Her story is her story. It's not mine to tell."

"Right. Sorry."

"But she's not the type to be offended if you ask her plainly. I'm sure she's comfortable enough with you to tell you."

Vincent yawned. "Mm. I don't want to pry."

"Of course, if you really *are* asking because you're interested in her, don't be afraid to proposition her."

"What? Are you joking?"

"Of course not."

He allowed her words to sink in, but couldn't quite accept their veracity. "I don't think so."

"You don't find her attractive?"

"On the contrary. I find her very attractive. That isn't the point."

"Wouldn't it be fun with all three of us?" Rhia said. Vincent tried *not* to think of it. Naturally, he failed. Rhia poked a finger at an area of the blanket that had suddenly billowed. "Evidently part of you thinks so." She smiled.

Vincent sighed in mock exasperation. "I admit it's an appealing fantasy, but..."

"But what?" she teased.

407

He pulled away. "Wait a minute. Are you trying to say that you'd actually *want* us to be lovers?"

She smiled at him. "Why not?" She fondled him, encouraging his arousal.

Vincent gently rebuffed her advances. "Rhia, don't! I'm serious, now. I really want to know what you're thinking."

She shrugged. "I was thinking it would be fun."

He shook his head. "You can pretend it's just sex you're after, but I can tell there's more to it than that. I know you love her. And I know you love me, even though you're afraid of admitting it to yourself, let alone me."

The witch looked him in the eye, then looked away. "I'm sorry."

"Don't be sorry. Just trust me enough to let me into your heart." Rhia sighed and relaxed into her pillow. She ran a hand through her hair, still not looking at him. "I'll try to understand," he said.

Now she cast a glance at him. "I know you will." Her faint smile faded quickly. "All right." She took a deep breath. "To understand it, you'll have to know more about the nature of witches." She paused, but he didn't prompt her. "Many witches live in covens. A coven is sort of a community." Vincent was familiar with the term, but felt it probably had a slightly different meaning here, so he let her continue. "It's a very personal, private community with little contact with outside society."

"And you were raised in such a community."

"For the first forty years of my life." She smiled wistfully. "It was pretty wonderful. All of us were so close."

"How many families were there?"

Rhia smiled as though inwardly amused. "Our concept of family is very different from that of outside society. When you use the word, you think of what? Parents and children, yes?"

Vincent shrugged. "Well, for the most part. Though sometimes there are extended families, where grandparents or other relatives live with them."

"But there is always a clear unit that you refer to as the family. All related by blood or bond."

"Right."

"Witches have no set structure as that. We choose the members of our families as suits us. Some do, indeed, choose just such a structure as you describe. There were some exclusive pairings in our coven that lasted for quite a while, but such were rare. Most families were larger, with perhaps six or eight adults living as a unit."

Vincent scratched his beard. "You're talking about group marriage or something like that? Sharing lovers?"

"Sharing? To me, that implies possession. You share something you possess with someone else. Witches do not regard other beings as possessions. In a coven, each witch in a family unit is an integral part of it. A group of equals. In fact, most families do not even have a formalized marriage arrangement. They are very open by design."

"What about children in these kinds of families?" Vincent asked.

"They were much loved. Children rarely thought of any two specific adults as their parents. I mean, we knew who our birth parents were, and felt toward them somewhat differently than the other adults, but we were raised by the whole coven."

"Sounds confusing for the kids."

"You're only thinking that because you were raised in a society with clearly defined parent-child relationships. If you'd been raised in a coven or similar community, you wouldn't find it confusing at all." He nodded in agreement. "In fact," she continued, "I remember what it was like when I first entered the outside society, how strange I felt their family customs were."

"Just like most people would find your family customs odd."

"Exactly."

"On Earth, most people would find your covens to be unnatural."

"Oh, it is the same here. In fact, many witches have been persecuted for exactly that reason. We are blamed for spreading immoral or obscene practices and vilified by those who put more stock in tradition than in reality."

Vincent thought of the plight of those on Earth who practiced alternative sexual lifestyles, finding yet another similarity between his two worlds. "That's a shame," he said. "So what's it like for you now that you're out on your own? Do you miss being part of a coven?"

"I miss certain aspects of it. I miss the closeness between people, the sense of unity. Few people in this outside society understand those things. They keep their feelings inside and allow jealousy and possessiveness to rule them. It's sad, really, but it seems to be the rule more than the exception."

"Not everyone is like that."

"Oh, I know. Felina isn't like that. And I don't think you are, either."

He shook his head. "I don't know. I'm not really experienced at 'traditional' sorts of relationships, let alone anything as unusual as what you're describing."

"Are you sure? You seem to have accepted my relationship with Felina in addition to my relationship to you."

Vincent didn't pursue that line of thought. Instead, he said, "So do you have a desire to someday form a coven of your own?"

Rhia's face softened and she looked him in the eye. "Would you be part of it?"

"Me?" Vincent said, shocked. "I'm not a witch."

"And I'm not traditional." She smiled. "I would love to have my family around me. You. Felina. And whoever else we chose. That would be my coven of choice. I would not want any other."

Vincent blushed a little at the thought, though he knew the concept would be in his mind a lot in days to come. He quickly changed the subject. "So why did you leave your coven?"

Rhia was quiet for a long time. When she spoke, her words were soft and Vincent could see the pain in her eyes. "I didn't exactly leave by choice."

Vincent frowned. "What do you mean? You were evicted?"

"You could say that. The coven elder council voted to do so."

"Why?"

"The elder council is a group you don't challenge, once their decisions are made."

"And you did."

Rhia chuckled. "To use an expression you're fond of, yes I did. Big time."

"What about?"

She gave a resigned shrug. "One member of our coven wasn't the nicest person you'd ever want to meet. She was not truly evil, mind you, but she could be decidedly single-minded when she wanted to be. And more often than not, her intentions were very self-serving. She lived in our coven for years, until she did something that was... Well, it was something that no one approved of. The elder council chose to cast her out."

"You disagreed with them?"

"Yes. I felt she should have been put to death."

Vincent raised his eyebrow. Such a sentence, pronounced so casually, was not something he ever expected to hear from her. "Wow," he said. "So, you challenged their decision and were evicted for it?"

"That sums it up, yes."

"So what did she do that caused you to wish her dead rather than shut out?"

Rhia hesitated, then blurted out, "She was caught practicing forbidden magicks."

"Forbidden?"

She nodded. "Those that dealt in the art of necromancy, primarily. Dealing with the dead." Vincent saw a hard expression form in Rhia's eyes. "She didn't even attempt to deny it when the accusations were made," Rhia said quietly.

Vincent could tell she did not want to talk further about this. He reached out a hand to comfort her and was somewhat surprised when she grasped it firmly and drew him to her. She buried her head in his shoulder and squeezed him tightly. He wrapped his other arm around her and held her. She did not cry. No sob escaped her. But Vincent knew she was wailing inside.

⁊ ⸙

Over the weeks that followed, Vincent spent much of his time observing the interactions between Rhia and Felina. It was easier, now that he had gotten to become friends with Felina, to appreciate the love that existed between them.

And he was oddly confused. Rhia, he knew, was a passionate woman. From everything he could tell, Felina was the same. Except that her passion was kept just below the surface. She cloaked herself in coolness, but underneath he knew she was a powder keg. She really was like a cat in that sense.

His confusion was from the fact that the relationship between these two passionate women seemed, to him, to be anything *but* passionate. The word that sprang to mind most readily was *comfortable*. The pair seemed to be so at ease with each other. This was evidenced by Felina's casual greeting of them the night of their arrival. He could only surmise that they'd been lovers for many years, to have achieved such a comfortable state between them.

Or maybe, he thought, maybe this was a love different than any he'd ever known. He supposed it could be that this type of romance was typical of a love shared by women. But that didn't seem to make sense. People were people. Didn't matter what their gender was. Just because they were both women didn't mean that their romance couldn't be stormy or giddy or whatever.

No, he decided. They must have been lovers for a long time. And that would make sense, given their ages. They only *looked* young, he had to continually remind himself. They could have been lovers for longer than Vincent had been alive.

Vincent spent a lot of time with Felina, as well. He liked her more and more as time went by. One night, as the two of them were sitting outside after Rhia had gone to bed, he decided to tell her of Earth. To his surprise, she confessed that Rhia had already told her. He didn't mind. In fact, he was impressed by the fact that she'd never brought it up to him.

And, after having spent several weeks there, he thought he'd finally memorized the names of all the cats around the place. There were a dozen of them, many of which had similar coloring. He was never quite sure if he was calling them by the correct name. But they were cats. They didn't come to him when he called, anyway, so he didn't lose any sleep over mistakes.

Trisket was by far the one who liked Vincent the most. He was never far from him. When he wasn't wrestling with Littlepuss, a smallish black cat with a tuft of white on her breast, he was in Vincent's lap. Or sleeping or eating, which were even more important than socializing with his pet human.

Kita maintained his air of indifference to the activities of humans. The kinship Vincent had once felt, or imagined he'd felt from the panther, was evidently temporary. The animal had little time to waste on paying attention to him. Sleeping was far more important.

The Season of Green passed into the Season of the Sun. Rhia spent more time gathering herbs in the forest then, leaving Vincent even more time to get to know Felina. They often spent time walking in the woods. Vincent enjoyed this immensely. In more ways than one.

"You're staring," she said to him one day as they trekked through the forest.

He shrugged and took his eyes off her body to meet her gaze. "Can't help it," he said. "That outfit is hard to ignore." He glanced again at her garb as she chuckled. She wore tight leggings of dark green. He couldn't figure out how they got to be so form-fitting in this elastic-less land. Her torso was covered only by a vest of soft leather lined with rabbit fur, matching the boots she wore. And there were her ever-present items of jewelry. Rings, armlets, and a necklace with a pendant that hung low over her small, firm breasts, the cleavage of which was visible above the top of the vest. The jewelry was all cat-oriented, as was the staff she used as a walking stick. It appeared to be made of solid silver, but had the strength of steel. Vincent had hefted its weight and wondered how a slight person such as Felina could wield it so casually. Atop it was a small cat's head carved out of what appeared to be onyx.

But Vincent's attention was on Felina's body, not the staff. Therefore, he did not notice her actions. She casually extended the staff so that he stumbled over it and sprawled in the dirt. She shook her head as she stood over him, a smile on her face. "Clumsy," she said.

Vincent paused in getting to his feet, a spear of pain shooting through him. He finished rising, but slowly. Any other word, he thought. Any other word and he'd be laughing along with her right now. He brushed the dirt from his clothes and tried to keep her from seeing the pain that he knew was in his eyes.

"What?" she asked.

He looked up at her, forcing a smile that he knew was lame. "Sorry. It's just that someone else used to call me that."

Felina nodded gently. "Ah. The other girl." Vincent looked at her sharply. She knew about her, too? "What was her name, again?"

"Ariaziane," he managed to whisper.

Again she nodded. "Rhia mentioned her. I've sensed your pain occasionally. It is very deep." Vincent gave her a questioning look. "Elves are somewhat empathic," she explained. "I'm sorry I caused you to think of her." Vincent was about to wave it off and say it was okay. But before he could, Felina said, "You are a good man, Vincent. It hurts me to know that you have such pain inside you. You should learn to let her go."

"Never," he answered.

Felina met his gaze for several seconds, then slowly nodded. They continued walking on, and Vincent decided to change the subject. "So, what exactly caused you to give up on men?"

Felina chuckled. "I was wondering when you'd ask. But I warn you. You might not like this story."

"If you'd rather not tell me..."

"I'm saying perhaps you'd rather not hear it." When Vincent didn't say anything, she continued. "A mage of my acquaintance had designs on me. We were lovers for a short time. But it wasn't a healthy relationship. Not to mention that I had my eye on someone else. So I broke it off with him." She shrugged. "He didn't like that."

"What did he do?"

"He cast a spell on me to make me fall in love with him." Vincent nodded, recalling how Sianon had enchanted Blade, early on. "Or rather," she continued, "a spell that gave the illusion of love. It wasn't real. It was control, pure and simple."

"So what happened?"

"Eventually, I was able to break the spell."

"How?"

"Mostly willpower. It is difficult. It helped that I knew he'd done it. He wasn't very secretive about it. If he had been, I might still be under his power today."

"Wow. How long ago was this?"

"Fifteen years or so."

"Geez. So, what did you do after you broke the spell?"

Felina fixed her gaze on him as they walked. "I punished him. Hopefully, it will teach him a lesson."

Vincent wasn't sure he wanted to know what form the punishment took. Had she Bobbitt-ized him? "So what was his name?"

A mischievous smile graced the corner of her mouth. "Kita."

Vincent blinked. Then he stopped walking as a chill ran through him. He stared at Felina as she turned to look at him. "You didn't."

The mage walked the few steps back toward him. "Oh, I most certainly did."

"Felina! You turned him into a *panther*?"

"Yes, and quite a handsome one, too, don't you think?"

"He's been like that for fifteen years?"

"More or less."

"Shit! *Felina!*"

"I warned you."

"That's inhuman!"

Felina smiled sweetly. "So am I, dear."

"Well, when are you changing him back?"

She raised her eyebrows. Then she laughed. "Now, why in the world would I do that?"

Vincent stood in front of her, wondering how anyone could do such a thing to another person for even a short period of time, let alone a decade and a half.

"You're judging me," Felina said flatly. "I suggest you not do so without having all the facts."

"Oh?"

She moved closer to him and he involuntarily stepped backward, ever so slightly.

"If you have never been under that sort of spell, that sort of control, you can't understand what it was like. I knew I was being controlled, but I couldn't change my actions. And let me tell you something. He wasn't content to let it go at that. He couldn't just accept that I would unquestioningly do anything he wanted while under his spell. He made me do disgusting things that I won't even describe. And he loved it. He made sure I knew how much he enjoyed degrading me." Vincent felt compassion replacing the revulsion inside him. Felina continued. "Tell me, Earth boy, how would you treat such a person on your world?"

He cleared his throat. "Well," he said softly, "I guess, if he were found guilty, he'd go to jail."

"Jail," she said distastefully. "Lock him up in a room for a while? You think that's punishment? You think that will make him see the error of his ways and maybe change?"

"Um, no. Not generally. The society I'm used to is more concerned with getting the offenders out of sight, rather than seeing them punished or rehabilitated."

"Well, then. You see the difference. Kita now has freedom, of a sort. He is imprisoned in a cat's body, true, but he is well cared for. And, since he still has his own mind, he is aware of what he did to me, and how I'm being much kinder to him, all things considered."

"Aren't you afraid of him breaking your spell the way you broke his?"

She shrugged. "Not particularly. Over the years, I've grown in my abilities, while he has been completely out of practice. The longer it goes on, the less likely he is to break it."

Suddenly, she froze, holding up a hand. Vincent's eyes followed hers, and then he saw it. Off to the west, about a hundred yards away, stood a girl. Vincent frowned. Two feelings washed over him, then. One was a feeling of dread, combined with the thought of Rhia. The other was a compulsion to go to the girl. He looked at Felina. From her face, he imagined she was feeling the same things, too.

Without speaking, they set off toward the girl, who merely waited for them. As they grew closer, Vincent was struck by the feeling that he'd met this girl before. She seemed awfully familiar. His first thought was that it was the same girl who had attacked him back in Port Remil, which had resulted in him being thrown down a mine shaft. But no. It couldn't be her. That girl was years younger than this one. Her sister, perhaps. The resemblance was striking.

At last, they stood in front of her, a mere ten feet away. The feeling of dread was now almost overwhelming inside him. He looked at the girl, noting what seemed to be a look of regret on her face. He opened his mouth to speak. But then, the world changed.

The trees around them shimmered, faded. The scene shifted, and they now stood in a clearing among the trees. Behind the girl, a great stone slab appeared, standing upright. Rhia was bound spread-eagled to the stone, her head drooping as though unconscious. No, not unconscious, Vincent realized. There was some movement. Not much, but some.

Burning torches rested in tall stands, a dozen or more forming a ring around them. And now, stepping out from behind the stone, a young man. Dressed all in black, bearded, he also reminded Vincent of the boy who had attacked him and stolen his gauntlets. Except, once again, this person seemed years older. He wore a wicked smile as he reached out and lifted Rhia's head by her chin. Her eyes slowly opened. Fury grew inside Vincent.

And a chill went through him as the boy spoke. "Good day, *Vincent*," he said, and his voice dripped with venom as he spoke the name. The girl stepped meekly behind him, her role in all this evidently complete.

Vincent clenched his jaw. "It seems you know me, friend. But I haven't a clue who you are."

"I know," he gloated. "And that's just fine with me. You see, I believe it would be much more fun for me to watch you suffer, rather than kill you outright." He giggled. "So I've decided to hurt those you love. That would include this red-haired specimen, here."

"I think not," rang Felina's strong voice.

And suddenly a flash of brightness leaped out. A searing bolt of flame that shot at the boy, engulfing him. Vincent covered his eyes at the brightness of it, turning his face toward Felina. She wore an expression of pure loathing, her arms spread out in front of her. Smoke issued from her fingertips when the blast was complete.

Vincent looked toward the stone. Since Rhia was directly behind the boy, he expected her to have been caught in the blast, too. But to his amazement, when the last remnants of the blaze disappeared, Rhia was unharmed. Her ropes were smoldering, but her body was intact.

Even more to his amazement, and dismay, was the fact that the boy was also unharmed. Rage contorted his face. "Elven bitch!" he screamed, and lashed out in return, battering back at Felina with a blast of bright green energy.

Felina had protection, however. The energy impacted against and illuminated a spherical field around the elf's body. Vincent sighed in relief as he saw this. But his expression grew concerned as the energy appeared to build in intensity. He saw Felina frown.

Then he gasped as he saw Felina's expression turn to one of alarm. She held her arms out in front of her, as though she were physically supporting her shields. But the energy kept battering at her. Vincent knew from his battle with Beltun Sagasht that her shields were failing. He could see it. He took a step toward her, wanting to help. She looked at him, shaking her head. And her concentration broke. The shields fell. And the green flare lashed through Felina. Vincent watched it as it struck her torso, and in an instant, spouted out her back. Her body flew backward to the ground, where she lay still.

The beam stopped. The boy's panting rage slowly faded, to be replaced by contented laughter. "That's one," he said.

Vincent gaped at Felina. Her chest was a mass of black blisters and green discoloration. Her face was frozen in that last look of alarm when he'd tried to help her.

She was dead. There was no question about it. She was dead, and it was his fault. He was to blame.

No, he told himself. Her shields were about to collapse. She knew it, too. You didn't kill her.

His eyes narrowed. No. He hadn't killed her. He turned to face the one who had.

"Oh, my," said the boy. "Look at that menacing expression, Sister! He means to kill me now!" And he laughed again. "This should be fun."

Vincent felt his heart pounding inside him, rage building. He wanted nothing more than to beat this punk senseless. But he wasn't blind to the fact that the boy was a mage. He remembered again the battle with Sagasht, how easily the mage could have killed him at any point. And he knew this boy could do the same.

Fighting down the ballistic urge, Vincent walked slowly toward the boy, who made no effort to get out of his way. Instead, he stood his ground, seeming to look forward to the confrontation.

"Normally," Vincent grated out, his voice choked with anger, "I would demand to know who you are, why you're out to hurt me, and all that." He stood in front of the boy. "But right now all I can think about is wringing your fucking neck."

The boy smiled in Vincent's face. "Wonderful! I like that! You want to beat me to a pulp, don't you?"

"Damn right."

"Be a lot easier to do with these, though, wouldn't it?" He held up his hands, now wearing gauntlets that Vincent recognized immediately.

His eyes grew wide. The gauntlets. Then these two really *were* the same kids who attacked him before. But their ages... He shook his head. He didn't understand, but at this point, he didn't really care.

Then another thought struck him. He looked at the boy's face again, and realized he was a bit late in thinking it. He had only a moment to absorb the grin on the boy's face before a magically enhanced fist drove into his stomach.

It blew the wind from his lungs. This had no real effect on him as far as breathing was concerned, but it still hurt like crazy. He buckled over, trying to keep his wits about him. A hand grasped him around the collar, lifting him up like a rag doll, and he knew he was in trouble. He sailed through the air, striking the stone between Rhia's legs with the side of his head.

He crumpled, feeling the blood running down his face, struggling to open his eyes as he lay there. He looked up, hearing the boy's laughter, still several feet away. What caught his attention even more was Rhia. Her eyes were open and aware, looking down at him. But it was a vacant look. Was she spellbound? No, he realized, when he saw a tear roll down her cheek. Not spellbound. She'd seen Felina's body.

The anger welled up inside him again and he rose to his feet. Immediately, he regretted the action, as he was hit with a wave of wooziness. Nausea ripped through him. The world spun and he braced himself against the rock. Briefly, he wondered if he'd gotten a concussion when he hit the stone. But then his thoughts were occupied by more pressing concerns. The boy approached and stood in front of him. As Vincent hoped, he drove another punch toward his stomach. At the last instant, Vincent sidestepped, and the boy's fist smashed into the rock.

But his voice carried laughter again, not pain. "Oh, was that supposed to hurt, punching the rock like that? Well, it didn't."

415

Vincent stared at him as he laughed. And then he noticed something. The ropes binding Rhia's legs had burned through. His heart soared as she kicked out with her foot, connecting with the young man's face. Blood spurted from his nose.

"Did *that?*" she asked.

Vincent didn't wait for his answer. He dove on top of the boy, going for his throat. But it was no use. The gauntlets gave him too much strength. Vincent flew back several feet, landing in a heap beside Felina's body.

His hand landed near her staff, which he immediately grasped and used to drag himself to his feet, just in time to see the boy lash out at Rhia. The same green flare, but noticeably weaker this time. His heart stopped as he watched his lover fry.

Except that she didn't fry. The energy seemed to be hitting a shield. But that was impossible. Then he noticed its source, at the same time the boy did. His sister was casting the spell of protection. So the siblings weren't necessarily of a like mind about things, Vincent thought.

And the next thing he knew, he was rushing forward, swinging the staff at the mage's head like a baseball bat. Just as the boy turned his attention to his sister, the staff connected. The effort drained Vincent, however, and he staggered back, leaning on the staff, his head ringing.

But the boy was down, sprawled a few feet from Vincent, roaring with pain and fury. The sister immediately assisted Rhia, severing the already fire-weakened ropes that held her wrists. If Rhia were recovered enough, it would now be three against one. Vincent's hopes began to rise. They had the son of a bitch now, he thought. He knew he lacked the energy to finish him. But Rhia could certainly waylay him. He hoped.

The boy evidently knew he was beaten, too. He rose and stood swaying next to Vincent, holding his head. Blood coated his face below his nose and around his ear. He glared at all of them, especially his sister. "Such betrayal," he said. "But I shouldn't be surprised, should I?"

"No," she said evenly. "Not at all."

"Your times will come," he said to the women. "Both of you." Then he turned back to Vincent. "And yours, last but most certainly not least." He smiled again. "Let me leave you something to remember me by." And with that, he whirled, leaping at Vincent, and laid a roundhouse punch to his head.

Vincent fell backward, his vision misting with red, fading to black, back to red again. He didn't feel himself hit the ground. He did see, however, the boy turn his attention briefly to the women, then smile. And in a burst of golden light, he disappeared.

"No!" he heard Rhia scream. At least, he assumed it was a scream, from the tone. The volume, however, was barely above a whisper. His ears were ringing and a searing pain was shooting through his skull. He deeply regretted not being knocked unconscious by the blow. I *used* to get knocked unconscious, he thought to himself. Not this time, of course. That would be too kind.

The sound of feet rushing past roused his awareness. He blinked, reducing the red glare a bit. Rhia was kneeling beside Felina's corpse, her stomach heaving. His heart went out to her, while mourning his friend's loss himself.

Then he noticed feet in front of him. The girl. She kneeled beside him, concern written on her beautiful face. He blinked at her, not sure how to react. She'd lured them into this trap, he realized. It was, indirectly, her fault that Felina was dead. But it seemed clear that she was forced into it. And she did save Rhia's life and probably his own. It was difficult to say that had evened the score, though.

He tried to blink away more of the annoying red mist, but this time it stayed. He felt woozy again. And the damn ringing in his ears! He lifted a heavy hand to his ear, hoping to stop the din. When he felt the blood, though, he knew his troubles weren't over.

Yup, he told himself. Definitely a concussion.

The girl said something, he couldn't tell what. But then Rhia was beside him. So quickly! Or had he blacked out for a moment? Rhia was peering into his face, frowning. He thought there were streaks of tears on her cheeks, but he couldn't be sure. He watched her shaking her head, then motion for him to get to his feet.

Yeah, right. Like he had the strength for that.

Then the girl put her hand on Rhia's arm, evidently indicating that she allow him to stay on the ground. Then the girl extended both her hands, placing one palm on his head, the other over his heart. He frowned. What was all this, now?

A warm, fuzzy feeling washed over him. Some of the pain lessened. He still had no energy, but didn't feel at death's door. He felt very detached from everything.

"He will recover," he thought he heard the girl say.

"He'd better," Rhia grated. "If I lose two friends today, I shall hold you personally responsible."

Vincent saw through eyes open momentarily that the girl had knelt now next to Felina. And, oddly enough, she was naked. Or maybe he was hallucinating.

She and Rhia exchanged words that Vincent couldn't make out. He closed his eyes again, then opened them. The women were gone.

He cast his gaze about, and saw them. They were *both* naked now. Rhia had straddled Felina's body, with her friend's forearms under her shins. She knelt facing the other girl.

Vincent thought momentarily that something decidedly on the sick side of kinky was going on, but then realized that magick was afoot.

Rhia leaned forward and placed her hands atop the girl's shoulders. Then, leaning forward more, they touched foreheads. They both spoke quietly, words that Vincent couldn't understand. He struggled to an upright position, the act making him dizzy and even weaker. But he hardly noticed, his attention not on himself.

When the ritual was spoken, Rhia leaned back, removing her hands from the girl's shoulders. She spread her arms wide, slightly above her head, as the girl began to chant.

The chanting grew louder and Vincent saw Felina's body start to twitch. Rhia's legs kept the elf's arms from flailing.

Soon Felina's body was thrashing violently. The girl's chant was becoming a scream, like a mad wail to her gods. And, much to Vincent's horror, the scream was joined by Felina's own death-wail. The body arched, the lungs hurling the anguish to the sky. It sounded to Vincent like the physical manifestation of the pain she must have felt as she was killed. Rhia shuddered and Vincent did, too. It was a shrill keening that pierced through the shouted spell of the girl, pierced through all the concentration that Rhia could possibly be focusing. Pierced through his very soul.

After an eternity, Felina's body collapsed. At the same time, the girl ended her spell. Rhia fell in a heap beside Felina, panting, sweat rolling off her body. The girl had slumped back on her heels, spent. And Felina...

Felina lay quietly beside her, her blackened chest rising and falling slowly, up and down, up and down.

✤ Thirty ✤

Vincent sat at the table in the rear of Felina's house, absently dipping his pen in and out of the inkwell, collecting his thoughts as he stared vacantly off into the distance. He had already written his account of what had transpired in the woods. But that was the easy part, he knew. The few days that followed were the ones difficult to describe. He sighed and turned his attention to the paper before him.

So much has happened, and yet, so little. Rhia and the girl somehow restored Felina to life. I don't know specifics, not having seen much of either of them since returning. But the truth of the matter is undeniable. Felina is alive. She's still unconscious, but her body is definitely alive.

It's so unnerving. I mean, I watched her die. I saw that bolt of green energy shoot through her body. I saw the blackened, bubbled flesh and her lifeless eyes. But now, that flesh is new and bright pink. Her eyes are closed, but I know there is a spark inside them.

The reason I haven't much information about the circumstances surrounding her resurrection is because the two responsible for it have been so busy. Rhia spends hours at Felina's side, casting healing spell after healing spell. And this is no healing done with herbs and stuff. This is raw magic that Rhia's using, which is why it drains her so. When she's drained, she wakes the girl and they talk for a bit. I assume they discuss Felina's progress, but I'm not privy to those discussions. I could eavesdrop, but I don't.

Then Rhia goes to sleep. While she sleeps, the girl sits with Felina, doing her own magic. They alternate, so that one of them is always with Felina. I've spoken for maybe a total of fifteen minutes with Rhia since the attack, and not at all with the girl.

I don't even know her name! I've tried to make conversation with her after she's done with Felina, but she always turns away or says she's too exhausted to talk. It's like she's avoiding me. But she's never rude about it. Possibly she's doing so out of guilt? Hard to say, since I can't talk with her.

There's no question in my mind that she is the same girl who attacked me back at the mine. Except that it wasn't really her who did the attacking, was it? Thinking back upon that episode, I remember her trying to prevent her brother from killing me, even then. She'd even so much as stated that she'd exacted a promise from him that he wouldn't kill me.

Kita hasn't left Felina's side since she was brought back. Except for calls of nature, that is. I imagine he's eaten, too, though I couldn't swear to it. It's strange. I get a definite sense of concern on his part. If it's true that the man inside the panther's body is fully aware of what's been done to him, I'd expect him to be happy about her being hurt. Perhaps her spell also included some sort of clause that prevents him from doing any harm to her. But I wouldn't think she'd have included something to instill such loyalty. That would sort of defeat the purpose she undoubtedly had in mind. So what's causing Kita to act this way? Yet another mystery on the pile.

And unsurprisingly, I find it very strange being around him, knowing he's really not a cat, but a human turned into a cat. It makes a certain amount of sense, now, all those times I felt Kita was empathetic to my situation. I guess he was. But I'll be damned if I know how to act around him, anymore.

It was late and the sunlight was beginning to fade, so Vincent capped his inkwell and pushed the paper aside. He debated whether to light all the torches around the perimeter or not. It was a pain in the butt, lighting a torch with flinty rocks. At home, he always kept an oil lamp burning, just to have a ready source of flame. Being a mage, Felina didn't need such a pilot light.

Just then, the door opened and Rhia stepped outside. She approached and sat beside him. Drawn and haggard though she was, she managed a smile and a hug for him.

"Hi, stranger," he said as they parted the embrace. "Nice to see you."

"You, too," she said wearily.

"I assume your new friend is with Felina now?"

Rhia shook her head. "Still sleeping. Felina is now to the point where her body can continue recuperating on its own. In fact, it needs to do so for awhile, lest it become too dependent upon our magical abilities."

Vincent frowned. Dependency on magical healing? Like addiction to prescription medication, he thought. "Geez," he muttered. "That would suck."

"Do not worry. She'll be fine."

"I'm glad to hear that," he said sincerely. He cleared his throat. "Look, I know you're really tired, but I have some questions."

"About what?"

"About this girl."

Rhia cut him off. "I know little more than you do, I'm afraid. And yes, I'm quite tired. Before I collapse onto the ground, I am going to bed. I just wanted to let you know Felina's condition."

Vincent let out an exasperated breath. "Okay," he said. "I'll see you in the morning." Rhia squeezed his hand before rising and heading back indoors.

He sat quietly for a while, absorbed in his thoughts, gathering up his writing materials. Then he took a deep breath, closed his eyes, and stretched out his senses. It was a ritual he'd kept to lately, finding it to be both stimulating and relaxing at the same time.

His hearing he turned toward the house. It relaxed him, listening to the purring of various cats. Sometimes he'd listen to Rhia or the girl while they slept. Their rhythmic breathing was peaceful. Just as he never eavesdropped on the discussions they had when both were awake, he never listened to the sessions either of them had with Felina. He'd heard part of one, once, and it was gibberish to him. Disturbing.

Felina would be alone, now, he thought, so he tuned in to her breathing. What he heard, though, wasn't the sound of breathing, but the soft, unmistakable sound of sobbing.

It could be Rhia, he thought as he rose quietly from his seat and headed for the door. He knew how traumatized she was over all this. But he saw, upon entering the house, that Rhia was asleep in bed. The girl, too, was sleeping in the room across the hall from Rhia's. He frowned, looking down the hallway to the doorway of Felina's room.

He approached as silently as he could, not knowing what he would find. He peered cautiously around the corner and his eyes widened at the sight.

A man, a naked man, was crouched over Felina's still form. His incredibly long, black hair hid his features, but it was definitely he who was sobbing. His body rose and fell gently to his quiet grief, his torso draped across Felina's. Vincent stepped into the room.

The man looked up abruptly, and Vincent looked into red-rimmed eyes. They were familiar eyes, haunted and knowing. Vincent's heart skipped a beat as awareness hit him.

The figure tore his gaze from Vincent and looked again at the elf's face. He reached out and touched it, caressed it.

"Does she know?" Vincent asked softly. In reply, the man gently shook his head. "But," Vincent began, but the man looked up at him sharply. His face was, at first, threatening, but softened to what Vincent could only interpret as pleading. Again the man shook his head. He didn't *want* her to know, Vincent realized. Then, with a final glance at Felina, the man quickly turned and dove through the open window head first. Vincent rushed to look outside, only to see Kita the panther looking back at him before turning and padding off into the woods.

Vincent stood staring after him for a minute, stunned by what he'd just seen. Then, shaking his head, he turned to Felina, moving to sit in the chair beside the head of her bed.

He had one concern he'd not voiced to anyone. Since he was in and out of consciousness through most of her resurrection, he wasn't sure how much time had passed between then and Felina's death. He worried that, although alive, the elf might turn out to be a vegetable. Had there been brain damage? He knew it only took a matter of minutes for oxygen deprivation to do its trick on brain cells. At least, on humans. On Earth. He had no idea how such things worked here. Maybe the spells that healed her also reversed any brain damage. He hoped so.

He was pulled out of these thoughts by a tickling at the back of his mind, that sensation he often got when someone was watching him. He turned around. "Oh," he said. "Hello." The girl turned her gaze to the floor, then to Felina, but said nothing. Vincent rose slowly from the chair. "Rhia says she needs to recuperate on her own, now."

The girl nodded. "Yes. She told me before I went to sleep that this was the case."

Vincent stared at her, knowing it was making her uncomfortable, but not really caring. He wasn't sure what to think of her. Should he thank her for her efforts in healing Felina, or berate her for helping arrange for her death in the first place? He sighed. No. It wasn't a hard decision after all.

"I want to thank you for everything you've done," he said.

The girl shook her head. "If not for me, she would not have needed anything done for her."

"If not for your brother, you mean. And I suspect he'd have accomplished his goals with or without your unwilling assistance. At least you were there to remedy his actions." She looked up at him, then, and Vincent was touched by the look in her eyes. She seemed so grateful for his words, as if she needed desperately to hear them. He imagined he would feel the same way. He could see, also, that she felt awkward around him. So often, he was the one who felt awkward around others. Self-conscious. Nervous. He hated that feeling and didn't want her to feel that way around him. He smiled. "We haven't been introduced," he said. "My name's Vincent. What's yours?"

She hesitated a moment, then shifted nervously. "If we are going to have a conversation, we should do so outside, so as not to disturb Rhia. Don't you agree?"

Vincent blinked. "Um, sure. I guess."

He fell into step behind her as she walked out of the bedroom. They stepped quietly past Rhia's room, then out into the darkening evening. He watched as she stepped over to the nearest torch in its tall stand and casually ignited it with a flick of her finger. Then she sat down at the round table that Vincent had so recently been using. He did likewise, looking at her expectantly.

After a few moments, she said, "Why do you keep staring at me?"

He shrugged. "Two reasons, really. I'm waiting for you to tell me your name, for one thing."

"And the other?" she asked.

Vincent cleared his throat and, despite himself, averted his gaze. "Well, the other reason should be obvious. I mean, you're quite attractive."

He glanced up at her as he said this, curious of her reaction. He saw her eyes widen slightly. "I am?"

"Yes!" he snorted. "Incredibly so. Don't tell me no one's ever told you that before."

She smiled shyly. "Never."

"I don't believe it."

"It's true." She smiled at him warmly. "Thank you."

He smiled back. "Is there a reason I shouldn't know your name?"

Her smile faded. "No."

Vincent waited, but she still said nothing. "Then what is it?"

She got a twinkle in her eye, then, and said, "I think you already know it."

"How could I?"

The girl smiled shyly and shrugged in what seemed a child-like way to Vincent. Slowly, she said, "You seem to be the type of person who could look at someone else and just *know* what their name should be."

He raised an eyebrow. "What an odd thing to think about someone," he said. All the more odd because he sometimes *did* feel that way. There were times when he could look at someone and say, for example, Yes, your name *should* be Jennifer. Your parents were right to name you that. But the way this girl said it to him, almost in anticipation, made him uncomfortable. With a frown, he said, "So you want me to guess your name?"

She nodded her head in what seemed like relief to him. "Yes!"

Finding it difficult to be annoyed at the game, he chuckled. "The chances of me guessing your name are very low, you must realize. For reasons you couldn't possibly know."

"Try anyway. Think real hard. Maybe it will just come to you."

He looked into her blue eyes, imagined running his hands through her dark brown hair. And as he gazed at her, a name started to form in his head. He blinked in surprise, then turned his eyes away to stare at nothing while he concentrated on the thoughts. Syllables came to him, like a voice through the fog. "Dar..." he said, and glanced at her. "Dar-something," he said. He saw an expression that seemed to be the same sort of surprise that he was feeling. He concentrated harder. "There's another syllable," he continued. "... La. Dar..." Suddenly, he looked back at her. "Darla?"

"Darla?" she repeated.

He chuckled again, shaking his head as if to clear cobwebs. "I told you I wouldn't guess it."

"But you did!" she said quickly. "My name *is* Darla!"

He looked at her suspiciously. "Baloney."

"What?" she said.

"If your name is Darla, then mine is Alfalfa. Seriously, what is your name?"

She looked into his eyes. "I swear to you, Vincent, my father named me Darla. If you insist on being called Alfalfa, then I will do so. But my name *is* Darla."

Vincent sat back in his chair. He listened for that little voice in his head to tell him that she was lying. But he heard nothing. But how could her father have given her such an Earth-like name? As quickly as he asked himself the question, he waved it off. Sianon's name, after all, was very much like the name Shannon, on Earth. Obviously there were some similarities between the two worlds.

He smiled faintly. "Well, then. Darla. It's nice to meet you."

She smiled in relief. "Thank you. It's nice to meet you, too."

"So," he said casually, tapping his fingers on the tabletop. "Silly question, but, why does your brother want to kill me?" Vincent saw her frown as she turned her eyes to stare at his tapping fingers.

"That's not an easy question to answer," she said softly.

Vincent shrugged. "I'm patient. When I need to be. The thing is, I don't know if I can afford to be patient right now. For all I know, he could pop in here in the next ten minutes and blast me the same way he blasted Felina."

"He wouldn't do that," she said. "Originally, he wanted you dead. But now, he wants to hurt you before killing you."

Her casual words caused his stomach to knot. He shook his head. "Darla, I'm not used to the idea of someone wanting me dead. I admit I could have made some enemies, but I don't remember ever meeting you or your brother before the day he stole my sword and gauntlets and tried to slice my head off. What did I ever do to him?"

The girl took a shaky breath. "Well," she began, "he had heard of you. You have, after all, made something of a name for yourself in some areas." Vincent nodded, knowing she was right, much as the fact astounded him. "My brother is vain, you see. He wished to prove himself by besting you."

"Why me, though?"

She shrugged. "Who can say why he got that idea into his head? Whatever the reason, he did choose you. And, with the gauntlets he took from you, he was able to track and observe you."

"How?"

"He was able to fixate on your life-force from the residue of it that lingered on the gauntlets. And the sword, too, but mostly the gauntlets."

Vincent nodded. "I see. And through tracking me, he was able to see my interactions with certain friends of mine. Rhia and Felina. Blade and that crew, I'm sure." His stomach twisted as a thought occurred to him.

"What is it?" Darla asked.

The dream he'd had, of Ariaziane being raped. That was after he'd been attacked at the mine, after the gauntlets had been stolen. After the boy had decided to hurt his friends to hurt him. Rhia had assured him it was just a dream, not reality. But still, she could have said that just to pacify him. Had Darla's brother caused her to be raped? Was he one of the actual rapists?

"What is wrong?" Darla asked, but he ignored her.

Or was it really just a dream? He had to admit that, if it were an actual event, the punk would have rubbed it in. He'd have bragged about it. Otherwise, he couldn't know for sure if the kid were responsible for it. And he'd not bragged about it, not mentioned it at all. This gave him some relief. It must have been just a dream. It *must* have.

"Vincent?" Darla said, her voice alarmed.

"I'm sorry," he said. "Just got caught up in thoughts." He shook his head. "Darla, his actions, his words, seemed filled with hatred. He doesn't seem to be only trying to best me to prove himself. Why does he hate me so much?"

Now it was her turn to fidget nervously. "My brother and I are twins," she said quietly. "But we are not very much alike. You might say we are opposites. And it seems that, the older we get, the more determined we are to show just how different we are. It almost seems we go out of our way to make *sure* that we are opposites."

"I don't see how that answers my question."

Darla hesitated, staring at the tabletop, before slowly answering. "It answers it very plainly, actually. He *hates* you... because I *love* you."

After a moment, Vincent closed his mouth. He blinked. "You what?"

Darla turned her eyes to meet his. "I love you," she repeated, quietly.

Vincent let out a breath he hadn't known he was holding. "But you don't know me," he said.

"Yes, I do," she insisted. "Better than you could imagine. I know you are an honest man, a trustworthy man. You are caring and kind and considerate. You put the welfare of others before your own. You arm yourself with a sword, but you wage more battles with your mind as a weapon. I know you love animals and the beauty of nature. And I know nothing makes you happier than knowing you've brought happiness to someone else. How could I *not* love you?"

Despite himself, Vincent felt his cheeks redden. He smiled self-consciously and cleared his throat. "Darla," he said kindly, "I'm very flattered. But while I can see how you might admire those qualities, perhaps greatly, that's still not the same as love."

"Isn't it?" she said, raising an eyebrow.

Vincent sighed. "Not really." And he looked at her, at her beauty. "Please don't think I'm brushing you off. I'm not. I just don't think you're quite sure of what you're saying."

Darla nodded her understanding. "Will you at least allow me the opportunity to prove it?"

He laughed. "Ah. Well, I can't say I wouldn't enjoy that," he said, smiling.

They spent the rest of the evening together, sitting at the table by the light of a single torch until it became too cold, then they moved inside. Rhia was still sleeping, and would throughout the entire night. Vincent and Darla sat in front of the fireplace, talking for hours, playing with the cats, and drinking mugs of steaming herbal brews.

Darla had so many questions for Vincent. He was amazed at how much she knew about his life. She inquired about particular events, including his days in the mine. She wanted to know, more than anything, what he was thinking and feeling throughout. She asked about the battle with Beltun Sagasht. About the freeing of the slaves out on the sea. About being blind.

Vincent knew he should be alarmed by these questions, by the fact that she knew so much about him, about events that took place before his gauntlets were stolen. And if she were familiar with these things, it was a safe bet that her brother was, too. That worried him. But he was so flattered by her attention, by her undisguised adoration, that he couldn't bring himself to spoil the mood by voicing his concerns. And after all, he couldn't change the fact that his life was an open book to her and her brother.

In the wee hours, slumber began to overtake them both. Vincent made himself comfortable among the pillows and furs on the floor. Darla snuggled up next to him, her arm across his chest, her fingers gently tangled in his long hair. He didn't mind a bit. "Good night," he whispered, closing his eyes.

"Good night," she whispered back, and leaned forward. Her lips were soft on his, startling him. He opened his eyes and allowed himself to respond to the kiss. It was gentle, but with a depth of passion that shocked him, for the passion wasn't just hers. They smiled at each other when their lips parted, said good night again, and snuggled into the furs. Sleep took Darla quickly, but for Vincent, it was a long time coming.

Felina regained consciousness the following day. Rhia had summoned Vincent and Darla inside at the first signs of activity. The three stood around Felina's bed, looking down expectantly, as Kita padded around, trying to obtain a clear view. Rhia spoke words of encouragement while Darla massaged Felina's hands. Finally, the elf's eyes opened. She took in her surroundings, her eyes lingering on all three of her visitors. Vincent saw in her eyes that she was rapidly remembering all the events. Her hand disengaged itself from Darla's and made its way up to her chest, where it lightly traced over the area where she'd been struck. Her face reflected the memory of the event. Then her features softened and, her gaze taking in all of them, she smiled faintly and said, "Ouch."

☙ ❧

It was quite emotional. All four of us cried. Then Darla and I left her alone with Rhia to care for her. She'll probably be asleep a lot over the coming days. But her body has recuperated enough to regain consciousness. And, to my relief, there seems to be no brain damage. All of us are happy, including Kita.

Rhia is sitting with Felina again today. They've been talking a lot. I haven't really heard what any of the conversation has been about, since I've been talking with Darla all day.

She and I grow closer daily. She's really very bright. And she's quite taken with me. It's very flattering. And she's gorgeous. I don't know, though. There's something about her that just seems odd. There's a strange feeling I get around her. Like a weight pressing down. It seems like she's had a really horrible life thus far, but I haven't really pried. I like being with her. And I know she likes being with me. I guess that's all I should care about right now.

As for Rhia, she's begun some sort of ritual fast. She's eaten nothing, to my knowledge. She drinks a lot of water, but that's all I've seen her consume. Tomorrow, she says, she starts to recharge. Whatever that means.

☙ ❧

What it meant was that Rhia sequestered herself away in a clearing in the woods. Darla went with her, and later described to him how Rhia had found the spot she wanted, then put down a pentagram in powdered chalk. Rhia disrobed and sat cross-legged in the center, then Darla wove a web of protection around her. It would protect Rhia from the elements, roaming animals, and physical attacks while she was in her trance state.

She remained there for one week, much to Vincent's dismay. He was assured by Darla of her safety from harm, but his concern was more for her nutritional well-being. She'd been without food for three days going into this, and would be without nourishment for the whole week. He failed to see how this would recharge her in any way.

But Darla explained to him that all the sustenance her body needed was being taken from the source of all nourishment, the world itself. Rhia, she told him, was now in perfect communion with the world. She was literally a part of it. Her body would absorb all the strength it was capable of storing during this period. Nourishment, she said, would be no issue whatsoever.

Vincent wasn't happy with this explanation, not seeing why she needed such an ordeal. He understood that she was drained from helping bring Felina back from the dead, but so was Darla, and Darla wasn't going through this ritual. But he said nothing to that effect. In the back of his mind, he felt that Rhia had her own plans. And though he was distressed because she was not making them known to him, he couldn't help but respect whatever they might be.

So he waited out the week, spending more time with Felina as her strength improved. Darla gave her a daily dose of magic to help her recovery, but not too much. By the end of the week, Felina was up and around, and Vincent went to great lengths to help her as much as possible, and to reinforce the friendship that had been growing between them since he and Rhia had first arrived.

Vincent's relationship with Darla grew stronger, too. Little mention of her brother was made, since speaking of him only made Vincent angrier and angrier. So angry, in fact, that it made his head hurt. He never even asked her brother's name. He didn't want to know. It made it easier to maintain a nice, rosy hatred for the man. Giving him a name would be making him more human. And he'd much rather hate something nameless.

Instead, he answered a barrage of questions from her. And, being comfortable with her, he told her of Earth, which brought forth even more questions. It bothered him, to a degree. She already knew so much about him, and was learning more every day. But he knew nearly nothing of her. It occurred to him that there really wasn't that much *to* know about her. She had lived a very secluded life up until recently. The life she described was a very boring one, growing up with only her brother and mother. The father, evidently, had left their mother before the twins were born.

When Darla was with Felina, Vincent had time for his own thoughts. And most of the time, they were of home. Not Earth. Home. His little house by the shore. He wanted nothing more at this point than to be back there, falling asleep at night to the sound of the surf, spending afternoons lying in the sun or throwing sticks for Blaise. Tending his garden. He was sick and tired of these confrontations. Ever since leaving home with Rhia, it had been one fight after another. The pirates on the sea. The brothers at the mine. The days in the mine itself. And now Darla's brother. He just wanted to wash his hands of the whole thing. He wanted it to be over.

But then, he told himself, he wanted a lot of things that he wasn't likely to get.

The day Rhia returned was cold and overcast, but the three of them were sitting outside at the table, despite the chill. Rhia walked out of the woods and stepped between the torches into the clearing. Their conversation stopped as they took notice of her.

Rhia's appearance seemed darker, though Vincent couldn't be sure. Her features were distinct, as though chiseled from stone or carved of wood. Her hair appeared to have deepened to the red of autumn leaves. Vincent only caught a glimpse of this, since she had the hood of her cloak pulled up, keeping her face in shadow. And she walked forward with a strength he'd never seen in her before. To Vincent, Rhia radiated the power of the earth itself.

And when she stood before them, her first words were, "It is time."

Vincent raised an eyebrow, but said nothing. He observed the others, first. Felina stood. After a moment of evident concern, she relaxed her face and gave a nod that Vincent interpreted as understanding.

Darla merely rose and embraced her. "Good luck," she said.

Vincent, too, got to his feet. "Time for what?" he demanded.

Felina and Darla exchanged glances and walked away, leaving the two alone. Rhia looked at Vincent, her eyes filled with sadness. "Time for me to take care of some business," she said quietly. "Alone."

"Business?" Vincent sputtered. "You must be joking. With all that's going on here, you're *leaving*?"

"Yes, I am. I'm sorry I couldn't tell you about this before, but it's something that must be done."

"What is?"

Rhia looked at him for several seconds. Finally, she said, "It is a witch matter. More than that, I cannot say. Please," she said, "do not ask. And do not be upset. I know you don't understand, and that's my fault. But you must trust me when I say this is necessary. Trust me as they do," she said, nodding her head at the others, who stood talking quietly several yards away.

"But what about Felina? She's still weak, certainly in no shape to defend herself if we're attacked by Darla's brother again."

"As long as she does not leave this area, her house and this compound, she'll be safe."

"Why?"

"It is quite well protected, magically. That is why we were attacked out in the woods, rather than here. The defenses Felina put up are powerful enough to prevent him from attacking here."

"Oh." Vincent stared at her for several seconds, frowning. Then he sighed, turning his gaze to the ground. He didn't like this one bit. However, Rhia had vanished from his life frequently in the past. He had no real reason to think such occurrences would cease, just because they were lovers. She'd come back, just like before. He looked up at her, his frown now gone. "Okay," he said simply. "I do trust you." He reached out and clasped her hand. "Do you know how long you'll be gone?"

She shook her head. "It could be a matter of days, or months. I have no way to know."

He nodded, absorbing this. "I see. So, when will you be leaving?"

"Right now."

He looked up at her sharply. "Now?" He sighed when she nodded. "Okay."

Rhia smiled faintly, then leaned in and kissed him. "Thank you," she whispered. Then she brushed past him and entered the house.

Vincent stood there for a moment, feeling the last tingles from the kiss slowly fade away. He licked his lips. Then he turned and stepped over to the others, hoping they could shed some light on what Rhia was up to. But Felina's expression told him right away that he shouldn't even bother to ask. It wasn't easy to fight down the resentment that this brought on. But he did.

He stood quietly for a time, staring at the door through which Rhia had entered the house. He wanted nothing more than to rush in, tell her not to go, or to take him with her. All the things he wanted to do... No, all the things he *had done* before Ariaziane left... They'd had no effect on her, but they might have an effect on Rhia. Rhia, after all, loved him. That had to count for something.

And it was as though the others knew his thoughts. Darla's arm reached out and her hand settled on his shoulder. "Don't," was all she said. Vincent looked at her and at Felina. Both wore expressions of concern on their faces. He grimaced. Then he shook off Darla's hand and strode quickly into the house.

He berated himself for doing it, but he needed to know if the others knew something that he didn't. So, once inside, he deliberately focused his hearing on the women outside as he went in search of Rhia.

"I knew this would be hard on him," he heard Felina say. "I told Rhia not to do this."

"I'm afraid for her."

"As am I. But Rhia is headstrong. There was no talking her out of it."

"Vincent is headstrong, as well," Darla replied, and he heard the door open and the women enter the house. "What do you think he will do?"

"What is there that he *can* do?"

By this time, Vincent had rushed through and peeked in every room of the house. Rhia was in none of them. "She's gone!" he said as he rushed out of the hallway into the living room. "I can't believe it! She's gone!" His voice was choked up and tears of anger fought with tears of sadness for the right to roll first down his cheek. "Why did she do it this way?" he said, mostly to himself, trying not to let the tears flow.

"Possibly because she knew your reaction would be one such as this," Felina offered. "She knows you well, Vincent. She knew you would try to stop her. Or join her."

The look he gave her was not one of fondness. But even as he glared, he knew she was right. He put a hand to his forehead, rubbing between the eyes where the headache was forming. Then he turned and walked slowly back to his room, where he flopped onto the bed.

For several minutes, he simply lay there, burying his head in the pillows, trying to tell himself that Rhia would return. He'd see her again.

He ignored the knock on his door. When there was a second knock, he frowned, then sat up, facing the door, his back to the wall.

"Vincent?" Darla said. "May I come in?"

When he didn't respond, she lifted the latch on the door and stepped inside.

He didn't look up, but stared at his open left palm as Darla stopped beside him. With his right index finger, he idly traced a path back and forth on the side of the hand, below the little finger. Darla sat gently on the bed near him, but not too near. "I went to a palm reader, once," he said in a hoarse voice.

"A what?"

"Someone who studies the lines, the creases, on your palm and can supposedly divine things about your life from doing so. I think it's a bunch of baloney," he said. Then he motioned her to look at the area of his palm below the little finger. "See those little lines there, on the side? The palmist said they indicated I would not have a single, stable romantic relationship in my life. I'd have a series of short ones." He smiled ironically. "Maybe I did get my twenty dollars' worth out of that, after all. I guess she was right."

"I don't understand."

"It's simple," he said, turning his attention from his hands to her face. "I was in love with Ariaziane. But she didn't fall in love with me. Or maybe she did. I don't know." He frowned. "It doesn't really matter, since I haven't seen her in two damn years, and maybe never will again. Then there was Rhia. I fell in love with her. And now she's gone, to return who knows when?" He paused, staring straight into her eyes. His voice was tinged with bitterness when he spoke again. "So. Are you next? When will you leave? I'd just like to have an idea, so I know how attached to you I should get." Darla looked at him, her mouth opening, then closing. Finally, she turned her face away. "That's what I thought," he said. And Darla stood and walked quickly from the room. Vincent heard her sob once, and tried to ignore the pain in his gut that it caused.

A minute later, Felina entered his room without knocking. She sat on the bed beside him. "So," she said. "Are you planning on staying around for a while longer, or will you be going home now?"

The question so took him by surprise that for a moment, he said nothing. Then he leaned forward, putting his elbows on his knees. "I hadn't really thought about it."

"Perhaps you should."

"You're saying you want me to leave."

"It would probably be for the best."

"Have I done something wrong? Something to offend you?"

She shook her head. "Not yet. But you're in pain. And in your pain, you've lashed out at someone who cares for you tremendously. You've hurt her. I don't want to be next." Before he could protest, she continued. "In addition to that, I do think it's time you left. Not because I want you away from here, but because you need to get on with things."

Vincent mulled over her words. "You make it sound as though I should accept the fact that Rhia's gone from my life forever and I should just get used to that."

"I certainly hope that is not the case. But if that's how you need to think of it in order to carry on with your life, then so be it. You cannot hold on to something that isn't there."

He looked up at her sharply. "But she is. She's here, inside my head and my heart. I can't forget about her. She's left before and has come back. She'll probably come back this time, too."

"Life is uncertain. If Darla hadn't been here, you and Rhia would now be long gone from here and mourning my death. And I, much to my surprise, would be dead. That's not something I'd have expected at my young age."

"Well, you're just a bundle of joy, aren't you?"

"Joy isn't found in bundles. Only in individual strands, as delicate as a spider's web. And as beautiful. Take what joy you happen upon, Vincent."

Tears welled up in his eyes again as he looked at her. "Are you well enough to be on your own, yet?"

She nodded. "Yes. We elves recuperate quickly."

Vincent was quiet for a moment. Then he said, "I just can't see how easily you let her go off like that, without a real explanation."

"Is she obliged to explain everything to us?"

"No, but you'd think she'd tell us! I mean, we're both... You know."

"Yes, we are very important to her. But ultimately, Vincent, everyone has things that are private, even from those they love. And we are showing our love for her by accepting that, understanding that, and trusting that she knows what she is doing. And, as you say, hoping for her safe return."

The headache beat against the inside of his skull and he put his face in his hands. He rubbed his eyes. "Yes," he whispered. "You're right. I'm being selfish. But it's hard not to be."

"True," she said. "Now, I'm going to go put together something to eat. And you, I think, need to talk to someone." She rose and was out of the room before he could even thank her. Taking a deep breath, he got off the bed and went outside to find Darla.

He found her easily enough, as she was sitting at the table in the back, Trisket curled up in her lap. The cat looked up with an inquiring whine as he approached. "Hiya, puss," he said. Darla didn't look up. He pulled out another chair and sat facing her. "Um, Darla..."

"You're right," she said flatly. "I can't tell you how attached to me you should become. I don't want to hurt you, but I can't say that it won't happen. In fact—"

"It's okay," he interrupted. "It doesn't matter. I'm sorry. I never should have said that in the first place."

She looked up at him, and he could see that she'd been crying. It drove a pain through his heart. "Vincent, I love you. I want to be with you. I *need* to be with you. But I know you don't share those feelings."

She was so beautiful, he thought. He melted when her eyes met his. And he knew he could never hurt her again, no matter how much he was hurting. He took her hands in his. "You'll have to put up with me sometimes talking about Rhia. And probably one other, too. That won't upset you?"

"How could it? I'm the outsider in your life. Rhia has been part of your life for a long time. And I would never begrudge you your feelings for her. She's very special to me, too."

"Darla, I'm going to be leaving soon. Felina has convinced me that it is probably for the best. I'm going to go home. I've been away for a while and need to get back.

Will you come with me?" She smiled and a happy tear rolled down her cheek. Trisket jumped down and scurried away as she surged forward and wrapped her arms around him.

❧ ❧

They left the following morning. Vincent hugged Felina good-bye, surprised at the hollow feeling it gave him to be leaving her behind. "You're sure you won't come, too?" he asked.

She shook her head. "No. I've things to do." She kissed him lightly on the cheek.

Darla and Felina exchanged good-byes. Then, with a final word of thanks, Vincent and Darla were off.

The journey to the nearest port was long. Darla wasn't the fastest of hikers. It took them four days.

The days were filled with talk, getting to know each other. Vincent found Darla to be very intelligent, but also very naïve. She knew very little when it came to people and the culture of the world, even less than he himself did. But, he reflected, he'd gotten around quite a bit in his five years here. He probably knew more about the different societal cultures than many people did.

Their nights were spent huddled together against the chilly temperatures. They were very awkward with each other. Darla seemed to love lying there, holding him. And though there were twinges of sexual desire, his emotions were in such turmoil over Rhia's departure that he could never really focus on them. Not that he honestly wanted to, anyway.

Finally, reaching port, they booked passage on the first ship heading west. There were fewer stops on this trip, compared to the voyage he and Rhia had made, making the trip considerably shorter.

On the fourth night of their sea voyage, Vincent found himself unable to sleep, so he dressed quietly and went up on deck. It was late. The breeze was steady, with some gusts that threatened to blow his hood back. The moon was high, reflecting beautifully off the waves. The aft deck, where he stood, was empty. He leaned against the railing, watching the silver reflections of moonlight as they were shattered in the wake of the ship's passing.

He gazed back, eyeing the dark shape of the shoreline off to the left. It made him think of where he'd been. Felina's. Blade's. So many things he'd done in five years here. So many things he'd seen. So many people he'd known. So many people he now missed.

Vincent shook his head. This was not what he needed, to be dwelling on the past. Felina was right about that. He turned and leaned his back against the rail, closing his eyes and allowing the wind to caress his face. It felt wonderful.

But for some occasional creaking of the boat, the only sounds were of wind and water. It was relaxing, peaceful. And those were sensations Vincent needed to feel. He breathed deeply and pretended that he wasn't on a boat at all. He imagined himself as a bird, skimming along the tops of the waves, feeling the spray in his face. Birds probably didn't dwell on their pasts. They were too busy looking forward, wondering where the next meal would be found.

Vincent sighed and opened his eyes. He needed to be looking to the future, too. No more fixating on the past, he vowed. And in a symbolic effort to keep the promise, he moved toward the foredeck, so he could look to see where they were headed, not where they'd been.

But as he approached the front of the ship, he noticed another person on deck. He stopped, frowning. Vincent wanted privacy, and, likely as not, so did the other person. He turned to go back to the rear of the ship, then stopped. His heart, inexplicably, began racing. And he felt as though he was being watched. Stealing a peek over his shoulder, he found the stranger staring directly at him. Vincent turned fully around, now, looking back.

The darkness was such that he could not discern any facial features. All he could make out was that he or she wore a long cloak with the hood thrown up against the cold, much as he himself was. But his instinct told him, from the stance and the few movements he saw, that it was a woman.

He wondered if it could possibly be Rhia. He gave in to his compulsions and headed slowly forward. The figure did not make any motion to depart, but when he approached to within a few yards, suddenly turned away from him. And he could have sworn he'd heard a gasp.

He puzzled over this. He couldn't have been recognized. His face was obscured by the darkness and his hood. His heart was still racing. Why? He leaned against the rail, also, facing the water. "A bit chilly tonight, isn't it?" he asked, watching for a reaction from the stranger. There was a nod, but no reply. Vincent frowned. Should he stay or not? He nearly chuckled aloud at the silly question. He had to stay, to see if the person really did know him.

He looked down at the rail. The moon cast enough light for him to see the person's hands clearly. And there was no question the delicate fingers belonged to a female. And no way they were Rhia's. Rhia's hands, while delicate, showed signs of being often used in gathering herbs and other growing things. They were also sprayed with freckles here and there. These hands, very delicate, showed no freckles, and certainly no evidence of gardening skills. And unlike this woman, Rhia wore no rings.

So it wasn't Rhia. Why, then, the feeling of familiarity? Why then, did she turn away as though she recognized him? A hard ball formed in his stomach. She hadn't seen his face, he was sure. She could see no more than what he could see. A cloaked figure. And his own cloak was held shut by a cloak pin. A very elaborate and unique cloak pin. One instantly recognizable. Especially by the person who had given it to him.

He looked back at the woman's hands, at the ring she wore. He could not tell the color of the stone in the dark, but the style was familiar to him. It was the same style as a ring from his horde of jewelry, a ring he'd given to Ariaziane.

He was speechless. His heart raced even faster. There could be no mistake. But he needed to see her face, just to add that visual confirmation. His mouth was dry. He couldn't speak, even if he had the slightest clue what to say to her. So instead, he stepped closer and reached out, placing his hand on hers.

She snatched her hand away, backing up a step. Then she folded her arms across her chest and turned so her back was to the rail, putting her face into slightly more shadow than before. Vincent still could not find words. He'd pulled his hand back after her reaction, and it now absently toyed with the cloak pin. Her eyes caught the

432

action and she turned her head enough to watch his fingers as they traced the shape of it.

Vincent watched carefully, hoping that he could see her face. He still could find no words to say. Just then, a gust of wind came. The woman's hood billowed for a second, then flew backwards, revealing her head. She quickly jerked it back up, but not before Vincent made out the long hair and finely sculpted features. Even in the silvery moonlight, he could see the fiery red of her tresses. Even in the shadow of night, he could make out the face he dreamed of so often. The confirmation made him swoon. He leaned heavily against the rail. He closed his eyes, regaining his composure.

When he opened them, she was gone.

The next morning, they docked at the port town of Tanrae. They were to spend an entire day and night there, departing again the following morning. Vincent spoke to the captain as they were docking. He described Ariaziane to him, insisting that he must know which cabin was hers. The captain seemed very reluctant to give the information to him, baron or no baron. A silver coin was enough for him to change his mind, however.

But when Vincent arrived at her cabin, she was not there. No matter, he thought. She'd obviously disembarked, as so many passengers had, so he and Darla did likewise. They spent the day in Tanrae, frequenting the tiny shops and eating each meal at a different establishment.

At sunset, they went back on board. Vincent once again found Ariaziane's cabin empty, so he went on deck and waited. He'd be there when she came back on board. He was queasy in anticipation.

"Baron," came a voice from behind him. He turned. "There you are," the captain said. "I trust you had an enjoyable day in town?" Vincent assured him that he had. "Good. Well, I wanted you to know that your friend, the woman you were looking for, has departed."

"Yes, I know. I'm waiting for her return."

"You misunderstand," the captain replied. "I mean to say that she has departed permanently. She returned at mid-day, taking her belongings." Vincent's world spun. He couldn't have heard him correctly. "She asked me to give you this," he said, holding out a folded slip of parchment.

Vincent took the paper and opened it. Inside was a brief message: *I'm sorry. Please do not hate me.* It was signed with the large, flowing "A" that he knew so well. Vincent squeezed his eyes shut. This couldn't be happening.

"Are you all right, Baron?" asked the captain. "Can I get you anything? A drink?"

Vincent waved him off. He thanked him for relaying the message. Then he made his unsteady way down to his cabin, where he collapsed in Darla's arms and, despite himself, cried himself to sleep.

The following weeks dragged by for Vincent. He found himself telling Darla every conceivable aspect of his life that she wanted to know about. The hardest part of this was telling her about Ariaziane. But he did. They spent the majority of their time in the cabin. It reminded him of the trip with Rhia, where they'd spent hours making love, even though he and Darla were not engaging in that activity.

He was very depressed. Rhia's departure and Ariaziane's reappearance then subsequent disappearance were too much for him to easily assimilate. He felt as though he was using Darla as an emotional crutch, but she didn't seem to mind. He couldn't quite figure out why this girl was so obviously devoted to him. She practically worshipped him. It made him uncomfortable, much as it flattered him.

So he quit trying to figure it out. He was, after all, quite human, and enjoyed having his ego stroked every bit as much as the next person. And Darla was, he would readily admit, quite an attractive piece of work. She was beautiful, smart, caring. And she was, it seemed, completely in love with him. And he cared quite a lot about her, too. He just couldn't shake the feeling that it was just a little too bizarre, how she dropped into his life like that with her feelings for him already so advanced. But, since he couldn't figure it out, he stopped worrying about it.

Finally, they reached Linnael. It was a cold, blustery day, overcast, with nary a hint of sun. They disembarked, happy that the journey was finally over. Rather than head straight home, Vincent took Darla to Aedriun's place. They spent several hours there, resting from the voyage, eating wonderfully prepared foods, and playing with Blaise. Aedriun naturally inquired about Vincent's journey, including who Darla was, and Vincent spent much time telling tales of everything that had happened over the past months.

They spent the night there, and in the morning, took a pair of horses and headed for home, Blaise bounding happily beside them as they rode. Vincent was of mixed feelings about returning home. It would be good to be home, but he wasn't happy about having the constant reminder of Ariaziane's house right next door. Especially after having seen her so recently. As it happened, however, his concerns were moot.

As he and Darla made their way toward Vincent's house, he got the feeling of something being terribly wrong. When they reached the point where the house could be seen in the distance, it didn't look quite right. The reason for this became quite evident as they neared.

Vincent broke into a gallop as he saw the damage. Both houses were leveled. Burned, crushed, destroyed. He dismounted when he reached his house. The damage was not new. None of the burnt timbers still smoldered at all. He walked through the blackened rubble, tears of anger streaming down his face. And then, in the center of all the wreckage, he saw something.

His guitar, or rather, just the neck of it, was stuck firmly in the ground. Attached to it by a ribbon was a piece of rolled up vellum. He removed it hastily and unrolled it. Though he'd never seen the handwriting before, he knew it belonged to Darla's brother. He could almost hear the boy's mocking laughter as Vincent read the short, two word note:

"Welcome Home!"

❧ ❧

Darella hated to leave the cave. There was probably more that she could have learned from the Seeker Portal. As it was, though, she'd learned plenty. She had theories about how it worked. She had even confirmed the existence of eight more Seeker Portals scattered throughout the world. Her goal was to locate these other portals in order to test her theories. To see if the portals were all identical, or if each had its own specific set of parameters under which it would operate. She was prone to believe the former, but wouldn't have put it past the druids to have made the latter case true.

And, she realized, sooner or later Rhia would track her down. She'd sensed Rhia probing for her over the past years. And now it seemed as though the child who'd betrayed her brother so recently could have revealed Darella's location to Rhia.

She frowned at the thought, but shrugged it off. She knew it had been a gamble, raising the children as she did. A gamble that had, sadly, failed. Interesting, though, how the two children had been failures in exactly the opposite ways.

The girl had evidently developed her own set of morals throughout her short life. Darella wasn't sure exactly how this happened, but couldn't deny the obvious. And it was clear the girl hated her. Darella wondered if she knew about the sacrificing of the baby. That sacrifice had fed her the power she'd needed to unlock many of the portal's secrets, though certainly the girl wouldn't have cared about that. She'd have been beyond outraged at the sacrifice. So many mothers were like that.

But no. The girl had been unconscious at the time.

Of course, the boy could have told her. It was the sort of nasty, callous thing he'd do. The boy was a failure because he refused to adopt any sort of ethics whatsoever. He was impatient. A witch could not be impatient. But she understood that part, at least. He knew he was living on borrowed time. Unfortunate that the spells that warded off the effects of time did not work on these two. She imagined she would have grown impatient, too. But sometimes she thought the boy was truly insane. She thought perhaps the realization of his impending death was too much for him to handle. It would certainly explain a lot.

As it was, she hardly saw him any more. He was always off doing his own thing. She'd given up on him months ago. Let him run amok and create mayhem. It was no concern of hers. Let him go after his father, kill him, make him suffer. That, too, was no concern of hers.

She knew her son wanted to utilize this portal for some purpose or another. He'd paid enough attention to her studies to learn a little about it. And she felt there could be no harm in allowing him to play with it. He had no prayer of harming it. She doubted he could even manage to operate it. He'd probably become completely frustrated within an hour of not being able to make it work. And he'd get angry and try to destroy it. But it was too well protected for that. No, she thought. He couldn't harm it. If she thought he could, well... She'd kill him if he even tried.

She advised the boy of her impending departure one day when he actually came to the cave. To no surprise of Darella's, he seemed quite pleased to know he'd have control of the portal in her absence. She let him believe that she would be returning at some point. Maybe that would prevent him from trying to destroy the portal when he found he couldn't utilize it.

She didn't bother putting up wards against Rhia's probable visit. It wouldn't be worth her time. Rhia could not possibly extract information from the portal in time to prevent any of Darella's actions. It had taken Darella many years to learn the secrets of the portal. Rhia wasn't likely to learn anything in less time than she had. And Darella didn't bother telling her son about the possibility of Rhia visiting. She knew she didn't need to. The boy had, after all, met her once already. She knew he'd not hesitate to kill her. And that was fine with Darella.

Book Five

Brothers in Arms

❧ Thirty-One ❧

Over a week had passed since his return. Vincent had salvaged what he could from the destroyed houses, and was surprised to find nothing missing. Not that there had been much to steal. He kept few valuables in the house. His trove of gems and cash were under Aedriun's protection. Vincent paid a crew to clean up the mess, disposing of the rubble. He'd been furious when he initially saw the damage. But, since there was nothing he could do about it, he got over it and set the ball rolling on having Ariaziane's house rebuilt, on the chance that she might, in fact, someday return.

He did not commission his own home to be rebuilt. He saw no reason to. His keep, he figured, should be finished sometime within the coming year. It was probably livable right now, but he didn't feel up to a move during the cold weather. He'd wait until the weather was warmer. The keep certainly wouldn't be as nice as his home here had been, nor nearly as luxurious as Aedriun's accommodations. In fact, it would be little more than bare stone walls at this point, but it would certainly do. He'd planned on residing at *The Yellow Beard* in town until that time, or possibly moving back to his cottage near Gnorrin, but Aedriun wouldn't hear of it. Vincent and Darla now had elegant rooms in Aedriun's household.

In fact, the splendor of Aedriun's home was a little too much for Vincent. He felt so odd being surrounded by people dressed in fine clothing all the time. He continued to kick around in his simple breeches and tunic. And though they were quality clothes, in good repair and with attractive trim, they were drab, compared to the clothes of most of the people he encountered. And they were about as fancy as he had the tolerance to wear.

Darla, though, was intrigued by the finery she saw, so Vincent made a point to purchase a few nice outfits for her. And the result pleased him. She was stunning. Everyone said so. During his second week back, Aedriun threw a ball in his honor. Darla was the center of attention. Her dark hair stood out sharply against the blue dress and gold necklace she wore.

To be more accurate, Darla was the center of attention out on the floor. Vincent, also dressed to the nines at Aedriun's insistence, drew crowds of his own, much to his amazement, not to mention discomfort. He shook hands with dozens of unfamiliar men, bowed over the hands of scores of unidentified women. Then, just after the meal, he saw someone he recognized.

The middle-aged man approached him warily, an expression of inquiry on his scarred face, as if asking silent permission to speak. He looked pretty awful, Vincent thought, with bad teeth and little hair. But Vincent knew the man. He was one of the slaves he'd freed from the pirate ship. Now Vincent understood why so many of the strangers this night had mentioned that particular feat.

The man bowed slightly. "Lord Vincent," he said. "Good to see ye again."

Vincent squirmed at the title. While technically appropriate when addressing a baron, the term "Lord" made him itch. He smiled politely and nodded. "And you as well, though I confess I cannot recall your name."

"Coldson, m'lord." he said.

"Coldson," he repeated. "I am glad to know you are in good health. How did you come to be here this evening?"

The man smiled broadly. "Did some investigatin' after you let us off at Luketsport," he said. "Found out ye lived here in Linnael. Met up with one of Lord Aedriun's men, who got me an appointment to see him. I told him how ye and yer lady friend rescued us all. He made me feel right at home, he did. Been here for over a month now, waiting for ye to come back."

Vincent frowned and made a mental note to ask Aedriun about this when they had some privacy. "Aedriun is a fine and considerate man," he told him. "I'm glad he's shared his generosity with you."

"I've signed on as a member of his guard," the man said proudly. "Until such time as I can be in yer service, that is. The baron knows that. When will ye be needin' us?"

Vincent shifted again. "Um..."

"From what ye said on the ship, I was figurin' ye'd be needin' us 'fore too long."

"Probably not until next year, if then." The man frowned, seeming about to protest his words, when Darla suddenly arrived. Vincent smiled in relief as she put her hand on his arm. He shrugged apologetically at the man. "Will you excuse me, my friend?"

The man nodded as Darla dragged him away. "Vincent," she said happily, "I just heard from one of the ladies that you're quite a dancer."

"What?" he gasped. "On the contrary!"

"She said that you invented a new dance right in this very room, and it has become very popular. Will you teach me? I know nothing about dancing. Teach me, please!"

Vincent grimaced, trying desperately to think of some excuse, when the quartet of musicians began their next piece, a sprightly number in 3/3 time. He glanced up to see the guests begin to dance, some of them looking in his direction, obviously hoping he'd join them. He looked at Darla's anxious face, and knew he was trapped.

His feet moved without conscious effort. The musicians' tune was lively and well-played. Darla picked up the steps very quickly and felt comfortable in his arms. But Vincent could not concentrate on dancing.

Instead, he thought about Ariaziane. Why had she not spoken to him on the ship? Why had she left after encountering him? These thoughts had haunted him for the remainder of his journey. At first, given his tendencies, he had only grown morose over the situation. Eventually, however, his emotions cleared enough for him to think about it. Once he was able to put himself in her shoes, so to speak, things became a little easier to understand.

His current feelings on the matter mostly revolved around the concept of Ariaziane feeling guilty about leaving him behind in the first place. It had hurt him, and she certainly knew it. Just the same, he knew she felt her quest or whatever it was still needed to be done, and still alone. Vincent's presence on the same ship was sheer coincidence, but she might not have thought so. She might believe he'd been following her and finally caught up. Or, if she didn't think that, she probably figured he'd try to convince her to let him accompany her again. And naturally, she'd want to avoid a repeat of their final day together two years ago. He couldn't blame her. And though saddened that she didn't even speak to him, he understood. At first, he thought it was a terribly rude thing for her to do. But speaking to him would only have made it harder for her to leave. He knew that now.

Maybe, too, he thought, she'd seen him aboard ship prior to that evening. Perhaps she'd seen him in the company of Darla and gotten the impression that he'd forgotten about her, or at least, found someone else. He really hoped that wasn't the case. If only she knew how much he still loved her. He hoped she knew. It was an ache always present. The pain was tolerable, but always known. And then there was the rape that might or might not have happened. If it had, who could say what it had done to her?

The song ended to the polite applause of the guests. Vincent snapped out of his reverie and smiled down at Darla, who positively glowed with excitement. As he escorted her off the dance floor toward the table of beverages, he thought about this girl.

Such a sheltered life she'd led, growing up with her brother and mother, far from any large town. Darla wasn't very open about her childhood, and Vincent never pressed her about it. It would only serve to bring forth memories of her brother. One thing Darla had let him know once was that her brother had effectively raped her repeatedly. She assured Vincent that, when they first started becoming sexually curious, they had experimented with each other willingly. Neither of them felt it was morally wrong in any way. The concept seemed alien to her. Vincent could understand that. Such a notion wasn't something people were born with, but learned as they grew up. Eventually, however, once her feelings for him started to become less than pleasant, he would force himself on her.

When she'd first told him this, he'd wanted nothing more than to track down her brother and kill him. His blood had boiled, listening to her words. But when it came right down to it, he knew there was nothing he could do. And once again, he let it pass. He tried not to think about it.

It amazed Vincent that any mother could know of sexual activity between her children and permit it to go on. But to know that her son was *raping* her daughter, and Darla seemed quite certain that her mother did know, this was beyond inconceivable to him. He had no desire to give Darla any reason to think about that particular part of her past. Better not to question her about any of it at all, rather than risk bringing back painful memories.

Oddly enough, it didn't really bother him that he didn't know much of her past. In fact, the more he thought about it, he realized that he didn't know much about Rhia's past, either. Or Ariaziane's. He was more concerned with learning who people were right now than with delving into their personal histories. He brooded on his own past too much to need to concern himself with those of others.

Sometimes he tried to analyze why he felt the way he did toward these three women. Ariaziane was the first female he had gotten to know here. She was fun, full of spirit, and slightly mischievous. She was beautiful and carefree, and he felt so alive when he was with her. Rhia, by comparison, was enigmatic, bold, and wise. She was sexy and strong, and he felt alive with her, too. Just in a different way. And Darla? Darla wasn't like either of them. She was quiet, reserved, innocent, decent, and loving. She was stunningly pretty. But he wasn't quite sure how he felt with her. He certainly enjoyed being with her. But he wasn't as caught up in the romance of it as he would have expected. But then, he imagined he'd feel a lot better about his relationship with her if there weren't so many other things on his mind.

Life was not being good to him. Rhia had left. Ariaziane had effectively shunned him. And some psychotic brother of his new interest was trying to kill him and those he loved. He rubbed his forehead, where a knot of pain was developing. He sighed.

Rhia had *left*. He couldn't get over that.

Aedriun's voice brought him back to the present. "If I could steal you away from this lovely young woman for just a moment, my friend?"

Vincent excused himself from Darla, leaving her to chat with Aedriun's nephew, Darvas. He walked with Aedriun out into the hallway outside the ballroom, following him through the halls and into one of his private chambers. Vincent took a seat in a comfortable chair, while Aedriun perched himself atop a large polished desk. "What's on your mind?" Vincent asked.

Aedriun stroked his mustache and grinned. "I was about to ask you the same thing. You have been very distracted this evening. Some of my guests have mentioned it." Vincent merely nodded as Aedriun went on. "I can certainly understand. From what I saw of the wreckage of your house, I'd be worried, too."

Vincent snorted as he ran his finger around the inside of his tight collar. "Aedriun, believe me, her brother isn't the only distraction I have right now. In fact, he's at about the bottom of the list." His friend looked at him strangely, and Vincent said, "What?"

The older man cleared his throat. "I do not know what these other matters are that occupy your thoughts. You've shared nothing with me that would be more dire than this. I am your friend, Vincent. I cannot help you if I do not know what you are going through."

"But I did tell you," he replied. "About Rhia leaving. And seeing Ariaziane on board the ship."

Aedriun scowled. "You cannot expect me to believe that those matters weigh more heavily in your mind than does the fact that someone is out to kill you."

Vincent sighed and rubbed at his forehead.

"What is it?" Aedriun asked.

"Headache."

"Another one?"

Vincent paused in his rubbing. He looked up at his friend. "What?"

"You seem to get these pains fairly often. This is the third time you've mentioned having one since you returned."

It was true, he realized. He had been getting headaches a lot lately. He had the momentary feeling that this meant something. But no, he thought. That was ridiculous. They were just headaches. Probably the result of too many blows to his skull over the past couple years. With a shrug, he said, "Well, like I said, I have a lot on my mind."

"But seriously, Vincent. You are more concerned over a wounded heart than about threats to your life?"

His head pounded furiously. "Yes!" he insisted. "Now can we change the subject, please?"

Aedriun was quiet for a time. Then he nodded and said softly, "I have nothing more to say. Please return to your lovely young lady."

Vincent rose and turned toward the door.

"If you'd be so kind," Aedriun said, "please send my nephew to see me."

Vincent did so, sending Darvas down the hall once he returned to the ballroom. He frowned when he saw Coldson. He'd forgotten to ask Aedriun about him. Coldson began to approach, but stopped when he saw Vincent conversing with Darla. Vincent was relieved, since he had little desire to put the man off again. He pulled Darla away from the crowd and told her that he was going to his room to lie down.

"What is wrong?" she asked.

"Head hurts," he said. "A short nap might help." He smiled at her, but the smile faded as he saw the look on her face. She had turned her eyes away from his, and he could swear he'd seen something that looked like pain on her face.

"I hope you feel better soon," she said. "This is your party, after all."

He lifted her chin, forcing her to face him. "I'll be fine. Don't worry about it." He kissed her lightly on the forehead and left the ballroom, heading for the stairs to the second level, where their rooms were.

Inside his room, he divested himself of the fine garments Aedriun had coerced him into wearing for the party. Since he had no intention of returning to the ballroom, he carefully hung the garments in the room's large closet, then climbed into bed.

As he fluffed the pillow under his aching head, his thoughts returned to the comparison he'd been doing earlier. There was something that still didn't sit right with him, something that seemed to be on the fringe of understanding, yet eluded him. Something he knew Darla would like him to get to the bottom of.

It was becoming clear to him that Darla's feelings had not abated. Whether or not she truly loved him wasn't something he could really tell. But he did know that she wanted to be closer to him. There was almost an urgency underlying her behavior. He didn't quite understand why, but that was the feeling he got.

And he couldn't say he wasn't tempted. He was very attracted to her, physically. But there wasn't a close enough bond between them for him to be comfortable with the idea of making love to her.

When he thought about it, that's what it boiled down to. The difference between having sex and making love. If he were to bed Darla right now, he would be having sex with her. He wouldn't be making love to her because he didn't love her. A simple difference, but one that was immensely important to him.

Darla never complained about this lack of sexual activity. Sometimes, when either of them needed physical intimacy, she would spend the night asleep beside him. He knew she liked that. For that matter, so did he. He just hoped that it would be enough to satisfy her until such time as he felt ready to go further. He also hoped he *could* eventually go further. He occasionally had his doubts.

And it wasn't all due to his remorse over Rhia's departure, or Ariaziane's, for that matter. It had to do with Darla herself. She was, without question, one of the most attractive girls he'd ever laid eyes on. But there was something that bothered him. Sometimes, when he looked at her, she felt familiar. Like he'd met her before. He kept telling himself that it was due to the encounter with Darla and her brother back in Port Remil. But something told him that wasn't it, either. Whatever it was, he found it quite disturbing.

But there was something else, too. Something about Darla that didn't seem quite right. And it bothered him, because he couldn't seem to put his finger on just what it was. And every time he tried to pinpoint it, it just made his head hurt. Like it did now, he realized.

He closed his eyes, hunkered down in the bed, and thought of Ariaziane. Thinking of her always seemed to rid him of his headaches. Specifically, he thought of the morning they'd gone for a walk through the ice-covered trees to their rock by the stream. And they sat and looked at the beauty around them. And he drank in the beauty beside him.

That was the first day he had realized that he was definitely in love with her.

He woke to the sound of his door opening quietly. He squinted against the glow of the bedside lamp, but did not stir. The scent told him it was Darla. A lack of party noises in the background told him it was late. He closed his eyes again, assuming she was just checking on him. And since he didn't feel like talking, he felt it best to feign slumber. Not that this was difficult. It felt so nice having his eyes closed. He heard her footsteps approach and stop beside his bed. But to his surprise, she didn't move away after a few moments.

To his even greater surprise, he soon heard the unmistakable faint sniffle that indicated weeping. Concern overrode his desire for privacy and he opened his eyes and focused on her. He frowned as she turned her face away and obviously debated leaving entirely. "What is it?" he said softly.

Darla hesitated, her head turning toward the floor. "Nothing. I'm sorry. I didn't mean to disturb you."

"No. Come here," he insisted, shifting in the bed to make room for her to sit beside him. He propped himself up on one elbow as she seated herself. "Look at me," he said, and she slowly turned to face him, dampness around her eyes. "Now tell me what is wrong."

Darla smiled slightly and shrugged her shoulders. "I'm just being silly," she said. "Really, it's nothing."

"Darla, I want to help you. But I don't know what I can do unless you tell me what's wrong."

She was quiet for some time. Vincent was struck by the tenderness in her eyes, the way she looked at him with a combination of longing and regret. "After Aedriun returned to the party, he seemed preoccupied. Naturally, I asked him what was wrong. And he said that he was concerned about you."

"He doesn't need to be," Vincent interrupted.

Darla ignored him. "But then he asked me, in a polite way, just what exactly our relationship was. He'd thought you and I were lovers, but..." She faded to silence, then finally said, "His question brought forth my own curiosity. I've been wondering lately how you feel about me. I don't... I don't expect you to be able to feel for me what I feel for you..."

"In time, it could happen," he said after a short pause. "Darla, I really haven't known you that long."

"I know," she said.

"And there have been other circumstances. Rhia's departure. I can't deny that it really hurt. I'm far from over that. And seeing Annie on the ship. That has," he admitted, "affected me more deeply than I thought it could."

"I know," she nodded. "I told you I'm just being silly."

"Silly? No. Impatient, perhaps, but not silly." He smiled as he said this, to let her know he was only kidding. But she didn't smile back. Instead, she turned her face away again. "It was a joke," he said, clasping her hand.

"No, it wasn't," she replied. "It was truth. But I can't help it."

"We're both young," he said. "Still plenty of time for things to develop. And for me to get over the things that I need to overcome."

Darla's only reaction was to turn to face him again. Her eyes held both an intensity and an emptiness. Vincent didn't understand the look, but whatever it meant, it made him very uncomfortable. After a few moments, though, she looked away, then rose from the bed. He was ashamed to admit that he was relieved.

He expected her to wish him a good night and leave for her room, then. Instead, she began undressing. He watched her do so, wishing then that the lamp cast more light. She really was beautiful and he enjoyed watching her take off the fine blue dress and jewelry. Finally, she turned back to face him, and he drank in once more the sight of her body.

She slipped into bed beside him and without another word, climbed on top of him, her legs straddling his hips. He began to protest, but couldn't find the words. His heart raced, but whether with alarm or desire, he couldn't say. Equal parts of both, he imagined. Her mouth on his felt like a dream and, despite himself, he surrendered to it. She was not an accomplished kisser, but her passion was undeniable. His hands roamed over her body, admiring every curve, every contour.

His headache returned and he ignored it as long as he could. But the more he tried to ignore it, the more intense the pain grew, until finally, he couldn't stand it. Even as Darla's hand found its way between his legs, he found himself thinking only of his pain. He stopped kissing Darla's throat and clenched his jaw. "Damn it," he spat.

Darla removed herself from atop his body and lay next to him, one hand gently stroking his forehead. "I'm sorry," they whispered simultaneously to each other. Then they both laughed and held each other for a time. Vincent cursed the throbbing in his skull, even as it slowly faded. He wasn't sure whether it had been a good thing or not that their activity had been interrupted. He tried not to analyze it to death. Eventually, weariness overtook him and he fell asleep in her arms.

❧ ❦

The following morning, Vincent sat at breakfast with Aedriun and Darla. It was a frequent occurrence, sometimes with Darvas joining them. Vincent assumed his absence this morning meant that his duties interfered. He drained his juice and gently returned the mug to the table. "I'm leaving," he said simply. The others looked at him. Darla's eyes, in particular, widening. "I need to get away for a bit," he continued. "To do some thinking. And to take care of some business," he added. He found himself looking only at Darla as he explained. Her face held a totally stricken expression, one that hurt him.

He imagined he'd worn that same expression when Ariaziane had announced her departure, so long ago. He saw written in Darla's face all the protests and questions he himself had voiced to Ariaziane. He didn't like feeling their pressure in her eyes and chided himself for making the announcement in this fashion. She deserved better.

"You need to monitor the progress on your keep," Aedriun said.

Vincent breathed a sigh of relief. "Yes," he said, glad for some shred of understanding from his friend. "Yes, I do. And I haven't seen Gnorrin in far too long. I thought to stop and visit with him on the way."

Aedriun raised an eyebrow. "Gnorrin is hardly 'on the way,' my friend."

Vincent shrugged. "I don't mind."

Aedriun nodded, then, evidently satisfied.

But Darla continued to gaze at him with beseeching eyes. They ripped into him and he felt his stomach flip-flop.

"It is because of me," she whispered, "is it not?"

He shook his head firmly. "No, no. I just need to do some thinking. I have quite a lot on my mind."

"And am I not part of that?"

"Well, yes," he admitted. "But..."

"I understand," she said, simply and without emotion.

Vincent said nothing for a moment, then, "Darla, I just don't know what to feel right now. I know how you claim to feel about me, and if the truth be known, I want to feel that way, too. But I don't. Yet. I need to clear my head before I can listen to my heart."

The girl nodded. "As I said, I understand." Her gaze now turned away from him, staring at the remains of her breakfast on the plate. "I assume you will be leaving today?"

Though he hadn't really thought that far ahead, Vincent nodded. "I think so."

Darla turned politely to Aedriun. "Will it pose a problem...?"

"Naturally you may stay," Aedriun stated. "You needn't have worried about that."

"It'll only be for a handful of weeks," Vincent blurted. "That's not so long."

Darla only looked at him. And once again, Vincent found that he could not interpret her gaze.

❧ ❦

One week later, late in the evening, Vincent arrived at the place he thought of as home. He stopped at his old cottage, smiling as he noted that Gnorrin had obviously been tending to the place. It was well kept. He thought briefly about laying in some firewood, but realized he would not need it. He'd stay with Gnorrin, in the spare room, and really do some reminiscing.

Gnorrin was shocked, but delighted, to see him. He bustled outside when he heard Vincent's voice calling him. The two embraced, Vincent having to go down on one knee in order to do so. After initial greetings and slaps on the back, Gnorrin held him at arm's length. "It's late to be on the road. Are you hungry, lad?"

"Only if it's stew," Vincent smiled, and began unloading his horse.

Gnorrin re-heated the stew pot and had another bowl himself. As they ate, Vincent related the many events that had taken place since last he'd seen him. Many of them were not news to Gnorrin. Vincent had occasionally written to him, sending the letters by one of Aedriun's couriers. So Gnorrin already knew of Ariaziane's second transformation and subsequent departure. He also knew of Rhia's return, though Vincent didn't recall telling him of that.

He told him of his visit to see Blade, only to find out that Blade had written of the visit in his own letters to Gnorrin. His friend asked him specifics about the battle with the pirates and Vincent obligingly filled in the details. Blade had evidently not, however, mentioned the situation he'd had with the three brothers. Gnorrin listened intently as Vincent explained about this, and how it was resolved. He seemed amused by the tale of Vincent's underground expedition.

He told him of the trip to visit Felina, of the attack that resulted in the elf's death, and of how Darla and Rhia had restored her to life. This prompted many questions, mostly about Darla. But Vincent didn't want to address those, yet. It made his head hurt. So he continued by briefly mentioning Rhia's departure and his return to Linnael.

Gnorrin collected the empty bowls and took them to the kitchen. After rinsing them, he returned to where Vincent relaxed on the floor in front of the fire. "And you have no idea why this boy is trying to kill you?" he asked, reclining in his chair.

Vincent shrugged. "Well," he said, turning his attention away from the flames, "Darla gave me her thoughts on the subject, but..." He rubbed his temple.

"But what?"

He frowned. "Didn't make a lot of sense to me. I think he's just nuts."

Gnorrin chuckled. "You and your Earth expressions," he said, shaking his head. Then, after a moment's silence, he leaned forward in his seat and said earnestly, "If I know you, my friend, and I think I do, you are more concerned over the pain in your heart rather than the threat to your life."

Vincent didn't reply for a moment. Then he turned his gaze from the fire to the floor. He nodded.

Gnorrin went on. "Well," he said quietly, "you certainly do manage to tally up the heartbreaks, don't you?" He rubbed his chin. "And what does Darla mean to you, exactly?"

Vincent fidgeted on the floor, then turned to face his friend. "I wish I knew. I think I'm just too overloaded with thoughts and emotions right now to be able to interpret my feelings for her. That's part of the reason I came to see you. I needed to distance myself from it. Hoping to get a more objective look at it."

"I imagine you would like to see the progress on your keep?"

"Yes, I would. I feel terrible that I haven't been around to attend to matters personally. I really appreciate your taking care of things for me."

"It is nothing. I think you will be pleased with the way it is progressing."

Vincent yawned. "Glad to hear it."

Gnorrin smiled. "You should sleep," he said, rising. "I'll prepare your room."

As his friend walked down the short hallway, Vincent stood and moved to his pack of traveling goods, which lay in a heap beside the door where he'd dropped them.

"Been a long time," came Gnorrin's voice, "since you last slept here."

"Yes, indeed," he agreed. He hefted the pack and moved back to the bedroom.

Gnorrin had lit the lamp and made up the bed. Vincent looked around in the room. It was, in fact, the first time he'd been in this room since he'd moved out of it.

Before Ariaziane moved in. He hadn't given that fact much thought, but now he wasn't sure staying here was such a good idea. He briefly considered heading down the road to his own cottage. But it was late, and it was cold. And he had no firewood there. And it would take a fire quite some time to heat the whole cottage.

"Is there anything you need?" Gnorrin asked.

Vincent smiled warmly. "Yes. Sleep." He sat on the edge of the small bed. "Thank you. It's great to see you again."

His friend nodded in agreement. "Rest well. See you in the morning."

After Gnorrin left the room, Vincent opened his pack. He withdrew his journal, pen, and inkwell. Then he undressed and climbed into bed. The sheets were cold and he shivered. He was tired, but not quite sleepy enough to fall off. Turning up the lamp, he prepared the journal for his entry.

Arrived at Gnorrin's about an hour after nightfall, he wrote, recalling with fondness the way the scratching of pen on paper sounded in this small room. *We talked for a couple hours, had some stew, and generally just caught up.*

It's strange being in this little room again. I can almost feel Annie's presence here. I'm not sure if I like that feeling or not.

We're planning on taking a trip to visit the keep, to check on the progress. I know I should be excited about this, but frankly, I can't seem to work up much enthusiasm for anything right now. I'm just so confused over things. I guess I shouldn't be so distraught over the way things have gone. But I can't help it. I miss Annie. I miss Rhia. I even miss Felina, and I barely got to know her. And Darla?

He paused and thought about that for a time, tapping his bearded chin with the end of the wooden pen. *Yes, I miss her, too. But it's not quite the same. Similar to the way I miss Felina, but not quite like that, either.*

I think what attracts me most about Darla, aside from her obvious physical charms, is the fact that she is insatiably curious about everything. It's almost as though she knows very little about the world, about people, and is drinking it all in like a parched person with water. Rather like me, when I stop to think about it. By contrast, my attraction to the others is my own curiosity about what they already know. Weird. I'm on the receiving end of that sort of attraction with Darla, and I don't like it as much.

I wonder if this is why no one has stuck around with me. Do they look upon me as being the curious one, not taking me seriously?

He thought for a long time about this idea, his brow furrowing. Then he dipped the pen in the well again. *If so, then I should take her attentions more seriously. Was it wrong of me to go off alone like this? Is that how I'm going to react every time something goes wrong in my life? Will I just run away by myself? That's not how I want people to see me. And it sure isn't how I want to think of myself.*

He capped the inkwell, wiped the pen's nib with his cleaning rag, and set the journal aside to dry. Then he lowered the wick in the lamp until it gave only a faint glow. As usual, sleep did not come quickly.

☙ ❧

Three days later, they prepared to journey to the keep. Vincent wasn't looking forward to another week on horseback. Longer, probably, since Gnorrin's little pony certainly couldn't keep up with Vincent's horse. He remembered traveling with Jaz on his flying carpet. He wished Gnorrin had one.

"Any chance you might be able to teleport us there, or make us fly there, or something?" he said, only half-jokingly, as they cleaned up after breakfast.

Gnorrin frowned. "I am not fond at all of flying," he said flatly. "This breakfast was far too tasty for me to want to lose it. And as for teleporting, let's just say that such a spell, for me, is used only in emergencies. It is far too powerful a spell to use for something insignificant like convenience of travel."

Vincent nodded. "Sorry. Guess I'm just spoiled."

"Oh, I certainly understand your concerns. Your keep isn't exactly down the road and around the corner. But fear not. We have an alternate mode of transportation that should suffice."

"We do?"

"Aye. In fact, it is waiting for us in front of the cottage even now."

Vincent blinked and turned toward the door. "Don't suppose it's a Jeep," he muttered. He opened the door and stepped outside. The sight that awaited him caused him to stop in his tracks.

Standing calmly near a tree, but not tethered to it, was a horse. Or what seemed to be a horse. Vincent shook himself out of his stupor and walked slowly toward the beast. The animal seemed to glow faintly. Its body was milky white, but with swirls of silver that seemed to move deep within it. The animal's head moved slowly to look at Vincent, then turned idly back to stare off into the distance again. There was no saddle or other harness on the animal. He couldn't imagine ever seeing such a creature disgraced with such trappings. It was, quite simply, the most amazing equine beast that Vincent had ever seen. Or expected to see.

"Wow," he whispered.

"Indeed," said Gnorrin, stepping outside, two packs in hand. He gave the larger one to Vincent, who thanked him. "It is quite a creature, isn't it?"

"What is it?"

Gnorrin straightened his bright orange breeches. "They're known by several names, the most familiar probably being Shadow Riders."

"Magical," Vincent said simply.

"Yes. I summoned this one while you slept this morning." Gnorrin donned his pack, but wore it in the front, rather than the back. Then he walked toward the horse, motioning for Vincent to come with him. "The beast must give its assent for you to ride upon it," he said to his friend.

The creature's head once again turned to size up Vincent as he approached. Vincent felt the animal's gaze looking him up and down. Their eyes met, and he felt as if the horse were looking into his soul. It gave him the chills.

Finally, the horse gave a slight nod, then looked away again. "Looks like you're in the guild," Gnorrin said, slapping Vincent on the back. "Now hoist me up there, if you would."

Vincent strapped on his pack and did as instructed, placing his friend on the animal's broad back, then climbed up behind him. The Shadow Rider felt very different than a normal horse. Vincent's legs tingled from the sense of power underneath him.

449

"Wait," he said to Gnorrin. "Aren't you going to seal up your house? And what about my horse?"

"Not to worry," said the gnome. "We shall not be gone long."

"What?" Vincent laughed. "But the keep is..."

The rest of his sentence trailed off as the horse began to move. Gnorrin guided them out onto the road. Vincent gasped as the horse picked up speed. They hurtled down the road, Vincent feeling nothing in the way of discomfort. It was as though the horse's feet never touched the ground. And the speed at which they traveled was astounding. In seconds, Gnorrin's cottage was lost from view.

"Wow," Vincent said once again. "This is amazing," he said into Gnorrin's ear. There was no rush of wind to whip his words away, however, so the gnome had no difficulty in hearing him.

"To use an expression of yours, my friend... You ain't seen nothing, yet!"

To Vincent's astonishment, the horse continued to gain in speed. And then things got decidedly strange. Everything around him seemed to bend, to flow together, to darken. Despite himself, Vincent felt his heart pounding in alarm.

"Oh, shit, we're going into hyperspace," he said. He closed his eyes, and then, at Gnorrin's bequest, he explained what he meant by hyperspace.

"Oh," said Gnorrin. "That's not far off, in fact. We're now traveling in a type of alternate dimension."

"And this is why we won't be gone long," Vincent surmised. "How long will the journey take?"

Gnorrin shrugged. "We should be there by nightfall."

Vincent blinked. A journey of a week compressed into a matter of less than ten hours. "Wow."

They continued in this fashion for several hours. The horse never tired, nor did Vincent find himself becoming as weary as he would have been on a horse of flesh and blood. The psychedelic flavor of the journey was, however, starting to jangle his nerves, like the paddle boat in *Willy Wonka and the Chocolate Factory*.

Nothing around him looked real, save Gnorrin. The landscape seemed to flow, like an evolving painting. Dali meets Escher. At first, it was amusing and vaguely fascinating. But after being surrounded by it for hours, it began to make him nauseous.

Finally, the effect began to lessen. Then it ceased altogether. And then they stopped.

Vincent looked around, trying to determine their location. Before him lay a river. And by the size of the mountains in the distance, he determined that this was the first of the two rivers they would have to cross on their way to his keep. This put them at slightly more than halfway there.

"Geez, how do you navigate during all that crap?"

"With difficulty, I admit. It takes considerable concentration. Once you get used to it, it isn't so bad, though." Gnorrin slid off the magical beast.

Vincent likewise dismounted. To his surprise, the horse then vanished in a puff of silver smoke.

"Don't worry," Gnorrin said. "I'll summon another before we depart." Vincent cast him a confused look and the gnome answered. "It also takes serious mental effort to control such a beast. I am tired and hungry. And the beast was unwilling to carry us further, anyway."

"Pardon?"

"It is a creature from another plane of existence. They are generally able to be controlled for a few hours, and they make excellent mounts, as you've seen."

Vincent reclined in the grass beside his friend, pulling out his own dinner rations. "I'm not sure I like the sound of that. *Controlled.* It sounds like you're enslaving them."

Gnorrin shook his head as he uncapped his canteen. "Not at all. Think of it more as an exchange. They serve as temporary transportation, and in return, they are able to spend a few hours here, observing this dimension, gaining information that they share with their fellows upon returning to their own plane."

Vincent paused in his chewing, then swallowed hard. "What do you mean by that? You mean those horses can talk?"

Gnorrin gazed at him with an expression Vincent couldn't understand. "You're jesting again?"

"What do you mean?"

"Why would you ask if they could communicate? Why should they be any different than any other beast?"

Vincent stared at him for a long moment. He put down his biscuit. "You're telling me that all animals can talk?"

Gnorrin frowned. "All animals can communicate. It is not the same as when you and I talk, certainly. Do not the animals in your world communicate?"

Vincent thought about it, then chuckled. "I guess so. The language of dolphins and the songs of whales are constantly being researched by people in the field. Dogs and cats seem to be able to communicate with each other. Sorry. Guess I was reading more into what you were saying. I thought you meant that they actually had a language that we could understand."

Gnorrin looked at him for a moment, then said, "And that is precisely what I meant."

Vincent merely stared in return, having no words that could capture his sense of astonishment.

"Oh, I personally cannot understand their meaning. Nor do I know of anyone who does. But there are those few gifted individuals who have learned to understand the languages of animals. It takes much more patience than I have, I can tell you."

Vincent shook his head as if to awaken from a dream. "Wait a minute. You're saying that there are people who could communicate with, say, my dog? Have a nice chat about the finer points of tinkling on trees?"

Gnorrin laughed. "Yes. But you must realize that, in addition to a totally different language, one is dealing with a totally different mentality. While a dog might, indeed, be interested in sharing its thoughts on tree watering, it is doubtful that it would wish to discuss things that have no relevance to it."

"Well, neither do I, for that matter."

Again his friend laughed. He waved his hand. "Be that as it may, it is doubtful that you will ever meet someone who could communicate with animals." He paused, scratching his chin. "I take that back. If ever there was anyone who *would* meet such a person, it would be you."

Vincent thought for a moment, remembering the apparent bonds that Felina displayed with her cats. There had been times he'd sworn he'd caught her talking to the animals. But he hadn't thought anything of it. He talked to Blaise, after all. Still, it wouldn't surprise him a bit if the elf actually was able to converse with the cats.

"Elves," he said. "They would have the patience necessary for that. Wouldn't they?"

"Possibly," Gnorrin conceded. "More than humans, at any rate." Gnorrin popped the last bit of biscuit into his mouth and began putting his pack together. "You're thinking of your cat woman, aren't you?"

Vincent nodded, swallowing some of the salted meat. "Yeah. I think she might."

"Perhaps you can ask her, when next you meet."

Vincent nodded, making a mental note to do so. Then he rose and headed into the trees.

A few minutes later, Vincent returned from relieving his bladder and found that Gnorrin had already summoned another of the horse creatures. "I wish you'd waited. I'd have loved to see how you did that."

The gnome shook his head. "This type of summoning works best when done alone." He was allowing the beast to check him out, the animal's nose sniffing around him. The beast concluded its inspection, showing no sign of disapproval. "Good," Gnorrin said. "Your turn, then."

Vincent approached and the beast repeated the process. Finally, it dipped its head, at which point Gnorrin said, "You pass again. These creatures obviously have low standards."

Vincent chuckled and lifted Gnorrin onto the animal's back. Then he joined him, adjusting his pack. "Okay," he said. "Ready when you are."

And off they rode. Vincent hoped the journey would be over quickly. Though he admitted to the usefulness of such a mount, he could hardly envision using one regularly. He didn't think he could ever get used to the bizarre visual effects of the ride.

On and on they rode, quietly, smoothly. Vincent tried to keep his eyes closed for much of the trip, but it was difficult. His curiosity always won out, and he would open them to see what strange shapes the landscape was taking.

Finally, they went through the slow-down process again. As the world resumed some semblance of reality, Vincent saw it was now dark. The next thing he noticed was that the mount beneath his legs was no longer white and silver, but black and silver. Gazing at it was like looking into space, seeing the tiny flecks and whorls of stars within it.

Then he looked up. Gnorrin had obviously guided the Shadow Rider up the mountain, because they stood now on the plateau. And in front of them was the face of Vincent's keep, tall and imposing, with two towers on the sides. Quickly, he dismounted, turning to look back out over the precipice, noting the trail they'd evidently traversed to get to the plateau.

He then helped Gnorrin off the mount, which promptly vanished. "Well, here we are," he said. "Looks like a keep."

Gnorrin nodded. "Aye. They're doing good work, as I've told you."

They approached the open front gate, Vincent admiring the huge wooden doors as they passed through. The interior was lit with torches, the main entrance hall having only enough to illuminate the way. The current work was being done deeper inside.

The entry hall was about eight feet wide and fifty feet long. At the end of the hall was a door, and a passage off to the right. The door led to what would become the audience chamber. The hall led to what would be the quarters for the keep's employees, once he got around to hiring a cook, a gardener, and so on. Also on this floor would be the kitchen and dining areas, the library, lots of storage space, and stables at the front of the keep.

The stairs were located inside the towers. They made their way to one of them and began climbing. The second floor was primarily sleeping quarters. Vincent's master bedroom was here, as were rooms he'd specifically set aside for his friends, including Gnorrin. Each room would eventually be decorated to suit that person. There were five rooms set aside for other guests, as well. In addition, there would be a smaller kitchen for late night snacks, a games room, a private study, the treasury, and baths. This was the floor where most of the workers were to be found this evening.

A pair of dwarves carrying long slabs of thin rock approached them in the corridor. The one in front nodded politely. "Master Gnorrin," he said. "How fare you this night?"

"Quite well, thank you," Gnorrin replied, coming to a stop a few feet from the pair. "Is Feletain near?"

"Inside here, in fact," the worker said, stepping back to allow Gnorrin and Vincent to enter the room.

"Thank you," Vincent said as they entered. He looked around inside. This was to be his private study, he realized. It was a decent sized room. Though now it wasn't much, eventually it would be quite pleasant. He watched the pair of workers carry the stone slabs to the rear of the room, where they began the task of affixing them in place. He frowned, not quite sure what purpose they served.

Feletain turned at the sound of Gnorrin clearing his throat. His eyes widened as he took notice of Vincent. "Well, hello," Feletain said, stepping over toward them. "I did not realize you'd intended a visit," he said to Vincent.

Tearing his gaze from the back wall, Vincent said, "It was a sudden decision. And not one that should alarm you. It is a very casual inspection, nothing of importance."

Feletain stiffened. "And if it were, you would be no more impressed, I'll wager. My crew has done an exemplary job, and it shows."

Vincent nodded. "It does. I am very pleased with what little I have seen so far. But I would enjoy a tour, if you don't mind."

The master builder beamed. "Right away!"

"In the morning," Vincent quickly corrected. "I am too tired right now to appreciate it." And it was true. Every bone in his body seemed weary. The ride had taken more out of him than he'd thought.

"Certainly," Feletain said. "It is a long journey. Come. I'll show you to some quarters." The dwarf led them out of the room and down the hall. "I apologize that a proper room for you is not available."

"Don't worry about that," Vincent assured him.

"How long will you be staying?"

"We'll be leaving after the tour tomorrow."

"So quickly?" Feletain shook his head. "You humans. Always in such a hurry." They arrived in front of the largest of the bedrooms. "This will be your master bedroom, per your instructions."

Vincent looked around the large room. He estimated it being twenty feet by perhaps thirty. It would be, when decorated, mighty impressive. The whole keep would, he knew. "Great," he said. "This will do fine." He unslung the pack from his back and dropped it on the floor.

"I'll fetch some extra coverings for you. Is there anything else you require?"

Gnorrin shook his head. "We'll be fine, my friend. Please wake us when you rise."

The dwarf nodded and departed.

Vincent pulled their bedrolls out of his pack and they began setting up for sleep. Momentarily, one of the workers arrived with furs for them. They thanked him, then made themselves comfortable.

"What is on your mind?" Gnorrin asked.

His friend blinked. "It shows that strongly?"

"At times, yes." Gnorrin shifted in his bedroll. "It is the girl, Darla, yes?"

Vincent paused for a moment, then nodded. "Mostly, yes. I think I'm being unfair."

Gnorrin snorted. "To whom?"

"To Darla."

"Rubbish! You cannot force feelings you do not have."

"It's not that simple," he said with a frown. "I've been doing a lot of thinking about myself, and her." He rubbed his temple. "Looking at myself from a different perspective, based on how I look at her." He was rambling, and he knew it. Making no sense.

"What is it?"

Vincent ignored the pounding in his skull. "I'm sorry. I can't put it into words."

"No, I meant that you seem to be in pain."

"Because I am. My head hurts."

"Again?"

He looked at his friend. "What do you mean?"

"You have complained of such pains before," Gnorrin said. "Yesterday, we were talking over dinner and you suddenly felt this ache in your head."

Vincent thought back. It was true. They'd been having stew, of course, with freshly baked bread. It was very tasty, Gnorrin having obtained some fresh herbs for the dinner. It had reminded him of Rhia's culinary skills, always with fresh herbs. And that had made him think of her departure, back at Felina's, which led him and Darla to return here. And suddenly he'd had a headache.

Vincent blinked. "Aedriun commented upon the frequency of them, too." He was silent a time, then shook his head. "It's puzzling, that's for sure." He yawned. "But I'm beat."

"Sleep well, then," said Gnorrin.

"You, too," Vincent replied. But he suspected he'd do nothing of the sort.

❧ ❧

Finally gone, he thought. His mother had finally departed. Now the portal was his to play with, his to use. He reveled in this knowledge.

His mother was a fool. She thought him unwise, too stupid to be able to operate the portal. She thought he hadn't paid attention to what she had tried to teach him. But she was wrong.

He'd watched, furtively, not wanting her to know exactly how much he did know. Had the time come when he'd needed to challenge her, he felt it in his best interests for her to think him inept.

Fortunately, that eventuality was now unnecessary. She'd left of her own accord to find the other portals, she told him. Fine with him. Let her go. He only needed one. And now he had it.

The question remained: What exactly was he going to do with it?

He had ideas. Several of them, in fact. But he hadn't decided which to pursue. He knew of different ways he could use the portal. He could use it to gain knowledge, scrying-fashion, like his mother used her crystal ball. He knew the portal also summoned forth beings from other worlds. He thought he could manipulate it into doing so, to his specifications. But even easier than that would be to cause it to move things around right here, to pick up beings and move them like gaming pieces from one land to the next.

This was a path he could easily follow, he knew. He had the urge to cause a lot of destruction. It seemed like a fun way to spend a little time. He'd start with that ugly keep that his father was building. After that, who knew?

But he needed to determine which beings to move. Where to find them and how, exactly, to relocate them. And there was the little matter of controlling them once they were moved.

These would take time to determine. Time wasn't in the greatest supply for him, however, and he knew he wasn't the most patient person. Still, he was sure he could figure it out. Patience he might not have. But ability... that was plentiful.

And any time spent in pursuit of his goal would be time well spent.

❧ Thirty-Two ❧

The following morning they rose early, packed their things, and joined Feletain for breakfast. This was served in the kitchen, down on the first floor. The meal was a thick, goopy mixture that Vincent had come to recognize over the years. The not-quite-oatmeal was hot and filling, but definitely lacking something in the way of flavor.

As they ate, Feletain gave Vincent a synopsis of the work completed thus far. Then, after giving instructions to a few of his workers, they set off.

They began on the first floor, leaving the dining area and turning up the hall to where Vincent's main reception area would be. Stepping through the door, Vincent eyed it carefully. It was much smaller than Aedriun's similar room. But that was just fine, since he had no desire to be as grandiose as Aedriun. That's why his keep was being built here in the mountains, rather than in a city. He wanted privacy, not publicity.

At the back end of the first floor were the quarters for the domestic servants. The cook, the stablehand, the gardener, and so on. Vincent thought fondly of Hennor, Jaz's manservant. Then he smirked. No, he couldn't see himself with someone in that capacity.

"Each floor," Feletain said, "will have garderobes, as per your instructions."

Vincent stood before one of the tiny rooms, opening the door and peering inside. It wasn't what you'd call a bathroom, since it had no bath, but it wasn't exactly a toilet, either. An indoor outhouse was how Vincent thought of it. Merely a hole with a seat over it.

"The holes are, as you instructed, very deep. At the bottom are creatures that feed on excrement."

"Feed on excrement," Vincent repeated flatly, as Gnorrin peered inside.

"Aye."

"Some life." He shook his head. "Are these creatures dangerous at all?"

"No," Feletain said, "even if they could climb up the walls of the hole. Which they cannot."

"So they just eat and breed, that's all?"

The dwarf shrugged. "As do many."

Vincent chuckled, despite himself. "But what about when the breeding gets out of control?"

"Periodically, about every three months, you will purge them by pouring oil into the hole, then dropping a torch inside. It does not smell pretty, but it is necessary. The fire won't kill all of them, but it will reduce them enough. And then you're ready for business again. So to speak."

The second floor, as Vincent had seen the previous night, contained primarily bedrooms. They spent little time on this floor.

"The third floor," Feletain explained briefly, "will be for your retainers."

"Pardon?"

"You will have men sworn to you, will you not? I understood that to be the case."

Vincent shook his head. "No."

Gnorrin cleared his throat. "Yes."

Vincent looked down at his friend, frowning. But he didn't feel like debating the point. "Whatever," he said.

They climbed the stairs to the fourth level. To call it a "floor" would have been inappropriate, since they emerged into open air. "The landscaping will be done later," Feletain said. "So it is not quite what you would like to see, I'm sure."

They stood on the upper plateau. The tops of the twin towers stood at one end of the area, one of which they'd just stepped out of. Short walls, perhaps eight feet high, headed back from them for about one hundred fifty feet or more, until the ground sloped steeply upward. The walls ended there. The area in which they now stood would eventually be flower gardens, reaching back to the slope. The gardens would have trails throughout, he pictured in his head.

"Over on this side," Feletain pointed, "is the path down to the lower level. Not too steep, fine for the horses in all but the nastiest weather."

Beyond the slope was a huge open area, perfect for the horses to graze in and for short rides. A few large trees adorned the area, plus a small stream. "Perfect," Vincent whispered. He turned back to Feletain. "I am very pleased," he said. "And we are on schedule for completion?"

"Aye," he replied. "Unforeseen disasters aside."

Vincent nodded. "Very good," he said quietly. "If you don't mind, I'd like some time alone. Thank you for the tour, Feletain. You may relieve your foreman now. I'll find my own way back."

The dwarf nodded, then Gnorrin spoke up. "Did you want some company, my friend?"

Vincent shook his head. "Not right now. If you and Feletain would like to go spend some time together to catch up, please feel free."

The gnome frowned, but said nothing more. He left with Feletain.

Once they were gone, Vincent walked back toward the sloping area of the field. The morning was cold, but he sat on the hard ground anyway. He lay down on the slope, arms beneath his head, looking at the sky. Clouds obscured the sun, but the light was still slightly painful to his eyes. So he closed them.

He could hear the gurgling of the stream in the distance. There were few other sounds. Mostly the far off calls of birds. The insects were mostly gone for the year, thankfully, and the ongoing construction had spooked most of the other inhabitants away. But in time, he knew, he'd see plenty of small fauna up here.

He knew this area would be his haven, his escape from it all. It was funny, in a way. Growing up on Earth, he had never been much of an outdoorsy person. He preferred closing himself in his bedroom with some music and a stack of comic books to just about anything his friends would suggest doing outside. But now, he felt in touch with nature. Rhia's influence? Probably.

He ran his hands through the grass, breathed deeply, and tried to relax. But Rhia made him think of Darla and that didn't help his mood. The thoughts he'd had, that first night back at Gnorrin's, hadn't faded. More and more, he felt as though he were serving Darla a grave injustice.

But other thoughts occurred to him as well. Aedriun's and Gnorrin's words, particularly about his headaches. Could there be more to it than his own view, that it was more than just stress, or various head injuries?

Yes, he thought. There certainly could be.

Darla might even know, he suddenly realized. Those times when she would look at him with an expression that seemed to be more than just sympathy. What was the other emotion?

And when did these headaches occur? When he thought about Darla?

No. He didn't have one now, and he was thinking about her. When did he last have one? Just last night, he realized. As he and Gnorrin were talking about her.

No. Not talking about Darla. They were talking about his feelings for her.

He frowned, realizing that he got headaches when he thought of Darla in a romantic or sexual way. But that wasn't the only time he got them, he thought. He got them whenever he thought about Darla's brother. Or rather, whenever he thought of how her brother had hurt her. He could think of him, and the boy's plans to kill him, and not care. He could even think of his murder of Felina and feel nothing more than a surge of anger.

He blinked, then sat up.

A surge of anger that quickly dissipated. Now why was that?

His head began to throb. The whole scenario hurt just to think about it. It confused him. He shook his head firmly to rid the thoughts. Then he stood, wiping dirt and grass from his clothing. Best not to think about it, then.

He'd taken no more than two steps before he stopped dead in his tracks and felt the blood drain from his face, realizing what he'd just done. Then he hurried to the tower stairs and headed down, first to grab their packs, then to find Gnorrin.

"Time to go," he said as he located his friend on the second floor. Gnorrin and Feletain looked up at him in surprise from where they stood watching the construction. "I'm sorry," he continued, "but something has come up and I must return immediately." Before Gnorrin could form a reply, Vincent handed him his pack and placed his hand on the gnome's back, urging him on. "Feletain, I am very pleased with the work." He pulled a small pouch from his own pack and tossed it to the dwarf. "A bonus for you and your men." The pouch jingled as it landed in the dwarf's hands. Gnorrin and Feletain muttered hasty goodbyes as Vincent proceeded toward the stairs.

Vincent was stalking around impatiently in front of the keep when Gnorrin emerged. "What is so urgent?" he demanded as he bustled outside. "What has gotten into you?"

"That's what I need to find out," Vincent said bitterly. "And I know of only one person who might be able to answer that question." He stopped pacing and motioned with his hands. "Okay, let's have one of those magic horses."

Gnorrin stopped a few paces from his friend and placed his hands on his orange-garbed hips. "Not until you tell me what is so important."

Vincent rubbed his temple and closed his eyes in pain. He took a deep breath. Then he shared his thoughts with Gnorrin, explaining everything as it had occurred to him just minutes before. Gnorrin listened attentively, rubbing his chin thoughtfully. When Vincent was finished, the gnome nodded. "It appears you and Darla need to speak. You'll wish to go directly to Linnael, then?"

"Would that be a problem?"

His friend shook his head. "Not at all. But I require privacy in order to summon the Shadow Rider."

Vincent nodded. Then Gnorrin walked back to the keep, entering the doors off to the side that led directly into the area that would eventually be the stables. Vincent paced for several minutes, trying to focus his thoughts without inducing a headache. He was only moderately successful.

Finally, the doors opened again and Gnorrin stepped outside, one of the magical mounts trailing close behind. Vincent stepped quickly over to them and, at Gnorrin's reminder, allowed the beast to check him out. When he'd passed muster, he helped Gnorrin onto the animal's back, then climbed up behind him.

Vincent hardly noted the passage of time during the trip. He closed his eyes to the kaleidoscope effects and tried to think about the conversation he would have with Darla. He had no idea how much time passed before they stopped for a rest. It was still daylight, though just barely. They ate from their dry rations and drank from their canteens. No conversation was shared. Then Gnorrin summoned another mount and they were off again.

The second half of the journey must have been even longer, Vincent realized when they finally stopped. He could tell it was quite late as they dismounted in front of Aedriun's residence. The normal hustle and bustle of his home generally lasted well into the night. But all was quiet now.

The distance from his keep to Linnael was a good stretch longer than it had been from Gnorrin's home to the mountains. He was exhausted and could only imagine how Gnorrin must be feeling. He watched the Shadow Rider dissipate back into its own dimension, then laid a hand on his friend's shoulder. "Thank you," he said.

"You can thank me by finding me a bed," said Gnorrin.

"Not a problem," Vincent said as they walked toward the gates. The guard recognized him and let the pair pass. As the gate closed behind them, Vincent raised an eyebrow as he saw a figure walking down the path toward them.

"Is that..." began Gnorrin.

"Yes," Vincent said, his heart racing with a multitude of emotions as he watched Darla walk calmly toward them. She stopped in front of them.

"I sensed you were returning," she said. "It was so sudden, waking me from my sleep."

"Yes," he said to her, not knowing what else to say. "Is Aedriun awake?"

Darla shook her head. "Aedriun is not here. He left days ago. I am not sure where he went."

Vincent introduced Darla and Gnorrin, then nodded in the direction of the building. "Let's go inside. Gnorrin needs to rest. And you and I need to talk. Privately."

Darla looked him in the eye for a moment. "I see," she said, then turned and walked quietly with them.

Inside, Vincent showed Gnorrin to one of the guest chambers. He thought briefly about saving the talk with Darla until the following day, since he was fairly exhausted, too. But he knew he couldn't. The issue was just too strongly in his mind. They bade goodnight to Gnorrin, then Vincent led Darla to a familiar private chamber.

Not so long ago, he'd sat in this very room with Aedriun. Looking back on that talk, he realized he'd been quite rude to his friend. Obviously, it was the spell he was under that had caused him to be in such a state. Looking at Darla, at the concerned expression on her face, he hesitated. She was so innocent, he thought. Certainly she couldn't have done what he was thinking. Then he took a deep breath and firmed his resolve.

"Darla," he said, leaning against Aedriun's desk. "I have a question to ask you. I don't really want to ask you, but I have to know what's going on. Forgive me if the question seems rude, but..." He trailed off, struggling over how to say it.

"What is it?" she asked cautiously.

Vincent hesitated for another moment, then blurted out, "Did you cast a spell on me?"

She stood looking at him, frowning oddly. "Of course," she said. Vincent blinked. She had! He couldn't believe it. "When my brother attacked you," she continued. "You remember. I cast a healing spell that stabilized you until you could heal on your own."

"No," Vincent said with a sigh. "I didn't mean that one. Did you cast another spell on me?"

She shook her head. "I've not cast any other spells on you."

He frowned, then, hoping his intuition would advise him that she was lying. But it did not. He dropped his forehead into his hands and rubbed his tired eyes. "Then who the hell did?" he whispered to himself.

There was a long silence. Then Darla quietly said, "Rhia."

Vincent slowly lifted his head. He stared at her. "What?" The girl seemed to visibly shrink, obviously not wanting to divulge any information. "*Rhia* did?"

Darla lowered herself into a chair, nodding faintly. "As you slept, the night before she went to commune."

It made no sense. Rhia couldn't possibly be afraid Darla would be a romantic threat. She herself had more than one lover. If she didn't care if he and Felina were to become lovers, why should she care if Vincent took Darla as one? Could Rhia really be that much of a hypocrite? He couldn't believe it, couldn't understand it.

But maybe Darla could.

"Why?" he asked.

Her response was slow and quiet. "There are some things that she did not wish you to discover."

"Like what?" he demanded.

"I believe her primary concern was that you not learn the whereabouts of my brother. She was afraid you would hunt him down and he would kill you."

Vincent absorbed the information. "And that gives her the right to put me under some enchantment that causes me pain every time I think of him? What is this? A *Clockwork Orange?*" He ignored Darla's confused look and ran a hand through his long hair. "Okay, but I also get headaches whenever I think of you in a sexual way. Is she trying to prevent us from sleeping together?"

"You forget that my brother is observing you. It could well be that our sexual involvement would infuriate him. Rhia no doubt feared that he would attack you again, were he to realize you were bedding his sister." She smiled weakly.

"Hm. Okay." That, he had to admit, was a very real possibility. "So can you remove the spell?"

"Possibly."

Vincent let out a relieved breath. "Good. Thank you."

"I did not say I would do so."

He looked at her sharply. "Excuse me?"

"I might not have approved of her methods, but I appreciate the result. If I remove this spell, you must give me your word that you will not attempt to locate my brother."

Vincent stared at her for a long moment. He really had no desire to hunt down the son of a bitch. Why did both women seem to think that was some great motive of his? "Fine," he said. "No problem. I'm just really getting tired of headaches, okay?"

"You swear to it?"

Vincent sighed. "I swear."

Darla rose and moved across the small room, motioning for Vincent to be seated. He made himself comfortable in the desk's chair, relaxing to her touch as she laid her fingers on his temples. Instantly, he felt calmer. Her touch always seemed to do that to him, though. Her fingers were so soft and gentle.

He heard her mumbling under her breath, her fingers moving from his temples to his forehead, then back. A tingling sensation began at the base of his skull, growing slowly to cover his entire scalp. He smiled faintly at the sensation. Then things grew dark.

Vincent woke late in the morning, feeling more refreshed than he could remember being in weeks. He vaguely recalled dozing off as Darla undid Rhia's spell, and seemed to remember her leading him up the stairs and helping him get undressed. He yawned and stretched and rubbed his eyes, then wrinkled his nose at the pasty feeling in his mouth.

Blaise yawned, too, from her position at the foot of the bed. Her happy tail thumped the mattress as she looked at him. "Hey, pup," he said, reaching out to her as she maneuvered to lick his face. "Good to see you, too."

He took a deep breath and decided to test Darla's job. He focused on the memory of their last night together before he traveled to Gnorrin's. He thought of her skin touching his, her lips on his. He was rewarded with a familiar stirring in his groin. But no headache.

Then he thought of her brother. He replayed the sight of Felina being seared by a green bolt, of Rhia tied to the rock. And his stomach tightened in fury. But his head remained free of pain.

He smiled. What a relief. He turned his attention back to the dog. "What do you say to some breakfast?"

The dog jumped off the bed as Vincent swung his legs over the side and stepped onto the cold stone of the floor. He washed quickly from the basin on his bureau, dressed, then made his way to the room where Gnorrin had slept. He found it empty, but heard the sound of his friend's voice downstairs.

Blaise led the way down. Vincent followed her into the dining area. Gnorrin and Darla were seated at a small table, halfway through their meal. "Good morning," he said.

"And to you," said Gnorrin. Darla simply smiled as Vincent sat.

Vincent stared at her for some time, a chill washing over him. It was as if he were seeing her clearly for the first time. She looked so much older than he remembered.

He shook his head. Surely it was because she was still tired from removing the spell from him. Nothing more. He turned to Gnorrin.

"Did you sleep well?" he asked the gnome.

"Well enough, it seems. Well enough to make the return trip as soon as you're ready." Vincent frowned as he picked up a biscuit. "Or had you forgotten that you have a horse at my cottage? Likely a very hungry one by now."

"Oh," Vincent replied. "In fact, yes. I had forgotten." He sighed. He wasn't looking forward to another long ride back to Linnael from Gnorrin's. "When did you wish to leave?"

"Any time before mid-day, I should think. We can arrive with a bit of light still left in the sky."

Vincent nodded and chewed his biscuit. Chesya, one of Aedriun's kitchen maids, entered carrying a pot of hot herbal brew. Then Darla said, "How do you feel this morning?"

He shrugged. "Okay, I guess. How long did that take, last night?"

"It was very complex. Rhia is much more skilled than I." She yawned. "Excuse me."

"How long did it take?" he asked again.

"All night," Gnorrin said. "She came downstairs no more than an hour ago."

"I took you to your room as soon as you started to fall asleep," she said. "It was probably easier for me that you were not awake. Your mind offered no resistance."

"I see." He knew how much such an investment of time must have cost her. He remembered seeing how drained she and Rhia both were after tending Felina during her recovery. "Thank you," he said.

"Please, do not thank me," she said. "I should have removed the spell as soon as Rhia told me she'd done it. I'm sorry. I never meant for you to suffer because of me."

"Hey, come on, now. I didn't suffer because of you."

Darla closed her eyes and took a deep breath. "I'm too weary to argue," she said. "But I wanted to make sure you were well this morning. I'm relieved that you are. But now I must sleep."

Vincent watched her as she rose. He didn't want her to leave, especially not in that frame of mind. But she was tired. "Okay," he said softly. "I'll see you when I return."

Her face brightened, then, and he saw a look in her eyes that spoke of love and gratitude. It made him feel awkward. She wished them both a safe journey before ascending the stairs.

Gnorrin tapped the rim of his mug with a thick finger. When she was out of earshot, he said, "I trust you have tested the effectiveness of her ministrations?"

Vincent nodded. "Yes. It seems to have worked perfectly."

His friend continued idly nibbling at his meal. "She told me she coaxed a promise from you. Something about not hunting down her brother."

"Yes," he said, tossing a bit of biscuit to Blaise. "I had no idea how difficult it would be for me to keep that promise. But already, I find myself wanting to track the bastard down." His voice was flat as he spoke. "And I haven't really been thinking about him. If I take the time to do so, I know I'll want to kill him."

Chesya stepped through the doorway with another tray of biscuits and a dish of the tart berry jam that Vincent liked so much. "You're too good to me," he said to her.

"Agreed," she said with a smile.

"Tell me, where is Aedriun?"

The maid wiped her hands on her apron. "I believe his destination was Goldenbrook, m'lord."

"I've warned you about calling me that," he teased.

"Idle threats and you know it," she tossed back with a smile.

"Mm. Perhaps," Vincent said.

"Will there be anything else you're needing?" Chesya asked.

"No. Thank you. Go spoil someone else for a while."

As Chesya left, Vincent turned to Gnorrin. "Goldenbrook. More politics, I'll bet."

"I'm sure I wouldn't know."

"Well, what good are you , then?" Vincent teased.

"Good for a ride home, it seems. Unless you'd prefer to walk."

"Ah... no."

The journey to Gnorrin's was brief, compared to the trip to Linnael the previous day. They arrived shortly before nightfall, stopping first at Vincent's cottage. Gnorrin had taken the horse there the morning they'd originally left for the keep, before Vincent had awoken. But he'd only provided grain for the animal to last a day or so. Water was not a problem, since the stream that ran behind the cottage also ran through a small part of the corral Vincent had built. Vincent fed the hungry beast, filling a feed bag from the large bin of grain that he kept near the stable. Then, after dropping their packs off at Gnorrin's cottage, they walked into town for dinner at the inn.

"What will you do now?" asked Gnorrin as they ate.

"About what?"

The gnome shrugged. "You have not said much since Darla removed Rhia's spell. It is most unlike you."

"How do you mean?"

"You have always been one to not only speak your mind, but to speak your heart. I am accustomed to knowing what you are thinking and feeling about things. Lately, however, you have been very silent on these matters."

Vincent poked his dinner absently with his fork. "I know," he said quietly. "I guess I'm just too confused right now."

"About what?"

"Everything." He leaned back in his chair, relishing the warmth of the fireplace. He thrust his hands into his cloak. "You know the only thing that made being stranded here acceptable was Ariaziane. When she left..." He stared with empty eyes at some nebulous point in the middle of the table. "I felt so lost. Abandoned."

"But then Rhia arrived."

Vincent smiled, filled with the memory of his early days with Rhia. But his thoughts ran too rapidly for him. They progressed through time, carrying him to the meeting with Felina, then Rhia's departure. His smile faded. "And then she left, too. Not only did she leave, but she cast a spell on my brain."

"You said you understood her reasons."

"I think so. But I still don't think she should have done it."

463

"Nor do I."

"Her actions after Felina's death and resurrection just seem so out of character. So inconsiderate."

Gnorrin sighed. "It is said that an attempt to understand the mind of a witch will end in severe frustration."

"On Earth we have a similar sentiment about women."

"Now that Rhia's spell has been removed, how do you feel about Darla? Are your feelings still clouded?"

Vincent sighed. "I'm afraid it's still overcast. I just don't know, Gnorrin. I feel like I know nothing about her. I mean, a little mystery is enticing. That was a big attraction with Rhia. But with Darla, it's not so much mystery, but more like there's really nothing there."

The gnome's brow knit. "What do you mean?"

He snorted. "That's just it. I don't know what I mean. I just get the feeling, sometimes, that I'm talking to someone with no past. And it's hard to get close to her. It's like there's not much to get close to. She has no real developed personality. So unlike Rhia. Or, for that matter, unlike Annie, too."

"I see."

A thought struck Vincent, then. He leaned forward, placing his hands on the table. "Gnorrin, you said you'd gotten occasional letters from Blade."

"Yes. Every three or four weeks he writes me."

Vincent licked his suddenly dry lips. "Have you ever gotten any correspondence from Ariaziane?"

Gnorrin looked down at his dinner and said simply, "Yes."

Vincent's heart skipped a few beats. "Why didn't you tell me?"

"Because she didn't want you to know."

"Why the hell not?" he demanded.

"You would worry."

"I would not! Well, okay. Yeah, I would. But so what?"

Gnorrin shrugged. "She loves you."

Vincent was silent for a while. Then he said, quietly, "She sure has a funny way of showing it." He took a deep breath. "Well, okay. What did she say in her letters?"

"I'll let you read them, if you like, when we return to my cottage."

"Great," Vincent said. "You done eating?"

Gnorrin chuckled and continued with his meal.

Vincent waited impatiently for him to finish, and when he'd done so, they left the inn and headed home. Once there, Gnorrin went straight to his room. He returned carrying a leather scroll tube and gave it to Vincent before taking a seat in his favorite chair.

Vincent quickly opened the tube and withdrew a stack of papers. Gnorrin had saved them all in one tube, he noted, rolling them together in the order of receipt. He quickly dove into the first letter.

"*Dear Gnorrin,*

"*I hope this letter finds you well.*

"*I'm sure Vincent has told you about my departure, and just as sure that it came as little surprise to you. You and I frequently spoke of my concerns about my first transformation. After I had a second, I knew I had to learn more about myself.*

"Sister Haleen at the abbey once told me that my parents were not native to that area, but had moved there from a town far to the northeast. That town was my first destination.

"I located, after much inquiry, a man and wife who were friends of my parents. They informed me, however, that Beren and Sascha were not my parents at all, but my grandparents! Their daughter, my mother, evidently died not long after giving birth to me. I asked how she died and they explained that she was a frail woman, and the pregnancy and birth were simply too much for her.

"This is certainly not uncommon, but I'm unsure whether to fully believe them. There was something about the telling of the tale that seemed... I do not know how to say it. Perhaps I have been around Vincent too long and am imagining that I have the ability to detect a lie, as he seems able to do.

"I miss Vincent. Many times I've thought that I was too hasty and that I should have allowed him to accompany me. But I couldn't. I need to do this myself.

"Please do not tell him I've written to you. I don't want him to make any attempt to find me. Not that I am asking you to lie for me, but... Well, use your own judgment.

"My next step is to try to determine who my real father was. It is possible that I could find a friend of my mother's who knew my father, too.

"I'll write again when I have more to tell. Take care of yourself."

The letter was signed with a large, ornate "A."

Vincent looked up at Gnorrin, who was sitting with his eyes closed and his hands behind his head. "Interesting. Her parents weren't her parents," he said as he shuffled pages to the second letter. Gnorrin grunted an acknowledgment.

"Dear Gnorrin,

"I apologize for the amount of time that has passed since my last letter. So much has happened that I found myself all caught up in it and kept putting off writing. I hope to never let that happen again.

"When last I wrote, I said that I would attempt to find a friend of my mother's. I succeeded. A woman who had been my mother's friend was able to add more curiosity to the ongoing puzzle. My mother, it seems, was not so frail as I had been led to believe. She was healthy and strong. Until the pregnancy, that is.

"My mother's friend said she watched as the pregnancy seemed to drain the life from her. The further into it she went, the weaker she became. This made no sense to her friend, who knew she was plenty strong enough to carry and birth a baby.

"By the time I was born, my mother was practically infirm. She died four weeks later.

"I know I should not feel guilty or responsible for her death, but I can't help but feel as though something about me caused her to die.

"Her friend, however, has another idea. She thinks my mother was under some sort of spell. It seems she was known to keep company with a mage in the area. Like mother, like daughter, eh, Gnorrin?

"I learned as much about this mage as I could. Not because I thought he had cast a spell on my mother, but because it's possible that he could have been my father. Mother's friend says she knew nothing of my father.

"So I traveled farther north in search of this mage, finally finding him about a week ago. His name is Sirrah, in case you have heard of him. Unfortunately, Sirrah has been unable to tell me anything of my father other than the fact that it isn't him. About my mother, however, he told me much.

"My mother was, in fact, beginning to learn the ways of magic from him. She'd not gotten very far when she suddenly seemed to lose interest. He questioned her about it and she assured him that her interest in magic was as strong as ever, but that her time was otherwise occupied. She'd met a man and had become quite smitten. The man must have been my father, since she became pregnant not long thereafter and ceased her studies altogether.

"Sirrah seems also to find it difficult to believe that a normal pregnancy would have killed my mother. He says she was far too strong for that. But he is without suggestions on what could have caused her death.

"I seem to be stuck, for now. But I can hear your voice telling me to stay and study with Sirrah, to learn more from him. And that is exactly what I am doing. I expect to be here for some time. He is a very kind man, Gnorrin. I expect you'd like him a great deal. I hope to learn much from him.

"I hope it will not be as long before I write again. Stay well, my friend. I miss you."

Vincent frowned as he moved the paper to the bottom of the pile. "Gnorrin," he said, "what do you think about the circumstances of her mother's death?"

"I do not know what to think about them," the gnome replied, opening his eyes and moving his hands to fold them across his belly.

Vincent rubbed his chin. "Felina once mentioned that similar deaths sometimes occur in cases where a human woman has mated with an elven male."

"Aye. That is true. The elven child requires more in the growing stages than a human does. Often, the baby will die before birth. But sometimes the mother will perish, it is true."

"Could Ariaziane be half elven?"

Gnorrin shook his head. "Not a chance."

"Why not? Elves don't look that different than humans."

"Not to you, perhaps. No, she's got as much elven blood in her as I do."

"Mm. So do you know this Sirrah guy?"

"I have not heard the name before, no."

Vincent nodded, trying to fight off a wave of jealousy that was bearing down on him. The thought of Ariaziane spending time with Sirrah didn't sit well with him. What if he tried something with her? What if she found herself drawn to him? He took a deep breath. Today, he told himself. Not tomorrow. He moved on to the next letter.

"Gnorrin,

"Vincent once explained the term 'irony' to me. It seems I have fallen victim to a good example of it.

"Sirrah taught me much during the months I stayed with him. He could have taught me more, but I grew impatient to continue with my original quest. I declined his offer to teach me spells in a certain field.

"That field was of a protective nature. I had assumed the basic protection spells you taught me would be enough. But I've learned that a spell is only good if you have the opportunity to cast it.

"I found myself in a situation recently wherein I could have avoided a good deal of anguish had I taken the time to learn more from Sirrah. The details are too disturbing to go into.

"Nevertheless, one day I will tell Vincent that I fully understand 'irony' in my life.

"I am about to trek north, a decision based on a combination of intuition and desperation. Some of the things told me by Sirrah, as well as my mother's friend, have led me to believe that my father was from an area north of here.

"I do not know when I will be able to write again."

Vincent frowned deeply as he read the letter. The tone was so unlike her other letters. And he knew why. His dream of Ariaziane being raped hadn't been just a dream. It had really happened, and he knew Darla's brother was responsible.

He felt Gnorrin's eyes on him as he swallowed past a lump of anger in his throat. But he didn't say anything. Instead, he moved on to the fourth letter.

"Dear Gnorrin,

"I am writing to you from an inn, on my way back to visit Sirrah. Many things have happened over the past several months. I do not, however, have time to write of them all in this letter. I have, fortunately, been keeping a journal of my travels, and you may read my accounts when I return.

"Two things of note, though, before I sleep. First, I found some very interesting underground caverns. They were obviously fashioned by a mage, or at least transformed by one from their natural state. The walls there were smooth as polished wood, but made of a material I have never seen before, as were the doors to different chambers. Many of these doors were magically sealed. I explored only a few, finding the oddest sleeping chambers you could imagine.

"I did not explore the entire cavern due to the second item of note. In one of the rooms, I discovered something. At first glance, it appeared to be a normal item of clothing. But it radiated such magic that I could not turn away from it. I have no idea what it is or does. That is why I am returning to Sirrah, in the hope that he might shed some light upon its nature.

"Another reason I didn't explore the caverns fully is because they were not entirely uninhabited. I did not recognize the creatures, but two things struck me. One was that they didn't seem to be the residents of the caverns, for they appeared to be exploring them just as I was. The other was that they seemed to radiate evil. I felt it was in my best interests to leave hastily. But you can be sure I'll return one day.

"As for what my plans are after visiting Sirrah again, I do not know. It could be that I'll return home. Only time will tell.

"Take care."

Vincent sighed as he finished reading. This letter, though a vast improvement from the one before, still didn't seem to accurately reflect Ariaziane's personality. Could it be, he wondered, that the rape had altered her so much that she had become a cold person? He certainly hoped not.

With slight trepidation, he moved on to the final letter.

"Dear Gnorrin,

"Once again, I'm very sorry it has been so long since my last letter. Sometimes I become so involved with my own situation that I don't stop to think of how my friends are affected. I know you understand how that can be, but I fear Vincent will not be so forgiving.

"I saw him recently. By purest coincidence, we were on the same ship. I was returning from seeing Sirrah, and I assume Vincent was sailing back to Linnael. We didn't speak. I just couldn't bring myself to do so. So much would have needed to be voiced. And I know that if I had begun, I would have told him far more than I would have planned.

"I would have told him how much I missed him. I would have told him that I loved him. That's one thing I've come to realize, Gnorrin. I do love him, very much. But I'll never be able to love him the way he deserves to be loved until I solve the puzzle that is Ariaziane.

"*However, it might be beside the point, even if I solve the mystery tomorrow. There was a woman with him on the ship. I watched them one day. It was clear that she loved him, too. Perhaps I have been right all along about his feelings for me.*

"*As for my progress with the aforementioned puzzle, it is not going as well as I had hoped. Sirrah was able, though, to solve the mystery of my new magical toy. You'll have to see it to believe it. But as for my original quest, I have learned nothing new since my last letter to you. Wish me luck that this should change.*

"*I do wish I could hear from you, impossible as that is. I hope you are in good health and that Vincent is not too angry with me. If he is, I can understand. I was terribly rude on the ship.*

"*Again, please do not tell him that I wrote to you. He would probably only be hurt that I did not write to him. I simply would not know what to say.*

"*I look forward to seeing all of you in the not too distant future. I miss you all very much.*"

Like the others, the letter was signed with a large "A" in fancy script. Vincent frowned in puzzlement as he finished the letter. What had she meant about being right about his feelings for her? He asked Gnorrin, but the gnome only shrugged.

Well, he told himself, at least she sounded like she was back to her old self. Perhaps enough time had passed that she was able to put the rape behind her. Then the thought struck him that perhaps her improved mood was due to Sirrah, and he found himself growing jealous at the thought. He frowned, then rolled the letters back up and sat quietly for a minute. Finally, he said, "Why did you allow me to read these when she asked you not to?"

Gnorrin yawned, then said, "I was not volunteering the information, but I was not about to deny it. Besides, I think you needed to know what she had written."

"Thank you. It's a lot for me to think on."

"You do that," his friend said. "I'll be in bed."

Vincent smiled and watched Gnorrin shuffle past. "See you in the morning," he said. And as Gnorrin prepared for sleep, Vincent read the letters again. And again.

In the morning, after breakfast, Vincent bade farewell to his friend and departed for Linnael. During his long days of riding, his mind was awhirl. His thoughts tumbled over one another. Thoughts of Ariaziane, Rhia, and Darla, and of the feelings he had for each of them.

Nights in his sleep sack were cold, but he barely noticed. His dreams, too, were full of images of these three women, occasionally graced with the presence of Felina, as well. His sleep wasn't restful. Pleasant as some of the dreams were, many found him waking to even more confusion in his mind than before.

Much of his thinking revolved around Ariaziane and her letters. He was glad his friend had allowed him to read them. But the letters disturbed him, too. Especially her mysterious reference to his feelings about her, and to unpleasant things that had happened. The rape. Now that Rhia's spell was gone, he could allow his hatred of the boy to overwhelm him. It was a relief to be able to do so without the accompanying headache, but the acid that welled up inside his stomach wasn't exactly a nice sensation.

And what about Rhia's spell itself? How did he really feel about that? He had to admit that he was angry. And it hurt to know that Rhia felt it necessary to resort to magic in order for him to obey her simple wish to refrain from trying to find Darla's brother. He was true to his word. If she'd simply asked him not to do so, he wouldn't have. But he also realized, feeling the bile churn inside, that perhaps he'd never have made such a promise to her. For he truly felt some viciousness toward the kid. He half regretted making the promise to Darla. He really wanted to make the boy suffer. Not a very enlightened attitude, he knew, but he couldn't seem to work up much of an argument against it.

Darla occupied the majority of his thoughts, however. He examined his feelings about the girl, trying not to focus on the physical. He knew there had to be more to her than he was seeing. Her innocence was appealing in its own way. But it wasn't really innocence, was it? Could she really be innocent after the abuses of her brother? Not to mention the things she knew. She was a witch, like Rhia. At least, he thought that's what she was. They'd never really talked about it.

And that was really the crux of everything, wasn't it? They'd never really talked. At all. This was something easily remedied, he thought. And it was something he wanted to do. Darla was, if nothing else, a very sweet girl. He could certainly do worse than her.

He couldn't count on the return of either Ariaziane or Rhia. Much as he wished otherwise, he had to accept that he might never see either of them again. Darla, on the other hand, was here. He'd be foolish to turn away her affections.

And so his journey passed, his mind finally becoming comfortable less than a day's ride from Linnael.

He arrived in Linnael in the late afternoon. It was a cold day, dreary and wet. The snows rarely touched the port town, but the Season of Sleep brought many chilly rains. Vincent dismounted outside Aedriun's gates. The guard recognized him and allowed him to enter. He walked his horse down the path, until a stablehand appeared and took the beast from him.

Inside, he headed straight for his room, where he removed his wet clothing. He wrapped a robe around himself and headed for the baths for a hot soak. He hung a pot of water over the fire, then filled a tub with rainwater from a barrel. When the pot was boiling, he dumped it into the tub. He tested with a toe, then stepped in.

It was deliciously relaxing. He closed his eyes and allowed the heat to draw the weariness out of his body and mind. He sighed deeply, thinking that he should relax in a hot tub more often than he did. He slipped down, allowing his head to submerge. The tub wasn't large enough for his full length, so he had to bend his legs and tuck them under each other in order to keep his entire body underwater. But it was worth it. Sort of his own little isolation tank.

He remained under for a long time, enjoying the feel of the hot water on his face and scalp and the unique, dreamy sound of being underwater. He could easily fall asleep like this, he knew. And as he thought about it, he thought it wasn't a bad idea at all.

In his sleep, he dreamed of Earth. He dreamed of arriving back home, years older, bearded and with hair so long it would give his dad a heart attack. In his dream, he entered his house and was greeted by a scream.

The scream belonged to someone he couldn't see. It was a shrill scream, interrupted by beseeching oaths to the gods. And then something grabbed his knee. He opened his eyes.

The scream was louder, now, but still somewhat distant. He sat up, water flowing out of the tub. He blinked at the chamber maid, who stopped screaming long enough to turn and run from the room.

Vincent laughed, despite her terror. He made a mental note not to fall asleep underwater when someone could come in and think he was a drowning victim.

The girl's screams caused some stirring downstairs, he could hear. He reached out with his hearing, past his immediate surroundings, ignoring the small splashes of water as drops fell from his wet hair, ignoring the crackle of the fire, searching for other sounds to feast upon.

Downstairs, he heard voices. The chamber maid was describing what she'd seen in the bath. Then Aedriun's roar of a laugh. Good, he thought. The baron was home.

Another sound caught his attention. Light footsteps, almost what he would call polite footsteps. He heard them as they climbed the stairs to the floor that held his room, then approached down the hall toward the baths. Darla's footsteps, he realized.

Closing his eyes again, he tried to relax. His mind suddenly swam with things he wanted to say to her, things he was afraid to say to her, and questions of what was truly right to say. To his surprise, his heart was racing.

The door opened and Darla stepped inside. "Hello," he said, before she'd rounded the corner.

"Welcome back," she said calmly. "I trust your trip was uneventful."

"Very much so," he said, opening his eyes finally. She stood nearby, gazing at him with an expressionless face. "I had nothing to occupy my time but my mind."

"Aedriun would say that you must have been quite bored, then."

He smiled. "On the contrary. I thought mostly of you."

"Oh?"

"Yes," he replied, but did not elaborate. He could not take his eyes off her. He remembered the morning after she had undone Rhia's spell. She'd looked so much older to him then than her years. He wasn't sure exactly how old she was, but it seemed only yesterday that he'd seen her and her brother in the forest. Yet she appeared so much older now than then. And he thought back even further, to when he first met the pair. They'd only looked in their mid-teens then. Now she appeared in her early twenties. It was very disconcerting.

Without a word, Darla moved toward the head of the tub. From a rack on the wall, she took a large leather bottle of shampoo. She knelt behind Vincent's head, and he obligingly lowered himself until his head was underwater, then rose. Darla gently worked his hair to a lather, her fingers massaging his scalp, making sure that none of the soap got into his eyes.

Vincent sighed as she washed his hair. It felt amazing. "You have a wonderful touch," he said.

"Thank you," she said softly. She lifted a small pitcher from the floor, filled it, then poured it over his head.

"Allow me," he said, and submerged himself again. He rinsed, then came up. "Thank you."

She smiled back. "You're welcome." She put down the pitcher and moved to the side, resting her chin atop her arms on the rim of the tub. "I've missed you."

"I've missed you, too."

"You have?"

He nodded, staring into her eyes. "Yeah. I did a lot of thinking on the trip back."

"Yes, so you said. Mostly of me, as I recall."

"Mostly, yes. I want to apologize for the way I've behaved."

"Why do you feel your behavior requires an apology?"

He shifted nervously. "I've been unfair to you," he said.

"On the contrary," she said, lowering her eyes. "It is I who have been unfair to you."

"No," he interrupted, but she quickly spoke again.

"I have," she insisted. "I pushed myself on you, hoping that my feelings for you would kindle similar feelings in you for me. I was foolish to think that such would be the case."

Vincent's heart went out to her. How many times in the past had he felt exactly the same way? He knew that one's love for another didn't obligate that person to love in return. It was a hard lesson he'd learned. And wouldn't it be grand if such returned feelings really did magically spring up? He sighed. Then he reached up and clasped her hand.

"Sometimes," he said slowly, "we do get what we hope for."

Darla looked at him, her brow furrowing. She opened her mouth to speak, then seemed to reconsider. She smiled abruptly and let out a brief chuckle before biting her lower lip coyly. "I'm not certain what you mean."

He smiled back at her. "I mean what you hope I mean." The smile vanished from her face, replaced with an expression of surprise. "I mean that I'm not putting you off any longer. I want to get to know you. I know you love me, odd as I find that to be. I've realized that I'm the one who's been foolish. I have no real reason to put off your affections."

Darla turned her face to the water, avoiding his gaze. "Do you love me?" she whispered.

Vincent felt a stab inside himself. "I don't know," he said truthfully. "I feel things for you that I don't understand. But I *want* to understand them. And I won't understand them on my own. I need to be with you to let them grow into whatever they will become."

The girl looked at him and smiled shyly. Then she leaned forward and kissed him tenderly. She leaned back, then stood. "Dinner will be served shortly. I must go and change my clothing."

Vincent nodded. "I'll not be much longer." He returned her smile as she left the room, but stared after her, a familiar feeling creeping over him again, a feeling of something being not quite right.

Aedriun looked up in surprise as Vincent entered the dining room. "Well, well," he drawled. "Look what the dragon coughed up."

Vincent chuckled and slapped his friend on the shoulder as he reached him. "Yes, well the dragon thought to improve the overall quality of your household."

"You seem in good spirits, my friend."

471

He nodded. "Better than before, rest assured. I hope my behavior recently hasn't been too awful to put up with. I'm sorry if I've been a pain."

Aedriun shook his head. "Think nothing of it. In fact, I was rather relieved to see you behaving like a boor. Your reputation was becoming too sterling for me."

"So how were things in Goldenbrook?"

"Oh, well enough," said the baron, and his tone told Vincent that this was all the answer he would receive.

"Fine, be that way," Vincent teased.

"I shall, thank you. Now sit down and eat, so that I may, as well."

Dinner passed with the usual jolly humor that Aedriun brought to most everything he did. Darla eyed Vincent frequently from across the table, and he smiled at her attention. He mentally berated himself. Surely his imagination had been playing tricks with him. Darla didn't look like a young girl, certainly, but he must have exaggerated in his mind the apparent age she displayed. Then again, he admitted, no matter what her age, she was stunningly pretty. He couldn't deny that.

The weeks passed. They were pleasant times, with Vincent and Aedriun spending a good deal of time together. Vincent learned more and more about different aspects of society that he never would have learned otherwise. Aedriun informed him of different guilds and other organizations. He explained the peerage of the realm, and gave brief insight into other realms.

He and Darvas became fairly good friends, too. The boy was perhaps a little too polite, but pleasant company.

And he found his feelings deepening for Darla, as well. He was falling in love with her, slowly but surely. The love wasn't the head-over-heels, rapid sort that it had been with Ariaziane. Nor was it the complex, multi-level type of love he felt for Rhia. But he did love her. He enjoyed every minute he spent with her.

Celebration Week arrived, bringing Vincent's twenty-third birthday with it. Aedriun had wanted to throw a party in honor of the occasion, but Vincent talked him out of it. "You always want to throw a party," he told the older man, who readily agreed that this was true.

Darla admitted that she had no idea what he meant by "birthday party," so Vincent had to explain it to her. She told him it sounded delightful and that he should allow Aedriun to host the party. But Vincent had his own ideas.

Instead, the pair went out on the town, enjoying the festivities of the holiday. They ate from the food vendors, watched the various entertainers and listened to the minstrels. After a day full of activity, they dined at *The Yellow Beard*. Their dinner was in a quiet corner of the inn, candle-lit and intimate.

All throughout the meal, Vincent sat mesmerized by her eyes. Darla was flushed with excitement from the day and quite giddy. She stared at him as they talked. And he found himself swallowed up by her beauty, her innocence, her tenderness.

They stayed at the inn for hours, following up the dinner with hot beverages and more conversation. Eventually, they departed, Vincent leaving a generous tip for the server. Hand in hand, they strolled the streets, now mostly empty of vendors and revelers. Street cleaners were in abundance, pushing brooms in front of them. They smiled and greeted them as they passed.

For a time, they stopped and watched the moonlight on the waves of the sea. When they finally returned to Aedriun's, it was very late. Aedriun himself had evidently retired for the evening. They made their way quietly up the stairs.

Inside his room, Vincent brushed a hand through her hair. He kissed her gently, sweetly, then began to remove her clothing. She stood nude in front of him, staring into his eyes. He disrobed and led her to the bed.

Vincent couldn't help but make mental comparisons during their lovemaking. Darla was far more submissive than Rhia. She seemed content to allow him to do most of the work, though she encouraged him with her soft moans and hands that roamed his body, pulling him closer, often bringing his head down for tender kisses.

They finished together, Vincent surprising himself with how much he'd needed the release. Darla pulled him down on top of her, embracing him tightly. Her hot breath warmed his ear and she sobbed, kissing his face and neck. "I love you," she said, over and over. He smiled and echoed the sentiment. Darla continued softly crying even after he moved to the side and held her in his arms. Eventually, she slept. And Vincent kept on holding her.

❧ ❧

He watched, anger growing, as his father bedded his sister. He used no crystal ball for this scrying, but the Seeker Portal itself. In the time since his mother had departed, he'd learned much of its abilities. There was much more still to learn, but he would. He had no doubt of that.

Some little part of his mind told him that he was overdoing it. His mother had mentioned the effects of the overuse of magic, but he'd paid little attention. If it got results, it was worth the price.

He looked down at his hands, at the bloody splits that covered them and his arms. They would heal, he told himself. It didn't matter that using the magic sometimes hurt.

The little voice needled him, saying that it hurt his mind, too. But he didn't care. All he cared about was destroying the man called Vincent.

He wanted nothing more than to tear his father's heart out, right this instant. But he couldn't leave the cave. If he did, then Rhia would have it all to herself.

She'd been watching him, he knew. But she was intelligent enough not to attack him. She surely knew he was the more powerful of the two.

So he let her watch. There was precious little she could learn from her distant vantage point. Soon enough, he'd be able to leave the cave permanently, once his plans were complete. And then, it wouldn't matter. The plans would be executed long before she could do anything to prevent them.

❧ Thirty-Three ❧

The Season of Green typically came early to Linnael, much to Vincent's pleasure. He spent a large amount of his time outdoors, going for long rides throughout the area. He also spent a good bit of time at his inn of choice, becoming on good terms with the proprietor and patrons of *The Yellow Beard*. Darvas occasionally joined him at the tavern.

Darvas was a good kid, Vincent thought. Though he had to admit he sometimes felt guilty when he thought of Darvas as a "kid." He really wasn't far from Vincent's own age. But since the boy's uncle Aedriun considered Vincent to be a peer, he tended to think of Darvas as being younger than he really was. Or was it that Vincent's life was just so much more complex than that of Darvas? He wasn't sure. And it didn't really matter.

Despite the assurances he knew Aedriun to be giving his nephew, Darvas took some time to really act at ease on these outings. One night, however, Darvas drank a little more than his usual, and his tongue loosened somewhat.

They sat at their traditional corner table near the fire, the nights still being on the cold side. It was late and the tavern was full. Vincent politely greeted the many regulars who addressed him. He wondered if this was how celebrities felt when going out in public.

Too many stories had been circulating about him. He'd heard some of them, and while grounded in truth, there were exaggerations that he frequently denied. But like most stories, there was no getting them back to the truth. The people seemed to want to believe the super-heroic deeds. In a way, he wasn't surprised. That seemed to be a facet of human nature, the need to believe the unbelievable.

"You never get drunk," Darvas said suddenly, his voice slightly slurred from his own drink.

Vincent smiled as he lowered his beverage to the table and nodded at the mug. "Getting drunk on this would be quite a feat." His drink of choice tonight was a frothy beverage similar to cocoa, but with a flavor more reminiscent of cinnamon than chocolate. "I don't drink alcohol."

"And why is that, my dear baron friend?"

"Well, to be honest, I don't really like most alcoholic drinks. I find the taste of ale pretty disgusting, for example."

"Then drink something that tastes good to you."

"Well, that's not my only reason. Listen to you, Darvas. You've drunk so much tonight that your tongue is thick. You'll probably continue, maybe even reach the point of not being able to stand without swaying."

"Quite possibly, yes," Darvas agreed with a smile.

"The very idea of not being in full control of my mind and body is utterly revolting to me. I can't imagine why anyone would deliberately do that to themselves."

Darvas shrugged and wiped condensation from his mug of ale. "Suppose. But you don't have to drink to get drunk." He frowned, apparently considering his words. "Well, yes you do, actually. But you don't have to get drunk. When you drink," he added as an afterthought. "One drink won't make you drunk."

"Not likely," Vincent agreed, "but it does affect you. Alcohol is a poison to your body. I'd rather avoid it altogether. Besides," he said, lifting his drink, "this tastes better."

His friend stared into his drink for a while, as if looking for something. Then he spoke, without looking up. "Your lady Darla is very beautiful."

Vincent felt a pang of guilt shoot through him. "Yes, she is," he said quietly.

Darvas looked up at him. "And she loves you very much."

"I know."

"So why are you avoiding her?"

There it was, the one question he didn't want to hear. He'd asked himself the same question so often lately. Since he didn't like his own answer, he didn't expect it would sound right to anyone else. But he needed to talk to someone about it. "Darvas," he said slowly, "do you find anything odd about Darla?"

The younger man frowned for a moment, then seemed embarrassed. "Yes."

"What, exactly? What seems unusual about her?"

Darvas considered this for a long time, looking into his mug as if for inspiration. Vincent didn't push. He knew how hard it was for himself, sober, to pinpoint exactly what he found to be odd. Finally, Darvas looked him in the eye. "Her face."

Vincent blinked. "Excuse me?"

"Her features. They seem different. Sharper. More, I don't know..."

"More mature?"

Darvas narrowed his eyes. "Possibly. Yes, that's it exactly." As Vincent chewed on that thought for a bit, Darvas continued. "Is that why you're away so much? Because you're disturbed by her face?"

Vincent laughed out loud. "Disturbed by her face?" He snorted. "Anything but." He allowed the smile to fade, then took a drink. "No," he said, "it is something a bit more profound than that."

"So tell me."

He smiled grimly. "You know, I tried to have this conversation with your uncle, not long ago." He shook his head.

"What?"

Now it was Vincent's turn to shrug. "Whenever I try to talk to him about my problems, he brushes them off. I don't know if he just doesn't take them seriously, or if it's something deeper."

Darvas leaned back in his chair. "Think I know."

"Oh? Please don't keep it a secret."

"I could be wrong," he drawled. Then, as though just realizing it, he said, "Or completely out of line, for that matter, but I think my uncle has too high an opinion of you." Vincent raised an eyebrow. "Uncle doesn't want to think you can have the same problems everyone else has. His image of you is..."

"Unrealistic?"

"Heroic."

Vincent rolled his eyes. "Great."

"And I can understand why."

"Oh, for crying out loud," Vincent muttered.

"No, I can!" Darvas insisted.

"Don't start," Vincent said firmly. "Just don't. If I hear one more time about how much I've accomplished since I've gotten here, and all that shit, I will absolutely scream."

Darvas blinked at him in bewilderment, then took another gulp of his ale. "All right," he said. After a long pause, he said, "Did I ask you a question?"

"Yes," Vincent said flatly.

Another pause, then, "Did you answer it?"

Vincent took a deep breath, letting it out slowly. "No. I'm sorry. I guess maybe part of my problem is that I don't really know what I'm feeling. Nothing seems clear. I feel something is wrong, but can't tell what, exactly. It's all very vague." He paused, stroking his beard for a moment. There was only one way he was going to easily solve this problem. He finished his drink. "Darvas, I think I'm going to cut this evening short." He stood and pulled some coins from his pouch. "Feel free to stay and drink yourself blind, if that's your plan."

His friend chuckled. "Why not? You're not the only one who can borrow my uncle's ring."

Vincent smiled, slapping Darvas on the shoulder as he passed, and headed for the door.

He found Darla alone in one of the smaller sitting rooms on the lower level of Aedriun's home, sitting on a sofa in front of a blazing fireplace, intent on some needlework, an art she'd learned from Chesya. Blaise lay on the floor at her feet. Both looked up as he entered the room. Blaise thumped her tail on the floor and Darla smiled.

"You're home early," she said.

"I missed you," he said, approaching the sofa.

Her face brightened. "Truly?"

He knelt, petting Blaise and glancing at the needlework. "I thought we could talk a bit."

"Certainly." She held up the linen for his inspection. "Do you like it so far?"

Vincent studied it. The colored threads showed a knotwork pattern around the border of the square. Inside was a stitched version of the stylized "V" that Ariaziane had designed. It was beautiful work, he could see already. But it made him slightly uneasy to know that someone other than Ariaziane was making it for him. "It looks great," he said honestly.

She lowered the fabric to her lap again. "What did you wish to talk about?"

He gave the dog a final scratch behind the ears, then joined Darla on the sofa. "I'd like to talk about you," he said simply.

"Oh," she said. "One of *those* talks." She put aside her stitching and turned sideways on the sofa to face him, tucking one leg under herself.

Vincent gazed into her anxious eyes and immediately regretted his need to have this conversation. He smiled tentatively. "I know it must get to be a bother, me asking you about yourself all the time." Darla turned her eyes to her hands and gave a minuscule shrug. "I'm sorry," he continued, clearing his throat. "Do you remember the first time we met?"

She looked back up at him, pain in her eyes. "When my brother stole your gauntlets."

Vincent nodded. "Yes. That's the occasion." He took a deep breath. "How old were you then?"

Darla blinked. "What?"

"Let me get to the point. That episode was less than two years ago. At the time, you and your brother appeared to be in your mid-teens. One year later, we met again, when your brother killed Felina. You seemed then to be about twenty, give or take a year. And now, you look around my age, if not older. What's the story?"

"I'm sorry," Darla said. "But I do not understand what you are saying."

"I'm saying that you *appear* to be aging more rapidly than you should, by a considerable degree. Did you and your brother magically make yourselves appear younger when I first encountered you? And if so, why?"

Darla shook her head. "There was no such disguise."

"Then you're saying..." He frowned. "What *are* you saying?"

"I wasn't aware I was saying anything. You are the one saying everything."

This was not the way he'd wanted the conversation to go. He sighed. "Don't you think there's anything unusual in what I'm talking about?"

"I'm not even certain what you *are* talking about."

"I'm talking about the fact that in the two years since I first set eyes on you, you appear to have aged half a dozen years or more!"

"Why should that be odd?" she shot back. "You have been here for over five years, but hardly seem to have aged half that many."

"Who told you that?" Vincent demanded.

Darla was silent for a moment. Then she shrugged, looking down at her needlework. "Rhia."

Vincent shook his head. "Seems Rhia does and says a lot of things without my knowledge. When did she mention this to you?"

"We often had discussions when we were aiding Felina in her recovery."

Vincent ran a hand through his hair. "Fine. Whatever. My aging, or alleged lack thereof, isn't really the issue. Yours is." He sighed and clasped her hand. "Darla, I'm just worried. What I see disturbs me. Do you have any idea what is causing it?"

She hesitated, as if debating her reply. Then she said, "I assume you do."

He shrugged. "No. I mean, there's a rare disease on my world, progeria, that affects children. It makes them appear quite old when they are, in fact, very young. But that disease is nothing like what you're going through. Sorry," he added when her eyes flared. "What you *seem* to be going through. Then again, that was on Earth. I have no idea what sorts of bizarre diseases you have here. This isn't my world."

"Isn't it?" she said, and Vincent looked at her sharply. "You've made this world your own, Vincent. You might not know everything about it, but that doesn't matter. You know enough to function, to succeed."

"True, but it hardly makes this my world. I've been here less than six years. I lived on Earth for three times that."

"And when you've been here for thirty years, will you still refer to Earth as your world, not this one?"

The thought seemed to pierce his heart. Homesickness struck him harder than it had in many months. But then her words registered in his mind more clearly. He knew she was right. A part of him would always think of Earth as his home. But this world was just as much "his" as Earth was. In some ways, more so. "I don't know," he muttered.

"Please just tell me what it is you want. What is bothering you? Is it Ariaziane? Rhia? Do you just not love me? I can accept that, if it be true."

"No! Not at all! I do love you."

She smiled with a hint of relief, but then frowned. "Why, then, have you been so distant lately? You spend more time away from me than with me."

"I know," he whispered. "I just..." His voice trailed off as he found his feelings impossible to convey.

She shifted slightly in her seat. "Vincent," she said softly, looking into his eyes. "I know you don't love me the way I love you. I understand that."

"Darla, no..."

"Please," she insisted. "Let me finish." She squeezed his hand reassuringly. "I know it is the truth. Please do not deny it simply to save my feelings from being hurt. I know I am not as fascinating as your Ariaziane. Or as interesting as dear Rhia. In fact, I must seem very shallow, compared to them. Like a child."

The words stung Vincent like a slap. He realized at that moment that he had, indeed, been thinking of her in such a way. As a child. He looked into her eyes. They were not the eyes of a child. He berated himself for thinking she could be so innocent. Not after the atrocities committed upon her by her brother.

He lowered his head. "I'm sorry," he whispered.

"My love, there is no need," she assured him, stroking his hand. "I understand. I am content to share a small part of your life. Whatever you deign to give me, I will accept gladly."

Vincent frowned. "Please don't say it that way. It makes me sound so condescending."

"All I meant was that I know I can never be as important to your life as Rhia or Ariaziane. I just hope I can be even half as special to you as you are to me."

Vincent said nothing, his eyes stinging with the threat of tears. He drew her into his arms and held her, rocking back and forth. But he knew it was more for his own comfort than for hers.

∾ ∾

I didn't know how to respond to her, he wrote the following day in his journal. *I just sat there, my heart beating like crazy, my mouth not moving. I held her for a long time. I know a tear or two of mine must have dampened her hair.*

I'm not sure if I feel better about things or not. I think I do, but there are nagging doubts. Then again, I have nagging doubts about damn near everything.

I know there are things she hasn't told me. But I don't feel it right to pry. For example, her abdomen shows stretch marks. She evidently was pregnant at one point. Obviously, the father was her brother. I can understand her not wanting to share that. But still, I have to wonder how much more she's not sharing. And it hurts to know that she doesn't feel she can share everything with me.

But I think what hurts the most is the realization that I've been thinking of her as sort of a child. It's unfair of me, but I can't seem to help it.

Not that I don't see incredible potential in her. She's obviously quite intelligent. She absorbs things quickly and has shown remarkable insight.

He paused in his writing, reading over the words. He frowned, shaking his head.

Listen to me. It sounds like I'm trying to justify my relationship with her. Trying to justify her as a person. It's ridiculous. Why am I doing this? Am I trying to convince myself that being involved with Darla is acceptable?

He stared at the page for a long time before admitting that he had no answer.

෮ ෯

The weeks flew by. Vincent spent more time with Darla and less time at the inn. He would still often go for his afternoon rides, but he would frequently take Darla along. She enjoyed the outdoors quite a bit and was fascinated to watch the ships out on the water as they skirted the coastline to or from Linnael.

He had received word from Gnorrin that his keep was effectively complete. Feletain's crew had done as much as they could per Vincent's instructions. Furnishing the keep was the next step, and bound to be both time-consuming and expensive. He knew it had to be done, though, and to that end, he sought out the advice of an expert.

Falconwall, Aedriun explained to him, was closer to Vincent's keep, but the prices of goods were high. Linnael, on the other hand, was a port town and received many goods right off the boats. Aedriun also volunteered his assistance in getting the lowest possible prices for Vincent. It would remain for the items to be transported across the kingdom, but overall, Aedriun assured him, it would be the less expensive way to do things.

So Aedriun and Darla helped Vincent do some shopping. For the next two months, they went with him on excursions to buy furniture, carpets, tableware, cooking utensils, paintings, and all the other embellishments that would make Vincent's keep look suitable for a baron.

By the time they were finished, or as finished as they were likely to be, Vincent knew it was going to take a virtual convoy of wagons to transport all the goods to his new home. And he didn't even want to think of how much money he'd spent.

Aedriun also handled the acquisition of the wagons, and in short order, everything was done. The wagons were packed, the guards hired. There was only one factor remaining to be dealt with.

"I'm scared shitless," Vincent said as he stood on the balcony of his room, looking down on the train of wagons in the early morning mist.

Darla stood beside him. "I agree that it is a big step for you. But what are you afraid of?"

He shrugged, looking off into the distance, toward the hills further inland. "I'm not sure. It's just not something I ever imagined I'd be doing. There will be a lot of responsibilities."

"But you've done so many things. I'm sure you never pictured yourself doing half of them."

"True. But most of the things I've done were things I just fell into. They weren't calculated or planned. Whenever I have something monumental like this, and time to contemplate it, I always get scared to death."

She nodded in understanding or compassion. He wasn't sure which. "I'm sure everything will be fine."

He was quiet for a moment. "King Breigar will likely be expecting me to fulfill my part of the agreement." He shook his head. "I know nothing about being a baron."

"I thought you already were a baron."

Vincent explained to her the agreement he'd made with the king, how he had gotten permission to build his keep in the mountains in return for the promise to at least consider assuming the duties of baron. "I guess that's what's really scaring me most," he said.

"You worry too much," Aedriun said as he turned the corner into the room. "It's a small parcel of land with few towns. Your work will be minimal. And Darla is correct. You will do fine."

Vincent nodded without turning around. "Great. I'll hold you to that. When I screw things up, I'll blame it on you."

"As you wish," Aedriun laughed. "But the train is ready. You should be on your way to make the most progress before nightfall."

Now Vincent turned. "I know. But this isn't easy, my friend. I hate to leave you and your wonderful hospitality."

"But I insist. I fully intend to avail myself of you and your hospitality at my earliest convenience. I cannot do that if you don't leave." He smiled widely.

Vincent chuckled as he and Darla turned and left the room with Aedriun.

"The kitchen staff has assembled some impressive provisions for you."

"Thank you," Vincent said as they descended the stairs. "I'm sure your men will appreciate that. Your cooks are excellent. I'm tempted to steal one."

The baron laughed. "Good luck in trying."

"Will you not be able to hire one from, say, Falconwall?" asked Darla.

"Most likely," Vincent said. "You know, one day I wouldn't mind running an inn, like *The Yellow Beard*," he said as they exited into the warm morning air. "It could be fun."

"And you think being a *baron* would be hard work." Aedriun laughed.

They stood in front of the wagon train, Vincent looking it over. There were ten wagons, each with four mounts to pull it. In addition to a driver for each, there were ten guards riding with them. Including Darvas, the men were on loan from Aedriun. All except Coldson, who was there of his own preference. Vincent greeted them all and thanked them for making this journey with him.

As the drivers and escorts mounted up, Vincent and Darla bade their farewells to Aedriun. For Vincent, it was nearly as difficult as saying goodbye to Blade had been. The baron had become a close friend. After some choked-up words, Vincent hugged him and slapped him on the back. He owed much to the man, from the restoration of his eyesight to the work he'd done in building houses for him and Ariaziane, as well as his kindness in allowing him and Darla to stay for so long.

"Take care," he said quietly as he let go of his friend. He climbed into the lead wagon, which was being driven by Coldson, Darla taking her seat beside him, and Blaise jumping in to join them.

"I always do," Aedriun said. "I'll be in touch. Sooner than you expect, I'll wager."

"Good," Vincent said with a wave as the wagon began to move.

The wagon train traveled, to Vincent's estimation, at approximately one-third the speed he would have made on his own. The days were accordingly fairly relaxed. So relaxed, in fact, that Vincent spent much of his time sleeping. The wagon that Coldson drove turned out to be, effectively, nothing more than a lavish car for the Baron Vincent and his lady Darla. And Blaise, though the dog often chose to run beside the wagons, making her way up and down the convoy as if conducting an inspection. Coldson told him the wagon had been done up at Aedriun's insistence. Vincent had frowned when he realized this was done, but didn't let it go to waste. He and Darla napped most of the day. At night, they stayed up.

There were many reasons for this, not the least of which was his sensitivity to sunlight. Another factor was that he simply didn't want to spend all that much time listening to Coldson's constant chatter. The man was nice enough, but his demeanor started to wear on Vincent during the first few days. Coldson was certainly sincere, but his incessant expressions of admiration were really more than he could take. Vincent had always preferred the night to the day, anyway.

He enjoyed the nights. It gave him time to be alone with Darla. Some of the men would stand guard near the fire, but for the most part, they had a good bit of privacy. They'd often take a blanket well away from the campsite and make love under the stars. Sometimes they'd just look at the sky. Vincent would tell her about the stars and planets, comets and nebulae. Darla's admiration for him was quite profound, too, but he somehow found it easier to accept than Coldson's.

There were times, when they would be talking at night, that he wanted desperately to delve deeper into her past. He wanted to know about her childhood. But he didn't want to force Darla to talk about her brother, which would be inevitable in talking about her past.

Their trip was, for quite a distance, an easy one. A major trade route existed between Linnael and Falconwall. The bulk of the journey was along this route, though they would eventually veer to the north after passing over the two rivers.

Crossing the first river was not as time-consuming as Vincent would have expected. Because they were traveling the trade route, the system worked very quickly and efficiently. A small town lay at the river's edge. There, they were able to spend the night in one of three lodging establishments, having a hot meal as well. On the river itself was a team of ferrymen. Their ferries were fairly large, big enough to hold four of Vincent's wagons. They were equipped with sails and huge rudders. If the wind was favorable, the ferries sailed straight across. If not, they were capable of tacking a short distance upriver and then crossing over as the current took them down river to the sister town that waited on the other side.

Vincent's train would take three crossings. Darvas and Coldson urged him to spend the night at an inn while they made sure the ferrying went properly. But he was too awake for that. They'd arrived late in the day, and he and Darla were fully alert by the time the sun went down. Instead, once on the other side, he sent everyone but Coldson to an inn. He was able to oversee the entire operation himself, leaving Coldson on the other side to take care of the wagons at that end.

It took several hours for the crossings. When they were done, he sent Coldson to get some sleep, too. He and Darla spent the rest of the night in one of the taverns, warming themselves by the fire and talking with other patrons. When morning came, they were on their way again, Vincent and Darla retiring to their customary position in the lead wagon.

Vincent had not studied the trade route on any maps before they left, but his memory of studying the maps he'd put together years before made him think that the route would pass not far south of Goldenbrook. His suspicions were confirmed on the second morning after crossing the river.

He woke to the urging of Coldson's harsh voice. He sat up slowly in the wagon, wiping sleep from his eyes. Sunlight filtered through the canopied top and he frowned. "What is it? I feel like I just got to sleep."

Coldson smiled apologetically. "That ye did, m'lord, but there's a messenger here to speak with ye."

"Messenger?"

"Aye. From the castle, he says."

Vincent blinked. He sighed, then dragged his weary body toward the front of the wagon, where he slumped over the back of the seat. He took brief notice of the horse and hooded rider before closing his eyes against the bright sunlight.

"You are Baron Vincent of Penn's Woods?" asked the messenger.

He nodded in reply. "Not generally at this hour, but yes. What's the message?"

"The message is that you should get your lazy bottom out of the wagon and say hello to an old friend."

Vincent knew that voice. He opened his eyes, then smiled. "Ghanol! How did you know it was me in this caravan?"

"Word gets around, Vincent," said the duke, throwing back his hood and moving his horse closer to the wagon. "In fact, I have been waiting for you. Do you have a day to spare? We would enjoy having you for a visit."

"Oh, but Ghan, I've got ten wagons here, more than twenty men..."

"I am able to count," he replied. "What does that matter?"

Vincent sighed, then smiled. "Fine, be that way. Coldson, follow the good duke here. We're having lunch with the king, it seems."

Coldson blinked in astonishment, then turned to face Ghanol. "Beggin' your pardon, Yer Dukeship, I had no idea."

Ghanol laughed. "Nor were you intended to, my good man. Please. Lead your fellow travelers along this road," he said, pointing northward. "I'll ride on ahead and tell my brother to expect you, Vincent."

"Yeah, as if he doesn't already," he smirked.

The duke rode off with a wave and Vincent turned back to the slowly waking Darla.

Coldson interrupted again. "Lunch with the king?" His voice was filled with disbelief.

"Yup. Probably wants to get an answer from me about the land baron thing." He yawned. Then, seeing Coldson's continual befuddlement, he told him the story of how he had acquired the title of Baron and King Breigar's desire for him to take over Ghanol's duties for the area in which his keep would be located. "I'm not real thrilled with the prospect, but I suppose I have little choice," he concluded.

Coldson nodded. "I heard the story of how ye saved the duke's life, stickin' that assassin from a hundred feet away. Impressive, but nothin' like what I saw ye do with my own eyes."

Vincent opened his mouth to correct the man's outrageous exaggeration of the sword throw. Then he shook his head, realizing it wasn't worth it. Twenty feet, fifty feet, a hundred. What difference did it make what he thought? "Let's get going," he said quietly. And as Coldson urged the horses into motion, Vincent joined Darla, snuggling up next to her for the rest of the journey.

Coldson woke them as they came within sight of the castle. Vincent had only been on the edge of sleep the whole way, so waking was not difficult. Darla was slower to do so. He looked at her as she tried to fight off her weariness. She'd not been sleeping well, lately. Her rest was plagued with nightmares, as Vincent knew from the many times her tossing and turning had awakened him. She evidently didn't take well to this type of travel, he thought.

He gazed out of the wagon toward the castle. It was still a magnificent sight to him, though his heart was heavy as he remembered the last time he was here. With Ariaziane. He shook his head, then moved up to sit next to Coldson.

The sun was a good bit higher in the sky now, and Vincent estimated that their side journey had taken something like three hours. He glanced over at his driver and noticed that Coldson's face betrayed his anxiety. "What is it?" he asked.

The man turned to face him, smiling sheepishly. "I'm a bit nervous about meetin' the king," he admitted. "I've no idea what to say. I'm not the type of person..."

"Oh, stop it," Vincent said. "Breigar struck me as being a really decent fellow. Don't worry about that." Vincent found himself looking at Coldson in a different light. He felt bad for having thought of the man as only a ruffian, uncouth and uneducated. This concern on his part, this worry over what someone else would think of him, served to remind Vincent that Coldson was every bit as human as the next person. It showed that he had a desire, if not an outright need, to be accepted. Coldson had low self-esteem, something Vincent could easily identify with. He clapped the man on the shoulder. "You'll be well received."

Coldson smiled, thanking him for his words. Then he frowned. "Ye should not call the king by just his name, though."

Vincent laughed.

Before long, they had passed through the outer gates of the walled city. An escort of six mounted knights accompanied them through the streets and up to the castle itself. Vincent noted with wry humor the way Coldson held himself so straight and proper as he guided the wagon.

The wagons were commandeered by stablehands as they reached the castle, and Vincent and his entourage were led inside by a page. Once inside, it was Darla to whom Vincent paid attention, as the girl stared wide-eyed at the castle's lavish trappings. The halls were decorated with colorful tapestries and torches in ornate sconces. Some of the doors were virtual works of art, with bas-relief carvings in the beautiful wood. She turned to him and said, "Is this how you intend your keep to appear?"

Vincent snorted. "Hardly. I don't need to impress visitors the way a king does."

"You're impressive enough as it is," she said.

"Stop it."

The page stood aside after leading them into the same audience chamber where Vincent and King Breigar had first met. This time, however, the king was already there, dressed in fancy robes and perched on his great chair. Duke Ghanol stood at his right.

They stopped several feet in front of his chair. Vincent stood with Darla on his right, Coldson on his left. Darvas stood at the head of the group of his uncle's men.

"Welcome to Goldenbrook Castle," Breigar said, his voice resonating in the chamber.

Vincent smiled and was about to thank him for the welcome when Coldson dropped to one knee and bowed his head.

The king raised a royal eyebrow. "Is your boot lace undone?" As Coldson looked up at him in puzzlement, the king added, "Otherwise, stand, my friend."

Vincent nearly burst out laughing, seeing the expression on Coldson's face when the king called him "friend." But he sobered when he realized that he was in no position to laugh. Since coming to this world, he had to admit that he'd had it pretty good. Would the king have been so friendly toward him had he not saved his brother's life? And people like Coldson... What chance did the common folks have of meeting kings? And Coldson himself had even had it worse than most, having been enslaved for quite a number of years. He couldn't blame the man for being overwhelmed by this. And he certainly couldn't laugh.

Coldson rose, bowing tiny little bows as he did so. "My 'pologies, Yer Highness. I didn't know..."

The king waved it off. "Vincent, I must say, you have the most amazing ability to bring gorgeous women with you when you visit."

With a smile, Vincent introduced her. "I am happy to introduce you to the Lady Darla."

The king nodded his head. "A pleasure. I look forward to talking with you over dinner."

Vincent continued. "This nervous gentleman is known as Coldson. I believe you already know Darvas, captain of my guard. Temporary guard, that is." The king greeted Darvas with a smile. "He and the rest of the men are on loan from Baron Aedriun, escorting me to my new residence."

The king nodded politely at the group. "It is a pleasure to have you all here. I hope you will enjoy your visit. You are free to stay as long as you like, though I'm sure you're anxious to get to your new home, Vincent. I insist you stay the night at the very least, however. First, I'm sure many of you would enjoy a hot soak. The baths are being prepared even now, as are rooms for each of you. An assortment of edibles will be laid out by the time you're done bathing. At sunset, there will be a feast." He addressed the page, standing quietly by the doorway. "Please give our guests the tour." He smiled again at them all. "Again, welcome to Goldenbrook. I look forward to seeing you later. Vincent," he said, his smile taking on a forced appearance, "I would speak privately with you."

Vincent nodded as the men started to file out. "I'll join up with you later," he said to Darla, kissing her cheek. Coldson bowed awkwardly again to the king before following the rest of the men out into the hallway. Vincent turned his attention to the king, who was rising from his chair with the assistance of an ornately carved cane. He followed the king, noting that the man's limp was more pronounced than he recalled, as Breigar led him to a small chamber behind the reception room. Comfortable chairs awaited them. As they sat, Vincent looked around the room. He'd had something like this constructed in his own keep. A private room where important matters, if there ever were any, could be discussed. He gazed admiringly at the beautifully drawn map affixed to one wall. It showed not only the realm ruled by Breigar, but of all the known realms, it seemed.

The king cleared his throat and Vincent braced himself, expecting a discussion about his upcoming duties as baron. But the king's words shocked him. "Some time ago," he began, "Aedriun came to seek my advice and assistance with something that was troubling him."

Vincent settled himself into the large armchair and frowned. "When was this?"

The king waved his hand, dismissing the question. "When it was is not important. But the matter at hand, or more specifically, what I've learned since then, is *very* important." Vincent nodded and waited for him to continue. "Aedriun is troubled by the fact that someone is out to kill a very dear friend of his. And that his friend is seemingly unconcerned by it."

Vincent heaved a great sigh. "Look, this is really nothing to be concerned about."

"Is it not?" the king said flatly. "I believe it is."

"Well, it's my life, Your Highness," he replied sharply. "If I'm not concerned about it, no one else needs to be. Yes, he wants to kill me. So what?"

"It is not just about you, my young baron. If this man carries out his intentions, there could be far more destruction than that of your body."

Vincent cocked his head. "What do you know of his intentions?"

"I know nothing," the king admitted. "However, I suspect much."

"What do you mean?"

"Words have been drifting to me from scouts in various locations for quite a while. Until Aedriun told me about this man and his abilities, I had no reason to think anything of the reports. But now..." He spread his hands.

Vincent snorted. "*Man,*" he repeated. "He's a boy, Your Highness."

The king frowned. "Aedriun told me he was your lady Darla's twin."

"Yes," he agreed slowly, afraid of what the king was going to say next.

"My eyes may not be as sharp as once they were, but Darla appears to be at least your age, perhaps a year or two older. By all accounts, you are a man. Therefore, he would be, also."

Vincent felt a familiar knot form in his stomach, that nagging sense that things weren't all copacetic with Darla's aging process. He tried his best to ignore it and turned his attention back to the king. "Whatever," he said. "But what reports had you heard?"

King Breigar nodded. "It is said that in the ice mountains to the north, snow giants are on the move."

Vincent raised an eyebrow. "I recall reading of giants in the books of my friend Gnorrin, but I confess to never having been fully clear on them."

"As their name implies, they are huge creatures. Similar to men, but beastly. The snow giants stand well over three times the height of a man. Incredibly strong, fiercely territorial. It is odd that they are migrating. They typically stay put once they've established a homeland."

"What are you saying?"

"I am saying I suspect something to be causing them to move."

"You don't think it could be just a coincidence? Or something totally unknown? You form your conclusion without any evidence, just a hunch of yours and Aedriun's paranoia?"

The king paused for a moment, looking evenly at him. Vincent fought down a surge of fear, thinking he'd just pissed off the most powerful man in the land, when Breigar finally spoke. "If it were only the snow giants, I would have thought it merely a puzzling event. But from other lands, creatures are moving."

After a moment, Vincent said, "And none of these are creatures I'd want to meet in a dark alley, I'd imagine."

"Nor an open plain at mid-day."

"And let me guess. They're all converging on where my keep is built."

At this the king cleared his throat. "In fact, no. That is the part that causes me to have only suspicions rather than being convinced. The others are going to other locations, the destinations of which I do not know."

A cold chill washed through Vincent. "Where?"

The king rose and, leaning heavily on his cane, stepped over to the map. He pointed to a spot on its surface, at the northernmost edge, due north of Vincent's keep. "This icy land is home to the snow giants. Four weeks ago, my scouts spied six of them here." He moved his finger south, to a great expanse of forest. "This is not wholly unusual, but they continued to move south. My last report, a few days ago, showed them here." Now Breigar's finger traced its way around a huge lake that lay between the arms of a mountain chain. It stopped at the crotch of the valley. "By now they should be past these hills and into the mountains themselves. They require little sleep, you see. They travel quickly. It is obvious that these giants are traveling toward your keep."

"Fine," Vincent said hurriedly, "but the others. You mentioned others."

"Aye," the king agreed. "Over here," he said, moving to the far eastern side of the map and toward the middle, "is a great marshy area. My scouts have seen a horde of trolls leaving the swamps and traveling through this forest directly west of it."

Vincent blanched. "How far have they gone?" he whispered.

"Oh, they would still be in the forest, as far as I can tell. It was a recent report. Do you know what their destination is?"

"Yes," he croaked as the boy's voice drifted back to him. "*... it would be much more fun for me to watch you suffer, rather than kill you outright. I've decided to hurt those you love.*" He firmed his jaw. "Yes," he repeated. "If your suspicion is correct, and I admit to the likelihood of it, then they are heading for Port Remil. They are heading for my friends." He sighed deeply, shaking his head. This couldn't really be happening. Was the kid really that powerful, that he could summon beasts from hundreds of leagues away? He looked back up at the map. "Across the bay from Port Remil, to the northwest. Are there any creatures heading toward that forest?"

The king frowned. "I'm afraid so," he said, moving his hand to the northeast of the forest some forty-five leagues. "Scouts near this hilly region have spotted a pack of mountain wolves moving toward that forest."

"Mountain wolves?" That was a new one to Vincent.

Breigar nodded. "Similar to the wolves you are no doubt familiar with, but much larger, more vicious, and quite a bit smarter."

"Dogs," Vincent whispered. "Against the cat-lady." He rubbed his head.

"Keep in mind," the king continued, "that there could be more. My scouts are not everywhere. There is also no reason to think that the six giants are the sum total of them. More could be following in their wake."

Vincent nodded, his heart sinking. Then he looked up at the king with a frown. "How are you able to obtain information so quickly from your scouts? Those areas you indicated on your map are many weeks' travel from here by the swiftest horse. Yet you seem to be right on top of the information."

King Breigar looked at him for a long time, as if considering whether to answer him or not. Then he smiled faintly. "I'll show you."

The king led Vincent to another private chamber, this one on the second level of the castle. It was a small room, not much larger than the one they'd just left, and there was minimal seating. One great chair sat in the middle of the back wall. Around the room stood what appeared to be dozens of mirrors, oval in shape, mounted on stands and facing the chair. King Breigar moved to the chair and sat, motioning Vincent to stand beside him. As he did so, Vincent noticed that the mirrors weren't mirrors at all, but seemed to be thin ovals of obsidian or some other glossy black stone. He frowned in confusion.

"What are these?" he asked. In reply, the king reached out a hand toward the nearest one. A pale beam of light surged forth from his outstretched fingertip, striking the black surface. Immediately, the oval began to glow with a light of its own. Breigar lowered his hand and they watched as an image coalesced into view. Vincent shot a look at the king. "You're a mage!"

"A very minor one," the king admitted. "My political skills far outstrip my magical abilities, let me assure you."

"Yes, Your Majesty," came a voice from the scrying stone that Breigar had brought to life.

Vincent turned and beheld a face looking out of the stone. He knew immediately that this was one of the king's many scouts.

"Good day, Alaris," said the king. "How fare you?"

"Quite well, my liege. How may I assist you?"

"Merely a social call today. I'd like you to meet my friend Baron Vincent. I'm giving him the show of my command room, as it were."

Alaris gave a slight bow, which made Vincent slightly uncomfortable. "Baron Vincent, it is an honor. Duke Ghanol is much loved by his men. We are indebted to you for preventing us from losing him."

"My pleasure," said Vincent.

The king nodded. "Very well, Alaris. Continue your excellent work."

"My liege, I shall."

And with that, the stone went dark. "How cool," Vincent said. "And all of these stones are somehow devoted to one specific scout of yours?"

"Not quite all. There are some I reserve for special occasions. I have spent many hours here over the past weeks, since Aedriun voiced his concerns."

"Quite impressive." Vincent frowned. "What do I do now? I have to warn my friends. They can't come to harm because of me. I'd never be able to live with myself."

"If you tell me how to find your friends, it should be possible for my scouts to reach them before they are attacked. My only concern is what might happen when it is discovered that your friends have departed."

"What do you mean?"

"You believe his goal is to harm your friends as a way to harm you, yes?" Vincent nodded in agreement. "If your friends run, will he have the creatures follow them, or will he have them wreak destruction on whomever and whatever they encounter?"

A good question, Vincent thought. There was no question that Darla's brother was mentally unstable. But he also seemed rather directed. "I don't think he would cause random destruction. He wants me. It's a personal thing."

King Breigar nodded. "I hope you are correct."

At the king's request, Vincent gave directions to the homes of Blade and Felina. He also asked for a scout to be sent to Gnorrin, just in case there were other creatures en route that they'd not discovered. He wished he knew where Ariaziane and Rhia were. He hated to think that his enemy might know their whereabouts when he himself did not. That thought was a cruel blow.

Breigar brought the appropriate stones to life and notified his scouts of their new duties. All of Vincent's friends would be notified of their impending danger and, at Breigar's suggestion, would make their way to Vincent's keep. Vincent didn't feel very happy about that decision, but admitted he could not think of a better idea. He knew that D'Ty would have to uproot his new family to run away from a danger brought on them only because he was Vincent's friend. It made him feel like crap.

After the last of the scouts had been notified and the stone faded to dark again, Vincent let out a long, depressed breath. "I should be on my way as early as possible tomorrow."

The king agreed. "Aye. But for now, you need to relax. Refresh yourself with a bath and have something to eat. There is a feast tonight and I would have you in good spirits for it."

Vincent sighed. "Easier said than done."

On the way to the room he was sharing with Darla, he grabbed a freshly baked roll and ate it as he climbed the stairs. And despite his doubts, he did relax in the bath. In fact, he fell asleep in the tub, it was so soothing. He hadn't realized how exhausted he'd been.

He woke some time later, the water now cool rather than steaming. He frowned at his shriveled fingers as he stepped out of the tub and wrapped the soft white robe around himself. Back in his room, Darla was dressing for the feast. She looked splendid in a deep green dress with white trim at the neck and sleeves. He embraced her, kissed her, then sat her down on the edge of the bed.

She needed to know what was happening. So he told her everything the king had said, explaining about the approaching minions of her brother. To Vincent's surprise, she became quite upset. "My fault," she whispered.

"Why your fault?" he asked. "It's me he wants to kill. How is that your fault?"

She looked up into his eyes. "Because he wants me. He wants to *kill* you, but he wants to *own* me." She looked down at her hands. "Mother once told me that she feared for his mind. That at some point he just…"

"Snapped?"

Darla raised her eyebrows. "A curious analogy, but a good one."

"It certainly seems like he's a bit unstable."

"And unfortunately, very powerful."

"Do you think I was right? Will he call off his attacks if my friends are gone?"

She thought about this for a moment. "I believe so. I hope so." She squeezed his leg and rose. "But you must ready for the feast. The king is expecting us shortly."

Vincent took a deep breath and stood, doffing the robe. "Must've slept longer than I thought."

"And you should stop sleeping in the bath. The bed is much more comfortable."

He chuckled as he drew on his tunic. "True, but I get more sleep in the tub than in bed with you."

"And what is that supposed to mean?"

"It means that when we're in bed together, we don't do a lot of sleeping."

Vincent was stepping into his breeches, one foot on the ground and the other in mid-pant leg, when Darla pushed him in mock indignation. He toppled over, caught his feet in the fabric, and landed roughly on the floor. He rolled onto his back, laughing. Darla giggled, too, then threw herself on top of him. Before long, they were well on their way to being late for the feast.

Vincent hated the fact that a page announced their arrival to the feast. They stood in the doorway to the feasting hall momentarily while eyes turned their way. Then they were escorted to the king's table. Breigar merely smiled knowingly at their flushed faces as they seated themselves.

Glancing around, Vincent noticed there were quite a few people present. All Aedriun's men, plus about fifty others. Members of the king's court, he assumed. A quartet of musicians played in a corner.

The king's table also seated Duke Ghanol, Darvas, several people Vincent did not know, and to the amazement of no one more than himself, Coldson. Vincent nearly laughed as he saw the look of sick anxiety on the man's face. The king introduced them to everyone at the table, and Vincent promptly forgot each and every name and title. He had too much on his mind to clutter it up with trivia.

The feast was mostly a blur to Vincent. If pressed later, he would be able to remember that there had been plenty of fresh baked goods, roasted fowl, and a thin, cool soup that tasted of mint and something akin to carrots. He would be able to state that the king spent several minutes speaking to Darvas, inquiring of Aedriun's health and activities. He would recall that he himself answered several questions from the strangers at the table.

But his attention was only on the words King Breigar had spoken to him earlier. And not just the news about the impending attacks. He also thought long and hard about what the king had said about Darla's apparent age. Was he wrong to keep ignoring it? Did he subconsciously know the truth, but was avoiding it by making excuses?

His train of thought was derailed suddenly by the king's words. "Tell us how you came into Baron Vincent's acquaintance, Coldson."

Coldson's discomfort faded. Or rather, Vincent thought, it hopped down the table to land squarely on Vincent's shoulders. He felt the butterflies in his stomach begin to flutter even as a large smile bloomed on the former slave's face.

Vincent smiled, too, but in an embarrassed, self-conscious way. He had to admit, though, that Coldson wasn't as prone to exaggeration as some people were. Then again, the story didn't need any embellishments.

"First thing we noticed," Coldson began, "was this noise. Like somethin' bangin' on the hull. From where I was, I couldn't see it, but the noise was from Lord Vincent's sword, pokin' right through the timbers!"

Vincent cringed, as usual, at the title Coldson had used. He began to be acutely aware of the eyes boring into him.

"We all stopped rowin', of course, because we just couldn't believe anyone could be so strong enough to stick his sword through the side of a ship. Then, when he'd made a circle of holes, he punched it out." Coldson paused, nodding at the murmurs around the table. "That's right! He punched it right out!" He clenched his fist to illustrate, then frowned. "Er... rather, he punched it right *in*, I suppose. At any rate, he came inside the hold and freed us all." He shook his head. "I missed a lot of what happened after that. But then his lady friend sunk the ship! She flew way up in the air and dropped a huge boulder at the deck!" Coldson was becoming quite animated now, which was fine with Vincent, since it took attention off himself. "It was amazing! It slammed down through the whole ship! This big fountain shot up out through the hole!" He paused then, his face growing concerned. "Trouble was, Lord Vincent was caught in some riggin' lines. When the boat sunk, he sunk with it. But nobody knew it."

The eyes returned to focus on him, now that Coldson had mentioned this particular fact. He smiled tentatively, shrugged his shoulders a bit. But he really wished the man would just shut up. He hated the fact that the king had requested the tale. Was Coldson's ease more important than his own?

"It was his lady friend who found him. She dove down and cut him loose. But it was a long time later. Longer'n any normal man could possibly hold his breath, even if he wasn't knocked out. We all knew he was dead when she dropped him on the deck of the other ship." Coldson looked down the table at him. His eyes were filled with admiration. "But he wasn't. Obviously."

There was much applause for Coldson's tale. Vincent sincerely hoped that most people considered it exactly that. A tale. Questions were aimed at him, but fortunately, dessert was served then. It was a baked pudding that seemed to melt in his mouth. It was so good that the questions died out. And as soon as the feast was over and people began to mingle and dance, Vincent and Darla excused themselves from the king and went to bed.

They left at first light, or shortly thereafter. Coldson, it seemed, had become the life of the party after they'd left, and had a little too much to drink. He was difficult to rouse in the morning and moved slowly even then. Vincent was thankful that the wagons practically drove themselves, once on the road. He expected Coldson to be snoozing much of the way today.

Breigar was not awake to see them off, but that was fine with Vincent. He was exhausted, too, and wanted only to crawl into his sleeping furs and rest. He hadn't slept much through the night, his mind racing with the images of what the king had said to him earlier in the day.

He slept as they drove, on and off. Darla napped with him, but also spent some time relieving Coldson at the reins. She seemed to enjoy it.

Day passed into night, into day, on and on. Another week went by, and each day, Vincent became more and more caught up in his thoughts. They passed the northern edge of a small forest, then the southern tip of a hilly region. On the tenth day after leaving Goldenbrook, they reached the second river.

No ferry was needed for this one, however. It was a dry time of year in this area and the water was shallow enough for the horses and wagons to traverse unaided. There were spots where the water nearly reached the bottoms of the wagons, but not quite. And as it was a narrow stretch of the river, it was over and done with before Vincent even had time to worry about it.

After crossing the river, they left the trade route. They turned north and followed the river, heading away from Falconwall. From here on, the journey would not be quite so easy. The roads were not as well traveled and the towns fewer and further between. Vincent began paying closer attention to the land. They would soon be entering *his* lands, those over which he would have charge. The thought made him at once proud and nauseous.

A few days later, Darla voiced her frustrations. "You've been so quiet and withdrawn. Are you upset about something?"

He looked her in the eyes and knew he had been wrong to keep everything inside. "Not upset," he said, "but yes, there have been things on my mind."

"I can understand that. I hope the king's scouts were able to persuade your friends to leave."

"I'm sure they were, but that wasn't my concern." He sighed. "I don't know how to bring it up, exactly. We've discussed it before."

"It is about my appearance again, isn't it?"

Vincent nodded. "Yes. Even the king commented on the fact that you look to be my age. Yet you first appeared years younger." He paused, then said, "Darla, how old are you?"

He saw her eyes widen ever so slightly. She turned her face away. "You would not believe me," she whispered.

"Look, if I can believe Rhia is over a hundred, I can believe you."

She looked up at him again, took a deep breath, and said, "I am six years old."

He blinked. Then he snorted in laughter. "Okay, you got me. Now really..."

Darla's eyes turned sad. "Vincent, I cannot lie to you. I am six years old. Believe me or not, it is still the truth."

There was no tingle in his brain to indicate a lie. He frowned, staring at her, rolling her words over again in his head. Six years old. The thought hit him like a blow. His mouth opened, closed, opened. Words formed slowly. "But, you look more like, I dunno, anywhere from twenty to twenty-five."

"I seem to age at approximately four times the rate of a normal human." As the light of understanding began dimly to glow in his head, Darla continued. In a soft voice, she said, "I had hoped you would never ask me that question, Vincent. The last thing I wanted to do was to hurt you."

491

He spoke slowly. "Why would you say that? You haven't hurt me. Okay. If you say you're six years old, you're six years old. But physically you aren't, so I can hardly be a pedophile."

"A what?"

"Sorry. A word on my world for someone who is fond of little children. *Very* fond of them, you might say." The light grew in his head. "Darla, if you're only six, how did you learn so much? How did you learn magic, for that matter?" He was growing more confused by the second.

"Our mother taught us magic and educated us using magic. Much of the knowledge we have was put into our heads by her, not by us. We did not learn to speak, for example, as a normal child would. Mother planted the words and the meanings of them in our heads, as she did with most everything. She thinks, and so do I, that this is partly why my brother went mad."

As understanding grew, Vincent's breath came in short gasps. His mind flashed back to the day he'd first really talked with Darla, back at Felina's. The day Darla asked him to guess her name. He remembered the sudden inspiration of syllables. *Dar... La...* He gasped sharply.

"Darella!" This realization also felt like a blow, but one wearing gauntlets of strength. Darella was her mother! He'd missed the middle syllable and latched onto "Darla." He'd said that name, and she'd agreed to it. Then she'd told him that her father had named her Darla. He turned wide, horror-stricken eyes upon her. She was six years old. He'd been in this world for slightly longer than that. And he'd had sex with Darella. "You're... You're muh... muh... my..."

Darla's voice was soft as she completed his sentence. "Daughter."

Vincent's breath came in great heaves as he heard the words. "You're my *daughter!*"

Coldson stirred in his seat, looking back over his shoulder, a puzzled frown on his face. "How's that, m'lord?"

Turning a panicked face to the man, he said, "What? Nothing! How's what?"

"Beg yer pardon. Thought to hear ye say the lady was yer daughter!" He laughed. "Ears be gettin' old," he said to himself as he turned back around.

"Vincent, my love," Darla began, her voice pleading.

"Don't call me that!" he blurted. "You can't call me that!"

"Why not?"

"Because! Because I'm..." He lowered his voice. "Because you're..." He sighed. "Because of our relationship."

"But..."

"No! Please." He ran sweaty hands through his hair. "Just let me get used to this, okay?" He let out a deep breath as Darla sat quietly, pulling her knees up under her chin. He stepped out beside Coldson, then to the side step on the wagon. He saw Darvas on his horse not far off and waved him down.

Darvas trotted over to the wagon. After a few words, they exchanged places, Darvas sitting with Coldson on the wagon and Vincent astride Darvas's mount. After thanking his friend, he took off, heading down the road well ahead of the wagon train.

He had a lot of thinking to do.

He stayed out on his own for the remainder of the day, deep in his thoughts. For most of the time, his brain was numb with shock. Darla was his daughter. The dream he'd had so long ago, the one Rhia said wasn't a dream. Here was proof that she was right. He'd copulated with Darella after coming through the portal. And, evidently only a few months later, she'd given birth to twins.

Darla and her brother. Two more dissimilar children one could not imagine. Darla was full of goodness, her brother evil incarnate.

Darla loved her father (and his mind shuddered to think how much) and her brother...his own son...wanted to kill him. Came very close to it on two occasions, in fact, he admitted.

The boy had killed a friend, his sister restored life to her.

He was a father. That thought alone was enough to floor him.

But he'd been having sex with his daughter! No, he corrected himself. He'd been making love to her. There was a difference, after all.

Nevertheless, that was behind him now. He had to accept the fact that it had happened, but it must never happen again. Not that he felt there was any danger of it. The idea had an effect quite the opposite of arousal.

Day grew into night and still he couldn't bring himself to return to the caravan. He sat on a small knoll, picking idly at the grass, fighting off the evening chill. Darvas' horse stood nearby, occasionally snorting. He gazed periodically at the wagons, perhaps five hundred yards away, and the campfire that looked so welcoming and warm.

His hyperactive hearing could pick up the jumble of conversation easily. If he tried, he was sure he could pick out individual conversations. Eventually, his curiosity got the better of him.

"... perhaps another three, four days..."

"... rain tomorrow, you think?"

"... gone this long." There, that was Darvas' voice. Vincent focused on it.

"He's deep troubled, that much is sure." Coldson, Vincent recognized.

"Aye. And he said nothing to you?"

There was a slight hesitation before Coldson replied. "Nothin', I'm afraid."

"Very puzzling."

Vincent could picture Darvas rubbing his chin as he so often did when trying to figure out a problem. He nearly smiled despite himself.

"I'm just worried about the lady Darla," Coldson said more quietly. "She's not come out of the wagon all day."

Vincent frowned, then tried to pinpoint Darla. It helped that he knew even the sound of her breathing. His heart sank as he heard another familiar sound. The sound of her softly crying.

He blotted it out, blotted them all out, put his hands over his ears and rocked back and forth. "Shut up!" he sobbed. "Shut up!" Soon enough, the only sound he could hear was his own sobbing.

He cried for many minutes, his tears coming from a multitude of sources. Not just the incestuous relationship he'd unknowingly been having, but from the pain of the loss of Rhia and Ariaziane. His life here was becoming unbearable. For the first time in many months, his thoughts turned strongly to Earth. He wanted to go home. Desperately wanted to go home.

And then, a thought struck him. The tears stopped and he looked up from his crouched position. He sniffled, then cleared his throat. The Seeker Portal.

Darla would know where the portal was. Rhia said that Darella would have stayed with the portal, studying it. Therefore, Darla and her brother would have been raised right there, in that cave. Surely she could tell him where it was, lead him to it.

He could go home! He could...

He could get creamed by her brother, that's what he could do.

Okay, he thought, so she would know where it was. It would take more than that knowledge to get him home. Still, it was a start.

He had to question her. Now. He shoved his other concerns out of his head, including the incest issue, got slowly to his feet, and began walking Darvas' horse back to the caravan.

Halfway there, he met Coldson, who greeted him formally, though not warmly.

"I was looking for ye," he said flatly. "Ye've got us all worried."

"I know," he admitted. "I'm sorry."

"Yer lady has been cryin' since sundown." Vincent swallowed the lump of guilt in his throat, but could find no words to say. "Vincent," Coldson went on, shocking him by not using any honorific, "I know I'm nothin' to ye. I'm no equal or peer. But I want ye to know that I'd do anything for ye."

"I know that," Vincent began.

"And that includes tellin' ye when ye're behavin' like a fool." Coldson lowered his eyes. "Forgive me, but that's just how it is."

"What do you mean?"

"Why did ye run off like that?"

"I really don't wish to discuss it."

"It has somethin' to do with what ye said this morning, doesn't it?"

A shock ran through him. "What did you hear?"

Though no one was within earshot, Coldson lowered his voice. "About Darla bein' yer daughter?"

Vincent forced a laugh. "That's preposterous. We're virtually the same age!"

"Aye. That's what most people believe." He paused. "Isn't it?"

Coldson had heard everything, Vincent suddenly realized. He knew everything. But he was keeping it to himself. He hadn't told Darvas, and he knew the man wouldn't tell anyone at all. Not even the king. He could see it in his eyes.

"I don't know what to say," he whispered.

Coldson smiled. "About what? Nothin' to say, I don't think. Except that we should get back. The men are concerned and yer lady Darla is still cryin'."

"She's not my lady any longer."

Coldson was quiet a moment, but finally said, "Is that wise, m'lord?"

"What do you mean?" Vincent fairly laughed. "How *can* she be?"

"No, I understand yer meanin'," the man continued. "But I'm thinking of the men. All they've seen is Darla in tears because ye went runnin' off. One reputation ye don't want tarnished is that of being a gentleman, if ye follow my meanin'."

"I'm afraid I don't. I don't give a damn about reputations, Coldson."

"Lord Vincent, please. Trust me. I know ye've no reason to, really. But I know what I'm talkin' about."

He stared at the man for many moments, then frowned. "Let's go," he said, and started walking.

For the remainder of the walk, Vincent pondered Coldson's words. Was the man right? Did he need to maintain some sort of image in front of Aedriun's men? He certainly didn't want Aedriun to think he was a dickhead or anything.

No, he thought. It didn't matter. Darla would help him find the portal and he'd be out of here post haste, as it were. It wouldn't matter what anyone thought.

But what if she wouldn't take him to it? What if she wouldn't even tell him where it was? What if her brother were still there, guarding it, as was likely to be the case? Darella, too, for that matter.

He picked up Darla's sobbing again, fainter this time, as though she were crying herself to sleep and had nearly achieved the goal. His heart ached to know that he had caused her this pain. His own pain was great, but obviously, hers was greater.

Somehow, it seemed that Darla found nothing wrong with having sex with her own father. That was no surprise, he realized when he thought about it. Darella wouldn't have wasted time planting societal mores into her kids' heads when other things were so much more important.

Nevertheless, whether what they had done was morally wrong or not, he knew he couldn't bear having caused such pain to her. This thought became stronger and stronger in his head and he began walking faster and faster. Finally, he tossed the reins of Darvas' horse to Coldson and broke into a run.

The men around the campfire saw him coming and all conversation abruptly ceased. Vincent ignored them, dashing straight for his wagon. He stopped as he reached it and stood there self-consciously. Then he climbed up and in.

Darla looked up as he entered, tears still wet on her cheeks and surprise in her eyes. She sat up, opened her mouth to speak, but Vincent shook his head. "No," he said quietly. "Don't speak. Allow me." He sat next to her and reached a hand out to wipe away tears. "I'm so sorry. I was just so shocked by what you told me. I had to get out, clear my head, you know?"

She nodded. "I understand," she said thickly. "Forgive me. I should have told you from the start."

"It's okay. I wouldn't have taken the news any better then."

"Yes, you would have. You wouldn't have bedded me."

He ignored the guilty twinge that produced. "True." He smiled grimly. "Forgive me for running out like that?"

"Already done," she said. She took a shaky breath. "Would you hold me?"

He wanted nothing more than to pick her brain about the portal. But that could wait. They had the rest of the journey to discuss that. And perhaps that would be better in private, anyway. "Sure," he said, and reached out to embrace her, trying to manufacture paternal feelings where lust had once been. It wasn't easy.

He held her tightly, just as tightly as she held him. She laid her head against his shoulder and nuzzled her face into his neck. "I'm sorry," she whispered again.

"It's okay," he replied, realizing that paternal feelings just weren't forthcoming. So he tried instead to ignore how nice her body felt next to his, how soft and warm and inviting. "I don't ever want to hurt you like that again."

"Nor I, you."

He chuckled slightly. "I really doubt that would be possible. You don't have any other deep, dark secrets, do you?" he joked.

To his surprise, he felt her stiffen against him. He frowned. She pulled back, still holding him, but looking into his face. "Yes."

A rush of panic swept through him. "What?"

She smiled meekly. "We're going to have a baby."

                           ❧ ❧

Perfect, he thought, the way things were proceeding. As he had hoped, his father's damnable luck had allowed him to discover the impending attacks on his friends. But that was fine. He'd expected it. Now, thanks to scouts sent forth from the king, Vincent's friends were packing up and moving out. Heading, if he were not mistaken, for their friend's newly constructed keep.

This was good. It would be so much nicer for him to be able to kill all his father's friends while Vincent helplessly watched. Knowing his friends were in danger and he could do nothing about it was one thing. But being helpless while nearby and watching was far more delicious.

So part one of his plan was complete. Soon he would confront his father in person. He toyed with the medallion he wore around his neck. This gift from his mother would be his most powerful defensive weapon. His father would not stand a chance. He'd gotten incredibly lucky in their last encounter. Plus there was the betrayal by his sister, for which she still had to pay.

This time, however, his father would die. Slowly. Painfully.

He smiled. How anxious he was for the games to begin.

❧ Thirty-Four ❧

The remainder of the trip was a blur to Vincent. After Darla's pregnancy revelation, he became quite ill. He was certain that it was all nerves, but that didn't change the fact that he had absolutely no appetite and chose to spend the majority of his time huddled into his sleeping furs. Finally, they arrived at the foot of the mountain into which Vincent's keep had been built. Coldson alerted him when they were near, and Vincent joined him at the front of the wagon. He looked up the face of the peak. It was, he had to admit, a striking sight. Twin towers rose up the face of the mountainside, seemingly carved out of the mountain's rock itself, rather than being attached to it. He allowed himself to feel a spark of satisfaction before falling back into his funk.

Climbing the trail up to the plateau was horrendously slow, but Vincent paid no attention to the time or effort involved. He sat numb in his seat, trying to rid himself of a three-day headache and attempting to make heads or tails of the family tree he'd planted. Darla was his daughter and she was pregnant. The baby would be his child as well as his grandchild. Easy enough to understand. Where it got bizarre was from the child's viewpoint. Its father would be its grandfather, while its mother would also be its grandmother, by virtue of being married to its grandfather, if in fact it came to marriage. Can't expect a kid to comprehend that kind of stuff, he told himself.

That thought never failed to bring him back to something like reality. It might actually be easier for the kid to think of Darla as his or her grandmother. By the time the child grew old enough to really notice such things, Darla's physical age would be well beyond Vincent's. And she would unfortunately die well before her time. It was a shame, he thought, that the little one would grow up without its mother for most of its life.

Then again, he thought, it could be that the child would age rapidly, too. Either way, it was a crime. The kid would be robbed of its mother quickly or they *both* would live accelerated lives.

Inside him, there was a war. On one side was the urge to do nothing but find his way home, to have Darla take him to the Seeker Portal and somehow make it send him to Earth. But on the other side was the need to take responsibility for his actions, to be a father and, yes, a husband, if that's what it took. That thought, however, made his stomach do even more flip-flops. He frowned, trying to push the conflict aside in order to deal with the present.

Eventually, all the wagons stood before the keep. Three doors faced them: one massive central door for the main entrance, and two smaller doors that led directly to the stables and some storage areas. It was through these doors that the wagons drove.

When Vincent's wagon was inside, he hopped down from his seat, then helped Darla descend. Blaise bounded out and immediately began her inspection of the other wagons, making sure everything was to her liking. The barren, cavernous area into which they'd drawn wasn't as dark as he'd expected. Since the front part of the keep extended out onto the plateau and was not totally surrounded by mountain, Feletain had put many small, shuttered windows in the walls through which sunlight streamed in. Coldson stepped down and faced him.

"I'll fetch some furs, then we'll get ye up to yer sleeping quarters. Ye need rest."

"I've been doing nothing but rest the last three days," he protested.

"Nay, ye've been doing nothin' but moan and sleep fitfully. Not much restin' been goin' on, m'lord."

"Coldson is correct," Darla said. "Please listen to him."

"Ye're home," Coldson continued. "Is there a rush in unpacking?"

"No, not as such," Vincent replied. Then he nodded to Darvas as he approached. Vincent addressed him. "You and your men are welcome to stay as long as you like. However, the lodgings won't be very comfortable. These loads are only the beginning, and I would not have your men sleeping on the stone floors."

Darvas cleared his throat. "Yes. Well, regarding that..." He reached inside his cloak and pulled out a sealed scroll. "My instructions were to present this to you upon our arrival."

Vincent took the scroll, recognizing Aedriun's signet imprint in the wax. With a suspicious glance at the slightly smiling Darvas, he broke the seal. He unrolled it, scanning quickly. "Oh, come on." He fixed Darvas with a penetrating look. "No. I won't have this."

"What is it?" Darla both said.

Darvas answered. "It is a document from my uncle stating that the men who accompanied you on this trip are now Vincent's men, including myself." He turned his attention back to Vincent. "A baron cannot function alone, you must realize. And I assure you it was a fairly done thing. My uncle asked for volunteers."

Vincent stared at him. "Volunteers?"

Darvas shrugged. "I cannot think of why they did so," he said sarcastically. "Perhaps they chose to be nearer to Falconwall."

"Why did you volunteer?"

"Sick of the smell of fish around Linnael," he said with a smile.

Vincent sighed deeply. "Well. First things first. I am going to take Coldson's advice and get some rest. I'll speak with you later about this situation." He shook the scroll in his young friend's face.

Darvas laughed. "Very good." He turned and headed back to the other wagons.

"I'll start settin' up the kitchen," said Coldson, who turned with a nod and headed toward the galley wagon.

"Thank you," Vincent said. "The men will be hungry before long."

After a few steps, Coldson stopped and turned back. "Er... Where is the kitchen?"

With a chuckle, Vincent gave him directions and the man continued with his task.

Once again in relative privacy, Darla said, "Aedriun is very generous in giving up some of his men for you. I do not think you should refuse him."

"I know," he replied softly. "But I feel guilty for so often taking advantage of the goodwill of others."

"Guilty?" Darla said, her eyebrows rising. "Why? You're one of the most generous people I've ever met. Would you have others feel guilty about accepting your generosity?"

"It's not the same, Darla."

"It is very much the same, and you know it. Why do you so often persist in denying that which is so readily apparent?"

He shrugged. "I dunno. I'm an idiot?"

Darla smiled. "Not quite. Just set in your ways."

"Who? Me?" Vincent teased. And just to see what it felt like, he made a valiant attempt to give her a fatherly hug. It was the first time in a while that he'd embraced her, which is why it didn't quite work the way he'd intended.

Darla beamed and returned the hug, then pulled his face down to hers and kissed him in a decidedly un-daughterlike fashion. "Go get some rest," she said with a smile that suddenly turned wicked, "Daddy."

As she walked away to assist Darvas and the others, Vincent felt the blood drain from his face. He frowned as he stepped to the back of the wagon he'd arrived in. Obviously, a father/daughter relationship would not work until Darla started acting like a daughter. He grabbed a few sleeping furs and a satchel from the wagon and headed to the main hallway of the keep's ground floor. Then again, he said to himself, what experience did she really have in being a daughter? Darella certainly couldn't have been much of a mother.

"Greetings, Baron," came a familiar voice behind him. He turned, looking up the hall to see Feletain approaching. "I apologize for not being here to greet you, but I was topside when you arrived."

"I had no idea you'd still be here," Vincent said. "I thought you said you'd be in Falconwall."

"My men are, taking a well-deserved rest, now things are complete."

Vincent nodded. "And why are you not with them?"

"I remained in order to make certain that all is to your satisfaction, naturally."

"Well, thank you. It is nice to see you, and I look forward to inspecting everything with you. But not right now. I am not feeling well and need to rest."

"I understand. Tomorrow, then?"

"Certainly. For now, however, I'd greatly appreciate if you would familiarize some people here with the keep's layout. A gentleman named Coldson is currently trying to locate the kitchen. And Darvas, the captain of the guard, is overseeing the unloading of the wagons. Would you mind?"

"I'll see to it. Rest well."

Vincent thanked him and made his way upstairs to his sleeping chamber. Stepping inside, he paused. "Whoa," he breathed. The room was beautiful. It still lacked furniture, but Feletain's crew had outdone themselves in every possible regard. The walls were all stone, but the stone was gorgeous. Unlike the grey rock of the mountain, the stone here was varying shades of brown. Colorful striations ran through, and somehow the dwarves had cut it in such a way as to make the natural beauty of the rock dominate the room. It was like having a suite in the Grand Canyon.

One wall had closets built into it, to Vincent's specification. Beautiful sliding doors of coarsely grained wood held deep storage space, full of hanging hooks and shelves. The doors had tiny wheels on the bottoms and rolled along in shallow grooves carved into the stone floor.

He tossed the furs on the floor, dropped his satchel and opened it. Inside were some fresh clothes, as well as certain necessary items. One of these was his journal. Arranging the furs, he made himself comfortable, then set about writing.

Well, here I am. My new home. Shame I can't seem to work up much excitement about it.

I'm still in shock, obviously. I mean, who could blame me? It's not every day you find out your lover is actually your daughter, and that you've gotten her pregnant. I'm amazed I didn't faint dead away when she told me. Nausea, yes. Oblivion, no.

I'd entertained the notion of just trying to go home, with Darla's assistance. But impending fatherhood sort of knocked that idea from my head. Like it or not, I'm going to be a daddy. I'll have to start getting used to it.

It's been a while since my brother's kids were babies. Wonder if I can remember how to deal with one.

And then there's Aedriun's men. Or rather, my men. All those who accompanied us on the trip, including Darvas, are now under my command, so to speak. On my payroll, anyway. I'm more than a little uncomfortable with that. Not the payroll part. The responsibility part.

I guess I just never expected to have a "command" at all. I pictured this keep in the mountains as some sort of fortress of solitude. I'd become a hermit or something and not worry about the affairs of the world outside. I still like that idea.

And, also like it or not, I might actually need these men. Darla's brother is mounting an attack on me. I certainly can't defend this place alone. I have no idea why he hates me so much. Well, that's not true. I have a theory, anyway.

He and Darla are twins. It's no secret that twins have a bond that is above and beyond that of most siblings. Darla has told me how close they were as children, how they'd seem to be thinking the same things, how they'd finish each others' sentences. Very close.

And I ripped them apart. Darla followed my life in her mother's crystal ball. Her brother didn't like this, as it reduced her time with him. He became insanely jealous, eventually with the emphasis decidedly on the insane part. The "education" Darella gave her kids couldn't have been easy on the psyche. His couldn't take it. Especially combined with the jealousy he was feeling and the onset of the horrible period of life known as puberty. Everything was stacked against him. And he couldn't handle it.

So he sees me as being the cause of it. Darla turned against him. He only really saw it the day he attacked Felina, but in truth, she'd done it long before. Perhaps he realizes that, too. Either way, I am the target of his revenge. Whether deserved or not, that's what it seems to be coming to.

☙ ❧

The following week was a bustle of activity. Feletain showed him around the keep and Vincent approved of everything he saw. Feletain fairly swelled with pride over his handiwork. Vincent delivered final payment to him, to be distributed to his crew in the city.

Vincent sent a courier to Jaz's keep with a letter inviting him to come down for a visit. Darvas took several empty wagons and a handful of men and made the trek south to Falconwall with the intention of purchasing bedding and other necessities for Vincent's new men. Feletain went with him, advising Vincent of where he could be found for quite a while, should he need to contact him for any reason. Darvas was also instructed to hire a chef for the keep, as well as any other help he could find.

While they were away, Vincent and the rest set up all the goods that they had brought with them. Vincent's chambers now held a bed and bureaus. The kitchen was stocked with dried goods and cooking utensils. And the main reception hall was decked with tapestries and a few paintings.

Vincent marveled at the variety of things that Coldson was capable of doing. He had been the main cook on duty all throughout the journey from Linnael. He still did all the cooking and was a natural when it came to supervising others. And he took on the role of being Vincent's advisor and confidante, even though Vincent felt he didn't need one. It still amazed Vincent that the man knew the truth of his relationship with Darla and kept it secret. Not only that, but he didn't seem to think much of it.

Was incest not taboo on this world? He had to admit that was a possibility. But if so, why then did Rhia not want him to know the relationship he had with Darla? And why go to such an extreme length to prevent him from learning the truth? It certainly seemed to be out of character for Rhia to do something so intrusive. Or was it?

If he knew Rhia, and he thought he did, at least as well as a human *could* know a witch, she likely had several things under consideration when she'd decided to cast the spell upon him. She probably had gleaned, from their many discussions of Earth and its culture, that incest was considered off-limits there, even if it weren't here. Then again, it certainly could be, here. He couldn't rule that out.

Then there was the fact that Darla was his daughter. Rhia knew that. She knew he'd try to persuade Darla to lead him to the Seeker Portal. If he'd done so, Darla's brother would have killed him. So there was obviously the concern for his own safety.

But was that enough? He couldn't say. What other factors were there?

Felina's death, for one. Despite the fact that she and Darla were able to revive the elf, it still didn't change the fact that Rhia had seen a lover die before her eyes. That had to have traumatized her.

He ran over things one more time. Incest. Safety. Trauma. Was this combination what caused her to act so much against her nature? He conceded the possibility.

He sighed. Why was he so preoccupied with it, anyway? For all he knew, Rhia herself could be dead. The thought sent a spasm of pain through him. No, he said to himself. She couldn't be dead. He couldn't bear that.

❧ ❦

One evening, Vincent and Coldson went for a walk topside and sat on the embankment near the stream. Vincent wanted Coldson to know how much he appreciated everything the man had been doing for him. It was a beautiful night, brisk and clear, with a bright swath of stars across the sky. Vincent gazed at it wistfully.

Coldson spoke up. "What are ye thinkin' when ye look at the stars like that?"

Vincent smiled ruefully and decided to play all his cards at once. "At the moment, I'm wondering whether that band of stars is the same galaxy I grew up in."

The older man frowned. "I'm not familiar with that term, m'lord."

"Please don't call me that." He wrapped his arms around his knees and looked at Coldson. "Do you know just what a star is?"

Coldson shrugged. "I've heard many ideas. Holes in the roof of the world. Torches of the gods. Spirits of warriors killed in battle. Things like that. But I suspect the stars are nothin' like what I've heard."

"Really? What would you suspect, then?"

"I've no clue. But I suspect if anyone knows for certain, that would be you."

Vincent paused for a long moment, studying Coldson's scarred face, then looked back to the stars. "You'd be right," he said finally. "A star, my friend, is a big ball of fire. And when I say it's big, I mean bigger than you could possibly imagine. So big that just an average sized one would dwarf the entire world you and I are sitting upon." He watched as Coldson turned a skeptical eye to the sky. "Yes, I'm serious. They look small because they are so very far away." He stopped, realizing that if he didn't, he'd wind up trying to explain things like the speed of light to the man. He turned the topic back to home. "The sun you see in the sky during the day is a star, just like the ones you're now looking at. But it's much closer. This world circles that star. In fact, this world isn't the only one circling this star. I've watched the night sky quite a bit over the last several years." Scanning the sky, he found a bright spot and pointed. "See that bright one right there?"

Coldson followed Vincent's finger and nodded. "Aye. Brighter than the rest."

"Yes. It's a planet, just like this." He slapped the ground beside him. "Well, probably not *just* like this. That particular planet probably doesn't have people living on it." He looked at his friend and saw the befuddlement there. "Too much information in one sitting, huh?"

Coldson looked at him. "Aye, but ye still have not told me what a galaxy is. Is it the group of planets going around the sun?"

"Nope. That's called a solar system. A galaxy is a huge group of stars. And I do mean huge. More than the fish in the sea huge."

The man blinked at him. "And each of the stars in the galaxy has planets around it?"

Vincent was pleased to see the connection of the concepts in Coldson's thoughts. "Probably not. Many of them, surely. And not all planets have life, of course. Still, quite a bunch must."

"Amazing."

"Oh, it gets better. As many stars as there are in a galaxy, there are probably just as many galaxies in the universe."

Coldson's eyes slowly widened. "God's teeth!"

Vincent raised his eyebrow at the oath, fighting back a chuckle. Then he looked to the stars again and tried to imagine having that kind of information thrust upon him in just a few minutes. He nodded. "Indeed."

"Ye come from one of those planets, don't ye?"

He smiled slightly. "Yeah. One of them." He heard Coldson's intake of breath. "But don't ask me how I got from there to here. I don't really know. I understand it involved magic, which is something we don't have on my world." He could tell from Coldson's expression that this was going to be a long talk, and that Coldson wouldn't be doing much of the talking. So he made himself comfortable on the grass and told the man everything.

He told him the whole story as he knew it, from his arrival to the present. He included information about Darella that he had only recently begun to fully understand himself. He omitted much personal information, namely about Ariaziane and Rhia. He mentioned them, but never the full extent of what they meant to him. At any rate, by the time he was finished, quite some time had passed. Coldson had asked many questions, not just about Earth, but about Vincent's deeds here. Finally, Vincent caught him up to the present.

"So now you know why I'm so distraught," he said. "Darla is my daughter. Where I come from, people would be totally appalled at what she and I have done, especially since a child will be the result of it."

"It is also frowned upon here, but it happens often."

"Oh?"

Coldson nodded matter-of-factly. "Aye. It's... er... conveniently overlooked when those involved are high rank, such as baron. People will talk, but they'll not stone ye, if that's yer worry. As I said, a worse crime would be to leave her."

"So you're saying I should maintain the illusion of being her lover? Just to prevent people from thinking I'm a horrible person? I'd hate living such a lie."

"How much of a lie? Have ye lost feeling for her?"

Vincent began to protest. "Lost? No. But it's changed! I mean..."

"I know. She's yer daughter. But ye've known that only since a few days afore our arrival here. How much longer were ye lovers? Yer feelings have changed that quickly? That completely?"

His mouth moved, but his brain was withholding the words. Finally, he gave up. "No," he whispered. "I can't help it. She's still the same person. When we're together, I feel exactly the same as I used to. But I keep telling myself I can't."

"Not that simple, though, is it?"

He shook his head. "No. And it doesn't help matters any that she doesn't seem inclined to feel differently about me. But then, why should she? She's known all along."

Coldson's voice became low and soft. "How much time do ye figure she's got? If ye don't mind me asking."

Vincent sighed. "Ten years. Fifteen at most."

The older man nodded slowly. "Be a shame if her short time left were spent alone." Vincent found he had nothing to say to that. His eyes were focused on nothing, and they stung. Then he heard Coldson say, "Ye're right."

Blinking away the stillborn tear, he looked up. "What?"

Coldson pointed. "The planet does move. It's over there, now."

Vincent smiled despite himself. "Yeah. They tend to do that."

After a moment, Coldson said, "I'm not surprised, y'know."

"About what?"

"About ye being from another world. I never thought someone from this world could do the things ye've done."

Vincent shook his head. "There's nothing spectacular about the things I've done. I've not even done all that much. I'm tired of hearing how great my deeds are. Because you know what? I wouldn't stand a chance against a mage. Or even a good swordsman. I'm nothing great, Coldson."

His friend was quiet for a long time, picking at the long grass between his feet. Then he looked Vincent in the eye and said, "When I was a little one, my father told me that greatness isn't measured by our abilities, but by what we do with 'em. And everythin' I've seen about ye, everythin' I've heard about ye, says that what ye do with yer abilities is always somethin' good. That makes ye great in my eyes. And others', too. Why do ye think all those men of Aedriun's volunteered to serve with ye?"

"I have no idea," he said honestly. "We're in the middle of nowhere, which is fine with me, but I'd expect these guys to want to stay in Linnael, where there's stuff to do. I mean, there's not an inn within five days' ride from here. What were they thinking?"

"Why don't ye believe that someone could want to serve ye just because of who ye are?"

He frowned, then said, "I just don't. Why should they? I sure don't think their careers are going to go very far by being stuck in this cave with me."

"I suspect they think different. But even so, not everyone is concerned about a career. Me, for example."

"You're an exceptional person, Coldson."

"Not so very," he replied. "I'm not the only one who is with ye just because of who ye are."

"Darla doesn't count."

"Didn't mean the lady."

"Well, Aedriun's men most certainly do care about their careers. Even Darvas, though I count him among my friends, too."

"Didn't mean them, neither."

"Then who?"

"The others ye freed along with me," he said simply. "They're gathered down in Falconwall. Darvas will be bringin' them back with him."

"What!"

"You didn't believe them, did ye? Or me, neither, I'd wager."

Vincent's mouth hung open. "How many?"

"About a dozen. Them that didn't have families to return to."

Falling back onto the embankment, he said, "Why? What do they think they're going to get out of this? I just don't understand."

"Wouldn't ye feel indebted to someone who'd freed ye from slavery?"

Vincent paused, closing his eyes against the stars. "Yes, I would. But I don't know that I would pledge my life in service to him. What am I going to have them do? I have no idea!"

Coldson cleared his throat. "Ye don't like having people sworn to ye?"

"Not particularly."

"And this is because ye feel put upon?"

He glanced over at Coldson. "Sort of. I guess." He paused. "I don't mean it to sound as harsh as that, though." Sitting up again, he said, "What do I do?"

"Well," the man drawled, "I think there's a way to make it work."

"Oh?"

"Aye. And it would be something ye'd be doing, anyhow."

"And what's that?"

"Well, ye've got a keep. Now ye need a town to go with it."

"A town?"

"Aye. At the base of the mountain, along the river."

Vincent pondered this. "Interesting. But there's something we're a bit short on, you realize."

"Women?"

"Women. The town will die without future generations to keep it going. And how do you expect we're going to attract women to this out of the way place?"

Coldson's face split in a grin. "One thing at a time. But trust me. We'll have women enough."

Vincent allowed his reservations to wash away in the light of the man's smile. "A town." He returned the smile. "Not bad. Not bad at all."

❧ ❦

As Coldson said, Darvas returned with thirteen of the men Rhia and I had freed from the pirate ship. At the moment, they're living here in the keep, and seem happy to be doing so. But I'm getting tired of the constant attention from them. They seem to have this burning need to do something for me, whatever I ask of them. I don't know what to say to them. There's nothing I want from them, really.

Darvas also brought back a good supply of provisions, plus bedding for himself and his companions. And the new men, too. A chef was hired. I don't even know what I'll be paying him. But all her meals so far have been outstanding, so I guess she's worth whatever price Darvas offered.

Another trip to Falconwall left today. This time Coldson went, along with some of the new men and some of the guardsmen. I imagine this will continue until the bad weather hits, which shouldn't be more than a few more weeks away. Hard to tell, though. We're pretty far south, after all. I'm sure we can get two more trips in. Maybe three.

Darvas and I spoke at length yesterday about Coldson's idea of establishing a town at the base of the mountain. He likes the idea and we threw a few concepts around. There are a lot of factors that I don't have a handle on, yet, but it could actually work. I suppose the king would like that. Another little area from which to extract taxes.

My growing friendship with Coldson makes me feel a little guilty. For so long, I'd not really thought of him as a person. I think I subconsciously thought of him only as the slave I freed. As though by having been enslaved, he'd been made less human. Or because he's uneducated, he wasn't worthy of my friendship. I can't believe I could have thought that way, but evidence dictates that I did. I'm rather ashamed of it. But I think I've rectified that. Coldson is someone I've learned to trust with anything. I like him. And more than that, I respect him.

I've also been really trying to maintain certain appearances, as Coldson recommended. Meaning with Darla. She's made it easy, I have to say. She knows what I'm going through over this. We even share a room. I'd prefer that we keep separate beds, but when I suggested that, the look in her eyes was just so... so stricken. So we share a bed. But I've insisted that both of us wear bedclothes of some sort. Daughter or not, she's still sexy as all get-out and I'd be lying if I said I fully trusted myself to keep my hands off her.

Sometimes I wonder what difference it would make. She's already pregnant and we've been lovers for quite a while. It's not like I believe in sin, anyway. I'm not worried about burning in some fictitious hell for this. No one's being hurt. So why am I so bothered by it?

Simple. I've been conditioned to be bothered by it. I grew up in a society that believed sexual relations between close relatives was a bad thing. And I don't mean incestuous rape, which is bad because all rapes are bad, but also consensual incest. Sure, there's always the genetic fear of the kid having nasty birth defects. But it's not as great a possibility as most people think.

My big concern about the kid to come isn't the possibility of genetic abnormalities. It's just the idea of being a father. It gives me the willies, frankly. I've never really wanted to have kids. Not that I dislike them or anything. Well, okay, I'm not real fond of the knee biters. Once they get to an age where they can carry on a conversation of sorts, then I like them.

I'm trying to look at the positive aspects of raising a child. I'm sure it must be a fascinating experience, watching a kid grow up, learning new things. I don't think I'll hate being a dad. But it scares me.

❧ ❧

Jaz arrived a few days after Coldson and crew left for Falconwall. Vincent gave him the grand tour, introducing him to Darla, Darvas, and the rest. He showed him a room for his use. "Rather drab," the mage said.

"Hey, we just moved in. Give us time to find a decorator." They laughed together as they moved on up to the top floor. "I don't think I'll ever have a place as nice as yours, Jaz."

"It took a long time for it to become as nice as it is," his friend assured him. "You're off to a good start, don't worry."

"How are Hennor and the others?"

"They are all well, thank you for asking. Ah. That reminds me. Hennor asked me to give you this." Jaz reached into his cloak. "Close your eyes."

Vincent frowned quizzically, but did as he was told. He heard a sound, and instinct took over. He stretched out his hand and laughed aloud, opening his eyes as the piece of fruit fell into his hand. "Very good. He has a sense of humor, after all." He tucked the fruit into his cloak pocket and smiled as he led Jaz out into the open aired space. "I'll have some gardens here, come the Season of Green," he said. "Lots of flowers, I hope."

"There are some beautiful ones in these mountains," Jaz said.

"Darvas put the word out for a gardener for me. Perhaps Coldson will bring one back when he returns."

"This is bigger than I remember it being," Jaz said with some puzzlement, gazing around the large open area.

"It is?"

"Definitely. When I flew in, I noticed. Have you gone the whole way back to the end?"

"Actually, no," he said, walking briskly toward the far end of the area. They crossed the stream and climbed the small rise that lay not far beyond it. Vincent expected to see the rear wall in the distance at this point, but it was nowhere in sight.

On and on they went, finally reaching the area where the wall should have been. They stopped. Remnants of wheel tracks remained from the builders. "There used to be a narrow gap here," Vincent said. "And now it's wide open." They stood and looked. A whole new area was opened up to them, a vast expanse of land. "How is this possible?" Vincent breathed.

Jaz shrugged. "Your keep was dug out of the mountain, Vincent. It seems Feletain and his men put the excess mass to good use."

"He never mentioned this! How far does it go? Could you tell?"

"Shall we go take a look?"

Vincent gazed outward. "It looks pretty big. I'm not in the mood for that great a hike right now."

"No hiking required," Jaz said, grasping Vincent by the wrist.

In seconds, they were above treetop level. Vincent's eyes bugged out and he felt his stomach do a loop. "Thanks so much for the warning."

"My pleasure."

They soared out over the area that Feletain's men had filled in. "That used to be a rocky mess, as I recall. With a bit of a drop, too."

Jaz dipped them lower, landing on the other side of the filled-in area. "And here there was no gap before," the mage pointed out. "It appears as though Feletain's crew took out a section of this ridge, then cleared the area beyond, which, as you can see, leads into another spacious area."

"Geez," was all Vincent could find to say. "Wonder how big it is."

Without another word, Jaz grabbed Vincent's arm again and they were aloft. They sailed lazily over the region, Vincent admiring the fact that it was fairly level. He soon spied another stream, larger than the first, then realized it was actually part of the same one. Closer to the source, he imagined. And soon, he found just that. "Whoa! Check it out!" he said.

They landed near a tiny lake, crystal clear and blue. "There is your water source," Jaz said. "There is a similar one not far from my keep. You should find it to be excellent drinking water. And mighty cold, too."

"And it's beautiful," Vincent breathed, watching the sunlight glint off the lake's surface, admiring the late colored foliage of the surrounding trees. Not all the trees were evergreens, much to his pleasure.

Jaz nodded. "That it is."

After soaking in the sight for another minute, Vincent said, "Feletain's getting another bonus."

His friend chuckled as they turned to walk back to the keep. "You do enjoy spending money."

"What good is it if you don't spend it?" They walked slowly, enjoying the weather and the scenery. "Jaz, I have a major favor to ask of you." He described then the set-up that King Breigar had for keeping track of his scouts. He also filled his friend in on the brewing situation with Darla's brother, advising him of events that had taken place since they were last together. "Can you help me?"

"Yes," Jaz drawled. "But if he's as powerful as you describe, with the resources you say he has... I'm not sure an observational ability will be much help. But magical protections would take too long."

"Well, it's better than nothing."

Jaz nodded. "I'll need certain items, first. I'll leave tomorrow morning for Falconwall. I should be back by the following day."

Vincent shook his head. "A solid week for the others to get there, another week back, and you make the round trip in a matter of hours. Seems grossly unfair," he laughed.

"Benefits of being a mage, my friend."

"Uh, huh. Any negative aspect of being a mage?"

"I don't meet many women. Always studying."

"I'm sure that's the reason. And speaking of studying, did anything come of all the stuff you acquired in Kurean's laboratory?"

"A bit, yes. I learned a few things, but for me, the appeal was that it was a glimpse into the life of one of the greatest mages in recent history. I've admired his works for many years and this opportunity was one I could not have dreamed of achieving. I owe you a lot for your help in that."

"Oh, rubbish. The little assistance I gave can't have equaled what you did for me."

Again, his friend shrugged. "Well. Since we disagree on matters of indebtedness, why don't we just forget about them?"

Vincent smiled. "Works for me. We're friends. Friends don't keep track of debts."

"Exactly. But I told you explicitly not to lose that sword!"

"Yeah, but you gave me a second one, just in case."

"That's not the point." The mage smiled.

"I'll get it back from him," Vincent said, sobering. "Somehow."

As predicted, Jaz returned from Falconwall the day after he'd departed. He and Vincent set about creating what Vincent half-humorously referred to as his "war room."

"I wasn't sure how many you'd need," Jaz said as he unwrapped the large bundle on the floor, "so I obtained six." Vincent looked at the slabs of shiny, black rock. Each oval was thin, about a foot in length and perhaps a quarter inch thick, polished to an almost mirror-like sheen. "And they're fancier than you need, but my choices were limited."

"Those most definitely are fancy," Vincent agreed, eyeing the ornate silver trim each slab sported.

"On the other hand, they make a matched set," Jaz said, unwrapping a smaller bundle. These were the portable versions that Vincent's scouts would carry. Virtually identical to the others except for size, these were affixed to silver chains that the scouts would wear around their necks. Each slab was about four inches in length and three in width, also trimmed in silver.

"Lovely," Vincent said. "Did you bother to shop around for less ornate ones, or look for bargains?"

"Of course not. It was your money."

"I see."

"What good is it if you don't spend it?" Jaz replied as he finished unwrapping the pieces.

The war room was located on the first floor, in the private room behind the main audience chamber, which itself lay at the end of the main entrance hall. Jaz had also returned with six stands for the magical eyes. Vincent drew upon his recollection of the king's set-up, placing the stands in an arc around his chair and desk. The slabs themselves would be clamped into the stands after Jaz finished enchanting them. The mage advised him that the enchanting process would take approximately four hours per slab. He'd enchant one set per day, so the war room could be operational in less than a week.

It was a difficult week for Vincent. Jaz was sequestered away during the day, working on the enchantments. In fact, the process took him an extra day, the seventh day being devoted to something that he would not disclose. Coldson was still in Falconwall, or on his way back. Darvas was overseeing the outfitting of the quarters for the men and the decoration of the main audience chamber, something he claimed was very important, though Vincent didn't exactly see why. He found himself spending much time alone, and most of the rest of the time with Darla.

Darla seemed to have changed a bit. Before, she'd seemed willing to allow Vincent the option of distancing himself, allowing himself time to adjust to the facts of their relationship. But now, Vincent noted, she seemed to have taken a more aggressive approach, a more assertive mentality.

"Good morning, Father," she would coyly say to him in the morning, before proceeding to kiss him passionately. And when he'd pale and disengage quickly, she'd giggle. It was as if she took particular delight in reminding him of the incest they'd jointly engaged in.

"Why do you insist on tormenting me like this?" he asked her one morning.

"Tormenting?" she replied. "Such is not my intention."

"Well, you must see that it bothers me. You seem to be proud of what we've done!"

"And why shouldn't I be?" she said, climbing out of bed. "I think you're a wonderful man and I'm very proud of you."

"Yes, but I'm your *father*, Darla!"

"And I'm very proud of that, too! I'm proud of you as a person, proud of you as a father. Why should I not be proud to have you as a lover and father of my child?"

Ignoring the wave of nausea that washed over him along with her words, he threw back the blankets and rose from bed. "Because!" He said it loudly, in the hopes that he might convince both of them by virtue of volume.

Darla laughed as she freshened herself from the wash basin. "That is the best you can reply?" She put the cloth back into the water, wrung it out, and handed it to him as he approached. "Why can't you just accept it?" she asked.

Vincent thanked her. "I don't know," he admitted as he swabbed his face. "I'm a prude, I guess."

She frowned. "I don't know that term."

He sighed and tossed the cloth back into the water, then dried his face with a towel. "Never mind. The point is, it's a very hard thing for me to accept. I know you can accept it easier because you weren't raised to think such things are in any way wrong, but I was."

"You've spoken of this before, but you've never explained to me just why it is considered wrong."

He frowned as they began to dress for the day. "It just is, okay?"

"No, it is not okay. I wish to know. Please help me understand."

Vincent pulled his tunic over his head, then sat on the edge of the bed. "I can't," he said simply. Emotions tore at him, frustration winning out. "The simple truth is that when it comes right down to it, there are no rational reasons behind it being wrong. The one legitimate factor involved, and that only has to do with the prospect of children, isn't even a big one."

"What about children?" she asked, her voice tinged with concern.

"When closely related people produce a child, there are higher chances of the baby being born with deformities of one sort or another."

"Deformities?" Darla said quietly.

"Yes. But don't worry about it. It's not a very great possibility. I didn't mean to frighten you."

Darla pulled on her dress and said, "Then you really do not have any reason other than some vague principle that has no foundation. And evidently you care more about societal approval than your own happiness." She said it simply, off-handedly. And Vincent was so taken aback by her attitude, by the simple truths she'd stated, that he just sat there while she finished dressing.

She didn't prompt for a response from him, which was a good thing, he felt, since he might just have voiced all the doubts that tugged at him. When she was dressed, she stood in front of him. "Going without trousers today? I rather fancy the idea, but I'm not sure everyone else would appreciate your hairy thighs." He took a deep breath, then picked up his breeches from the floor. "I'll meet you downstairs," she said, and with a swirl of her dress, she was gone.

It was several minutes before Vincent put on his pants.

❧ ❧

Coldson and the caravan eventually returned, bringing more provisions for the keep, including more dry and preserved goods for the coming cold season, more feed for the horses, bolts of fabric, seeds for planting once the weather warmed again, and a wide variety of tools. Coldson had hired a gardener and a stablehand, as well. A very practical trip, Vincent felt, which didn't surprise him, since Coldson had been in charge.

Darvas soon prepared for the third trip to Falconwall. Vincent gave him one of the magic eye necklaces, as he called them.

No sooner had the caravan left than Jaz took Vincent aside. "If King Breigar's approximations are correct, it is time we seriously looked at the threat of these snow giants. I am going to fly north and attempt to locate them. I've got one of the necklaces. I'll contact you periodically."

"Fine, but am I supposed to live in the war room waiting for your call?"

The mage smiled and pulled a small ring from his finger. It was silver, carved in a pattern similar to the trim of the necklaces. "This is what I worked on after I finished with the eyes. All six of the necklaces are tuned to this ring, as well as to their individual larger counterparts. When someone with one of the necklaces is trying to reach you, the ring will vibrate."

"Great. A pager to go with the cell phones."

"Eh?"

"Forget it." He frowned. "Wait a minute. How would Darvas, for example, contact me?"

"Right now, he can't. For that matter, right now you can't contact him, either. You both need to be taught how to operate these. It is a simple spell."

"Whoa!" Vincent said. "A spell? I'm not a mage, Jaz!"

His friend laughed. "Nor will you be one after I teach you how to do this. As I said, activating these requires but a simple spell, one I can teach you in an hour or so. The magic is contained within the talisman, not within you. More accurately, you will be activating the magic within the device, not truly casting a spell upon it."

Vincent was doubtful, but said, "If you say so."

510

"I do say so. Meet me in your war chamber after the mid-day meal. I'll instruct you then. Afterward, I'll be off. I have some things to do at my own home before I go further north."

The mid-day meal was a quiet gathering. Vincent sat beside Darla at the table, paying little attention to the conversations going on near him. His thoughts were only on Darla. He stole glances at her between bites of food, always averting his gaze whenever she caught him.

His thoughts were awhirl with an internal conflict that he felt he should have been accustomed to. The liberal side of him thought only of his love for her, of how he felt being with her, of how natural it all seemed. And the conservative side of him focused only on how appalled he felt at the nature of their relationship, how wrong it was.

It was easy, he realized, to think only of the conservative side when he wasn't with her. Just as it was simple to think only of the liberal side when they were together. He frowned as he toyed with his food. He turned his eye to the other side of the table and found Coldson studying him. The man smiled slightly and nodded.

Coldson could tell what was going through his head, Vincent knew. It seemed the old man was his primary confidante these days. Whenever they would bump into each other, Coldson would ask, "How are things?" And by that, he always meant with regard to this very problem.

Darla laughed at something said further down the table. He looked at her face, at the way her eyes danced as she laughed. Her cheeks flushed slightly, her lips glistened with the juice she'd been drinking. So beautiful, he thought.

His heart tightened inside and his breathing grew funny. He stared at her until her eyes moved toward him. The laughter gradually faded and she looked self-consciously at him through lowered lashes. And in her eyes he saw many things. Trepidation. Concern. Insecurity. But mostly, adoration. His eyes began to sting, then, and he put down his fork. The things he saw in her eyes were exactly the same things he felt inside himself. He wasn't sure if all conversation at the table really stopped, or if he was just no longer aware of it. Gently, he reached for her face.

He cupped her chin with a finger and lifted it slightly. She looked back at him with uncertainty, her lips parting as if to ask him what he was doing. And then he kissed her. Incest be damned, he thought. Happiness was more important than the approval of society, he decided.

After a moment's shocked hesitation, she returned the kiss fully. Then her arms were around his neck and his around her body. Breaking from the kiss, he pulled her close and whispered into her ear, "I'm so sorry, Darla. I love you."

He felt her response in the form of warm tears on his neck as they embraced.

Vincent entered the war room, finding Jaz waiting impatiently for him. He smiled sheepishly. "Sorry I'm late. I was um... occupied."

The mage shook his head. "You young people and your urges," he muttered.

"Oh, like you're so old yourself," Vincent began. Then he stopped. "Okay, I've learned my lesson in that regard. So how old are you?"

Jaz rose from Vincent's chair and allowed him to take his seat. "Younger than most of your friends, never fear. Now. Shall we begin?"

Vincent sighed. "I guess so. If you're so sure you can teach me how to do this."

"I could teach Blaise how to do this."

"Oh, that's all I would need, having this ring tingle my finger every time she wanted to go for a walk or wanted a bone or wanted to play."

His friend chuckled. "On the other hand, you could give a necklace to Darla. Then you'd get a tingle every time she wanted..."

"Stop it," Vincent interrupted, smiling.

"Your hand would probably go numb."

"Can we just get on with it?" Vincent laughed.

Jaz nodded to the closest stand. "The magic, as I said, is contained in the device itself. It is much easier to draw the magic forth from the device rather than from thin air, as it were."

"Which is why," Vincent said, "there are so many magical rings and wands and things, right?"

"Exactly. With a little practice, nearly anyone can utilize a magical device. Well, most magical devices, that is."

"Okay, so how do I tap into it?"

Jaz smiled. "You must learn how to feel it. Again, with a device, this isn't difficult. Place your hand over its face," he suggested. Vincent reached out, his palm over the flat, black surface. "All right," Jaz said, "now simply—"

"Cool," Vincent said, his hand lingering over the device. A tingly sensation tickled his palm.

The mage frowned, then slowly smiled. "Of course. I should have thought of this before. Your heightened senses. This will not take as long as I expected." He nodded. "Feeling the power is the most difficult step. All you need to do now is picture yourself drawing the energy inside of you. Imagine a connection between your mind and your hand, between your hand and the energy, the energy and the stone face."

Vincent concentrated for a bit. "Okay, so I've got a connection. What do I do with it?"

"You merely will the stone to show you what you wish to see, which in this case is the person on the other end. Your friend Darvas."

"Far out," Vincent murmured. "Base to Darvas, come in, Darvas," he droned. Then, to his surprise, the face of the stone began to brighten. He jerked his hand back in shock. "Whoa!" The stone faded to black again.

"Excellent! But you must maintain the concentration."

"It worked! Sort of. I mean, I guess I just didn't expect it to work, you know?"

Jaz smiled. "In fact, I do. I still remember the feeling of casting my first successful spell. I was so amazed I nearly fainted."

"Well, let's try this again," Vincent said. Extending his hand again, he instantly felt the buzz of energy that was the magic within. He imagined it becoming part of him, then pictured the stone fading in like a movie cut. And this time, when it swirled to brightness, he didn't panic.

The face of his friend slowly sharpened in the stone. "Darvas! Dude! How are you?"

Darvas smiled and chuckled slightly. "Baron," he nodded. "Your new toy evidently works." His voice came to him not from the stone, as Vincent would have expected, but from the air all around him. It was almost as if Darvas were standing right there. "Is this a social call, or was there something you required?"

Vincent smiled broadly. "Just testing the equipment, so to speak. I trust all is well?"

"We are less than a day into the journey," replied the young man. "No one is homesick just yet." He smiled as Vincent laughed. "If I may say so, you seem to be in much better spirits than when I left."

Feeling a softness in his chest and remembering the tender moments spent with Darla before he came to the war room, Vincent nodded. "To say the least. Well. I'll be speaking with you later."

Darvas nodded in the silver-framed oval. Vincent turned to Jaz. "How do I hang up?" And in that moment, the disc went black. "Oh," he said. "Like that."

"So much for taking an hour to teach you how to operate this," the mage said. "All the better. I can be on my way, now." He paused, stroking his beard and facing his friend. "You know, Vincent, despite your age, you might consider taking up the study of magic. I suspect you'd learn quickly."

Vincent shook his head. "Don't think so. I'm really not all that interested in it. I mean, I'm fascinated by what you can do, and I'm curious about how you do it, but I just don't think I'd want to learn to do it."

Jaz shrugged. "As you wish. Seems a waste, though. You've got ability."

"Perhaps. But just because I have ability does not obligate me to use it."

They retrieved Jaz's belongings from his room, then climbed one of the towers to the uppermost level of the keep. "I'll check in periodically," the mage reminded him when they stepped outside. "Anything I discover, I'll let you know."

"I appreciate it," Vincent said. He clapped his friend on the shoulder. "Thanks."

Jaz smiled as he unrolled his magic carpet, seated himself upon it, and sailed away. Vincent watched him go, waiting until he was a speck in the distance before returning indoors.

In bed that night, Vincent broached the subject to Darla. "What's it like to learn magic?" he asked.

To his surprise, Darla's response was bitter. "You should probably ask someone who really learned it, rather than had it forced into them."

"But you took that knowledge and did new things with it. Being able to revive Felina, for example. Darella wouldn't have taught you that."

Darla propped herself up onto one elbow and faced him. "If someone were to hand you a poem, would you not be able to recognize the patterns and rearrange them into a different rhyme?"

"Well, yeah," Vincent said slowly. "I guess."

"But would you really have created something new? Would you really have learned anything?"

"A little."

"Exactly," she said. "A little. But not much. Not enough for a clear understanding." Vincent pondered this for a moment, but Darla continued before he could comment. "Besides that, there is the fact that I intentionally stopped learning after a while. I would reject anything she put in my head."

"Why?"

"Because I hated her. I thought that her magic inside me would make me like her. And I didn't want that. I wanted to be as unlike her as I could." She smiled slightly, then said, "Why do you ask, though, about the magic?"

"Oh, just something Jaz said to me before he left. He said I'd probably be good at it."

Darla looked at him in confusion. "Why did he say 'probably?' I'd say you are."

He returned the look. "What do you mean? I don't know any magic. I mean, aside from what Jaz just showed me."

"You don't?"

He laughed. "No!"

"Then what do you call what you can do with your eyes closed?"

Vincent shrugged. "Sleeping?"

"No, silly. I mean how you can 'see' without using your eyes. Isn't that magic?"

Shaking his head, he said, "It's just using the senses we all have. I learned to use my ears and nose a lot more when I was blind. There's nothing magical, it's simply a matter of paying more attention to what's there, in all ways, rather than the one we're most used to."

Darla smiled, leaned over, and kissed him. "Jaz is right. You *would* make a good mage."

He was about to protest, but she kissed him again, this time more than just a peck. And he knew that more talk was probably not forthcoming.

❧ ❦

The first report from Jaz came two days later. Vincent sat in his chair in the war room, speaking with his friend through one of the devices. "There are at least a dozen of them," the mage said. "They've traveled quickly, if the king's scout was accurate in giving their positions."

Vincent frowned. A dozen! This wasn't the kind of news he wanted to hear. "What do you suggest we do?" he asked.

Jaz raised an eyebrow. "I suggest we rid ourselves of the threat."

"How dangerous are these snow giants?"

"To whom?" the mage said with a smile.

Vincent chuckled. "That means you can handle them yourself?"

"I would imagine so."

"The Great and Powerful Jaz has spoken," Vincent laughed.

"It puzzles me that her brother would take this approach, summoning various creatures."

"Everything puzzles me about his actions. Nothing makes sense," Vincent said. "But speaking of that, do you think you could check on the progress of the other creatures, too?"

"Certainly. Let me handle this situation first. I'll contact you later."

And with that, Jaz's image faded to black. Glancing over the array of magic eyes, Vincent had to wonder if he'd wasted a lot of money and a lot of Jaz's time in putting this war room together. If Jaz could dispatch a dozen snow giants with little effort, then he could certainly handle a pack of wolves and a bunch of trolls.

Jaz's curiosity still echoed in his own mind. He'd not gone into it with his friend because he didn't like to think about it. Obviously, the boy wanted Vincent's friends dead or hurt, so as to hurt Vincent himself. What he'd seemingly planned as simultaneous attacks on Felina and Blade would have been impossible for Vincent to prevent alone. And then there was the fact that the snow giants had been sent toward his new keep. Was this just a psychological torture? Did he want to see his father torn, deciding whether to save his home or his friends? And if he'd had to choose, which friend?

He shook his head. It didn't matter, now. He didn't have to worry. Jaz would take care of things.

He rose to leave, but had gotten no further than the door when the ring on his finger began to vibrate. He frowned, then returned to his chair, where he activated Jaz's connection again.

"What's up?" he asked when his friend's face appeared.

The mage appeared troubled. "Ah," he said, looking away and below him. "This could be more of a problem than I'd expected."

"Why?"

Jaz turned to face his friend. "It seems the creatures are highly resistant to magic."

Vincent lowered himself into his chair. "What do you mean by that?"

Jaz opened his mouth to reply, then his face vanished from the stone. Vincent saw something flash past on the screen before his friend's visage returned. "Sorry," the mage said.

"What was that?"

"A very large rock," Jaz said calmly. "As I was saying, my magic isn't affecting the giants as it should. They have some sort of protection, the nature of which I do not know. I do know, however, that I'm feeling rather inadequate at the moment." Jaz reared back as another rock hurtled past, then looked down at the snow giants and calmly said, "Stop that."

Despite himself, Vincent laughed. Then he sobered, realizing the significance of his words. "Okay. How about you do the reconnaissance for me? Check out the locations of the wolves and the trolls." He waited, noticing Jaz's hesitation. "Is that not a good idea?"

"My concern is that they are headed toward my keep."

"Oh."

Jaz shook his head. "Well. I can do your scouting and be back before they reach it. Perhaps I can even work out a plan of attack while doing so."

"Are you sure? If you need to stay to protect your home, I'll certainly understand."

"I don't believe they are at all interested in my residence. Or rather, I hope they are not. Let me be off, then. I'll contact you when I have news."

"Fly safely," Vincent said with a thankful smile. And then the stone went dark again. No sooner had it darkened than there was a knock at his war room door. "Come in," he said.

The door opened and Coldson appeared. "Sorry to disturb," he said, "but ye have a visitor."

"A visitor?" He frowned in puzzlement as he rose and strode toward the door. "Who?"

"Short little man," Coldson said, turning and walking down the hall with Vincent. "Didn't catch his name, though. Some odd accent he has."

Vincent smiled, despite the heavy mood brought on by Jaz's news. "Gnorrin!" he said.

"Aye, that could've been it," Coldson said.

They reached the audience chamber to find the gnome wandering around, looking at the paintings on the walls. He turned as Vincent entered. "I would think I could find more urgently needed things to buy upon first moving into a keep," Gnorrin said.

Vincent's smile broadened. "Good to see you, too. What brings you here?"

"I thought you might be in the dark," he replied. "I seem to recall a conversation some time ago about you needing some illumination for this cave you've dug out for yourself."

"Ah," Vincent chuckled. "Yes. Well, as you can see, Jaz has already helped me with that."

Gnorrin made a face. "Jaz has little appreciation of lighting, then. Look here," he said, pointing to the twin globes casting magical light down from the ceiling. "This is your audience chamber. You want your guests to feel welcome and secure. These are harsh, penetrating." Gnorrin pointed his hands at one of the globes, muttered under his breath, and the orbs lowered themselves from the ceiling to hover on each side of Vincent's great chair, about eight feet from the floor. Then they dimmed, casting a mellow glow throughout the chamber, rather than the bright illumination they'd previously given. "There," Gnorrin said. "Comfortable."

Vincent nodded. "That's quite nice. Feels homey."

"Yes, well, if you're going to live in a cave, the least you can do is try to have light that appears natural."

"Gnorrin," he said soberly, "I'm glad you're here. I could really use your help."

"So I would imagine," his friend said.

Briefly, Vincent told him of the overall situation, finishing by summarizing Jaz's latest communication. "I know next to nothing about magic, as you realize. What do we do about these giants?"

"First of all, did your friend say they were totally unaffected, or just were not affected as much as he had expected?"

"He said the magic was not affecting them as it should."

"Well, that's something, at least." Gnorrin rubbed his chin. "I wish he had told you what sort of spells he had cast upon them."

"Why?"

"Because resistance to magic often takes specific forms. Much like that ring you wear. Fire does not harm you. The ring imparts a resistance, or in this case an immunity, to one specific group of spells. Fire."

"Not to mention non-magical fire. Remember, I learned of its abilities by being knocked into my campfire by the boar."

"Exactly. But you see my point. If your efreeti friend had attacked you with anything other than fire, you would have died."

"So you're saying that Jaz just chose the wrong spells to cast?"

"That's one possibility. You have to understand, too, that the vast majority of mages choose a particular branch of magic to study. From what you've told me about

Jaz, and from his fascination with the arts of Kurean, I'd say he's probably inclined to the same studies. Elemental spells, predominantly fire-based."

Vincent frowned. "But..."

"What?"

"Well, it would just seem to me that when one fights against a snow giant, fire would be the sensible choice for a spell."

Gnorrin nodded gravely. "Aye. So it would seem."

"Jaz will be back in a few days, I think. You can question him then, unless it's urgent. We could contact him now if need be."

His friend shook his head. "How's that?"

Vincent told him about the magical communications that he'd first seen of the king's and how Jaz gave him a similar setup. Gnorrin expressed his interest in seeing it, so Vincent took him there. They selected the stone that was attuned to Jaz's necklace and Gnorrin activated it. After a friendly re-introduction, Vincent left the two of them alone to discuss things magical.

Before dinner, Vincent sat with Gnorrin and Darla in the sparsely furnished sitting room. Eventually he would fill the room with comfortable chairs and all the bound books he could get his hands on. For now, it had a few straight-backed chairs around a blazing fireplace.

"It is nice to see you again," Darla said to Gnorrin.

"You, as well," Gnorrin replied.

Vincent cleared his throat and said to the gnome, "We have some news to share with you."

"Is that so?" said Gnorrin with a smile. "You're planning to wed, aren't you?"

Darla blushed. Vincent raised his eyebrows. "Well, not at the moment. I'm not sure that would be..." He frowned. "I learned something about Darla not long ago. Since you're my oldest friend here, I think you should know." Gnorrin sat expectantly, idly toying with the end of the green and purple sash tied below his yellow tunic. Vincent took a deep breath. "Darla is my daughter," he said.

Gnorrin blinked at him, the polite smile still frozen in place. Then he frowned in confusion. "Is this Earth humor? You know how I have difficulty with it."

So Vincent told him the whole story, Darla sitting quietly as he did so. Gnorrin absorbed the information, toying less and less with his sash as the story unfolded. By the time Vincent had caught him up to the present, Gnorrin was very still in his chair.

"By my grandfather's grave, Vincent," he said, "I swear there has never been a more unusual life than yours lived in this world." He chuckled and rubbed his chin, then turned to Darla. "I'd say I could see the resemblance between you, but I cannot. You are far too lovely to be the offspring of this beast."

"On the contrary," Darla said, smiling. "Our eyes are much alike. His are prettier, though."

Vincent snorted at this, feeling some relief that his friend was so understanding about the situation. "As I'm sure you can imagine," he said, "the news was quite a shock to me." Gnorrin nodded at his words. "But so was the announcement that Darla is carrying my child."

At this, the gnome's eyes grew wide. "I repeat my earlier proclamation." Then he looked into Vincent's eyes. "What? Are you looking for some sort of blessing from me?"

To his shock, Vincent realized that, in a way, he was. "I'm sorry," he said.

"You have feelings of guilt over this."

Vincent glanced self-consciously at Darla, saw the words bite into her. She looked away. "Yeah, I guess that's pretty obvious. I mean..."

"I know what you mean. But this is not something I can help you with." And as Vincent nodded, Gnorrin said, "Besides, I'm too hungry to think of such matters. Will we be dining soon?"

Vincent took a deep breath and stood. "Whenever you're ready." The others joined and followed him out of the room.

"What are we having tonight?" Darla asked. "Something special in honor of Gnorrin's visit, you said."

"Well, 'special' is a subjective term," he said to her. "I hope you like stew."

❧ ❦

A week later, Darvas returned with the caravan, bringing more foodstuffs, tools, winter clothing, blankets, and weapons. Vincent frowned when he saw box after box of crossbow bolts being unloaded, but realized Darvas was being sensible.

He was worried, though, that he had heard no word from Jaz since he had shown Gnorrin his war room setup. He'd been tempted to contact the mage through the stones, but didn't want to disturb his friend just to appease his own curiosity.

The weather was turning colder and frost lay heavily on the morning ground. There were occasional flurries of snow, but no accumulation, yet. He found himself questioning why he'd chosen to build his keep in the mountains. He really wasn't looking forward to the weather he knew was coming.

But he knew why he'd done it. It was a bittersweet realization, though. His mind drifted back to a snow-covered morning, glistening with ice, when he'd walked and talked with a beautiful young girl with black hair and violet eyes. That was the morning, he knew, that he'd lost his heart to Ariaziane.

Or part of it, anyway, he thought. For he'd lost another part of his heart to Rhia. And to Darla. He remembered the pain of Ariaziane's and Rhia's departures. And knowing that Darla's time in this world was growing shorter at quadruple the normal rate, he wondered just how much of his heart was left.

Another week passed, still with no word from Jaz. But Vincent's concerns were at least partially put aside by the arrival of Blade, Sianon, D'Ty, and Felina. He was half-expecting them to arrive, given the fact that King Breigar had sent warnings to them, but he didn't expect Felina to arrive with the others.

She explained that she'd come upon the others during her flight, and recognized them from the descriptions he and Rhia had given. They were well acquainted now, having spent the last three weeks traveling together.

Vincent was surprised that D'Ty had come along. "I owe you at least that," he said in return. "You've done much toward my present happiness in life," D'Ty said.

"As you have for all of us," Blade said, and Sianon nodded her agreement.

518

"Tisen and the baby?" Vincent asked.

"With Tisen's mother," D'Ty explained, and Vincent nodded.

Gnorrin was delighted to see his old friend, and pleased to see D'Ty and Sianon again. He was polite to Felina, but formally so, in Vincent's opinion. "I don't fully trust elves," he said privately to Vincent later.

Vincent didn't go into it with him. After all, Felina had turned a former lover into a big cat. He certainly couldn't allay his friend's distrust based on a character assessment.

Marshalling his courage again, Vincent introduced Darla to those she had yet to meet. He didn't hold back anything. As he had done with Gnorrin, he told the full story.

"Ah," Felina said. "That explains much about Rhia's behavior."

Before he could question what she meant, Sianon spoke up. "Wait, wait, wait. I obviously didn't hear that right," she said. "Did you really just tell us that this woman, who is carrying your baby, is your daughter?"

Vincent shrugged and smiled briefly. "Evidence would indicate."

Sianon held up her hand, palm out toward him, turning her head away. "That's more information than I require, thank you."

D'Ty wore a sympathetic smile on his face, but said nothing. Blade wore a frown, much to Vincent's dismay. The tall man stared at him, and Vincent was afraid that his friend was about to condemn him. But the more he looked into Blade's eyes, the clearer it became. He was trying to assess how Vincent felt about this. Vincent took a deep breath and looked back into those grey eyes, trying to convey that everything was all right, that he was accepting of the situation.

"It's a shame Tisen isn't here," he said to D'Ty. "I thought maybe she and Darla could discuss names together."

"Seems to be plenty of time for that, yet," D'Ty said, indicating the non-protruding state of Darla's belly. "Perhaps when the Season of Green arrives, we can get them together."

Vincent nodded. "Perhaps."

The group spent the rest of the day together, catching up on events. Vincent spent a good deal of time in reflection, wondering why it was that he felt the need to tell his friends about Darla's true relation to him. He hadn't told Jaz, however. But that was because he himself hadn't been comfortable with the truth at that time. Perhaps when the mage returned, he would have a talk with him.

After the evening meal, they went topside, Vincent showing off his great outdoors. A light snow was falling, and Vincent breathed in the chilly air with a mix of nostalgia and peace. It was during this idyllic moment that Jaz came swooping in on his carpet. His face was grim as he stepped off and faced them. "I hope no one here has plans for the near future," he said quickly.

"Why?" said Vincent.

"My friend," Jaz sighed, "you are soon to have your first taste of siege warfare."

❧ Thirty-Five ❧

Vincent stood staring at Jaz, the mage's words ringing heavily in his ears. *Siege warfare*. He shook his head. Jaz couldn't have meant what Vincent pictured when he heard the term. He stepped closer to his friend. "What, exactly, did you mean by that?"

"I mean that I have assessed the situation and, to put it in a way that you'll not misunderstand..." He spread his hands. "It sucks." He began walking toward the entrance to the keep. "Now if you don't mind, I've been flying for hours. I'd much prefer to talk around a warm hearth."

Inside they went, Vincent's anxiety worsening with every step. The others followed behind, quietly. Once gathered around the fireplace, Vincent quickly introduced Jaz to his newly arrived friends. Then he said, "Okay, so what's the situation?"

Jaz took a deep breath. "All the creatures that had been converging upon your friends," and he nodded at them all, "are now coming here. It took some time, but I was able to locate them. I found the wolves first. The pack grows as it progresses. There were at least forty when I saw them. As for the trolls, there are perhaps twenty of them. They seem somehow to be summoning others to join them as they travel."

"And the resistance to magic?" Gnorrin prompted.

"Present in all groups," Jaz confirmed. "Gnorrin, I tried spells from every discipline I know, but I only affected perhaps one or two with every spell."

"Just as with the snow giants," Gnorrin said. "Remarkable."

"Maybe not," Vincent said. "Darla says he's probably using the portal to manipulate these creatures. Gnorrin, you said yourself that the portal probably imparts some sort of protection, since I wandered through untold areas without harm before I was found by you."

"What is remarkable," the gnome countered, "is that this protection is extending to all the creatures, even those that later joined the few original ones summoned with the portal. If, indeed, the originals *were* summoned with the portal."

Vincent blinked. "Oh."

"I feel certain we could defeat them if they were stationary, in a region where we had resources to draw from," Jaz continued.

"Such as?" D'Ty asked.

"Something physical. A landslide down this mountain, for example. Drowning them. Surrounding them with non-magical fire."

"Dropping pianos on them?" Vincent offered. The others stared at him. "Sorry," he said.

"Perhaps you should not be," said Felina. "I do not know what a piano is, but as Rhia demonstrated to you, dropping a heavy object upon something can be quite effective. But once again, as Jaz says, they are moving too quickly."

"Oh, come on," Vincent said. "A room full of mages and we can't figure out a way to just stop these things? Throw up a magical wall or something! *Then* drop the pianos."

"Are you not listening?" Jaz said. "They are resistant to magic. They would pass right through a magical wall."

"Right, right, okay. I'm a moron," he said, nodding his head.

"Not a bad idea," said Felina. The others looked at her. She waved off their questioning eyes. "I shall handle the wolves. They were sent after me, so that would be proper." The others started to question, but again she waved them off. "The trolls, on the other hand, are what worry me. Wolves are one thing, but trolls another."

"What's so bad about trolls?" Vincent said.

Jaz fixed him with a serious look. "They regenerate from their wounds," he said flatly.

"Excuse me?"

"Strike one with your sword," Gnorrin expanded, "and within moments, the wound is closed and healing. Sever a limb, and within minutes it has regrown."

"Shit," Vincent breathed. "What kills them, then?"

"Fire," said Jaz. "My specialty." Then he frowned. "Sadly, magical fire hasn't had any effect."

"Normal fire would?"

"Presumably, yes. But that's considerably harder to accomplish. Once again, we would need to halt their movement."

"Well, I'm sure all you geniuses can think of something," Vincent said somewhat bitterly. He didn't really want to be discussing warfare, killing, death and destruction. He stood abruptly. "Excuse me," he said, and quickly left the room.

He felt claustrophobic, suffocated, all of a sudden. Climbing the stairwell, he headed for his room and stepped out onto the balcony. He drank in the cold, night air, his eyes shut and mind racing. This was, effectively, a *war* they were talking about. The very concept nauseated him. He was about to see people, friends, put their lives at risk. For him. And that was the last thing he wanted.

Who knew what other surprises his son was cooking up? The snow giants, the trolls, and the mountain wolves could all be just a small part of his plan. What if he summoned something worse? Or several somethings?

He looked out over the valley. It was, he admitted, a beautiful sight. He could see no details of the valley in the dark, but the stars were brilliant. One of them could be Sol, he realized. And circling around it, Earth. On Earth, he would not be worrying about battles and killing. He'd be... With a sigh, he realized he had no idea what he'd be doing now. It had been six years since his arrival here. He'd have graduated college. Well, he chided himself, he assumed he'd have graduated if he'd finally mastered calculus. Maybe he'd be working on his Master's degree. Or maybe he'd have gotten a job as an assistant in an observatory, studying stars and planets, nebulae and galaxies.

Or he'd have screwed it up, like he did most things, and wound up working in a factory, or flipping burgers. He frowned at this thought. Not a very pleasant image, but certainly better than planning for a war, for death.

He shook his head. He had to stop dwelling on this. But how? Huge lungfuls of chilly air weren't clearing his head. The claustrophobic feeling was gone, but his mind still felt fuzzy. He heard a noise behind him, soft footfalls. He turned, expecting Darla, but it was Felina.

"I hope I'm not interrupting," she said.

"Not really."

She stepped over and joined him on the balcony. "Are you angry with me?" she asked, leaning beside him against the stone railing.

He frowned. "Why would I be angry with you?"

The elf shrugged. "I wasn't overly polite to you during our last days together, back at my home. I'm sorry if I seemed rude."

"It's okay," he smiled. "You'd been through a lot. And I wasn't behaving very well, either."

"Neither of us was. And you'd been through a lot, also." She leaned against the rail and stared outward, as Vincent was doing.

"They could be anywhere," he said softly.

"Aye," she agreed. "And they could be anything, too."

"I don't know what to do," he confessed. "This isn't anything I ever dreamed could happen to me."

Felina glanced up at him, a slight expression of consternation on her face. "Your life seems to be full of such happenings, however, doesn't it?"

Despite his mood, Vincent laughed. "I can't deny that." He smiled down at her, then said, "Felina, I never really got a chance to properly thank you."

"For what?"

"For clearing things up with me, concerning Rhia. You know, before I knew about the age thing, and all that."

She waved it off. "Oh, don't thank me for that. I just made you aware of things you didn't know."

He nodded. "Well. Either way. Thanks."

"You're welcome."

"How's Kita?"

Felina smiled mischievously as she gazed out across the valley. "Still a panther."

"Mm," Vincent replied, wondering if she'd ever learn the truth about that.

"Are you expecting company?" she said suddenly.

Vincent frowned, looking out to the valley again. "No. Why?" He saw nothing, but imagined his vision was nothing like that of an elf.

"Because there is a campfire out on the horizon." He strained his eyes, but still saw nothing. "Oh, do not worry," she said. "It's there. I would not expect you to see it. Whoever it is still has several hours' journey before reaching you."

"But who could it be?" He felt a surge of panic go through him, then fought it down. Wolves and trolls wouldn't be stopping to build a campfire.

"I would say you'll know by mid-morning," she said casually.

Vincent frowned. "I hate waiting."

Felina smirked. "Humans."

"Yeah, so sue me." He waved off her puzzled expression, then sighed and turned his eyes back to the stars, trying not to think of anything in particular. No approaching visitors, no approaching marauders, no approaching anxieties of any sort. It might even have worked, were it not for the feeling of eyes on him. He glanced over at Felina, noting that she was, indeed, staring at him. "What?" he asked.

She smiled. "You were thinking about Rhia." With a shock, he realized she was right. He'd meant to simply clear his mind, but instead he'd been remembering happier times. Times with Rhia. "I don't blame you," she continued. "I think of her often, too."

"I wonder if I'll ever see her again."

"You will."

He snorted. "You're that certain?"

"Yes," she said firmly. And something in the tone of her voice made him look at her differently. Did she know something he didn't? Well, obviously, he berated himself. She was an elf, a mage, and almost six times his age. She would know quite a bit more than he did. But did she really know that he would see Rhia again? Or was it just optimistic thinking? He didn't want to push it. He was grateful for the words, no matter the truth behind them.

"Thank you," he said.

They stood together, looking out over the valley until Felina eventually decided to go to bed. Not long after her departure, Darla entered the room behind him.

"Are you well?" she asked.

He nodded, turning from the balcony to meet her with a hug. "Yeah. Thanks."

"Did you and Felina have a good talk?"

"We did. Is that why you waited until now to follow me up here?"

"Yes. She is your friend. You haven't seen her for a long time, and this is the first opportunity you've had to talk privately with her since her arrival."

He smiled. "You're wonderful, you know that?"

"I try," she said.

As he held her, he thought of how much he loved her. It was a nice feeling inside, but Rhia sat prominently in his thoughts, too. She filled his heart with an ache. Despite Felina's words, he had no overwhelming feeling that he'd ever see her again. And no amount of Darla's love could ever erase that pain completely.

Morning found him standing on his balcony again, watching for any approaching travelers. It was still early. Darla had stirred in bed when he rose, but did not wake. Vincent shivered in the chill and wrapped his cloak tighter around himself. He was impressed with the fact that his bedroom was warm. The doors Feletain had installed between the room and the balcony had no drafts.

It had snowed overnight. Perhaps an inch or so lay atop the railing of the balcony and across the valley. He had been standing there for the better part of an hour and only now could see the faintest hint of something moving in the distance.

A suspicion had been growing in his head, an idea regarding the identity of the approaching visitor. It wasn't an idea that thrilled him, given the circumstances. He shook his head. War. This wasn't something he could handle. No way. He was, when it came down to it, a peaceful person. He still had nightmares sometimes about the man he'd killed by punching him in the nose while wearing the gauntlets. In a bizarre way, he was rather happy that his son had stolen those things from him. No more accidents like that one.

He didn't want to see anyone hurt, with the possible exception of his son. The mages could probably take care of themselves, he knew. If he could send Felina, Jaz, Sianon, and Gnorrin out to handle the approaching nasties, they could probably do so without any real risk to themselves. Felina seemed sure she could handle the wolves, for example. The others should be able to take care of the giants and the trolls, and whatever else came along. But he would not allow the others to be put at risk. Blade, D'Ty, Darvas and the men. Or Aedriun, if this truly were him approaching.

He turned away from the balcony and quietly opened the door, stepping quickly inside. Darla continued to sleep peacefully. He stood near the crackling fire for a few minutes, warming himself and thinking of what he wanted to do. Then he headed downstairs.

At one time, he would have frowned at the bare walls and mostly empty rooms that he passed. He would have thought about what sorts of furniture would look good in the rooms and what kinds of artwork should adorn the walls. But not now. Now he had no interest in the keep, except for the passing thought of who might live in the structure when he was gone.

He reached the lower level and went to the kitchen. Food was the farthest thing from his mind, but a mug of something hot would hopefully soothe his jangled nerves. To his surprise, he heard the soft sounds of voices as he approached. In the kitchen, he found Felina, Jaz, and Gnorrin. They looked up as he entered. Felina smiled and pulled down a mug for him and proceeded to fill it with freshly brewed tea, or its near equivalent.

"Morning," he said to them, then thanked Felina as she handed him the cup. "I'm guessing you're planning on getting started."

Jaz elected himself spokesmage. "If our magic is going to be only slightly effective, we will need repeated attacks. Therefore we should begin now, before they approach much further."

Vincent nodded. "Logical. I trust you'll all keep your distance, too. I don't want you getting hurt."

"Yes, Father," said Gnorrin, causing the others to laugh.

"Sianon will not be assisting you?"

Jaz shook his head. "Sianon's magical abilities are nowhere near as well-developed as ours, to be honest. And it would not do to keep you totally without magical protection here."

"Do not worry about me," he said. "Perhaps Sianon could do some reconnaissance. I'm concerned that there could be other surprises in store for us."

"As are we," Felina said. "We know the boy is devious."

"So who is handling what? I know you're taking the wolves," he said to Felina.

"I'll be working on the snow giants," Jaz said. "They are in my territory, after all."

"And I've dealt with trolls before," said Gnorrin.

Vincent let out a sigh, then nodded. "Okay," he said softly. "But I want each of you to take one of the necklaces Jaz made for me. I want to be able to monitor your progress." He sipped at his drink and inhaled the soothing aroma. He was tired, and the stress of this situation wasn't helping matters any.

Jaz excused himself to fetch the necklaces. Gnorrin busied himself with preparing something to eat, pulling out biscuits and butter. Felina stepped over to Vincent and surprised him by kissing him warmly. "That's for being so concerned about our safety."

He felt the blood rushing to his cheeks and cleared his throat. "Um. Thank you."

Felina chuckled to herself and swept her long hair back from her forehead. "You're funny, Vincent."

"I try," he said.

Jaz returned with the necklaces. Gnorrin and Felina put them on. Then Felina said, "I believe I'll be on my way, then."

The others bade her farewell and good luck. She brushed up against Vincent, catlike, as she left. He could have sworn she'd purred, too.

"You are comfortable with the scrying disks?" Jaz asked.

Vincent nodded. "Yeah, I'll be fine. Don't worry about that."

"Simply being certain." He paused, as if contemplating another statement, then shook his head. "Well. Advise Sianon that the southern regions are those I did not thoroughly examine, but..."

"But what?"

He smiled faintly. "No matter. Just be alert." He clapped Vincent's back. "I'll be in touch." He said goodbye to Gnorrin, then departed.

Gnorrin idly buttered a biscuit as Jaz left. When he was gone, he said, "You do realize, don't you," he said, "that these are mere diversions?"

Vincent's head dropped, his eyes closing. "Yes," he whispered.

"That's what Jaz was trying to say. He didn't wish to worry you, however."

Taking a deep breath, Vincent said, "All I care about is that no one gets hurt. If the three of you can't stop these creatures, then they'll converge here. If they do that, I know Darvas will take the men into battle against them. I also believe Aedriun is on his way here to offer his assistance. If they all go against them, some of them will die, and I do *not* want their blood on my hands."

Gnorrin's reply was not immediately forthcoming. He brushed crumbs from his orange tunic, then crossed his arms over his chest. "It is noble of you to be concerned for their safety. But can you not see that all of us are equally as concerned for your safety? Personally, I do not like going off to fight trolls. I'd much rather make certain you are safe."

"And I'd much rather have you here, believe me. I don't stand a chance against him, you know."

His friend nodded. "Aye. My fear is that you will be attacked while we are out."

"And yet, if you do not go, he will wait until all the diversions aren't diversions any longer. They'll be here, attacking with him."

"Yes. A nice quandary."

"No kidding." He sighed and put his hand on Gnorrin's shoulder. "Good luck. And thank you."

"I imagine I shall be speaking with you soon," he said as he toyed with the necklace. "I imagine I should be off, eh?"

Vincent smiled grimly. "I imagine."

"Hold down the keep, as they say," Gnorrin said as he departed. "Everything will be well."

He watched his friend leave, then drained the last of his now lukewarm beverage. He soaked in the warmth from the wood stove as he tried to put things in order in his head. It didn't work very well. He poured another mug from the kettle on the stove, then walked into the small adjoining dining room and sat at a table.

He looked around at the room. So empty, he thought. When finished, it would have many more tables, plus lots of wall decorations. As it was, it was barren. Cold. Ugly. Rather like circumstances, he thought as he put his head down on his folded arms. He wondered how long it would take Aedriun to cover the remaining distance to the keep. And then, he fell asleep.

He woke to an annoying sensation. His hand was tingling. He blinked, sitting upright. His neck was sore and obviously, his hand had fallen asleep. Then his hand tingled again. With a shock, he realized it was the ring, indicating that someone was attempting to contact him. He spilled the mug's cold contents across the tabletop as he sprang to his feet and hurried to his war room.

One of the scrying disks was swirling with grey as he took his seat. He had no idea which of the mages was trying to contact him, since Jaz didn't tell him which necklaces were being taken. He impatiently reached toward the stone and concentrated. Soon, a face coalesced into view.

"About time, handsome," Felina said when the image was complete.

"Sorry," he said, wiping sleep from his eyes. "What's your situation?"

"The situation is that you have a pack of mountain wolves approaching and I'm going to try to stop them."

"Tell me something I don't know," he drawled.

Felina smirked, and the view changed. Vincent could now see down toward the ground, his scene obscured only slightly by what Vincent realized was part of Felina's belt. She'd tucked the necklace in before going into action.

He watched as her spell generated a wall of ice. Though magically generated, Vincent knew the ice itself was very real. It appeared to be tall enough so the wolves could not jump over, and thick enough so they could not break through. He frowned, though, because there were so many of them. He wasn't sure her wall could be made sufficiently wide quickly enough to hold them all.

The view shifted as Felina moved, and Vincent now saw the wall curving around, forming a circle. His hopes rose, then, for he saw the wall complete, and all but a couple of the wolves were caught inside. They paced back and forth restlessly, angrily.

Then Felina began another spell. Vincent watched, wondering what she was up to. At first, nothing happened, then he saw hail begin to fall. Small stones, at first, but growing larger. In a minute's time, the stones were the size of bricks, hurtling down from the sky.

The wolves began to take a pounding, and despite his knowledge of what their goal was, he couldn't help but feel bad for them. They were, after all, pawns in this game.

But then, his heart stuttered. Three of the wolves stood together, facing the wall. And the others, taking a running start, jumped onto their backs, then vaulted over the wall to freedom. Soon, the stream of wolves was running across the open plain again.

Felina watched helplessly, her hailstorm fading away to a gentle snowfall. Five wolves lay bloody in the snow inside the ice circle. Five, Vincent thought bitterly. Out of forty or more. "Shit," he breathed.

But then the scene blurred. Felina was chasing them, flying to get ahead of them. Once again, she began the wall, this time higher. Vincent strained, looking into the stone, trying to see what the wolves were doing. He shook his head. It wasn't going to work, he knew. The wolves were gaining speed. Felina couldn't build a wall fast enough. The animals would go around it before it was big enough. With the plains being wide open, they could alter their trajectory any way they wished to avoid it.

After two failures, Felina let them proceed, then settled to the ground. Her face came into view in Vincent's stone. He saw the frustration on her face even before he heard it in her voice. "Mountain wolves are not that resourceful," she said.

Vincent suspected that his son was probably aiding them somehow. He waved off her comment. "They have to sleep sometime," he said. "Track them until they settle down for the night, then take care of it."

"I was thinking similar thoughts," she replied. "I suppose that's my only option at this point."

"Keep me posted," he said, just before she ended the connection. He slumped back in his seat, frowning. His eyes wandered over the remaining scrying stones. Who would be next to check in? Would any of them fare better than Felina had? Somehow, he doubted it. His eyelids drooped in weariness and frustration, and soon he was asleep again.

He woke when Darla entered the room. He stretched, smiling at her. "You didn't sleep last night, did you?" she asked.

"Not very well, no."

"How long have you been down here?"

Briefly, he told her of the departure of the mages, as well as Felina's initial failures. "I'm waiting for the next round," he said. "Also, I believe Aedriun is approaching."

Darla shook her head. "No. He's here. That's why I sought you out."

Vincent frowned in mock petulance. "You didn't come for me just because you wanted to see me?"

She smiled and kissed his cheek. "I would have, yes. But Coldson woke me when Aedriun arrived, so I didn't have the chance to find you for my own selfish purpose."

"And what would that purpose have been?"

"Mm, why ruin the surprise?"

"I like the sound of that," he said, grinning. "But I suppose I should welcome Baron Aedriun to my humble home, shouldn't I?"

Darla nodded, holding out a hand to assist him. He grasped it, rising, and walked hand-in-hand with her as they left the war room. She led him to the kitchen, explaining that she felt it was a more proper place to greet morning visitors, especially when they are friends.

Aedriun was seated at a small table, happily shoveling eggs and toast into his mouth. "Ah!" he said, spying Vincent. He laughed heartily, mopping at his mustache with a napkin as he rose from his seat. "How good to see you!" He strode forward and clasped Vincent's hand and upper arm.

"And you, my friend. Enjoying your breakfast?"

"Very much so," he said, returning to his seat. "Your cook was most gracious to me."

Vincent looked over at the woman. "That looks positively wonderful. Would you mind?"

"Not at all," she replied, placing the skillet atop the cooking fire again. Vincent watched as she put an inch of water in the bottom of the skillet, then carefully cracked eggs into it when it was hot. A separate, dry skillet heated the thick slices of buttered bread. Aedriun had finished his meal by the time Vincent and Darla were served theirs.

"You must have left quite early this morning to get here so soon," Vincent said.

Aedriun nodded, peeling his gaze from Darla back to his friend. "Aye. Very early. Before the sun."

"You didn't travel alone, did you?"

The baron shot him a look that Vincent didn't quite comprehend, then shook his head. "I brought two of my men. They are unloading our wagon."

Vincent nodded as he ate. "It is very good to see you," he repeated, "but I must protest you coming all this way. I know why you're here. And I won't have you putting yourself at risk for my sake."

Aedriun toyed with the ends of his mustache. "If it comes to that, I am quite willing to fight for you. We brought arms for such purpose. But that is not my real reason for being here."

Surprised, Vincent said, "Oh? Then what is the reason?"

His friend smiled in a puzzled fashion. "I cannot say." He shook his head as if he couldn't believe what he was about to say. "Vincent, I suddenly got the feeling that if I didn't come, I would never see you again."

Darla looked at Aedriun in alarm, then at Vincent, then back to Aedriun. "What do you mean by that? You had a premonition of his death?"

"No, not at all," Aedriun assured her. "I do not know how to put it. A feeling of... of *absence*, I suppose."

Vincent didn't think too hard about these words, for they simultaneously filled him with dread and hope. Dread, for the same reason Darla was alarmed. He didn't want to die, that was certain. And hope, because it begged the possibility that he might actually find his way home. And he certainly didn't want to get his hopes up, only to have them dashed.

He swallowed a mouthful of poached egg and pushed a thick piece of toast through warm yolk on his plate. "Whatever your reasons, I'm glad to see you. But," he said seriously, "you will not be fighting for me. Nor will your men."

Aedriun raised his eyebrows and shrugged. "I do not think it will be necessary. You have some heavy magical assistance—"

"—that is failing," Vincent finished for him. "But even so, even if all the nasty beasties get through, you are not fighting for me."

The baron narrowed his eyes and frowned. "And why is that?" he asked.

Vincent finished his last bite of toast and put his fork down. "Because," he said simply, wiping his mouth, "I forbid it." Aedriun began to protest, but Vincent cut him off. "No one will put themselves in danger because of me. Gnorrin and the others can attack from complete safety, which is why I had no problem with them going off on their individual missions. But I will not have anyone going into close-quarters combat against these creatures simply to defend me or my property. That is unacceptable."

The older man stared at him over his steepled fingers for several seconds. Finally, he said, "Have you considered that you and your property might not be the only things at risk? If the snow giants, for example, overrun your keep, do you not think that all inside would perish? Or, gods forbid, what if they are directed not to attack you, but an outlying town?"

With his words, all Vincent's bravado dissipated. He *hadn't* considered those scenarios. He dropped his face into his hands. "You see, Aedriun? Breigar was foolish to make me a baron. I've got no head for this sort of thing."

Before his friend could reply, the ring on Vincent's finger started vibrating. He jerked upright, startled. "What?" Aedriun asked.

Vincent clenched his fist against the sensation. "Follow me," he said as he stood.

Once in the war room, he activated the swirling stone. As he sat in his chair, Aedriun and Darla at his sides, Jaz's face came into view. He wasn't smiling.

"What's the word, Jaz?"

The mage frowned. "How about 'futile'? That would seem to apply." He sighed, then seemed to notice the others. "Good morning, Darla. Greetings, Aedriun."

The pair greeted him, then Vincent said, "How futile?"

Jaz shrugged. "On the encouraging side, from my perspective, they seem to be ignoring my property. They are near it, but continuing past. On the discouraging side, I've been unable to slow them."

"At all?"

"Not to any degree of significance. Vincent, I have never seen resistance to magic like this. Heat, you know, is something snow giants dislike. I've used every fire-based spell in my head, and none have done more than singe their hairs. It is as if my previous attacks upon them only served to accustom them to my magic."

"That would be magical fire, though, right?"

"What else would you have me do? Start a fire in the forest in front of them?"

"No, nothing so extreme. But don't you have lamp oil or something that you can douse them with and ignite?"

The mage smiled ruefully. "I did, yes. That was, in fact, my first attack."

"They're immune to normal fire, too?" Aedriun said, shocked.

"No, not at all. However, no sooner had I set one of them ablaze than the others proceeded to extinguish the flames. The end result was of no consequence. I would need to have a tremendous amount of oil on hand to accomplish the task of halting even one of them. And, doubtless, I would succeed in starting that forest fire I mentioned."

Vincent rubbed a hand over his face, sighing. "Okay, so now what? What is your next plan?"

"Other spells, of course. I'm certainly not going to take a sword to them."

"What about cold-based spells?"

"Aye, I am working on that. They are not my specialty, but I know a few. Your reasoning is that they have been fortified against the spells that do them the most harm, but not against those that harm them little, yes?"

"Exactly."

"Let us hope your reasoning is sound. I'll be back in touch."

Vincent thanked him and ended the connection. But no sooner had the stone faded to black than his finger was vibrating. Gnorrin came into view as Vincent activated another stone.

"Don't tell me," Vincent began. "The trolls aren't being affected by your spells." Gnorrin raised an eyebrow. Vincent shook his head. "Sorry. Just a little frustrated."

Gnorrin nodded. "Understandable. Unfortunately, you are correct in your assumption. My spells have been fairly ineffectual."

Aedriun interjected, saving Vincent the trouble of thinking of something to say. "Gnorrin, good to see you again, if even under these circumstances."

"And you, Baron."

"What results have you had?"

The gnome frowned. "These trolls are exhibiting behavior I have never seen in trolls before. These are creatures that live in hordes, but are not especially fond of each other. One will not go out of its way to assist another. They gather in hordes for the safety factor it gives, not to mention the intimidation it represents." He paused, stroking his chin. "This group, on the other hand, is showing almost a group mentality. I attack one, the others rally to its defense. It's almost as if..."

"As if someone were directing them," Darla finished.

There was a long silence. Vincent studied Gnorrin's face and knew he'd been thinking exactly that. Aedriun's expression was one of concern. A feeling of helplessness began to wash over Vincent. "Just how powerful is your brother?" he whispered.

Darla's brow furrowed. "More than I thought," she said.

"More than any of us thought, it seems," Gnorrin added, somewhat needlessly, in Vincent's opinion.

"Okay," Vincent said. "Do whatever you can, Gnorrin. Check in with any progress reports." He paused, then said, "In the event that you don't discover some way to stop them, when would you expect they'd arrive here?"

Gnorrin looked him in the eye. "Most likely by tomorrow night."

The words pierced Vincent to the bone. "I had no idea they were that close."

He thought briefly of summoning Jaz and Felina on the stones, to ask the same question of them, but he knew what the answer would be. His son wasn't stupid. He'd have them all arrive simultaneously, or pretty close to it.

"All right," he said to Gnorrin. "Thanks. Good luck."

The gnome nodded, then the stone went dark.

Vincent felt Darla's hand on his shoulder, squeezing compassionately. He smiled fondly at her, though he felt horrible. His stomach had a pit that kept growing and growing.

"It seems you might be requiring the services of men-at-arms, whether you like it or not," Aedriun said.

His words only made the pit churn. He knew Aedriun was right, but that didn't mean he had to permit it, if he could help it.

"So it would seem," he said.

"If I may, I would oversee the readying of the men."

Vincent nodded, feeling defeated. "As you wish."

As Aedriun left the war room, Darla knelt beside Vincent's chair. "You do not intend to allow the men to fight."

"Nope."

She smiled at him. "Your compassion for others is a beautiful thing," she said. "It will probably get you killed, but it is very beautiful."

"If your brother wants me dead, I'm dead. Aedriun and the others fighting his distractions will not prevent it. For that matter, if he wants all of us dead, it's conceivable that he could pull that off, too."

Darla frowned. "Against all your mage friends? I would not think so."

"Perhaps not. I guess I'm just feeling very helpless and frustrated. While others fight my battles for me, all I can do is wait for your brother to arrive."

Darla said nothing, but wrapped her arms around him. He leaned against her, wishing against all evidence that his friends would find some way to defeat the invading beasts, so they could be here with him when his son showed up. He wished for this with all his might. But he knew it was in vain.

He spent much of the remainder of the day speaking with D'Ty. The two of them stood on the upper level of the keep, outside. They climbed up onto the wall and stood looking out over the valley. Vincent was looking for some sign of the approaching creatures, but they were still too far off. Perhaps this time tomorrow, he thought, there might be some sign of them. Or perhaps not.

"What am I going to do? How can I hope to fight against him?"

His friend frowned in dismay. "I have no idea."

"Great," he muttered. "I'm toast."

D'Ty looked at him, his face bemused. Then, to Vincent's amazement, the man snorted and began laughing hysterically. Immediately, he tried to stop laughing, which only made matters worse.

Despite himself, Vincent chuckled. "Thanks so much," he said sarcastically. "I'm about to die and you think it's hilarious."

"I'm sorry," D'Ty managed to say between guffaws. "I am not taking this lightly. But," he said, then laughed louder. "'*Toast?*'" He regained his composure briefly. "I just had this vision of you covered with butter and fruit."

"Pervert."

"It was not appetizing in the least," D'Ty said, and resumed laughing.

"Ha, ha," Vincent said flatly. "You can bite me."

As his friend laughed quietly to himself, Vincent leaned against the top of the stone wall and gazed out over the valley again. He welcomed the bit of levity, but its usefulness to him was over, now. He'd smiled for perhaps the first time all day, and he was glad that D'Ty was enjoying himself, anyway. But the feeling of dread came back to him. Hard.

Suddenly he turned, frowning. "Something's wrong," he said.

Instantly, D'Ty was all business. "What?"

"I don't know. Come on." He hurried back into the keep, D'Ty right behind him.

They found Sianon speaking with Darla in one of the smaller rooms on the first floor. Both women looked up in alarm as the men burst into the room. "I need an eye in the sky," Vincent blurted. "Sianon, can you?"

"Yes. What is wrong?"

"Please take a look to the south. It's the only direction not accounted for, and I have a horrible feeling that something's coming from that direction."

"I didn't know you were prone to such visions."

"It's not a vision, just a hunch. Please take one of the necklaces with you and let me know immediately whatever you learn."

After a brief goodbye, she was gone, D'Ty going with her to the war room to fetch one of the necklaces.

"Do you have any idea of what it could be?" Darla asked.

"No. Just a strange feeling. Almost like a message sent to me." His thoughts turned to Rhia, then. He'd been able to send messages to her, subconsciously. Was this a warning from her, wherever she was?

Blaise yawned and stretched near the fireplace. He shook his head. "I'm glad someone is still relaxed through all of this." He took Darla's hands in his and kissed them lightly. "I'm going to the war room to wait for Sianon's message."

"I'll join you shortly." She smiled as he let go of her hands and departed.

In the war room, he sat nervously in his chair. Blaise had followed him inside, though she seemed to regret it. The war room had no fireplace, and she sniffed around dejectedly for a while before planting herself at his feet. She yawned again and promptly fell asleep.

True to her word, Darla soon joined him. She carried a tray with sliced meat and cheese, plus a mug of hot spiced cider. He thanked her when she put the tray down on a small table to the left of his seat. "I'm afraid my stomach is too wound up to tolerate food."

"It is there if you change your mind." Darla then proceeded to climb into his lap and put her arms around him. "I love you."

For just a moment, his mind left his worries behind. He smiled. "I love you, too." It was in the middle of their kiss that Vincent's ring began vibrating. He jerked away from Darla. "Sorry," he whispered, squeezing her hand. She got up from his lap as he activated the scrying stone. Sianon's expressionless face came into view. "What's up?" he asked quickly.

In response, Sianon turned the necklace outward, allowing him to look through it as if he were looking through a telescope. What he saw made his stomach hurt even worse. On the horizon was a small army of men. They were approaching on foot, weapons of all sorts carried with them: swords, bows, spears, pikes, flails...

"Sianon, how far away from the keep are you?"

"Not far enough," was her reply.

Vincent's mouth was dry. His heart pounded in his chest. "How many?" he whispered.

"At least fifty," Sianon replied. Before he could ask, she answered his next question. "I can take some of them, Vincent, but not all."

"I don't want you to kill any of them," he said quickly.

Sianon raised an eyebrow. "Fine. I'll just make faces at them. Maybe they'll run away."

He hadn't the heart to argue with her or be upset at her sarcasm. His voice was barely above a whisper when he spoke. "I just don't want anyone hurt."

"It's either them or us, Vincent," Sianon said.

"I know! I know." He fretted for a minute. Then, defeatedly, he said, "Do what you have to do."

"I shall. But as I said, I can't handle all of them. You'd best alert your men."

The stone went black, then, leaving Vincent to deal with her words. He looked at Darla, whose expression was so sorrowful that it nearly brought tears to his eyes. "I'm sorry," she said.

"There you are." D'Ty strode into the war room, Blade, Aedriun and Darvas with him.

"My brother says you had a vision," Blade said.

Vincent shook his head. "No. Just a feeling. One that has been confirmed."

"Already?" Aedriun said. He nodded, then told them of his contact from Sianon. "All right," said Aedriun. "I'll gather the men."

"You'll do no such thing," Vincent said, causing all to stare at him. All but Darla, he noted with some gratitude. "I told you before. I won't allow it."

"You have no choice, Vincent," Aedriun insisted. "Come, my friends. My men will fight with me."

"*Your* men, Aedriun?" The baron turned at Vincent's cold words. He stared at him. "I thought they were *my* men, now. Which is it? Darvas. Which of us do you serve?"

Darvas looked from Vincent to his uncle. Aedriun ignored his glance, continuing to stare at Vincent. "I serve you, m'lord," he said to Vincent. "But I agree with my uncle. You must fight them or be overrun. And I'll not stand idly by and allow that to happen."

Vincent felt as though all his energy left him, then. It had been his one hope, that he could order the men not to fight. "Fine," he said softly. "If you'll not obey my demands, then would you consider it as a favor to me? I'm asking you in the name of our friendship. Please. Don't do this."

For a long moment, the four men looked at him and amongst themselves. Aedriun was the first to leave. Darvas lingered momentarily, then with one last look of apology at Vincent, followed his uncle out. D'Ty frowned and folded his arms across his chest, obviously waiting to see what his brother would do. Vincent looked expectantly at Blade.

The tall man shook his head. "What do you hope to gain by not allowing the men to defend themselves?"

"I have no problem with them defending themselves. I just don't want them putting their lives at risk defending *me*. And that's what they're doing."

"They're doing both. Surely you see that."

Vincent opened his mouth to protest, but then his finger began vibrating. He sighed in exasperation, then activated the stone that he knew corresponded to Jaz. Blade and D'Ty took advantage of the distraction and left the room. Blade grabbed the remaining necklaces on his way out.

Jaz's face peered at him from the stone. "Greetings, again," he said. "I'm afraid I have unpleasant news."

"That makes two of us."

The mage paused. "Oh? What has happened?"

"Hang on a second." He activated the stones for Felina and Gnorrin, then waited for them to acknowledge. When all three were present, he told them all of the development that Sianon had discovered.

Felina was the first to speak. "Do you wish us to return, or to continue our valiant, but ineffective, efforts?"

"I have no idea," Vincent admitted. "Aedriun is gathering the men even now, to take them into the field against this new threat. I didn't want him to, but there was no stopping him."

"His actions would seem prudent, given the circumstances," said Jaz.

"You know that Jaz is correct," said Gnorrin, "but I understand your reasons. I'm sorry."

"Okay, fine. So what do you guys think? Should you stay or come here?"

Jaz stroked his beard. "I, for one, would like to continue with my task at hand. At least for a little while longer."

"To be honest, I'm out of ideas," Felina said. "I'd just as soon return."

"Whatever is your wish," Gnorrin put in.

Vincent heaved a sigh. "Well, shit."

"Goddess!" Felina gasped.

"What?" Vincent snapped.

"The wolves! They're gone!"

"What do you mean?"

"She means," Jaz put in, "that her dogs have disappeared. As have my giants."

"And my trolls," added Gnorrin.

"What, they just vanished?" Vincent blurted.

"No," Darla said ominously. "They're being moved along by my brother." Her words struck everyone silent. "He's coming," she said.

As Vincent listened to the sounds of warriors leaving the keep to face the oncoming horde, his friends vanished, one by one, from the scrying stones. He knew they'd ended the connections and were headed this way. He glanced at Darla. She looked terrible.

"It's all my fault," she said.

"What is?"

"It's my fault that he has become what he has, my fault that he's trying to destroy you."

"And how do you figure that?"

"Because he's angry. He's angry that I fell in love with you. Angry that I left him for you. It's me that he wants. If I go back to him, he might stop all this."

Vincent didn't like the look in her eye. "I don't think so. He's obsessed, now."

"But I have to try!"

"Try what?" he said in exasperation. "You're not seriously considering facing him, are you?"

She turned sad eyes upon him. "I love you," she said. "I do this for you." And before Vincent could say a word, she raised her arms and disappeared in a flash of blue light.

A wave of panic swept over him as he surged from his chair. He ran from the room, but realized he had no chance of finding her. She wasn't in the keep any longer, he knew.

He hurried down the hall, then up the stairs to his room. There, he gathered his weapons. Sitting in his war room was accomplishing nothing. He was a dead man and he knew it. No sense in pretending that people weren't going to die. But Sianon was right. Better the "bad guys" than the "good guys."

He stepped out onto his balcony for an aerial view of whatever might be going on. He looked down into the notch of the valley at the foot of the mountain and saw nothing. Sweeping his gaze outward, he saw tiny specks in the distance. It was hard to say what they were from this distance, though. The approaching horde from the south could not be seen from this angle, and that bothered him, since that was the attack he dreaded the most.

He started to turn back into the room, when another speck of darkness caught his attention. But this speck was airborne. He frowned, looking off into the distance. The speck was growing at an impressive rate. It was rushing toward the keep, beginning to take on human form. But before it was near enough for him to discern details, it vanished.

His hands clenched on the stone railing as he searched the skies for some sign of whatever or whoever it was. Then he froze, as a burst of blue light flashed behind him. A chill washed over him and he turned slowly.

"She was half correct, you realize," came the hated voice. "I *am* angry that she left me for you." Vincent stared at the boy, and a double shock went through him. The first was because of the boy's resemblance to himself, even as far as age. The other was that the young man's face was scarred, faint traces of recent injury criss-crossing over his cheeks and nose. A voice at the back of his head told him that it was self-induced. Not intentionally, but from the overuse of magic, as Hennor had once explained it to him. The mages had wondered at how powerful the boy was, seemingly able to unlock the secrets of a Seeker Portal. Evidently, he had gone a little too far. Vincent also wondered at the effect this must have had on his mind.

He shook his head, trying to stop staring at the boy. Darla was in his arms, limp. His son placed her on Vincent's bed. "I know it's unusual," he said to his sister, "being *above* the sheets rather than *between* them, most likely with your legs spread for Father," he rambled, paying no attention to Vincent. "But new experiences make life interesting, don't they?"

"If she's hurt," Vincent began, trying to muster a threat to his voice.

"Of course she's hurt, you ignorant lout. She's unconscious, or are you still blind?" He whirled on Vincent and strode toward him. "That's the problem with women," he spat. "None of them can take a solid blow to the head." He laughed. "Not like you, obviously! You've taken some spectacular blows! I almost admire you, Father!"

Every time he used the word "father," Vincent flinched. It nauseated him to know that something as vile as this could have been born of him. He studied the boy. He looked different, and not just because he was older now than when he'd seen him last. He looked a bit ragged around the edges. And, he realized sadly, he radiated power. His hopes faded. He knew he'd stand no chance whatsoever against him. Still, he had no intention of just giving in. "You said she was 'half correct,'" he said. "What was she wrong about?"

"Oh, well, she was deranged to think that her return to me would cause me to stop my little game of 'Destroying Daddy.' It's far too much fun to stop."

Vincent clenched his teeth. "Fine. Then finish the game." He knew it was going to end, and how. His son was a very powerful, if insane, mage. He had a magical sword at his side, one that he'd stolen from Vincent. And he had the gauntlets on. Vincent knew he didn't stand a chance and simply wanted it to be over. Perhaps, he reasoned, if he were to die now, then his friends might live. It was Darla's theory turned sideways.

But his son shook his head and smiled. "The game is just beginning. But let us take a closer look, shall we?"

He stepped forward and grasped Vincent's tunic with one hand as he headed for the balcony. In a few quick strides, he leaped off, sailing up into the air.

"Get your fucking hands off me!" Vincent yelled and planted his fist in his son's face.

Eyes flaring, the boy slapped Vincent's face with a gauntleted hand, nearly rendering him unconscious. A wash of red appeared before Vincent's eyes. "That was impolite," came the voice. "But if you insist."

He was falling. His eyes cleared and he saw how high he was. A moment of panic struck him before the magical ring's power came into effect, slowing his descent and lowering him gently toward the ground.

Levitating above him, his son said, "Oh, now that is most unfair." He sailed down and grabbed him again before he could hit the ground. Then they were sailing up over the keep, out over the open sanctuary Feletain had opened for him, back through wooded areas to the lake.

And Vincent's stomach finished its fall.

Two armies were clashing. Sianon circled above, shooting bursts of flame down into the crowd at frequent intervals, all the while dodging arrows and crossbow bolts. Dead and injured were already littering the field. "Let's see how you fare." His son sailed over the thick of the battle. Then he dropped him.

"No!" Vincent yelled, but even as he protested, he was pulling out his sword. The boy knew how to hurt him. There was nothing in the world Vincent wanted less than to kill, with the possible exception of dying himself. And here he was, floating down into the middle of a battle, where he would have to choose one or the other.

Time seemed to take on a life of its own, as soon as he touched down. Men began to assail him with a variety of weapons, and Vincent's subconscious took over. He fought as if someone else controlled his actions. All the while, his eyes darted around, looking for his friends.

He reduced the enemy to shadows. If a figure attacked him, he dealt with it. He did not give it a face, or even a race. It was a shadow, to be dispatched coldly, quickly, without remorse or, indeed, without thought. Blood was flying onto him from all angles, but so far, none of it was his own.

Darvas. That was Darvas ahead of him. His relief at seeing the boy alive was shattered as he saw a shadow with a long, sharp pike approach him from behind. He tried to shout a warning, but the voice that erupted was Aedriun's. And it was too late. The weapon entered Darvas's back and pushed through to emerge just below his breastbone. Vincent's heart nearly burst as he saw the look on Aedriun's face as he watched his nephew die. His cry hung in the air seemingly forever. And then the shadows were on him again, blurry now through Vincent's tears.

Time warped again as his sword flew around him. He shut down his mind. They were not people. Most certainly, they were not innocent people being manipulated by his son. If he thought of them that way, he'd lower his sword and allow himself to share Darvas' fate. And that wasn't something he was willing to do, yet.

He became a cold, heartless, fighting machine, dispatching foe after foe. Blows struck him, but he ignored them. He was numb, feeling none of the small sword cuts, few of the strikes of mace or hammer. Arrows didn't touch him, thanks to the magical necklace that Ariaziane had given him, so long ago. At least, so far. She'd warned him it wouldn't last but for a dozen arrows. Who knew when the thirteenth would come?

He stumbled, once, as a sword cut through the flesh of his left calf. He landed on one hand, his sword still parrying above him. And his eyes widened as he saw Coldson's body, stuck with several arrows, an expression of anguish on his still face.

His sword arm fell, then, and he looked up to see the death blow begin to fall. It would be a flail that killed him, he realized as he recognized the weapon. Some called it a morning star. He found the astronomical analogy oddly appropriate. The spiked ball flew toward him at the end of its chain, the long wooden handle grasped firmly in the hands of a man who didn't seem strong enough to wield such a weapon. Vincent resigned himself to it, closing his eyes with a sigh.

Just then, there was a wrenching sensation and he flew backward, then upward, his body stiff and motionless.

"Now, now, no one kills my father but me," said his son, who floated before him. Vincent looked down at the battle, gripping his sword even tighter in his hands. "But I need a bit more fun with you before you die," the boy continued.

"Fuck you," Vincent grated.

"I don't know what that means, but I suspect it is insulting. Oh, now I have an idea!" he said brightly. "Let's check on some of your friends."

They swooped over the battle until they were near Sianon. His son waved a hand toward her and Vincent watched as black bands materialized in the air and wrapped themselves around her arms, legs, and face. She plummeted from the sky, landing harshly on the ground just outside the circle of battle.

Blade began hacking his way through the crowd toward her, ignoring the many attacks upon himself. D'Ty was right behind him. Vincent felt his throat constrict in fear.

Blade reached Sianon's side and began cutting at the black bands. Vincent stiffened as a tall man leaped at his friend's vulnerable back with his sword poised to strike. But before the sword could reach its target, D'Ty was there, deflecting the blow. Vincent relaxed slightly, but then gasped as a second attacker ran his sword through D'Ty's abdomen. Blade retaliated then, his sword severing the second attacker's arm. But then he, too, was struck down, the first man's sword plunging into him from the side.

Sianon now freed herself of the remaining bonds and immediately incinerated the man before he could take off Blade's head. She then grabbed both brothers with a spell and flew off with them trailing in her wake.

"Oh, now that *was* fun!" the hated voice said in his ear. "Couldn't you just watch that sort of thing all day?" He looked into Vincent's face for a reaction, but Vincent only clenched his jaw and remained silent. His son pouted. "You're not being fun anymore." He clasped his father by the shoulders and looked him seriously in the eye. "I don't look well, do I?" Vincent didn't reply, so the boy continued. "It's this power," he said almost in annoyance. "I've drawn so much of it from the portal into myself that I just don't know if my body can contain it all. I need to let some of it out." He paused, then inched closer. "Do you want to end this now?"

Vincent's eyes narrowed. "Damn right."

There was a bright flash and suddenly they were standing on the plain out in front and below Vincent's keep. He fell to the ground as his son released him from whatever spell he'd been under. He looked up to see the boy backing off a little, pulling out a familiar sword. "I assume you'd like to have the chance to run me through with your sword. This could be amusing, so let's have a go at it."

Standing, Vincent sized up his situation. The boy still wore the gauntlets. One blow of the sword wielded by those fists would probably go through his own sword parry and his body, too. He had to avoid the attacks completely, not parry them. And for the life of him, he couldn't see how he could expect to do so for very long. He was wounded from the battle. Not severely, but he was beginning to feel the injuries.

He hated this boy for what he'd done, forcing him to watch friends die, forcing him to kill others or be killed himself. He hated him for what he'd done to Darla. And he hated him for smaller things, for acting so superior, for having no thoughts for the welfare of anyone other than himself... basically, for being an asshole.

Vincent didn't care, anymore. He'd sworn never to kill again, but he was sure he'd done in several unfortunate souls just now. He didn't want to think about that. All he could think about was ending it. And if that meant that he had to kill his own son, unlikely as that possibility was, then so be it.

The only way, he knew, that he could get the drop on the boy was to use trickery. But what that would consist of, he wasn't sure. He felt defeated already. It was no use. There was nothing he could do but attack him in vain and wait for death.

"You hesitate. Why?" Before Vincent could reply, he went on. "Ah, I understand. You are thinking that you stand no chance against me. What can I say?" he said with a shrug. "You don't." He frowned. "Still, there must be something I can do to make this more enjoyable for me. You haven't been very cooperative, you know. I had hoped that you would have been more disturbed by the battle we just left." He crossed his arms and tapped his fingers idly against his cheek, the sword dangling limply from one hand. "Let me think."

Vincent nervously flexed his hand around the grip of his sword. "Naturally I am concerned. You have the ability to use magic against me. I stand no chance against that, just as you stand no chance against me in the use of swords alone."

The boy raised an eyebrow. "I do not?"

Continuing his ploy, Vincent forced a laugh. "How could you? For that matter, you would not stand a chance against me in hand-to-hand combat if you weren't wearing the gauntlets."

"You are correct," he replied flatly. "I have spent all my time in learning the ways of magic, including how to manipulate the portal that brought you to this world. I have had no time or inclination to learn the ways of the sword or the fist. Still, your tactic was sound, to play on my own pride. A pity I am above that."

Vincent's hopes crashed, then. That had been the best he could come up with, pathetic as it was. He clenched his jaw and calmly walked toward the boy. "Let's end it, then." When he was within striking distance of the smirking face, he lashed out, bringing the sword up in a vicious cut at his neck.

But there was no neck to connect with as the sword continued in its arc. With a flash, the boy disappeared, reappearing with a second flash directly behind him. The flat of the boy's sword crashed into Vincent's rear end, sending him sprawling forward with the force of the blow. It was painful and humiliating, and as he lay there, staring up at the laughing boy, he knew his chances of defeating him were even lower than he'd thought.

"Please stand up," the boy said with mock politeness. "Here, let me help you." He reached down and grabbed Vincent's arm, yanking him roughly to his feet.

Vincent felt the arm wrench in its socket and winced from the pain. But he was clearheaded enough to take advantage of the boy's actions and bring the sword crashing down again.

And once again, his hopes were dashed as the sword bounced harmlessly from some invisible protection that his son had erected around himself. He saw the grin on his enemy's face.

"That wasn't very nice," the boy said, his amusement turning to anger. His grip on Vincent's arm grew, and Vincent knew that the gauntlets could easily snap his bones. "What kind of father are you, Vincent?" the boy rasped.

Vincent's knees buckled as he strained against him. The pain was overwhelming. He was about to cry out in agony when there was a bright flash of blue light behind him. Then a searing bolt of green rushed over Vincent's head and slammed into his son.

Or rather, it slammed into his son's shields. The shock was enough for him to let go of Vincent's arm, however. He fell back, heaving a sigh of relief as the pain in his arm disappeared. He turned, confirming his suspicion. The attack had come from Darla, who stood shakily behind him. He was overjoyed that she was not seriously hurt, but wondered how long that state would last. He looked up to ascertain what damage, if any, she had done to her brother, only to see the boy vanish again.

Instinctively, he turned around, expecting the boy to appear behind him. And he wasn't surprised. He materialized behind Darla, quickly reaching around to grasp both her arms, yanking them roughly behind her. She cried out in pain and surprise as Vincent struggled to his feet.

"So nice of you to join us, dear sister," the boy said. Vincent watched as the boy raised one hand and clenched Darla's neck as he held her wrists with the other hand. He knew the gauntlets could snap her neck with just a simple twist of her brother's wrist, just as he could have broken Vincent's arm. The question was whether he was really crazy enough to kill his own sister. Darla had assured him that he'd never do that, but Vincent didn't think he was quite the same brother she remembered. During their time apart, he had gone further and further away from sanity.

He saw Darla cringe as her brother leaned in close to her and slowly licked her ear. Vincent's eyes narrowed in anger, but he was helpless. His sword lowered impotently, which didn't really matter. He was too exhausted and hurt to use it effectively. The boy extended a finger from Darla's throat and the sword flew from Vincent's hand. He watched in alarm as it sailed behind his son, sticking harmlessly into the ground. "That's two of your swords I have in my possession, Father. I'm building quite a collection, wouldn't you say?" He paused, the mirth vanishing from his face. "But that still doesn't come close to equaling what you've taken from me." His face darkened and he pushed Darla toward Vincent. "Now," he said, "kiss her."

"What?" he replied, dumbfounded.

"Kiss her, *Father*." He pushed her closer toward him, the grip on her neck never seeming to lessen. "I want to see how my father kisses his daughter." Vincent's pulse began to race. Something in that voice scared him. "*Now!*" he yelled.

Vincent swallowed hard, focusing on Darla's eyes. The terror on her face told him that she, too, no longer knew the man who had his fingers digging into her. Slowly, their lips met. Darla whimpered, tears beginning to form.

"Kiss her like you do when you're bedding her," he growled. "You, too, sister. I want to see this spectacular passion that tore you away from me."

Darla's tears were flowing freely, now. Unsurprised, Vincent realized his were, too. His mind raced, trying to grasp upon something that could turn this confrontation around, get Darla to safety. But nothing came to him.

"*Do it!*" the boy screamed.

Darla yelped in pain, then sobbed. And she did kiss him. Not as her brother had ordered though, not passionately. No. Her kiss was that of someone saying goodbye.

"I love you," she sobbed.

Vincent felt the bottom drop from his stomach as she said the words. He stole a glance at her brother and saw his face grow dark with fury. "Say it again, sister," he hissed.

"I love you," she said more firmly, looking deeply into Vincent's eyes. Then her face was thrust forward. They kissed again, her tears flowing all the while.

And as Vincent panicked, heart beating like a jackhammer, his son's other hand came up, grasping him behind the head, holding his face to Darla's. For what seemed an eternity, their lips were mashed together, almost painfully. Darla's tears and Vincent's panic grew proportionately to the pressure the boy was exerting on them.

Then there was a grinding snap. And Darla stopped crying.

Vincent's eyes widened as he felt the sudden twist against his lips. Panic surged through him. He started to scream, but it came out muffled, his mouth pressed against Darla's still, lifeless lips.

"Oh, dear," said his son, and his face came into view. "I seem to have broken her."

Suddenly, the boy let go of both their heads. Vincent staggered backward as Darla's body dropped to the ground. His son stood there, watching it for a moment, then turned away, pinching the area between his eyes as though he had a headache.

Vincent dropped to his knees beside her body, feeling the sting of tears as he looked upon her wide open eyes and parted mouth. His mouth still tingled with the sensation of her death, as all movement had suddenly stopped. His stomach heaved at the thought, but he fought it down. He stroked her face as the tears fell. Then his hand moved down to rest on her abdomen.

"Oh," came the voice. Vincent looked up to see his son crouched beside him. "Were you going to be a father again?" He smiled sickeningly. "I'm terribly sorry."

Fury replaced remorse inside him, then, and Vincent lunged at his son. They toppled backward, Vincent landing on top of the boy. But no sooner had he accomplished this than gauntleted hands were against his chest. The next thing he knew, he was landing solidly on his back.

He struggled to get up. Looking back, he saw that he'd been thrown at least twenty-five feet. His son now stood motionless, looking down at the body of his sister. Vincent rose to his feet, his vision blurring in berserk anger. All control went from him. His lips curled back and from the depths of his being came a primal scream of pure rage. He ran at the boy, no conscious thoughts muddling his brain, just instincts and emotion.

As he raced forward, he saw an inexplicable look of shock on his son's face as he saw Vincent barreling down on him. Vincent could almost see each muscle in his face moving to cause the alarmed expression. He was aware of the scent of the boy. He could hear his slight gasp. But more than that. He could see something else.

Or perhaps it was more than sight. It was as though he could detect the presence of something else with all of his senses, and none of his senses. It was all around him, under his feet, brushing against his face, tickling at his fingertips. He made a fist, felt it tingling like electricity on his palm, felt it flowing out between his fingers, trying to escape. It was like a thing alive in his grip. And when that fist hit the boy's face, it was as though Vincent were wearing the gauntlets of strength, not his son.

The boy flew backward, sprawling on the ground. Immediately, Vincent was upon him, landing squarely on his chest. Some instinct he couldn't identify caused him to grab a golden chain that lay about the boy's neck. In a moment, he was thrown back again by gauntleted hands, but this time he took something with him.

The chain snapped and Vincent held a necklace in his hands. Instantly it began to levitate, and Vincent saw that the boy was trying to pull the necklace back to himself. Vincent tightened his grip on the chain and grabbed the pendant that hung at the end of it. He could see the power radiating in and around it, and he still felt the energy surrounding him. He channeled some of it into the pendant, willing his fist to become tighter and tighter. He heard his son scream as he felt the pendant crush in his hand.

There was an explosion of force that knocked him backward, stunning him. When he shook off the effects of the blast, his son was standing over him, weaving unsteadily, holding his head in pain, but with a sword held high. Vincent rolled out of the way of the swing, then kicked out with his foot. It caught the boy in the side of the knee and he stumbled and fell, staring in anger at Vincent.

He wondered why the boy wasn't attacking him with magic, then remembered the scream when the pendant was crushed. It was the teleportation device, he knew. The boy must have shared some sort of link with it. Perhaps because he was willing the necklace to come to him, perhaps something else. But it was clear that, between Darla's attack, Vincent's seemingly magically-enhanced blow, and the crushing of the medallion, the boy was as off-balance as he was likely to be.

Vincent tried to summon the magic again, but he'd lost it. He was too excited, he knew, too filled with the possibility of living through this battle, to be able to see the force he needed to tap into. He pushed questions from his mind about how he'd been able to see it in the first place, and whether this meant that Jaz was right about him being mage material. He didn't want to think about anything other than defeating his son. He could have no distractions. He knew he had to continue the attack, not allow the boy to regain his senses.

He had to play dirty. If he had the chance, anyway.

They were both on their feet, now, the boy with his sword held unsteadily in front of him. Vincent had no weapon at the ready and had only two remaining on him. One was his dagger, which he drew from his belt sheath. Against the sword, it was nothing, but it was the only thing that might prove useful right now.

To his surprise, the boy began to back away. Probably hoping to regain his composure, to renew his magical attack, he realized. Vincent stood still, watching him back away. He took the opportunity to draw forth his other weapon, the hand-held crossbow that had been intended for use in assassinating Duke Ghanol so long ago. He quickly drew back the string, locked it into place, and set a bolt into position. He saw his son's eyes widen, then narrow.

Did that mean he no longer had shields? His foot had connected, but that meant little, Vincent knew, since most shield spells were designed against specific things, such as projectiles or blades. Well, he thought, he'd find out soon enough.

Calmly, he pointed the crossbow at his son. To his surprise, the boy charged him. In his shock, he pulled the trigger of the crossbow and the bolt sailed harmlessly past the onrushing youth. The boy raised the sword to strike and Vincent's eyes never left it. He watched as it began its downward stroke and in that moment, he, too, charged.

His lunge brought Vincent inside the arc of the boy's swing. The sword didn't touch him, but the boy's arms did, and the blow knocked him easily to the ground. He landed roughly, wrenching his arm painfully underneath him. With a shock, he realized he no longer had hold of his dagger. He looked up in alarm, expecting a follow-up strike from the sword. Instead, the boy was standing in shock, looking down at his abdomen, to where Vincent's dagger protruded. He silently pulled it from his body and snapped it in half.

That answers one question, Vincent thought dispassionately as he painfully lifted the crossbow again and loaded it, rising to his feet as he did so. His son stood motionless, staring at him. For just an instant, there was a yellow glow around him. Vincent frowned as the boy smiled. The shields were back, he knew. The crossbow would be useless, now.

As his son slowly advanced upon him, Vincent relaxed. His only hope was to tap into the magic again. The problem was, he didn't know how he'd done it in the first place, so how could he do it again? He stared at the boy, extending his senses as he'd done before. He remembered that had been part of it. He'd been hyper-aware of everything. He tried to extend his range of vision, as he extended other senses.

To his surprise, he quickly saw again the yellow glow of the boy's defenses. Fighting back the excitement, he looked away from the boy, trying to see the energy that was the magical force all around them. And there was something. Not as clear as it had been before, but there was something.

He had no understanding of it, no knowledge of what to do with it. There was no way he could tap into it the way his son could. He couldn't make fire from it or anything as delicate or complex as some of the things he'd seen his friends do. But maybe, just maybe, he could push it around.

He remembered the fight with Beltun Sagasht, how he'd kept pounding on the mage's shields until they finally buckled. But he'd had the gauntlets, then. Any pummeling he did now would be pretty futile. But if he could hammer at him with something other than his fists, that might just work.

Taking a deep breath, he pushed with his mind, imagining a wall between them, plowing into his son. The boy hesitated for a moment, a puzzled expression crossing his face briefly, then he laughed. "Father thinks he's a mage, now, does he?" His voice was ragged, to Vincent's satisfaction. "There's more to it than you think, I'm afraid."

Again, he reached out with his mind, picturing an invisible wrecking ball swinging toward his son. As the imaginary ball struck, the boy staggered slightly. This time, the expression on his face was one of annoyance. "Allow me to demonstrate how it is done," he said coldly.

There was a sudden rush of wind and then a tremendous weight crushed into Vincent from behind. He flew forward, the breath knocked from his lungs, and slid in a heap at his son's feet. Then he was picked up, as though by a giant, invisible hand,

and slammed to the ground. He felt things move about inside himself that he felt sure should stay in place. Blow after blow rained upon him, pounding his head, his back, his stomach.

And then, the beating stopped.

He looked up at the boy through a fog of red. His son stood over him, slowly lowering the point of his sword so that it rested gently, just above Vincent's breastbone. Vincent was gasping for breath, but recovering now that the blows had ceased. The boy smiled insanely down at him.

"You put up a good fight, Father. I don't know how you did that, destroying my necklace. That was very painful, you know." He frowned for a moment, then smiled again. "It's been fun," he said, paying close attention to Vincent's responses, "to watch you suffer. And do you know what my favorite part was?"

Vincent did not acknowledge the question, merely stared up into his son's face, trying to find some way out of this mess.

"Do you?" the boy screamed, jabbing the point of his sword a little closer to Vincent's throat.

"No," he grated in reply.

The boy smiled gleefully. "Oh, well, I'll tell you. It was that girl. You know, the one who went away." Vincent's blood turned to ice at the words. "It was so much fun to do her! Oh, I knew she was a mage. That's why I had the men bind her hands and gag her and slap her face. She couldn't concentrate on anything, and she certainly wasn't strong enough to free herself from those big men. Certainly wasn't strong enough to prevent me from going between her legs and plowing into her over and over and over again."

Without realizing it, Vincent had stopped breathing as he fought to hear anything but his son's words, fought to prevent the picture from forming in his mind of Ariaziane being raped. But it wasn't working. His rage grew and grew until it was beyond hot. It grew until he was overwhelmed. His mind went into shock, turning off all sensation. His rage grew freezing cold.

"When I was done, the others had her. Did you know that?"

That was enough. He felt something snap inside himself. And in one swift move, Vincent slapped the blade of the sword and lurched his body to the side. As expected, his son plunged down with the sword, but Vincent's movement was enough that it pierced only the muscle above his collarbone. He ignored the searing pain.

The instant the sword was withdrawn for a second strike, Vincent lashed out, kicking the boy's legs out from under him. As he fell, Vincent threw himself forward, snatching up the crossbow from where it lay, still loaded. He pounced upon the boy's sword arm, momentarily holding it down. Hoping against hope that the shock might have caused his shields to drop, Vincent pulled the trigger on the crossbow. To his satisfaction, the bolt plunged through the boy's forearm, pinning it to the ground.

As his son screamed in an agony that Vincent remembered all too well, he wrenched the sword from his son's now loose grip. Then, with great calmness, he brought the sword down, severing the pinned arm at the elbow. The boy bellowed with pain and rage. Vincent was surprised he didn't pass out from the shock. And a sick part of him, deep inside where he kept such things, was glad his son was still conscious, for he wanted him to suffer.

He picked up the incomplete limb and gently pulled the gauntlet from the limp hand, then tucked it into his belt. He looked coldly at the boy, who was now sitting up, clenching the stub of his arm with the other hand, stanching the flow of blood with the magical grip of the gauntlet. "Damn you, Father!" he screamed, his voice raw and grating. "May all the gods in existence damn you!"

The rage in his son's eyes was fierce beyond anything Vincent had ever seen before, but he didn't care. He was no longer afraid for his own life. No, that wasn't quite right. He no longer *cared* about his own life, he corrected. That was different.

The boy stumbled to his feet, lurching forward at Vincent, cursing him the entire time. The sword's next target was the boy's groin, the blade swinging upward to slice deeply into his crotch. Now, he fell and didn't get up. He lay there, writhing in pain. But that wasn't enough for Vincent. He wanted to give the bastard more.

He dropped, sitting on the boy's stomach, eliciting a groan and more cursing from the boy. To his amazement, Vincent realized that his son was still completely conscious, with no evidence of shock. He was in agony, but his eyes were clear and fixed upon him. A small part of his mind reminded him that the boy had endured much suffering while manipulating the portal. Doubtless he'd acquired a certain tolerance for agony.

Vincent leaned forward, placing one hand on the back of the boy's head, the other on his chin. "I'm tired of your mouth," he said, then shoved the jaw to one side. It made a popping noise like a huge light bulb breaking.

The boy gurgled in additional pain, if such was possible. Vincent watched calmly as the boy's remaining hand slowly made its way toward him, gauntlet open wide in an attempt to grasp at something. "Let me help you," he said sarcastically, then leaned forward and put his neck into the open hand. His son squeezed, but was so weak from pain and blood loss that the pressure was next to nothing.

"You're weak," Vincent taunted him without emotion. "You're nothing. You're helpless. How do you like it?" The words enraged the boy, who began to flail about under him. Vincent allowed him to do so, until the boy was out of strength.

He stared coldly down at him. "None of your wounds are fatal," he said. "When you heal, you will be merely lacking part of an arm, with a ruined jaw, and somewhat reduced capacities in the lower portions of your anatomy." He was silent a moment. "Then again, I know from experience that it is possible to grow new body parts, given certain magical circumstances. And I wouldn't put it past you to know how to do so. Therefore..."

He tore open his son's tunic and found the spot on his abdomen where the dagger had penetrated. He inserted two fingers into the wound, then savagely thrust forward. Flesh stretched and tore, blood spurted, as Vincent's entire hand made its way inside. As his son gasped, Vincent pushed his hand upward through the body, past various organs, until he found the heart. He wrapped his fingers around it and looked into his dying son's terror-stricken face. He stared at him until he saw complete comprehension settle into his son's eyes.

Only then did he squeeze.

He wasn't sure how much time passed before he removed his arm from the corpse. He had passed out, he realized. He removed the other gauntlet from his son's intact arm and tucked it beside the one in his belt. Then he stood, blood dripping from his arm, and staggered away, feeling every injury he'd received this day.

Not far off, he saw her, lying still and lifeless on the ground. He made his way over to her side and knelt, crumpled over Darla's body. His stomach threatened to send its entire contents up and out, but Vincent fought it down. Grief overwhelmed him and he sobbed until it hurt. Everywhere he looked, there was death. Darla was dead. Her brother, dead. Darvas, Coldson, Blade, D'Ty, and who knew how many others?

Finally, the convulsions passed and he fell limply across her body. Everything seemed grey to him. All he could think about was how empty he felt, how numb. There was nothing for him, here. Nothing but death.

When at last his breathing returned to normal, he sat up, looking around himself. Every muscle in his body hurt and blood caked everywhere around his wounds. Then he lifted Darla's body into his arms, and made his way toward the trail leading up to his keep.

She wasn't heavy, but he was terribly weak. He knew the gauntlets would make his task much easier, but this wasn't something he wanted to be easy. He wanted to struggle with it. It was far less than he deserved. This girl had loved him and what had he given her? Death. True, he'd given her life, too, but that wasn't the point, he told himself.

It took him an hour to climb to the plateau, an hour of panting, sweating, stumbling. An hour of self-deprecation and self-loathing. And when he finally reached the top, it was to continue struggling. He carried her into the keep, up the tower stairs to the second floor, to his bedroom. There, he lay her on the bed, then collapsed to his knees on the floor beside it. He kept hold of Darla's hand as he leaned against the bed. The hand was so cold, he thought. So still.

Rhia. He needed Rhia here. He began to sob again, screaming in his mind for her to come to him. He cried for many minutes, until no more tears would come. Rhia, his mind cried, over and over, until he slept.

❧ Thirty-Six ❦

Vincent stood leaning on the stone railing of his balcony, numb, trapped in the same stupor he'd been in for the past day. The crisp, early morning breeze coming off the mountainside did little to refresh him. He had no energy, or any real desire, to pull himself out of his torment.

So much death, so much pain. He couldn't shake the images, the memories, from his mind. In there, the grisly scenes replayed themselves without end... Darvas being impaled on a pike... Aedriun's wail of remorse... Coldson's arrow-ridden body... Over and over, he re-lived the horror of seeing D'Ty struck down while saving his brother's life, and Blade's subsequent felling while avenging his brother. Though neither of them had died, they were both grievously hurt. Sianon's quick rescue saved their lives. That, at least, was something to be thankful for.

His own injuries were healing well enough, he supposed. Frankly, he paid little attention to them. The pain in his heart overshadowed his physical aches. His body could heal or not. He cared little, either way.

He did find one injury interesting—his right arm. From the elbow down, it hurt, much like a severe sunburn hurt. He assumed this was from his brief manipulation of magical forces when battling his son. Like the side effects that overuse of magic could cause, unfamiliarity with magic must do something similar, he reasoned.

The others had given him details of the battles they'd been involved in. Much of it didn't make sense to him, especially the reports from the mages. Felina had said that she'd finally caught up to the mountain wolves, only to find them in the process of running away, as if being chased. From a distance, Gnorrin saw trolls stop dead in their tracks, then slowly turn and wander off. As for the snow giants, they seemed to have simply given up and began returning to their northern lands. Jaz suggested that they might no longer have been under the control of Vincent's son by this point. Without his guidance, they had no reason to remain. It was a good explanation, and Vincent thought it probably true. But he didn't think that was the complete story. From Felina's account, for example, the mountain wolves seemed frightened of something.

It didn't matter, though. He had too many other things on his mind to care about such details.

Vincent's clothing and skin were still stained with blood. His right arm in particular was stained a deep red from elbow to fingertips. But he couldn't seem to work up any enthusiasm for washing.

He had killed his son, and didn't even regret it. The boy was insane, violently so. He was vicious and cruel. And the bastard had killed his sister, Vincent's daughter, Darla. And their unborn child. He grieved over the lost potential of that fact, but the most painful memory of all was that of his daughter, his lover, dying in his embrace. The sudden shock that ran through her. Her last breath gasping into his mouth. Her body going limp... What happened after that was a blur to him. But he knew what he'd done. Every sick bit of it.

And he still didn't regret it.

He shook his head, ridding it of the horrible thoughts.

A noise caused him to glance idly over his shoulder. Gnorrin and Aedriun stepped into the room. He turned to face them, wishing they'd go away, but knowing they wouldn't. He knew they were concerned. And he also knew that no one, not even his closest friends, looked at him the same way now. They'd seen his son's body on the field.

"Good morning," said Aedriun quietly, more as a courtesy, Vincent knew, than because he felt it was.

"Hardly," he replied in a voice barely above a whisper.

His friends stole glances at the bed, where Darla's body still lay. Aedriun shook his head, but said nothing. Gnorrin's face screwed up with concern. "Vincent," he began softly, still looking at the corpse.

"Don't start," he said flatly.

"My friend, she is dead. Let it go."

"Shut up!" Vincent stormed. "We will not discuss this!"

Gnorrin sighed and wrung his hands. "You are unwell," he said sadly.

Vincent allowed the anger to trickle away. His voice was hollow as he answered. "I'm not unwell, Gnorrin, I'm empty. There's nothing inside me. Nothing outside of me, either. Just... Nothing."

Aedriun spoke up again, his voice slightly harsh. "You are not the only one to have lost, here, Vincent."

He nodded. "I know. I'm sorry about Darvas."

"'Sorry,'" Aedriun repeated, his temper fraying. "That's all you can say? My nephew died in your service and all you can say is that you're sorry? I have to tell my sister that her child is dead, and you're sorry?"

Vincent turned vacant eyes upon the baron. "I did not ask your nephew to serve me."

"No, you did not, but he gladly volunteered!" Gnorrin tried to shush him, but Aedriun's anger flared. "It seems to me that you could strive to show a tiny bit of appreciation for what he and others have done for you!"

Something snapped inside Vincent, then. The anger he'd allowed to die just moments before returned in full force. "Appreciation? For what? Dying? I didn't want them to do *anything* for me!" he screamed. "How dare you stand there and accuse me of not appreciating their sacrifices? I didn't *want* their sacrifices! *I* was the target of all this! Not you! Not Darvas! Not anyone but me! *I* should be the one lying dead, no one else!" The anger faded, to be replaced with weariness and a heavy heart. "I would gladly exchange my life for those who were killed." His voice was soft and choked. "I begged you not to fight for me, or have you forgotten that?"

Aedriun was quiet as Vincent spoke. Finally, he nodded his head and turned his sad face to the floor. Then Gnorrin spoke up. "Vincent, I understand the pain inside you."

"Not likely," Vincent said bitterly.

"But you must look at the other side of the coin in your hand. Do not overlook what you have gained, what you have retained."

"What?" Vincent flared. "Just what was gained by this senselessness?"

"Not in this battle, my friend," said Aedriun, composed now. "He means, look at what you've gained since arriving here."

"*I don't give a shit!*" Vincent bellowed. "Take the damn money! Screw the status! I don't care about any of that! Take this damn hole in the mountain, take every stupid thing I own. It wouldn't matter. It just wouldn't matter." He turned his back on his friends. "Ever since arriving here, it's been nothing but a lot of pain mixed with brief hints of pleasure. I've been injured time and again, shot with arrows and crossbow bolts, blinded by sword cuts. The only things I've ever truly wanted since coming here have been mine only temporarily. Ariaziane left, years ago. Rhia has gone off on her own, probably never to be seen again. Darla..." He paused, fighting down the nausea that threatened to overwhelm him, then turned to face them again. "And you, my friends. I've caused you pain, robbed you of loved ones. None of this has been for the best. I can't feel good about it. The only other thing I've ever wanted since coming here has been to go home. And I can't even have that."

"In fact," came a female voice, "I wouldn't be so certain of that."

All three looked up to see Rhia standing in the doorway. Vincent nearly swooned as he recognized her and a spark of hope ignited within him. Aedriun and Gnorrin moved aside as Vincent crossed the floor to where she stood.

"You came," he whispered.

"How could I not?" she replied. "The anguish in your call was overwhelming."

Vincent strode across the room, grabbed her arm, and rushed her over to Darla's side. "Bring her back," he said frantically.

Rhia's face clouded as she looked down at the body. "Vincent, I..."

"Bring her back!" he demanded. "Damn it, bring her back!"

She sighed, reaching out to touch the girl's lifeless cheek. She ran a hand over the brow, the hair. And a single tear rolled down Rhia's cheek and fell to the bedclothes. "I can't," she whispered.

"Why not?" he demanded.

"She is too far gone." She turned slowly and faced him. "Because it must be done quickly. In her case, especially quickly, considering the way she aged. Too much time has passed for her."

"If you'd been here, you could have brought her back!" he accused. "Damn you!"

But Rhia shook her head. "No."

"No, what?" he said, flustered.

"Even had I been here, such a spell is beyond me. I could not have done it without assistance. And there was no one to assist."

"Felina!" he said desperately. "She could have helped!"

Again, she shook her head. "Felina knows nothing about that form of magic."

"Well, Jaz, then!" He turned to face Gnorrin. "Or..." But Gnorrin and Aedriun had slipped out.

"No," Rhia said, and she placed a hand on his arm.

The touch sent him reeling. He spun back around, his mind whirling with conflicting emotions. He staggered, caught himself on the bedpost, then slowly sank to the floor. Sobbing wracked his body and Rhia knelt and comforted him.

"I'm so sorry," she whispered as she embraced him, more tears falling from her eyes.

"I've lost everything," he choked out. "Annie, you, Darla."

"I'm here."

"But you won't stay!" he wailed and pushed himself away from her. "You'll leave again." His voice faded. "You always do."

Rhia was silent for a time, avoiding his eyes. Finally, she said, "I cannot promise to always be with you. I cannot promise you that kind of stability, if that is what you need. But I am here for you now."

Vincent sniffed and wiped his eyes. He breathed deeply, running his hands over his face.

He sat quietly for a minute, accepting the finality of Darla's death for the first time. Rhia knelt at his side, running her fingers through his hair. He leaned against her and sobbed.

Eventually, he stopped. He squeezed Rhia's hand and said, "I have so many questions to ask you."

"I know," she replied. "And I'm sure one of them is about what I did to you."

Vincent shrugged, feeling drained, but oddly clear-headed now. "You didn't want me to find the portal because her brother was there." Rhia nodded. "Or was it that you expected Darla and I would become lovers, and you knew I'd be freaked out over the incest thing?"

Rhia smiled ruefully. "I suspected the incestuous aspect would bother you. I had hoped you'd never learn the truth, but knew it was a vain hope."

"It's okay," he said. "I came to accept it." His eyes filled with tears he didn't know were still in him. "I'm sorry... I haven't quite been myself, lately."

She was silent for a time, holding his hand as they sat on the floor. "Did you hear what I said when I entered the room?"

He nodded. "I take it you've discovered how to send me home."

She was slow in answering. "I'm fairly certain, yes. When I arrived at the portal, Darella had gone. Her son was there, however, but rather than confront him, I waited. After he'd gone, I used all my energies to unlock the secrets of the portal."

"But Darla said it had taken her mother many years to do that."

Rhia nodded. "And had I just discovered the portal, it would have taken me even longer. But I knew what it was. Darla had told me much about it, and I'd studied how her brother manipulated it, heard what spells he cast. Darella did all the hard work."

"What about her? Will she return to it?"

"I have no idea, but it wouldn't surprise me in the least. I can't imagine her being away from such a powerful artifact for long."

"So you're saying I need to make a decision quickly."

"I'm afraid so."

He looked at her for only a moment. He ran a hand through his hair and let out a long sigh. "Well," he said. "Then let's get me out of here."

He bathed, deciding it might be nice to arrive back home in a relatively clean state. Besides, he thought, he'd been covered with the blood of others long enough. He had to scrub his arm for a long time before it came clean.

Then he dressed in his Earth clothes. The T-shirt and jeans hung loose on him, a reminder of the physical changes he'd been through during his time here. A rope secured the pants well enough.

When he was done, he packed some souvenirs. Obviously, since he'd arrived fully clothed and with his tape player, the Seeker Portal would allow him to return with it, and hopefully other items as well. He took the cloak pin Ariaziane had made for him, his rings, the gauntlets, the necklaces from Gnorrin and Ariaziane, and his swords. He'd been warned that the magical items would most likely prove totally incapable of performing their magic on Earth, but he didn't really care. His journal he packed with great tenderness. Here was a written reminder of his years in this world, he thought, for those days ahead when memory would begin to fail. And, not being entirely without common sense, he filled his pockets and pouches with as many gold coins as he could comfortably carry. No reason he should be destitute upon returning home.

The others insisted on journeying to the cave with him and he didn't argue. Though he hated good-byes, he loved these people. They were his friends and he would never see them again. The good-byes were necessary. But before they left, there were things to do.

He stood on the balcony of his bedroom once he was ready. Far below, he watched as Aedriun's men dug graves for those who'd perished. They would be buried there, in a small graveyard to be seen by all who ventured here. All but Darvas, whose body would accompany Aedriun back to Linnael. In fact, Aedriun would have preferred to have them buried on the plain upon which they'd fallen, but down there was more appropriate, Vincent felt. If, indeed, a town ever grew in the valley, the graves would be seen by all, a reminder of their selfless sacrifices.

A deep wave of regret flowed through his body. This world had been home to him for a handful of years. Once or twice, he'd even felt comfortable here. But those were times when he had someone special to share life with.

Now he had no real reason to stay. Doing so would undoubtedly only cause more harm to his friends and total strangers. And he'd caused enough of that already. He couldn't stand more death, more pain, on his conscience. True, it wasn't exactly his fault. But the fact remained that those who were dead were dead only because they knew him. Darvas, Coldson, and the others would be alive and well today if it weren't for their misfortune in meeting him.

Coldson could still be a slave, too, another part of his brain said. He told that part of his brain to shut up.

With a sigh, he turned away from the view and returned indoors.

Aedriun spoke tearful words as his men, Vincent's men, were interred. Vincent's tears flowed, but he had no more sobbing grief inside. He stood silently by as the dirt was thrown onto the shrouded bodies.

Coldson was buried next, and Vincent felt his heart wrenching as he spoke a farewell. He couldn't hear his own words, his mind filled with memories of the talks he'd had with the older man. He ended with, "Thank you. I'm sorry."

Lastly, they burned Darla's body topside. No words were spoken, though Rhia did perform some sort of ritual over the body, ending by kissing the girl on the forehead. Vincent saw tears in her eyes as she backed away from the body. Gnorrin proceeded to levitate the corpse, then Jaz shot a burst of flame that engulfed the body. Felina summoned a wind that swept the ashes and smoke high into the sky. Vincent watched through teary eyes as the body shriveled and eventually vanished.

When the last of the smoke and ash disappeared into the sky, Vincent dropped his head and whispered one final farewell before turning and slowly heading back inside.

Blade and D'Ty were next on his list. They lay recuperating in one of the bedrooms on the second level. Sianon looked up from Blade's side as he entered the room, alone. He stepped over to his barely conscious friend, who opened his eyes slowly and smiled.

"Hi," Vincent said.

Blade appraised him, his breathing shallow, but his perceptions still keen. The smile faded from his face. "Rhia visited me earlier. I understand she has accomplished the task for which I hired her," he said flatly and a little sadly.

Vincent felt a lump form in his throat and began to realize just how difficult these farewells would be. "Yeah," he said quietly. "It's a 'now or never' kinda thing."

"What does that mean?" Sianon said suspiciously.

"It means our friend is going home," Blade said, his eyes never leaving Vincent's.

Sianon turned her shocked expression on Vincent. "You're what?" she demanded.

"I have to, Sianon," he said, forcing a smile. "There are just too many..." He paused, fighting back the urge to weep. "There are too many painful memories for me here."

"I know all about painful memories, Vincent."

"Dear," Blade rasped, "stop." They both looked at him. "It is his decision. Do not make it more difficult for him than it already has been."

Sianon let out a sigh and frowned petulantly. But she heeded Blade's request and said no more. Instead she hugged him tightly, and when they let go, Vincent could see the gratefulness in her eyes.

He swallowed past the lump and reached down to clasp Blade's hand. "I owe you a great deal, my friend."

Blade shook his head. "No more than I owe you." He smiled faintly. "I will miss you."

"Ooh," Vincent said, fighting back emotions, "now *you* stop." His friend nodded and let go of his hand. Vincent looked over at D'Ty, still unconscious from his wounds. "Your brother's a good guy, Blade. Please apologize to him for my sudden departure when he comes around."

"Certainly."

Vincent stood there for a moment longer, eyes locked with Blade's, countless silent words flowing between them. Finally, he nodded, then quietly departed.

Outside, in front of the keep, he knelt in front of Blaise. She whined, confused by the gathering. "Goodbye, girl," he whispered to her. "I wish I could take you with me." He held her tightly, feeling the tears well up as she turned her head and licked his cheek. Rhia had warned that trying to send the dog with him would make success not as likely. "Gnorrin will take good care of you," he said.

Then he stood, taking one last look up at the place that was meant to be his home. The place he'd dreamed of sharing with Darla, with Rhia, and just maybe one day, with Ariaziane. For that matter, with all of his friends, whenever they wished.

It had been such a lovely idea, full of warmth. But the stone face of the keep only stood there, dappled with cold snow. There was no warmth left in the dream.

The others stood waiting for him: Gnorrin, Rhia, Aedriun, Jaz, and Felina. With four magic-wielding individuals among the six of them, he didn't expect the trip to the cave would take long at all.

And he was correct. Rhia stood flanked by Jaz and Felina, acting as the center, each of them holding one of her hands. Gnorrin brought forth some sort of bubble that surrounded them all. Aedriun and Vincent braced themselves. There was a bright flash of light, a momentary sensation of horrible nausea, and then they stood in front of the entrance of a cave.

He looked at the mouth of the cave, a feeling of familiarity washing over him. He turned and looked away, taking in the surroundings. Though he didn't remember the actual events, he knew this was where he'd descended the hill, made his way through the wilderness, eventually to be discovered by Gnorrin and Blade.

For several minutes, he stood staring out across the landscape. He saw a town in the distance. Was it outside of there that Gnorrin's cottage lay, as well as his own? It was too far away to tell. He shook his head. It didn't matter, he told himself. Taking a deep breath, he turned back to face the cave. Glancing at his friends, he started toward it.

Rhia walked beside him. "The cave is deep," she said, "and the Seeker Portal is at the far end."

Vincent nodded as they entered. Inside, he saw signs of habitation. There were tiny globes of light scattered around the roof of the cave and functional furniture that didn't look very comfortable. And he smelled the scent of his son. His eyes narrowed at this, his jaw clenching.

And there at the back was the Seeker Portal. It stood nearly from floor to ceiling, its face a dull and dark grey, bordered by a thick, sculpted stone relief. The sight made his heart skip a beat. "So this is it, huh?" Vincent ran his hands over the stones and lightly touched the grey surface. "This is what brought me here." His friends were silent, allowing his introspection. Finally, he turned and looked at Rhia.

"Whenever you're ready," she whispered.

The rest of his friends had been keeping a respectful distance behind him. Now he turned and stepped back to them. He smiled, though it was forced. "I guess this is it," he said quietly, his voice echoing hollowly in the cave.

One by one, he bade them farewell, first to Felina. "I'm sorry we didn't have the chance to get to know each other better," he said.

The elf nodded. "As am I, but I'm pleased to have known you at all."

He hugged her, drinking in her exotic scent. "Don't let Rhia forget me, okay?" he whispered in her ear.

"Not a chance," she replied.

Next was Jaz. "I have no idea what to say to you. I feel like I'm leaving a brother behind."

"Oh, stop being so sentimental," the mage said, clasping his hand and gripping his upper arm with the other. "It's been rather remarkable, hasn't it?"

Vincent smiled, this time having no need to force it. "It sure has. Take care of yourself, okay?"

"I always do."

To Aedriun, Vincent said, "Sorry I didn't turn out the way you'd expected, Baron."

The older man smiled, his eyes crinkling. "And who says you didn't, Baron?"

They shook hands warmly. "Look," Vincent continued, "I'm sorry about how I was behaving earlier."

But his friend cut him off. "Please." He smiled understandingly. "I wasn't acting with my usual decorum, either." Then Aedriun firmed his jaw and said, "It has been an honor."

"Definitely," said Vincent and squeezed his hand firmly.

Lastly, he knelt on one knee in front of Gnorrin, bringing himself just slightly below the gnome's eye level. He embraced him, holding his friend close for a long time. To his shock, the gnome had tears in his eyes when they broke. Emotion welled up in him again. "Words can't say how much I'll miss you, Gnorrin," he said, his voice a whisper.

"Then don't bother trying," came the hoarse reply.

"Take good care of Blaise for me."

"I shall."

He nodded. Then, clearing his throat, he said, "Um... If you, ah... If you see her..."

Gnorrin nodded, patting him on the shoulder. "Of course. Of course." He pulled out an orange handkerchief and blew his nose. "Now go on."

Vincent squeezed his friend's arm one final time, then stood. He took a deep breath, gazing again at each of his friends before turning back to Rhia and the portal.

He took Rhia's hand and held it at his side. "I love you," he said.

"And you know I love you." They stared into each other's eyes for a moment, then kissed warmly. He shut his eyes against the tears. "If it hurts so much, why are you doing it?" she said very faintly as he buried his head in her shoulder.

"Because," he whispered, "it hurts too much not to."

Finally, they separated, but continued to hold hands. They approached the Seeker Portal, Vincent's heart racing. They stood there, an arm's length from it. And Vincent did as she instructed him, reaching out with his mind, picturing his world, his home. He was surprised at how easy it was, but perhaps that was due to Jaz's instruction on how to use the magic eyes.

He began by picturing Earth in his head, the entire globe, green and blue, spinning slowly in space. The others gasped behind him as the scene came to life in the portal. Rhia, in contact with his mind, guiding him, translated for them. "Earth," she said quietly.

Vincent pictured himself as a camera, zooming in on the planet. "North America," Rhia whispered, reading his thoughts. Then, "Pennsylvania."

He pictured it as a map, zooming along toward the northwestern part of the state. Amazement washed over him and he knew he was really looking at his home, not just his own recreation of it. He knew rough geography of the area surrounding his home town, but not in this much detail. He searched for landmarks, swooping in low. His friends muttered in shock at the things they were seeing: cars, paved roads, trains, office buildings and more.

He spotted a road sign he recognized and zipped along the roads, coming at last to his hometown. He pulled back, taking it all in. It was winter. Snow lay everywhere. Plows were clearing the roads, bringing more amazed noises from his friends. With a shock, he realized it was Christmas. The street lamps were decorated with the gaudy snowmen and bells he remembered so well.

Finally, he moved to his street, to his house. He let the view hang there, looking down at the modest, two-story home with three cars parked in front. He didn't recognize any of them. But his father had a habit of trading his car in every few years. One of them was undoubtedly his dad's latest vehicle. One could be his sister's, home for the holiday. The other certainly could be his brother's.

"Home," Rhia said. She squeezed his hand tighter. He loved her for that. Slowly, he lowered the perspective, inching closer and closer to the large front window of the house. From this angle, he could see the decorated tree in the corner, lights blinking merrily. His father's face came into view, white-haired and smiling, looking down at the floor where, Vincent assumed, one of his brother's children played with a new toy.

"Dad," he whispered, and felt Rhia's hand clench tighter. His heart threatened to fill his throat. He glanced at Rhia. "How do I... um..."

She took a deep breath. "The easiest way," she said, quietly and somewhat sadly, he thought, "is to imagine the portal as an actual doorway. A hole in a wall through which you'll step." Her voice cracked as she said, "And then, just do it."

He stood there, watching his house, watching his father return to sit in his recliner chair, a cup of ever-present coffee in his hand. He looked just the same as when he'd last seen him.

Vincent sighed and looked down at his own body, wondering what his family would think of him now. Unlike his father, his appearance was very different. Muscles lay underneath his clothing, where only fat had been before. Muscles honed by the years of fighting and hard work here in this world.

He thought of his friends at home, and his friends here. He thought of his future on Earth, and his future here. He was so tired, so drained.

He stood there for many minutes, thinking of these things. The pull of the portal was a thrumming, seething oscillation of power. A thought came into his head, then, and he knew it was from Rhia. The portal could not remain open like this for long. He had to act soon.

Staring again at his home, at the festive and happy people milling about inside, thoughts whirled inside his head. Doubts and fears pulled him in conflicting directions. He waited until he knew he had to act, Rhia's mental prodding becoming more urgent. Then, firming his jaw, he opened his eyes and stared at the portal, willing the scene to shift, to change. Earth vanished, to be replaced by something else. Something burning.

Rhia's hand went slack in his own. He heard his friends mutter and gasp behind him. Quickly, he thought to himself. This must be done quickly. He stole a glance at the portal and saw its view glowing red, exactly as he had hoped. He let go of Rhia's hand and stepped forward, pulling the gauntlets from his belt and quickly slipping them on.

"No!" she yelled.

Without hesitation, he thrust his head and one arm through the portal. It was a very odd sensation, tingly and gelatinous at the same time. "Help me!" he yelled to the other side. Then he felt something grab his arm and with all his strength, Vincent pulled.

Yells of alarm and wonder came from his friends. Rhia was in a panic. He ignored them all as he fell back onto the ground, barely noticing that his friends jumped back further. He was about to stand when he heard Rhia's fearful cry, "Down!"

There was a deep rumbling noise. Looking up, Vincent saw the Seeker Portal begin to disintegrate. Rhia threw her arms up, a shimmering incandescence appearing briefly in front of her. A split-second later, the portal exploded. He saw the shimmer bulge outward, then disappear. Shards of rubble sprayed forth. Rhia screamed and fell. Vincent ducked his head, turning his eyes toward his friends. He saw Gnorrin had thrown up a shield of his own and the shards bounced off harmlessly. Then Felina yelled Rhia's name and leaped forward.

He jerked his head back around. "Oh, no," he whispered, scrambling frantically to rise. He rushed forward, fighting through clouds of dust to where Rhia lay. She was bloody from a hundred cuts, her breath ragged, but she was alive and conscious. In an instant, Felina was there, pushing him aside. The witch smiled wanly, reaching to hold Felina's hand.

Vincent rose from his crouched position, knowing Felina would be of more help to Rhia than he would be. He stepped away, facing the figure that slowly rose to tower over him, having to duck from the low ceiling in the cave. Vincent smiled, empty though the gesture was. "Hey, stranger."

The efreeti stopped examining its surroundings and turned its head to face Vincent. A slow, but huge, smile spread across its red face. Then it began to laugh, a deep, booming noise. "By my horns, Vincent! I cannot believe it!"

"I keep my promises," Vincent said without emotion. "Now please, excuse me." He brushed past the creature, and his friends, and rushed into the open, where he stood gulping air.

His heart raced and he couldn't breathe. The fact that he didn't *need* to breathe didn't make his panic any less pronounced. What had he done? He'd destroyed the portal. Now he'd *never* get home! But he'd known that pulling the efreeti through might forfeit his chances. He'd still done it.

Slowly, he regained his composure. He stood for several minutes looking over the landscape, down the path that he must have taken, years ago, when he arrived on this world. He'd somehow made it the whole way to Gnorrin's where he was taken in by the gnome, befriended by him and Blade. And thus had begun the most amazing handful of years of his life.

And now, to his surprise, he had destroyed the Seeker Portal. Why had it blown up?

"Several possibilities," came the efreeti's deep voice behind him, "but I believe it was predominantly a matter of incompatibility."

"What do you mean?" Vincent asked, without turning, clamping down on his thoughts.

"According to legend, the druids created nine of these portals, scattered throughout the lands. Each portal was designed to seek out individuals of certain disposition, so to speak. If this is indeed the portal you were summoned through, then it was obviously designed to select those with your disposition. What you did, however, was force the portal to summon me through it. And you and I, my young friend, are of much different dispositions."

Now he turned, puzzled, and looked at the creature. "When you say 'disposition,' what exactly do you mean?"

"The druids believed in certain basic traits. For example, good and evil. Order and chaos. And naturally, they favored neutrality. Everyone, so they felt, was disposed toward either good or evil, also order or chaos. Or neutral, in either of those traits. Therefore, there could be a total of nine basic combinations. Nine Seeker Portals." The efreeti smiled. "You, obviously, are disposed to good. My race is not, especially. This created the incompatibility within the portal, went against its original design." The creature rubbed its chin thoughtfully. "Not to mention the fact that you were *forcing* the portal to function, rather than it operating of its own accord. That could not have helped matters any."

Vincent absorbed all this silently. There were ramifications there that he didn't especially want to think about. Fortunately, the efreeti continued, allowing him to put the thoughts aside.

"Vincent," it said, "your gnome friend spoke to me before I joined you out here. I must know the answer to something."

"Sure," he said flatly, turning again to survey the horizon.

"He claims that you had been using the portal with the intention of returning to your own world."

"True."

"He says, further, that you had not only located your world within the portal, but had even viewed your own home. Is this so?"

Vincent merely nodded, his back to the efreeti.

"And you chose to free me, for which I am, of course, eternally grateful. I assume you were planning to use the portal to return home after freeing me?"

Vincent blinked, watching the sun begin to set in the distance. He tried not to attach any symbolism to it, though it was easy to draw the analogy of the sunset being the fading of his hopes of returning home. When the efreeti prompted him again for a response, he broke from his reverie. "No," he whispered.

The efreeti frowned. "I do not understand."

Vincent ran a hand through his scraggly hair, then sighed and looked up at the creature. "I'm not sure I can explain." He looked at the creature's puzzled face and realized that it really did wish to understand. He shrugged. "I'm not the same person who left there when I was seventeen. I wouldn't fit back into my old life so well." He heaved a sigh, wishing he could explain it better, to himself as well as his friend.

"What have you done?" Vincent was startled by the sudden shriek from inside the cave. He did not recognize the voice, but he dashed inside, knowing instinctively that danger awaited him.

He stopped short as he came upon the scene. His friends stood in a semi-circle, tense with anticipation. Felina still crouched beside Rhia on the floor of the cave. Rhia was sitting upright, and the look on her face was one of pure fear. Her eyes, and all others, were upon the figure that stood in the center, looking in horror upon the remains of the Seeker Portal.

"You," he said flatly, his instincts telling him who it was.

Darella looked up at him, as if surprised to see him. She frowned. "This destruction was not caused by your departure?" She looked at Rhia, who stood in just as much shock as the others. "I am most impressed that you determined how to operate the device, daughter."

The words struck him like a blow. Rhia was Darella's daughter? He'd had no idea! She'd never indicated this to be the case in all the times they'd spoken of the woman. But that would have made Darla Rhia's sister! His pain was doubled, knowing this fact. Rhia had known all along. And now she'd lost a sibling.

Darella looked back at Vincent when Rhia had no response. "Before I rid myself of the annoyance of all of you, tell me how this happened!"

Despite the bravado of the boast, Vincent had little doubt that she could accomplish the task. A cave full of mages notwithstanding, the scope of Darella's power was all too evident. It put the chill of fear into him. He couldn't form words, and Darella was becoming impatient. She moved forward, stepping over Rhia's injured body.

"I do not *require* this answer before I kill you," she said directly to him. "It would merely be pleasant to know. Since you seem inclined to keep it a secret, however, I will be content to bypass it altogether."

"*I* will give you an answer," came a deep voice from behind Vincent. He smiled as he saw Darella look up to the source of the voice. Her face paled.

"Bones of the dead," she whispered.

The efreeti smiled broadly, displaying gleaming white fangs. "Cross with me and it would be an interesting battle, I admit. Yet against all of us, you would stand no chance."

Darella straightened in what Vincent had to call a prim fashion, as if she wouldn't sully herself with a response. She turned her back on them both and looked at the spot where the Seeker Portal had been. "Very well," she said. "You shall live." Then she turned back to Vincent and smiled. "I do so hope you fully realize what you've done." And with that, she crossed her arms casually across her chest and vanished.

It was as though a spell had broken, then. The others began to move and talk amongst themselves. Vincent's eyes went straight to Rhia's and he stepped over to her. She was clearly relieved as she looked back at him, smiling sheepishly. "My mother," she said weakly. "I believe you've met."

He shook his head, smiling despite the poor attempt at humor. "Why didn't you tell me?"

She managed a shrug. "Would *you* admit to it? I'm sorry if it bothers you."

"No," he said, clasping her hand. After a moment, he said, "But what did she mean just now?"

Rhia's smile faded and she averted her gaze. It was the efreeti who answered. "She meant that, although this portal has been destroyed, the others are still functioning." All eyes turned to the creature at the other end of the cave. "As I told you, Vincent," it continued, "each portal is attuned to a particular disposition. One of the 'good' portals is now gone. The balance is now in the favor of the 'evil' portals."

Vincent frowned. "But if the portals were designed to monitor and maintain such a balance, would they not 'know' that this portal is not functioning and operate accordingly?"

"Yes," Rhia said, and all eyes turned to her, now. "If the master portal, the true neutral portal, were operating properly. But the fact that Darella knew something had happened to this portal, causing her to arrive here, indicates to me that something must have gone terribly wrong."

"Indeed," said the efreeti, and once again, heads turned.

"Would you mind moving over here?" Vincent said. "I feel like I'm at a tennis match."

The creature cast him an odd look, but accommodated his request, ducking its head and moving closer. "As I told you outside," it went on, "when you brought me through the portal, you went against the basic intention of the device. This doubtless caused some greater disturbance throughout the web of portals, like ripples in a pond."

"And," Rhia added, "the portal was considerably weakened due to the manipulations done by your son. Pulling your efreeti friend through was simply too much for it to accommodate."

Vincent sighed heavily. "So," he said, "this means that there's a task remaining."

"Aye," Aedriun said. "One of the 'evil' portals must be destroyed to maintain the balance."

"Except," Jaz said, "that we would have to know precisely which one to destroy, the one that corresponds with this one."

"Not to mention knowing *how* to destroy it," Gnorrin put in.

"No," Vincent said, and everyone looked at him questioningly. "We destroy *all* the remaining portals. Get rid of all of them." Seeing the confused looks on the faces of his friends, he explained. "Life, no matter what its 'disposition,' must not be by design of someone, druid or otherwise. The world will go its own way for a change."

The others were silent for several moments, his friends absorbing his words, some of them nodding. Vincent glanced over at the efreeti and found the creature smiling. "Very wise," it said.

Vincent turned his gaze to Rhia again. "What do you think?"

She looked at him, and he knew the pain in her eyes wasn't from her injuries. She smiled. "I think I love you," she said softly.

His heart throbbed as she said this, but they weren't words he wanted to hear at this point. "You know I love you, too. But is this the right decision? Destroying all the portals?"

"Of course it is."

He kissed her on the cheek. "Thank you."

As his friends prepared for the magical jaunt back to the keep, Vincent returned outside. He stood staring out over the plain again, eyeing the small town in the distance. A sound caused him to turn. The efreeti joined him. "What an unusual turn of events," it said.

"And this surprises you, somehow?" Vincent replied.

The efreeti chuckled. "Not where you're concerned." The creature paused, then said. "I wish to thank you again for freeing me from my imprisonment. I've said before that you were a remarkable human, and I repeat the sentiment."

"Don't mention it," he said.

"Very well. I shall not. But I also shall not forget it. Now, if there is nothing I can do for you at the present time, I would return to my own people. I have a most interesting tale to tell them. One which may perhaps cause the efreet to think differently of other races."

Vincent looked up at the giant with a forced smile. "So, will we meet again?"

The efreeti's eyes twinkled. "It would not surprise me in the least. Be well." And with that, the creature vanished in a puff of red smoke.

Gnorrin's voice came to him from the mouth of the cave. "Are you ready?"

With a last gaze out over the plains, he nodded. Then he joined his friends for the magical trip back to his keep.

⁊ ⸲

Aedriun departed the following day, taking Darvas's body with him to Linnael. He and Vincent apologized again to each other for their behavior, and their friendship was as solid as ever by the time Aedriun left.

Jaz left the same day, but promised to visit often.

Rhia's minor wounds healed quickly and she left with Felina within a week. She and Vincent had several long talks before she left. He explained to her, even though he knew he didn't need to, that he needed time alone. He had a lot of healing to do, himself. Once he felt human again, he promised to find her.

Sianon tended to Blade and D'Ty in Vincent's keep. D'Ty recovered consciousness within days and both were well enough to travel in about three weeks. Their departures were difficult for Vincent, since he had no idea when he'd see them again. He wished they didn't live so far away.

Gnorrin was the last to leave. He stayed with Vincent for an additional two weeks after Blade, Sianon, and D'Ty left. In many ways, Vincent considered Gnorrin to be his closest friend. Perhaps it was because he was the first to truly befriend him when he arrived in this world. Perhaps it was because Gnorrin was almost like a father figure to him. He didn't know, or care. All he knew was that he was grateful for his friend's presence, even when he didn't feel like spending time with him. When Gnorrin left, Vincent promised him he'd come to visit as soon as he felt up to it.

Once his friends were all gone, Vincent had to turn even more attention to the maintenance of his keep. Like it or not, he still had mouths to feed. Not all those who'd sworn service to him had died in the battle against the forces gathered by his son. There were plenty left, some who'd been Aedriun's men, and some of the freed slaves.

Fortunately, they seemed to get along pretty well without much attention from him. Much effort was being put into the design of a town at the base of the mountain. Vincent wasn't too interested in the details of this, trusting the people to know more about towns on this world than he would.

And of course, when he wasn't dealing with such mundane issues, he was dealing with the mending of a broken heart. The weight of his experiences bore down on him like the world on the shoulders of Atlas. He blamed himself for the deaths of Darla and the others. He constantly second-guessed himself. Was he right in not wanting anyone to fight on his behalf? Should they have put together some sort of search party to locate his son, long before things escalated to their horrible finale? Should he have done more to prevent an attack on himself and his friends? So many questions, so many doubts, plagued him.

But mostly, he dealt with the sorrow of having lost Darla, as well as the child they would have had together in a handful of months. This was not an easy task. No matter how many times he had to get over the loss of a love, he knew he'd never be any better at it. He still mourned the loss of Ariaziane. He still felt the pangs of being separated from Rhia. Nothing ever prepared you for it, he realized. No matter how many times it happened, or in how many different ways. It still hurt.

Most of the Season of Sleep passed, and every day, Vincent felt a little bit better. Jaz visited him once during this period, and this cheered Vincent more than he'd expected. The pair flew to Falconwall, enjoyed some theater and fine restaurants, and conversed long into the evenings. By the time Jaz flew back home, Vincent knew he was ready to see other friends.

First on that list, as promised, was Gnorrin. As Celebration Week approached, Vincent loaded up a horse and set off on the journey. It wasn't the best time of year to be traveling, but he made the best of it. He ignored the chill as he camped in the snow and tried to imagine the taste of Gnorrin's stew as he chewed on hard biscuits and jerky.

Finally, he reached his former residence. It was midday when he arrived at his cottage. He stopped in the road, just looking at the structure in the pale light of the season.

It seemed so long ago that he'd lived here. In many ways, it was a lifetime ago. So much had happened to him since he and Ariaziane had moved from here to the outskirts of Linnael, where he'd had their houses built. So many strange, terrible, and wonderful things. His life today bore only the most superficial resemblance to his life when he'd lived here.

But the place seemed in good repair. Gnorrin must have been keeping an eye on it. He dismounted, then stabled his horse. Gnorrin didn't have a full-size stable, so the animal would stay here. Then he went up to the cottage, opened the door and stepped inside. He smiled, both from nostalgia and bemusement. Had he really lived in a place as small as this?

He wandered around for a bit, remembering. He remembered cooking in this tiny kitchen. He opened the spigot of his sink, finding that it still worked. He quenched his thirst with icy cold water, glad that the weather wasn't so cold that his basin had frozen.

The bedroom brought back memories, too, especially of the night of Ariaziane's change. He remembered sitting with her as she'd slept, as she tossed and turned in pain, as she screamed into the pillow. Let's not go down that road, he thought. Those weren't the memories he wanted to deal with right now.

He took a deep breath, then left the cottage, heading down the road to Gnorrin's place. Memories there would be more pleasant, he was sure. He noted how barren everything here looked during this season, and how lovely it was for most of the rest of the year.

Vincent smiled as he reached the spot on the road where he'd collapsed, only to be taken in by Gnorrin and Blade. He stood there for a moment, gazing at the cottage before him. The gaming table wasn't under the tree, now. Gnorrin took care of that table, keeping it inside during the cold months.

He didn't go into the cottage immediately, though. It was a nice day, and he felt like stretching his legs. He wasn't used to riding such long periods on horseback. So he went for a walk out behind the cottage, on a path very familiar to him. The path that ran alongside the small stream. The path where he'd first met Ariaziane.

Looks like we're going down that road no matter what I think about, he mused. Then he berated himself. This was where he had met her, gotten to know her, fallen in love with her. How could he expect to visit here, especially in this nostalgic mood, and *not* think of her?

The large stone was just as he remembered it. Huge and rounded. He remembered lying in the sun here, drying out after falling into the creek when he'd first met her. He remembered sitting here many times with her, especially that snowy morning when he realized just how crazy he was about her.

He sat there for many minutes, until the cold rock began to numb his rear end. Perhaps, since he was set on depressing himself, he should walk down to the abbey where she'd lived. Maybe cut across into town, too, and see if old Mepis were still around.

He heaved himself off the rock, but stumbled in the act. He fell to the ground, landing roughly on his stomach. It shocked him more than it hurt him, like most falls. But what shocked him more was what he heard after he fell.

There was a sigh, then one word. "Clumsy."

Before he could even register what he'd heard, there were feet in front of his face. He studied the soft leather, his eyes slowly rising, his level of disbelief doing so, also. The boots led up to dark blue leggings, wrapped with leather thongs.

"And I didn't push you *this* time, either."

He saw a tunic of the same color peeking from under a fur-lined, tan leather vest. One pale hand clasped a staff of light colored wood. Long cascades of red hair fell from under the tunic's hood.

Vincent lay there on the ground, staring into piercing blue eyes the color of sapphires. Ariaziane was looking down at him, her expression a mixture of tenderness and humor. "Are you going to stay down there all day?" She extended her hand to help him rise.

Still stunned, he reached out and grasped it, and as he rose, he held it tightly. "It's you," he whispered, though he didn't really believe it.

"Oh, I'll wager you say that to everyone." She smiled, then the humor left her voice. "You can do better than that," she said softly.

"No, probably not," he said, suddenly understanding. "I'm not used to conversing with hallucinations. I don't know the protocol."

"I'm no hallucination, Vincent."

"Of course you are. And it's no surprise, considering everything I've been through. My mind was bound to snap eventually."

"Can hallucinations be nervous?"

The question caused him to pause. "Nervous about what?"

"About seeing you. Talking to you. Being with you."

She fidgeted as she said this, a movement Vincent remembered all too well. He took a deep breath, staring at her. He didn't *feel* like he was hallucinating. Maybe this *was* real.

"Don't you have anything to say?" she asked.

"No. I mean..." He took a deep breath and let it out slowly. "I have more things to say to you than I could count. But I have no idea which to say first."

"How about 'hello'?"

He smiled weakly. "Hello," he said. Then he surged forward and embraced her, squeezing her close to his body. To his tremendous relief, she didn't disappear in a puff of imagination. She was solid. She was real. But words still wouldn't come, so he simply continued to hold her, happy that she returned the embrace, though perhaps not as desperately as he did. Finally, he let go and stood at arm's length. "You're really back."

"I really am," she said with a gentle smile.

"I wasn't sure I'd ever see you again."

She sat down on the rock, and he joined her. "I know," she said apologetically. "You have no idea how bad I feel for having hurt you."

Vincent gave a weak shrug. "It was just the first of many hurts. I survived." He looked into her eyes, then, and saw in them a world of hurt that was hers alone. He remembered the rape, then, and thought he understood. But mentioning it could open up too many questions and possibly too many painful memories on her part. Instead, he clasped her hand tightly and continued the conversation. "You *are* back to stay, aren't you?"

She hesitated. "Is that what you'd like?" she asked.

He snorted. "You have to ask?" When the girl shrugged, Vincent was reminded of her words. "I read your letters to Gnorrin," he said.

She nodded. "I expected you would."

"You said something about your thoughts on my feelings for you. What did you mean?"

Ariaziane turned her eyes to the ground. She was slow to respond. "I meant that I never truly believed that you were in love with me. I always assumed you were just infatuated with me."

"How could you have thought that?" Vincent gasped. "What did I do to give that impression?"

"Nothing. No, it wasn't you. It was me." She smiled ruefully. "I've come to realize many things about myself, including the fact that I've never had a very high self-image. I never believed you really loved me because I never viewed myself as being the kind of person anyone could love."

"That's ridiculous."

Again she shrugged. "Perhaps. I'm working on that." She looked him in the eye, sadness on her face. "I know you've been with someone else. And I know what happened to her. I'm sorry."

"Thank you," he said. The thought briefly crossed his mind to apologize, to beg her forgiveness for not waiting for her. But he quickly dismissed it. He had no regrets along those lines, and certainly nothing for which he needed to apologize. Instead, he said, "I missed you."

Ariaziane squeezed his hand. "I started missing you the day I left, and all it did was grow in intensity. There were times when I would have given anything for you to have been there with me."

"I know how that feels."

"However," she went on, "I do have unfinished business, and I'd like very much if you'd accompany me. Eventually. There's no rush."

He nodded. "You know I'd be more than happy to."

Ariaziane nodded. "I want to tell you all about my travels, show you what I've found and what I've learned. And I want to know all you've experienced, too. Obviously, you've had a lot more going on in your life than I have in mine. I've heard some, from Gnorrin, but want to hear more. But not right now. Right now, I just want to be with you, to help you recover from your losses."

He smiled slowly. "I like the sound of that." Then the smile faded. "You've been here with Gnorrin? For how long?"

Ariaziane paused, as though she were hesitant to reply. "Since coming here from your keep."

Vincent blinked. "What?"

"I went home," she said. "Months ago. When I arrived, I found your home gone and mine in a partial state of rebuilding. I went to see Baron Aedriun and he explained much to me, including the news about your keep. And," she said quietly, "that you were with Darla." She paused again, then continued. "I stayed with Aedriun for a time, then journeyed with him when he made the trip to your keep. On the way, he told me all he knew about your situation."

"You were with Aedriun?" She nodded, and Vincent remembered how the baron had always looked admiringly at her. He wondered if the two of them... No, he thought, shaking his head. He was being paranoid. "He never mentioned it," he said.

"I asked him not to. At that point, I had no idea if my presence would be welcome. After all, you were with someone."

"So. You rode with Aedriun," he said, turning the conversation away from those memories.

"We parted ways in the morning before he arrived at your keep. I went off and assisted as best I could."

"Ah, it was you," he said. "You drove off the mountain wolves." She nodded. "How?"

"The mountain wolf's natural enemy is the blue wolf. Are you familiar with them?"

"I've heard of them. Bigger, meaner, with glossy black fur that hints of blue in the moonlight."

"And exceedingly vicious. Fiercely territorial. They'll accept no other wolves in their domain. Have you ever seen one?"

"Fortunately, no."

Ariaziane smiled. "Close your eyes." He did so, then opened them at her command a moment later. "That's one over there," she said.

"Whoa, mother!" Vincent nearly jumped to his feet in alarm as he spied the biggest wolf he'd ever seen in his life. It was just as he'd described, though bigger than he'd expected, with nasty-looking teeth that protruded many inches around the snout. "Where'd *that* come from?"

"My head," she said, and with a wave of her hand, it vanished. "It's an illusion. Just as the other hundred or so were that the mountain wolves saw waiting for them."

"Damn," he breathed. "And the trolls? Did you affect them, too?"

"Yes. As they crested a hill, they saw a huge forest fire before them, stretching across the whole width of the valley."

"Wait," he said. "We tried magical fire on them, to no effect. How did yours succeed?"

"The magical fire failed because they are immune to it. When it struck them, it did no damage. They realized this, and were no longer afraid. They are not immune to real fire, though. And without wading into my illusion, they had no way of knowing whether it was real or not. The illusion also mimicked heat, you see. And though trolls aren't too bright, they're not stupid enough to walk into a burning forest just to see if it's real."

Vincent nodded. "Tricky. But wait. Gnorrin didn't say anything about seeing this forest fire of yours. He saw the trolls turn back, though." Ariaziane looked at him, and suddenly Vincent knew. Gnorrin had seen the fire. He'd even seen Ariaziane.

"I swore him to silence," she said. "I didn't think you needed me on your mind at that point in time."

"I see," he said, not sure how to process this bit of information. "So this is the field of magic that you've pursued over the years? Illusion?"

"Mostly. I think it's fascinating."

"And useful. So then what did you do after that?"

Her face grew sad, then. "I returned to you. But I arrived too late to save your... to save Darla. If I had come sooner, maybe..."

But Vincent shook his head. "Stop. You helped my men. Without your assistance, chances are they'd all have died. I can never thank you enough for that."

Ariaziane continued after a moment. "I arrived just before you killed him."

Vincent's stomach dropped. "Oh." He didn't like that she'd witnessed such a hideous event. "I guess you were right about all that repressed anger."

She brushed his comment aside. "Forgive me for that, please. I was young and foolish, then. You are a good man, Vincent. You'd never take your anger out on another person unless... Well, unless it was a situation like what you found yourself in."

He wondered briefly just how much of it she'd seen. Had she heard his son's confession of rape? Did she know that he now knew about it? One day, he knew, it would come up in conversation, and he'd admit to knowing. But that was for another time. "Why did you wait so long to reveal yourself?" he asked.

"I didn't think it would be right. After the battle, you were distraught. What was I to do? Jump back into your life and expect to make everything all better?" She shook her head. "I didn't think I could do that. I still don't." She took a deep breath. "I stayed by your side the whole time, trying to work up the courage to face you, trying to be sure I should." She shrugged. "Then you decided to go home, and I just accepted that as fate."

"But I wouldn't have gone, had I known you were back."

"Again, I didn't want to influence you while you were in such a state." Vincent frowned, but could see the wisdom of her words. "When you went to the cave, I had no idea where you were going. But I found Blade inside the keep, and he knew. The one named Rhia had told him where the portal was, roughly." She looked him in the eye. "You love her, don't you?"

"Yes," he said. "Very much."

Ariaziane nodded, then continued. "I arrived there just before you pulled the efreeti through. And when I realized what you'd done, I was both thrilled and crushed. Thrilled for purely selfish reasons. I didn't want you to go. And crushed because I knew how it must have made you feel."

Vincent frowned. "I think you should tell me just how you're able to do all this, Annie. I thought at first that you meant you were there, but invisible. But I'd still have known someone was near."

"Not only invisible, but insubstantial. At least, from your perspective." She lifted the hem of her tunic and pulled it upward. Vincent tore his gaze from the creamy flesh of her abdomen to focus on a belt of intricately swirled silver metal. "This is what makes it possible," she said. "I acquired it on my travels, and I'll tell you all about that, later." Then she uttered a syllable he didn't quite catch, and promptly vanished.

Vincent looked around, then reached out to the space where she had been. His hand encountered only air. Then, a moment later, she reappeared, on the other side of the stream.

"Ah, teleportation."

"No," she said, and vanished again. A few seconds later, she appeared, seated beside him. "Nothing quite as useful as that. What happens is that I go into another plane of existence. You are unable to sense me at all, because I don't exist on this plane any longer. I am able to see and hear you, however, due to the magic in this belt. As for travel, it is still by foot. I walked across the stream just now, no differently than I would have without the belt."

"Except your feet didn't get wet."

"Because my feet were in another dimension than the water. I cannot touch anything here in the physical realm while in the other."

"But why didn't you come to me in all the time since then?"

"I nearly did. But Gnorrin is wise, as you know. He convinced me that you would come here when your heart was ready. The last thing I wanted to do was to get in the way of your healing."

Vincent nodded. "I see." Then he paused, staring at her. "You're really back, aren't you?"

"Yes."

He shook his head. "This still seems so unreal, like a dream."

"I'm as real as I ever was."

He snorted. "That's no help. I always thought you were a bit on the unreal side."

"What is that supposed to mean?" she laughed.

"Well, I think it comes down to the fact that I've idealized you in my mind. Made you seem almost perfect or something." He smiled faintly. "Dream or not, though, I've really missed you."

He looked into her eyes, then, as she looked into his. From the expression on her face, he knew she was seeing years of pain reflected there. Especially the recent pains, the loss of Darla and their unborn baby, the deaths of friends, and the possibly irrational but nonetheless real thought that it was somehow all his fault.

"Do you know what I'd like?" Ariaziane asked suddenly.

"What?"

There was a spark in her eyes that reminded him of their days together half a decade ago. "I'd like to ride. For old times' sake." She jumped to her feet and faced him. "Ride with me, Vincent!"

"I don't have a horse."

"Nor do I. But," she said mischievously, "I know where to get them!" She reached out and grabbed him by the wrist, yanking him off the stone, and led the way down the path along the stream. They ran for many minutes, eventually coming out at the rear of the abbey. They stood together at the split rail fence. Ariaziane whistled and a pair of horses turned in their stables to looked at her. She smiled, then leaped the fence and dashed across the field.

Vincent watched, smiling, as she unlatched the stable doors and led the horses outside. She mounted one and urged it into a trot, leading the other one. To his amazement, she caused them both to jump the fence. Another whistle brought the second horse up short before it could run off. Then they were beside Vincent and he was climbing up onto the second animal.

And they rode. They rode down the old road they'd always ridden in the past. Memories washed over him, memories of the early days, when he was full of hopelessness over having been transported to this world. Memories of how that hopelessness was lessened by the entrance into his life by a feisty, cute, black-haired girl named Ariaziane.

He remembered her humor, her spirit, her shyness. He remembered her fascination with magic and their first exploit together, to Kurean's old keep. He remembered her concern when she thought he might be hurt or killed by the man they encountered in the corridor.

He remembered when she got sick, and the morning she woke to find her black hair was auburn and her violet eyes now indigo. He remembered her panic and his helplessness in answering her questions.

He remembered her astonishment at his behavior when they'd encountered the efreeti. He remembered dancing with her at Aedriun's. He remembered watching her undress in her room at an inn in Goldenbrook. Vincent chuckled as they rode. He remembered getting *caught* watching her undress in that room in Goldenbrook.

He remembered her passion for the ocean, and building houses for the two of them near Linnael. And he remembered her second transformation, to red hair and sapphire eyes.

And he remembered her departure. He remembered the tree under which they'd stopped. She'd kissed him. But she'd still gone alone.

Vincent shook his head. No more thinking about the bad things, the sad things. He'd dwelled upon them long enough. Unfortunate events happened all the time, but so did pleasant ones. Why did he always focus on the unpleasant?

Watching her riding slightly ahead of him, he saw that her hood had flown back and her red hair was flowing freely in the wind, long and lustrous. If anything, she was even more beautiful than ever.

Love rekindled in his heart, and he knew it was so easily done because it had never been extinguished. He'd always loved her, and he always would, just as he'd always love Rhia and Darla.

She looked back over her shoulder and smiled at him. It was a dazzling smile and he came alive under its spell. He took in deep breaths of air and urged his mount to go faster and faster, until he was directly beside her.

They smiled at each other, and as if they read each other's minds, reached out a hand to the other. They rode that way, hands clenched and smiling.

He laughed out loud, squeezing her hand tighter. She squeezed back, looking at him in a way that held untold promise. And though his heart was still heavy from recent events, no longer did the world appear so grim.

He still had a lot of healing to do. But he *would* heal. His friends would help him, he knew. And though one love was gone from his life, Rhia was sure to re-enter now and again. And now Ariaziane was back, and who knew where that would go?

Life would go on, and he'd do his best to make it good. And for just this moment, the ride was everything he wanted from life... racing the wind with Ariaziane by his side.

And never slowing down.

About the Author

Vincent M. Wales grew up in the small town of Brockway, in northwestern Pennsylvania. He attended the Pennsylvania State University, where he was a founding member of the Penn State Writers Club and head of its Fiction Writers Group.

During a decade in the western suburbs of Philadelphia, he started the *Polyamory Awareness and Acceptance Ribbon Campaign*, which is devoted to de-stigmatizing the lifestyle of responsible non-monogamy.

While a resident of Utah, he formed the *Freethought Society of Northern Utah*, an organization dedicated to supporting First Amendment rights and presenting the positive aspects of lifestyles based on reason rather than faith, among other things.

Currently, he teaches a series of fiction writing classes for The Learning Exchange in Sacramento, and sits on the boards of both *Northern California Publishers & Authors* and *Atheists & Other Freethinkers*. He is also answers questions at AllExperts.com on the topics of atheism, polyamory, and writing books.

He lives in northern California with his wife, Lori.

Visit his webpage at *www.vincentmwales.com*, and his blog – AUTHORIAL VOICE – at *vincentmwales.blogspot.com*.

www.ingramcontent.com/pod-product-compliance
Lightning Source LLC
Chambersburg PA
CBHW030751260626
47169CB00001B/1